D1129730

This special limited edition of
The Machinery of Night
is limited to 1,500 signed copies.

THE
MACHINERY
OF NIGHT

For Lori —
Turn on the
machinery —

[signature]

THE
MACHINERY
OF NIGHT

Douglas Clegg

CEMETERY DANCE PUBLICATIONS

Baltimore
❖ 2004 ❖

Signed Hardcover Edition   ISBN 1-58767-088-7

Cemetery Dance Publications
132-B Industry Lane
Unit 7
Forest Hill, MD 21050
Email: info@cemeterydance.com

www.cemeterydance.com

For Ellen Datlow, one of the best short story editors out there, and a beloved friend.

Extraordinary love and everything else to Raul Silva who lived through just about every single one of these stories. Additional thanks to Matt Johnson for coming up with the idea of this collection in the first place, and to Richard Chizmar for the phenomenon that he is.

Table of Contents

FOREWORD

1

Horror is where we see it. And where it exists.

The tale of horror is one that doesn't necessarily scare, nor does it necessarily disturb.

Instead, I believe, the tale of horror haunts.

2

The first short story I can remember setting down to paper for public consumption had to do with snakes and blood.

In third grade, at a school that happened to be called Sleepy Hollow, I had an extremely bright and creative teacher named Miss Clark. She was not young, but she had the vibrancy of the young. Alive with intelligence and creativity, she had us writing and reading constantly. In March, we were asked to write a story around St. Patrick's Day.

I wish I'd saved that story.

I wrote about how this guy named Patrick went to the streets of Dublin when blood ran in rivulets in the gutter. Perhaps I wouldn't have used the word "rivulet" back then. I probably wrote: "Blood poured all over the street." The snakes of Ireland, you see, slaughtered Dubliners right and left. Then Patrick arrived, and began a campaign to get rid of the snakes.

Only problem: one of the snakes remained behind. Waiting. Heh heh.

Hey, I was eight years old—what do you want?

3

I had wanted to be an artist, first.

My mother was a somewhat frustrated artist. By the time I was three, she had me sketching vases and flowers and dogs and trees. My brothers were singing and, along with my sister, playing pianos and guitars all over the house, while I was most likely in my room, drawing. I drew so much that I did more drawing than note-taking in my classes, clear through high school. This may explain why math often eluded me.

So I figured I'd be an artist, and as I got more into kid-dom, I wanted to be some kind of cartoonist. And a fine artist. Both. I wanted to be Paul Gauguin as well as Charles Schultz. Or draw for *Mad* magazine while painting great art (Frederic Edwin Church being my favorite—as I grew older, I'd go to the nearby National Gallery and sit in front of his "Morning in the Tropics" when I wanted to escape my troubles). As a kid I had high—and low—aspirations.

When I was about eight, we had this pet mockingbird. Inadvertantly, I had led it to its death. I'd been playing with it—as it flew around our rec room—and it landed on the floor, where the family dog went over and bit it. I still feel guilty about this, and have at least one sibling who occasionally would remind me of the bird's death for the next twenty years of my life.

My mother knew I felt bad. She told me to paint the bird. I did—I sketched it, and then painted around my sketch. Then, she got me a typewriter, and asked me to tell her about the mockingbird by writing it out.

So, I typed up a one-page report, which seemed ridiculously hard to do. One whole page! Since I'd never typed before, it was labor. And the typewriter didn't just type. It had nothing but uppercase letters so I WROTE LIKE THIS WHEN I WROTE THE STORY. In red ink.

Foreword

I knew when I wrote that piece of journalism about the pet mockingbird's life: I was going to be a writer.

I just knew it. I began reading even more voraciously than I had before. I began writing in private. Never showing what I had written to anyone. I wrote about whatever I felt like writing about. It became its own engine within me, and then a well, and sometimes a fountain. I wrote lyrics and poems and plays and stories and novels of about twenty pages. I'd often tear these up, because they weren't right yet. They didn't say exactly what I wanted to say in the way I wanted to say things, or in the precise way I had observed something and wanted to relay it through words.

But I wrote and typed and scribbled and doodled—until writing a story, telling a tale, creating a scene, became second nature to me.

4

When I was in my early 20s, I sat in a café in Paris, wanting to be a writer. I mean, a novelist and short story writer. To be published. To be "real." I wrote diligently in that city—every day for months. Drinking *espresso* after *espresso,* then *vin blanc* after *vin blanc,* I wrote and wrote. When I felt I'd written a goodly amount, I looked at my handwritten sheets of paper. At least two hundred pages.

And I threw it all out. Into the trash. No copies. Nothing.

I returned to the U.S., sure that I was not going to be able to write despite my having worked toward the goal of being a writer for many years. Eventually, I learned that throwing pages out was as important to storytelling as putting pages in a novel or story.

I found that I didn't need a café in Paris. What I needed was a solid table for writing, and a story. Not even a room with a view. Just a room. Maybe a typewriter with lowercase as well as uppercase.

It took me several more years to find out what a story was, and what it was not. Serving a story is like serving the most difficult dinner guest. You have to bow and scrape and then clean up and serve again. Readers don't always like where a story goes. Well, truth is, neither do writers. I believe stories go where they're meant to go, and the writer's job is to craft it as much as possible, and then get out of the way.

It is the most psychologically rewarding activity I've ever encountered.

5

Sex! Death! Love!

These are, to me, my themes. I'm laughing at myself as I write this.

And by sex, I don't just mean the act and the Big O, I mean birth, as well. And affection. The physical life. Reminds me of a great story I once heard about a famous elderly writer of great lit who was asked by her editor if she could just add a bit more sex to the book, since there was none, and sex helped sell books. So the writer turned in the book with a very long scene of labor and birth.

Sex is a great motivator, a harbor of fears, a well of intimacies, a place of deceit, a beautiful…well, you get the idea. We are born from it. We can be destroyed by it. Some get addicted to it. Others become predatory with it. Still others find a great symbolic fountain within it. Children are born from it. Some live for it. Some die from it.

There's a lot of room for storytelling in the desires and consequences of the flesh.

Likewise, Death is, hands down, the most complex and yet simple notion that all of us must somehow incorporate into daily living. I write from a position of some authority. I've been around Death. I've heard tell, and seen some of its work, and I've railed against it, and wished for its extinction. And still, it is a hard idea to swallow. In 2001, my father died, my uncle died, my dog died, one of my editors died, a good friend died, and then I watched the towers of the World Trade Center come down, just a few miles from my rooftop. My mother just died in the fall of 2002, as if she fully intended to follow my dad on whatever journey comes next. I had a death-dream before my beloved dog, Randy, died. I dreamed that I was in a strange, dark house. Randy came up the stairs from below, whimpering. My father stood beside me, and he no longer had the

FOREWORD

Alzheimer's Disease that had plagued his final years. He told me, "It's all right now. Randy will be with me. I'll take care of him." But, in the dream, I was frantic. I yelled that we had to get the dog to the vet. I couldn't find a phone book to call the vet, but my dad's calming voice kept telling me not to worry, that he'd make sure that Randy was with him.

I awoke from this dream, and my dog died a few hours later.

What do I make of such a dream? That my mind was working out death? That my dog, who had been sick, would die, and my mind had somehow made it psychologically safe for me to deal with that fact?

Yet, ask anyone who has had this kind of dream, and they'll probably tell you what I will tell you: it felt like more than that. It felt like I had a glimpse of something very real, in a brief moment.

The mystery of anything beyond our lives. Maybe. Maybe not.

So Death, to me, is something that rules in fiction as it does in life—it changes our perceptions, our dreams, our daily lives. It creates an awareness of what matters and what does not. It takes away, yet doesn't take away.

And finally, love.

Crazy that a guy known for writing horror and suspense stories is writing about love, right?

Yep, but to me, the greatest mystery, the most powerful force—for both creation and destruction—is love, and the unknown depths and pinnacles of the human heart. That we love who we love is enough of a mystery. That we give love to those deemed unworthy by others, and take it without regard, and offer it when least expected, and ignore it when most needed—it is the force that, I believe, overcomes the payment that Death asks of us. Love, like Death, settles all debts. It is bewildering in its capacity. It is insane in its single-mindedness. It makes no sense, and yet to be without it, one is bereft.

How could I not write fiction that often centers on sex, death, and love? How can one live life without increasing our experience with those three aspects of who we are and where we are going?

My sense of horror comes from my sense of love—for I believe the world is a chaotic place. A place where horrifying things will happen. And yet I believe that it is also a place of benevolence.

What saves us in this is our sense of love, our sense that we are all, under the skin, somehow the same being. That none of us is separate in a tragedy. That our point of connection is a kind of love that is hard to deny once you've felt it. I have known people who have risen above the most wretched of circumstances, and it is their love for both themselves and others that has allowed them to overcome the obstacles that might blow away many of us. I've also seen people willing to destroy themselves and others because of love—or hate, its mirror.

If you look at my stories carefully, I think you'll see where that point of connection comes, within love. Sometimes, it brings a horror. Sometimes, it brings redemption. Sometimes, both.

6

When I began writing fiction, I did not embark on the undertaking as a short story writer. I began with a novel called *Goat Dance*, and then wrote a few novels before I ever wrote my first publishable short story. That story was called "Where Flies Are Born," and was followed in short order by another called "People Who Love Life," both of which are included in this collection.

For writers here, as well as readers, I figure I might as well dredge up some recollections for how I came to write short stories at all.

First, I didn't think I'd be able to write any. I'd made a couple of attempts at short fiction in my 20s, but those two turned into novels—they weren't short stories at all. One became my novel, *You Come When I Call You*. Dave Silva, an excellent writer, used to run a great magazine called *The Horror Show*. I submitted the story to him, and he wrote back a brief but encouraging note that the story, called "You Come When I Call You," was not quite developed enough. He was right. I ended up taking more than a decade to develop it into the novel that was finally published in the year 2000.

FOREWORD

In my 20s, I was not quite ready to write short fiction—the longer forms came more easily to me (as they continue to do).

But, having then finished my second novel, and nearly finished with my third, I decided that I had stories that needed to be short. Only one problem: I had no idea how to keep them short. The late Richard Laymon encouraged me. I used to go to his house and hang out with Dick, Ann, and Kelly Laymon, like my second home, and Dick would give me advice and ways of approaching the writing of short fiction. I doubt I would've written one short story at the time without his suggestions. My friend, Chelsea Quinn Yarbro, also gave me really great advice on the creation of a short story.

So, I set out to write a short story for this cool magazine called *Cemetery Dance*. I stayed up all night, a bit shivery from this one story. I submitted it to *Cemetery Dance* magazine.

And it was rejected all too quickly.

The main reason I'm mentioning that story is that sometimes young or new writers think that all of us who have had several books published had it easy at the start of our careers. Nothing could be further from the truth.

And, honestly, the story I wrote sucked. I just didn't know it at the time. When I looked at it a month later, I thought: this story is terrible. No wonder Chizmar, this faceless publisher who I thought would never buy any writing of mine, rejected it.

Then, I began writing another story. This one was about something that bothered me—a doctor, a friend at the time, told me about someone who he thought was dead, but it turned out this person was alive. I said to the doctor, "How did you find out he was alive?" And the doctor said, "Well, how do we know someone's alive, ever? Usually some movement."

I began to think: Is movement enough to make us happy with life? Is that all there is to it?

My mother, rest her soul, used to call wrestling "wrassling," and so I wrassled with the futility of the idea that movement alone defines what life is, at its most basic.

Then, I had a nightmare. In it, I saw three children, with flies coming from their mouths. But their mouths and eyes were sewn up with threads; the flies had broken through the threads. Upon waking, I recalled having a small wooden toy as a kid, into which you put a fly. As the fly jumped around, the wooden toy moved. The toy seemed to be alive because it moved around. I never used the toy because I would've felt bad for the housefly, but this was the theory of it. A bug torture chamber, basically.

Additionally, one time I sat on a train between Washington, D.C. and New York City, and we were stuck because of snow on the tracks. Someone next to me said, "Thank god we're stuck here. We can go to a nice hotel. If we'd gotten stuck forty miles back, we'd be in the boonies."

Yep, all of these things came together, and I began writing this story about a woman who escaped an abusive husband, with her little boy. A train gets stuck out in the middle of nowhere, and this woman finds out about the grief—and terror—of some good country people. This became, "Where Flies Are Born," and as soon as I had the title, the whole story came together. A small but significant journal of the horror genre (at the time) called *Tekeli-Li!* bought it, and published it.

Then, another great journal of its time, *The Scream Factory*, bought my next story. It was called "People Who Love Life." I had the title long before I knew what the story would be. Years before, I had known too many people in their early 20s who seemed to like to overcomplicate their lives and sort of wallow in ennui. I said to a friend, "We've got to start hanging around with people who love life." For some reason, that phrase stuck with me awhile. It struck me as a funny way to look at things. It begged the question: what if someone really didn't love life? And why? And what if…well, I won't tell you more. I began to write this story about a particular woman who has good reason not to love life.

Ellen Datlow, then the fiction editor of OMNI magazine, and an editor of many anthologies, said a few good words about the story. As any new writer knows, particularly in the genres of science fiction, fantasy, and horror, Ellen is one of those editors whose word can be gold. And it was—suddenly, people were asking to see more stories from me.

FOREWORD

Around this time, I was in a Sargasso Sea with my then-publisher, Pocket Books, for various reasons. I had a break between novels, and decided to devote significant time to writing short stories and sending them out. My next story was called "Damned, If You Do." I'm still not sure what this one's about, but I went for a walk with a friend of mine in Fullerton, California. We passed the backyard of an old man, digging holes in his backyard, and taking a break to sip lemonade. I said, "It looks like a Norman Rockwell moment. What if he's burying his children back there?" I went back and wrote the story, sent it off to *Cemetery Dance* magazine, and it was my first sale to the very publisher who is now bringing out this edition. An artist named Keith Minnion illustrated it with beautiful drawings that were perfect for the tale.

From this point on, I wrote story after story after story for awhile. Editors like Marty Greenberg, Ellen Datlow, Rich Chizmar, Ed Gorman, and others, began asking me for stories. I began to consider the writing of short fiction to be my way of cheating on whatever novel begged to be written.

I also began to love writing short stories, as demanding as they can be.

7

A couple of the stories here are not my favorites. I've included them because people have asked for them. Some are experimental. Some are sketches. "Mrs. Feely" was originally called "Mrs. Phelan" for a completely ridiculous reason. The editor of the anthology in which it originally appeared knew that I had had a creative disagreement with a guy who was a reviewer, whose last name happened to be Feeley. My story, which was written long before I ever crossed sentences with Feeley online, had the title "Mrs. Feely" for a specific and highly personal reason (and involved someone named Feely from the 1930s who is now dead and gone). I loved the name. But the editor felt that, despite the fact that Mr. Feeley and I were not enemies, even if we'd disagreed, by naming the story something else, the anthology might not get a bad review somewhere. Hey, I was younger then (I say this nearly every year when I look back at the bad decisions I made the year before). I went along with this absurd notion because I was too passive to fight about it, allowed the title to be changed to "Mrs. Phelan." Well, damn it, it's going back to "Mrs. Feely" right now. In this collection. It was silly to allow the title to be changed in the first place.

Now, having said that, I don't love the story. It's a slice of life about family madness. Sometimes I write a story from a very murky place, and can't figure it out. When this happens, and it is rare, the story comes out like — well, like "Mrs. Feely." It's not a horror story and it's not a suspense story. It is a prolonged character sketch. I've included it here because there's still something within it that resonates with me. Whenever I write a story where I truly want to live imaginatively within the confines of that story, I usually like it, even for perverse reasons.

(I fully expect a few critics of this volume to pull that one out as, "Clegg himself admits that his stories are not really much as stories, as in the case of his truly execrable 'Mrs. Feely,' a tale that goes nowhere, signifying nothing." But I got here first. I am telling you, the story is just not very good.)

Additionally, there are some short stories here that have never before been published. One, called "The Skin of the World," is one of my favorites. I wrote it early in my career, and then just put it aside and forgot about it. Going through some older files, I found it, and still enjoyed something about it enough to include it here.

There are three poems of sorts here. One, "Medea" is about, well, Medea, at her most vulnerable and yet most brutal. Another, "Why My Doll Is Evil," came from one of those murky places I mentioned earlier. There is one story that's so short and clipped that it's really halfway between a poem and a story. It's called "Subway Turnstile," and is neither quite a short story nor quite a poem.

And now, more sex!

Now and then, I get to write about sex and sexuality in fiction, and I enjoy doing so, because I find aspects of sexual attraction and sexual consummation to be disturbing, lurid, and altogether too seductive. And then I get letters from readers telling me that all I do

18

is write about sex. It ain't so. When sexuality is my subject matter, I tend toward the disturbances of sex, not the allure.

It's also damn hard to write about without crossing the line into titilation (a word that contains the seed of its own titilation). Nobody really likes writing about sex as it is. Most writers I read who write about sex tend toward sexual fantasy—the way we want sex to be, but not necessarily the reality with both the good and the bad parts of it, the meaningful and the meaningless. I suspect the problem is that sex feels to the participants very different than it looks or perhaps actually is, without the feelings. I think I write somewhere in between the mythology of sex and the reality. (A story, to me, is a way to "lie the truth," as a character in the strange and disturbing movie, *The Fourth Man*, says.)

"Ice Palace," which originally appeared in Ellen Datlow's *Little Deaths,* is about a college man's initiation into a different fraternity—a fraternity that I believe exists for some men. I've known some of them—they live double lives, even in the 21st century. They go underground for their secrets. The story is sexual, and deliberately not about what it appears to be about. That is my favorite kind of story to write. "Piercing Men," is about a guy who, though married, finds an aggressive sexual outlet with a neighbor, and from there, something really terrible occurs. It was originally published in an anthology that Michael Rowe edited, called *Queer Fear*, which was a bit of a landmark collection of stories about horror with gay themes.

Sex plays a role in "I Am Infinite; I Contain Multitudes," as well. In it, an inmate-prisoner has a truly unusual sexual kink (although I've always been of the crowd to say, "as long as you're happy and no chickens are harmed, go for it"), something I'd have a hard time understanding—yet, in writing the story, I began to understand about the different ways someone you love can get under your skin. "The Night Before Alec Got Married," also has a bit of sex in it, although I'd probably label it as something other than sex—maybe the predatory and yet strangely consumerish nature of certain folks.

Among my favorites in this collection: "Fries With That?" —mainly because I liked the way these girls started with a simple, if devious, scheme, that then changes course.

"White Chapel," which is, without a doubt, the best short story I've written so far. Don't ask me where it came from. My friend Poppy Z. Brite invited me to write for her wonderful anthology, *Love In Vein*. I have always loved all things Indian, and feel that if I'd been reincarnated in the past, I was in India. So I wrote a story that came out of that sense and went into a nightmarish journey with it.

"The Fruit of Her Womb" is a favorite for personal reasons that I probably won't reveal anytime soon, as is "O, Rare and Most Exquisite."

On another front, outside of thematic notions, I wanted to write stories that fit in with a modern sensibility—and a structure of fiction—that still had its roots in gothic literature. By gothic, I don't mean Goth in the late 20th century terminology, but in the sense of the gothic literature that still has a foothold, even in the 21st century. Thus, in "White Chapel," the human monster is very much a product of his era, but he finds his meaning within the prison of an ancient deity. In "265 and Heaven," the main character, Paul, is a cop in a small city, but finds the secrets of the world within a mythological wood. Or, perhaps, it's heaven.

The story from which this collection takes its title, "The Machinery of Night," is a modern gothic tale: it is the story of molecules and madness, and of the fragile nature of perception as it goes from dusk to nightfall. It is also one of my favorites, because it is concerned with love, and sex, and death. And horror.

Of course.

§

Thirteen of these short stories appeared in the paperback collection, *The Nightmare Chronicles*. The rest do not. My novelette, *The Dark Game*, is here. This is a strange one—and I want to ask that you don't read it unless you've first read my novel, *The Hour Before Dark*. Why? This novelette is a coda of sorts to that novel.

FOREWORD

My novella, *Purity*, is also here. *Purity* came out in a hardcover edition in 2000, and then went on to an ebook edition that managed to reach about 100,000 people. It is still one of my favorites, mainly because I just like Owen, the main character, so much, with his sociopathic heart.

Within these pages, you'll find the beautiful and the damned, the gross and the subtle, the quiet terror and the screaming calm. You're exploring my imagination when you read this, but you're also bringing your own into the stories. If they scare you, it's something that's already within you that brings the scares. These are merely stories of human beings and extraordinary moments, love, death, sex. If they disturb you, I suspect the disturbance is yours. Nothing in the stories has ever happened. At least, not the way I tell it.

If you find yourself haunted, then I appreciate the company.

Douglas Clegg
January 1, 2003

21

Halloween Memory
age Four, Hawaii, 1961

I am beginning this collection, not with a short story at all, but with a brief remembrance from my childhood in Hawaii. Originally published in October Dreams, *an enormous book that recently came out in paperback, this is a true story that I have never been able to grow out of. I saw what I saw. You can't convince me otherwise.*

When I was four years old, I lived with my family in Hawaii; I have especially vivid memories from this time, but only in moments, like a camera's snapshot, but with sixty seconds of movement. I remember my hostility toward one of the nursery school teachers, and my love of one of the other ones; and I remember riding my father's shoulders on some trip through a garden, watching my mother, who was as beautiful as the garden itself, walk ahead of us; I remember how I'd go to the ocean with my father, lugging my large plastic fish and my black cat puppet; he'd show me how to body surf, although I doubt I ventured more than a foot out from shore. But one of the most distinct memories—and it's as if it just happened, even though this took place around 1961, was the Halloween night when I saw a witch.

At four, there isn't a lot to remember beyond specific details, so I'll begin with those. We had a lanai with a straw mat hanging down, and my godmother was visiting. My godmother and my mother always seemed to have adventures together, which they took me on (once I went to a movie with the two of them and they told me to look down at my lap, full of gumdrops, during the movie. I did as I had been told, but for a second, I looked up and saw a man sticking a hypodermic needle into a bikini-clad woman's foot, right under the heel. I never looked up at the movie again). But my memory of my first Halloween is my most vivid—my first conscious Halloween, where I knew Halloween and knew it was something special, and felt it in the air and in the stories the other kids told.

It was Halloween night, and I had heard the legends of witches and goblins and mummies. The enjoyable, enthusiastic terror was in me as I went out to the backyard and looked up at the sky.

There, flying across the face of the moon, was a witch, astride a broomstick.

Now, I knew even at four that this wasn't something you were supposed to tell grown-ups. I'm fairly sure I kept it to myself. The witch was shadowy, but she definitely rode a broom.

As a four-year-old, this didn't seem that out of the ordinary. I fully expected it on Halloween night.

I remember nothing else of that night, and I can't quite recall other Halloweens as a child, except for a few parties, a few collections for UNICEF, a few masks that smothered me as I trudged with a jack-o-lantern flashlight from house to house; my last year of trick-or-treating, in which I could only go to a couple of houses before heading off with my older brothers and sister and my father to a local football game, all the while thinking how much I'd rather be trick-or-treating with friends.

The image of that witch on her broom stayed with me for years.

We moved to Connecticut sometime after Halloween—I'm not sure how long after, but by the time I entered kindergarten, I was out of Hawaii. But each Halloween, I would go outside and look up at the sky and wonder if I'd see a witch or two again. I never did. But I always will believe that flying witches exist.

Halloween Memory

In fact, I'm certain that I clung to that memory for many years, and, at least until puberty struck with its unwanted lightning, I kept the secret of what I had seen. I felt I was protecting the witch. Well, I knew it was foolish. There were, after all, no such things as witches. And flying on brooms?

The witch never came back, but I have to tell you: it was enough. You only need to see the witch once, on her broom, sweeping the sky, to understand both what Halloween is about, and to understand how the world is never enough for someone who has seen the magic. I know there are people who will tell me that witches don't do that, or witches don't exist, or that kids have wild imaginations and that the magic isn't real like that. But no one can convince me that at four I didn't see what I know I saw.

I have not gotten too far from that little boy, standing barefoot in his swimming trunks, crew cut, brown eyes soaking up the night with all its wonder and possibilities; his brothers and sister gone out to trick-or-treat, his mother and godmother and father and godfather in the house or nearby; geckos running along the walls; the Hawaiian darkness as mysterious as the legends and stories that boy must have heard; and it's not just any night, but a magic night, a night that is like no other; a night when any and all things are possible.

Why do I have a feeling that I'll see her again, my good omen for future life? She's an assurance that what those around me tell me is true about the world is not everything, is not all true, is not the complete wisdom of the world; why do I feel that one Halloween night, perhaps in another forty years, I'll see her flying across the moon, and will let her sweep me alongside her? Maybe then I'll ride the night and the moon and the sky before the Day of the Dead comes my way, and some little kid will look up and see us on the broom against the moon and will grow into someone who believes that there is no end to what the world can dream up.

Where Flies Are Born

The train stopped suddenly, and Ellen sat there and watched her son fill in the coloring book with the three Crayolas left to him: aquamarine, burnt sienna, and silver. She was doing this for him: she could put up with Frank and his tirades and possessiveness, but not when he tried to hurt Joey. No. She would make sure that Joey had a better life. Ellen turned to the crossword puzzle in the back of the magazine section to pass the time. She tried not to think of what they'd left behind. She was a patient woman, and so it didn't annoy her that it was another hour before anyone told the passengers that it would be a three hour stop, or more. *Or more*, translating into six hours. Then her patience wore thin and Joey was whining. The problem with the train, it soon became apparent, was one which would require disembarking. The town, if it could be called that, was a quarter mile ahead, and so they would be put up somewhere for the night. So this was to be their Great Escape. February third in a mountain town at thirty below. Frank would find them for sure; only a day's journey from Springfield. Frank would hunt them down, as he'd done last time, and bring them back to his little castle and she would make it okay for another five years before she went crazy again and had to run. *No.* She would make sure he wouldn't hurt Joey. She would kill him first. She would, with her bare hands, stop him from ever touching their son again.

Joey said, "Can't we just stay on the train? It's cold out there."

"You'll live," she said, bringing out the overnight case and following in a line with the other passengers out of the car. They trudged along the snowy tracks to the short strip of junction, where each was directed to a different motel or private house.

"I wanted a motel," she told the conductor. She and Joey were to be overnight guests of the Neesons', a farm family. "This isn't what I paid for," she said, "it's not what I expected at all."

"You can sleep in the station, you like," the man said, but she passed on that after looking around the filthy room with its greasy benches. "Anyway, the Neesons run a bed-and-breakfast, so you'll do fine there."

The Neesons arrived shortly in a four-wheel drive, looking just past the curve of middle age, tooth-rotted, with *country* indelibly sprayed across their grins and friendly winks. Mama Neeson, in her late fifties, spoke of the snow, of their warm house "where we'll all be safe as kittens in a minute," of the soup she'd been making. Papa Neeson was older (*old enough to be my father*, Ellen thought) and balder, eyes of a rodent, face of a baby-left-too-long-in-bathwater. Mama Neeson cooed over Joey, who was already asleep. *Damn you, Joey, for abandoning me to Neeson-talk.* Papa Neeson spoke of the snowfall and the roads. Ellen said very little, other than to thank them for putting her up.

"Our pleasure," Mama Neeson said, "the little ones will love the company."

"You have children?" Ellen winced at her inflection. She didn't *mean* it to sound as if Mama Neeson was too old to have what could be called "little ones."

"Adopted, you could say," Papa Neeson grumbled, "Mama, she loves kids, can't get enough of them, you get the instinct, you see, the sniffs for babies and you got to have them whether your body gives 'em up or not."

Ellen, embarrassed for his wife, shifted uncomfortably in the seat. What a rude man. This was what Frank would be like, under the skin, talking about women and their "sniffs," their "hankerings." Poor Mama Neeson, a houseful of babies and *this man*.

"I have three little ones," she said, "all under nine. How old's yours?"

"Six."

"He's an angel. Papa, ain't he just a little angel sent down from heaven?"

Papa Neeson glanced over to Joey, curled up in a ball against Ellen's side. "Don't say much, do he?"

The landscape was white and black; Ellen watched for ice patches in the road, but they went over it all smoothly. Woods rose up suddenly, parting for an empty flat stretch of land. They drove down a fenced road, snow piled all the way to the top of the fenceposts. Then, as with a barn behind. *We better not be sleeping in the barn.*

Mama Neeson sighed, "Hope they're in bed. Put them to bed hours ago, but you know how they romp…"

"They love to romp," Papa Neeson said.

29

The bed was large and she and Joey sank into it as soon as they had the door closed behind them. Ellen was too tired to think, and Joey was still dreaming. Sleep came quickly, and was black and white, full of snowdrifts. She awoke, thirsty, before dawn. She was half-asleep, but lifted her head towards the window: the sound of animals crunching in the snow outside. She looked out—had to open the window because of the frost on the pane. A hazy purple light brushed across the whiteness of the hills—the sun was somewhere rising beyond the treetops. A large brown bear sniffed along the porch rail. Bears should've frightened her, but this one seemed friendly and stupid, as it lumbered along in the tugging snow, nostrils wiggling. Sniffing the air; Mama Neeson would be up—four thirty—frying bacon, flipping hotcakes on the griddle, buttering toast. Country mama. The little ones would rise from their quilts and trundle beds, ready to go out and milk cows or some such farm thing, and Papa Neeson would get out his shotgun to scare off the bear that came sniffing. She remembered Papa's phrase: "the sniffs for babies," and it gave her a discomforting thought about the bear.

She lay back on the bed, stroking Joey's fine hair, with this thought in her mind of the bear sniffing for the babies, when she saw a housefly circle above her head; then, another, coming from some corner of the room, joining its mate. Three more arrived. Finally, she was restless to swat them. She got out of bed and went to her overnight bag for hairspray. This was her favorite method of disposing of houseflies. She shook the can, and then sprayed in the direction of the (count them: nine) fat black houseflies. They buzzed in curves of infinity. In a minute, they began dropping, one by one, to the rug. Ellen enjoyed taking her boots and slapping each fly into the next life.

Her dry throat and heavy bladder sent her out to the hallway. Feeling along the wall for the light switch or the door to the bathroom—whichever came first. When she found the switch, she flicked it up, and a single unadorned bulb hummed into dull light.

30

A little girl stood at the end of the hall, too old for the diaper she wore; her stringy hair falling wildly almost to her feet; her skin bruised in several places—particularly around her mouth, which was swollen on the upper lip. In her small pudgy fingers was a length of thread. Ellen was so shocked by this sight that she could not say a word—the girl was only seven or so, and what her appearance indicated about the Neesons...

Papa Neeson was like Frank. Likes to beat people. Likes to beat children. Joey and his black eyes, this girl and her bruised face. I could kill them both.

The little girl's eyes crinkled up as if she were about to cry, wrinkled her forehead and nose, parted her swollen lips.

From the black and white canyon of her mouth a fat green fly crawled the length of her lower lip, and then flew toward the light bulb above Ellen's head.

Where Flies Are Born

Later, when the sun was up, and the snow outside her window was blinding, Ellen knew she must've been half-dreaming, or perhaps it was a trick that the children played—for she'd seen all of them, the two-year-old, the five-year-old, and the girl. The boys had trooped out from the shadows of the hall. All wearing the filthy diapers, all bruised from beatings or worse. The only difference with the two younger boys was they had not yet torn the thread that had been used to sew their mouths and eyes and ears and nostrils closed. Such child abuse was beyond imagining. Ellen had seen them only briefly, and afterwards wondered if perhaps she hadn't *seen* wrong. But it was a dream, a very bad one, because the little girl had flicked the light off again. When Ellen reached to turn it back on, they had retreated into the shadows and the feeling of a surreal waking state came upon her. *The Neesons could not possibly be this evil.* With the light on, and her vision readjusting from the darkness, she saw only houseflies sweeping motes of dust through the heavy air.

At breakfast, Joey devoured his scrambled eggs like he hadn't eaten in days; Ellen had to admit they tasted better than she'd ever had before. "You live close to the earth," Papa Neeson said, "and it gives up its treasures."

Joey said, "Eggs come from chickens."

"Chickens come from eggs," Papa Neeson laughed, "and eggs are the beginning of all life. But we all gather our life from the earth, boy. You city folks don't feel it because you're removed. Out here, well, we get it under our fingernails, birth, death, and what comes in between."

"You're something of a philosopher," Ellen said, trying to hide her uneasiness. The image of the children still in her head, like a half-remembered dream. She was eager to get on her way, because that dream was beginning to seem more real. She had spent a half-hour in the shower trying to talk herself out of having seen the children and what had been done to them: then, ten minutes drying off, positive that she had seen what she'd seen. It was Frank's legacy: he had taught her to doubt what was right before her eyes. She wondered if Papa Neeson performed darker needlework on his babies.

31

"I'm a realist," Papa Neeson said. His eyes were bright and kind—it shocked her to look into them and think about what he might/might not have done.

Mama Neeson, sinking the last skillet into a washtub next to the stove, turned and said, "Papa just has a talent for making things work, Missus, for putting two and two together. That's how he grows, and that's how he gathers. Why if it weren't for him, where would my children be?"

"Where are they?" Joey asked.

Ellen, after her dream slash hallucination slash mind-your-own-business, was a bit apprehensive. She would be happy not to meet Mama Neeson's brood at all. "We have to get back to the train," she said. "They said by eleven."

Papa Neeson raised his eyebrows in an aside to his wife. "I saw some flies at the windows," he said. "They been bad again."

Mama Neeson shrugged her broad shoulders. "They got to let them out at times or they'd be bursting, now, wouldn't they. Must tickle something awful." She wiped her dripping hands on the flowerprint apron, back and forth like she could never get dry enough. Ellen saw a shining in the old woman's eyes like tears and hurt.

Joey clanked his fork on his plate; Ellen felt a lump in her throat, and imaginary spiders and flies crawling up the back of her neck. Something in the atmosphere had changed, and she didn't want to spend one more minute in this house with these people.

Joey clapped a fly between his hands, catching it mid-air.

"Mama's sorry you didn't see the kids," Papa Neeson said, steering over a slick patch on the newly plowed road.

"But you're not," Ellen said. She was feeling brave. She hated this man like she hated Frank. Maybe she'd report him to some child welfare agency when she got back to the train station. She could see herself killing this man.

"No," Papa Neeson nodded. "I'm not. Mama, she don't understand about other people, but I do."

"Well, I saw them. All three. What did you do to them?"

Papa Neeson sighed, pulling over and parking at the side of the road. "You don't understand. Don't know if I should waste my breath."

Joey was in the backseat, bundled up in blankets. He yawned, "Why we stopping?"

Ellen directed him to turn around and sit quietly. He was a good boy. "I have a husband who hits children, too."

Papa Neeson snapped, "I don't hit the kids, lady, and how dare you think I do, why you can just get out of my car right now if that's your attitude."

"I told you, I saw them," she said defiantly.

"You see the threads?"

Ellen could barely stand his smug attitude.

"You see 'em? You know *why* my kids look like that?"

Ellen reached for the door handle. She was going to get out. Fucking country people and their torture masked as discipline. Men, how she hated their power trips. Blood was boiling now; she was capable of anything, like two days ago when she took the baseball bat and slammed it against Frank's chest, hearing ribs cracking. She was not going to let a man hurt her child like that. Never again. The rage was rising up inside her the way it had only done twice in her life before, both times with Frank, both times protecting Joey.

Papa Neeson reached out and grabbed her wrist.

"*Don't hold me like that,*" she snarled.

He let go.

Papa Neeson began crying, pressing his head into the steering wheel. "She just wanted them so bad, I had to go dig 'em up. I love her so much, and I didn't want her to die from hurting, so I just dug 'em up and I figured out what to do and did it."

When he calmed, he sat back up, looking straight ahead. "We better get to the junction. Train'll be ready. You got your life moving ahead with it, don't you?"

She said, "Tell me about your children. What's wrong with them?"

He looked her straight in the eyes, making her flinch because of his intensity. "Nothing, except they been dead for a good twenty to thirty years now, and my wife, she loves 'em like they're her own. I dig 'em up, see, I thought she was gonna die from grief not having none of her own, and I figured it out, you know, about the maggots and the flies, how they make things move if you put enough of 'em inside the bodies. I didn't count on 'em lasting this long, but what if they do? What if they *do*, lady? Mama, she loves those babies. We're only humans, lady, and humans need to hold babies, they need to love something other than themselves, don't they? Don't you? You got your boy, you know how much that's worth? Love beyond choosing, ain't it? Love that don't die. You know what it's like to hug a child when you never got to hug one before? So I figured and I figured some more, and I thought about what makes things live, how we know something's alive, and I figured, when it moves it's alive, and when it don't move, it's dead. So Mama, I had her sew the flies in, but they keep laying eggs and more and more, and the kids, they got the minds of flies, and sometimes they rip out the threads, so sometimes flies get out, but it's a tiny price, ain't it, lady? When you need to love little ones, and you ain't got none, it's a tiny price, a day in hell's all, but then sunshine and children and love, lady, ain't it worth that?"

34

Ellen had a migraine by the time Papa Neeson dropped them off down at the junction. She barked at Joey. Apologized for it. Bought him a Pepsi from the machine by the restroom. People were boarding the train. She went to the restroom to wipe cold water across her face—made Joey promise to stand outside it and not go anywhere. The mirror in the bathroom was warped, and she thought she looked stunning: brown eyes circled with sleeplessness, the throbbing vein to the left side of her forehead, the dry, cracked lips. She thought of the threads, of the children tugging at them, popping them out to let the flies go. Ran a finger over her lips, imagining

Where Flies Are Born

Mama Neeson taking her needle and thread, breaking the skin with tiny holes. Ears, nostrils, eyes, mouth, other openings, other places where flies could escape. Flies and life, sewn up into the bodies of dead children, buried by other grieving parents, brought back by the country folks who ran the bed-and-breakfast, and who spoke of children that no one ever saw much of.

And when they did…

So here was Ellen's last happy image in the mountain town she and her son were briefly stranded in:

Mama Neeson kissing the bruised cheek of her little girl, tears in her squinty eyes, tears of joy for having children to love.

Behind her, someone opened the door.

Stood there.

Waiting for her to turn around.

"Look who I found," Frank said, dragging Joey behind him into the women's room.

Two weeks later, she was on the train again, with Joey, but it was better weather—snow was melting, the sun was exhaustingly bright, and she got off at the junction because she wanted to be there. *Frank was dead.* She could think it. She could remember the feel of the knife in her hands. No jury would convict her. She had been defending herself. Defending her son. Frank had come at Joey with his own toy dump truck. She had grabbed the carving knife—as she'd been planning to do since Frank had hauled them back to Springfield. She had gone with the knowledge of what she would have to do to keep Frank out of her little boy's life forever. Then, she had just waited for his temper to flare. She kept the knife with her, and when she saw him slamming the truck against Joey's scalp, she let the boiling blood and rage take her down with them. The blade went in hard, and she thought it would break when it hit bone. But she twisted it until Frank dropped the dump truck, and then she scraped it down like she was deboning a chicken.

All for Joey.

She lifted him in her arms as she stepped off the train, careful on the concrete because there was still some ice. Joey, wrapped in a blanket, sunglasses on his face, "sleeping," she told the nice lady who had been sitting across from them; Ellen, also wearing sunglasses and too much make-up, a scarf around her head, a heavy wool sweater around her shoulders, exhausted and determined.

Joey's not dead. Not really.

It hadn't been hard to track down the Neesons. She had called them before she got on the train, and they were not surprised to hear from her. "It happens this way," Mama Neeson told her, "our calling."

Ellen was not sure what to make of that comment, but she was so tired and confused that she let it go. Later, she might think that something of the Neeson's had perhaps rubbed off on her and her son. That, perhaps just *meeting* them might be like inviting something into life that hadn't been considered before. *Something under your fingernails.*

She carried Joey to the payphone and dropped a quarter in. Joey was not waking up. She did not have to cry anymore. She told herself that, and was comforted. Things change, people move on, but some things could stay as they were. Good things.

"Mr. Neeson?"

"You're here already?" he asked. He sounded relieved.

"I took an early train."

"Mama's still asleep. She was up all night. Worries, you know. Upset for you."

"Well...."

"I'll be down there in a few minutes, then," he said, adding, "you're sure this is what you want?"

"Love beyond choosing," she reminded him. A spool of white thread fell out from Joey's curled hands, bouncing once, twice, on the ground, unraveling as it rolled.

People Who Love Life

Why did he always have to follow her wherever she went and bring her back? Irene liked to go down to the schoolyard because of the children, the little children. Their faces, *their faces*, their tiny hands, their dresses and shorts and shirts and shoes, so small, so perfect. It bothered her when he volunteered to go, too, because the edge of the schoolyard was her special place, the children were there, and he didn't know anything about children. Children had that edge; they could *smell* things when they were bad, and they weren't afraid to say it. And when things were truly good, children sensed that, too. Children were the thing.

"Oh, but when *we* were children," the girl had said in the kitchen, and Irene had had to stare at her younger sister long and hard before she realized that she wasn't a girl at all, but a woman in her early forties: Gretchen was still pretty and adolescent, even with her slightly etched face and graying hair. Irene could not stand her sometimes, although Gretchen on her own was one thing— sweetness and light even though she *knew*, but Gretchen with this man she'd married was quite another. Irene had never really enjoyed his company, although she couldn't ever tell Gretchen how she felt; and so, she was often stuck with him, this William person, and yes, even when she went to the schoolyard to watch her children play.

"When *we* were children," Irene had replied, "good lord, I can't even remember, barely."

Gretchen was loading the dishwasher. "I remember like yesterday. Days like today, just like today. Look outside the window, it's just like when we were children and mother was in here cleaning, looking out at us." But, of course, there were no children out the window now. Gretchen was the most self-assured person that Irene had ever known, but she lied. Irene knew that about Gretchen: she lied. Gretchen could not possibly remember their childhood accurately, she had no head for memories. She blocked them purposefully, like closing doors on useless rooms. Irene remembered just about everything, but she had lied, also. Irene was not fond of remembering: *days like today, indeed. All days, like today. Unending. I just want to leave. Why won't they just let me leave?* They had been a family of liars, and had never quite grown out of it, although Irene was tired, today, lying to herself about what she felt and what she wanted. Truly wanted. *I just want to go by myself.*

"You were undoubtedly two of the most spoiled girls in creation, all those toys and the way your mother used to dress you up for Sunday school like little dolls," William had said, and Irene had thought: *why do you live here with us when you're so awful to Gretchen? How you did to her what you did, let alone how I must pay for it, is beyond imagining. But you have no imagination, do you? You think it is the way you see it. In front of your face. The way you see it, with no one else allowed to look.* He was an old man who pretended to be young, but she saw right through that, right to that middle-aged heart with its bloodless beating. He pretended things were all right, that there was good to every purpose.

"We were never really spoiled," Gretchen said, "but there's always been someone to watch out for us."

"Amen to that," William said, clasping his hands together.

He had decided to come with her this day, and so there he was at her right arm, helping her every few steps as if she were a complete cripple. "I can handle the steps quite well, thank you, William," she said, and knew she sounded testy. Her right leg twisted as she stepped down to the sidewalk. Again, she had lied; stairs were difficult for her, the way her feet went, one moving almost against the other, but once she was on flat ground she was fine. But she was tired of his help.

"All right, then," he said, and he was being humorous, *that voice,* so much like he was winking conspiratorially. She could not stand people who spoke like that. People who made fun of everything. People who love life. If only he'd let her *go* sometimes, instead of following after her like a yappy dog.

"I am not so far gone," she told him, "that I can't walk by myself. You know that, don't you?"

"Oh, Irene, I was trying to be helpful."

"Don't think me ungrateful. You and Gretchen have been kind, since the accident. More than kind. But I don't want kindness, not anymore." She had given up on direct sarcasm, and never thought he would get it, anyway. Why couldn't he just let her go?

"You're almost all healed." He reached over and touched around her face. Irene gasped. He was always close to touching her, and *there* of all places, but he had never accomplished more than the slightest graze. She stood still as if he were pulling a stray hair from her forehead. He began reading her scars the way blind people read books in Braille. His fingers were soft along the place where the skin had bubbled and obscured the vision of her left eye. Why did his fingers seem so warm, when she knew him to be so cold, so empty? Was he laughing at her, the way he laughed at the whole of creation?

But his eyes were closed. He was really *feeling* her, and she felt like he was violating her face. But it would be nothing to him. William violated people.

Finally, he removed his hand. "Does it hurt?"

"Not now. Like a headache, sometimes, but the pills take care of that, but please, let's not talk about it, I feel all talked out, and I see it in the mirror every morning, so I don't find it interesting." Would that shut him up? She would like to just have a nice day and watch the children in the schoolyard.

"God loves you, you know, Irene. He really does, and in His infinite wisdom," and he would've gone on with his smug little litany, too.

But she spat at him, "I don't care for your God, William, and I don't care for you. I was going to spend the day alone, in my own way, and you have to come along with your almighty creator and ruin everything once again."

"I know you don't mean that," he whispered, like a hurt child. "I know you're saying it because of great pain."

"You," she said, "you are my great pain. You and your miracles."

He was walking several steps behind her, and she thought of trying to lose him in the village, but she really must go and see the children when they went out to the playground. She must not miss them. Perhaps she'd stop in for a cup of coffee, but only for a minute, because the children would be waiting to see her. Only the children knew how to treat her, how to respect her wishes. They had almost come through for her last time: their tiny hands, so willing, so lovely. It was because children knew things instinctively, they had gut reactions, they were so close to the real pulse of life. Grownups had lost it all, and certainly men like this William person that Gretchen had married were so out of touch, so *clueless*, that everything was like a car: maintenance and repair, tinkering around with things that were best left to the junkyard. And always the male need for possession, possession. *Well, I do not belong to you.*

She limped another quarter mile through the village, and it was empty. It had been mostly empty when she and Gretchen had been girls, and it was empty when they were in their twenties and thirties, and now it was desolate. She had wanted to leave the village for as long as she could remember, but she'd never had the nerve. Now she knew of only one route, and damn him, he was going to shadow her.

The sunlight was flat and nothing escaped it: she saw her reflection in the secondhand bookstore window. The scars weren't healing at all, they were simply drying. Her mouth looked terrible, and she couldn't bring herself to look at her jaw. Her hair was mostly gone, but the scarf hid that. The clerk in the bookstore was pretending not to stare at her from behind his counter, but she saw him stealing glances. *I don't mind*, she thought, nodding to him, *let this be a lesson to you. When it's time, it's time.*

William was behind her. She saw his reflection. "My sister told me once that life was precious," Irene said aloud, knowing he would hear her, "and I believed her. But she meant something different than this."

"Life is the greatest gift," he said. He sometimes had a voice like nails on wood, and in the county they said he had a voice like thunder, but he sounded to her most like teeth grinding. Nothing more than teeth, one bone wearing away at another.

She turned to face him. She counted to ten, silently. Her tongue went dry in her mouth. Sometimes, yes, she was at a loss for words. "I am going to have some coffee, and I want to be alone."

He said nothing, and she walked on down the sidewalk, trying to stay in the shade. She passed Fred Smith, whom she hadn't seen since just after the accident when the town meeting was called, and he actually tipped his baseball cap to her, which seemed a rather pleasant gallantry, considering what he'd said about her in the past. *"Way I see it, you belong somewhere between a freak show and a wienie roast," Fred had muttered from the safety of his pick-up truck, but she hadn't blamed him because he was right.* "Well, hey, Miz Hart," he said this time, but he didn't look at her, not directly. Her shoes, yes, but not her face. She didn't blame him: she was surprised that the young man in the bookstore had tried. *They're all afraid they're going to turn to stone.*

She went past him, into the Five & Dime, but not before she heard Fred say, more stiffly than when he'd greeted her, "Hello, preacher."

And William's absurdly heartfelt reply, "This is the day the Lord has made, Fred, rejoice."

"Yeah, well…" Fred's voice died like the wind had died, too.

The lunch counter was grease-spattered and vacant, as it usually was on Thursdays. Ever since the freeway had been built closer to Blowing Rock, the village didn't even have the trucks coming through. *As if the world knew not to come through here. Like it's a cursed place. Unclean, like in biblical days.* Jeannie Stamp came out from the washroom and leaned over the counter, nodding when Irene sat on the stool.

"It's dying, all my business is gone, just about," Jeannie said as she poured out the coffee. "Black, you like it? I told that old fart Harry to make sure the county money got thrown our way, but he said wait wait, and look what's happened now we been waiting long enough, we ain't even on the map. Used to be, ten, twelve people in here by noon, and now, just you and me, Renie." Jeannie never looked at her directly, either, but Jeannie was always nicer than the rest of the village. She had been to school with Jeannie, and had never thought in all her youth that she would ever depend upon her for friendship, but it was the best that was offered these days.

"I'm going to the school," Irene told her, leaning her elbows on the counter, sipping her coffee. It was lukewarm and smelled like dirty socks, but this was the only place to get coffee in town since the trouble when they'd burned down the ice cream shop. It was the older kids, just going crazy and setting fire to things. Even the teenagers knew when something was wrong, when things needed to be torn down. *Maybe the whole village will go. If I can't leave, maybe it will leave me.*

"You think that's a smart move?"

Irene shrugged. "What's smart?"

"School. All them kids I heard about the other day. What happened."

"*Almost* happened, *almost.*"

"Well, it could."

"Yes, hon, it could," Irene set the half-empty cup down and could not decide if she should go out in the summer heat again and face Gretchen's husband, or if she should wait another fifteen minutes. The children would be in the playground soon, and if she didn't see them today, it would be tomorrow, and if it didn't happen today, they might get used to her presence and never do what she knew they wanted to, never be free to be children, *just be children.* Less than twenty children left in the village at all.

"Preacher's talked about the Lord in our lives," Jeannie said. "He says we should be grateful, that God shines His light on us, even here, to the lowliest."

I am so tired of this fundamentalist town. Irene felt a headache coming on, and all her pills were back at the house, so the headache would just have to hammer away at her. *Gretchen and I should've left long ago, back when we had choices, back when we wanted to get out in the world. I should've learned to drive when I was in my twenties. Not wait until I was forty-six and in a stickshift with a sixteen-year-old. But they would've laughed at me. Luke was the only one who could teach me, the only one I could trust not to tell William, or even Gretchen. They would've laughed, and then he would've wondered why I wanted to leave so badly, and he would've stopped it. He did stop it. And I should never have been pulled from the car. Not back to this godforsaken place.* "If that's true, Jeannie, about God, what about Luke?"

43

Jeannie looked like a girl who had been scolded. "That's different. Preacher says God helps those He chooses."

"Who chooses? God, or the preacher?"

"Preacher don't have a choice, way I see it. He just got the gift. Always been miracles, always will be. Ain't you happy, being so special and all?"

Irene put two quarters on the counter. "Look me in the eye and ask me that."

"Oh," Jeannie said, "you know I can't do that. You know what happens. You don't want it to happen, do you?"

Irene waved to William as she came back out, into the sunlight. No one else was on the street, and there he was with his grin, his hopeful grin, like a dog waiting to be kicked. He had that charm, that she found so dull, but in a village like this one, he would be king, he would be adored, and so he had come here and found Gretchen. He was the big fish in the small pond. He was Preacher, and this was his Flock. She had once liked him, a little, but not at all since the accident. She had not even been feeling kindly towards her sister. "I don't understand you," she'd told Gretchen, "why do you even want me here? Isn't it painful?" But Gretchen was so brainwashed by this William person, by his laying on of hands and speaking in tongues, that she was not really the same girl that Irene had grown up with. Gretchen could not see her way out of things, never had been able to; for Gretchen, things were the way they were. Only once had Gretchen asked her about that day, about what happened. And Irene had pretended to have forgotten, as if the accident and the darkness had wiped it away.

"Irene," William called out, his hands tucked almost sheepishly in his pockets; he was rocking back and forth on his heels, "I was afraid I'd lost you." He stepped into the street and crossed over to her. He walked like a boy, all bounce and uncertainty.

"I'm going to see the children."

"I like walking with you."

"Do what you like," she closed her eyes and he touched her elbow with his hand. The bone was broken there, and had not healed where it poked out from her skin. She could move it fine, but she didn't like to be reminded of it. She wondered how he could touch her the way he did; she sensed his discomfort each time he was close, but now, this day, he seemed more relaxed, as if he were no longer fearful of what had happened to her body. She often wondered: *Do you like what you see? Does it please you to be so close to this monster? Do you love life this much, even when it looks this way?* But she had never been beautiful; Gretchen was always the pretty one, which bothered her until the accident, because afterwards, Irene was happy with Gretchen's beauty. She felt her little sister *should* be the lovely one, the one whose flesh was pleasant and fragrant and satisfying. Irene needed no beauty, she needed nothing. What she longed for was death, truly, and in death, an escape from this ravaged flesh.

"You're beautiful in God's eyes," he said, his breath like a warm humid wind along her neck.

"You should have left me."

"I couldn't."

"The children, the ones in the ice cream shop. Told me."

"Liars."

"You let him die."

"Those children are liars."

"Your own son."

"God called me to you. To save you."

"But Luke was still *alive*. You could've saved him," she was exasperated. He was so dense, he was so stupid. He only saw what he wanted to see. She moaned in frustration, wanting to hit him as hard as she could. "I was dead. Why can't you just let me go?"

The schoolyard was empty, and she went to sit on a swing. Of course, he followed her, but he hadn't said a word, so she acted as if he were not there. The school was small, and was made up of six rooms; the village had always been a small one, and the population had only diminished over the years. *This would be a place for miracles*. She smelled the dying honeysuckles, the drying grass. She saw their faces in the schoolroom windows, staring and pointing, some calling. She knew their parents. Places like this, you know everyone, you had no secrets.

"It could happen again," he said, and she tried to will him away, but he was standing beside the chain link fence near the Monkey Bars. "You should come home with me now."

When she didn't respond, he said, "You want it to happen, don't you?"

Irene watched the children in the windows: some of them had been at the ice cream shop when the car had smashed into the truck, and the fire had started. She remembered their faces, fascinated, their screaming, excited voices, as they watched the burning wreck. Her last sight had been of them holding their ice cream cones, and she had felt a peace, even in the pain of death, the numbing cold of fire, a peace from those lovely faces, knowing that the world would pass on without her there, that she would leave them, and they would still eat ice cream, and still talk out of turn, and still grow up into the world without some woman they barely knew by sight named Irene Hart who had stayed her whole dull life in the village. Her last thought had been, *children*. It had been a death she enjoyed, and the suffering had only come when she was pulled from the darkness, and opened her eyes to hear him, this man that Gretchen had married, saying, "And as Christ brought Lazarus from the dead, so I call His servant, Irene Hart, come, come to us, live again in the flesh with us."

Irene sat on the swing and began crying. She felt the weight of his hand on her shoulder. She could not help herself, and in spite of her repulsion at his touch, she asked, "Children are closer to God, aren't they? Closer than us? 'Suffer the little children to come unto me,' isn't that the quote?"

"God is close to all of us. All who believe, anyway."

"Oh," she stopped crying and laughed. He came and stood in front of her. She hadn't laughed in ages, and he smiled, probably thinking he was finally seeing the light within her. "Oh, that explains it, *that's it*. It's not God who lifted me up from the burning car, it's something else entirely. It was Luke who God took care of, not me. I get it now, oh, William, you should've told me at the time. It was Luke that God loved, not me."

"Irene, you don't know what you're saying."

"Well, if it's not true, why didn't you save your son? Why did you raise me up?"

William looked her in the eye, and she almost fainted because no one had done that since the accident. He whispered something, but she knew it before he whispered it, and she wanted to stop up his mouth before the words had formed, "Because I love you," and she knew he was ashamed and humiliated to have to say it in a schoolyard, in the light of day. *"Ever since I saw you, I loved you. I want to be near you. I never want to let you go."*

So that was it. That was all.

Love.

"You go home now," she said softly, "you go home now." She turned away from him, swinging to the side, her heels scraping the dirt, happy that he had let that awful feeling out, what he called love, out to evaporate in the shimmering heat of August. It had burned all these years within him, and she had been singed by his fire. She had

46

not known what to call it, and she knew that it was not love, not love at all, but desire. Had it been only his desire that had brought her back from the dead? *Well*, she thought, *let desire die, then, and let it have no resurrection.*

"I'll see you at supper," he said, and she heard his footsteps on the soft grass as he headed back to the street.

The swing sagged beneath her weight: *it was made for a child and I am not meant to be here. The children will know, too*, she thought.

The bell rang, and the children poured out onto the playground, and some saw her and some were involved in their games. Children like golden light on the grassy field, coming slowly, curiously towards her. They called her the names she knew children called, their small, delicate hands, and their wondrous faces, their perfect thoughts. She had come before, and they had been close to it, but they had not done what they longed to do. Their hands, their eyes, their instinct so much a part of their flesh.

But today.

Today.

One of the little boys was bold, she thought he must be twelve, and he came up and stared at her fiercely. "You're ugly," he said, "my daddy said you should be dead. You look dead. You even smell dead."

She looked him in the eye, and did not even flinch.

One of the children behind this boy picked up a small stone and threw it at her, hitting her just above her left eye. Irene smiled, *the children know what to do, they are closer to things, to nature.*

She felt another stone, this one larger, hit the back of her head, and then she was surrounded by beautiful, joyful children, and she waited for the darkness as they looked her in the eye and knew what she was.

Sweet darkness blossomed from stones.

It was later, when she thought the Kingdom was opening for her that she regained sight, and she welcomed whatever Kingdom there was, whatever light there was as the place where she belonged, but it was nothing other than the beam of a flashlight, and the lid of a

47

coffin opening, and a madman above her who had scrambled in the earth to dig up a grave, only to say, "Come to us, live again in the flesh with us."

48

Damned If You Do

Calhoun was sweating up a storm, and it was only ten, but this was La Mesa in summer, and he actually found the talk radio soothing while he worked. He could hear, beyond the chattering radio, the children in the schoolyard across the street, all yelling and pounding the blacktop while they played dodgeball. He could smell the jaw-aching sweet stink of the fat lemons in the trees that Patsy had planted when they'd first moved into the bungalow, ten years before. The old shepherd, Vix, was chewing on a lemon, which made the dog whine with sour hurt as the juice got into his gums — and still, he wouldn't let go of a lemon once he got hold of it.

Cal's beard itched, too, another annoyance on a particularly annoying day, and his shovel struck the flat rock again, or maybe it was a pipe this time, for sure the sewage system ran this way and that across the back of the property, and who the hell knew why since the toilets were always backing up, and the garbage disposal ran rusty brown nine times out of ten.

"Mother—" he began, and then held his tongue, laughed because Patsy didn't like strong language or strong drink in her house.

Her house.

It's my house as well as yours.

He had been digging for twenty minutes—the ground was dry and hard, and there weren't many places left.

Not that he'd left any markers, but he had a memory like a trap, and once he saw something, he always remembered it.

I remember you, you and you, he thought, blinking his eyes in the sun, looking from one patch of garden to another, or there, in the mulch pile.

He went back in for a Pepsi and one last piece of apple pie—she baked it the night before, and he had had one too many pieces, but he loved her pies. The radio was louder in the kitchen, echoing, and a man was on it talking about his problems with his wife, and how he wanted to leave but couldn't because he loved her.

The call-in DJ, who claimed to be a therapist, although she doled out advice about as bad as any Cal had ever heard, the Radio Lady, as Patsy called her, said, "Love is not just a state of being, but an active, everyday thing, you know—know what I mean? Like you maintain your house and your car, you also have to everyday maintain your relationship, like a tune-up...."

Patsy always had that thing blaring, always talk radio, from morning til night til morning.

The Radio Lady jabbering, nattering, bantering.

He wanted to turn it off, but if he did then they'd know.

The neighbors.

They'd know.

Old Fat Broad over the high wall with her arms of beef and face of jug, always leaning over and saying, "Whatcha doin'?" Or that brat of hers trying to get over to pick lemons, looking in the windows, trying to slide through the casement windows into his woodshop.

Mr. Erickson, who Patsy called Ear-Ache, complaining about the volume of the radio, wouldn't he think it strange when the radio went off? Ear-Ache once came over to be neighborly, and asked Cal, "So, you're retired now, what was your business, anyway?"

Damned If You Do

And Cal had told the truth, although he sometimes lied because he hated when people pried, "I used to be a principal of a school down in Dauber's Mill, back before they consolidated. I liked teaching better, more hands-on work, but they needed a principal more than they needed a woodshop teacher, so I had at it for a good fifteen years."

Ear-Ache and Fat Broad, eyes, ears and mind on him all the time, wondering if they were looking, if they were watching.

He never did his work at midnight or in the wee morning hours, because he had learned in his sixty-three years that you could do anything you wanted in life as long as you did it in broad daylight, when nobody believed what they saw, anyway.

He took a bite of pie and a swig of soda, and looked out across the lawn at the shallow trench he had begun.

Maybe I'll just put her with that pig-tailly girl, in the mulch.

The problem with the mulch pile, or with any mulch pile, is you couldn't put anything salty in it or you'd ruin it for sure. No bacon drippings, no skin, nothing that had a high salt content. The pig-tailly girl was easy enough to scrape, and even though she still had plenty of salt in her, he just had to bury her deep and hope for the best. Dead mice you could put on the mulch, and even dead birds, but nothing too much larger or you had a pile of shit that was just a pile of shit.

Cal set the can of soda down, stroked his walrus moustache, scratched his chest through his sweat-stained t-shirt.

Can't scrape Patsy, though. Can't do it.

Take much too long, and then, I'd have to flush too much scrapings. More back up in the toilets, maybe too much, and maybe they'd have to come out and dig up the lawn to check on the sewage pipes, and then what?

"No more woodshop, for sure," he said aloud.

He whistled for Vix to come inside, and then he turned and went down the narrow hallway with its family pictures tattooed on the wall, all the kids they'd had in all those years. The radio noise got louder, this time just a commercial. He hated the way on T.V. and radio, how they made the commercials louder than the shows.

They were advertising for Squeaky Kleen, a deodorant. Cal didn't use deodorants, although he made an excellent natural soap in his woodshop, using an old recipe he'd found in a book from the turn of the century. It was a little bit of lye and a little bit of animal fat, and it got skin so clean it practically took the hair right off, with a fresh smell, like children on their birthdays.

He went into Patsy's room—they had separate rooms, ever since he'd retired, because she wouldn't put up with his night fears anymore. So he had the little guestroom, what used to be the nursery off the second bathroom, and she kept the master bedroom that looked out over the backyard. She was simple in her tastes, which is what he always liked about her, anyway, and difficult in her emotions. She had a bed, a table with a reading light, her mother's rocking chair, and the radio. It was an old one, a big jobbie that she'd had since the fifties, hell, it took four big fat batteries to run it, and like his old Royal typewriter, she had it repaired constantly rather than replace it with something newer and easier to use.

On the radio, a woman began crying, and the dj-lady said, "It's all right, it's good to cry, hey, I'd cry, too, if that happened to me. But you do have a choice, sweetie, you can walk right out that door and get a life! It's the thing to do in the '90s, get...a...life. It's easy. When you do it, you'll see. You'll call a friend, or a family member, and see if you can't stay with them for awhile, until you've got your feet on the ground, and then you'll get a life. Sound good?"

The woman on the line said, "I guess. I thought this *was* my life."

"What you described is not a life, I know it hurts to hear this, but it's why you called in, isn't it? It's not a life, I repeat. A life is something you participate in and draw some satisfaction from. Capiche?"

Cal wanted to shut that damn radio off more than anything, but he knew if he did, someone somewhere nearby would think something, would wonder about something, might even look in a window somewhere.

Patsy's eyes were wide, but the tape had held on her mouth. The wire around her ankles had cut into the flesh, but not too far, and they held well, strung around the frame of the rocker. She'd exhausted herself all night rocking back and forth, trying to get over to the window; he'd had to pick her up twice between eleven and two when she'd spilled forward and slammed her head into the parquet. He'd wiped the blood from her nose, and kissed at her tears, and used his heart to try and unscramble a message to her, to help explain what he was doing and why he had to, but she was too busy listening to talk radio. She never got the messages he sent from his heart, but he always followed his heart and tried to get her to understand the direction it took him. It was no use talking to her, because she only understood normal everyday problems and emotions, not the kind that made a man do what he had to do, a place beyond words, a territory of pure obligation.

Maybe if she still went to her job downtown, maybe she never would've noticed.

But she, too, had retired, just had the retirement party at the Sportsman's Lodge down on Edison and Fourth last Friday night. He was going to wait until she went to run some errands or whatever— and maybe if she hadn't given up liquor so suddenly, and gotten religion in one lightning bolt of revelation, maybe she would've been so self-involved she would've missed what he did.

What he'd been doing for twenty-five years.

He remembered his mother's words, so many years back, on her death-bed. Her advice, her comfort. He repeated them, whispering, although Patsy would not hear them, she would hear the radio, radio, nothing but radio. "I know it's terrible to watch your mother die like this, Cal. But far worse is it for me to go to my glory without knowing that you are taken care of. I want you to be happy, but I know the pain life brings. We've all had it visited upon us. Happy is the man who buries his own children, for in his pain, in his burden, is the care and comfort that he laid them to rest before their spirits could be crushed."

The sunlight burned the windowsill, beneath the translucent shade, and he heard old Vix whining from the kitchen—still chewing that lemon.

Patsy smelled, and her face glowed with sweat.

Nine children in twenty-five years.

Someone was bound to find out, one day, but he never imagined it would be his wife. She had used the soap, she had used the candles, she had blown on the whistle he made out of bone, the whistle with the little sparrow carved into the side, the whistle like ivory. She had stood by him when he spoke with the police about each one running away, about the troubles boys and girls like that faced, not feeling that their biological parents had claimed them, not feeling at home, not feeling safe.

Not feeling cared for.

On the radio, a teen-aged girl giggled and talked about not having her first period until she was sixteen.

He had promised Patsy, too, that he would care for her, until death. Perhaps this was Providence stepping in and making sure he was as good as his word, although he didn't believe in fate or God or karma.

Soon, he'd have to stop old Vix's breath, too, for what would a dog do if his master were to die?

I've been dying for years, Patsy, his heart said, and I've cared for my own.

It wasn't fun, never, he wasn't one of those who enjoyed doing his duty. It was like being a soldier, shooting his brother, but the weight of his obligation was great.

His mother, too, he had taken care of her in her last moments.

He had no choice, back then, when he was sixteen, because she had been the one with the gun in her hand, and it had taken a good half-hour to wrestle it from her.

Mother was trying to take care of him, but Cal had known, even then, that it was a man's job. He knew he was damned, but it was a damned if you do, damned if you don't sort of proposition when you came into this world.

Patsy's eyes were bulging, and he never liked to see her worried or in pain, but he had wanted to give her time to think it over and make her peace. Life is meant to work out the way it works itself out, and maybe Patsy, maybe she would die within the next decade

54

anyway, and if something happened to him, who would care for her?

The weight of duty was heavy, for sure.

The Radio Lady said, "We are given free choice when it comes to our own behavior, and we can only change someone else insofar as we can change ourselves, you know?"

He looked around for her needles, the long thick ones.

He didn't like to prolong pain, and he remembered how peaceful his mother had been, how the gasp from her bosom, and the stench, and the *relief* in the act itself, were like opening a sewer pipe of flesh to release gas and what was trapped inside the gutter of the body.

It was noon before her heart stopped, and nearly one when he'd taken her down to his woodshop. He laid her across the bench, her neck in a vise because it helped keep the rest of the body stable if the spine held.

Then he went to work, and he cried, as he always did, and he drowned out the sound of talk radio with his instruments.

The sky clouded over by two-thirty. The children were let out of school, and he had to wait until the last yellow bus took off, and the last child had finished walking home, peeking over the wall to taunt Vix into barking, before he could go out and dig some more. He went to the mulch pile, which was still moist and humid with dead grass and sour milk and the fish heads from Tuesday's supper. Vix lay down beside him, and let a lemon roll from his mouth. The old dog looked at the lemon, and pawed it. Cal noticed there were ants crawling across it.

He bent over, his back hurt, picked it up, was about to toss the rotting, chewed, ant-cursed lemon into Fat Broad's yard, when he figured, what the hell, and dumped it down beside him. Then he pitched the shovel in deep, trying to keep in mind where he'd buried the pig-tailly girl from two years back. When he felt he had dug

55

down far enough, he went and got several of Patsy's parcels, and plopped them in, and then checked the wall for a spy, saw no one, and went and got the rest.

Vix sniffed the hole he'd dug, but the dog was more attached to lemons than anything else out in the yard. "Find another one, Vix, this one," Cal nudged the rotting lemon by his foot, "this one's all wormy. Good boy."

He took the radio, too, shut it off, finally, and dropped it in, kicked in the wormy lemon and some fish heads, and covered the whole mess up.

Then he went into the kitchen, sat at the small glass table, and actually missed the sound of talk radio for once in his life. He went and turned on the little Japanese radio he'd bought for Patsy, the one she'd never used. He turned it to the talk radio station, and kept the volume up.

"I just loved that last call—didn't you?" The Radio Lady said, "It's a day brightener to hear something like that in these times. Imagine, rescuing a cat and someone's grandmother in the same hour. Gosh, sometimes life is difficult, but it's always fascinating isn't it?"

Cal looked at the telephone hanging from the wall.

At the radio.

Wonder if Patsy ever called in.

She wasn't one for discussing her life.

Miss her, even so.

The Radio Lady announced the number to call in, and Cal went and dialed it.

After seven rings, a man picked up, and Cal hung up quickly.

Then he dialed again, got the man who mentioned he was screening calls, and asked Cal what his problem was.

"It's about my wife and kids. I have trouble, sometimes, taking care of them."

The man on the phone told him he'd be on in about two minutes.

Two minutes turned to four, when the Radio Lady came on. Cal had to turn the radio down to hear her. "What can I help you with?"

"Well," he said, and then thought he might hang up.

"Don't be shy," she said.

"I've been listening to you for a long time. Years."

"Well, I've been here four years so far, so thanks for the compliment."

"Hmm. I thought it was longer. Well, it's about my wife and my kids."

"Is it good or bad?"

"Neither. Just about life. What I've learned. I'm sixty-three, you know."

"Congratulations. Hey, isn't it great that you people still call in?"

"My wife, I miss her, and the kids. Most of the kids."

"How many do you have?"

"Nine."

"Holy cow, nine kids. And you raised them all?"

"I cared for each and every last one of them to the best of my ability."

"Well, you deserve a pat on the back for that. These days, too many people are abandoning their children."

"That's right," Cal said, "most of my kids were like that. Foster kids. But my wife and I took them in. Loved them. Gave them a home. And I fulfilled my obligation to them, too."

"I wish I could meet a man like you," the Radio Lady said, "I'll bet a *lot* of women in my audience would. So what are you calling about, you catch?"

Cal paused. "I'm tired of burying them. I miss them."

The Radio Lady said nothing.

Cal said, "Oh, they live on, in things, in day-to-day objects, when I wash sometimes, I can smell their skin. Fresh. So fresh, the way only a child can smell."

The Radio Lady said nothing.

And then, Cal realized why.

She was crying. "Oh, you poor wonderful man, God bless you, God bless you."

"Thank you," Cal said, and hung up.

He went and turned off the little Japanese radio. He couldn't cry anymore. Except for taking care of Vix, he had fulfilled his obligations. He just couldn't take care of Vix, not yet.

In the morning, the roses needed hosing down because he had been hoping it would rain and had left them dry for days. He washed with the sunken-eyed boy soap, and remembered the tight little curl to the child's fingers (although he couldn't for the life of him remember names much anymore). Then he went outside, turned the hose on, and sprayed down Vix while he flooded the roses. Ants crawled out from the soaked earth, and crawled up the garden wall. Fat Broad was out in a muumuu and barbed-wire curlers with her yorkshire terrier, getting the ball of stringy fur to yap, yap. Before he could take cover, she'd spotted him, and called out, "Your wife—is she all right?"

Cal kept the hose spraying, and pretended not to hear.

She thinks I'm ancient, so being deaf isn't much of a stretch.

Fat Broad, and her yorkie, toddled over to the wall, and he smiled, and then dropped the smile like a turd.

She said, "I don't hear the radio. The talk shows."

"Radio broke. Wife won't listen to any other radio. She's a peculiar woman. Thirty-five years of marriage."

"I'm not surprised it broke. Good heavens, she played it night and day. You must be happy it broke."

He scrunched up his face angrily. "Not at all, woman. I was used to it."

"Well, it's nice to have the quiet so I can hear my wind chimes."

"Doesn't get too windy," Cal said, stepping as far from the wall as he could without getting too muddy in the puddles he'd created with the garden hose. Vix put his forepaws up on the wall and began barking at Fat Broad and her yorkie, so she went back to her own business.

He went and checked the bougainvillea, which hadn't been growing well this year, although the Mexican Trumpet Vine was in full bloom, with hummingbirds darting in and out of its blossoms.

I take care of my own. My family, my garden.
My obligations.

Oh, but he missed them, their kisses, their hands, their love.

Even his mother, with that friendship of blood that transcended all others.

It's over, he thought. *It's done.*

Someone, in another yard, somewhere, he thought, *just beyond Fat Broad's turned up their radio loud as if to fill the void left by Patsy's blaster.*

He could faintly hear the Radio Lady say, "You're on the air, caller? You're on the air."

A child's voice said, "Hi...um...I don't know if I'm s'posed to call you...but I listen to you all the time."

The Radio Lady said something, although Cal couldn't quite hear it.

The boy said, "I ain't—I mean, I guess, I *haven't* ever called in. Not like this."

Another voice, a girl's, said, "Hello? Wow. This is cool. Hello? Is someone there?"

"You're talking with the Radio Lady," the other voice said, and although faint, Cal recognized it. It was Patsy.

He went and called Fat Broad back over to the wall. She came over, shuffling like she was all bound up inside that oversized dress, and curled up her nose at him like he stank.

"You hear that?" he asked her.

"What?"

"Listen," he held a finger to his lips.

Fat Broad was silent for a moment, cocking her head to the side like she was trying to roll that last marble right out from her eardrum.

Another boy, about six, said, "I scared."

The girl, the pig-tailly girl, Cal was sure, said, "Don't be scared. We're all taken care of. Aren't we?"

The Radio Lady said, "That we are."

Fat Broad interrupted Cal's listening, "I don't hear nothing. Is it a siren or something? If you tell me what I'm listening for, maybe I can hear it."

Cal was angry that she was talking so much while the talk radio was going on. "No," he said. "I won't tell you. If you don't hear it, I won't."

"I hear things sometimes," Fat Broad said, nodding, "maybe you're hearing a ghost."

Cal looked at her sharply. "I don't believe in ghosts."

"I don't mean that kind, I mean like on T.V. when you have a ghost image. Or now that your wife's radio broke, you're so used to hearing it, that you still think it's playing." But the woman saw that Cal was paying no attention to her, so she tramped across her own pansy bed to reprimand her son for leaving his trike out overnight.

Cal listened, and noticed that Vix, covered with mud in the garden, seemed to be listening, too.

He couldn't fall asleep. He went to Patsy's room and rocked back and forth in the chair, smelling her smell. He had the curtains pulled to the window, and he looked out at the backyard. The radio had gotten louder, just a bit, but still not to the volume it had been up to when Patsy had been around. He listened to each of his nine children talk with their mother, and he listened to her words of comfort, but he was still very sad.

At least I have one comfort, he thought, *at least I can hear them.*

And then, around three a.m., just as he was nodding off, he heard a voice on the radio which did not belong to any of his children, nor to his wife.

It was a woman with such an impediment to her speech, it sounded like a toad was sitting beneath her tongue. "Ca-hoo, Ca-hoo, heh-up mee, Ca-hoo."

He got out of the rocker and went to the window. He rolled the side windows open wider, and smelled the sweet rosewater and the scent of moist earth.

"Mother?" he asked, peering out into the dark.

"Cay-uh, cay-uh," she said, and then was lost in the static of the radio.

She had said, "Care," he was sure.

Care.

Even though she wasn't buried in the yard, but in a cemetery twenty-five miles away, she had traveled through the groundwaves, through the sewage pipes of the dead to speak to him.

He knew why her voice was strange, because of what he'd had to do to her mouth.

He wished now he hadn't. He would like to understand her better, for she was a person of enormous wisdom.

He watched the darkness, listening for her voice again on the radio, but all was silent.

He drank several shots of whiskey, not his style at all, and slept late. He dreamed of the sound of machines roaring and dogs barking, and awoke at nine-thirty when someone tapped him on the shoulder.

He smelled mud and flowers, and looked into the empty eyes of his mother, her face dripping with mud and sewage. She opened her scarred mouth, the one that had burned so well when he stretched the electric cord across her lips, between her teeth, and switched on the juice. The scars took the form of a star pattern, and when she parted her lips, dry leaves and dead grass dropped out.

She took his hand, and led him to the woodshop, where the sound of talk radio drowned out the other sounds, the sounds of the care one human being shows for another.

The Radio Lady said, "Happy is the man who fulfills his obligations in this life."

61

THE PARTY

The knife went into his back, and he thought that it would hurt, but he had no pain. He wandered through the party, between the two women who laughed at each other's jokes, and alongside the old man who conducted a very serious conversation with a younger man who seemed too drunk to understand. The numbness along his spine made him drop. He crawled between legs, wondering if the sight of shiny black shoes would be the last thing he would see before he died.

Then, one of the laughing women with the gin breath and the high forehead crouched down next to him. She put her hand on his shoulder, still giggling from a joke. He felt another knife go into his back. The force pushed him hard into the carpet, and he turned on his side just in time to see the old man lean over him, pressing the edge of a blade between his ribs.

The old man needed help getting up.

Not feeling pain but just a coldness. The laughing woman took a middle-aged man's hand who helped her up. He had seconds, perhaps, left of life, and he saw, standing over by the mirror, near the window, between the bar and the table of food, his oldest friend in the world, who nursed a drink and just watched him. He saw a little sadness in his friend's eyes. His friend turned to talk to a young woman in black slacks and a tan sleeveless top, and the party continued.

Becoming Men

Becoming Men was originally published in an anthology called
Subterranean Gallery. *There have been these boot camps for kids,
where parents who can't control their kids and feel their kids need
the toughest of tough love, send their kids to be in a genuine working
prison of sorts. Perhaps these are good things. I don't know. When
I was a kid, I was sent off to a really tough basketball camp. I'm
sure it was fun for the kids who loved basketball. In fact, I had loved
basketball before I arrived there. By the end of my time at this camp,
I hated the sport. And worse, I hated coaches. They were okay to
me, but I saw them victimize the so-called weakest of the group, and
it made me dislike men who used their authority to step on people
too young or inexperienced to fight back. I used the idea of this as a
backdrop for how we come to accept our own inner drives, for better
or worse.*

In the case of Ralph and his friends, it's for worse, of course.

It was like fire in his mind, in all their minds, it was a great
bonfire reaching up to the sky, and Ralph knew that when it reached
the sun, he'd wake up from it—a fever dream. The night had seemed
to last forever, and they would all remember it for years to come,

they knew, if there were years ahead of them and not mere hours. Shadows flickered around them, the darkness itself illuminated by a brilliant moon grown hazy with the canvas that stretched above their heads. The smells were sweat and farts and hidden tears—the fear was in all their mouths, in their nostrils, like smoke from a catching fire. The bunks and cots were shadowy with the other boys, some of them moaning in real or imagined pain, others huddled together like the small group Ralph found himself in, a circle of boys sitting up on two cots and sprawled on the wood floor of the Hut.

A match lit, the tiny yellow flame illuminated the circle of boys, casting their faces in flickering. It was like camp, that's what Ralph thought, it was like camp only it wasn't camp, it was the nightmare of what camp was to children much younger than them. Part of him felt as if he were still four years old and he'd been left all alone at the playground, his mother had not come to get him after school, and all the other children were gone, no one needed him enough to be there. No one wanted him enough. No one cared. But he was older now. He had to let the memory of that turn to ash. He needed to tell what had happened. He had to break the silence so the other boys around him could break theirs, too, so they could find relief from this night.

Ralph went first, his breath coming slowly because he still hadn't recovered from the way they'd held him down, his asthma had kicked in slightly and they'd taken away his inhaler so he had to be careful. Slow, deep breaths. His eyes hurt just from the memory of the interrogation's bright lights and then the bitter tears that followed his confession. Was he still crying? Even *he* wasn't sure, but he tried to hold it in as much as possible, to hold in the little boy inside him who threatened to burst out and show the others that he was what he'd always feared himself to be: a weakling. The darting matchlight slapped yellow war-paint on all of their features. They were Indians in a sweat lodge. He closed his eyes and began, "I had just barely gotten to sleep—halfway in a dream and it was all kind of like a dream when I heard all the shouting, it was my dad, he was shouting like crazy."

Becoming Men

Jesus DeMiranda, the smallest boy of thirteen that Ralph had ever seen, said nothing, but his eyes widened, and he had a curious curl to his lips like he was about to say something, even wanted to, but could not. There was something compelling to his face, something withdrawn yet very proud. Ralph tried not to only look at him, because it made him feel little and ready to break down crying again, so he laughed like it didn't matter, "And my dad is such a loud son of a bitch."

Jack jumped in, "My dad didn't say a word. The bastard."

Hugh coughed. "My dad went nuts, he was just shouting, and my mom was crying, but even when the big guy grabbed me—"

"The big black guy," Jack added, then glanced at the others. The match died. Another one burst to life immediately; Ralph and his matchbook again.

"A big white guy," Marsh said, slapping Jack across the top of the head.

"Yeah, a big white guy, wearing camouflage shit and his face was all green, it was freaky, I tell ya," Ralph continued, holding the piss-colored fire in his hands like a delicate small bird in front of the others so they could all see their own fear, "and I was so scared I pissed my underwear and my dad, when I saw him, he was practically crying but since I could tell they weren't beat up I knew somehow that they had something to do with this, and it had something to do with that thing with my cousin from three days before and maybe with the fire that burned down this old shack, but I never really thought they'd do something like this, I mean, shit, this kind of Nazi bullshit—"

"It's scary," Marsh said, and his voice seemed too small for his six-foot tall frame. He grasped his elbows, leaning forward on his knees. "I just smoked some pot. That was it. Not half as much as my friends."

"What did you do that got you sent here?" Ralph asked Jack.

A silence.

Match died.

"Ralph," someone said in the dark, Ralph wasn't sure who it was, but he waited in the dark for a moment because the ghosts of their faces still hung there, photographed by the last light of the match.

Scraped another one against the matchbook.

Marsh continued, "With me, I thought they'd killed my folks and my sister and they were gonna do something terrible to me. And then I wished it was a dream. All of it."

"They hit you hard?" Hugh asked, nodding towards him.

Marsh shrugged. "They hit me. That's all. I barely felt it by then. I just figured they were gonna kill me. I figured if I just concentrated or something it would all happen and then it would be over. I thought it was because of the time I bought pot and got more than I paid for. That's what I thought. I didn't even think. I just figured that was it. It was over."

"And it's worse than that," Jack said. "You know what I heard my mother say when they put the blindfold on me? I heard her say—"

"No one cares," Ralph spat. "They all lied."

The boys fell silent for a minute.

"I thought it was gonna be like ToughLove or something."

"They sold us up a river."

Jesus opened his mouth as if to speak, but closed it again. Fear had sealed his lips.

"They did it because they love me," Jack said, but he was crying, he was fourteen and crying like a baby and Ralph decided then and there that he didn't care what the others thought. He leaned over and threw his arm over Jack's shoulder. It reminded him of when his little brother got scared of lightning or of nightmares, and even though Jack was his age, it seemed okay, it seemed like it was the only thing to do. Jack leaned his head against Ralph's neck, and wept while the others watched, not shocked, not confused, but with longing for someone to let them cry on his shoulder, too.

Jesus DeMiranda wept, too, softly. Ralph asked him why, and he said it was because he was afraid of the dark. Ralph gave him one match to keep. "For an emergency," he said, and all the boys watched as the little DeMiranda boy put it in his pocket, as if the match were hope and someone needed to keep it.

Becoming Men

Ralph kept lighting his matches as other boys gathered around in the darkness and told their stories of woe, and wept, and gave up what fight they had in them.

By the time Ralph's last match had died, morning had come, and with it, no sound until the foghorn blasted its wake up call.

TO BE A MAN

YOU MUST KILL THE CHILD

YOU MUST BURY THE CHILD

YOU MUST GROW UP

YOU MUST ACCEPT RESPONSIBILITY FOR YOUR ACTIONS

YOU MUST TAKE ON THE RESPONSIBILITIES OF OTHERS

YOU MUST BURN

YOU MUST FREEZE

YOU MUST GIVE YOURSELF TO US

The words were emblazoned on the side of the barrack wall, and every morning, Ralph knew, he would see those words, every morning, no matter how hard he tried to resist them, they would enter his soul. In the line up, they had to shout out the words, they had to shout them out loud, louder, I can't hear you, louder, over and over until it seemed as if those words were God.

"Number one!" the big man named Cleft shouted so loud it rang in their ears, pounding his chest hard as if he were beating it into his heart, "I am your priest, your father, your only authority, understand? I am Sergeant Cleft, and my colleagues and I, your superiors in every way, are here to drill you until you break. We are not interested in bolstering your gutless egos. We are not interested in making men out of you. You are the worst kinds of boys imaginable, every one of your families has disowned you, and we intend to break you down as far as is humanly possible to go. Then, if you have what it takes, you will build yourself up from the tools we give you here. Right now, this is Hell to you. But when we are through grinding your bones and spirits, this will be heaven. I don't want any quitters, either. You never give up, do you understand me, grunts? Never ever give up! This isn't a camp for sissies and pansies, and you aren't here because you been good little boys! You got sent here because you are headed for destruction! You got sent here because you couldn't cut it like others your age! You got sent here before someone sent you to jail! Before you destroyed your families! Before you could keep up your stupid anti-social ways!" His barks sailed over them, for by dawn, even the terrified ones were ready to put up some resistance, even Ralph's tears were dry and he spent the time imagining how to escape from this island in the middle of nowhere, how to get a message out to the authorities that he'd been kidnapped against his will, and then he was going to sue his parents for kidnapping, endangerment, and trauma. He looked at Cleft with cold eyes, and wished the big man dead. Cleft was musclebound, large, a baton in his beltstrap, pepperspray too, and something that looked like a stungun looped at his back. Ralph glanced around at the others, the twenty-three boys, all with dark-encircled eyes, all looking scrawny from a night of no sleep and dreadful fear, and he shouted inside his mind. How could they do this? How could all these parents do this to their children? What kind of world was this?

Morning had come too soon, and they'd been roused and tossed in the open showers (like the Jews, Ralph thought remembering the show on the History channel, like the Jews being thrown in showers and gassed, or hosed down before they started on their back-breaking labor, treated not like people but like cattle), and then they all had been given uniforms, and the boys had complied. It struck Ralph as strange how everyone accepted it all; as if this was the Hell they were all consigned to, and there was no way around it. The uniforms were brown like shit, that's what Cleft had told them, "Like you, you are shit, and you will look like shit until we make men out of you!" Then no breakfast, but barrels of water just outside the showers, and each boy, if thirsty, had to stick his head in the barrel like an animal and drink. Some didn't, but Ralph did. He wanted water badly, he wanted to drink the entire barrel despite the other boys' spit he saw floating in it, and the insects that had fallen in. The bugs were everywhere, from sucking mosquitoes to huge dark winged beetles that flew at the screen door on the barracks. And what kind of island was it? Where? Was it the Caribbean? Ralph thought it might be off the coast of Mexico somewhere, something about the light of the sky, something about the water, but his experience was limited. He knew the island was flat where they stood, raised like a plateau. There were cliffs diving down to the sea, he'd seen them when the helicopter had brought him in the night, when the blindfold had slipped slightly and he'd glimpsed the rocky cliffs and the crashing waves far below.

"Grunt!" Cleft shouted, and Ralph looked up. Cleft pushed his way through the front line of boys in their shit-colored uniforms, and found him. Cleft looked like a parody of a Marine, a steroid joke, a pit bull-human love child, and when he stood right in front of Ralph, Ralph wished he would wake up. Just wake up, he told himself. It's a dream. It has to be a dream. Piss your pants. Roll out of bed.

Cleft barked, "You worthless sack of owl dung, you keep your eyes on me, you understand? I seen a lot of boys come through here, and you are the sorriest ass piece of shit I ever saw. You hear me?"

Ralph kept his gaze forward, staring at a place just below Cleft's eyebrows, not *in* the eyes, but between them.

"I said, you hear me?"

Ralph trembled slightly, feeling his knees buckle. Hunger grew from a place not in his gut, but in his extremities, his fingers, toes, the top of his head, it was like a spider tingling along his skin, squeezing his nerves. His mouth felt dry.

"I hear you like to set fires, Pig Boy," Cleft almost whispered, but a whisper that boomed across the heads of all the other boys. "I hear you did something really nasty to another boy back home. I heard you—" Ralph shut his eyes for a second and in his mind he was flying over all the others, he was going up to the cottony clouds. He felt hunger leave him, he felt tension leave him, he felt everything fly away from his body.

With a sickening feeling, he opened his wet eyes.

Then Cleft glanced down from Ralph's face to his chest, then his crotch. Cleft laughed, a nasty sound. "Baby Pig Boy here has pissed his panties!" Cleft clapped his hands together. "He's pissed his panties like a big Baby Pig Boy, haw! You can put out a lot of fires with that piss, can't you Pig Boy?"

Then, Cleft shoved him hard in the chest, so hard Ralph fell backwards on his ass. He looked up at the big man, the bulging muscles, the sharp crewcut, the hawk nose, and gleaming teeth. "Let me show you how to put out a fire, men!" Cleft laughed as he spoke, unzipping his pants and Ralph screeched at first, like an owl, as the piss hit his face. Cleft continued shouting, telling him that to be a man, one had to first prove himself worthy of manhood, one had to accept humiliation at the hands of one's superior, one had to take what one deserved whether one liked it or not, one had to know one's place—"You like to set things on fire, grunt, but you need a man to put out the fire inside you!"

Just kill me, Ralph thought. *Just kill me.*

We are just like the Jews in the concentration camps, Ralph thought, glancing to the others who still had their eyes forward, their lips drawn downward, looking scrawnier and weaker than boys of thirteen to sixteen should look, looking like they would all have been happy to not have Cleft pissing on *them*, happy that Ralph was the first sacrifice of the day, happy to just die.

Just die.

It became a routine that they neither looked forward to, nor complained about, and the others who had sat up with Ralph the first night never spoke together again. Ralph would give Marsh a knowing look, and Marsh would return it, but for a millisecond before his eyes glazed over in what Ralph came to think of as "Clefteye." It was the zombie-like way they were all getting, Ralph included. When he lay asleep in his lower bunk, he could hear Hugh weeping in his sleep, then whimpering like a puppy, and sometimes Ralph stayed up all night listening for Hugh to cry, and it would help him fall asleep if only for an hour or two. Food got better, but not good. From the first two days of water only, they went to bread and water. By the end of the first week, they were having beans, rice, water, bread, and an apple. By the second week, it was beans, rice, water, bread, milk, apple, and some tasteless fish. Ralph noticed that his diarrhea had stopped by the third week, as did most of the boys'.

Becoming Men

The labor was grueling, but Ralph didn't mind it because while he hacked at the logs, or while he chipped at stone with what seemed to be the most primitive of tools, he remembered his family and home and his dog, and it was, after awhile, almost like being with them until the workday was over. The maneuvers began at night. Cleft, and the six others who ran the camp, had them running obstacle courses in the stench of evening when the mosquitoes were at their worst, when the mud was hot and slick, when the sweat could almost speak as it ran down his back. Wriggling like snakes beneath barbed wire, climbing ropes to dizzying heights, leaping from those heights into mud, running across narrow, stripped logs, piled end to end, it all became second nature after the initial falls and screams. Foghorn, as they called a large boy in Hut D, fell and broke his leg the first day of the obstacle course, and Jesus, the little boy that Ralph had never heard say so much as a word, got cut on the barbed wire, badly, across his shoulders, and then got an infection when it went untreated. After the third week, none of the boys saw Jesus anymore. Some said he'd been sent back home. Some said he'd died. Some said he'd run off. Some said it was all bullshit and he was probably back with his dad in New York City, lucky bastard, with a scar on his shoulder, and an excuse for not being in Camp Hell.

73

Rumors circulated that Jack and Marsh had been caught jacking each other off. The next time Ralph saw them, he also noticed bruises around their eyes and on their arms. Boys had ganged up on them, but Ralph didn't want to know about it. He was somewhere else. He didn't need to be among any of them, he was in a place of family and fire in his head, and although his muscles felt like they were tearing open when he lay down in his bunk at night, he knew that he was growing stronger both inside and outside.

And then, one day, Jack came to him.

"Got any more matches?"

Ralph opened his eyes. It had to be four a.m., just an hour to First Call.

The shadow over him gradually revealed itself in the purple haze of pre-dawn.

"What the—"

"Matches?" Jack asked again. "You're like the fireboy, right?"

"No."

"Liar. Come on, wake up. We have something to show you."

"I don't care. Leave me alone." Ralph turned on his side, shutting his eyes.

"He pissed on you. Don't you hate him?"

Ralph kept his vision dark. If he didn't open his eyes, it might all go away. "I don't care."

"You will care," Jack said. The next thing Ralph knew, it was morning, the horn blasted, the rush of ice cold showers, the sting of harsh soap, the barrels of water and then chow. Out in the gravel pit, shoveling, someone tossed pebbles across Ralph's back. He looked over his shoulder.

"Leave me alone," Ralph spat, the dirt-sweat sliding across his eyes; he dropped his shovel, looking back at Jack.

"You set fires back home, I know that," Jack whispered. "We all know it. It's all right. It's what you love. Don't let them kill that. We need you."

"Yeah, well, we all did something. What did you do to get you sent here?"

Jack said nothing for a moment.

Then, "We found Jesus," Jack said, and tears erupted in his eyes. Ralph wanted to shout at him not to cry anymore, there was no reason to cry, that he was weak to cry, just like Cleft said—

Ralph asked, "Where is he?"

"Dead," Jack said. "They killed him. They killed him and they hid him so we couldn't find him. Did you know he was only ten years old?"

"Bullshit," Ralph gasped. "He's thirteen."

"Ten years old and his father sent him here after he left his mother. His father sent him because his father didn't give a damn about him. You, Ralph, you set fires. And me, I maybe did some stuff I'm not real proud of. But Jesus, all he did was get born in the wrong family. And they killed him."

Becoming Men

Ralph closed his eyes. Tried to conjure up the vision of his family and home again, and the beautiful fires he had set at the old shack in the woods, the fires that had made him feel weak and strong all at once and connected with the world. But only darkness filled his mind. Opened his eyes. Jack's face, the bruises lightening, his eyes deep and blue, the dark tan bringing out the depth of the color of those eyes, a God blue. "Dead?"

"Yep." Jack said this without any hostility.

We are all zombies here. "How?"

Jack glanced over at Red Chief and the Commodore, the two thugs disguised as Marine-types who stood above the gravel pit, barking at some of the slower boys. "Keep digging, and I'll tell you, but do you know what I think we're digging?"

Ralph cocked his head to the side, trying to guess.

"Our own graves."

"Me and Marsh been trying to find a way out every single night. We wait till three-thirty, when the goons are asleep with only one on watch, and we get mud all over us, and we do the snake thing and Marsh and me get away from the barracks until we go out on the island, and we see that there's no way anybody's getting off this island without killing themselves, that's why security ain't so tight. It's a nothing island, maybe two square miles at the most, with nothing. The thugs' huts are in the east, and between those and ours and the workpits, there ain't a hell of a whole lot. But we find this thin crack opening between these rocks just beyond the thug huts, and we squeeze in—that's all the bruises—"

"I thought you got beat up."

Jack held his temper. "That's what we said, dumbshit, so nobody would know."

"I thought you two...."

Jack cut in. "We spread that story, fool. So we squeeze through the opening, and it's too dark to see, and this cave that we're hoping will take us out ends within six feet of entering it, only we feel something there in the dark, we feel something all mushy and stinky and only when Marsh falls on it and screams does he realize it's a body."

It was Jesus DeMiranda, the littlest boy at camp, dead not from an infection but from something that smashed his hands up and his knees, too. Ralph heard the rest, tried to process it, but it made him sick. "Where the fuck are we?" he whispered, leaning in to Jack.

"All I know is, I think we're all dead."

"All?"

"I think," Jack said. "I think they're going to just kill all of us. I don't think any of us are leaving." Jack stuck four small rocks in the back of Ralph's shorts, and then put some in his own pockets. Ralph looked at him, but Jack betrayed nothing in his eyes. "Later. They'll be useful," Jack said.

"Just like the Concentration Camps," Ralph whispered, and then Commodore shouted at him, and he returned to shoveling while the blistering sun poured lava on his back.

"I said get up here, you worthless Pig Boy!" Commodore yelled.

By the time Ralph made it up from the pit, crawling along the edges, he had scraped his knees up badly, and he was out of breath.

"Something you want to share with the rest of us?" Commodore said, his eyes invisible behind his mirrored sunglasses. His head was completely shaved, and he had green camouflage make-up striping across his face. "I saw you chattering down there, Pig Boy."

"Don't call me that," Ralph coughed, his breathing becoming more tense.

"Something wrong?"

Ralph covered his mouth, hearing the balloon-hiss of air from his lungs. "Asthma," he gasped. "I don't have…my inhaler…."

"It's all in your tiny brain, Pig Boy, you don't need some inhaler like a mama's boy, you just need to focus. You need to be a man, Pig Boy," Commodore laughed, and shoved Ralph down in the dirt. Ralph felt his windpipe closing up, felt his lungs fight for air.

He could not even cough. His eyes watered up, and he opened his mouth, sucking at air.

Commodore lifted him up again, bringing his face in line with Ralph's. Eye to eye, Commodore snarled, "Breathe, damn you!"

Ralph gasped. He knew he would die. He knew his lungs would stop. His vision darkened until all he could see were the man's brown eyes. He thought of little Jesus, dead, his hands smashed into bloody clay. Dust seemed to fill his mouth.

"Breathe!" Commodore continued, and reached over, pressing his hand down hard on Ralph's chest. "You want to be a man, Pig Boy, you breathe like a man, open up those lungs, make 'em work," and suddenly, air whooshed into Ralph's mouth, he gulped, gulped again. The darkness at the edge of his vision erased itself into the light of day.

Ralph sucked at the air like he was starving for it.

"There," Commodore said, and pushed Ralph back down in the dirt. "You boys, you think you can create the world in your own image. That's your problem. You think you can keep from growing up. Well, growing up means accepting the burden just like the rest of us. Accept it, accept the truth, and you'll thrive. Keep doing what you've been doing, and you'll die."

Ralph sat on the ground, staring up at the man. The air tasted pure. He gulped it down, feeling his lungs burn.

TO BE A MAN

YOU MUST KILL THE CHILD

YOU MUST BURY THE CHILD

YOU MUST GROW UP

YOU MUST ACCEPT RESPONSIBILITY FOR YOUR ACTIONS

YOU MUST TAKE ON THE RESPONSIBILITIES OF OTHERS

YOU MUST BURN

YOU MUST FREEZE

YOU MUST GIVE YOURSELF TO US

They shouted it in the morning, still shivering from the icy waters that erased their dreams, standing in the shimmering day, a mirage of day, for in their hearts, they never felt dawn. At night, Last Call, the bells ringing three times, running for the piss trough, running for a last cold shower, running for two minutes in the latrine, and then Light's Out.

"He's under the Hut," Jack said. He'd gathered Hugh, Marsh, a boy named Gary, a boy named Lou, and Ralph wanted to see, too, to see if they were telling the truth about Jesus. At three a.m., they all hunkered down, crawling like it was another maneuver under barbed wire to get out of the Hut unnoticed; then under the Hut's raised floor, down a narrow tunnel that might've been dug out by jackals. Jack and Marsh had dug an entrance that led down into a larger hole, and there, in the dark, they all felt Jesus' body, smelled it, some vomited, others gagged. Ralph reached into the dead boy's pocket and drew out the last match, the one he'd given the little boy the first night they'd met to keep him from the dark.

Ralph struck the match against a rock, and it sputtered into crackling light.

They all looked at Jesus, at the rotting, the insects already devouring his puffy face, the way his hands were bloody pulps, his kneecaps all but destroyed.

"Holy—"

"—Shit."

"They did it," Jack said.

"Mother—"

"Yeah—"

"Holy—"

"Is that really him?" Gary asked.

"It has to be," Marsh said.

"Who else?" Ralph said, and then the last match died.

Sitting in the dark, the stink of the boy's corpse filling them, Ralph said, "If we let this go, we all are gonna die. You all know about concentration camps in World War II. You all know what happens. This is just like it."

"Yeah," Lou said. "They killed him. Man, I can't believe it. I can't believe my mom would send me here. I can't believe...."

"Believe," Jack said. Ralph felt Jack's hand give Ralph a squeeze. "Maybe our folks don't know what they do here. Shit, I doubt Jesus' father even knows."

"I can't believe it either," Ralph said. "They're monsters."

"They aren't human, that's for sure," Marsh added.

"What are we gonna do?" Jack asked the darkness.

"What can we do?" Ralph countered.

"Someone should do something," Gary moaned.

Then, they crawled out of the ground, up to their Hut. The diffuse moonlight spattered the yard, lit the barracks and huts and showers and the boy's faces were somehow different in the night, flatter, more alike than Ralph had remembered them being. Before they went inside, Jack turned to Ralph and said, "Too bad you wasted that match. We could've set fire to this place with it."

Ralph said almost to himself, "I've never needed a match to set a fire."

In the morning, a quiet permeated the camp, and when the boys trooped out to shout their pledge of allegiance to the dawn, their mouths stopped up as if their tongues had been cut off.

On the side of the barrack wall, the words:

TO BE A GOD
YOU MUST KILL THE ENEMY
YOU MUST BURY THE ENEMY
YOU MUST NEVER GROW UP
YOU MUST BURN THEM
YOU MUST FREEZE THEM
YOU MUST GIVE YOURSELF TO THE CAUSE OF JESUS

There, besides the hastily scrawled revision, written in rough chalk, the body of Jesus DeMiranda, held up by barbed wire twisting like vines around his limbs and torso.

Ralph glanced at Jack, who laughed, and then to Marsh who had a tear in his eye. Behind them, Cleft came striding, whistle in his mouth, wearing a green baseball cap and green fatigues. "Into the showers, you pansy ass bitches!" Cleft shouted, blowing the whistle intermittently, and then seeing what they'd done, the writing, the body. The whistle dropped from his mouth. He reached up and drew his baseball cap off, dropping it.

And then the rocks. Jack had made sure there were enough, just enough, for ten of the boys, Ralph included and they leapt on Cleft, stronger now, their own biceps built up from weeks of labor. Cleft tried to reach for the pepperspray, but he had to raise his hands defensively to ward off the blows. Cleft was like a mad bull, tossing them off to the side, but the rocks slammed and slashed at his face, tearing his hawk nose open, a gash above his eye blinding him with bloodflow, and as the red explosions on his face increased, Ralph felt something overpowering within him. He became the most ferocious, ramming at Cleft with all his weight, cutting deep into Cleft's shoulder with the sharp edge of a rock, loving the smell of the man as he went down on his knees. Ralph grabbed for Cleft's belt, tearing it off the loops, holding up the pepperspray and stungun and baton. Tossing the gun and spray to others, he lifted the baton in the air and brought it down hard on Cleft's skull.

It hit loud, a crack like a break in rock when a pickaxe hit, and blood flowed anew.

And then all of the boys were upon Cleft.

"YES!" Ralph shouted, high-fiving Jack, running like a pack of wolves with the others, across the muddy ground, through the steamy heat, rocks held high, Cleft's pepper spray in Ralph's left hand. Jack held the stungun, and Marsh, the fastest runner of them all was in the lead, waving the baton that still had Cleft's fresh blood on it. They shrieked the words of rebellion, twisted from the Wall. Several of the boys had taken down the body of Jesus DeMiranda and were carrying it like a battering ram between them as they flew to the sergeants' barracks. They caught the masters in their showers, mid-coffee, shaving, cutting at them with their own razors, scalding them, beating them, until two more were dead, and the others unconscious. But the last thing Ralph remembered was the feeling of all of them, all the boys together, moving as one, storming the island, like lava overflowing a volcano. The rest was nothing to him, the hurting and maiming and all the rest, all the war cries and whoops and barbaric ki-yi's that stung the air—it was nothing to him, for his mind was overflowing.

When it was all over and night covered them, Ralph leaned forward to Commodore—the man was tied to a chair, his great muscles caught in wire. Ralph held out a cigarette lighter—a souvenir from a downed sergeant. Stepping forward to Commodore, Ralph struck the lighter up, the flame coming forth.

"Arsonist, murderer," Commodore said, his eyes bloodshot, his face a mass of bruises.

"Shut up or I'll cut out your tongue," Jack laughed. Ralph looked back at him, and wondered if, like Jack, he was covered with blood as well. He heard the shouts of the other boys as they raided the food supply.

"We didn't kill that little boy, you dumbfuck," Commodore said.

"Okay, here goes the tongue," Jack said, coming up to the bound man, clippers in hand.

"Liar," Ralph said, twisting the lighter in front of Commodore's face.

"One of you must've done it," Commodore spat, but it was the last thing he said, for Jack had the clippers in his mouth. Ralph couldn't look, it wasn't something he enjoyed, but Jack had that glow on him, his whole body radiated with his joy.

The man didn't even try to scream.

Ralph looked at the blood on Jack's hands.

"Jesus, Jack," Ralph said, feeling the spinning world come back to him, the world of sanity that had somehow gotten out of control. "Jesus, Jack."

"What?" Jack laughed, dropping the clippers, clapping his red hands together.

Ralph looked back at the man, his mouth a blossom of bright red.

The man's eyes did not leave Ralph's face.

Ralph was amazed that the man didn't cry out in pain, that he kept his eyes forward, on Ralph, not pleading, not begging, but as if he were trying to let some truth up from his soul.

"Jack," Ralph went over to his friend, his blood-covered friend, his friend who had helped him get through this time in Hell. "Was he lying?"

"Yep," Jack said, averting his gaze. The blood ran down his face like tears. "He's one of them. They always lied to us."

"You sure?"

Jack closed his eyes. "Yep."

Then, "Did you and Marsh kill Jesus?"

Jack opened his eyes, staring straight at him. "If that were true, would it change anything? Jesus is dead. He came here. They did all this."

Ralph felt his heart stop for a moment, and then the beating in his chest became more rapid.

"We're just like them," Ralph whispered, mostly to himself.

"No," Jack grinned, blood staining his teeth. "They're weak. We're strong. Their time is up. Ours is just beginning."

"What did you do that got you sent here?" Ralph asked for the last time.

"Nothing," Jack said. "Nothing that you need to know about."

"You killed someone, didn't you?"

"It was nothing, believe me," Jack smiled. "And you've done some killing yourself today, haven't you?"

"I wouldn't have if—"

"You'll never know," Jack slapped Ralph on the back. "But it's okay. I understand."

Later, the man they called Commodore died.

Before morning, Jack came to where Ralph sat on a bench outside the barracks. He put his arm over Ralph's shoulders and whispered, "Now we can go home. We can go home and make them all pay."

Becoming Men

"Are we men yet?" Ralph asked, feeling an icy hand grab him around the chest, under his skin, closing up his throat until his voice was barely a whimper.

"No," Jack said. "We're better than men. We're gods. Come on, let's play with fire. You'll feel better after that, won't you?" He stood, drawing Ralph up by the hand. "You're good at fires, Ralph. We need you. I need you."

"I don't know," Ralph said. "Yesterday it was one thing. It seemed different. Jesus was dead. They were like the Nazis."

"I need you," Jack repeated, squeezing Ralph's hand tight, warm, covering Ralph's fingers in his. "You as you are, Ralph. Not what they wanted. As you are. I want you."

Ralph felt his fingers curl slightly under the weight of Jack's. He looked down at their hands and then up at Jack's face. "I can't."

"No shame," Jack said. "Let's set it all on fire. Glorious fire. Let's make it burn all the way up to the sun."

"That's my dream," Ralph whispered, a shock of recognition in Jack's words, a secret between the most intimate of friends. "How did you know my dream? My first night here, I saw it in my mind, a fire going all the way to the sun."

They stood there, frozen for a moment; then, Jack slowly let go of Ralph's hand, leaving in his palm a silver lighter. "Go set fires across the land."

Before the sun rose from the sea into an empty sky, the fires got out of hand. Ralph realized, putting aside other considerations, that it was the most beautiful thing he had ever seen in his young life, the way fire could take away what was right in front of his eyes, just burn it away with no reason other than its own hunger. Jack told him it was the best day he'd ever had, and when the burning was done, the boys went and had their showers, all except for Ralph who went in search of something new to burn.

Something Terrible Is Always Happening

On a window ledge
Brick and brownstone cracks,
Calico cat sleeps.
Smoke rises within,
Behind the open window.

Behind the cat, a woman curses into a telephone.
On the wall beside the woman, a stain grows on the yellow wall.

The cat stirs, and drops into the garden,
Leaps into the window.
Behind the cat,
A man paints a red landscape upon the wall.

He dips his brush into the torn body of another man.
Who looks up at the artist,
Who dips his brush again into the paint that pools
Between the dying man's ribs.

The artist paints the cat, sitting on window ledge,
Behind the cat, in the painting, a woman is cursing into a phone.

Behind the woman, a blossoming stain.

The Cabinet-Maker's Wife

"The Cabinet-Maker's Wife" is one of the stories whereby I could look at the subject of infidelity and what someone does to keep her marriage together, basically. With a little murder thrown in.

1

She had been raised to be somewhat old-fashioned, and she made no apologies to anyone for it. Linda had her hobbies, and reading, and although she was still fairly young (just turned thirty-two), she had no interest in getting out into the world much, preferring instead to stay home and cook and read, or, in the spring, to walk through the woods. She had known no other man, and was devoted to her husband, who was an artist of sorts who designed and made furniture. Linda's husband, Stephen, liked to work in oak best, but only when it came to furniture, for the cabinets he was best-known for were done in pine. His finest piece of work was the wardrobe he'd made for Linda on the eve of their wedding. It was made from knotty pine, and had a top shelf within its cupboard, and six drawers on one side, with a place to hang things on the other. On the outside he'd carved some beautiful designs—birds and baskets of fruit with grape vines dangling between. But every piece of furniture in the house was hand-made—the corner display cabinet in the dining room, the secretary in the den, the cocktail cabinet, the linen chest, the chiffonier in the bedroom. He was such a talented man, and his business used to just thrive, but then the economy had dived and, well, no one really needed hand-carved expensive furniture when they couldn't make a house payment. So he had begun brooding, again, as he had when she'd first met him in his late teens, brooding because there was nothing to keep his hands occupied. He continued working, for a while, on cabinets and chairs and other furnishings, but he'd had to store the excess down below, in the crawlspace basement in order to have room in the house just to sit.

And it was to that place, beneath the oriental rug that covered the trap door to the basement, that Linda went in search of a little corner chair, something small enough for a child—her sister had just had a baby, and she wanted to send along some token. It wasn't much, but it was sturdy and made from white pine, and when the baby was two or three, he would be able to go sit in it.

She rolled the rug back, and had to get a screwdriver to lift the wooden trap. It was heavier than she had remembered—usually she would call Stephen for some help, but he was out of earshot at the moment. She managed to slip her fingers beneath the flat wooden trap, and with a great heave, shoved it off onto the dark wood floor.

She didn't enjoy going down there, for it was a place of filters and the hot water heater and the storage furniture, a place where skunks sometimes crawled into and let off a terrible stink. Linda was not fond of spiders, and it was winter—there would be webs near the heater. She took a small flashlight with her, and a broom, and slid down through the square opening. When her feet touched the cold concrete floor, she ducked down and turned on the flashlight. There, in the middle of the room, was a single naked bulb, its flayed string hanging. She stepped around an overturned dresser and pulled on the string. The bulb gave feeble light, but it was enough to look around. She thought she heard some scuffling over near the enormous boxes that Stephen kept for no good reason, and turned her flashlight on them.

Nothing. No skunks in evidence, no spider webs, for that

matter.

She glanced about at the cloth-shrouded forms: the tables and chairs and dressers. Where would it be? That adorable little chair, that little doll chair of a type that had once been so popular with Stephen's customers…. It smelled like a dead animal, just a bit, as she moved across the room, keeping her head tucked under, lest she hit it against the low ceiling. There was a noise, too, not the scuffling she thought she'd heard, but a steady tap-tap-tap like a faucet dripping, or the tattoo of some dull object, a rock, say, or a book, against another. There was an enormous chest next to the hot water heater, and this seemed to be the source of the sound. The chest was a prize; it was originally commissioned for a family of six, and it would be used to store their treasures, but the family reneged, and Stephen was stuck with something that he couldn't possibly use.

There was that tap-tap-tap sound again.

She knew she should go get Stephen, but he had been brooding so much, she hated to bother him over what was possibly only a rat or squirrel.

Could it have gotten stuck in the chest?

She shined the flashlight all over the area around it—the dust had been disturbed, and the dropcloth had been drawn tight around the chest, rather than just thrown over it as had been done with all the others. Unlike Linda, Stephen was rather sloppy in his habits, meticulous as he was in his work.

Some animal had come in through the low casement windows and had gotten into the chest.

But the cloth was so tight around the chest, it was as if someone had tucked the chest in with it.

She took a step forward in her stocking feet, the cold of the floor now feeling like hot coals, for she was frightened easily by things. Animals could terrify her, dogs and cats, but also wild things like skunks and squirrels and rats. The basement was normally Stephen's domain, although she had come down here once before to re-light the hot water heater and had seen a nest of spiders. Linda was timid, this she knew, and even the thought that she might find a dying rat huddled against the beautiful mahogany, among cedar chips, made her wish she was somewhere else. What if it bit her?

Like a shock, Stephen said, "Hey, what're you doing?"

Linda turned about—he was kneeling above the trap opening, his head upside down, his hair hanging straight—he needed a cut, she didn't like him looking too shaggy and unprofessional. "I'm looking for that chair. The doll chair. For Susie's baby."

"It's in the garage, you knew that," he said, his voice accusing her of what he liked least about her: her snoopiness.

"I looked there. Trust me, if I didn't have to, I wouldn't come down here at all," she said, relieved that he was here with her, in spite of that tone in his voice.

"It's in the garage, Linda," he repeated. It was his sour mood. A man could only go without work so long before going a little crazy. He had turned from boy genius to middle-aged babyface past his prime between the ages of thirty-two and thirty-five; and the winter was hard on both of them. Her work sometimes required her to travel for miles, and when the snow fell she was stuck in some motel in Outer Mongolia, New Hampshire, while he was at home in the woods all by himself, living off Campbell's soup and drop biscuits until the snowplows came through. She'd been taking a week off work just to make him feel cared for a little—how like a child he could be, what a mixture of ups and downs and pouts and perkiness. He was an artisan, a craftsman, and there were so few around anymore, and look how the world treated him.

"I said, it's in the garage."

"Okay. Jesus, Stephen, you'd think I'd just found your secret garden or something." And then, she heard it again.

Tap-tap-tap-tap-tap.

More frantic, the dying rat in the chest scratching its paws against the wood grain.

"Hear that?" she asked.

Stephen listened for a few seconds, and shook his head. "It's the branches outside—scraping the wall above. Got to cut those some day—after the ice melts. After this goddamned winter is over."

Linda made dinner at six, but Stephen told her he was going down the road for a beer while the road was still open. She was hurt he didn't ask her along, although she wouldn't've gone to The Wily Trapper, which was the roadhouse out on House Mountain, just six miles outside of town—she didn't like bars, nor did she enjoy his drinking, although she understood his need for a few beers. She understood what he was going through. It was a lot of work on her part, maintaining the marriage while he was so down about everything, but she figured if two years were bad out of a lifetime, what was that? A breath, that was all, just a breath out of an eternity of breathing. The sex had fallen by the wayside, too, but she had never placed much value on sex or sexuality, and she had always felt that he was watching her for signs of putting on weight or getting older whenever she had to take off her clothes in front of him, and she especially hadn't liked the unflattering angles he'd be viewing her from when he mounted her. She knew that he had diminished desire, now, especially in winter, in relative unemployment; her parents' sexuality had been reserved for child-bearing years, and since she and Stephen had decided on no children, what would foregoing that uncomfortable and sometimes humiliating pleasure matter?

Still, she longed for his touch, for that kind of wincing pleasure when he took her, as he had in their first months together, when he took her and held her so tight that she wondered if he might smother her. And then, the wave upon wave of electrical current running between their bodies, as if they would generate their own power— that sparking second when she forgot how unattractive she felt, when the pleasure was more than just a response, when something seemed to be created between them like nothing could ever break it, and then her mind, gone, gone, a blue spark in a yellow field of emanations, his fingers about her throat, his groans, the tears in his eyes which made him seem so sensitive to her, the way he cried like a baby when he was spent. That last thing had been better than her own pleasure, for she always retained some home-learned guilt about her body, but that last thing, her arms around him, his head in her breasts, the feeling of his tears against her nipples like a mother with her child…she missed that most of all.

After she ate her split pea soup and ham sandwich, she watched the news. The weatherman mentioned the possibility of snow, so she called down to The Wily Trapper to get a message to Stephen, but the bartender said that he hadn't been in all night.

2

It didn't surprise her as much as she thought it would, this bit of information. Her father had an affair at least once, and her mother had told her years later. Her mother had said, "I wanted to leave him, but I wasn't sure."

"You didn't just ask him? I would've," Linda said, shocked and saddened at the time.

Her mother shook her head, "No, in marriage things are different than in other things. If I had confronted him, and he had told me he was having an affair, I would've stood by my principles and left him then. If he told me he wasn't having one, I wouldn't have believed him, and I would've acted crazy. I had a bad year, then, wondering, but I'm glad I stayed."

"Why?"

"Because there are rewards, Linda, other rewards for staying in a marriage."

"But you must've lost respect for him. And trust."

"I guess I did, but there are other rewards. You'll understand when you get married. You have to go through some hurt in life, no matter who you're with. But if you stick with it, things will grow."

She hadn't understood then, but now, in her thirties, she did, and she sat and watched the snow fall outside the kitchen window, thinking about the other rewards of staying in a marriage, the ones other than happiness.

The snow piled up in enormous drifts by nine, and the wind shrieked through the windows where the plastic sheeting had come untaped. By ten, when the wind died, and the vacuum silence of snow was interrupted only by the distant sound of trucks out on the interstate, Linda had already gone through the pockets of his jackets and pants, plundered his desk drawers, and the strong box where he kept his records and receipts. She slipped on a pair of boots and his down jacket and braved the cold and two feet of snow to go to his workshop. It had once been a stable, for the previous owner had kept three horses, but over the six years they'd lived there, Stephen had turned it into his dreamplace. His drill press, circular saw, bench saw, vises and braces, all the drill bits arranged neatly, and a half dozen or more planes, hammers, nails, carving tools. It smelled of fresh-cut wood, as if the tree had been shaved right there, within the hour, and the scent of pine sap almost on her lips, just breathing the vivid air. She went over to his worktable. He had stopped making a small chest of drawers, the kind that would be suitable for jewelry or scarves—the chest was done, but not finished, and the drawers were cut and carved but required some assembly. He did beautiful work, and for all his troubles, she admired the man for his talent.

But inside the chest was a woman's bra, wadded up.

She picked it up, and, without knowing why, sniffed it. It smelled like perfume, the cheap dimestore kind. The kind teenage girls wore. The bra was small. Was he screwing some sixteen-year-old from the local high school? There had been that girl, Willa, who had helped around the house, two summers back when Linda had been on the road a lot with work. But Willa's breasts were enormous for a girl, so much so that she bent forward. This was not Willa's bra.

As she was turning to go, feeling angry, betrayed, *but not surprised*, Linda saw the other thing, hanging from a nail above the door.

It was a girl's purse, small, also cheap, dimestore bought.

She reached up and lifted it off the nail. She hesitated a moment before looking inside it. Was she going too far? Her mother hadn't investigated her father's affair. Her parents seemed to have a wonderful marriage, especially now that they were in their sixties.

But she undid the clasp, and inside were some Kleenex. She moved these around. A set of keys. A pack of Wrigley's. A tampon.

A driver's license.

The girl was only nineteen. At least he wasn't going for underage girls. At least her competition could never provide Stephen with a *life, not like me. I am his life. What would he do without me?* Her name was Mary Anne Lamprette. It was a Vermont driver's license.

Why would a girl leave her purse behind?

There was six dollars all wadded up, and some change, too. Another tampon—this one bloody, with a Kleenex wrapped around it. She closed the purse, and set it back on the nail.

Inside the house again, she looked up the name in the phone book, and found Mary Anne Lamprette living on Copper Road. Linda dialed the number, and after four rings, the machine answered. The girl's voice was sweet and perky. The voice said, "Hey, it's Mary Anne. Nobody's here, or maybe I am only I'm just fooling around. So keep talking, or you may never hear from me again."

Linda hung the phone up.

94

She couldn't sleep that night, and she wondered about that chest in the basement. The dropcloth around it, how it had been so neatly tucked. The house was freezing at this point, so she went to turn the heat up to eighty, and kept the down jacket on. She imagined that Stephen was pressing himself into the doughy form of his beloved Mary Anne, leaving the impression in her skin of his grubby fingers, his paunchy belly, his dick expanding the poor girl's inner geometry until her innards would prolapse into a dodecahedron. What would that feel like? It had been so long since they'd made love, since she was feeling like a pretty young girl. Would he put his hand about her throat like a necklace, tightening while the shimmering blue pleasure spread across her thighs, across her belly, through her hardened, small nipples? *Don't think about sex. It doesn't matter. He loves you, and Mary Anne is just a diversion, a release from his anxiety.*

Then, as she lay thinking about the chest, and sex, she heard what sounded like a cat in heat screeching for a brief second.

Then, the silent world of a snow-covered house.

She got the trap door up again, and slid down to the cold floor of the basement. The tapping began again, as if whatever was inside the chest had heard her coming. Then a sound like sexual awakening, a gasp, or a moan of pain. She turned on the bulb, and, shivering, stepped around the boxes and overturned tables until she got to the chest. She pulled the dropcloth back. The chest was locked. Linda had no idea where the key might be. She rapped on the top of the chest.

Something tapped back, the same sequence of raps.

"Hello?" Linda asked, something dawning on her, something terrible, although her mind was becoming clouded with the confusion of conflicting emotions.

"Aauraught," the voice within the box said. The tapping became more rapid.

"My God." Linda stood there, shaking, and she dropped the flashlight—its crash to the concrete floor echoed through the house.

And then, she asked the box, "Mary Anne?"

The thing in the box answered with a series of desperate, splintery scratches.

3

Stephen was in by noon the next day. "Tried to call," he lied, "but the phones were down. Stayed overnight at Joe Ball's. Slept in his daughter's bed. She's away at UMass. Majoring in journalism or something. Hard to believe she's eighteen already. Paula sends her best."

Linda was reading one of his Louis L'Amours, trying to block his lies out. She chewed her lip as he spoke; he went on and on about the Ball family, how Paula was getting a little down because of the harsh winter, how Joe couldn't get his plow to start, how Billy, the youngest, was flunking chemistry. Finally, Linda looked up from her book. "I know about her," she said.

Stephen didn't even change his expression, although he looked a bit like a deer caught in headlights just before the impact. "Who? What do you mean?"

"That's all I'm going to say. I spoke to her last night while you were gone."

He blinked, turned his head to the side as if he could read something on the wall near the family pictures. Then he turned completely around, looking out the living room window. "Things in your head again, Linda, you've got to get out more. This week off from work was the wrong thing. We've been under so much stress." He was so much like a little boy caught doing something naughty, scrambling with stories to get out of it.

"I couldn't find the key, but I talked to her anyway."

And then Stephen held his breath, then exhaled after a long minute. He knew he was caught, he had that erratic breathing of a captured liar.

He said, "Which one did you talk to?"

Linda asked, "How many have there been?"

4

He kept the keys to the chests and cabinets with him at all times. "You don't really want to see her, do you?" But then he saw the look on Linda's face—she would brook no nonsense. "She's not pretty. Not like you. But she…."

"She what?"

He shuddered, again reminding her of a little boy having to reveal his most humiliating secret. He said, "She lies real still." He turned to face her, tears in his eyes.

Linda took this in; the scope of it; what it meant. What it meant that Stephen *liked*. She felt a wave of nausea, to have *lived* with this man, to have *shared*…so much time, so much energy, so much damn *work*. She remembered, with a certain amount of horror, how, when they made love he had wanted her quiet and still, his hands about her throat when he came inside her, her eyes closed, her breathing stilled, briefly. Four young women around the property, all in boxes and crates and chests and wardrobes, and perhaps another—he couldn't quite remember—down at the old store where he had run his business before hard times hit.

But the worst for her, still, was the word that she couldn't contain. "Unfaithful," she spat out. "How dare you lie to me, live the way we lived, deny me a loving, sexual relationship, while you were out finding these…tramps! How dare you, after all I've done for you, after all the sacrifices. Christ! Jesus, Stephen, you have some kind of sickness. You need help."

He cast his glance down to his muddy shoes; his hands slid into the pockets of his jeans; he was so rumpled looking, his flannel shirt bunching around his waist, his hair a mess, his sorrow amplified by the snow that still melted from his clothes. He said something almost silently.

"What?" She asked.

He looked into her eyes. "It's not so bad, I said. It's not so bad. When they're dead. Completely dead, I mean. They give me pleasure."

Linda followed him into the basement, flicked on the light, watched as he clicked the key into the lock on the chest, and turned it.

"You sure?" he asked.

She nodded.

He lifted the lid up; its hinges creaked against the wood.

The girl was curled in a fetal position, as if she'd fallen asleep. She was naked except for the pink silk panties, but her arms covered her breasts demurely. The smell of cedar chips and rotten meat came up to Linda's nostrils, and she began breathing through her mouth to avoid the smell. Mary Anne Lamprette was a pretty girl, but she looked older than nineteen. What sort of life would she have anyway? Having affairs with married men, working in some tavern or in a dress shop waiting on the depressed and downtrodden in town. What sort of life would that have been? Linda would not have wanted that life at all. Linda said, "She was alive last night."

Stephen said, "Sometimes it takes a week. I leave them in the chips to help with the smell."

Linda said, "And that's how you like to make love?"

Stephen said nothing.

"And you didn't touch these girls—this girl—before she died?"

"I wouldn't," he said, "I just couldn't."

Linda looked from the dead girl to her husband, to the beautiful furniture, some covered, some not. "Stephen. Stephen?"

"Yes?"

"What is it that you like so much—about this. This *hang up*, or whatever you'd call it?"

"You really want to know?"

She nodded.

He said, "It's going to sound silly."

"Try me."

"Okay. They get cold on the outside. Their skin. Their hair, even. But on the inside. On the *inside*. It's like a warm wet velvet glove." He said this as if it was the most important feeling in the entire world, and a shred of sanity came back to her while she listened to him, *really* listened, and the nausea in her stomach, in her *soul*, came up her throat.

She barely noticed his arm coming up and then down, the metal of the flashlight gleaming in the feeble basement light.

5

She awoke to darkness. Smell of cedar chips. She touched the sides of the chest to check its dimensions.

Too small to move about much.

"Stephen?"

No answer.

She pushed on the lid, but it was locked, and perhaps even weighted down, too.

She heard his voice, on the other side of the wood. "Linda, Linda."

"Please, Stephen, I'm frightened."

"Oh, Linda, you know you're the only woman I really love."

"I know that, sweetheart. Now let me out. LET ME OUT."

"I can't. I saw that look on your face."

"I was jealous. Your affairs. The pretty girls."

"They meant nothing to me. Just sensation, that was all."

"Stephen? What's going to happen?"

"You'll get hungry, then thirsty. Then you'll fall asleep. You'll scratch some. Maybe it'll hurt. I'm not sure. I try to stay away from the boxes for at least four days. I usually hit the girls harder though.

Maybe it'll take longer with you. I don't know."

Linda listened to him, cried, prayed, thought of her mother, and within the hour began hallucinating, until even the hallucinations seemed to shrink and dry up and she knew death was coming to her. She had no concept of days, how many had passed, or how many times Stephen had come to talk to her.

He said, "It's always been my dream to have you. Like this. Always."

Do the dead feel? When they are taken by the passion of the living, do they buck and grind and moan and delight, if only in the stillness of their flesh and bones?

His dream, she thought, facing along a wavelength of sputtering darkness, *I am his dream*. She felt the moment come upon her, the wave of pleasure, the overlapping sensations of pain and opening, of the river of ultimate love and touch, the stormy gusts of the opening doors and windows of eternity, of the stillness of creation.

She smelled the ozone of fading consciousness, and then bore witness to the blue heralded spark of the machinery of flesh, drying, set in new motion.

99

6

Stephen drew her from the chest, and knew true and faithful love for the first time in his life.

The snow beyond the house piled in hills and across the span of forests, and cutting through the ice wooden silence, was the fierce cry of human joy.

Do the dead feel? When the body is no longer occupied with shared consciousness, do the nerve endings long to twitch and spur the body onward? When his fingers found her, stroking gently and then with roughness, did she lay there, somewhere in that body that could have no expression, and remember what the girl, Mary Anne, had told her?

"Please," the dying girl had said through the wood, *"please."*

Had that been her last wish?

It is the commandment of physical love, that one word, and some who dwell in the flesh will follow its law even unto the darkest of places.

Fries With That?

"Fries With That?" is my attempt to write a fun story about friendship, jealousy, and my memories of girls I knew in high school, twisted to the nth degree. If I were going to describe this as anything, it would be as a horror comedy, although it's really not very funny, what these girls do to each other.

When we got interviewed by *People* magazine, Maggy said that I'd always known about my talent, but that isn't true. She didn't say it to the guy interviewing us, just to me in private. She told him that the gun had felt good and warm in her hand. "Like a kiss," she said. "Everytime I took a shot."

Mags doesn't tell the truth in interviews.

The truth is, I never really knew about my talent much until things started to happen over a long period of time. My gramma didn't even know for sure, at first, at least not till I told her. Now, I wish I had listened to that old woman. She knew how bad it could get.

My mom should've known, too, after that cat. But she didn't catch on too quick, and now, look at the mess. Sure, we could hire good lawyers because of how much both my mom and dad make, and who my dad knows, and we did what we could for Maggy. She's not mad at me or anything, but every now and then she gives me that glare.

But gramma knew, once I told her about the cat and other things. She told me without really telling me about how bad it could get.

Mags said it would've happened anyway, what she did.

I have to admit, it was fun going on television, and meeting big celebrities like Jenny Jones and Jerry Springer and Oprah Winfrey. They were all nice and really sweet. I thought I looked ugly in that white dress my dad made me wear. He told me that young ladies going on T.V. should look virginal, as if this has ever been a problem for me. Maggy only wore her usual black, from head to toe. I call it her witch phase, although she thinks she looks thinner like that. She doesn't like me calling her a witch or a bitch, mainly because she's both—she hasn't been to church since confirmation, and the bitch part...well, if you saw her on television, you'd understand. When she started yelling back at the studio audience on Jerry Springer, I just about died. But it figures. She was up there flailing her arms around and cursing and I know her grandmother just about had a cow watching on the old RCA T.V. back at the trailer park.

Maggy doesn't like being called trailer trash either, but that's really what started it all when she and I were showering off after field hockey (which is neither, since we have to play it on what might best be referred to as a gravel pit, and our team has always been lame). It was before fourth period, and Alison Gall had stolen Maggy's clothes. Alison, who is the kind of bitch that no one ever calls bitch, is not exactly the cheerleader type even though she made the squad finally after years of trying. It was her mother pushing her that made her crack the squad, and ever since then she's just been looking for scapegoats for unresolved anger all the time. So she calls Mags a trailer trash dyke, and Mags throws her against the tiles. And Mags, sounding like some otherworldly monster, says, "I'm gonna kill you someday, Alison, and when I do, you're gonna wish you'd never been born."

Alison picked on a lot of girls, but mainly Mags. Maggy is a good scapegoat since she doesn't quite fit into Glasgow High (named for Ellen Glasgow, who I know was a famous writer, like

I want to be someday soon, a woman who apparently has fallen into the obscurity of this millennial bullshit). Maggy is not exactly Glasgow material. She smokes too much, tells everyone but me to fuck off, and sometimes me, and she has what Mr. Herlihy writes on her report card as "An unusual sense of justice." Mr. Herlihy's easy going, which is why we like him. But Mr. Green always writes, "Margaret has trouble forming bonds with other students due to issues."

Issues.

Such bullshit.

All of this was read aloud on those talk shows, and then some gooney psychotherapist came out and told Mags what was wrong with her.

Besides which, Maggy and I formed a bond in third grade when she was the kick ass new girl who talked back to old Mrs. Burley.

And Mr. Green, or anyone for that matter, calling her Margaret when in fact she was christened Maggy Mae after an old song… Nowhere on her birth certificate is the word, "Margaret." And that word would not describe Mags anyway (I can call her Mags. I've earned the right over all these years. You, and others, cannot).

In third grade, she was just this dark thing. That's all I can tell you. I was, of course, that whole blond-blue eyes-ribbon in her hair kind of nice little girl who laughed at boys' jokes as if I knew what the hell they were talking about. But Mags, she was already taller than the tallest kid, with long dark hair that obscured most of her face, what I like to call cigarette lips—big pouty vaginal lips right under her nose. But I didn't think so then, not back in my nice little girl phase. Back then I thought she looked like NOT A NICE LITTLE GIRL. She looked like trouble and trash, but I got over it fast. I went out to clap the erasers for Mrs. Burley, and there Mags was, behind the dumpster, smoking a Camel.

"What the fuck are you staring at?" she asked. I had never before heard a girl use the F word. She had a dark voice. Everything about her back in third grade was dark.

I was too scared to say anything. Truth be told, I peed my panties right there. I thought she was going to eat me or something. She just sucked back that cigarette till there was nothing but ash, and eyed me with those dark eyes.

"I asked you a goddamned question," she said.

"I'm...not staring...I'm really not," I said.

She shook her head in disgust. I saw the rest of her face for the first time when she pulled back her hair a little. She had a tattoo on her left cheek, just next to her earlobe. Just a small star. "Like it?" she asked, when she caught me staring.

"Not really," I said. Back then I had a mouse squeak voice. I was pretty much a little nothing who had pretty handwriting and a yes'm attitude. Just a little pleasing machine. But I did not like dark thoughts or tattoos. Yet.

"I like it," Mags said, letting her hair drop. "You're probably stuck up like every other girl here, ain't you?"

I shook my head. "No. I'm not. Really."

"Here," she said, extending her hand, the next cigarette already lit. "Have a smoke."

"I...uh...no thanks."

"Have a goddamn smoke," she said. She reached out and grabbed my hand. She thrust the cigarette between my fingers. I stared down at it.

"My mother used to smoke," I squeaked.

"It's good for you."

"No it isn't, the Surgeon General said—"

"You believe that government tool? Smoke," she said.

It was a command.

I delicately put the cigarette between my lips. I thought she was going to kill me if I disobeyed her.

"Inhale, come on, inhale," she commanded.

I sucked back the smoke, and coughed, and sucked, and coughed, and pretty soon I was hooked on the damn things, and I still am. One of life's little pleasures. Come to Marlboro Country. Get the Most Out of Life.

Sure, Mags corrupted me thoroughly. She taught me all about smoking and drinking and why it was important for a boy to have a big one. It took me three years to figure out what big ones were, but

FRIES WITH THAT?

I was happy Mags had warned me ahead of time. The vodka helped with that, too. I hid most of it from my mom and dad, who weren't too cool. They were church going types, and basically so was I. Unfortunately, I was also heavily into sin as both a concept and an action. After church, I'd sneak off down to the alley behind the Meat Market in town, and me and Mags would smoke and have a few beers and then go out and raise hell. I'm sure God in His Heaven didn't give a rat's ass if we got into trouble now and then.

Sin was not new to my family. My mother once cheated on my father with Dr. Van Graaf, my orthodontist. How do I know? Dad was away on business, and Mom and Dr. Van Graaf were upstairs in bed, that's how I know. My mother is no stranger to sin herself. She didn't want me to know, and in fact, I was supposed to be staying at Mags' for the night. But that had just been a ruse. I was really going to spend the night with Billy Alcott in his backyard tent, along with a bottle of Stoli and a carton of menthols. But Billy was acting like a creep, so I told him I was having my period and he ran like hell. All boys do, the wimps. His tent sucked, anyway, barely enough room to move your elbows let alone have some teenager on top of you trying to tell you how much he loved you when you knew he didn't give a flyer and had been doing it with Missy Hanscomb three nights before.

But my mother and Billy and Dr. Van Graaf have very little to do with this, my confession.

Yeah, I know, if you saw us on T.V. or read *People* or maybe that little piece in the *New York Times* or in our local rag, you might know the rest of it. Six kids all lobotomized and hemorrhaging in the middle of Glasgow High School with their signed yearbooks at their feet. Bullets flying. It was something, I'll tell you.

Gramma would've told me, maybe, how to stop it, but she wasn't around by then.

There's always more to this stuff than meets the eye. *60 Minutes* is doing this thing on us in about a month, and I'm sure it will be more lies. I'm really holding out for Barbara Walters for the interview. Her people haven't contacted me yet. I figure when school starts up in the fall, and things like November Sweeps are going on, she will. Mags thinks Barbara Walters and her people don't give a flyer about two girls from Minnesota who were suspected of mass murder at the end of their junior year. But I think based on the coverage we've gotten so far, we're worth the Sweeps Month and maybe even a retro thingy in the spring. I would even say we've put Carthage, Minnesota, on the map, except there was that movie star who did that back in the seventies before he got eaten up by heroin and a nasty car wreck. I know that once we get Barbara Walters to interview us—and not just one of her *20/20* interviews, but one of those Specials she does that are so good—the record will be set straight. I'm having trouble convincing Mags to wait till then to tell everything, since we really didn't get a chance on the talk show circuit. Too much yelling and screaming and myth-making. My mother didn't even call them talk shows, she called them Freak Shows of the Very Vapid. I kind of like that. Mom has a way with words. But Oprah and Jerry and Jenny weren't like that. They all have a lot of heart. They were sweet. Mags was hilarious on them. I was just doing my Pretty Nothing act, because I didn't want to let the world know the truth yet. I was the Loyal Best Friend. Mom'd totally freak herself if she knew I was writing down what really happened, but Mags is in trouble over this now, and the truth is, she's just protecting me.

All right, Mom has known all along, but she is really good at denying reality. Even when it slaps her in the face. I wish I could do that.

She's known ever since I was about four. She saw what I did to the cat. Now, first off, I've never liked cats. Please don't hold that against me. I've just never met one that liked me. They all act like little bitches around me, they don't purr, they don't preen, they just growl and slash at my ankles. So it's no surprise to me that I did the Fries With That? thing. That's what Mags calls it. When we were in fourth grade and I did it to this one kid, Mags said to me, "Fries with that?" She meant it as a double joke. First, because at Burger King and McDonald's and Wendy's and all those hamburger fast food places the guy on the speaker says, "Fries with that?" no matter what the fuck you order. You could order shit on a stick, and he'd say, "Duh, fries with that?"

That's part of it.

The other part is that Fries word. All its meanings.

But wait, back to the cat when I was little. Mom said that the cat was hissing at me, as usual. I was sitting on the kitchen floor. I just stared at the cat long and hard and suddenly like my eyes rolled back into my head and I turned all pale and started speaking in tongues. Well, Mom is a fundamentalist, and even though she knows it probably was not her beloved Holy Ghost talking through me, she always likes to think the best. In fact, I think Mom turned to church-going because of the talent, and gramma had it, as it turns out. After that, Mom said that cat was not right, and would just walk in circles. Which cracks me up to think of a cat walking in circles all the time. And again, for you cat lovers, it's not that I hate cats, it's that they never like me. I suppose one day I may meet one who likes me, and then I may take cats on a case-by-case basis. Until then, we really have nothing to do with each other whenever possible.

I told Mags about the cat in eighth grade when I knew for sure she was my absolutely best friend of all friends.

We went from smoking a pack a day to three packs a day each by the time we entered high school. The liquor didn't really kick into high gear till junior year. We hung out in the girls' room a lot, smoking of course and writing nasty things about girls like Alison Gall and some of the other girls of what we called the Canine Corps. All cheerleaders were a little too kissy face for our tastes, even though they had to go down on the filthy football players. I really shouldn't have hated Alison so much—that's half my problem. I would obsess on girls and boys I hated, and then I would have no control sometimes. I actually had excellent control, up until the beginning of June when we raised the hell to end all hells, but who knew?

Not me or Mags back when we were scratching our Bic pens into the toilet stall wall. "Alison Sucks Donkeys," I read my exquisite poetry aloud while I scratched.

"No, more sophisticated," Mags said with that smoke-scraped throat of hers. Then, she lifted her Swiss Army knife and scratched, "ALISON'S DICK IS BIGGER THAN JOEY'S."

"That's so fourth grade," I said, grabbing the cigarette from between Mags' lips and stuffing it in my greedy mouth. I sucked back the smoke and whooshed it out through my nostrils. "Besides which, everybody's dick is bigger than Joey's."

Mags laughed. The stall was tiny, but since we're both pretty skinny, it wasn't too bad. The toilet bowl was almost full of our cigarette butts.

"What is it she ever did to either of us that makes us hate her so much?" Mags asked. "I almost forget."

"She's just so Alison," I said. Suddenly, Mags thrust her hand over my mouth.

She lipped, *Someone just came in*. The cigarette dropped from her mouth into the toilet, pronto.

The girl's bathroom door swung shut, and we heard little mouse steps over to the sink.

I glanced at Mags, who released her hold on my mouth.

We both knew who it was. Janine Cunligger—and yeah, it was her real name. I could not make up a name that good even if I tried.

Janine was spooky, but not in the same way that Mags is scary. Janine was one of those girls you knew would one day turn psycho on everybody, or else she'd invent the cure for the Common Cold. Maybe she'll end up revolutionizing software or something. She's that kind of girl. Despite the last name Cunligger, she was called Gyro because of her scientific and mathematical bent. Mags nicknamed her this in sixth grade, after Mags got tired of all the boys calling Janine by a not-so-nice revision of her last name. Mags originally called her Gyroscopa, Goddess of Science Nerds, but eventually this became Gyro until Janine herself used it when she introduced herself to new kids.

Janine was also plug ugly, at least as far as any of us knew. Unlike Mags who had the cool hip urban look of dark hair on dark clothes and dark heart, Janine a.k.a. Gyro had a frizz and thick glasses and Pippi Longstocking legs and was flat as a pancake even at sixteen when the rest of us had pretty much Jiffy Popped to our full bra sizes.

And as Mags and I stood silently in the toilet stall, we heard the saddest most mournful sound coming from the sink where Gyro stood letting water run over her hands.

"Jesus," Mags gasped, closing her eyes.

Gyro was sobbing up a storm, and the running water didn't hide it.

I was the first out of the stall. I stood back a ways from Gyro, because she still was a bit spooky in my opinion. I had never really warmed up to her after I'd been held back a year in Chemistry and she had moved on with Honors.

She saw me in the mirror over the sink. Her headband was askew. Her frizz of hair seemed frizzier.

"You okay?" I asked. I felt Mags' hand on my shoulder, as if trying to pull me back.

Gyro leaned over the sink again, pulling her glasses off. "Yeah, fine. Just got some dirt in my eyes."

"You were crying," I said.

"We heard you," Mags added. "What's up?"

Gyro kept pretending until Mags just went up to her and threw her arms around her. "It's okay," Mags said, "We're not gonna hurt you or anything."

Gyro pulled away, shrugging away from her. "Yes you are. You're like all the rest of them."

"To hell we are," Mags said.

"That's right," I volunteered weakly. Truth was, I didn't really care to delve into Gyro's problems. She was one of those girls I didn't want to get to know too well because: a) we had nothing in common and b) there was nothing I was going to gain by being friends with her. Now my b) choice may seem cold and unfeeling, but I learned years ago that there's no point in making friends if it doesn't help you in some way. I don't mean namby-pamby help, I mean, if a friendship doesn't take you to a new level, or open up a different world, or feed you in some way, why have it?

All right, maybe I am a bit cold. I got burned by some of those other girls and boys enough to know that you are lucky if you can make one good friend in your lifetime.

Mags was that friend.

But Mags has a better soul. She managed to wrestle her arms around Gyro's shoulders again. Gyro started crying again. I went and hopped up on the edge of the sink. I brought another cig out from the pack, lit it, puffed, and passed it to Gyro. Gyro didn't hesitate. She snapped it out of my hand and took a long drag on it. I reached into my fanny pack and brought out some Kleenex for her. Then, I drew the flask out. It was rum and Coke, and not a lot of rum so please don't get the idea I was drunk twenty-four hours a day. Mags is the one with the bar in her locker at school, not me.

"So what's the deal?" I asked.

Gyro sucked back another lungful of smoke. On exhaling, she said, "It's Alison Gall."

I looked at Mags.

"We were just talking about her," I said, with glee.

"What's she done to you?" Mags asked. Mags really has the milk of human kindness in her veins. She looks dark and nasty, and she talks like a whore sometimes, but she really is the kind of person who would save a gnat on the ass of a weasel.

And then, Gyro told us. All of it.

It's not really important what she told us. In fact, I think it would hurt her feelings if she knew that I was writing this, and knew that it probably would get published someday since we're so famous now. But let me put it this way: Alison did something to Gyro that was so terrible, something that is the worst thing one girl can do to another girl. I do not make this stuff up. If you're female, you know what that is. If you're male, you probably don't have a clue. But when you're sixteen, and a girl, and another girl does to you what Alison Gall did to Gyro, you would feel on the inside like all the joy in life had been extinguished—no, stolen from you by the worst kind of thief. Boys sometimes do this to girls, but they don't have a clue. Girls sort of accept that boys do this because boys don't understand

what it means. But for a girl to do it to another girl is the lowest form
of life.

So then and there, the three of us made a pact, Gyro, me and
Mags.

We set our plan into motion before Friday, the day of the Prom.

It was easy enough to lure Alison Gall to the old farm off Route
7. Not that she was exactly a Four-H girl, but we knew that the guy
she really wanted to ball was Quent Appenino, the Italian Stallion
quarterback who had transferred from some California school when
his folks got divorced. Quent was built, and had good buns and a
great smile. If he weren't such a tardo when it came to school, I'd
have lusted after him, too. But he was a big pretty guy and since
he'd arrived he'd been going steady with Susie Malloy. Quent was
a good boy, too, and didn't cheat, and this drove Alison nuts. So
what we did was we told Quent that it was Susie's birthday, and we
had this card for her. We wanted him to be the first to personalize
and sign it. So he takes up like half the card, the dufus, and writes,
You know how much I care for you, baby. You + Me=4-Ever. Then,
pretending I'd forgotten the way out to the farm—which Quent's
grandfather owned—I asked him to write down directions on this
really thin piece of paper. "I want to drive out with my dad this
weekend just for fresh air."

Quent really was a dumshit. He didn't question this at all.

He just wrote out the directions.

Then, Mags, who is a genius at this, carefully traced his note
about the directions. Again, trying to imitate his handwriting, which
she did about perfectly, she scrawled at the bottom: *Before the
Prom, 4 p.m. I want you. Quent.*

"She's going to melt," I said.

Gyro nodded. "But what do we do when we get her out there?"

"Don't even worry about it. We do what we do," Mags said,
passing another cigarette to her. Gyro had a bad jones for cigs, it
turned out. I discovered that at least we had that in common.

Okay, now here's where it gets hazy. Not that the Prom coming
up was any big deal to us since we weren't seniors. We didn't have
steadies, and I'm not big on wearing a big poofy dress with my hair

111

up like Cinderella. Maybe my third grade pre-Mags self would've been into that crap, but I was more of a let's get drunk and break into the arcade kind of girl by junior year. If I wanted a boy sexually, I didn't need all that filler: just give me the guy. The bad influence of my best friend again.

She always said I was the real bad influence, back when we were little. It was that fourth grade thing, when Jonathan Rice was on the monkey bars and Mags and I were stepping on his hands as he swung around. Jonathan was, I think, a budding masochist, or else he liked to look up my skirt. Back in fourth grade I wore what Mags still calls the Betsy-Wetsy outfits where "You looked like one of those American Girl dolls." But Jonathan grabbed my ankle. I slipped, landing on my tailbone on the cold metal of the monkey bars, which hurt bad enough, but then I lost my balance and fell down into the gravel.

It was the first time I realized you could actually see stars when you slammed into the earth hard enough. I thought my brain had been knocked to my shins. Now, maybe Jonathan jogged something in my head a little more than it should've been, or maybe what I did to that cat when I was four just got worse the closer I got to puberty.

Or maybe it was just fate.

That was the first day Mags had ever used the term Fries With That? about what I can do. I don't do it often, and, in fact, I never planned on doing it.

But I almost fried poor little Jonathan Rice right there on the playground during recess. He came over to me, kneeling down to see if I was okay.

And I just went blank. Like the white dot that's left on the T.V. when you turn it off sometimes. I went down this winding tunnel in my head. I figured I must be dying or something.

When I came to, Mags described the whole thing to me.

"Damn, it was scary as shit," she said. "Jonathan was crying about you, and you start showing the whites of your eyes and frothing at the mouth, and breaking out in rashes all over your face. Then your mouth opens wider than I figured it could go, like a wide-mouthed bass screaming or something, and your tongue starts waggling, and then…"

Mags paused here for effect. Her eyes widened.

"Then…all these words I never heard of come out of your mouth, words that are almost like English but aren't quite, and you're shaking, and I break out in goosebumps all over, and Jonathan starts making choking sounds and then I smell what seems to me to be the smell of toast burning in a toaster, and then it doesn't smell like toast but it smells like when the dentist drills in your mouth at a cavity and how it doesn't hurt because of the Novocaine but this weird burning smell comes up…And I look at Jonathan and his face is all red and then the color in his eyes just kind of melts into nothing."

That was the description, but nobody ever blamed me for what happened to Jonathan Rice. At first, they called it stress blindness, then shock, and then autism for a little while. But Mags and I knew he just got the Fries With That? treatment. She called him Fried Rice. One day, when Jonathan Rice was in seventh grade, now at a special school for autistic kids, he took a long walk off a short pier. I've always felt a little guilty about that.

I asked my mother about it then, and she was cagey, but she did allow that gramma had it. So I go to the nursing home where gramma lays sputtering through her nostrils, god love her, and I tell her what mom told me.

Gramma had these curious eyes back then, pale blue, covered with a translucent milkiness. Her skin was as thin as tracing paper, and you could see all these blue veins under the surface. I loved my grandmother, even though she had to wheeze when she breathed. I snuck her cigarettes, too, and played Hearts with her sometimes for hours. She might have been the only human being I ever cared for, at least that was blood. She was always wonderful to me, and I felt warmly towards her.

But this time, when I tell her about Jonathan Rice, and then the cat, her eyes well up with tears. Gramma was from Ireland, and she wells up with tears easily, from hearing "I'll Bring You A Daisy A Day," to when she thinks of County Clare and all its green pastures and blue skies. Harp ale does it for her, also. She reached for my shoulder to steady herself as she rose up on the bed. "You have the Evil Eye, then," she said, her voice all soft and wispy like cotton candy. "I knew it would show again."

"It's not my eyes," I said. "I speak and stuff too."

"It's through the eyes," she nodded, ignoring me. She pointed to the pale blue of her eyes. "Look, you and I have the old blue. Your hair is blond like your daddy's, but you got the old ways in your spirit. They say we're descended from fairies, but we are from the original people of the islands. We have the eyes, and we have the talent."

"Evil Eye?" I asked. "But I didn't mean to hurt Jonathan." I began crying, still somewhat in my Pretty Little Nothing phase.

"No, it's what others have called it. It's a vision that takes over. It's a reshaper of minds, it's a molder of people's insides." Then, gramma hugged me close. Her breath was terrible, like a cat's. Her light whiskers scratched my cheek, but her warmth was not to be denied. I lay there, letting her hold me, the sticky warmth between us, until it grew dark. Before I left, she asked me to learn to focus. "Through craft," she said. "Talent is nothing but wildness without craft."

"Like witch-craft?" I asked.

"Nothing like that, dearie," Gramma said, her voice going raspy from the long day and the illicit cigarette-smoking. "The craft of your art. Your art is there, and now you must make it sing. But one thing," she whispered, "stay away from the dead. It's not meant to be near them."

"Why?" I asked.

"Oh," she said, "you're too young to know. Let me just tell you that your great-great-grandmother Irene had it, and once, she was at a wake. She thought she heard her dead uncle knocking at his coffin after she'd danced around it a bit."

"Cool," I said.

"Not so cool," Gramma whispered. "Not so cool at all."

She fell asleep soon after, and then a few months later, before I could actually ask her how I was to go about perfecting this so-called craft, Gramma died. The day she died, it felt like someone kicked me in the gut. Death does that to you. I imagine it didn't feel so wonderful to my grandmother, either.

Because I didn't like to think of myself as Evil (I was a God-fearing little Jesus freak back then for the most part, although I was moving closer to my ultimate embrace of hormones and sin as time went on), I dropped the whole Evil Eye phrase. I went with Mags' Fries With That? designation.

So, when Mags said to Gyro, the afternoon of the Prom, "Don't worry. We do what we do," I was a little afraid of the Fries With That? syndrome coming through.

Mags assured me this was next to impossible. "I mean, it hasn't happened since you were in fourth grade. For all we know, Jonathan Rice just went brain dead right then because of some interior alarm clock."

"Freud said there are no accidents," Gyro cautioned, although she could not possibly have known about what I accidentally did to Jonathan Rice in fourth grade.

"Freud has been dead a long time. It's the millennium," Mags said, without a trace of irony.

We repeated a lot of this as we stood over poor Alison Gall, whom we had most heinously trapped at Quent Appenino's grandfather's farm out in the middle of Bumfuck. She had worn a cute little yellow pullover that showed her melons to their best advantage, and her little tight-ass cheerleader skirt, knee socks, cute little black shoes, and no underwear to speak of. Need I mention what a shock she had received when she entered the old barn that had yet-another forged love note tacked to its door? Three furies standing there in the semi-dark of the barn, with rope, duct tape, and gun.

Okay, the gun was a last minute thing.

Gyro's older brother Lance was a cop wannabe. He was too smart for the local police force, apparently, but still he kept a major stash of Glocks and Smiths & Wessons and big old rifles, none of which Gyro knew much about. Mags picked out the Glock 17. "I've seen this on *NYPD Blue*," she said. "At least, I think I've seen this."

"I don't think we need a gun, do we?" I had asked as we stood shivering in Gyro's brother's room, knowing the fearful act we were to perform a few hours down the road. And then, it was Alison Gall's turn to shiver, which is what I expected when she saw the gun.

Instead, she was the bitch of bitches. "What the hell kind of joke is this?" she asked, and then, looking at the gun, she laughed. "You all planning on going to prison for the rest of your lives?"

Mags laughed. She had that great throaty laugh, the kind that old movie stars have, or old cigarette smokers. "Listen, Alison, we're minors, get real. Gyro's dad is a brain surgeon, and Nora's dad is a tax lawyer. Who do you think's going to go to prison?"

"You, trailer trash girl," Alison huffed.

"Shut up," I said.

"Shut up yourself, geek."

"Don't make me bitch slap you," Mags said. She meant business, particularly after the trailer trash comment. "My dad may not be some big professional, but he's been known to spring a few dudes from prison. I doubt girl's reform school is going to take a major army to overcome."

Alison quieted down. She glanced at me, then at Gyro. "Is this a lesbian thing or something?"

I laughed. "You'll wish when it's over."

"No," Gyro said. "We just want you out of the way until after the Prom."

"No way!" Alison shouted, and for a moment I felt sorry for the poor thing. Alison Gall lived for major social events. She never missed a Football Party, or a dance, or a chance to show off her cheering skills. She was a debutante in the big cotillion up in St. Paul. For just a second there, I saw the sad little girl beneath the make up and the dye job and the "Look How Cute I Am" clothes. She was just like I was years ago. A Pretty Little Nothing. Trying to make do. Trying to please other people. No wonder she was so nasty to us girls all the time—we were the one group she didn't have to please.

I was about to call the gag off, but this was Gyro's game. Gyro stepped forward with the rope. After the initial scuffle, we got Alison's hands behind her back. I only had to hit her once. By the time the duct tape went over her mouth, Alison's eyes were red from tears. Mascara ran down her cheeks.

"I should shoot you just for being a cheerleader," Mags said, pointing the gun directly at her forehead.

Alison didn't even flinch. I knew why. She was such a Pretty Little Nothing that she thought death was not more terrifying or hurtful than missing the biggest dance of the year. Maybe this was shallow of her, I don't know. We all want something out of life, don't we? We all want something, and to someone else, it probably sounds stupid and shallow and empty, but to each of us, it's the shining moment that we can always have at the center of our lives.

And the Prom was going to be Alison's shining moment.

Here she was a senior, probably going to the local college next year, if at all, and her entire future life depended upon looking back on high school as that peak, that golden moment.

We were taking that away from her.

Mags must've guessed my shift in sympathies. "Don't forget what she did to Gyro," she said.

I shined my flashlight over at Gyro, fury still in her eyes. She carefully wrapped the remainder of her rope around Alison's ankles.

I shut my flashlight off. I no longer wanted to look at our captive.

I no longer wanted to look at any of us.

And that's when Gyro rose up and took the gun from Mags' hand and aimed it at the side of Alison Gall's head and shot her at point-blank range.

Sometimes there are things you do in life and you know when you're doing them that later on you'll hate yourself, or you'll want to go back and erase part of the picture of that moment.

In that millisecond when Gyro fired into Alison's skull, I tried to, at least in my mind, turn the clock back by a minute so I could grab the gun before Gyro could get it.

I know neither Mags nor I had intended to use that gun. It was just a scare tactic. But Gyro, I think, probably had planned Alison's death for at least a week, from at least that moment when she entered the bathroom sobbing, from the moment that we told her that we'd seek a suitable revenge for her humiliation.

The silence afterwards was like a roar of locusts in my head. I thought I heard lightbulbs sparking and popping all around us. I thought it was the Fourth of July, from the crashes and booms inside my head.

Alison lay on her side, half her scalp blown off. Part of her face was on the dirt, as if the bullet had unmasked her.

Mags was the first to speak. "Oh, Christ, Gyro."

"Yeah," Gyro nodded, tossing the gun down. "I know. I shouldn't have. But I had to before it went the other way."

"Went the other way?" I asked.

But I knew what she meant.

If you didn't put a bullet in the head of the one who tormented you, you put the bullet in your own head. It was always either-or when it came to vengeance.

"All right, now, we're fucked," Mags said. "Now we're really fucked." She slapped the side of her face. "Christ, my heart is beating like it's gonna jump out from my chest."

"Funny," Gyro said, almost kindly. "I've never felt this calm. You?" She looked up at me as if it was important what I was feeling.

"I have no idea what I'm feeling."

"As long as she doesn't get the Fries With That? feeling, we're fine," Mags managed a joke.

FRIES WITH THAT?

Long after the Prom was over, we sat in that dark barn with the corpse, passing cigarettes around until our six packs were empty.

"Gyro," I said, passing her my flask. "You may go to jail for a long time for this."

Mags waved the last of her cigarette, tracing a red line in the air. "We're accomplices. Or accessories."

"Accessories," Gyro gasped after taking a long swig of my special brew. "But I'm the killer."

"People loved her," Mags whispered, reverentially. "I don't know why, but boys and parents and local business people, and little kids all loved her. Alison Gall, the bitch." Then she laughed. "I can't believe we're sitting here with a cheerleader's body drinking bad rum and Coke from a cheap flask on Prom Night."

"It does lead one to suspect we're insane," I said, drunkenly. The flask was dry by the next go round.

"Almost insane. If we were insane, we'd probably play with her or something," Gyro said.

"Yuck," I said.

"That is disgusting," Mags agreed. "One thing, though. We need a plan of action now."

Out back was that duck pond, empty of ducks at two a.m., and Mags was the first of us to shed her clothes. She grabbed the old rope swing, and swung out over the middle of the pond before dropping.

The splash was huge, and Mags bobbed up laughing. Gyro told me she wasn't in the mood, but I convinced her we should go in because of how filthy and stinky we'd all gotten since she shot Alison Gall in the head. Soon, all three of us were in the pond, splashing and laughing and trying to forget the millisecond of bad judgment when we decided to set any of this in motion in the first place.

In the moonlight, Gyro came up from the water, and both Mags and I gasped.

"What is it? What's wrong?" Gyro asked.

I looked at Mags and she at me, and both back at Gyro. With her frizz brought down by the water, and her glasses off, and naked so we could see her breasts—

She was beautiful.

"You are the most beautiful girl in school," I said.

"No kidding. Why do you hide under all that other shit?" Mags asked.

Gyro covered her breasts with her hands. "You're making fun of me."

"No," I said. "I swear, Gyro—"

"Janine," Mags corrected me. "No girl who looks like this could be named Gyro. Jesus, Janine, you look beautiful. And you've got those champagne glass breasts."

"And not the fluted kind," I joked.

"You're embarrassing me," Gyro said. "Seriously. Call me Gyro, I don't like being called Janine."

"I can't anymore," Mags said. "No way. Christ, Janine. You're a murderess and a beauty. Surprises galore."

"Please," Gyro began sobbing. She swam over to the muddy shore.

There was nothing to do, or at least, we didn't figure out what the hell we were going to do yet. We sure as shit couldn't go home. We couldn't just leave Alison's body there in the barn. We toyed with the idea of pinning the murder on Quent Appenino, because the notes would be in his handwriting. And he was stupid. But that story would probably have flaws we couldn't figure out. We thought about saying some strange man did it, but what if some innocent guy matching the description we gave got the chair over this or something? We still had shreds and scraps of conscience, after all.

Then, 'round about five thirty, just as the first pink rays of June sunlight came up to the east, Mags slapped me on the shoulder. "You!" she cried out.

"What the—"

"Fries With That?!" Mags began dancing around in a circle, her blouse still not buttoned up so her breasts kind of swung out like ripe pears about to fall.

"What's that mean?" Gyro asked.

I shrugged.

Mags clapped her hands together and stood still. "It's her thing. It's like an ability. It's like a magic thingy."

"No it isn't. It's like the Evil Eye."

"No negative thoughts today," Mags announced boldly. "Now, Nora, you can fry people's brains, right?"

I shrugged again. "Animals, people. Only done it twice that I know of."

"What?" Gyro asked, her beauty still apparent in the early light.

"Okay," Mags said. She paced in a circle around me like some mad professor. "Okay. So! You know how this ability of yours works?"

"Nope," I said. "It's an inherited characteristic."

"Like a recessive gene," Gyro volunteered, still with a confused look on her face.

"Exactly, and it's there. It's inside you. It's sleeping, but," Mags stopped pacing and stood almost nose to nose with me. Her breath was sour. Her voice dropped to a whisper. "Ever tried it on a dead girl?"

Gyro probably whined about not understanding us or something, and Mags probably went on with her ravings, but actually the idea burst within me as Mags said that one sentence.

Ever tried it on a dead girl?

Yeah, my gramma's words came back to me then. *"Stay away from the dead."*

Then I remembered what she'd told me about my great-great grandmother. How something had been knocking from inside her uncle's coffin....

Birds began singing before the light was fully up that morning. We were worried about when the farm folk would come out to their barn, even though there were no animals to be seen in it, only the basics of farm machinery. So, we took Alison up, using Mags' sweatshirt to jam her face against her skull. Any little bloody bits, we covered up with straw and dirt. We took her back to her car, and put her in the trunk. It was a cute little Toyota Camry. Alison had been so spoiled in her lifetime.

So Mags and Gyro drove Alison's car, and I drove my mother's Buick, back to my house. My house was the biggest, and my room was the furthest from the front door and the closest to two side doors. We would not be noticed by my parents at all, given that it was Saturday morning which meant Country Club B.S. for both of them.

They laid Alison on my bed, keeping her bloodied head on Mags' sweatshirt.

Gyro looked at me gravely. "I don't know if I can believe all the stuff she told me in the car, but if you can do anything, it might help."

I looked at Mags. My best friend in the whole world. Better than best. Best of the best. She seemed small and vulnerable now. The way I felt on the inside.

I looked down at poor Alison.

"It's not working," I said after a few minutes.

"How does it work?" Gyro asked.

"I need to get mad at her."

"Stimulus, response," Gyro nodded. "And between stimulus and response there's a pause. In the pause, we decide what the response will be."

"Huh?" Mags asked.

Gyro nodded again to herself, and I could practically see the little wheels turning. Hesitating only a moment, she walked over to me, leaned close, and whispered something in my ear.

The explosion from inside my head seemed to knock me back against the wall. The room began spinning, and I swear—I swear—I saw a fire burst across the wallpaper, ripping and devouring the flower print, until the walls were charred—

And I was there with Alison's corpse, Alison's bloodied corpse, but poison spewed from inside me, and then my vision blackened.

When I awoke, I was on the floor, fever in my head, and Mags kneeling beside me. "What the fuck did she whisper?" she asked.

I looked at Mags, wondering for a moment where I was. Gyro stood beside the bed, looking down at it.

"What made you so mad at Alison again?"

Fries With That?

My mind returned from blankness. "She said...she said..."

I could barely recall the words that Gyro had whispered to me.

"Please...help...oh god," Alison's voice came like a scratched up old cat from the thing on the bed.

How long we all stood in the room, waiting for what was to come, I'm not sure. My memory is spotty on this.

But Alison, her face still sliding off, eventually sat up, and all of us saw what my Fries With That? had brought back from the dead: a bitch who looked like hell.

I don't need to go into a lot of the rest. I'm waiting for the Barbara Walters interview, and I want to give her an exclusive. Suffice it to say that we had one week left of school, and Alison Gall was alive again. No need to go into the surgery that Gyro did using some medical equipment we grabbed from her father's office, or the fact that Alison was there inside her body, but just not on the surface yet the way most of us are. She was down deep. Somehow I had rewired some circuits in her, while others had been permanently damaged. She barely said more than squat anymore.

We made up a story for her mother about how we rescued her at the Prom, how she'd fallen down some stairs drunk after coming in with some boy from out of town. Her now ex-boyfriend believed this, as did most everyone else. Thus the stitches, thus her slowness, thus the fact that while she still performed routine tasks, like getting up in the morning, showering, eating, dressing for school, even cheerleader practice, Alison Gall was, for all intents and purposes, not all there.

She was hideous to see, too. Her face, with the tiny threads, her hair a bit lopsided. From the neck down she was still gorgeous, but the meaner boys started calling her a two-bagger hump, "in case the bag falls off her head, you still have one on."

Now and then, in the last days of school that year, I would sit across from her, and a little shriek like a seagull makes would come from deep down in her throat.

Mags and Gyro and I didn't talk much, but nodded to each other in the halls every now and then. I smoked in the girl's bathroom sometimes, hoping Mags would come in, but she never did.

And then on the last day of school, Alison Gall, walking in her daze down the hallway, turned towards her ex-boyfriend Joey Hoskins and I saw it coming.

I don't know why I didn't think of it before, but I should've.

We all should've wondered what would happen if Alison came back.

What she might be able to do if her brain got Fries With That? from death to life.

I saw her pupils go up under her eyelids, I saw the rash spread across her face, and I saw her mouth open impossibly wide.

She had it now, too. Whatever I had endowed her with, it had opened up something in her, too. Maybe we all have it within us, and only some of us have it at the surface.

She had Fries With That?

Shit, I thought. *It's contagious. Shit. Just like gramma said to me. "Stay away from the dead."*

And now, she did it to Joey. His body began twitching, and the blue of his eyes melted across his face like punctured egg yolks.

Like lightning, it passed around the hall, five other kids, some innocent of past association with Alison, some not so innocent. All shaking and shivering, foaming at the mouths, their eyes rolling up in their heads.

Five kids, and Mags came down the hall and watched it, too. Others came out, but ran when they saw the jolts and smelled the burning.

Mags turns to me, shaking her head. Not at me, I guess, but at our bad decision. At our bad cover up of Gyro's killing of Alison and us as accomplices in murder. There was a lot of love in her gaze as she looked at me.

It was either-or, I could tell.

Either it ended right there, or it goes on, and who knows how many brains would fry because I have this little talent inherited from my gramma's side, a little talent that no doctor has figured out yet though god knows they probed and poked inside my head enough these past couple months.

I know what she's going to do, and I'm wondering why she still has it on her. Why she carries it.

And that's when Mags pulled out the Glock from the inside pocket on her black denim jacket and started firing at all the kids who were fizzling into the Fryer that Alison is beaming at them.

I guess she just didn't want to take it anymore.

Later on, when she was taken in, I went to visit her. "Don't tell them what happened," she told me. "I'll be out in a couple of years anyway. I'm sixteen. How much can they do?"

"But it's not your fault," I said.

"Look," Mags said. "I'm from the trailers. You and Gyro are Country Club Acres girls. Like Alison. You wouldn't survive what I'm going through right now."

Then, the tears welled in her eyes. "You are my best friend. It's no big deal for me to be here."

We both had a good cry that afternoon. I felt like I did when my gramma had been alive. That kind of warmth. There were times when I wanted to hug Mags tight and never let her go. I could watch her face, the way her eyes sink into it, the way her dark hair hangs like a canopy over and around it, I could watch her face for hours. She has this perfect way of being. Even when she's going through hell.

Then I asked her why she had done it. I mean, I knew why, really. I knew that we had started something that wouldn't stop on its own.

But Mags surprised me. She said, "Because I have wanted to shoot those kids since the third grade when I first met any of them. Fried brains or no."

Mags is probably the most bold person I know.

Bold as they come.

But her boldness is losing its edge. I think jail did that to her.

Later, all the talk shows started, and then Mags was let off because Alison had recovered from her wounds and was living on some machines and spilled a fake story about someone other than

Mags doing the shooting. Even though it was an obvious lie I was happy to know that Alison had regained her speech a bit more, and I was happy that Mags was no longer the prime suspect.

Then, of course, we all found out that Alison somehow escaped the hospital, pulling out all her wires. There's a story that she wrote something in blood on the hospital wall, about coming after each of us, me, Mags and Gyro, but I'm not going to sit around getting scared over this. Life is too short. She's probably doing some zombie strip show up in Duluth or something by now.

Gyro has stayed out of the limelight, but occasionally she calls after midnight. Crying, whispering, full of fear and rumors of things that might happen. She's afraid of Alison, but I think Alison probably did what she should've done before we even had decided to abduct her.

Got the hell out of town.

Dead or alive, it's all any of us wants to do.

126

Of course, this is the true story. Mags is covering for Gyro when she tells it her way. Her way has me as an insaniac and Gyro as an innocent and Alison Gall as the bitch goddess. Mags says the truth is that she and I went nuts one day in school. That she had stolen Gyro's brother's gun. That I laughed while she fired the shots at Alison and the others.

Sometimes, she tells me on the phone that she doesn't really believe the truth anymore.

She told me, "It couldn't happen the way we saw it. It just couldn't. It had to be us, Nora. You and me. Maybe we just got too fucked up in life to know what was really happening around us. I don't know. I'm not smart enough."

She lost her courage somewhere since all the T.V. shows and the newspapers and *People* magazine. She's still my best friend, and I admire the hell out of her, I really do.

But I wish she'd face the truth.

Fries With That?

Yeah, there's more, like what Alison did to humiliate Gyro. And what Gyro whispered in my ear to make me so mad I could focus my Fries With That? on poor dead Alison.

I mean, even thinking it again makes me mad enough to spit, but I'm saving it for when Barbara Walters' people call me.

THE MACHINERY OF NIGHT

All I can really say about The Machinery of Night is: I've done a fair amount of research of forensics hospitals, the ones that house the criminally insane population. I also have a sense about molecules that allows them to be—possibly—more fluid than the way we perceive them.

1

He thinks: it is our thoughts that make us solid. And daylight. Daylight affects our vision so we believe in solids, in mass, in the religion of material and weight. But when the night washes over us like a flood, it draws back the veil. Pagans knew this; Buddhists knew this; maybe even some Christians know it, which is why they fear the devil and all his works so much. The devil is night. The devil is low definition. The devil is where one ends and another begins and all of it a great stream. The devil is darkness. It's a mechanism for seeing without seeing. Starlight reveals how fluid we are. How there is no beginning and end. Christ said I am the Alpha and the Omega, but the darkness says there is no beginning and end; there is only world without end, world without definition, world without boundary. How to erase the lines between the boundaries is the thing.

Then he stops thinking. Light, somewhere, light spitting out of the hole in the sky.

The night recedes again, the world hardens. Walls arise, windows, doors, beds, restraints.

2

"Who did this?"

"The ones who come in the night."

"Stop that. Who did this? Tell me right now. I mean now. Come on. One of you did this."

"I told you. It doesn't surprise me you don't believe us. You don't believe in much, do you?"

Human feces spread like a post-modern landscape across the green wall.

The words: I FORGIVE YOU SON in curly-cue shit paint.

Layton glanced at the three of them, knowing that not one man among them would confess. All it meant was more work for him. More cleaning, more scrubbing, all the things he hated about his job. Meanwhile, the world spun—outside the window, he could see the river as it ran beside the spindly trees, the flooding having subsided three days earlier; the sun through morning mist; the gray doves like children's paper airplanes floating on the nearly-insubstantial breeze, finally landing on the outer wall, beyond the razor-wired fence. He wanted to be there. He wanted to quit his job that day, but he was still waiting for things to happen—he waited for the other offer from a better hospital, or even a nice administrative position at the Cancer Society. Anything but here, this place where no one ever seemed to get better, where the depressed remained bleary-eyed, their blood nearly all Thorazine and Prozac at this point; or the criminals, the ones who had done terrible things out there in the world and now were with him, with Layton Conner, behind these walls; and who, after all, were any of them? It was said that even one of the nurses had ended up in a bed down on Ward Six, her mind scrambled because she let them in, she let the patients' world engulf her own until she didn't know there was an Outside.

Look outside when they get to you. Just for a second. You need to do this to keep yourself safe. When they are getting inside you, look out the nearest window for a second, look at your shoes, look at anything that will take your mind away from them for a moment so they won't own you.

He wished he'd had a cigarette on his break. He felt the addiction kicking in, and even with the patch on his arm, it wasn't enough drug to keep him sane in this environment. He glanced from the window to the three men—Nix, Hopper, and Dreiling, each with his secret history, secret insanity, secret darkness. Then, he looked beyond them to the far wall where one of them had taken their excrement and had written the words. Dreiling, who had prettier hair than any of the others in the ward, shook his locks out and grinned. "It's music," he said, and the interminable humming began; Nix clapped his hands in the air, catching the imaginary, or perhaps keeping time with Dreiling's annoying tune. Hopper, who was rather nice in Layton's opinion, gave an 'aw, shucks,' look, shook his head, and whispered something to himself.

"You can't do this anymore," Layton said, easing away from his own frustration. "It's not going to help when Dr. Glover comes in and sees this. It's not going to keep you free."

At the mention of the psych director's name, all three shivered slightly, as if a ghost had kissed them on the neck right at that moment, and Layton felt a little powerful invoking the name of the dreaded man.

Nix's face broke out in sweaty beads, and he put his hand up to his throat. "I...I can't swallow...."

"Of course you can, now, Nix, come on, take a deep breath," Layton stepped forward, bringing his hand up to pry Nix's fingers loose. "Let go. You can swallow just fine."

"I can't," Nix said somewhat despondently, but in fact, he could. "I hate Dr. Glover. And Dr. Harper. And you nurses."

"Do you ever think she'll stop?" Hopper asked later while Layton guided him back to his own room for the daily dose of meds.

"What's that?"

"She dreams all of it, her and the baby, and the old man, all of them." Hopper whispered, a secret, and Layton nodded as if he knew what the hell the tattooed man was babbling about, and then he gave him the little pink drink from the little white cups, and eventually, Hopper fell asleep on the cot while Layton fastened the restraints to his arms.

"This is not everything I'm about," Layton said to the girl in the pub later, leaning against the bar, a mug moving swiftly to his lips. He had bored her with his day. She was cute. She laughed at his jokes; she smiled at the stories of Nix, Hopper, Dr. Glover, Shea, Shaw, and Rogers and the Night Nurse. It was getting on towards evening, and he had stopped in for a quick drink or two before heading back to his place on Chrome Street. The day had been long, and there had been two eruptions, as Hansen called them, between inmates—first in the showers, what had begun as a rape between two very violent individuals had turned into a near-riot with six of the patients; and then, when Layton was clearly off his shift, he'd heard the screams from Room 47, and had run to intervene with Daisy, the Flowergirl, when she didn't want to get her sponge-bath. Daisy was sweet, and Layton hated seeing her get hurt, particularly from the techs and nurses on the floor, all of whom seemed to loathe the woman for no apparent reason. Once he'd calmed her down, she'd gone to her bath fairly easily; he watched while they held her and then he had taken the sponge himself, frothy with soap, and had spread it across her neck and arms and along her back before the female nurse had taken over. He felt bad for poor Daisy, but still, she had made him stay an extra two hours over his shift before he got his freedom again.

And now, the bar, the beer, and the pretty girl who could not be more than twenty-two; even so she worked hard to exude girlishness. Her skirt too short, her laugh too tinkly, her eyes much too shadowed. "But the insane, that's who you work with?"

He shrugged. "That's one way of looking at them. They're ordinary people who have had something go wrong. Sometimes, what went wrong is small and nearly unimportant, but it's enough to make them want to attempt suicide. Sometimes, it's a big wrong, and a few of them have murdered or harmed others. Sad thing is, bottom line, they're there to be protected from themselves more than anything."

"Crazy people," she shook her head. "I can't imagine. My mother went crazy during the storms…"

"They were bad," he grinned, noticing that something seemed to be ripening about her right there, in the bar, at nine o'clock in the evening, fertility swept her hair and lifted her breasts and reddened her lips like a Nile goddess. He wanted her. He wanted to touch her.

"When the river flooded, we had to go to my grandfather's place in the hills, and we almost didn't get my mother out in time," she laughed, shaking her head. He bought her a beer, she sipped it, and he had another one, and it seemed as if he'd just ordered another one when he was in the dark with her, in a small bed, and he was almost inhaling her skin and kissing down and up the smoothness of her. Even when they made love, he looked beyond her, out the arched window of the bedroom in her mother's house, at the moon casting nets of light across the river, sparkling like fish on its rumbling surface; across from them, up the third hill, the asylum waited to snatch his days. He smoked three cigarettes afterward, and fell asleep in the crook of her arm.

"I can't offer you coffee," she said. Angela. That was her name. Out the window, it was still night. He smiled, almost afraid he would forget her name. "Mom would throw a fit if she knew you were here. Got to be quiet."

"How old are you?"

"Nineteen," she said.

Shit, he thought.

"You?" she asked.

"Twenty-eight."

"When you were ten," she said.

"I know, you weren't even walking."

"When you were ten," she repeated, "you found your father crawling on all fours and braying like a mule."

"How did you know that?" he gasped.

"You told me last night. Remember? You wept."

"I wept?"

She kissed his cheek as he buttoned his shirt. "I thought it was sweet. It's why you became a nurse. Remember? Your father attacked you finally and you had to somehow take care of it all. I can only imagine."

Layton laughed, hugging her. "My god, what was in that beer?"

"Shh," she said, covering his lips with her hand. "I have to get her breakfast and then get ready for class. You need to go."

"What time is it?" He glanced at the clock on the table. It was nearly six; not quite light out. "Damn it."

3

"A lot can happen in twenty minutes," Sheila said, her starched blouse looking like white armor covering her starched soul. "In twenty minutes I could've been home in bed already."

"Sorry. I'll come in early tomorrow." Layton took up one of the pens from the cup, and signed his name on the yellow paper next to her hand.

"I am exhausted." Her eyes would not meet his—typical—and she signed off on her papers, her shift done, passing him the clipboard. "Jones and Marshall are on today, and at nine, Harper comes in to do meds. Glover is over at State for three days. You need to do better on sharps check; I found this," she drew something from her pocket. Passed it to him. He glanced at the thing in his hand—a safety pin. Her voice was gravel and rain. "Nix had it. Don't know how he got it. Said something about some people giving it to him. He's been known to kill with things like that."

"I can imagine," Layton said, trying to keep it light. Sheila could be a bitch if she felt like it, and she was senior staff and stupid, a terrible combination. She had Doc Ellis's ear, and that meant she could make sure his review bit the dust, no raise, and no promotion to an easier ward. He grinned. "Thanks for covering for me. Twenty minutes is too much. Had a car issue."

"Oh," Sheila said, her voice now all sleet. "That's twice in six weeks. Better get it into the shop."

After she left—making sure to check his keys for him like he was a baby—he started on the basic rounds with one of the psych techs. Sharps check, whites check, laundry baskets rolled out as more staffers arrived, coffee in the vending room, twice-told jokes about the boy who grew trees on his back, complaints from Shaw and Rogers about their treatment, a backed-up toilet on two, followed by basic bed check—Rance had the sniffles, and Layton quickly checked his temp only to find a high fever and then, oh shit, the day was screwed. Harper arrived and began a mini-quarantine to make sure it wasn't anything worse than the flu—six ended up in Rance's room, all with fevers, all beginning to moan about the demons who were scratching at them or their skin falling off, or any number of odd complaints. Diarrhea on the floor, dripping, spitting, and Layton going between them with juice and toast, just hoping for once they'd all get the plague and die.

When he finally got to Nix's room, he unstrapped him. "I thought Shaw would've done this by now, damn it," Layton said, muttering to himself, but Nix laughed.

"That's the first time you've ever said anything that made sense, Mr. Conner," Nix said, "and now, if you don't mind, a little privacy?"

Layton nodded and turned his back. He watched the wall and tried to ignore the pissing sounds coming from the toilet in the corner.

"All done," Nix said.

"Glad to see no writing on the wall today," Layton said, turning.

Nix had a face that was a genetic mix of wise child and prematurely old troll—Layton had never noticed 'til now that Nix had a scar on his chin, or that he was beginning to go bald. His blond hair receded from a point on his crown. How old was he? Layton thought he was forty, but he might've been mid-thirties. It was on his chart, but who looked at the charts anymore? Administrative bullshit.

"She finally stopped," Nix said, getting fidgety. His face became stormy—his brows twitched, his lips curled, his skin began wrinkling with nervous spasms.

135

Needs his meds. "You sleep okay?"

"Not really," Nix giggled, his fingers beginning their familiar snapping—

Where the fuck is Rogers and the med cart?

"Couldn't sleep—"

"At all?" Layton asked.

"The baby kept me up, so I had to wander," Nix said, and then went to the sink and began washing up. He shook like a drunk. Where the hell was the med cart? Layton watched him in the steel mirror. "I went out and had a drink or two and then made friends."

"Oh did you," Layton nodded. He glanced at the open door. The squeaking whine of the med cart wheels echoed along the green corridor. Somewhere a fly buzzed. Out the window? He glanced outside, through the bars and glass, past the pavement, the fences, to the river and the valley—God, he just wanted to be there. Layton went and sat down on the mattress. It was clean—unlike other patients' rooms. "Another night on the town?"

Nix turned slowly, his face shiny with water. "Oh yes. I met someone and we spent the night together."

"Well," Layton grinned. "Not a total loss then." Stretched his arms out, and hopped up again. Nix was an easy patient for the most part; violent when he was on the outside, but inside he was pretty much a kitten. Nix never went for the eyes. He spoke sensibly except when he went into some delusional talk. Layton went to the sink and brought up a towel for him.

Taking the towel, wiping his hands slowly, Nix said, "Not a total loss at all. But then…that baby was still wailing. She hadn't changed him, that's why. She doesn't know how important it is. See, the thing is, she can understand all this movement, this jumble of molecules, but he's just a baby, his mind hasn't quite sorted it out. She thinks because he's a baby he's better at it. I had to change him myself."

"Is that how you got the safety pin?"

"The what?" Covering his face in the white towel, Nix's features came through the cloth. Layton shivered slightly. Something about the towel on the face reminded him of his father's madness. The form without expression. The open mouth without sound.

"Nurse Allen found it, this little pin," Layton grabbed the towel back, rolling it into a ball. "She took it from you. Last night."

"Oh, that," Nix swept a hand in the air. "That night nurse is no good. She's a brick. She finds that and she thinks I'm just plotting to stab her in the neck twenty times with it or plunge it into her heart and extract it. She's crazy."

Layton wanted to add: *it's what you did to two women on the Outside, Nix. Why wouldn't she think you'd use it on her, too?*

4

Layton met Angela again the following Saturday, they got a little drunk again, ended up down on the muddy bank of the river, found a dry rock, kissed, almost began to make love, but she said she just wasn't in the right mood. "It's my mother," she said. "She's been giving me hell lately."

"I keep forgetting you're nineteen."

"I turned twenty."

"When?"

"Thursday."

"Happy Birthday."

"I don't care about birthdays or age. Or anything. It's all this proof. It means nothing. If I told you I was twenty-seven, you wouldn't really know the difference. It's just revolutions of the earth. Years go by. Gravity pulls. We all buy into it." Angela reached into her breast pocket and withdrew a pack of cigarettes. She offered him one—he snapped it up—and then sucked one up between her lips, lit it, puffed, and sighed. "All learning is about trapping. Keeps you trapped inside this…vehicle…we call a body. We learn that we're flesh and bone, but somewhere it's all particles. Somehow the particles convince us we're solid. I took molecular biology last semester and barely understood a word, but the way I see it, we're all just convincing ourselves that anything we are or see is solid, but it's not. It's confetti. Bits and pieces and then it's all like this river. Look at the river—silt and fish and water and amoebas and all kinds of things, and we call it river, but it's all one thing, and who's really to say that the fish actually moves or if it becomes water and in the next second is fish again only because it was water?"

"Well," he said, nibbling on her ear, "college and beer are doing you good I see."

"Well, it's hard to swallow some of the bullshit."

"Yeah, tell me about it. It's like being raised Catholic."

"You? Catholic?"

He laughed. "Yeah, you know all that belief shit. Even science is full of its little beliefs, and half the problem is buying into them or not. Just like you said."

"Well," she shrugged, "I believe in a lot of what you'd probably call belief shit."

"I gave up believing in anything I can't see when my father died," he said quietly. He wanted to laugh and make a joke of this, but he couldn't.

She opened her mouth to speak, but smoke came out. She stubbed the cigarette out on the rock.

"My mother is basically dying," Angela began, almost inaudibly. She said it again a bit louder. Layton had nothing to add. He wanted to say something wise and kind, but no words came to mind. "She's dying, and I'm just getting started on life. She's a nightmare at times. I've wished her dead with each surgery. For her own sake. I've wished her gone. Can't imagine having a daughter like me." She brightened for a second. "Change the subject, quick. I don't want to think about it."

"I had a boring week," he said. "You don't want to hear about it. I'm sorry about—"

"I really mean it. Change the subject. Poor baby. Boredom is worse than dying. Change the subject. Your work, your boyhood, your religious awakening, anything."

"In my job, boredom is good."

"Well, then." She lit another cigarette. "Tell me how it was boring."

"No attacks, no riots, no bizarre rituals involving stray cats, no eyes getting popped out."

"Something to celebrate."

"Along with your birthday."

"Now I feel like it," she said, leaning into him, and he felt her ripen again, as if she wanted him to open her, to be part of her. The cigarette went into the mud, his hands found their way beneath her blouse, her hands encircled his back. Nature took over—he found himself making love to her on the rock, in the torn fingernail of light along the banks of the flooded river. They dozed afterward for just a few minutes; then she said something; he opened his eyes but was still in a half-dream.

"You see? You're in it, too. You think you're outside but you're really in," she said. When he asked her what she meant by that, she acted as if he had dreamed it. It was two a.m. when he walked her home, and kissed her on the forehead. She looked surprised. "You took all my passion," he laughed.

"Ah," she nodded. "Well, I best get some sleep. I have a Physics exam on Monday, bright and early."

"Physics? Ouch," Layton grinned. "My worst subject."

"I kind of like it. We have a bizarre professor who talks about string theory and molecular shake ups and why we can't just go through chairs and things."

"Okay," Layton nodded. "You lost me. I'm just a nurse."

"Don't play dumb," she swatted him playfully. "Hey, wait, before you go, you need to give me something."

"Oh I think I did already."

"Not that, you cad," she whisper-giggled. "Something to show you care."

He reached into his pockets, "Christ, I've got nothing. No mementos at all. Wait," he brought up a half-roll of Lifesavers. "There you go. To save your life with." He pressed it into her hand, and she giggled and told him that until they met again she would treasure each and every tropical fruit flavor.

5

"Where did you get those?" Layton asked. It was a few weeks later, and Angela had not been answering his calls and no one answered her door, and now he was at work feeling the worst heartache of his life—and Nix the Needle had a half-roll of tropical fruit Lifesavers in his hand.

"You going to take those off me?" Nix asked, tugging at the restraints that held his hands to the bed. "Don't I even have a right to candy?"

"Give it to me," Layton said, plucking the roll from the man's hands. "Where did you get—"

Nix looked up into his eyes, deeply, soulfully, and whispered in a soft voice, "She's dying, and I'm just getting started on life. She's a nightmare at times. I've wished her dead with each surgery. For her own sake. I've wished her gone. Can't imagine having a daughter like me. Change the subject, quick. I don't want to think about it."

6

"I'm afraid for you," Dr. Glover said. It was mid-afternoon and Layton was going off-shift soon. "I'm afraid in a way that I was afraid for Molly Sternberg."

"Please. Molly had a history of—"

"All of us have histories," Glover said. "None of us is immune to this. You work with mentally unstable people—sociopaths as well—and you become enmeshed. You begin to experience a similar dissociation from reality that they also experience. It is not that unusual. It is somewhat expected." Glover scratched at the side of his head. "Don't worry, Conner, I'm not going to put you away. You haven't identified yourself as insane. But it would not surprise me that you might just need a little distance. When was your last vacation?"

"Three months ago."

"Perhaps this is just one of those things," Glover added.

"Those things? You're a psychiatrist," Layton nodded his head slightly hoping that the doctor would laugh it off.

"Because I'm trained in a way of handling medical issues doesn't mean I have all the answers. Sometimes the unexplainable occurs. Sometimes it's a delusion. Sometimes it happens. I've been here long enough to realize that there's more to the world than has been catalogued in the medical texts. Now, what did Nicholas say?"

"He said exactly what this woman I know said the previous weekend."

"Precisely?"

"As precisely as I could recall it."

"You could recall it?"

"Christ," Layton said. He stood up. "I'd like a few days off."

"Speak to your supervisor; as far as I'm concerned, take any amount of time you want off. Your job is secure." Glover glanced over to his bookshelf. "You know, Conner, you've been here a few years. You know your ward inside and out. You've seen a lot. You've handled a lot. On the one hand, this could be your mind playing tricks on you." Glover reached beneath his glasses and rubbed two fingers along the bridge of his nose. He shut his eyes for a moment. "On the other hand, sometimes there are things that come through the patients. I'm not even sure what I mean by that." He took his glasses off. "Without my glasses, you are blurred." He put them back on. "Now I see you clearly. Does that mean that when I see you blurred that you are in fact blurred and that my vision is perfect but your image is in flux?"

"Sir?"

"All I'm saying is, we can't know everything. Assuming that Nicholas Holland said what you heard, perhaps he did know what this woman said to you. Perhaps he made it up and by some strange coincidence, for the first time in his own history, he said the exact words to disturb you. But I've learned in twenty-eight years as a psychiatrist handling the more extreme cases of human insanity, that—" and here Glover leaned forward, and Layton knew he would whisper, and he stepped forward to the edge of the desk, "we know nothing of the human mind. We are still in the Dark Ages of psychiatry. We are fumbling. Do you know what Nicholas said to me when he first entered this place? He told me that when the night came, the mechanisms changed, and that while I was eating supper the night before with my wife, he had already seen to it that the pie in the kitchen had fallen to the floor."

Layton, caught up for a moment, asked, "Did it?"

Glover drew back, laughing. "No, of course not. And we hadn't had any dessert. It was a complete fabrication. But how was I to know?" The laughter stopped. "I didn't even mention it to my wife, I thought it was just a rambling delusion on his part. But a year or so later, I was at a dinner party at a colleague's home, and some of the doctors were telling tales out of school. The usual—patients who sat up in the middle of operations, the near-malpractice suits that managed to get cleaned up in some hilarious way, the patients who hallucinated bizarre images—and so I had my glass of wine and told the story about Nicholas claiming to break into the house. I had them rolling mainly because I recalled all the details he added—how he sipped milk from the fridge, how he peed in the sink. And then I mentioned the pie claim, I said, and he then told me that he dropped a pie on the kitchen floor just so I wouldn't eat it. And Layton? I saw it in my wife's face, out of the corner of my eye, even then I saw that she had gone white as if something dreadful had come over her. She said nothing at dinner, but on the way home she told me that she had bought a pie at the A&P and had warmed it in the oven for a bit before letting it cool on the cutting board by the sink. 'And,' I asked, 'did it fall on the floor?' She told me it had not, but that someone had broken the crust, a man, she thought, because the handprint was big. Handprint? Yes, she said. It scared her because it was nearly perfect, almost as if someone had baked his hand into the crust. She threw it out, not wanting to even think about it. So, you see, perhaps Nicholas knew something. Perhaps he didn't. How could he? I am a man of some education and knowledge of science, Layton, but I have no basic explanation for this—or for you. Except to say: take a few days off and let this go."

7

And then, on his day off, he saw her again.

It was just after nine, and the rain began, and he was going to have a late dinner at the Hong Kong Moon restaurant when he saw her walking out of the Quickie Mart with a small bag of groceries. When he caught up to her at her car, she didn't look happy to see him at all. He wanted to ask about the Lifesavers, but it seemed trivial and stupid now.

"Oh, hi Layton," she said. "I'm sorry I haven't been around. My mother died. There was a lot to take care of."

"God, I'm sorry."

She got in the VW, rolling the window up against the rain.

He stood there, the blur of the rain on the car window obscuring her features, feeling the shiver of the end of love—not real love, but new love, the moment when it is over.

And then, she began laughing.

For just a second—was it the rain? His tears?—he thought that it all shimmered.

Not just her, but the rain and the glass and the metal of the car.

8

It took Layton twenty minutes to get up the hill, flash his badge at the guards, nod to the night nurse who was surprised to see him, and make his way down the ward. He found Nix sitting up on his mattress, his hair soaked. Nix glanced up, then back down to his own upturned palms. "My nerves are all tingly," Nix said.

"Tell me everything," Layton said.

Nix didn't look up from his hands. Then he licked his lips like a hungry child. "You don't know this for sure, Conner, what you're thinking. Whatever it is you're thinking."

"Do you know who Angela is?"

Nix grinned. "I have known many angels."

"Angela. She's the one who gave you the Lifesavers."

"I have saved many many lives," Nix said.

Layton rushed over and grabbed him by the shoulders, lifting him to his feet. They stared eye to eye; sweat ran down Nix's face. "What is it you do? What is it about the baby crying and the woman and the things that you babble about?"

Nix's grin faded. "It's the machinery. It's how it works. It's how we work. It's how the world changes in the dark, Conner. It's how when light particles are lessened, it's not just about seeing, it's about how in absolute darkness it can change. We can change."

Layton pushed him back down on the bed. "Half an hour ago you were a woman in a car."

"Was I?" Nix asked, almost slyly. "Was I? Well, then, Nurse Conner, you have already begun your journey. Do you remember being inside her, this Angela? How you pushed in, how she opened, how she made those little noises that made you push to greater and greater heights, how she turned twenty one week and how she told you all about her dying mother and how you fell in love and how she broke your heart one night in the rain? Do you remember playing with her body, or asking her to do something that you find in your heart of hearts to be repulsive and lowly but which brings you great pleasure? Do you remember when she told you all her secrets, even the one about her uncle, or the time you both laughed at once over something you seemed to think of at the same time, as if you had so much in common, Nurse Conner, that this might just be the girl for you, this might just be Miss Right and you just might be the luckiest man in the world? And then you told her that awful secret, the dark secret, the one you thought you could trust her with, the one about your father's madness, about how it pushed you to the edge and how one night you—"

Later, when two psych techs pulled him off Nix, Layton could not remember raising his fists, let alone bringing them down near forty times over Nix's head, nor could he remember through the trial that even after he'd begun to break the skin of Nix's face, long after the patient was dead, particles of bone from the patient's jaw and nose had splintered and some had gone, needle-like, into the palm of Layton's hand.

9

Nearly a year later, Layton tried to sit up in bed, but the restraints held him fast. He wanted to shout for the night nurse, but whom could he trust? He knew them all, he knew they thought he was one of the many criminally insane, but he knew the staff well, and he didn't understand why they should restrain him when he had only tried to kill himself once, and had botched the job anyway.

The Machinery of Night

It was the whisper of night coming up under the barred window, the last light of day was nearly vanished, and he still felt drowsy from the last med administered at two. The nights were the worst, because of the people who moved through it, who came and went and he watched in horror as they did what had to be done. Even Nix, even he came through, his face sometimes a bloody tangle, a forest of twisted flesh and bone, sometimes it was just his face, beads of sweat on his forehead, that trollish look, that milky complexion. The machinery hummed and if he could just believe strongly enough, he could slip through the restraints and join them, he could go and be anywhere and anyone, but it never seemed to happen. Some of the other patients came and went; the walls rippled like a flooding river; the air itself became vivid with the movement of nearly invisible molecules as they went like clouds of mosquitoes, forming and splitting apart again.

Layton, in restraints, tried to pray to what he could not see for freedom. His heartbeat raced as he watched a swollen bubble of glass move along the window.

"It's belief," he whispered. "Belief makes it move. It's absolute belief," but it wasn't coming for him, the molecules weren't changing, the mechanism of darkness was not clicking into place. "Please let me go. Please," he begged, and then, as happened nightly, his voice became louder, sobs and screams. One of the nurses came by with another med, and as she wiped the sweat from his forehead, he told her how they left nightly, how when the sun went down the machinery of night made it happen and their molecules swirled and how even the two men he had killed in his life, his father and Nix, sometimes came to him and made him do terrible things in the dark. "And the woman who spoke to the courts? Her name was Angela, but she's really one of the men I killed, only you can't ever really kill anyone, you can't, it's just a rearrangement of molecules and at night they can change again or if they want they can stay as they were that night for a whole day and they can even come to your trial and talk about you and things you told them and how you seemed to be going slowly mad only you never ever went mad, if anything it's complete sanity, it's the kind of sanity that's like the sun at noon all bright and sharp and please don't turn off the light, that's all I ask, when you leave and I get sleepy from the pills, please leave the lights on," his voice softened, and the nurse nodded. When he awoke later—when the meds were beginning to wear off—the room was dark and he felt the brush of a thousand particles that whispered with the voice of his father.

265 and Heaven

This is possibly the saddest story I have ever written, because it's about the lengths to which we humans might go just for brief moments of happiness. I believe a lot of people live for brief moments of heaven, whether it's from a drug, a drink, or something more brutal, as it is in this tale of Paul and Fabbo.

Alan Clark had a picture of a fantastic woodland house, with birds and lizards and a very beautiful but haunted look to it. This gave me the image of heaven for this story, and was used to "literate" his picture in the anthology, Imagination Fully Dilated.

1

What do we all live for? the bird asks.
This.
A glimpse of heaven.

2

The town at night seemed all crumbling brick and leaky gutters, alleyways washed clean by the summer rain, the stink of underground swamp, and grease from burger joints in the air. He was always on shift at night, and so it was the town he grew to know: the rain, the steam, the smells, the red brown of bricks piled up to make buildings, the hazy white of streetlamps. The same haunted faces downtown at night—the lonely crowd, the happy crowd, the people who went from diner to movie to home without walking more than a few feet, the kids in their souped-up cars, the old men walking with canes, the brief flare of life in the all-night drug stores.

All of it he saw, and it was for him the world.

But then one night, he saw something else.

It began as a routine call about an old drunk out at the trash cans. Paul was six-months new to the uniform, having only seen a couple of drug busts of the non-violent variety and one DUI. It was that kind of town—one murder in the past six years, and one cop killed in the line of duty since 1957. He and his little sister had lived there five years, and picked it because it was fairly quiet and calm, a good hospital, good visiting nurses' association, and no one to remember them from nine years before. He had been a security guard back in St. Chapelle right after college, but it had been his dream to be a cop, and now he was, and it was good, most nights. Most nights, he and his partner just trolled the streets for small-time hookers and signs of domestic violence. Sometimes they arrived too late at a jumper out on the Pawtuxet Bridge. Sometimes, they watched the jump.

Paul couldn't shake the vision out of his head of the kid who had jumped two weeks ago. Damn lemmings, some of these kids were. Just wanting to get out of town so bad they couldn't wait for the bus.

"Some guy's over in front of the Swan Street apartments knocking over cans and covered with blood," the smooth voice of the dispatcher said.

"Christ," Paul muttered. "Swan Street. Why does everything seem to happen over there?" He glanced at his watch. Nearly midnight.

His partner, Beth, sighed and shook her head when the call came from dispatch. "I bet I know this guy," she said, "Jesus, I bet it's this old clown." She turned left at Wilcox, and took two quick rights until they were on Canal Road. The night fairly steamed with humidity, and the sky threatened more rain. Paul wiped the back of his neck, feeling the slickness.

"He used to be with the circus, a real carny-type." As she spoke, Beth managed to reach across the dash, grab a cigarette from the pack, thrust it between her lips and punch in the lighter while still keeping her eye on the road. "He spends half the year God knows where and then comes back here in the summer. We had to ship him out twice last year."

"What a night," Paul said, barely hiding the disgust in his voice. The flat-topped brick buildings, dim blue windows, dark alleys of downtown bled by as he looked out the window. The streets were dead.

When Beth pulled the patrol car to the curb, Paul saw him. A fringe of gray hair around a shiny bald scalp, the checkered shirttail flapping, the saggy brown pants halfway down his butt. The guy stood beneath the streetlamp, his hands over his crotch. "He jerking off or what?" Beth asked, snorting.

"Poor old bastard," Paul said. "Can we get him to the station?"

"Easy," she said, "you just tell him we're taking him for some free drinks." As she opened her door, she shouted, "Hey! Fazzo! It's your friend!"

The old man turned, letting go of his crotch. He hadn't been masturbating; but a dark stain grew where he'd touched. He cried out, "Friends? My friends!" He opened his arms as if to embrace the very darkness beyond the streetlamp.

Paul got out, too, and jogged over to him. "Buddy, what you up to tonight?"

Looking at his uniform, the guy said, "I don't got nothing against cops. Believe you me. Cops are gold in my book."

Paul turned to Beth, whispering, "His breath. Jesus."

She gave him a look like he was being less than professional. He was new enough to the job to not want to get that kind of look.

The guy said, "I just been having a drink."

"Or two," Beth said. "Look, Fazzo..."

"Fazzo the Fabulous," the guy said, and did a mock-spin. "The greatest magician in the tri-state area."

"We got to take you to another bar."

"You buying?" he asked her.

"Yeah sure. You got a place up here?" Beth nodded towards the flophouse apartments beyond the streetlamp.

Fazzo nodded. "Renting it for thirty-five years. Number 265."

Paul shined his flashlight all over Fazzo. "I don't see any blood on him."

"It's the piss," Beth whispered, "someone reported it as blood. It happens sometimes. Poor old guy."

Beth escorted Fazzo to the car. She turned and nodded towards Paul; he took the signal. He went over to the back staircase. The door was open. He walked inside—the carpeting was damp and stank of mildew. A junkie sat six steps up, skinny to the bone, leaning against the peeling wallpaper, muttering some junkie incantation. Paul stepped around him. The hallway above was narrow, its paint all but stripped off by time. The smell of curry—someone was cooking, and it permeated the hall. When he got to 265, he knocked. The door was already ajar, and his fist opened it on the first knock.

There was a light somewhere to the back of the apartment. Paul called out to see if anyone was there. He gagged when he inhaled the fetid air.

All he could see were shadows and shapes, as if the old guy's furniture had been swathed in dropcloths. He felt along the wall for the light switch. When he found it, he turned on the light. It was a twenty-five watt bulb which fizzled to life from the center of the living room ceiling. Its light barely illuminated the ceiling itself. The chairs and couch in the room were covered with old newspapers, some of them damp from urine. The old man hadn't even bothered to make it to the bathroom anymore. There was human excrement behind the couch. Empty whiskey bottles along the floor in front of the television set.

Paul didn't notice the strong stink once he'd stayed in the apartment for a few minutes.

Beth arrived at that point. "I got him cuffed, not that he needs it. He fell asleep as soon as I sat him down in the car. Jesus!" She covered her mouth and nose. "I thought he'd been living on the street." Her eyes widened as she took in the other sights.

"Look at this," Paul pointed to the windowsill, shining his flashlight across it.

It was black with dead flies, two or three layers thick.

He continued on to the kitchen. "Should I open the fridge, you think?"

"Sure," Beth said. "Looks like Fazzo the Fabulous is going to end up in state hospital for awhile. What the hell?" She picked something up off a shelf and held it up. "Paul, look at this."

In her hands, what looked like a wig with long, thin hair. "You think Fazzo steps out on Saturday night in pearls and pumps?"

Paul shook his head, and turned back to the refrigerator. He opened the door, slowly. A blue light within it came on. The refrigerator was stacked three trays high with old meat—clotted steaks, green hamburger, what looked like a roast with a fine coating of mold on it. "Shit," he said, noticing the flies that were dead and stuck against the wet film that glazed the shinier cuts of meat. "This guy's lost it. He's not just a drunk. He needs serious help."

Beth walked into the bathroom, and started laughing.

"What's up?" he asked, moving around the boxes in the kitchen. Paul glanced to the open door.

The bathroom light was bright.

"It's clean in here. It's so clean you can eat off it. It must be the one room he never goes in." Beth leaned through the open doorway and gestured for Paul to come around the corner. "This is amazing."

Paul almost tripped over a long-dead plant as he made it over to where she stood.

The bathroom mirror was sparkling, as was the toilet, the pink tiles. Blue and pink guest soap were laid out in fake seashells on either side of the brass spigots of the faucet.

Written in lipstick on the mirror: a phone number.

For a second, he thought he saw something small and green skitter across the shiny tiles and dive behind the shower curtain. A lizard?

151

Paul went to pull the shower curtain aside, and that's when he found the woman's torso.

3

Paul washed his face six times that night, back at the sheriff's office. He wished he hadn't found it, he wished it had been Beth, or some other cop, someone who could take that kind of thing. It was the sort of image he had only seen in forensics textbooks, never in living color, never that muddy rainbow effect, never all the snake-like turns and twists...he had to put it out of his mind. He did not want to think about what was left of the woman in the tub.

He had not seen her face, and he was glad. She wasn't entirely human to him without a face.

Her name was Shirley, Fazzo the Fabulous told him. "Shirley Chastain. She was from the Clearwater District. She ran a dry cleaners with her mother. I thought she was a nice sort of girl right up until I cut her. I dug deep in her. She had a gut like a wet velvet curtain, thick, but smooth, smooth, smooth. She had a funny laugh. A tinkly bell kind of laugh." He had sobered up and was sitting in county jail. Paul stood outside his cell with the county coroner, who took notes as Fazzo spoke. "She had excellent taste in shoes, but no real sense of style. Her skin was like sponge cake."

"You eat her skin?" the coroner asked.

Fazzo laughed. "Hell, no. I'm not some damn Jeffrey Dahmer wannabe. I mean it *felt* like sponge cake. The way sponge cake used to be, like foam, like perfect foam when you pull it apart." He kneaded the air with his fingers. "I'm not a freakin' cannibal."

Paul asked, "You were a clown or something? Back in your circus days, I mean?"

"No, sir. I wasn't anything like that. I was the world's greatest magician. Even Harry Blackstone told me, when I was a kid, he said, 'Fazzo, you're gonna be the biggest, you got what it takes.' Didn't mean shit, but my oh my it sure did feel good to hear it from him."

"I guess you must've been something," Paul said.

Fazzo glanced from the coroner to Paul. "Why you here, kid? You busted me. What are you gawking for?"

"I don't know," Paul said. "You kind of remind me of my dad I guess." It was a joke; Paul glanced at the coroner, and then back at Fazzo. Last time Paul saw his dad, his dad's face was split open from the impact of the crash.

"Shit," the old guy dismissed this with a wave. "I know all about your old man, kid. It's like tattoos on your body. Everybody's story is on their body. Dad and Mom in car wreck, but you were driving. Little sister, too, thrown out of the car. I see it all, kid. You got a secret don't you? That's right, I can see it plain as day. You shouldn'ta never gone in 265, cause you're the type it wants. You're here because you got caught."

"*I* got caught?"

"You went in 265 and you got caught. I pass it to you, kid. You get the door-prize."

"You're some sick puppy," Paul said, turning away.

Fazzo shouted after him, "Don't ever go back there, kid. You can always get caught and get away. Just like a fish on the hook. Just don't fight it. That always reels 'em in!" Paul glanced back at Fazzo. The old man's eyes became slivers. "It's magic, kid. Real magic. Not the kind on stage or the kind in storybooks, but the real kind. It costs life sometimes to make magic. You're already caught, though. Don't go back there. Next time, it's you." Then Fazzo closed his eyes, and began humming to himself as if to block out some other noise.

It sickened Paul further, thinking what a waste of a life. What a waste of a damned life, not just the dead woman, but this old clown. Paul said, "Why'd you do it?"

Fazzo stopped his humming. He pointed his finger at Paul and said, "I was like you, kid. I didn't believe in anything. That's why it gets you. You believe in something, it can't get you. You don't believe, and it knows you got an empty space in your heart just waiting to be filled. You believe in heaven, kid?"

Paul remained silent.

"It's gonna get you, then, kid. You got to believe in heaven if you want to get out of 265."

Then, Fazzo told his story. Paul would've left, but Fazzo had a way of talking that hooked you. Paul leaned against the wall, thinking he'd take off any minute, but he listened.

4

I was famous, kid, sure, back before you were born, and I toured with the Seven Stars of Atlantis Circus, doing some sideshow skit like sword-swallowing and fire-eating before I got the brilliant idea to start bringing up pretty girls to saw in half or make disappear. This was way back when, kid, and there wasn't a lot of entertainment in towns with names like Wolf Creek or Cedar Bend or Silk Hope. The Seven Stars was the best they got, and I turned my act into a showcase. I was hot, kid. I blew in like a nor'easter and blew up like a firecracker. Imagine these hands—these hands—as I directed the greatest magic show in the tri-state area, the illusions, kid, the tricks of the trade, the boxes with trapdoors that opened below the stage, the nights of shooting stars as I exploded one girl-filled cage after another—they turned into white doves flying out across the stunned faces of children and middle-aged women and old men who had lost their dreams but found them inside the tent. Found them in my magic show! It was colossal, stupendous, magnificent! I gave them a night of fucking heaven, kid. We turned a dog into a great woolly mammoth, we turned a horse into a unicorn, we turned a heron into a boy and then into a lizard, all within twenty minutes, and then when it was all done, the boy became a rabbit and I handed it to some thrilled little girl in the audience to take home for a pet or for supper. Once, traveling during a rainy spring, the whole troupe got caught in mud, and I used my knowledge of traps and springs to get us all out of there—and was rewarded with becoming the Master of Ceremonies. It was practically religious, kid, and I was the high priest!

But the problem was, at least for me, that I believed in none of it. I could not swallow my own lies. The magic was a fake. I knew where the animals were hid away to be sprung up, and the little boy bounced down into a pile of sawdust while a snowy egret took his place, or an iguana popped up wearing a shirt just like the one the

154

boy had on. The boy could take it, he was good. Best assistant I ever had. The woman, too, she was great—saw her in half and she screamed like she was giving birth right on the table—not a beauty except in the legs. She had legs that didn't stop at the ass but went right on up to her chin.

When she got hit by the bus in Memphis, everything changed for me, and I didn't want to do the act again. Joey wanted to keep going, but I told him we were finished. I loved that kid. So, we quit the act, and I went to do a little entertaining in clubs, mostly strip joints. Tell a couple jokes, do a few tricks with feather fans—voila! Naked girls appear from behind my cape! It was not the grandeur of the carnival, but it paid the rent, and Joey had a roof over his head and we both had food in our mouths.

One month I was a little late on the rent, and we got thrown out. That's when I came here, and we got the little place on Swan Street. Well, we didn't get it, it got us.

But it got you, too, didn't it, kid? It wasn't just you walking in to 265, it was that you been preparing your whole life for 265. That other cop, she lives in another world already, 265 couldn't grab her. But it could grab you, and it did, huh?

I knew as soon as I saw you under the streetlamp.

I recognized you from before.

You remember before?

Hey, you want to know why I killed that woman? You really want to know?

Watch both my hands when I tell you. Remember, I'm a born prestidigitator.

Here's why: sometimes, you get caught in the doorway.

Sometimes, when the door comes down, someone doesn't get all the way out.

You want to find the other half of her body?

It's in 265.

Only no one's gonna find it but you, kid.

You're a member of the club.

5

Paul was off-shift at two, and went to grab a beer at the Salty Dog minutes before it closed. Jacko and Ronny got there ahead of him and bought the first round.

"Shit," Paul said, "it was like he sawed her in two."

"He saw her in two? What's that mean?" Jacko asked. He was already drunk.

"No, he sawed her in two. He was a magician. A real loser," Paul shook his head, shivering. "You should've seen it."

Jacko turned to Ronny, winking. "He saw her sawed and we should've seen it."

"Cut it out. It was...unimaginable."

Ronny tipped his glass. "Here's to you, Paulie boy. You got your first glimpse of the real world. It ain't pretty."

Jacko guzzled his beer, coughing when he came up for air. "Yeah, I remember my first torso. Man, it was hacked bad."

"I thought nothing like that happened around here," Paul said. "I thought this was a quiet town."

Jacko laughed, slapping him on the back. "It doesn't happen much, kid. But it always happens once. You got to see hell just to know how good the rest of this bullshit is."

Paul took a sip of beer. It tasted sour. He set the mug down. "He called it heaven." But was that really what Fazzo the Fabulous had said? Heaven? Or had he said you had to believe in heaven for 265 to not touch you?

Jacko said, "Christ, forget about it Paulie. Hey, how's that little Marie?"

Paul inhaled the smoke of the bar, like he needed something more inside him than the thought of 265. "She's okay."

6

When he got home to their little place on Grove, with the front porch light on, he saw her silhouette in the front window. He unlocked the front door, noticing that the stone step had gotten scummy from damp and moss. The early morning was strung with humid mist, the kind that got under skin, the kind that permeated apartments and houses and alleys. Humid like an emotion. Inside, only the bathroom light was on. He walked in, glancing at her, sitting in the living room.

"Marie," he said.

"I couldn't get the T.V. to work," her voice was humid.

"Sorry, kid," he said, trying not to show exhaustion. "I'll get it fixed tomorrow. You should be asleep."

"I should be," she said.

"Well, try and get some," he whispered. He went into the darkened living room, careful not to trip over the books she always left on the rug, or the Coke bottles, or the newspapers open to the comics pages. As he knelt beside her, he touched the top of her head. "How was Mrs. Jackson?"

"Oh, she was something," Marie said, and Paul was always amazed at her acerbic way of saying things. But it was nearly three a.m. on a Friday. No school tomorrow. Nothing for Marie but a vast day of nothing to do.

"How's the pain?"

She didn't answer.

Paul kissed his little sister on the forehead. "Well I need to go to bed. You should too."

Marie pulled away, turning her chair back towards the window. "I hate what you did to me," she whispered.

She said this more than he cared to remember.

"I hate it, too," he said. Trying not to remember why she could say it in the first place. "You keep your oxygen on all day?"

She may have nodded, he couldn't tell in the dim light.

"I hate what I did to myself," she whispered, but he wasn't sure. She may have said, "I hate what I do to myself." Or, "I hate what I want to do to myself." It was late. He'd had a couple of beers. She had whispered.

The three possibilities of what she had said played like a broken record through his mind every now and then, and in the next few days—staying up late, staring at the ceiling, hearing the hum of the machine that helped keep his beautiful twenty-year-old sister alive, he was sure she'd said the last thing.

I hate what I want to do to myself.

7

Clean up crew had been through, photographers had been through, the apartment was cordoned off, but not picked over much—with a full confession from Fazzo there wasn't much need of serious evidence. Paul stood in the doorway, nodding to one of the detectives in a silent hello.

He glanced around the apartment—it was trashed. Just a crazy old drunk's shit-hole.

The bathroom light seeped like pink liquid from under the door.

He didn't go in.

He didn't want to.

He wanted to not think about the torso or the magician or even the lizard he'd seen scuttle into the bathtub.

But it was all he thought about for the next six months.

8

158

On his nights off, he'd sit in the living room with Marie and watch television. Marie loved television, and besides her reading, it was the only thing that got her out of herself. "I saw a great movie last night," she told him.

He glanced at her. The small thin plastic tubing of the oxygen like a Fu-Manchu mustache hanging from beneath her nostrils, hooked up to the R2D2 Machine. The braces on her arms that connected to the metal brace that had become her spine and ribs. The wheelchair with its electric buzzes whenever she moved across the floor.

Still, she looked like Marie under all the metal and wire and tubing.

Pretty. Blond hair cut short. Her eyes bright, occasionally. Sometimes, he thought, she was happy.

"Yeah?" he asked.

"Yeah. It was amazing. A man and woman so in love, but they were divided by time and space. But he wanted her so badly. He sacrificed his life for her. But they had this one...moment. I cried and cried."

"You should be watching happy movies," Paul said, somewhat cheerfully.

"Happy or sad doesn't matter," Marie said. "That's where you mix things up too much. Happy and sad are symptoms. It's the thing about movies and books. It's that glimpse of heaven. No one loves anyone like they do in movies and books. No one hurts as wonderfully. I saw a movie about a woman in a car wreck just like ours, and she couldn't move from the waist down. Her family spurned her. A friend had to take care of her. She thought of killing herself. Then, the house caught on fire. She had to crawl out of the house. A little boy helped her. The little boy couldn't talk, and they became friends. I cried and cried."

"I don't like things that make you sad," he said. He meant it.

"This," Marie nodded to the machines and the walls. "This makes me sad. The stories get me out of this. They get me into heaven. Even if it's only for a few minutes, it's enough. You want to know why people cry at movies even when the movie is happy? I've thought about this a lot. It's because life is never that good. They know that when the screen goes dark, they have to go back to the life off-screen where nothing is as good. People who have cancer in movies have moments of heaven. People who have cancer in real life just have cancer. People in car wrecks in movies and stories get heaven. In real life..."

159

She didn't finish the thought.

"So you feel like you're in heaven when you read a story?"

She nodded. "Or see a good movie. Not the whole movie, just a few minutes. But a few minutes of heaven is better than no heaven at all. You know what I dream of at night?"

"No machines?" he said, hoping she would not be depressed by this comment.

She shook her head. "No. I dream that everything is exactly like it is, only it's absolutely wonderful. Then, I wake up."

They were silent for a moment. The movie on television continued.

Then she said, "I know why people kill themselves. It isn't because they hate anyone. It isn't because they want to escape.

It's because they think there's no heaven. Why go on if there's no heaven to get to?"

9

Paul went to see Fazzo the Fabulous on Death Row. Fazzo had gained some weight in prison, and looked healthier.

"I have to know something," he said.

"Yeah, kid?" Fazzo looked at him carefully. "You want to know all about 265, don't you? You been there since I got arrested?"

Paul nodded. Then, as if this were a revelation, he said, "You're sober."

"I have to be in here. No choice. The twelve-step program of incarceration...Let me tell you, 265 is a living breathing thing. It's not getting rented out any time soon, either. It waits for the one it marked. You're it, kid. It's waiting for you, and you know it. And there's no use resisting its charms."

"Why did you kill that woman?"

"The forty million dollar question, kid. The forty million dollar question."

"Forget it then."

"Okay, you look like a decent kid. I'll tell you. She was a sweet girl, but she wanted too much heaven. She and me both. Life's job is not to give you too much heaven. But she got a taste for it, just like I did. You get addicted to it. So," Fazzo gestured with his hands in a sawing motion. "She got in but the door came down. I mean, I know I cut into her, using my hands. I know that. Only I wasn't trying to cut into her. I liked her. She was sweet. I was trying to keep it from slamming down so hard on her. They thought I was insane at first, and were going to put me in one of those hospitals. But all the doctors pretty much confirmed that my marbles were around. Only all that boozing I did made me sound nuts." Fazzo leaned over. "You got someone you love, kid?"

Paul shrugged. "I got my little sister. She's it."

"No other family?"

"I got cousins out of state. Why?"

"No folks?"

Paul shook his head.

"Okay, now it's clear why 265 chose you, kid. You're like me, practically no strings, right? But one beloved in your life. Me, I had Joey."

Paul grimaced.

"Hey!" Fazzo flared up. "It wasn't like that! Joey was a kid whose family threw him out with the garbage. I gave him shelter, and that was it. Wasn't nothing funny about it. Sick thing to think." Then, after a minute he calmed. "I gave Joey what was in 265 and everything was good for awhile. Joey, he had some problems."

"Like—"

Fazzo shrugged. "We all got problems. Joey, he had leukemia. He was gonna die." Then it was as if a light blinked on in the old man's eyes. "You know about Joey, don't you? It touched you in there, and it let you know about him. Am I right? When it touches you, it lets you know about who's there and who's not, and maybe about who's coming soon. You know about Joey?"

Paul shook his head.

Fazzo seemed disappointed. "Sometimes I think it was all an illusion, like my bag of tricks. In here, all these bricks and bars and grays—sometimes I forget what it was like to go through the door."

"What happened to Joey?"

"He's still there. I put him there."

"You killed him?"

"Holy shit, kid, you think I'd kill a little boy I loved as if he were my own son? I told you, I put him there, through 265. He's okay there. They treat him decent."

"He's not in the apartment," Paul said, as if trying to grasp something.

"You want me to spell it out for you, kid? 265 is the door to Heaven. You don't have to believe me, and it ain't the Heaven from Jesus Loves Me Yes I Know. It's a better Heaven than that. It's the Heaven to beat all Heavens." Fazzo spat at the glass that separated them. "You come here with questions like a damn reporter and you don't want answers. You want answers you go into that place. You won't like what you find, but it's too late for you. 265 is yours, kid.

Go get it. And whoever it is you love, if it's that sister of yours, make sure she gets in it. Make sure she gets Heaven. Maybe that's what it's all about. Maybe for someone to get Heaven, someone else has to get Hell."

"Like that woman?"

Fazzo did not say a word. He closed his eyes and began humming.

Startled, he opened his eyes again and said, "Kid! You got to get home now!"

"What?"

"NOW!" Fazzo shouted and smashed his fist against the glass. The guard standing in the corner behind him rushed up to him, grabbing him by the wrists. "Kid, it's your sister it wants, not you. You got caught, but it's your sister it wants. And there's only one way to get into heaven! Only one way, kid! Go get her now!"

10

Paul didn't rush home—he didn't like giving Fazzo the benefit of the doubt. He'd be on shift in another hour, and usually he spent this time by catching a burger and a Coke before going into the station. But he drove the murky streets as the sun lowered behind the stacks of castle-like apartment buildings on Third Street. The wind brushed the sky overhead with oncoming clouds, and it looked as if it would rain in a few minutes. Trash lay in heaps around the alleys, and he saw the faces of the walking wounded along the stretch of boulevards that were Sunday afternoon empty. He passed the apartments on Swan Street, doing his best not to glance up to the window on the second floor—265, its three small windows boarded up. No one would live there, not after a woman's torso was found in the bathtub. Even squatters would stay away.

He dropped by his apartment, leaving the car to idle. He just wanted to see if she was watching her movies or reading.

He didn't believe the old man.

Fazzo the Fucked Up.

In the living room, her books, the television on.

Soft music playing in the bathroom.

Paul knocked on the door. "Marie?"

After four knocks, he opened it. His heart beat fast, and seemed to be, not in his chest, but on the surface of his skin—

The machines were off, and she lay in the tub of pink water. On her back, her face beneath the water's surface like a picture he'd seen once, when they'd both been children, of a mermaid in a lake.

Scratched crudely on the tile with the edge of the scissors she'd used to cut herself free from the flesh, the words:

I don't believe in heaven.

11

It was only years later, when he saw the item in the papers about Fazzo the Fabulous finally getting the chair, after years of living on Death Row, that he thought about 265 again. He heard, too, that the apartments on Swan Street were being torn down within a week of Fazzo's execution.

In his forties, Paul had led what he would've called a quiet life. He'd been on the force for fifteen years, and the town had not erupted in anything more than the occasional domestic battle or crack house fire. He kept Marie's machines in his apartment, and often watched television in the living room feeling as if he were less alone.

But one evening, he went down there, down to Swan Street, down the rows of slums and squats where the city had turned off even the streetlamps.

Standing in front of the old apartments, he glanced at the windows of 265. The boards had come out, and the windows were empty sockets in the face of brick.

He carefully walked up the half-burnt staircase, around the rubble of bricks and pulpy cardboard, stepping over the fallen boards with the nails sticking straight up.

The apartment no longer had a door. When he went inside, the place had been stripped of all appliances.

The stink of urine and feces permeated the apartment, and he saw the residue of countless squatters who had spent nights within the walls of 265.

Graffiti covered half the wall by the bathroom—spraypainted cuss words, kids' names, lovers' names...

Scrawled in blue across the doorway to the bathroom, the words: THE SEVEN STARS.

The bathroom had been less worked-over. The shower curtain had been torn down, as had the medicine cabinet. But the toilet, cracked and brown, still remained, as did the bathtub and shower nozzle.

Paul closed his eyes, remembering the woman's bloody torso in the tub.

Remembering Marie in the pink water.

When he opened his eyes, he said, "All right. You have me. You took Marie. What is it you want?"

He sat on the edge of the tub, waiting for something. He laughed to himself, thinking of how stupid this was, how he was old enough to know better...how Fazzo the Fabulous had butchered some woman up here, and that was all. How Marie had killed herself at their home, and that was all.

There was no heaven.

He laughed for awhile, to himself. Reached in his pocket and drew out a pack of cigarettes. Lit one up, and inhaled. The night came as he sat there, and with it darkness.

Sometime, just after midnight, he heard the humming of the flies, and the drip drop of rusty water as it splashed into the tub.

In a moment, he saw the light come up from the edge of the forest, near the great tree, and two iguanas scuttled across the moss-covered rocks. It came in flashes at first, as if the skin of the world were being stripped away layer by layer, until the white bone of life came through, and then the green of a deep wood. The boy was there, and Paul recognized him without ever having seen his picture.

"You've finally come to join us, then," the boy said. "Marie told me all about you."

"Marie? Is she here?" Paul's tongue dried in his mouth, knowing that this was pure hallucination, but wanting it to be true.

The boy—and it was Joey, Fazzo's friend—nodded, holding his hand out.

The world had turned liquid around him, and for a moment he felt he was refocusing a camera in his mind, as the world solidified again. The great white birds stood like sentries off at some distance. A deer in the wood glanced up at the new intruder. Through them, as if they were translucent, he saw something else—like a veil through which he could see another person, or a thin curtain, someone watching him from the other side of the gossamer fabric. Lightning flashed across the green sky. A face emerged in the forest—the trees and the fern and the birds and the lizards all seemed part of it. A face that was neither kind nor cruel.

And then, he saw her, running towards him so fast it took his breath away. She was still twenty, but she had none of the deformities of body, and the machines no longer purred beside her. "Paul! You've come! I knew you would!"

She grabbed his hand, squeezing it. "I've waited forever for you, you should've come earlier."

Joey nodded. "See? I told you he'd come eventually."

Paul grabbed his sister in his arms, pressing as close to her as he could. Tears burst from his eyes, and he felt the warmth of her skin, the smell of her hair, the smell of her—the fragrance of his beautiful, vibrant sister. He no longer cared what illusion had produced this, he did not ever want to let go of her.

But she pulled back, finally. "Paul, you're crying. Don't." She reached up and touched the edge of his cheek.

"I thought I'd never see you again, I thought—" he said, but covered his face to stop the tears.

"Yes, you did," Marie said. "You believed in 265 all along. They told me you did. They knew you did."

"Who are they?" he asked.

Marie glanced at Joey. "I can't tell you."

"No names," Joey whispered a warning.

The rain splintered through the forest cover like slivers of glass, all around them, and the puddles that formed were small mirror shards reflecting the sky.

Marie grasped Paul's hand.

He could not get over her warmth. "How...how did you get here?"

She put a finger to her lips. "Shh. Isn't it enough that we're here now, together?"

Paul nodded his head.

"It won't last long," Marie said, curiously looking up at the glassy rain as it poured around them.

"The rain?" he asked, feeling that this was better than any heaven he could imagine. This was the Heaven of all heavens.

"No, you being here. Each time is only a glimpse. Like striking a match, it only burns for a short while."

"I don't understand," Paul said.

Marie looked up at him, and all he felt was joy. He had never remembered feeling so alive, so much part of the world, so warm with love. Again, his eyes blurred with tears.

"It's only a glimpse," she whispered. "Each time. When Fazzo was executed, he was the sacrifice. But they need another one. This time, they want the sacrifice to be here, on the threshold. It works longer that way. Just one. Each time, for you to be here."

Then, her mood changed, as she smiled like a child on his birthday. "Oh, but Paul, it's so wonderful to see you. Next time you come I'll show you the rivers of gold, and the way the trees whisper the secret of immortality. The birds can guide us across the fire mountains. And I have friends here, too, I want you to meet."

"I don't understand," Paul whispered, but the rain began coming down harder, and a glass wall of rain turned shiny and then melted, as he felt her hand grab for him through the glass—

He was sitting in the darkness of the bathroom at 265, a young woman's hand in his, cut off at the wrist because the door had come down too hard, too soon.

12

For Paul, the hardest one was the first one. He found her down in Brickton, near the factories. She was not pretty, and looked to him to be at the end of her days from drugs and too many men and too many pimps beating her up. She had burn marks on her arms, and when she got into his car, he thought: I won't be doing anything too awful. Not too awful. It'll be like putting an animal out of its misery.

"You a cop?" she asked.

He shook his head. "No way. I'm just a very desperate guy."

He told her he knew this place, an old apartment, not real pretty, but it was private and it got him off. When they reached Swan Street, she laughed. "I been in these apartments before. Christ, they look better now than I remember them."

He nodded. "Will you be impressed if I tell you I own them?"

"Really? Wow. You must be loaded."

Paul shrugged. "They went for cheap. The city was going to tear them down, but I got that blocked, bought them up and fixed them up a bit."

"They look empty."

"Just started getting them ready for tenants," he said.

They went upstairs, the green lights of the hallway like haloes around her red hair. Inside the apartment, he offered her a drink.

"All right," she said.

"Need to use the bathroom?" he asked, opening the freezer door to pull out the ice tray.

"If you don't mind," she said.

"Go ahead. Take a shower if you feel like it."

"Well, you're buying," the woman said.

When he heard the bathroom door close, he went and took the key from the dresser. Standing in front of the bathroom door, he waited until he heard the shower turn on.

He checked his watch.

It was two minutes to midnight.

From the shower, she shouted, "Honey? You mind bringing my drink in and scrubbing my back?"

He opened the bathroom door. Steam poured from under the shower curtain. When he was inside the bathroom, he turned and locked the door. He put the key in his breast pocket.

"That you?" she asked.

"Yeah," he said. "I'll join you in just a few seconds."

He crouched down. Beneath the sink, a large wooden box. Opening it, he lifted the cloth within. He grabbed the hand-ax and then closed the box.

He set the small ax on top of the sink. He unbuttoned his shirt, and took it off. He hung it on the hook by the door. Then, he stepped out of his shoes. Undid his belt, and let his trousers fall to the floor.

"Baby?" she asked.

"In a minute," he said. "We'll have some fun."

Pulling off his socks, and then his briefs. Grabbing the hand-ax. Looking at himself naked in the mirror, ax in fist.

For a second, the glass flashed like lightning, and he saw her face there.

A glimpse.

Then, he pulled back the shower curtain and began opening the door to Heaven.

Mrs. Feely

My father told me the story of a woman he'd known as a child, whose lover, in his teens, had ridden his horse up to the front porch to knock down the door because he wanted to come get her. My father was about four at the time, which places the story in the 1920s. I wanted to overly-fictionalize this moment and morph it into a story of a father and son and a memory that somehow began the father's journey into nightmare. Ultimately, "Mrs. Feely" is a character sketch, and I will be the first to admit that it just ends where it ends.

1

No event of significance arrives full-blown without something in the past, a secret, perhaps, which has been kept, and which was the birth of the future event. When a man kills for pleasure, for instance, it is not a new thing for him. He has learned this somewhere and kept it away from the eyes of the world. In 1938, a woman was found dead in a secluded area of Vermont, her body had been stuffed with corn cobs and apples, all dried, hard and rotting, as if her skin was meant to be a mattress. This had been done to her while she'd still been alive; one of her ribs had been sawed from her side, also. The man thought responsible for this heinous act was found dead, too. There was no great mystery to this crime, because the murderer involved had killed someone a few years earlier and had been hiding in the woods until his own death, which was, apparently, at the hands of Nature, in Her wisdom.

In 1985, a man in his early sixties was arrested for the alleged murder of a prostitute in upstate New York. The woman had been kept in a freezer for several weeks; other corpses were later found. If you remember the news stories of that year, the man was white of hair and handsome; his eyes were brown; he looked like the nice man you see standing beside you in line at the bank, or sitting opposite you on the bus or train, in a gray suit, a man who served in Korea, and who raised four sons.

That man was my father.

I could not believe that such a kind and gentle man could've been so evil. He had never raised a hand to me or my brothers in all the years we lived beneath his roof. He had been a devoted husband up until my mother's death from ovarian cancer in 1969. He attended Mass on Sundays, and worked with the Literacy First campaign in the Genessee Valley for twelve years; he had only recently retired from the accounting firm of which he was a founding partner. He was almost blind—he had, within four months of incarceration, begun to only distinguish shadows and slow, steady movement.

I met him at the hospital, before the conviction, and asked him to try to help me understand. He smiled and said, "I've always been a killer, son. I don't know why. They say it's better to be killed physically than to have your spirit killed, and I think that's true. You can only get killed once, but your spirit can be crushed so many times, in so many ways, it's beyond understanding. It's beyond words. I'll tell it to you like a riddle. You're the tree, and the floor's the sky, only upside-down and backwards. The dirt's the clouds, and the dust is the snow coming down from heaven."

I was not the first to think that my father had lost his sanity.

And then he told me about the woman in the 1930s.

Mrs. Feely

The love of his life.

Mrs. Feely.

2

"You're the tree, boy, and the floor's the sky, only upside-down and backwards," Mrs. Feely said to Jim, handing him the broom, doing her Irish dance that had a hint of gypsy to it. She was a show-off, Mrs. Feely was, with her eye-paint and her wigs, the biggest flirt in all of Vermont. Jim knew all about her from his father who had warned him to mind her over the holidays, but "not to mind her in every way." She was like the land of Canaan that he'd heard about in church, for she seemed always to be full of milk and honey, happy, her larder was alway stuffed, and she always had a way with Jim like no one else. Jim was just eight, it was the last gasp of 1929, the final day of December, and Jim's father and stepmother were driving down to Leadham for the Carcassone's big New Year's Eve party. His father had remarried just last year; his real mother had died when Jim was born, and although he was happy that his father had married someone who could keep house and such, he wasn't sure if he would ever call his father's wife, "Mommy." Jim was given to tantrums around the stepmother, who was at her wit's end most of the time; Jim's father decided that he and his wife should have a few nights out on their own, and that Jim should be briefly farmed out over New Year's with the couple that had, at one time, been servants in Jim's grandfather's house.

Mr. Feely was already in bed, having imbibed too much of holiday cheer, and now it was left to Jim and the Mrs. to stay up and usher in the year 1930. Jim wore his Christmas vest, still, along with the cowboy hat with the broad brim, and galoshes that were two sizes too big because they had belonged to Mrs. Feely's son, Ernest, who'd gotten hit three years back by the trains just on the other side of the property. Jim's Uncle Alan worked the trains, but had not been on the one that took out Ernest Feely; if he had, he surely would've saved the boy (that was what Mrs. Feely always said, anyway). Jim had wondered what Ernest had been doing on the tracks, all by himself; Jim and Ernest were as close as brothers, and Jim didn't think that Ernest ever went anywhere by himself. Jim often thought of poor dead Ernest, mashed by the train; he would look out the window when he heard the train whistle, and think of him. The woods outside were caked in snow; the light was from the oil lamps, because the cabin had nothing else, not even a fireplace; and the moon was snuffed out that night, as if God had forgotten to fill it with oil.

Mrs. Feely turned the radio up, so that the music was louder, with someone playing the ukelele and singing about a lost straw hat. Mrs. Feely tapped her toes in time. Jim asked, "Won't we wake up Mr. Feely?"

"He's out like a log," she said, turning around in a shuffle and fan. "I like music when I clean, makes it go ever so much faster. Now get to work, my Janitor's Boy, and be quick about it." She called him her Janitor's Boy from a poem she loved ("Oh, I'm in love with the Janitor's Boy..." it began).

Jim was put to sweeping; like Mrs. Feely'd said, he was the tree, and the broom was his branch, and the floor was the sky. "Dirt's the clouds," he said to her.

Mrs. Feely had already returned to the big sink full of dishes. She looked around. "It is, and the dust's the snow coming down from heaven." There was a big thump, like someone had just taken a paper bag filled with air and had burst it, but when Jim turned to look, it was only Mrs. Feely clapping to a Rag that she swung her generous hips in time with (they called her "Snake Hips Sally" in town); she turned the music up even louder for the rest of the song, and Jim hoped that old Mr. Feely slept sound and sauced, because he could get a temper on him sometimes, and Jim didn't like to be around for it.

Jim swept all the dirt and dust into the corner. He grabbed the lamp that hung near the door—it looked like the lamp that the boy named Aladdin had when he called forth his genie—he held the flame down low so he could see if he had done a good job or not. He never had to clean so much back home in Connecticut, but he knew that Mrs. Feely liked things tidy. She glanced over now and again, her eyes moving from his face to the broom to the floor to the dustcatcher. He worked very hard; when he came across a bit of dirt that wouldn't come up, he scraped at it with his nails until it was embedded beneath them. When this was done, his next chore was to go outside in the snow, and walk around to the side of the cabin. There, he would find logs that were as long as he was, nearly. "The stove's dying," Mrs. Feely said, "if we're to last the night, we must feed it, my sweet Janitor's Boy." She laid out, on the dining table, a tin of sardines (which were a great delicacy to her, and which she only ate on holidays), two bottles of beer (he'd be allowed three long sips, if he was a good boy), and a pen and paper for the writing of New Year's Resolutions.

The front porch was slippery, so Jim clung to the railings along its periphery for balance. His hat fell off, and then he fell, also, into the snow, feeling the wetness go up inside his pant leg. When he finally found his hat, it was wet, and he left it at the last step of the porch rather than soak his head with it. Although there was no moon, the lights from within the cabin, as well as an incipient light from the white snow itself, provided a soft haze of illumination which made the woods seem black, the cabin blue, and the driveway and road a muddled indigo and light gray. He went to get the logs, but as he turned right at the side of the house, another light blinded him.

Jim put his gloved fingers up to his face, and then the light lowered.

He looked up. For a second, he thought it was an angel, for the man was wearing white, and seemed to have a halo around his head.

But it was only an illusion, because in the next second, there was no halo, and no white garment: only the farm-boy who worked in the fields in the summer and fall. He was sixteen, lanky, with a long face as if it had once been short and made of taffy until someone pulled on it. His hair fell on either side of his forehead, and hadn't been cut in awhile. He wore a coat that went from his neck almost to his toes. In one hand, a lantern.

In the other, something that Jim thought might be a gun.

"Hey, you're the Welsher," the older boy said.

Jim didn't respond.

"I 'member you from summer. You give my little sister the fishing rod and you tuck it back. You made her pull her dress over her head."

"What're you doin' here?" Jim asked. He looked at the gun. Jim knew that the farm-boy was dangerous because in the summer, the farm-boy had ridden his horse right up to the porch of the cabin and had tried to kick the door down, calling out to Mrs. Feely that he was going to get her, that he wanted her right then and there. Jim had huddled with Mrs. Feely on the other side of the door, hoping it would hold against the hooves. Within a few minutes, the farm-boy had gone off down the road, but Jim still shivered sometimes, when he thought about it. Jim kept looking back at the gun. He was sure it was a gun, just like the kind his grandfather had in Boston.

The farm-boy grinned. In the lantern's light, he looked like a mule with a million teeth. "I ain't here, boy, and you're dreamin'. Must be the cold. Must be the dark. You ain't never seen me here tonight."

"I'm gonna scream for Mrs. Feely."

"Do that, Welsher, boy, go ahead and squeal. I'm only here to take what's mine by nature. But you go on and squeal." The farm-boy ignored Jim, and walked past him. Jim just stood there, open-mouthed until the chill got to his teeth. He watched the farm-boy tromp on down the drive to the road.

Jim went to get a log, but as he lifted it, he thought he smelled kerosene. He sniffed the log. Soaked in kerosene. He dropped the log. Jim wasn't sure if this was important or not, but he went around to the front door and pushed it open.

"Mrs. Feely," he said.

She was sitting in her rocker, next to the radio. It was playing some dance music. She was working on her needle-point.

"That farm-boy was here," Jim said, pointing back towards the open door.

Mrs. Feely stood; her right hand pressed just beneath her left breast; she walked carefully to the door. She looked out into the darkness of Vermont winter.

MRS. FEELY

"He was here and he had a gun I think and he put kerosene on the logs."

Mrs. Feely didn't look at Jim, but kept watch in front. The cold air blew in, and Jim had to put a blanket around his shoulders. Mrs. Feely said, "Randy was here? He came tonight?" Then, she called him to her side. She put her hand on top of his scalp, stroking her fingers through his hair, gently, like he was a puppy. "You sure you saw him?"

"Yes'm, and I couldn't get the wood 'cause it smelled like kerosene."

"Well, we don't need anymore wood tonight, Jim, we'll be fine."

When she moved away from the door, a full hour later, tatters of snow drifted in, and Jim ran to the window to watch as the sky began sweeping the trees with white, as the wind spread the dust of heaven across the windowpane.

175

He awoke at four, when his parents came into the room, smelling like gin, and then he awoke at six fifteen, when Mrs. Feely started screaming.

Jim didn't see Mrs. Feely much for the next three years, and what he learned, he learned slowly, and through eavesdropping on the grown-ups or from putting together, gradually, what had gone on that night that he had missed. He was in court before he figured it all out. Mr. Feely had been shot sometime in the night, and Mrs. Feely had slept right next to him all night long, not knowing that half the mattress was soaked in blood. So, the men in court had asked him about that night, and he had told them about the farm-boy with the gun, and the logs that smelled like kerosene. The farm-boy, named Randy Fordell, had killed Mr. Feely because Mr. Feely had not paid him for the past season's work. Randy was a wicked boy, and had been known to kill cats in the field when they got in the way of his work; he was also hot-headed, impetuous, rakishly handsome in spite of his mulish smile (as Jim's stepmother had observed often enough when the men worked in the field), and had sworn to one of his buddies that he would "get what Feely owed him even if he had to take it in blood." Most of Randy's friends told similar tales. All of this information sifted through Jim piece-meal, but it turned out that he was the star witness, even though everyone told him that he was only a little boy. Randy Fordell was never caught; they said he rode to Canada on his horse, and was living in the mountains. Mrs. Feely took to her bed for many months after this, rarely coming out of the house except to buy food in town, or to pick up her husband's pension check at the Post Office.

Jim and his parents didn't go up to see her again until 1933, and this time, in late September.

3

The fields were high and yellow and wild, for no one cut them anymore. The woods seemed thick with shiny golds and yellows bursting across the trees' branches. An arrow flock of geese passed overhead; the Ford took the bumps in the hard-packed road badly; Jim was jostled in the rumble seat—his mother had to warn his father to slow down. But Jim didn't mind—he was big for his age, and muscular, and could take a bit of jostling. He had shot up just in the past year, and some girls thought he was fifteen. He didn't feel fifteen—he felt his age—but he liked to think other people thought he was mature. When they arrived at the cabin, Jim was first out, and went running up the steps. He pounded on the door. "Mrs. Feely! Mrs. Feely! It's your Janitor's Boy!"

He exhausted himself at this awhile, and then bounded back down the steps, to the field. He was sure she must be in the barn, and he ran through the grass with its burrs clinging to him, and the last bees of autumn cursing about his ears. He was out of breath by the time he got to the barn, and shoved at the door—it wouldn't budge. He knew of an opening at the back, where Mrs. Feely stored her apples. Jim ran around to it, and pushed at the two boards. They pressed inwards, and he slipped beneath them. The barn was dark, and empty, but there was a small light coming from up where the tackle, and some of the sharper tools, were hung. He climbed up the ladder to the loft, and there was a lantern, and there was Mrs. Feely, all greasy and naked and shiny in the light, and above her, the farm-boy who'd killed Mr. Feely, slapping her with his stomach, holding her hands down, pressing himself against her as if he were trying to kill her by smothering her body. Mrs. Feely was grunting and moaning, and she turned her face toward Jim, her eyes widening in what Jim could tell was terror, and Jim was up the last rungs of that ladder faster than a polecat. He grabbed the big shovel and slammed it into the back of the farm-boy's shoulders until the blade had dug in deep just below the neck. The farm-boy's body kept bucking, his hips moving further in between Mrs. Feely's legs.

Mrs. Feely began shouting out, "No, Jim, no, oh, god, Randy, yes, oh, dear god, yes," her legs clutching his buttocks as he rammed her.

Jim let go of the shovel; it dropped beside him.

The farm-boy's head lolled forward; blood spat from his shoulderblades.

Mrs. Feely's eyes seemed to go white for a second, and she shuddered and shivered and shook.

Jim watched her, frozen.

The body on top of her fell to the side.

Mrs. Feely's forehead was slick with sweat.

Jim heard his parents calling from outside; they were trying to find a way into the barn.

He looked at Mrs. Feely. At Randy Fordell who was crying a river of blood onto the gray wood.

At the shovel; shiny dark red at its tip, with a scraping of flesh.

The farm-boy had not been attacking Mrs. Feely.

It had been something else, entirely.

Mrs. Feely had liked what the farm-boy was doing to her.

She had looked like she was in heaven.

Jim was almost twelve; he was beginning to understand some things in life that adults took for granted, but which he found terrifying.

The farm-boy kept crying.

177

Mrs. Feely covered herself with a bit of blanket, and said, "Get out of here, get out of here, right now, right now, Jim, before I kill you," and he could tell that she was weeping, too.

4

He caught his breath; coming back down from the loft had been like running for miles. He heard his father calling from outside. He managed to open the barn door from the inside. His stepmother and father stood just on the other side of it, smiling expectantly. His stepmother asked, "Did you find her?"

Jim looked through them to the yellow field. He tasted something sour in the back of his throat. "No," he said, "she must be in town."

His father said, "And you go running around here making a jackass out of yourself, you're too old for that, young man, and I hope that you won't be bothering the poor woman too much while we're gone."

Jim didn't bother looking at his father. "No, sir," he said, "I won't."

Mrs. Feely showed up at the front porch a half hour later. She had a small wildflower thrust behind her ear, and she was wearing a flower-print dress; in her arms, bunches of pussy-willow. She was barefoot. "Well, look who's here, and me off hunting a centerpiece." She gave Jim a head-pat, and his stepmother a kiss on her cheek. He couldn't believe how she wasn't going to tell on him; but then, he knew that she'd been doing something very wicked. When he did wicked things, he didn't like to admit it to people, either. Mrs. Feely said, "I knew I'd get behind on things, just cleaning out the place all day long, and wandering over to the creek for these." She held out the long stems with their furry pearl buds for Jim's inspection. "Pussy-willows, my Janitor's Boy, just like a cat's fur, feel them, feel them, don't be shy."

Jim put his hand out and touched one of the buds. It was soft and warm.

His stepmother said, "We'll be back on Monday morning."

"Do you think," Mrs. Feely said, "you could pick me up something while you're there?"

His stepmother glanced at his father, then back to Mrs. Feely. "I don't see a reason why not."

Mrs. Feely said, "No, never mind, it's too much trouble. You two need to go have some fun, enjoy it a bit."

"No, really," his stepmother said.

"We insist," his father said.

"There's a cookie they make there. Called Sarah Bernhardts. Haven't had them since I was a girl. Make me fat, they will. But, no, not for cookies, don't stop for cookies when you two have so many more—"

"Sarah Bernhardts," his father said, "of course we'll stop."

"I don't see how stopping for cookies will do us harm," his stepmother said, by way of politeness.

"Well, then," Mrs. Feely said, "Jim and I will be fine. Just fine. And we shall all have Sarah Bernhardts come Monday."

His stepmother didn't bother hugging him, like she had when he'd been younger. There was a chill between them, something that Jim encouraged. He didn't have any feelings for her, his stepmother, and if someone were to push her under a train, he might just not mind at all. She gave him a half-smile, probably more glad to be rid of him for awhile than anything, and his father tipped his hat to both Jim and Mrs. Feely. They'd left the car running. It was another four hours to their destination; it would be dark soon. Jim wanted to run to both of them, but knew that they would not believe a word he said; not with Mrs. Feely right there. His stepmother had caught him in too many lies already. Nobody would believe what he'd seen in the loft.

And if they did believe him, perhaps he would be in the worst trouble of his life.

Jim watched them leave, and wondered if he would ever see them again now that he was a murderer.

Mrs. Feely touched him lightly on the shoulder. "He's only hurt, Janitor's Boy, he's not dead."

Jim did not want to turn to face her. He kept his sights on the road, the trees, the jagged clouds that scraped the darkening sky.

"When you're all grown up, you'll understand things better." She watched him for a response, like she was his school-teacher.

He said, "I think I understand things now."

"Oh, you do?" She said this as if it were all a lark: the death of her husband, what the farm-boy had been doing to her up in the loft. "Well," she continued, "why don't you just tell me what you understand?"

She walked around in front of him, dropping the pussy-willow at his feet like an offering. She knelt down on one knee, grasped his arms, looked up into his face. Her skin smelled like freshly-turned earth. In the few years since he'd seen her, she'd somehow managed to look less like someone's mother and more like a woman. He thought of her body up in the loft; the way the farm-boy was pumping at her. Jim felt warm. A little scared. He liked his body, and was only starting to get over a certain self-consciousness he'd had in early childhood. He thought about what his body would be like, pressed against her. He wondered what that part of her smelled like. He wanted to put his fingers into it. He wanted to find out how far up it went inside her. Her furnace. She had a kind of power there, between her legs, a power that he could only imagine because he'd never really seen one except on a six year old, and that was hardly anything.

Mrs. Feely's power, emanating from her hips, seemed as strong as steel to him.

But this didn't keep him from speaking his mind. "I thought the farm-boy was attacking you, but that's not it at all. You wanted him like that because you're dirty. My grandfather works in Boston and says that there are a lot of dirty people there. You used to work in his house, didn't you? When you were seventeen, he told me, he told me that your mother was one of those people, one of those women. He says there are women who are called 'wars' and they do indecent things."

"Wars?" Mrs Feely laughed, sweetly. "I think you mean 'whores'. That's a rude sort of language to use around me."

Jim said, "I doubt it. I think you're like those women. Wars."

"Dirty?"

"Yes."

"You're a brave one, Janitor's Boy, to throw that name in my face. My mother was not a whore, rest assured, she was merely Irish, and to your grandfather, it's the same thing."

Jim felt a heat in his body that didn't seem to be localized anywhere.

He drew back from her; took three steps away. She remained where she was, gazing at him. Her eyes were like the glass beads his mother had on her dressing table: green and small and shaped like diamonds.

Jim said, "I know what happened that night. Now. I know."

"You were always too smart for me, Jim."

"You knew he was going to kill Mr. Feely. That's why I was there. So I would see him do it. So I'd tell people."

She shook her head. "Oh, sweet butterscotch pudding, child. You read too many intrigues. Neither of us wanted you to see him. Someday, you may understand about life. About what a man can do to a woman."

"Like in the barn."

"No, not like the barn. I mean, hitting and shouting and killing the spirit. Sometimes you'd rather get hit than hear the words, those terrible, foul words, the way they can break a spirit in two like a twig snapping under your foot. You'd rather have someone break your arm in two, it would be sweeter, than what a man can do to your spirit. You'd rather be skinned alive, so long as he didn't touch your fire. It was what Mr. Feely did..." Now she had tears in her glass bead eyes. Her lips trembled. Then, the tears were sucked back somewhere; the lips, stilled. Her mood shifted. "If I need to confess, I've got a good priest in Father Murphy not six miles away. I am a grown up, and you are a boy. You may never understand these things."

She got to her feet, clumsily, and walked past him, back towards the barn.

Jim watched her, without a thought in his head: his confusion was immense.

Then, he ran after her.

In the barn loft, Randy Fordell lay on his side in the straw. A bandage had been made of his shirt, and wrapped around his shoulderblades; it was soaked with blood. Mrs. Feely wiped a damp towel across his forehead. The farm-boy was shivering.

Jim sat in a corner, and watched.

Mrs. Feely glanced over at him now and then, but didn't seem to care if he was there or not. Finally, she said, "It's deep. If I don't get him to a doctor, there'll be trouble."

Jim said, "I'm sorry."

Mrs. Feely smiled at this, nodding.

He closed his eyes and thought of her greasy, shiny body moving like it was an engine being stoked with coals, shoveling into it, and the engine picking up steam, moving faster and faster beneath the farm-boy, getting stoked with what was between his legs, the furnace, from which she drew her power.

The three days were quiet.

Randy slept most of the time in Mrs. Feely's bed, and when he was awake, it was to sip chicken soup from a large green tureen. He had a fever. Mrs. Feely and Jim both knew that, given the past, and the murdering of Mr. Feely, they could not send for the doctor for aid or relief. Mrs. Feely knew some things about herbs, so she rubbed myrrh into his back, and this provided some relief for him. She also knew of a stimulating tonic that required bees—in autumn, they still buzzed around the fallen apples, so Jim collected six of them easily in a jar. Mrs. Feely took the jar, shook it, and set it down on Randy's back. Two bees stung him immediately; Jim winced at this. Mrs. Feely removed the jar from the farm-boy's back, and plucked the stingers out after a few minutes. "It's an old remedy from my great-gramma's day, but it works. Gets the blood flowing; gets the bones and muscles going about their business."

The last night, Jim couldn't sleep.

He lay on the narrow bed in the second room, wondering if Mrs. Feely was touching the farm-boy in those places where he'd stoked her.

He wondered if what Mrs. Feely had said about Mr. Feely were true.

His peter got hard. It had begun doing that a lot within the past few months, and he'd had no idea exactly what it meant. He had learned to rub pillows against it, and that seemed to make it go away after awhile. But he knew that it was somehow connected to Mrs. Feely and what she'd let the farm-boy do in the loft. He began stroking it with his hand, curled into a small fist. It felt good, but it made him ashamed, too. Yet it was hard to stop doing it, because it felt too good and it made pictures in his head of Mrs. Feely and the farm-boy whacking each other with their hips, his peter in the raw gash that ripped the seams of her flesh there where he had never seen a woman before.

On the last night, he heard the moaning through the walls, and could not take it anymore.

He pulled his pants on, and stomped out of the room, went over and banged on the door to Mrs. Feely's room.

The moaning continued unabated.

Jim was sweating as if he were the one with the fever; when Mrs. Feely opened her bedroom door, he saw in the lamplight that the farm-boy was moaning from pain. Mrs. Feely said, "What is it?"

Jim stood there for what seemed like the longest time until he knew that if he didn't do something right away that he would burst or start screaming because his mind could no longer control his body. He wanted something from her so badly, but he wasn't sure what it was. He just knew it had to do with stoking the magnificent

183

furnace between her legs, that gap that he could only imagine, her greasy, sweaty body.

He raised his fist and slammed it across Mrs. Feely's face, just beneath her right eye.

"You damn war," he said, "look what you're doing to me."

She grabbed his fist just after he hit her, and twisted his arm around behind his back, "Wicked boy!" she shouted. "Don't you ever do that again, not to me, not to anyone, what is wrong with you, Jim, what in god's name has gotten into you?"

He felt then like he'd been released from his body, for he watched as if from the ceiling as his body crumpled, and she held him, and the tears pumped out of him like they were his life-blood.

Mrs. Feely said, "I don't need you to be like this, my Janitor's Boy, I need your help, oh, god, my sweet little boy," and she, too, began weeping. "If we don't help him, he's going to die, boy, and I love him so much."

She kissed Jim on the cheek, and he felt a surge of power run through him.

He knew what to do.

The train's whistle, from out in the pines, pierced the room, and then died.

5

When he was sixteen, Jim ran away from home, for the third time, and hopped the trains that ran to Canada; in two days, he leapt off a boxcar, landing hard on some rocks. He rolled down an embankment, and was knocked unconscious for a few minutes. It was winter, and the snow was heavy, but he was free of an even greater chill. His father had died six months before, the father who had told him about a moral compass which would always point a boy in the right direction if he would only find it within himself. After his father's funeral, he had thought about his moral compass, the one within his heart; his stepmother was already talking about how a young man of his age should be out in the world, for there was no love lost between them. So, in a dream, he knew where to go, where the hand of the compass pointed, to a small cabin in Vermont, to Mrs. Feely, whom he hadn't seen since they'd buried the farm-boy out back in the woods when he'd been twelve.

It was dark, but he had known where to jump by the mountains, how they sloped just so, and maybe he'd had some help from his inner compass, too, for he followed a trail that led right to Mrs. Feely's place. He stomped his boots on the porch, and set his sack down to dry by the front door. She had heard him, and looked out through the window, holding the chintz curtains to the side. She didn't recognize him, so he called to her through the door. "It's your Janitor's Boy!"

She dropped the curtain, but did not answer the door.

He knocked again, "Mrs. Feely! It's me, it's Jim, it's freezing out here."

She opened the door, and he noticed, for the first time, her age, for she must've been close to his father's age, but it had been harder for her getting there. After he'd gone in, and she'd brought him a beer, she said, "How did he go?"

"Father?"

She nodded.

"It was his throat. They said it was the cigars and the pipes. Ate his mouth and throat up."

She sighed, closing her eyes; she brought a beer to her lips, and sipped it. She said, "If you're hungry, I've got plenty of food in the larder. Corn, apples, and I canned some pears. There's a bit of ham, too, if you like." She seemed to be wishing him away.

"You thought it was me," he said.

She kept her eyes closed. "I didn't know what it was, Jim."

"You're wishing I hadn't come," he said.

She opened her eyes, but looked past him. "You are the only one I want to see these days, but I was scared you'd come back."

"I wouldn't hurt you, Mrs. Feely."

She whispered, "No, I don't think you would. But you would hurt others, Jim. And it's my doing. My sins. My wickedness. What you did to Ernest..."

Jim set his beer down. He remembered Mrs. Feely's son going to the train tracks. "I told him not to play out there. I told him it was dangerous."

"I knew it was you, then, not when Ernest died, but with Randy. I knew it was you."

"I didn't kill him. He was dead. I told you. He was dead. You saw him. You knew. He had a bad infection."

"Just stop your mouth up, Jim. I don't want to hear it. You been a liar since as far as I can recollect. You put Ernest there, under the train, I don't know how, but you did. And I found blood on the pillow-case, after you left. You musta pressed it over Randy's face."

Jim said nothing. He glanced around the cabin; little had changed—she still used oil lamps even though they now seemed like antiques to him. "I left home," he said.

She drank her beer fast, and when she'd finished it, she set it down on the table beside her, wiped her mouth with her hand, and said, "You can sleep the night here. But I want you gone after breakfast, you hear?"

Mrs. Feely rose, and wobbled on unsure feet to her room, shutting the door.

Jim sat there, drank two more beers, then went into the other room to lie down.

He stared at the ceiling for the longest time; the moonlight lit the landscape outside to a shining brilliance. He remembered her body, how it shone, also, with sweat and lust as the farm-boy ploughed into her. Her swampy place, down there, that he'd seen briefly, wet and smelly and open, strings of hair like Spanish moss dangling from the mound. He wanted that more than anything; he was sixteen, and he felt the need for sexual relief constantly, although shame and fear of exposure had kept him from ever trying it with any of the girls he knew—and they weren't like Mrs. Feely, for even with the age on her face, she had the curves and the hills and valleys that he longed to sink his hands into—she wasn't like those nice girls he knew, she was bad, the kind of woman who liked men to do it to her.

He thought of her as a kind of goddess, and he lay there not even realizing that his hands had stroked down his chest, pinching his nipples slightly, and then gliding feather-light down his stomach, beneath his boxer shorts to the fat penis that was just beginning to grow. He remembered, as he always did when he beat off, climbing the loft, and even that was arousing for him, climbing the wooden slats of the loft ladder, the smell of hay (he could sometimes ejaculate suddenly if he smelled hay, still), the stink of the barn. The farm-boy's muscular back, the buttocks with the dimples on each side, thrusting, slamming, and Mrs. Feely's meaty legs wrapped around the boy, her skin liquid and turning like it was molding itself to the farm-boy, and the moans, the moans that were like an ache from the heart.

Jim let go of his penis; he sat up in bed, and drew his boxers off. His prick was as hard as he had ever seen it, fatter and longer than he thought possible; he wanted Mrs. Feely now, he wanted her the way the farm-boy had her.

He turned on the light in her room.

Like a dream.

She was just opening her eyes.

He grabbed her, and pressed himself into her just like he was stabbing at a wound and sinking into it with a knife between his legs. He covered her mouth with his hand, and told her how much he loved her and how good it felt.

When it was over, he lay there beside her, and she began laughing.

Laughing, as the light of morning came up slowly from the window, casting a lavender shadow across the curves of her skin.

She didn't stop laughing until he slapped her, and even then she smiled.

She told him something, a secret she had kept all the years he had known her, she told him something and hoped that it would drive him mad.

6

And, according to my father, it did, although he knew that he had already started down that road to insanity years before she'd told him.

But what she had told him pushed him across the line, into a country from which he would never again return.

My father, who told me the story about Mrs. Feely, about how he had killed her lover, and then raped her, told me that he would take the secret she revealed to him to his grave, and he almost did. He died soon after being transferred to a prison for the criminally insane; he was, after all, in his seventies and had a bad heart.

I went to visit his grave seldom, for I wanted to put it all behind me, the fact that my father was the most brutal of killers, that his face was on playing cards now, that there was talk of a horror movie loosely based on his life, the quiet accountant from Boston who sliced and skinned eight women in his lifetime.

But then, one weekend I was lecturing at Dartmouth, and my wife suggested we take a drive through New Hampshire and Vermont the following day. As if following some internal map, I found that I was driving right to the town outside of which had been Mrs. Feely's cabin. I didn't tell my wife that I recognized the name of the town, and as they sold excellent blown glass there, she investigated the shops, while I wandered the streets trying to forget about Mrs. Feely and my father.

They say the sins of the father are visited upon the children, and I had felt that since my father's trial, that somehow, just having been his seed, I was tainted with the blood legacy of a sociopathic murderer. I found myself often going to churches, and so I entered the small Catholic church in that town. I knelt to pray, and the local minister stepped out at the altar to fix some arrangement of hymn numbers on a board. He was elderly and Irish, with ears that stuck out to give his face an almost monkeyish appearance, his thick glasses expanded his eyes to the size of saucers, but he smiled at me, and when I'd risen came out to extend his hand to me. We introduced ourselves, and luckily, he didn't recognize the surname which had, over a period of a year, become synonymous with the Bogeyman.

I had to ask him, "Did you know the Feelys?"

He shook his head, but then I asked him about the history of the place, for he was an avid historian, as was I. He was roughly my father's age, and so, instead of names, which he seemed to have no memory for, I asked him about scandals.

The old man lit up at this, and we went into his office for some tea. "We have had a famous murder, back when I was a boy."

"Oh," I feigned ignorance.

"Yes, a woman was brutally killed out in the country. A horrible thing. And her lover, you see, died, too, for they found him in the spring of the same year, in the thaw, although his body was so badly decomposed, barely anything left after the animals had gotten to it—pardon me if I'm a bit gruesome, but it was quite a sensational case for the time. Nothing like what's on the news these days, but quite a horror show for 1938. The woman was a bit of an outcast, see, at least that's what I heard from my mother when it hit the papers. She was not proper, she was what they used to call fast. I still call it fast, although, who can judge? They say she'd come to town under a cloud of disgrace—you see, she'd been a maid at a house in Boston or New York, and, when she'd been seventeen had gotten with child by a man. She married—but the story was, it was not the man who'd fathered her child. She was considered something of a trollop around these parts. After she had her second child, the stories died down about her."

"A second child?" I asked.

He looked at me squarely. "You know this story, perhaps?"

"Some of it," I said, hating to lie to a priest.

"Well, sympathy in town was there for her when her boy died in an accident, but she was again the scandal when a local boy murdered her husband—a trial and everything—and although she was considered innocent, she was thought to have been involved in the murder. See, she twisted things, that woman did. At least, that was the gossip."

"Twisted?"

"They said she was different people—the way Sybil was, you know, different personalities and such. Some people up in these hills thought she was possessed, but most people, including my own parents, believed she was suffering from illness since the death of her child."

"What about the other child?"

"Which?"

"The one that was still alive?"

"Oh," he said, taking off his glasses to rub his eyes, "the first, you mean. Nobody knew. You see, she and her new husband had come here to have the baby so the scandal from her former employer would die down. But, after it's birth, it was gone. Adopted probably. Some people thought she killed it, or maybe it died at birth, and others said that the father had come for it and had raised it himself. I favor the latter story. I met the father once, the man who had fathered her first child—he came into town to answer questions after the woman's husband had been killed by the local boy. He wasn't much older than me, but he seemed a decent sort, in spite of his past mistake. Although he wasn't Catholic, he would talk to the priest before me, Father Murphy, at some length."

"Is Father Murphy still around?"

The priest shook his head. "Died in '64. Eighty years old. Long enough, he said a few days before he went. Seems like you've got a lot of questions for someone who isn't from the area."

"I guess I do," I said. Then, "Was she pretty?"

He looked startled by the question. "She was the most beautiful girl I had ever seen in my life," he said, "bar none, she was the Irish Helen of Troy. But you're hiding something from me, aren't you?"

I nodded. "She was my grandmother."

I met my wife in the late afternoon; she had a box of beautiful crystal champagne glasses she'd seen at one of the shops. I carried the box, and held her hand tightly. She looked at me, curiously. "What have you been up to?" she asked.

But it was my father's secret, and I let it die there, in that town, all the misery and pain and, yes, even insanity. We walked to the old graveyard, and I found Mrs. Feely's marker. We had a picnic upon the grave, and I told my wife nothing of the misery and terror, but only of the fact that my grandmother was buried there.

"And what did you inherit from her?" my wife asked, innocently.

I thought about it for a minute or so, and then said, "My spirit."

Ice Palace

When I was in college, my fraternity did all kinds of hazing rituals, and one was called "ice palace." It involved sitting in your underwear in a big bucket of ice (the kind of bucket that could hold beer kegs), in the middle of winter, in the snow, and telling the entire fraternity jokes until every single one of them laughed. I was fairly quick with jokes, so I was out of the ice palace in seconds, but some guys turned blue because they just could not tell a joke.

This story, "Ice Palace," has very little to do with that ritual. This is about another hazing ritual I heard about, where some frat boys had taken a freshman to the local graveyard and paid a local scary drunk to watch the freshman all night and make sure he stayed tied up at the graveyard. But, then, this story is really about something else, isn't it?

1

I once helped murder a boy, when I was nineteen, only we didn't think of ourselves as boys back then. It was in college, at a university in the mountains of Virginia, when the snow had piled up and the parties were in full swing. I lived with my brothers—we weren't blood relations, except through the college fraternity system. It was February, and certain aspects of fraternity hazing were not yet complete. It was always in the harshest part of the season that the sadistic rituals took place on campus, from paddling to raiding to a particularly cruel torture called Ice Palace.

I was just buttoning up my shirt, about to start shaving, when Nate Wick, known as the Wicked Wick or the Flaccid Wick, grabbed me by the collar and slammed me against the wall; the whole world shook and I cussed him out something fierce; his face was all scrunched up like he was about to cry. He had hair growing from his ears even at twenty-one, and fat cheeks like a cherub gone to seed. I socked him in the jaw, 'cause he could be crazy sometimes, even if he *was* my fraternity brother. He took the blow pretty good, and my fist ached like a son of a bitch, and he dropped on my bed, right on the wet towel, so it made a smack kind of sound, and if he hadn't been naked I'd've grabbed *him* by *his* collar and heave-hoed him right onto the balcony, where it was twenty below and iced smooth.

"Damn it, Wick," I said, "you drive me, you know that? You drive me, Christ."

"Drive you what? Nuts?"

"You just drive me, that's all," I said, finally catching my breath.

Nate said, slyly, "I know what you want, Underdog. I know what you want." I felt my face going red. Something disturbed me about his comment.

"What the jizz you shittin'?" Stan, ever the poet, said from the doorway to my room. Stan was naked, too, which was pretty much how the guys went around on a Saturday morning in February when the nearest open road to the girls' college was ten miles away. It was funny, being as generally modest as I was, how I'd got used to all this flaunted nakedness in the ice-cold mornings. Myself, I never got out of the showers except with a big blue towel around my waist, and never left my room except with a shirt and khakis on.

Nate began laughing, and I figured given his jug-face that I hadn't even caused him a moment's pain; but I was still mad 'cause I hated being surprised like that. Everything in that frat house was a surprise attack, especially on Big Weekends. Nate was on-edge on account of his girl might not be making it down for Fancy Dress, so there was a chance he might be the dateless wonder. Nate said, "Look, Underdog, we got the pledges coming over for Ice Palace, and you look like a queer from Lynchburg."

"If that's what you think, jerk-off, then you better not lie naked on my bed too long with that come-hither look on your face," I said. I went back to shaving in the bowl I'd put beneath the mirror in my room for privacy; it saved me from running to the communal and much-pissed-upon bathroom every time I needed to shave or wash.

Stan said, "Fuck the fuck it very." It was a line he said often, sober or drunk, and I couldn't figure it out for the life of me. He had patches of hair up and down his body, armpits to knees, like he had some ape pattern-baldness problem. "I can't wait for tonight, girls, I'm gonna get me some fine pussy, fine pussy."

"Underdog," Nate addressed me in his usual manner, "the Hose Queen's coming down tonight. You want to get laid?"

"No thanks, and get out of here, willya?"

This particular winter semester, in my second year, Nate, who was my big brother in the House, wanted me to learn how to be a man as only Nate knew how. It wasn't enough that I was flunking Physics for Poets because of the midweek grain parties, nor that I had no interest in cow-punching or whore-hopping. Nate was a wild man and rich redneck from Alabama, and his life was something to marvel at. He had learned the ropes of human sexuality at twelve from his baby-sitter; at seventeen, he'd saved an entire boatload of immigrants off the coast of Bermuda—losing three toes in the process. He *knew* life, how to live it, what paths to go down, when and where to get a hard-on and what to do about it and with whom. The bizarre part was, he was an honors student, his old man ran one of the growing tobacco companies, and he never, *ever* had a hangover.

193

Somebody stuck a condom in the scrambled eggs that morning, a typical frat joke, so I passed on breakfast and headed up to the Hill to do some studying on campus. I didn't have a date for the Fancy Dress Ball that night, even though I'd bought two tickets well in advance thinking this girl I knew from high school, Colleen, might want to go, or maybe I'd meet someone else last minute. But Colleen was not to be wooed down to what she called the "last bastion of the old South." I called three girls I knew Down the Road, but each had had a date since October. One of them was kind enough to say she could set me up with this really homely girl who was a chem. major. I passed, and figured I'd get some studying done for once, and let them all go to hell. I was determined to spend the day studying, not scrounging for dates or hazing freshmen.

But Nate was not one to give up easily in his quest to keep me from doing anything productive. He hunted me down on campus, shut my American History book for me, sat on the edge of my desk, and said, "You missed Ice Palace."

"Big deal. Jesus H., quit following me around like some kind of retriever."

"Jonno told a good one. Got us laughing right-off. Bug Boy practically froze to death, we had to let him off after about half an hour, just 'cause we were getting bored watching his lips turn purple. Only one part left."

I groaned. "Yeah, yeah, the crowning of the King. It's like being with Nazis in kindergarten."

"Hey, it takes a special kind of guy to be King of the Palace." Nate Wick had a snarly way of talking that was both seductive and distancing, as if he were an untamed dog waiting for the right master. "Ice Palace is almost as good as fish dunking."

"I hate the whole thing. Ice Palace could make one of them sick."

"You liked it well enough last year."

"Well, I was drunk last year. I liked lots of things then."

"Well, piss on you, Underdog. Sometimes I wish the old you would come back, the one that would stay out all night and really howl." But his mood changed again. "We're gonna kidnap Lewis," he said, like he was planning out the day in his head. He grinned so bright I thought the sun had come out from the gray sky outside the window.

"When?"

"This afternoon. Few hours."

"Shit," I said. "Jesus, of all days. He's your King? Christ, Wick, that poor son of a bitch won't last three hours in the cold. He's got bronchial asthma, he'll come down with something." The truth was, I was protective of Stewart Lewis, who didn't even have the hapless luck to be a brain, for he was skinny and homely and not too bright; if he hadn't been a legacy, he would've gotten blackballed by 60 percent of the House. But his old man was a major brother back in the fifties, so the frat had no choice, because it was in the charter to take legacies no matter what. I had known Stewart Lewis back at St. Sebastian's, the Episcopal school I'd gone to before college. Lewis was always a weinie, always sick, always a mama's boy, always something not so good.

Nate dismissed Lewis with a snap, and then a slap on the desk. "He's a Spam, don't worry about him. We're gonna take him to Crawford's Dump, stick him in the snow, pay Donkeyman to watch him, tie him up, nothing bad. We won't leave him there all night, you fiend. Just a couple of hours, and then I'll go get him in time for Fancy Dress. I doubt he's got a date, though. He's such a Spam. Maybe we'll write on him. The usual. Scare the kid a little. Just a shit speck. He'll get to wear his Jockeys, whatta you want? Whatta you want?"

"You always sound homo to me when you talk about it," I said, hoping to get him angry. I was only a sophomore, but I'd hated hazing so much from the year before—I'd been too blotto to protest much—that I felt very protective of the poor freshmen pledges who went along with any idiotic torture that seniors like Nate devised.

"Maybe I am homo, Underdog. Wanta suck it to find out?" Here he whipped out his thing, which was not the most unusual sight between frat brothers, and was, perhaps, a big reason why we were all so homophobic. Then he put it back in his trousers, zipped up, and said, "You gonna go tonight?"

"Why? You want to buy my ticket?"

195

"Just wondering. I'm not always as insensitive as I seem, buttface."

It started to snow again, and the wind picked up outside, whistling around the old brick and columns along the colonnade; feather flakes seesawed beyond the beveled glass of the windows. It was an ancient campus, from the 1700s, all columns and Greek Parthenon-types and mountain vistas, and I wished I was somewhere, anywhere, else.

"Look," Nate said, "Helen's coming up from Hollins. She likes you. She said she wants to see you." Helen was his girlfriend, a pretty girl who, for some reason, idolized Nate, possibly because she was more unbalanced than she seemed—there was a hint of this in her Sylvia Plath-like scribblings. I thought she was too good for him.

"That's nice," I said. "Look, Nate, I don't want Lewis to go to Ice Palace. He'll get sick. If Dean Trask hears about it, we could get shut down. Think about that. I mean, a half hour of Ice Palace is one thing, but three or four hours, and it's snowing…it's not that funny."

Nate laughed, drumming his fists into the desk. I'd seen him pummel a stray dog like that once, just because the dog was in his way. That was how he used his fists most of the time. He said, "I think it's a goddamn laugh riot."

I avoided the frat house until six, when hunger got the best of me. I was wary of most of my brothers, because I wasn't good at taking any kind of teasing, and that seemed to be their primary business in college. When I entered the foyer, I smelled the steaks— it was a special night, Fancy Dress Ball and all that, and so our cook was doing it up good, steak and asparagus and biscuits and potatoes and fruit and Jell-O and apple pie. Most of the brothers had taken their dates out to dinner, but the poorer among us sat at the long tables, not yet dressed in black tie, with dates astride hard-backed chairs. Plain girls, too, for the most part, until, upstairs, in a guarded bathroom, they would make up and spray, Vaseline their teeth for smiles and for other, more urgent desires, later; spruced with expensive, oversize gowns, and their mother's Shalimar or L'Air du Temps, transforming from ordinary faces and bodies to creatures of unconscionable beauty, perhaps gaudy in the garish light of the upstairs bathroom, but almost mythic, the Woman in All Her Glorious Aspects, in the dimmed, squinting light over at the student center, where the ball would be held.

Nate called out, "Underdog!" He was at the last table, with Helen at his side. She looked up briefly, and then down at her plate again, a flash of curiosity about me, about what I'd been up to since last summer, dying in her face. She was skinny—looked like she had starved herself for this one night—and she'd greased her hair back around her ears with some sort of conditioner.

I went over and took a chair, grabbed some slop, and lopped it on my plate. "Helen," I said.

"Hey, Charlie," she said sweetly, her accent growing more Southern with each year she spent in Virginia. She did not look up from her plate; it was obvious she hadn't eaten.

Nate lip-farted. "Call him Underdog. Humble but lovable."

I smiled at Nate. "Things go okay with Lewis?"

Nate winked. "Fine, fine."

"He around?"

"Yeah. I don't know. I guess he was upset."

I wasn't sure whether to believe Nate or not, but Helen must've detected my doubt. She said, "He said he was going to a movie. He was very upset. Y'all are so dang insensitive. It's what I hate, absolutely hate, about y'all being in a fraternity and all."

"Helen's on the rag," Nate half-whispered, loud enough for all six tables to hear.

I looked to Helen, and reached my hand across to touch hers because I felt so bad for her at that moment, stuck with Nate, Nate who bragged about doing her on his water bed, about muff-diving her in the backseat of her father's Continental, taking her every which way but loose up in the carillon tower of chapel when she didn't want it but loved it anyway. I didn't know Helen well, but I wanted to touch her more than anything.

Helen glanced up at me, her eyes dry. Nate was clanking his fork on the side of his plate. He was always jealous when it came to Helen, and he must've seen the way she looked at me.

"Why don't you just fuck her?" he asked, shoving himself away from the table, his chair falling backward. He was drunk; so that was it. He stomped across the room, and went upstairs.

Helen said, "I hate him."

"Nah," I said, "he's a jerk sometimes. But he has his good side."

Helen laughed. "No, he doesn't. I don't know why I'm even here."

She shut her eyes, her face taut, her hands in fists. Then she opened her eyes, unclenched, and said, "Because I'm a good girl. Because I do what I'm told." She said it like it was taking her medicine, an antidote to some other, more profound venom. And then, "Will you go with me tonight? I don't want to go with him."

198

2

There are certain humiliations we will withstand when we are young, if it means that we can become part of something bigger than just ourselves, by ourselves. This notion upheld all the tortures of hazing.

Ice Palace was a peculiar ritual, in which a tunnel at least the length of a man's body was dug out in the snow. The pledges had to dig it, for they were virtual slaves to the upperclassmen, and it always reminded me a bit of stories I'd heard about the Jews digging their own graves before the Nazi guard. Then, one at a time, the pledges were stripped down to their underwear. Each was then hosed down with water, and sent into the tunnel, which was now deemed the Ice Palace. The pledge had to sit back in the freezing ice and tell a joke until every upperclassman present laughed. When I had gone through Ice Palace, I had got them laughing within ten minutes, so it hadn't been too hard on me. There had even been something of a respite from the outer world when I had crawled into that ice cave, shivering for sure, but also experiencing a strange pleasure, as if I were protected in a way I didn't quite understand. Some pledges could not tell a joke to save their lives, however, and so it could be a painful, if not simply a chilling, experience. This was one of the least pleasant aspects of hazing. The other rituals (egg-yolk passing from mouth to mouth, or fish dunking in a toilet) were disgusting, but essentially harmless. Even paddling was child's play, with the only casualty being a sore butt for a few days.

But Ice Palace...I thought of Stewart Lewis, with his taped-up glasses on his beaky nose, his small pea-pod eyes, that squirmy way he had of moving as if he had worms or something, and of the humiliation of the whole ritual, particularly of being chosen to be the King of Ice Palace, as he had been. King of Ice Palace: the honor at the shit end of life's stick, the pledge chosen basically because he was commonly known as the Spam, the Nerd, the Loser, the Meat. There was always one pledge who fit this bill— almost as if, each year, the brothers decided to admit someone they could torture, someone who was so desperate to be accepted that he would take it.

The King's hands and feet were roped together, and he was to be sealed up in Ice Palace until someone came to get him out. Cold water was hosed over the entire tunnel in order to truly give it a thick layer of ice. Then, after a set period of time, the Brother High Alpha, which in our case was Nate, would break open the door to Ice Palace. The King would come forth from his white chamber, freezing and cursing, yet somehow stronger, and more part of the group than he could ever be through ordinary means. If the chosen one tried to get out early, there was Donkeyman, the local wino. He was as scary as any nightmare, his face elongated, his ears out and pointy like a mule's, only three teeth in his head, and barely a nose at all, just two flared nostrils exhaling frosty clouds of carbon dioxide. The freshmen weren't familiar enough with the university to have seen Donkeyman yet, for Donkeyman was a creature of alleyways and Dumpsters. He was perfectly harmless, but he looked like a demon lover of donkeys.

Ice Palace was a fraternity secret and, by all accounts, illegal, at least as far as the college went. If it had been known that it was an ongoing ritual, the entire fraternity system, which was then enjoying a rebirth in popularity, would have been shut down.

There was a story that back in the late fifties a boy had died in Ice Palace.

3

"That's the boy," Helen whispered in my ear. We were slow dancing, off the dance floor. She had abandoned Nate to his drunken fury earlier in the evening, and because I owned my own tux, she had grabbed me and driven me up to the student center and the ball before I could protest too much. I felt a little guilty for snaking my big brother's date, but she was pretty, and he was acting like an asshole, anyway.

I glanced up from her shoulder, for I had been watching the bone there, beneath the skin, so delicate, so feminine. Smelling her, too, like jasmine with the snow just on the other side of the walls, and here, there were flowers and sandalwood. "Huh?" I asked.

"That boy," she said, dreamily, "the one they put in the snow."

We stopped dancing, and I turned around to look at Stewart Lewis. "I didn't know he was going to be—" I said, but then, there was no Stewart.

Just Stan the Man, who came over and slapped me on the back. "Fuck the fuck it very," he said, his breath stinking of whiskey. "So, Underdoggie, you got Nate's squeeze, bravo, good job, didn't deserve her, the Flaccid Wick didn't, my god, this wine tastes like cow jism." His eyes barely registered either of us; his date, Marlene, stood off to the side, avoiding just about everyone.

"Stan wasn't Ice Palace King," I told Helen. "Is that who you saw in Ice Palace?"

"I didn't see him." Helen turned away from me, waved to a friend. "Nate told me it was him. Isn't that Stewart?" and then, to Stan, "Aren't you Stewart Lewis?"

"The Spamster?" Stan guffawed. "Lawdy, no, Miss Scarlett, I don't know nothing about birthin' no babies."

"He's too drunk to make sense," I said. "Nate told you?"

Helen shrugged. "I thought this guy was Stewart. You boys all look alike with your khakis and down jackets. Are you sure you're not Stewart?"

Stan grinned, but wobbled back to Marlene, who apparently scolded him for something.

"Jesus, I wonder if he ever let Lewis out," I said. "Look, Helen, you wait here, I'll be back in a while."

"Charlie," Helen said, not even startled. "Charlie."

"What?" I snapped, and then blurted, "My god. My god. It'll kill Lewis. It'll kill him." I left her there, and ran through the make-out room just beyond the dance floor, out through the French doors, down the icy steps, almost slipping on the concrete pavement. The town was a small one, almost a town in miniature, and I didn't own a car. It would be a ten-minute jog down Stonewall Drive to get to the House, and to Nate, if he was still there. The night was a furious one, for although the snow had quieted to shavings from trees, the wind had picked up, and had dropped the temperature at least twenty degrees. I was a decent runner then, but I'd had two beers, and this, with the wind, seemed to slow all motion down by half, so I felt like a half-hour had passed before I was coming into the frat house from the back entrance. The lights were off in the kitchen; I flicked them up. The place was a mess, like a child's giant toy box overturned, but this was usual. What was unusual were the marks on the wall, as if someone had tried finger painting with bacon grease—which there was plenty of around, for it was stored and used in another hazing ritual.

"Nate! Wick! Where the fuck are you?" I took the stairs two at a time, and came to his room on the second floor.

He lay in bed, with the light on. He was wearing his tux. He opened his eyes. "Underdog."

"Where's Lewis?"

"Lewis? Who the fuck cares? That human spittoon. You stole my girl, Underdog. You stole my girl." He rolled over, away from me, facing the wall. "You stole my girl. But fuck it. Like Stan says, fuck the fuck it very."

I couldn't believe that even Nate would leave Lewis in Ice Palace for the eight hours he would've been in it by now. I almost laughed at myself for worrying. I caught my breath, my hands on my knees, bent over slightly. I looked at the poster of the naked girl with the snake that Nate had on his wall. She was some movie actress, I don't remember who, but her belly seemed to meet the boa constrictor in an almost motherly caress. "Whew, Nate. Whoa, boy. You almost had me going. You know, you miserable—you know I ran all the way down here from Fancy Dress, just to…just to—"

"He's still in it." He didn't turn to face me, but his voice was smug. "And I'm the only one who knows where he is."

"You're joking."

"I'm joking, but the joke's on Lewis. Or should I say, you can now find Spam in the freezer section of your local supermarket."

I went over and grabbed him by the back of his collar and hauled him off the bed. When he turned to face me, I slapped his face four times. "Where is he?"

Calmly, Nate said, "What the hell do you care?" There were tears in his eyes. "What the hell do you care? It might as well be me in there, for all any of you care. Why don't you like me, Underdog? Why?" His tears were both a shock and a revelation to me: he was only a nine-year-old in a twenty-one-year-old's body, the jug-face was a mask, the rough talk, a cover, the attitude, a sham.

And I said what I felt, although I regretted it within the hour.

I said, "Because you're not even human."

4

We took his car, but I drove. "You said you were doing Ice Palace at Crawford's Dump," I said, "so we'll go there first. You better hope to god Lewis had the sense to break out of there."

"I don't know," he said, a singsong to his voice. "I gave Donkeyman some Chivas to do double duty. I told him to hit Spam on the head with the shovel if he tried to get out. We hosed it down pretty good. Twenty below. Nice thick ice. Ice you could skate on. Ice Palazzo." Nate was still crying, bawling like a baby, and singing;

he had cracked; he was drunk; he kept trying to grab the wheel while I was driving.

Crawford's Dump was the old graveyard just outside town, but there were few markers, and even fewer showed through the heavy snow. I skidded the Volkswagen to a stop on the slick shoulder of the pot-holed, salt-strewn road, and left the headlights on. We tromped in our tuxes through the Styrofoam crunch of snow, and each time Nate tried to pull away I socked him in the shoulder and cussed him out. The snow and a clouded moon provided a soft light, making the dumping ground of the dead romantic, beautiful, sublime. Even Nate, when I spat my fury at him, looked beautiful, too, with the tears streaming, and his eyes always on me. The dump descended into a small valley, where the entire cemetery spread out all around us.

"Where?"

Nate shrugged. His tears ceased. The wind, too, died, but we heard it howling around us, up the hill. Trucks out on the interstate blew their horns, one to another, and even the music from the Fancy Dress Ball, playing "The Swing," could be made out.

"Where, Nate? Tell me."

"Wherever Donkeyman is. You stole my girl, Underdog."

"Look, asshole, Lewis is going to die. You hear me? You will have murdered a human being. Don't you get it? You tell me where that stupid Ice Palace is, or I will kill you with my bare hands."

Nate blinked twice. "Suck my dick."

I got a good clear shot at his jaw, my second in one day, and then a knee in the groin before he swung back; he only clipped me, but I was off-balance, and fell into the snow.

I thought for a second—just a second—I felt a gentle tugging.

There, in the snow.

Like a soft mitten, pulling me down.

Nate jumped on top of me, spitting all over my face as he spoke. "You are my best friend, Underdog, you are my best friend in the world. Who the fuck cares about Lewis? Are you in love with him or something? Are you? Is that all you want? Lewis? Why are you doing this to me?" He began boxing my ears with snow, until I felt them go numb; I tried to heave him off me, but the mother was heavy; I felt that gentle tugging again. Soft. Like kittens on my back.

And then, something I had always known would happen, did happen. I just had never had a clue as to the form it would take.

Nate Wick kissed me on the lips as warmly and sweetly as any lover ever had.

Something clicked for me then, and for the longest minute in the world, I shut my eyes and just felt the warmth of those lips, and the even tempo of my own breathing through my nostrils. I was somewhere else, and the cold of the snow was almost burning now, like a bed of warm coals against my tuxedo. His hands remained around my ears, and the sound of distant music, and trucks, too — their own music — voices up on the hillside, passersby to whom we were invisible. The whiteness of snow, the indigo sky, all there, but without me seeing or hearing. His lips were rough and chapped, and I felt my own lips opening like a purse that had been kept too long shut; his upper lip grazed my teeth. His breath was a caustic brewery, but I held each one for as long as I could. I hated this boy, this man, so much; I hated him, and yet tied like this, together, unnaturally if we were to believe those who ran the world, we were perverse brothers, children playing. The blood rushed to my face, an unbearable burning sensation. I opened my eyes; his remained closed. I kissed a corner of his lips, and then the other. He made a deep noise, a churning machine somewhere within his gut, or igniting along his spine, as he rose and fell again, softly, like the tugging I felt in the rabbit-fur snow beneath my back. The knob of desire, or prick, or dick, or wang, whatever we had called it through all the shared moments of college life, pressed from his pants against mine. I shivered as much from embarrassment as from lust; but there was no one around, you see, no one within miles. I remembered him in the showers, soaping his underarms like he was scrubbing a saddle, tender and quick and then sandpapering at the last; the tumescence he had, which I noticed only peripherally. I hated him. I hated him.

He pressed the side of his face against mine, and it was like holding someone for the first time, this boy, this innocent, angry, drunken boy. I wrapped my arms around him. "I love you," he whispered, and even though I smelled the alcohol, I sighed.

He said, "Lewis was nothing. He was nothing."

And then my mind came back to me, through this physical revelation, through this lightning-swift understanding of all I had done before in my life, as well as much of what Nate himself had done.

Lewis.

Stewart Lewis. The freshman that Nate Wick had chosen as King of Ice Palace.

"You fucked Lewis," I said. "You fucked him and then you buried him. Get the fuck off me!" I shoved hard, and he rolled back.

"No," he said, rather meekly, not breaking eye contact with me. "I didn't. He wouldn't let me. He...he didn't want me."

205

I would've liked to have died right there, my secret self that I had worked so hard to hide buried forever in snow, but I was worried about Lewis. The kiss had made me forget him, briefly, but the reality of who and what Nate Wick was came back to me, a sour taste in the back of my throat. "Get up, get up." I stood, kicking him in the side. But he looked forlornly up at the moon, which had swept off its clouds; the lover's moon, I thought, the horny poking male moon, the prick of light, the howling desire of man's madness. I felt dirty, and picked up fresh snow and rubbed it on my face, my lips, to get that awful taste of *him* off me.

"It's so white," Nate said, snow in his hands too, packing a snowball, which he threw at me as I wandered the valley.

At last, I saw a solitary figure, a minute man standing guard: the illustrious Donkeyman, his shovel stuck firmly into a heap of snow. He was the whitest man I had ever seen, and even at night, the pink eyes, the white hair, the chin stretched like putty, the ears demonic; blubbery lips, nostrils drippy with snot. He grinned, and brayed some greeting—the bottle of Chivas Regal lay empty beside him, along with several piss stains at his feet. "Preppy boy, how you?" he asked congenially, waving the flashlight that he held tight in his gloved left hand. He had a hunter's flap-down hat on, and an oversize tan duster around his shoulders, one that one of my frat brothers had no doubt loaned him for the night. "King a Ice Palace in there. I done my job. Got you another bottle?"

I took the shovel up and asked, "Where?"

"I said, got you another bottle? Donkeyman done his job. Icy Palace, nobody goes in, nobody goes out." He was pleased with himself, for he took pride in such work.

I threatened him with the shovel, until he pointed out the mound, not three feet away. I tapped it with the edge of the shovel. Hard as a rock. The ice of its outer layer gleamed, for Donkeyman shone his flashlight upon it.

"Lewis?" I shouted. "Lewis!"

I listened, but there was only the adenoidal sniggering of Donkeyman as he lit himself a Camel and puckered his lips at the first puff.

"King a Icy Palace ain't been talkin' since about six, seven. Done a good damn job. Best. You boys know it, too." He spat a brown lungie in the snow.

I took the shovel up, down, up, down. The blade struck the outer edge of the Ice Palace. It was like breaking rocks in two. The ice finally creaked and cracked where I struck, and snow began to fall rapidly as I worked.

5

I looked through the opening I had dug. Nate was already there at my side, perhaps sobering up a bit, because he seemed nervous and worried. Donkeyman patted me on the back now and again in my labor, cheering me on. We were some crew.

"Lewis? Stewart!" I shouted into the tunnel.

Silence.

"I only had him make it maybe six feet in," Nate said, with some regret.

I grabbed Donkeyman's flashlight, and shone it into Ice Palace. The tunnel in the ice and snow did go about six feet or so, but then there seemed to be a twist. Hand prints in the ice, too, along the shiny white and silver walls. There were the ropes. "He got out," I said, almost relieved. "He got out."

"He got out," Nate said, solemnly.

"Thank god, thank you god for saving Lewis's life." I stood, leaning against the shovel.

Donkeyman said, "He got out?"

"Underdog. Charlie," Nate said.

"Thank god, you better thank god, Wick, because if he had died in there...well, you are one lucky SOB."

Nate looked stunned. "He didn't get out, Charlie." Finally, for the first time in his life, calling me by my real name.

"What do you mean?"

"I mean what I said. He didn't get out."

"He must've. See for yourself." I showed him the tunnel, and swirled the flashlight around to show the shape of the curve, to the left, barely visible. "He got loose and dug around that way. The lucky bastard must've gone for about six yards or something, and then tunneled up."

"He didn't get out," Nate repeated. He shoved me aside, and crawled into Ice Palace. I watched his ass shimmy through the thin tunnel, blocking my light.

"Nate, get out of there," I called after him.

I heard his words echo through Ice Palace. "I'm telling you, he didn't get out. I put him here, Charlie, I put him here, so I should know."

"What's he mean by that?" I asked Donkeyman, as if he would have a coherent answer.

Donkeyman scratched his scalp beneath his cap and said, "Don't know. The boy already done got Icy Palaced by the time the Donkeyman show up."

I crawled in a ways, shining the flashlight first up ahead, and then to the frozen walls. Lewis's hand prints, as if he'd pressed against the snow to try and push his way out here. But he must've realized that this end of the tunnel would be iced over from the water that Nate would toss over it. So Lewis—you smart dog—you figured on digging farther, I thought, you miserable lucky nerd! Nate turned left, at the twist in the tunnel. I noticed a certain indentation in the inner wall. Letters of a word. I held the flashlight at an angle to make them out.

RESUR

Then, a hint of red. A bit of fingernail. Lewis had cut his fingers in the stiff snow. He had stopped writing.

"Nate?" I called, but there was no answer, so I shuffled on my hands and knees, my back low but still pressing the ceiling, to catch up with him.

I turned the corner to the left, and stopped, for something was

different.

I shone the flashlight all around.

I couldn't see Nate at all, anywhere; the tunnel seemed to descend at the turn, rather than do the logical thing, which was to move forward and up. If Lewis were to escape, surely he would've tried to push *up*?

"Nate?" I cried through what now seemed an eternal tunnel of ice. "Nate!"

My voice echoed.

There were other hand prints there, in the ice, none of them the same. All were smeared, and some seemed impossibly thin; in one indentation, I saw what might've been a silken patch of the thinnest skin. I began to back up, to get out of the tunnel. As I reversed as far as I could, I turned a bit, shining the flashlight back toward the entrance.

It was once again sealed.

"Donkeyman!" I shouted. "Donkeyman!"

I thought I heard him laughing, but perhaps it was not on the outside, but within this chamber, this tapeworm that had no end. This chamber of ice. I slammed my fist into the ceiling, but succeeded only in skinning my knuckles. Somehow, Donkeyman had sealed us in there again. I moved forward, the only place to go, past the hieroglyphs of hands and the sides of smooth bony faces, a thread of skin here, a spray of torn hair under my knees. The tunnel descended and then widened, so I could move about a bit more; there was less air here, and what there was of it began to stink like sewage.

And then something grabbed me by the wrist, and shook the flashlight out of my hand. It rolled to the side, shining its light against the wall, casting gray-white-yellow shadow.

I was in a room with others.

Nate whispered, "I killed him, Charlie. I killed Lewis."

I was too numb to be shocked by what seemed inevitable, for I'd had a feeling from the beginning of the day that Nate would kill Stewart Lewis.

Nate leaned over and kissed me gently on the cheek, then my right ear. Something moved in front of us. "I love you, Charlie. I'm scared. I mean, I'm really scared. I never been this scared." His face shuddered, and I drew away from his caress.

I leaned forward, picking up the flashlight, and shot its beam directly in front of us.

"Oh god," Nate said.

It was Stewart Lewis, hunched in a wider chamber, his white oxford-cloth shirt torn and bloody, with red and black slices through the skin of his chest. His khakis were muddy and soaked. I had never seen him without his glasses, but he seemed handsomer, with his hair slicked back, and a pale cast to his face. Around him, others, young men all, young and decayed, slashes along their arms, or blue flesh as if their blood were frozen, half-naked, tendons dangling from some, others as beautiful as if they were alive, and in some respects I knew they were, and in some respects they had not lived in a very long time.

Nate said, "King of Ice Palace."

Lewis grinned, naughtily, and leaned into us, until his lips were practically an inch from my face. "Pleasures beyond life, Charlie, beyond the snow. The warmth of life, the sun within the flesh."

Lewis turned his face toward Nate, who clung to my sleeve. "One of you," he said, his voice the same hopeless soprano of an undeveloped choirboy, but the face, full of fierce authority, his lips drawn back, his eyes ice ice ice. "One of you," he said, "is mine."

Nate let go of my arm, recoiling from me, and said, "Him. Charlie. You can fuck him. You can do whatever you want to him."

"Oh, Nate," Lewis said, "you wanted me, in the woods, you held the knife to my throat because you wanted me."

"I'm not like that," Nate said, pressing himself back against the wall. "He is. Charlie's like that. It was because you wanted me to do it. That was all. I have a girlfriend. *Charlie*, tell him about Helen. *Tell him.*"

"You miserable—" I said, pushing at him. And then I turned to Stewart Lewis. "Lewis, what happened, what...what...are you?"

"King of Ice Palace, Charlie, just the way Nate wanted me. Frozen, consenting, helpless. Nate, give me your tongue, give me your wet sweet tongue, give me the fire of your breath, give me the secret you." Lewis leaned into Nate, and I moved to the side, but could not get too far from them. Lewis and Nate had locked mouths, and I heard a gurgling, but not of terror or pain. It turned into a tender moan, like a kitten searching for its mother's milk. I watched in the white chamber as Nate's color changed to a peach on his face, for this love was being passed between them, this frozen and glorious and fearful love.

All the young and dead men in the chamber watched as Nate pushed himself against the wall as if trying to break out of there. His hand traced a line along the shiny wall, gripping, becoming a clench of delight as Lewis leaned forward into him. Stewart Lewis was only newly resurrected, but it made me think how beautiful physical love could be, between two people, a doorway between two separate entities, that submission on both parts, that surrender to the warmth and the gasps of physical contact. I knew then why men enjoyed watching the sexual act almost as much as participating in it.

Because it is a celebration of the perverse, no matter the context—the thrusting buttocks, the muscular legs tight and kicking as if in combat, the slobbering mouth, the exquisite beauty of lost consciousness.

That can happen to me, yes, and that, too, you think when you watch one enter the other, one clasp his hands around the other's shuddering flesh.

I loved Nate Wick, and I loved Stewart Lewis, and I loved the boys who had died, for the ritual of the ice had been known since before I came into the world.

All of them, crowned for a season through years of winter, Kings of Ice Palace.

6

Leaving Ice Palace, while difficult, is not impossible, for the King is not a tyrant, neither is his court a prison. Nate never followed me out to the other side when the morning broke, but I think he was safer in there. I did not run from that place, but departed after having left my own hand prints along its white walls.

I helped murder a boy once, or perhaps he had just become a man that night and did not want to return to the warming climates. He was my brother, although he was no blood relation. I do not believe that he is, in any real sense, dead, although his family has given up on him, as has his girl friend, Helen.

Ice Palace: I do not wish to live there, not yet, although I venture into its white, secret chamber often on dark winter nights.

It is a secret chamber, Ice Palace.

Ice Palace.

But, even so, it is never as cold or as lonely as my days in the world above.

211

The Five

I once lived in an apartment building where a feral cat went in and had her babies in the walls of the building. We heard meows constantly once the kittens got older. The landlord had to bust down some walls to get the kittens out so that they wouldn't die in there – the fear was that the mother might not come back one day from her daily hunt, and then the kittens would be doomed. So, the kittens were rescued, homes were found for them, and the remaining opening, that the mother cat had originally found, was sealed up.

I began this story thinking of that, and also of what it was like being a child who could not communicate well with grownups. "The Five" grew from there. It originally appeared an anthology edited by Ellen Datlow called Twists of the Tail.

1

The wall was up against the carport, and Naomi, who was just beginning the gangly phase, stretched out across it like she was trying to climb up the side of the house to the roof. She heard the sound first. She knew about the cat, the wild one that lived out in the Wash. Somehow, it had survived the pack of coyotes that roamed there, and she had thought she saw it come near the house a few times before.

But there was no mistaking the sounds of kitten mewling, and so she presented the problem to her father. "They'll die in there."

"No," he said. "The mother cat knows what she's doing. She's got the kittens there so the coyotes won't get them. When they're old enough, she'll bring them out. They're animals, Nomy, they go by instinct and nature. The mother cat knows best. The wall's sturdy enough, too. Walls are good, safe places from predators."

"What's a predator?"

"Anything that's a threat. Anything that might eat a cat."

"Like a coyote?"

"Exactly."

"Where's the father cat?"

"At work."

He showed Naomi where the weak part of the wall was, and how to press her ear up against it with a glass. Her eyes went wide and squinty, alternately, and she accidentally dropped the glass, which broke.

He said, "You'll have to clean that up."

She was barefoot and had to step carefully around it, and the oil spots from the car, over to get the broom. She took a few swipes at the broken glass, and then leaned against the wall again. Her father was, by this time, just starting up the lawn mower in the side yard. She wanted to ask him more about the cat, but he was preoccupied, and since (she'd been warned) this was one of his few days off for the summer, she decided not to bother him. She went indoors and told her mother about the cat and the kittens and her mother was more concerned. Her mother had helped her rescue a family of opossums at the roadside out near Hemet—the mother opossum had been hit by a car, and although Naomi knew intellectually that the babies were probably doomed, she and her mother gathered them up in a grocery bag and took them to a nearby vet who promised to do his best and that had been that. Her mother was much more sentimental about animals than her father, and went outside with her immediately to examine the wall.

"There's the hole near the drainpipe. I don't know how she did it, but she squeezed in there. Good for her. She protected her children." Naomi's mother pointed up to beneath the eaves, where the pipe only partially covered a hole that her father had put into the wall accidentally when he was repairing the roof.

"I've seen her before," Naomi said, "the mother cat. She watches gophers over in the field. She's very tough looking. My father says she's doing it because of instinct."

Her mother looked from Naomi over to her husband, mowing. "It's his day off and he mows. We see him at breakfast and before bed, and on his day off he mows."

"It's his instinct," Naomi said. The air was smoky with lawn mower exhaust and fresh-drawn grass; motes of dust and dandelion fluff sprayed across the yellow day.

She thought about the kittens all afternoon, and wondered how many there were.

"I think several," her mother told her. "Maybe five."

"Why don't people have babies all at once like that?"

Her mother laughed, "Some do. They're crazy. Trust me, when you're ready to have children, you won't want several at once."

"I can't wait to have babies," Naomi said. "When I have babies, I'll protect them just like the Mom cat."

"You're much too young to think that."

"You had me when you were eighteen."

"So, you have nine more years to go and you need to pick up a husband along the way."

Her father, who had been listening to all this even while he read the paper, said, "I don't think it's right to encourage her, Jean."

Her mother glanced at her father, and then back at Naomi.

The living room was all done in blues, and Naomi sometimes felt it was a vast sea, and she was floating on a cushion, and her parents were miles away, underwater.

Her father, his voice bubbling and indistinct, said something about something or other that they'd told her before about something to do with something, but Naomi had known when to block him out, when to put him beneath the waves.

She climbed the drainpipe just after dinner, with a flashlight held in her mouth making her feel like she would throw up any second. She grasped one edge of the roof, and cut her fingers on the sharp metal of the pipe, and lodged her left foot in the space between the pipe and the wall. She directed the flashlight down the hole, and saw a pair of fierce red eyes, and movement. Nothing more than that. The eyes scared her a bit, and she tried to pull her foot free so she could shimmy down, but her foot was caught. The mother cat moved up into the hole until its face was right near hers. Naomi heard a low growl which didn't sound like a cat at all. She dropped the flashlight, and felt a claw swipe across her face. She managed to get her foot free, and dropped five feet to the ground, landing on her rear. She felt a sharp pain in her legs.

Her mother came outside at the noise, and ran to get her. "Damn it," her mother gasped, "what in god's name are you doing?" She rushed to Naomi, lifting her up.

"My leg." It hurt so much she didn't want to move at all, but her mother carried her into the light of the carport. She was trailing blood. It didn't spurt out like she thought it might, but just came in drips and drabs like the rain when it was spitting.

"It's glass," her mother said. She removed it; Naomi didn't have time to cry out. Tears were seeping from her eyes. The pain in her leg, just along the calf, was burning.

Her father had heard the shouting, and he came out, too. He was in white boxer shorts and a faded gray T-shirt. He said, "What's going on here?"

"She cut herself," her mother said.

"I told her to sweep up the glass," he said, and then turned to her, and more softly said, "didn't I tell you to clean up the broken glass, Nomy?"

Naomi could barely see him for her tears. She looked from one to the other, and then back, but it was all a blur.

"We've got to take her to the emergency room."

Her father said, "Yeah, and who's coming up with the three hundred bucks?"

"Insurance."

"Canceled."

Her mother said nothing.

"We can sew it up here, can't we?"

Her mother seemed about to say something. Almost a sound came out of her mouth. Then, after a moment, she said, "I guess I could. Jesus, Dan. What if this were worse?"

"It's just a cut. It's only glass. You know how to put in stitches."

Her mother asked her, "Sweetie, is that all right with you?"

"If it's what my father wants," she said.

Her father said, "She always calls me that. Isn't that strange? 'My father'. Why is she like this?"

Her mother ignored him. She felt the warmth of her mother's hand on her damp cheek. "It's okay to cry when things hurt."

"She never looks me in the eye, either. You ever notice that? You're Mommy, but I get 'my father'. Christ." Her father said something else, but even the sounds were starting to blur because Naomi thought she heard the kittens mewling in the wall, just the other side, and they were getting louder and louder.

Even later, when her mother took out her sewing kit and told her it wouldn't hurt as much as it looked like, even then, she thought she heard them.

2

The stitches came out a week later, and although there was a broad white scar, it wasn't so bad. She could still jump rope, although she felt a gentle tugging. She hadn't been outside much—she'd got a fever, which, according to her mother, was from an infection in her leg. But all she'd had to do was lie around and watch *I Love Lucy* re-runs, and eat Saltines and guzzle cola. Not the worst thing, she figured. As soon as she was able, she went out to check on the kittens.

She had a can of tuna with her—she knew cats loved it, and her mother would never miss it. She set up the step ladder, and climbed up.

But the hole was no longer there.

It had been sealed up. White plaster was spread across it.

She asked her mother about it.

"They got old enough to leave," her mother said, "and so the Mom cat took them back out to the field to hunt mice."

"What about the coyotes?"

"Wild cats are usually smarter than coyotes. Really, honey. They're fine."

3

Although she wasn't ever supposed to go into the field that adjoined her father's property, Naomi untangled her way through the blackberry and boysenberry vines, and went anyway. The grass in the field was high and yellow; foxtails shot out at her and embedded themselves in her socks. She picked them out carefully. There was an old rusted-out tractor in the middle of the field, and she found several small stiff balloons near it, and a pipe made completely of brass. She kept searching through the grass. Something moved along the mound where the grass grew thickest. A great tree, dead from lightning, stood guardian of this spot. A peregrine falcon sat at its highest point. She looked up and down, and all around, which was something she'd once heard about. The grass quivered. The falcon flew off across the field, down towards the orange groves.

She saw two ears rise slowly above the grass.

A coyote was not four feet away from her. Its yellow-brown head came into view. It was beautiful.

She stood still for several seconds.

She had never seen a coyote this close.

And then, the animal turned and ran off down the field, towards the Wash.

Naomi had been holding her breath the whole time, not realizing it. The sun was up and boiling, and she looked back across to her house. It seemed too far away. She sat down in the grass for a minute, feeling the left-over heat of fever break across her forehead.

THE FIVE

She cupped her hands together like she was praying, and lay her head against them. She whispered into the dry earth, "Don't let anything hurt the kittens."

When she awoke, the sun was all the way across the sky. Ants crawled across her hands; some were in her hair. She had to brush them out. She felt like she'd been sleeping for years, it had been that peaceful. Her mother was calling to her from the back yard. She stood, brushed dirt and insects from her, and ran in the direction of the familiar voice. She jumped around the thorny vines, but her leg started to hurt again, so she ended up limping her way up the driveway. She went along the side of the carport to get to the back gate, when something leapt out in front of her.

It was the mother cat. Snarling.

Naomi froze.

The mother cat watched her.

Naomi looked around for the kittens but saw none.

And then she heard them.

She followed the sound.

Pressed her ear against the carport wall.

She heard them.

Inside the wall.

The five.

4

When her father got home from work, he went in and sat in front of the television to watch the ten o'clock news. Naomi was supposed to be getting ready for bed, but she had been pressing herself up against the wall in the living room, because she thought she heard something moving behind it. She wandered into the den, following the sounds. Her father glanced at her, then at the television. The noise in the wall seemed to stop at the entrance to the den.

Naomi stood there, leaning against the door jamb. "You didn't take the kittens out, did you?"

He looked at her. His eyes seemed to be sunken into the shriveled skin around them; his eyeglasses magnified them until she felt he was staring right through her.

"Nomy?" he asked.

"You left them in the wall."

He grinned. "Don't be silly. I took them out. All five. Set them down. The mother carried them into the vines. Don't be silly."

"I heard them. I saw the big cat. She was angry."

"Don't be silly," he said, more firmly. He took his glasses off.

She realized that she was alone in the room with him, and she didn't like it. She never liked being alone with him. Not inside the house.

She ran down the hall to her mother's room. Her mother was lying on the bed in her slip, reading a book. She set it down.

Naomi climbed up on the bed. "Mommy, I have a question."

Her mother patted a space beside her. Naomi scooted closer. She lay down, resting her head on her mother's arm.

"It's about the kittens in the wall."

Naomi looked up at the ceiling, which was all white, and thought she saw clouds moving across it, almost forming a face.

"What I want to know," she said, "is, did the cat take the kittens out before he covered the hole?"

Her mother said, "Why?"

"I heard the kittens earlier."

"Before dinner?"

Naomi nodded. The cloud face in the ceiling melted away.

"You didn't tell me you heard them."

"I was really angry. I thought you lied to me."

"I wouldn't lie to you."

"I asked my father, and he said I was being silly."

"Well, it's not silly if you thought you heard them. But you must've imagined it. I saw them leave. With the Mom cat."

"I saw her, too. She looked angry. She looked like she was mad at me for letting her babies get put in the wall like that."

"Oh," her mother said, stroking her fine, dark hair, "cats don't think things like that. She was probably just asking for milk. Maybe she's getting tamer. Maybe one day she and all the kittens, grown up, will come back because you were so nice to them."

"I was sure I heard them."

"Maybe you wanted to hear them."

Naomi was fairly confused, but had never known her mother to lie.

Her mother said, "You got sunburned today."

"I saw a coyote in the field."

"You went in the field?"

"I was looking for the kittens."

"Oh, you. Don't tell your father."

In the morning, she returned to the carport wall. She pressed a drinking glass to it, and then applied her ear.

Nothing.

No sound.

She tapped on the wall with her fingers.

No sound.

And then...something.

Almost nothing.

Almost a whine.

And then, as if a dam had burst, the screaming, shrieking of small kittens, and the sound of frantic clawing.

She almost dropped the glass, but remembering her leg, she caught it in time. *I wouldn't lie to you*, she heard her mother say, a memory.

I wouldn't lie to you.

She put the glass up to the wall.

Nothing.

Silence.

Sound of her own heart, beating rapidly.

5

That night, she lay in bed, unable to sleep. In the daylight, she would be all right, but at night she had to stay up because of things in the dark. She thought she had forgotten how to breathe; then realized, she was still inhaling and exhaling.

About one in the morning, her door opened.

Someone stood there, so she had to close her eyes.

She counted her breaths, and hoped it wouldn't be him.

She felt the kiss on her forehead.

That, and the touching her on the outside of the blanket, was all he ever did, the nighttime father, but it was enough to make her wish she were dead and wonder where her mother was to protect her.

But as she lay there, she heard them again.

The kittens.

Mewling sweetly, for tuna or milk.

They had traveled to find her, through the small spaces within the walls, to find her and tell her they were all right.

She fell asleep before the door opened again, listening to them, wondering if they were happy, if they were catching the mice that she knew occasionally crawled into other holes and vents and cracks. The five were still there, her kittens, her kittens, and she knew it would turn out fine now.

6

"What's wrong with her?"

"Well, Dan, if we'd taken her to the hospital instead of letting the infection go like that..."

"And somebody would've accused us of child abuse. That's all that ever happens anymore. And it's not some infection, Jean. Look at her. Why is she doing that?"

"I think she's sick. Her fever's back."

"What's gotten into her?"

Naomi heard them, but paid no attention, because the kittens were getting louder. They were three months old now, and they sounded more like cats. They played there, behind the diamond shaped wallpaper in the kitchen, just behind the toaster. One had caught a mouse or something, and they were playing with it—she could hear the frightened squeaks. She pressed the palms of her hands against the wallpaper, trying to open up the wall, but no matter how much she pressed, nothing gave.

Her father said, "She shouldn't be crawling around like that. She looks like an animal."

"Sweetie," her mother said, stroking her hair, "don't you think you need to get back in bed?"

She glanced up at her mother, "I love them," she said, unable to control an enormous smile, "I love them so much, Mommy."

Her mother wasn't looking at her. She said, "I'm taking her to a doctor right now."

"Hello, Naomi." The doctor was bald and sweet looking, like a grandfather.

"Hello," she replied.

"That leg's healing okay. Looks like whoever stitched it, did it right."

"Mommy did it. She used to be a nurse."

"I know. She used to work with me. Did you know that?"

No reply.

"What seems to be the problem?" he asked. He put the stethoscope against her chest. She breathed in and out. Then, a funny looking thermometer, which he called a "gun," went in her ear. Lights in her eyes. A tongue depressor slipped to the back of her throat almost gagging her.

"I don't know," she said, finally.

"Your Mommy's really worried."

"I don't know why."

"She says you listen to the walls."

Naomi shook her head. "Not the walls. The five."

"Five what?"

"Kittens. Each of them know me. I love them so much."

"How did the kittens get there?"

She looked at him, unsure if she should trust him. "I can't tell you."

"All right, then."

He gave her a shot in the arm, which she didn't feel at all. She thought that was strange, so she told him.

"Not at all?"

"I didn't even feel it."

He put his hand under his chin. Then he reached to her arm and pinched.

"Did you feel that?"

She shook her head.

Then, he went over to a counter on the other side of the room. He returned with a plastic bottle. He took the lid off and held it under her nose. "Smell this."

She sniffed.

"Sniff again," he said.

She sniffed hard.

"What does it smell like?"

"I dunno. Water, maybe?"

He was trying to smile at her response, she could tell, but couldn't quite do it. "Is there anything you want to tell me?" he asked.

"About what?"

"Anything. Your Mommy or Daddy. How you feel about things."

She thought a minute, "Nope."

And that was it, he took her out to the waiting area where her mother was sitting. Then, she was asked to sit and wait while her mother had a check-up, too.

On the way home, in the car, her mother was in a mood. "Are you playing games?"

"Uh uh."

"I think you are. Are you trying to destroy this family? Because if you are, young lady, if you are...." Her mother's hands were shaking so hard, she had to pull the car over to the side of the road and park.

Naomi began to say something, but she saw that her mother wasn't listening, so she shut her mouth.

And as her mother started lecturing her, Naomi realized that she could barely hear a word her mother said.

7

The nights were peaceful. She could press her ear against the wall, and hear them, playing and hunting and crawling around one another. She kept trying to think up good names for them, but each time she came up with something, she forgot which was which.

Then, when the bedroom door opened—which didn't happen very often anymore—she listened to the cats (for they had grown in size), and sometimes, if she closed her eyes really tight, she could almost imagine what they looked like. All gray tabbies like their mother, of course, but one with a little bit of white in a star pattern on its chest, and two of them had green eyes, while the rest had blue. One had gotten very fat from all the mice and roaches it had devoured over the past weeks, and another seemed all skin and bones, and yet, not deprived at all.

225

8

One day, a woman in a suit came by. She had some manila files in her hand. Naomi's mother and father were very tense.

The woman asked several questions, mainly to her parents, but Naomi was listening for the sound of the five.

"Naomi?" her father said. "Answer the lady, please."

Naomi looked up; her father's voice had gotten really small, like it was caught in a jar somewhere and couldn't get out. She looked at the lady, and then to her mother. Her mother's forehead held beads of sweat.

"Yes, ma'am." She looked back to the lady.

"How are you feeling, dear?"

Naomi said, "Fine."

"You were sick for awhile."

Naomi nodded. "I'm better now. It was the flu."

"Have you had a good summer vacation?"

Naomi cocked her head to the side; she squinted her eyes. "Can you hear them?"

The lady said, "Who?"

"All of them. They just caught something. Maybe a mouse. Maybe a sparrow got in. I thought I heard one. Do you think that's possible?"

9

After the lady left, her father exploded with rage. "I am so sick and tired of you running our lives like this!"

Who was he talking to? Naomi heard the runt of the litter tearing at the bird's wings, feathers flying. The five could be brutal, sometimes. They stalked their prey like lions, and brought a bird or mouse down quickly, but then played with it until the small creature died of fear more than anything. Something beautiful about that—about taking something so small, and playing with it.

"There are no fucking cats in the fucking walls," her father's voice intruded. He came over to her; lifted her up from under her arms. "I am going to tell you what happened to those kittens, right now," he said.

Her mother said, "Jesus, Dan, you're going to hurt her like that," but the voices rushed beneath some invisible glass, caught, silent.

Her father began screaming something—she knew by the movements of his mouth—but all she heard was the one she was calling Scamp tussle over the sparrow's head. Yowler tore at the beak with her claws, but lost most of the skull, which Scamp took down in one gulp. Hugo ignored them—he was not one to join in when food was being torn apart—he preferred to lick the bones clean later, after the carcass was stripped.

"I'm going to show you once and for all," her father's voice came back, and she was being dragged out the backdoor, around to the carport wall. He dropped her to the ground, and went around the wall, into the carport; she heard Fiona whisper something to Zelda about some centipedes that she had trapped in a spider web behind the wall at the back of the refrigerator.

Her father came back around the corner with a large hammer.

"You just watch what you see," he said, and slammed the hammer into the wall, down where the kittens had once been born. Back and forth, he worked the hammer, chips of wall flew up, and beneath them, chicken wire, and there, in a small mound, surrounded with bits of cloth and newspaper were small dried things.

"See?" her father said, poking at them with his hammer. From one, a dozen wriggling gray-white maggots emerged. "Do you fucking see them?" He shouted, his voice receding again.

She looked at them, all stiff and bony and withered like apricots. Her heart was beating fast; she thought something wet came up her throat; light was flickering. Were they the bodies of the mice that the five had caught, in storage for a future meal?

And then she thought she was going to faint. She saw pinpricks of darkness play along the edge of her vision, and then an eclipse came over the sun. The world faded; her father faded; and she reached her hand into the new hole in the wall, and pressed her head through, too. Her whole body seemed to move forward, and she saw pipes and wires and dust as she went.

227

10

"I can hear her," her mother said, "I think she made a noise."

Her father said nothing. After a minute, "For three days, she does her weird, unintelligible sounds, and now she snarls her upper lip and you think she's on the road to recovery."

"She said something. Honey? Are you trying to say something?"

But Naomi didn't care to speak with them at the moment. She held Hugo in her lap, stroking him carefully, carefully, because he didn't like his fur ruffled. Scamp was playing with the ball of thread; the others slept, piled together.

"Look at her," her father said.

"Sweetie?" her mother said, beyond the wall. "Are you trying to talk? Is there something you want to say?"

"You think holding her is going to help?" her father said. "You think she's ever going to get better if you coddle her like that? All that rocking back and forth—she knows what she's doing. She's not stupid."

Zelda rolled on her back and stretched out, a great yawn escaping her jaws. Her whiskers brushed against Naomi's ankle. It tickled.

"Sweetie?" her mother asked.

"She's just doing this," her father said, "for attention. And look at you, giving it to her. She's just doing this to hurt us."

"No, look at her lips. She's trying to say something, look, Dan. My god, she's trying to talk. Oh, sweetie, Nomy, baby, tell Mommy what's wrong. Are you okay? Baby?"

On the other side of the wall, Naomi pressed her face into the dust-covered fur, and listened to the purring, the gentle and steady hum beneath the skin that was like a lullaby. It was warm there, with the five, with the walls around them.

Her father said, "My god, she's starting in again."

"Shut up, Dan. Let her."

"I can't stand this. How can you sit there and cradle her and not scream out loud when she does this?"

"Maybe I care about her," her mother said.

Naomi mewled and rocked and mewled and rocked, safe from predators, safe in the wall.

She watched as one of the cats sat up, her hackles rising, hunting some creature which had the misfortune of entering this most secret and wonderful domain.

Freshman Survey
English Lit Beowulf to
Jonathan Swift

We got so drunk that night, we ended up at Prof Morris's place, playing Beatles records, watching the prof get stoned while he talked about literary theory and how his third wife was a danger to herself and others. I left early with Jack. Had to go back to get my gloves. That's when I heard Barrett telling Morris he thought I was a complete dimwit. Morris only slightly defended me. They didn't know I was standing in the front hall. Jack told me later that I shouldn't worry about Barrett and his opinions, and that I wasn't meant to hear that, anyway.

"But I heard it," I said, and went to take a leak in the snow while Jack started talking about how he was going to do something amazing with his life.

Next day, after class, I sat in Morris's office with him, shooting the breeze about nothing in particular, and somewhere in there I said something about Barrett stealing my notes. Morris laughed at first, and then asked if I were telling the truth. I told him Barrett stole notes in order to get through his classes.

"He needs to stop that kind of stuff," Morris said.

When I ran into Barrett at the art department's big show, he told me that I should just shut up about my notes and that I was a lousy note-taker.

"The thing about college that's really awful is that you're just stuck here all winter long with everyone else who's stuck," I told him.

Before the end of February, Barrett got brought up on honor violations. Turned out, he didn't just steal notes from study carrels in the library, he also stole tests from the professors' offices. Jack told me, "Well, I guess he's more of a rat than we all thought."

Barrett missed a class, and Morris got angry because Barrett had a presentation on Chaucer to give. The next day, we all heard that Barrett had put a gun in his mouth and pulled the trigger, maybe because things had come to light about him and it included some pretty heavy stuff. I felt bad for having ever said anything to Morris in the first place.

When Jack and I and Morris got together for drinks down at the Pit, I said, "Man, poor Barrett, who knew?"

Morris nodded. "Well, he wrote some decent fiction. We're going to try and publish it in the literary magazine. It had something, what he wrote."

Jack said, "That's how it goes. Undiscovered genius. If he hadn't killed himself, nobody would've found his stories and they would never be published. Sometimes I wonder what it is about life that's so great."

Once published, I read his stories—they were good. I could read between the lines and see that Barrett had been in love with me in a screwed-up Freshman-at-an-all-male-college crush way, and it made me miss him a little.

WHite CHapeL

*All I can say as way of introducing White Chapel is that it is
the story that keeps haunting me.*

I

"You are a saint," the leper said, reaching her hand out to
clutch the saffron-dyed robe of the great man of Calcutta, known
from his miracle workings in America to his world-fame as a holy
man throughout the world. The sick woman said, in perfect English,
"My name is Jane. I need a miracle. I can't hold it any longer. It
is eating away at me. They are." She labored to breathe with each
word she spoke.

"Who?" the man asked.

"The lovers. Oh, god, two years keeping them from escaping.
Imprisoned inside me."

"You are possessed by demons?"

She smiled, and he saw a glimmer of humanity in the torn skin.
"Chose me because I was good at it. At suffering. That is whom the
gods chose. I escaped, but had no money, my friends were dead.
Where could I go? I became a home for every manner of disease."

"My child," the saint said, leaning forward to draw the rags away from the leper's face. "May God shine His countenance upon you."

"Don't look upon me, then, my life is nearly over," the leper said, but the great man had already brought his face near hers. It was too late. Involuntarily, the leper pressed her face against the saint's, lips bursting with fire-heat. An attendant of the saint's came over and pulled the leper away, swatting the beggar on the shoulder.

The great man drew back, wiping his lips with his sleeve.

The leper grinned, her teeth shiny with droplets of blood. "The taste of purity," she said, her dark hair falling to the side of her face. "Forgive me. I could not resist. The pain. Too much."

The saint continued down the narrow alley, back into the marketplace of what was called the City of Joy, as the smell of fires and dung and decay came up in dry gusts against the yellow sky.

The leper-woman leaned against the stone wall, and began to ease out of the cage of her flesh. The memory of this body, like a book, written upon the nerves and sinews, the pathways of blood and bone, opened for a moment, and the saint felt it, too, as the leper lay dying.

My name is Jane, a brief memory of identity, but had no other past to recall, her breath stopped.

The saint reached up to feel the edge of his lips, his face, and wondered what had touched him.

What could cause the arousal he felt.

II

"He rescued five children from the pit, only to flay them alive, slowly. They said he savored every moment, and kept them breathing for as long as he was able. He initialed them. Kept their faces." This was overheard at a party in London, five years before Jane Boone would ever go to White Chapel, but it aroused her journalist's curiosity, for it was not spoken with a sense of dread, but with something approaching awe and wonder, too. The man of whom it was spoken had already become a legend.

Then, a few months before the entire idea sparked in her mind, she saw an item in the *Bangkok Post* about the woman whose face had been scraped off with what appeared to be a sort of makeshift scouring pad. Written upon her back, the name, *Meritt*. This woman also suffered from amnesia concerning everything that had occurred to her prior to losing the outer skin of her face; she was like a blank slate.

Jane had a friend in Thailand, a professor at the University, and she called him to find out if there was anything he could add to the story of the faceless woman. "Not much, I'm afraid," he said, aware of her passion for the bizarre story, "they sold tickets to see her, you know. I assume she's a fraud, playing off the myth of the white devil who traveled to India, collecting skins as he went. Don't waste your time on this one. Poor bastards are so desperate to eat, they'll do anything to themselves to put something in their stomachs. You know the most unbelievable part of her story?"

Jane was silent.

He continued, "This woman, face scraped off, nothing human left to her features, claimed that she was thankful that it had happened. She not only forgave him, she said, she blessed him. If it had really happened as she said, who would possibly bless this man? How could one find forgiveness for such a cruel act? And the other thing, too. Not in the papers. Her vagina, mutilated, as if he'd taken a machete to open her up. She didn't hold a grudge on that count, either."

233

In wartime, men will often commit atrocities they would cringe at in their everyday life. Jane Boone knew about this dark side to the male animal, but she still weathered the journey to White Chapel, because she wanted the whole story from the mouth of the very man who had committed what was known, in the latter part of the century, as the most unconscionable crime, without remorse. If the man did indeed live among the Khou-dali at the furthest point along the great dark river, it was said that perhaps he sought to atone for his past—White Chapel was neither white nor a chapel, but a brutal outpost which had been conquered and destroyed from one century to the next since before recorded history. Always to self-resurrect from its own ashes, only to be destroyed again. The British had anglicized the name at some sober point in their rule, although the original name, *Y-Cha-Pa* when translated, was Monkey God Night, referring to the ancient temple and celebration of the divine possession on certain nights of the dry season when the god needed to inhabit the faithful. The temple had mostly been reduced to ashes and fallen stone, although the ruins of its gates still stood to the south-east.

Jane was thirty-two, and had already written a book about the camps to the North, with their starvation and torture, although she had not been well-reviewed stateside. Still, she intended to follow the trail of Nathan Meritt, the man who had deserted his men at the height of the famous massacre. He had been a war hero, who, by those court-martialed later, was said to have been the most vicious of torturers. The press had labeled him, in mocking Joseph Campbell's study, *The Hero With A Thousand Faces*, "The Hero Who Skinned A Thousand Faces." The war had been over for a good twenty years, but Nathan was said to have fled to White Chapel. There were reports that he had taken on a Khou-dali wife and fathered several children over the two decades since his disappearance. Nathan Meritt had been the most decorated hero in the war—children in America had been named for him. And then the massacre, and the stories of his love of torture, of his rituals of skin and bone...it was the most fascinating story she had ever come across, and she was shocked that no other writer, other than one who couched the whole tale in a wide swath of fiction, had sought out this living myth. While Jane couldn't get any of her usual magazines to send her gratis, she had convinced a major publishing house to at least foot expenses until she could gather some solid information.

To get to White Chapel, one had to travel by boat down a brown river in intolerable heat. Mosquitoes were as plentiful as air, and the river stank of human waste. Jane kept the netting around her face at all times, and her boatman took to calling her Nettie. There were three other travelers with her: Rex, her photographer, and a

British man and wife, named Greer and Lucy. Rex was not faring well—he'd left Kathmandu in August, and had lost twenty pounds in just a few weeks. He looked like a balding scarecrow, with skin as pale as the moon, and eyes wise and weary like those of some old man. He was always complaining about how little money he had, which apparently compounded for him his phsyical miseries. She had known him for seven years, and only had recently come to understand his mood swings and fevers. Greer was fashionably unkempt, always in a tie and jacket, but mottled with sweat stains, and wrinkled; Lucy kept her hair up in a straw hat, and disliked all women. She also expressed a fear of water, which amazed one and all since every trip she took began with a journey across an ocean or down a river. Jane enjoyed talking with Greer, as long as she didn't have to second guess his inordinate interest in children. She found Lucy to be about as interesting as a toothache.

The boatman wanted to be called Jim, because of a movie he had once seen, and so, after morning coffee (bought at a dock), Jane said, "Well, Jim, we're beyond help now, aren't we?"

Jim grinned, his small dark eyes sharp, his face wrinkled from too much sun. "We make White Chapel by night, Nettie. Very nice place to sleep, too. In town."

Greer brought out his book of quotes, and read, "'Of the things that are man's achievements, the greatest is suffering.'" He glanced to his wife, and then to Jane, skipping Rex altogether who lay against his pillows, moaning softly.

"I know," Lucy said, sipping from the bowl, "it's Churchill."

"No, dear, it's not. Jane, any idea?"

Jane thought a moment. The coffee tasted quite good, which was a constant surprise to her, as she had been told by those who had been through this region before that it was bitter. "I don't know. Maybe—Rousseau?"

Greer shook his head. "It's Hadriman the Third. The Scourge of Y-Cha."

"Who's Y-Cha?" Rex asked.

Jane said, "The Monkey God. The temple is in the jungles ahead. Hadriman the Third skinned every monkey he could get his hand on, and left them hanging around the original city to show his power over the great god. This subdued the locals, who believed their only guardian had been vanquished. The legend is that he took the skin of the god, too, so that it might not interfere in the affairs of men ever again. White Chapel has been the site of many scourges throughout history, but Hadriman was the only one to profane the temple."

Lucy put her hand to her mouth, in a feigned delicacy. "Is it...a decent place?" Greer and Lucy spent their lives mainly traveling, and Jane assumed it was because they had internal problems all their own which kept them seeking out the exotic, the foreign, rather than staying with anything too familiar. They were rich, too, the way that only an upperclass Brit of the Old School could be and not have that guilt about it: to have inherited lots of money and to be perfectly content to spend it as it pleased themselves without a care for the rest of mankind. Greer had a particular problem which Jane recognized without being able to understand: he had a fascination with children, which she knew must be of the sexual variety, although she could've been wrong—it was just something about him, about the way he referred to children in his speech, even the way he looked at her sometimes which made her uncomfortable. She didn't fathom his marriage to Lucy at all, but she fathomed very few marriages. While Greer had witnessed the Bokai Ritual of Circumcision and the Resurrection Hut Fire in Calcutta, Lucy had been reading Joan Didion novels and painting portraits of women weaving baskets. They had money to burn, however, inherited on both sides, and when Greer had spoken, by chance to Jane at the hotel, he had found her story of going to White Chapel fascinating; and he, in turn, was paying for the boat and boatman for the two day trip.

Jane said, in response to Lucy, "White Chapel's decent enough. Remember, British rule, and then a little bit of France. Most of them can speak English, and there'll be a hotel that should meet your standards."

"I didn't tell you this," Greer said, to both Jane and Lucy, "but my grandfather was stationed in White Chapel for half a year. Taxes. Very unpopular job, as you can imagine."

236

"I'm starved," Lucy said, suddenly, as if there were nothing else to think of, "do we still have some of those nice sandwiches, Jim?" She turned to the boatman, smiling. She had a way of looking about the boat, eyes partly downcast, which kept her from having to see the water—like a child pretending to be self-contained in her bed, not recognizing anything beyond her own small imagined world.

He nodded, and pointed toward the palm leaf basket.

While Lucy crawled across the boat—she was too unbalanced, Greer often said, to stand without tipping the whole thing and this was, coincidentally, her great terror—Greer leaned over to Jane and whispered, "Lucy doesn't know why you're going. She thinks it's for some kind of *National Geographic* article," but he had to stop himself for fear that his wife would hear.

Jane was thinking about the woman in Thailand who claimed to have forgiven the man who tore her face off. And the children from the massacre, not just murdered, but obliterated. She had seen the pictures in *Life*. *Faceless children. Skinned from ear to ear.*

She closed her eyes and tried to think of less unpleasant images.

All she remembered was her father looking down at her as she slept.

She opened her eyes, glancing about. The heat and smells revived her from dark memories. She said, "Rex, look, don't you think that would be a good one for a photo?" She pointed to one of the characteristic barges that floated about the river, selling mostly rotting meat, and stuffed lizards, although the twentieth century had intruded, for there were televisions on some of the rafts and a Hibachi barbeque.

Rex lifted his Nikon up in response, but was overcome by a fit of coughing.

"Rex," Lucy said, leaning over to feel his forehead, "my god, you're burning up," then, turning to her husband, "he's very sick."

"He's seen a doctor, dear," Greer said, but looked concerned.

"When we get there," Jane said, "we'll find another doctor. Rex? Should we turn around?"

237

"No, I'm feeling better. I have my pills." He lay his head back down on his pillow, and fanned mosquitoes back from his face with a palm frond.

"He survived malaria and dengue fever, Lucy, he'll survive the flu. He's not one to suffer greatly."

"So many viruses," Lucy shook her head, looking about the river, "isn't this where AIDS began?"

"I think that may have been Africa," Greer said in such a way that it shut his wife up completely, and she ate her sandwich and watched the barges and the other boatmen as though she were watching a *National Geographic Special*.

"Are you dying on me?" Jane asked, flashing a smile through the mosquito net veil.

"I'm not gonna die," Rex said adamantly. His face took on an aspect of boyishness, and he managed the kind of grin she hadn't seen since they'd first started working together several years back— before he had discovered needles. "Jesus, I'm just down for a couple of days. Don't talk about me like that."

Jim, his scrawny arms turning the rudder as the river ran, said, "this is the River of Gods, no one die here. All live forever. The Great Pig God, he live in Kanaput, and the Snake God live in Jurukat. Protect people. No one die in paradise of Gods." Jim nodded towards points that lay ahead along the river.

"And what about the Monkey God?" Jane asked.

Jim smiled, showing surprisingly perfect teeth which he popped out for just a moment because he was so proud of the newly made dentures. When he had secured them into his upper gum again, he said, "Monkey God trick all. Monkey God live where river goes white. Have necklace of heads of childs. You die only once with Monkey God, and no come back. Jealous god, Monkey God. She not like other gods."

"Monkey God is female," Jane said. "I assumed she was a he. Well, good for her. I wonder what's she's jealous of?"

Greer tried for a joke, "Oh, probably because we have skins, and hers got taken away. You know women."

Jane didn't even attempt to acknowledge this comment.

Jim shook his head, "Monkey God give blood at rainy times, then white river goes red. But she in chains, no longer so bad, I think. She buried alive in White Chapel by mortal lover. Hear her screams, sometime, when monsoon come, when flood come. See her blood when mating season come."

"You know," Greer looked at the boatman quizzically, "you speak with a bit of an accent. Who did you learn English from?"

Jim said, "Dale Carnegie tapes, Mister Greer. *How To Win Friends And Influence People.*"

Jane was more exhilirated than exhausted by the time the boat docked in the little bay at White Chapel. There was the Colonial British influence to the port, with guard booths, now mainly taken over by beggars, and an empty customs house. The place had fallen into beloved disrepair, for the great elephant statues, given for the god Ganesh, were overcome with vines, and cracked in places; and the lilies had all but taken over the dock. Old petrol storage cans floated along the pylons, strung together, with a net knotted between the cans: someone was out to catch eels or some shade-dwelling scavenger. A nervous man with a straw hat and a bright red cloth tied around his loins ran to the edge of the dock to greet them; he carried a long fat plank, which he swept over the water's edge to the boat, pulling it closer in. A ladder was lowered to them.

The company disembarked carefully. Rex, the weakest, had to be pulled up by Jim and Jane both. Lucy proved the most difficult, however, because of her terror of water—Jim the boatman pushed her from behind to get her up to the dock, which was only four rungs up on the ladder. Then, Jane didn't feel like haggling with anyone, and so, after she tipped Jim, she left the others to find their ways to the King George Hotel by the one taxi cab in White Chapel. She chose instead to walk off her excitement, and perhaps get a feel for the place.

She knew from her previous explorations that there was a serendipity to experience—she might, by pure chance, find what she was looking for. But the walk proved futile, for the village—it

239

was not properly a town—was dark and silent, and except for the lights from the King George, about a mile up the road, the place looked like no one lived there. Occasionally, she passed the open door to a hut through which she saw the red embers of the fire, and the accompanying stench of the manure that was used to stoke the flame. Birds, too, she imagined them to be crows, gathered around huts, kicking up dirt and waste.

She saw the headlights of a car, and stepped back against a stone wall. It was the taxi taking the others to the hotel, and she didn't want them to see her.

The light was on inside the taxi, and she saw Rex up front with the driver, half-asleep. In back, Lucy, too, had her eyes closed; but, Greer, however, was staring out into the night, as if searching for something, perhaps even expecting something. His eyes were wide, not with fear, but with a kind of feverish excitement.

He's here for a reason. He wants what White Chapel has to offer, she thought, *like he's a hunter*. And what did it have to offer? Darkness, superstition, jungle, disease, and a man who could tear the faces off children. A man who had become a legend because of his monstrosity.

After the car passed, and was just two sets of red lights going up the narrow street, she continued her journey up the hill.

When she got to the hotel, she went to the bar. Greer sat at one end; he had changed into a lounging jacket that seemed to be right out of the First World War. "The concierge gave it to me," Greer said, pulling at the sleeves which were just short of his wrists, "I imagine they've had it since my grandfather's day," then, looking at Jane, "you look dead to the world. Have a gin tonic."

Jane signaled to the barman. "Coca-Cola?" When she had her glass, she took a sip, and sighed. "I never thought I would cherish a Coke so much. Lucy's asleep?"

Greer nodded, "Like a baby. And I helped with Rex, too. His fever's come down."

"Good. It wasn't flu."

"I know. I can detect the D.T.s at twenty paces. Was it morphine?"

Jane nodded. "That and other things. I brought him with me mainly because he needed someone to take him away from it. It's too easy to buy where he's from. As skinny as he is, he's actually gained some weight in the past few days. So, what about you?" She didn't mean for the question to be so fraught with unspoken meaning, but there it was: out there.

"You mean, why am I here?"

She could not hold her smile. There was something cold, almost reptilian about him now, as if, in the boat, he had worn a mask, and now had removed it to reveal rough skin and scales.

"Well, there aren't that many places in the world...quite so...."

"Open? Permissive?"

Greer looked at her, and she knew he understood. "It's been a few months. We all have habits that need to be overcome. You're very intuitive. Most women I know aren't. Lucy spends her hours denying that reality exists."

"If I had known when we started this trip...."

"I know. You wouldn't have let me join you, or even fund this expedition. You think I'm sick. I suppose I am—I've never been a man to delude himself. You're very—shall I say—*liberal* to allow me to come even now."

"It's just very hard for me to understand," she said. "I guess this continent caters to men like you more than Europe does. I understand for two pounds sterling you can buy a child at this end of the river. Maybe a few."

"You'd be surprised. Jane. I'm not proud of my interest. It just exists. Men are often entertained by perversity. I'm not saying it's right. It's one of the great mysteries—" he stopped mid-sentence, reached over, touching the side of her face.

She drew back from his fingers.

In his eyes, a fatherly kindness. "Yes," he said, "I knew. When we met. It's always in the eyes, my dear. I can find them in the streets, pick them out of a group, out of a schoolyard. Just like yours, those eyes."

Jane felt her face go red, and wished she had never met this man who had seemed so civil earlier.

"Was it a relative?" he asked. "Your father? An uncle?"

She didn't answer, but took another sip of Coke.

"It doesn't matter, though, does it? It's always the same pain," he said, reaching in the pockets of the jacket and coming up with a gold cigarette case. He opened it, offered her one, and then drew one out for himself. Before he lit it, with the match burning near his lips, he said, "I always see it in their faces, that pain, that hurt. And it's what attracts me to them, Jane. As difficult as it must be to understand, for I don't pretend to, myself, it's that caged animal in the eyes that—how shall I say—excites me?"

She said, with regret, "You're very sick. I don't think this is a good place for you."

"Oh," he replied, the light flaring in his eyes, "but this is just the place for me. And for you, too. Two halves of the same coin, Jane. Without one, the other could not exist. I'm capable of inflicting pain, and you, you're capable of bearing a great deal of suffering, aren't you?"

"I don't want to stay here," she told Rex in the morning. They had just finished a breakfast of a spicy tea and *shuvai*, with poached duck eggs on the side, and were walking in the direction of the village center.

"We have to go back?" Rex asked, combing his hands through what was left of his hair, "I—I don't think I'm ready, Janey, not yet. I'm starting to feel a little stronger. If I go back...and what about the book?"

"I mean, I don't want to stay at the hotel. Not with those people. He's a child molester. No, make that child rapist. He as much admitted it to me last night."

"Holy shit," Rex screwed his face up, "you sure?"

Jane looked at him, and he turned away. There was so much boy in Rex that still wasn't used to dealing with the complexities of the adult world—she almost hated to burst his bubble about people.

They stopped at a market, and she went to the first stall, which offered up some sort of eely thing. Speaking a pidgin version of Khou-dali, or at least the Northern dialect which she had learned, Jane asked the vendor, "Is there another hotel? Not the English one, but maybe one run by Khou-dali?"

He directed her to the west, and said a few words. She grabbed Rex's hand, and whispered, "It may be some kind of whorehouse, but I can avoid Greer for at least one night. And that stupid wife of his."

Rex took photos of just about everyone and everything they passed, including the monkey stalls. He was feeling much better, and Jane was thrilled that he was standing tall, with color in his cheeks, no longer dependent on a drug to energize him. He took one of her with a dead monkey. "I thought these people worshipped monkeys."

Jane said, "I think it's the image of the monkey, not the animal itself." She set the dead animal back on the platform with several other carcasses. Without meaning to, she blurted, "Human beings are horrible."

"Smile when you say that," Rex snapped another picture.

"We kill, kill, kill. Flesh, spirit, whatever gets in our way. It's like our whole purpose is to extinguish life. And for those who live, there's memory, like a curse. We're such a mixture of frailty and cruelty."

The stooped-back woman who stood at the stall said, in perfect English, "Who is to say, miss, that our entire purpose here on Earth is perhaps to perform such tasks? Frailty and cruelty are our gifts to the world. Who is to say that suffering is not the greatest of all gifts from the gods?"

Her Khou-dali name was long and unpronounceable, but her English name was Mary-Rose. Her grandmother had been British; her brothers had gone to London and married, while she, the only daughter, had remained behind to care for an ailing mother until the old woman's death. And then, she told them, she did not have any ambition for leaving her ancestral home. She had the roughened features of a young woman turned old by poverty and excessive labor and no vanity whatsoever about her. Probably from some embarrassment at hygiene, she kept her mouth fairly closed when she spoke. Her skin, rough as it was, possessed a kind of glow that was similar to the women Jane had seen who had face-lifts—although clearly, this was from living in White Chapel with its humidity. Something in her eyes approached real beauty, like sacred jewels pressed there. She had a vigor in her glance and speech; her face was otherwise expressionless, as if set in stone. She was wrapped in several cloths, each dyed clay red, and wrapped from her shoulders down to her ankles; a purple cloth was wrapped about her head like a nun's wimple. It was so hot and steamy, that Jane was surprised she didn't go as some of the local women did—with a certain discreet amount of nakedness. "If you are looking for a place, I can give you a room. Very cheap. Clean. Breakfast included." She named a low price, and Jane immediately took her up on it. "You help me with English, and I make coffee, too. None of this tea. We are all dizzy with tea. Good coffee. All the way from America, too. From Maxwell's house."

Mary-Rose lived beyond the village, just off the place where the river forked. She had a stream running beside her house, which was a two-room shack. It had been patched together from ancient stones from the ruined Y-Cha temple, and tar paper coupled with hardened clay and straw had been used to fill in the gaps. Rex didn't need to be told to get his camera ready: the temple stones had hieroglyphic-like images scrawled into them. He began snapping pictures as soon as he saw them.

"It's a story," Jane said, following stone to stone. "Some of it's missing."

"Yes," Mary-Rose said, "it tells of Y-Cha and her conquests, of her consorts. She fucked many mortals." Jane almost laughed when Rose said "fucked" because her speech seemed so refined up until that point. No doubt, whoever had taught Rose to speak, had not bothered to separate out vulgarities. "When she fucks them, very painful, very hurting, but also very much pleasure. No one believes in her much no more. She is in exile. Skin stolen away. They say she could mount a believer and ride him for hours, but in the end, he dies, and she must withdraw. The White Devil, he keeps her locked up. All silly stories, of course, because Y-Cha is just so much lah-dee-dah."

Jane looked at Rex. She said nothing.

Rex turned the camera to take a picture of Mary-Rose, but she quickly hid her features with her shawl. "Please, no," she said.

He lowered the camera.

"Mary-Rose," Jane said, measuring her words, "do you know where the White Devil lives?"

Seeing that she was safe from being photographed, she lowered the cloth. Her hair spilled out from under it—pure white, almost dazzlingly so. Only the very old women in the village had hair even approaching gray. She smiled broadly, and her teeth were rotted and yellow. Tiny holes had been drilled into the front teeth. "White Devil, he cannot be found, I am afraid."

"He's dead, then. Or gone," Rex said.

"No, not that," she said, looking directly into Jane's eyes, "you can't find him. He finds you. And when he finds you, you are no longer who you are. You are no longer who you were. You *become*."

245

Jane spent the afternoon writing in her notebooks.

Nathan Meritt may be dead. He would be, what, fifty? Could he have really survived here all this time? Wouldn't he self-destruct, given his proclivities? I want him to exist. I want to believe he is what the locals say he is. The White Devil. Destruction and Creation in mortal form. Supplanted the local goddess. Legend beyond what a human is capable of. The woman with the scoured face. The children without skins. The trail of stories that followed him through this wilderness. Settling in White Chapel, his spiritual home. White Chapel—where Jack the Ripper killed the prostitutes in London. The name of a church. Y-Cha, the Monkey God, with her fury and fertility and her absolute weakness. White—they say the river runs white at times, like milk, it is part of Y-Cha. Whiteness. The white of bones strung along in her neckless. The white of the scoured woman—her featureless face white with infection.

Can any man exist who matches the implications of this?

The Hero Who Skinned A Thousand Faces.

And why?

What does he intend with this madness, if he does still exist, if the stories are true?

And why am I searching for him?

And then, she wrote:

Greer's eyes looking into me. Knowing about my father. Knowing because of a memory of hurt somehow etched into my own eyes.

The excitement when he was looking out from the taxi.

Like a bogeyman on holiday, a bag of sweeties in one hand, and the other, out to grab a child's hand.

Frailty and cruelty. Suffering as a gift.

What he said, Two halves of the same coin. Without one, the other could not exist. Capable of great suffering.

White Chapel, and its surrounding wilderness, came to life just after midnight. The extremes of its climate: chilly at dawn, steamy from ten in the morning 'til eight or nine at night, and then hot, but less humid, as darkness fell, led to a brain-fever siesta between noon and ten o'clock at night. Then, families awoke, and made the night meal, baths were taken, love was made—all in preparation for the more sociable and bearable hours of one a.m. to about six or seven, when most physical labor, lit by torch and flare, was done, or when hunting the precious monkey and other creatures more easily caught just before dawn. Jane was not suprised at this. Most of the nearby cultures followed a similar pattern based on climate and not daylight. What did impress her was the silence of the place while work and play began.

Mary-Rose had a small fire going just outside the doorway; the dull orange light of the slow-burning manure cast spinning shadows as Mary-Rose knelt beside it and stirred a pan. "Fried bread," she said, as Jane sat up from her mat. "Are you hungry?"

"How long did I sleep?"

"Five, six hours, maybe."

The frying dough smelled delicious. Mary-Rose had a jar of honey in one hand, which tipped, carefully, across the pan.

Jane glanced through the shadows, trying to see if Rex was in the corner on his mat.

"Your friend," Mary-Rose said, "he left. He said he wanted to catch some local color. That is precisely what he said."

"He left his equipment," Jane said.

"Yes, I can't tell you why. But," the other woman said, flipping the puffed-up circle of bread, and then dropping it onto a thin cloth, "I can tell you something about the village. There are certain entertainments which are forbidden to women which many men who come here desire. Men are like monkeys, do you not think so? They frolic, and fight, and even destroy, but if you can entertain them with pleasure, they will put other thoughts aside. A woman is different. A woman cannot be entertained by the forbidden."

"I don't believe that. I don't believe that things are forbidden to women, anyway."

Mary-Rose shrugged. "What I meant, Miss Boone, is that a woman is the forbidden. Man is monkey, but woman is Monkey God." She apparently didn't care what Jane thought one way or another. Jane had to suppress an urge to smile, because Mary-Rose seemed so set in her knowledge of life, and had only seen the jungles of Y-Cha. She brought the bread in to the shack, and set it down in front of Jane. "Your friend, Rex, he is sick from some fever. But it is fever that drives a man. He went to find what would cool the fever. There is a man skilled with needles and medicines in the jungle. It is to this man that your friend has traveled tonight."

Jane said, "I don't believe you."

Mary-Rose grinned. The small holes in her teeth had been filled with tiny jewels. "What fever drives you, Miss Jane Boone?"

"I want to find him. Meritt. The White Devil."

"What intrigues you about him?"

Jane wasn't sure whether or not she should answer truthfully. "I want to do a book about him. If he really exists. I find the legend fascinating."

"Many legends are fascinating. Would someone travel as far as you have for fascination? I wonder."

"All right. There's more. I believe, if he exists, if he is the legend, that he is either some master sociopath, or something else. What I have found in my research of his travels, is that the victims, the ones who have lived, are thankful of their torture and mutilation. It is as if they've been—I'm not sure—baptized or consecrated by the pain. Even the parents of those children—the ones who were skinned—even they forgave him. Why? Why would you forgive a man of such unconscionable acts?" Jane tasted the fried bread; it was like a doughnut. The honey that dripped across its surface stung her lips—it wasn't honey at all, but had a bitter taste to it. *Some kind of herb mixed with sap?*

It felt as if fire ants were biting her lips, along her chin where the thick liquid dripped; her tongue felt large, clumsy, as if she'd been shot up with Novocain. She didn't immediately think that she had been drugged, only that she was, perhaps, allergic to this food. She managed to say, "I just want to meet him. Talk with him," before her mouth seemed inoperable, and she felt a stiffness to her throat.

Mary-Rose's eyes squinted, as if assessing this demand. She whispered, "Are you not sure that you do not seek him in order to know what he has known?" She leaned across to where the image of the household god sat on its wooden haunches—not a monkey, but some misshapen imp. Sunken into the head of this imp, something akin to a votive candle. Mary-Rose lit this with a match. The yellow-blue flame came up small, and she cupped the idol in her hand as if it were a delicate bird.

And then she reached up with her free hand, and touched the edges of her lips—it looked as if she were about to laugh.

"Miss Jane Boone. You look for what does not look for you. This is the essence of truth. And so, you have found what you should run from, the hunter is become the hunted," she said, and began tearing at the curve of her lip, peeling back the reddened skin, unrolling the flesh that covered her chin like parchment.

Beneath this, another face. Unraveling like skeins of thread through some imperfect tapesty, the sallow cheeks, the aquiline nose, the shriveled bags beneath the eyes, even the white hair came out strand by strand. The air around her grew acrid with the smoke from the candle, as bits of ashen skin fluttered across its flame.

A young man of nineteen or twenty emerged from beneath the last of the skin of Mary-Rose. His lips and cheeks were slick with dark blood, as if he'd just pressed his face into wine. "I am the man," he said.

The burning yellow-blue flame wavered, and hissed with snowflake-fine motes of flesh.

Jane Boone watched it, unmoving.

Paralyzed.

Her eyes grew heavy. As she closed them, she heard Nathan Meritt clap his hands and say to someone, "She is ready. Take her to *Sedri-Y-Cha-Sampon*. It is time for Y-Cha-Pa."

The last part she could translate: Monkey God Night.

She was passing out, but slowly. She could just feel someone's hands reaching beneath her armpits to lift her. *I am Jane Boone, an American citizen, a journalist, I am Jane Boone, you can't do this to me,* her feeble mind shouted while her lips remained silent.

249

III

Two years later, the saint lay down in the evening, and tried to put the leper he had met that day out of his mind. The lips, so warm, drawing blood from his own without puncturing the skin.

Or had it been her *blood that he had drunk?*

Beside his simple cot was a basin and a ewer of water. He reached over, dipping his fingers into it, and brought the lukewarm droplets up to his face.

He was, perhaps, developing a fever.

The city was always hot in this season, though, so he could not be certain. He wondered if his fear of the leper-woman was creating an illness within his flesh. But the saint did not believe that he could contract anything from these people. He was only in Calcutta to do good. Even Mother Teresa had recognized his purity of heart and soul; the Buddhist and Hindu monks, likewise, saw in him a great teacher.

The saint's forehead broke a sweat.

He reached for the ewer, but it slipped from his sweaty hands, and shattered against the floor.

He sat up, and bent down to collect the pieces.

The darkness was growing around him.

He cut his finger on a porcelain shard.

He squeezed the blood, and wiped it across the over-sized cotton blouse he wore to bed.

He held the shard in his hand.

There were times when even a saint held too much remembered pain within him.

Desires, once acted upon in days of innocence and childhood, which now seemed dark and animal and howling.

He brought the shard up to his lips, his cheek, pressing.

In the reflecting glass of the window, a face he did not recognize, a hand he had not seen, scraping a broken piece of a pitcher up and down and up and down the way he had seen his father shaving himself when the saint was a little boy in Biloxi, the way he himself shaved, the way men could touch themselves with steel, leaning into mirrors to admire how close one could get to skin such as this. Had any ever gone so far beneath his skin?

The saint tasted his blood.

Tasted his skin.

Began slicing clumsily at flesh.

IV

Jane Boone sensed movement.

She even felt the coolness of something upon her head—a damp towel?

She was looking up at a thin, interrupted line of slate gray sky emerging between the leaning trees and vines; she heard the cries of exotic birds; a creaking, as of wood on water.

I'm in a boat, she thought.

Someone came over to her, leaning forward. She saw his face. It was Jim, the boatman who had brought her from upriver. "Hello, Nettie," he said, calling her by the nickname they'd laughed about before, "you are seeing now, yes? Good. It is nearly the morning. Very warm. But very cool in temple. Very cool."

She tried to say something, but her mouth wasn't working; it hurt to even try to move her lips.

Jim said, apparently noticing the distress on her face, "No try to talk now. Later. We on sacred water. Y-Cha carry us in." Then, he moved away. She watched the sky above her grow darker; the further the boat went on this river, the deeper the jungle.

She closed her eyes, feeling weak.

Ice cold water splashed across her face.

"You go back to sleep, no," Jim said, standing above her again, "trip is over." He poled the boat up against the muddy bank. When he had secured it, he returned to her, lifting her from beneath her armpits. She felt like every bone had been removed from her body. She barely felt her feet touch the ground as he dragged her up a narrow path. All she had the energy to do was watch the immense green darkness enfold about her, even while day burst with searing heat and light beyond them.

When she felt the pins-and-needles feeling coming into her legs and arms, she had been set down upon a round stone wheel, laid flat upon a smooth floor. Several candles were lit about the large room, all set upon the yellowed skulls of monkeys, somehow attached to the walls. Alongside the skulls, small bits of leaf and paper taped or nailed or glued to the wall; scrawled across these, she knew from her experience in other similar temples, were petitions and prayers to the local god.

On one of the walls, written in a dark ink that could only have been blood, were words in the local dialect. Jane was not good at deciphering the language.

A man's voice, strong and pleasant, said, "'Flesh of my flesh, blood of my blood, I delight in your offering'. It's an incantation to the great one, the Y-Cha."

He emerged from the flickering darkness. Just as he had seemed beneath the skin of Mary-Rose, Nathan Meritt was young, but she recognized his face from his college photographs. He was not merely handsome, but he had a radiance that came from beneath his skin, as if something fiery lit him, and his eyes, blue and almost transparent, enflamed. "She is not native to this land, you know. She was an import from Asia. Did battle in her own way with Kali, and won this small acre before the village came to be. Gods are not as we think in the West, Jane, they are creatures with desires and loves and weaknesses like you or I. They do not come to us, or reveal themselves to us. No, it is we who approach them, we who must entertain them with our lives. You are a woman, as is the Y-Cha. Feelings that you have, natural rhythms, all of these, she is prey to, also."

Jane opened her mouth, but barely a sound emerged.

Meritt put his finger to his lips. "In a little while. They used to use it to stun the monkeys—what the bread was dipped in. It's called *hanu,* and does little harm, although you may experience a hangover. The reason for the secrecy? I needed to meet you, Miss Boone, before you met me. You are not the first person to come looking for me. But you are different from the others who have come."

He stepped further into the light, and she saw that he was naked. His skin glistened with grease, and his body was clean-shaven except for his scalp, from which grew long dark hair.

Jane managed a whisper, "What about me? I don't understand. Different? Others?"

"Oh," he said, a smile growing on his face, "you are capable of much suffering, Miss Boone. That is a rare talent in human beings. Some are weak, and murder their souls and bodies, and some die too soon in pain. Your friend Rex—he suffers much, but of the garden variety. I have already played with him—don't be upset. He had his needles and his drugs, and in return, he gave me that rare gift, that," Meritt's nostrils flared, inhaling, as if recalling some wonderful perfume, "moment of mastery. It's like nothing else, believe me. I used to skin children, you know, but they die too soon, they whine and cry, and they don't understand, and the pleasure they offer...."

"Please," Jane said. She felt strength seeping back into her muscles and joints. She knew she could run, but would not know to what exit, or where it would take her. She had heard about the temple having an underground labyrinth, and she didn't wish to lose herself within it.

But more than that, she didn't feel any physical threat from Nathan Meritt.

"You're so young," she said.

"Not really."

"You look like you're twenty. I never would've believed in magic, but..."

He laughed, and when he spoke, spoke in the measured cadences of Mary-Rose, "Skin? Flesh? It is our clothing, Miss Jane Boone, it is the tent that shelters us from the reality of life. This is not my skin, see," he reached up and drew back a section of his face from the left side of his nose to his left ear, and it came up like damp leaves, and beneath it, the chalk white of bone. "It may conform to my bones, but it is another's. It's what I learned from her, from the Y-Cha. Neither do I have blood, Miss Boone. When you prick me, I don't spill."

He seemed almost friendly; he came and sat beside her.

She shivered, in spite of the familiarity.

"You mustn't be scared of me," he said, in a rigid British accent, "we're two halves of the same coin."

Jane Boone looked in his eyes, and saw Greer there, a smiling, gentle Greer. The Greer who had funded her trip to White Chapel, the Greer who had politely revealed his interest in children.

"I met them in Tibet, Greer and Lucy," Meritt said, resuming his American accent. "He wanted children, we had that in common, although his interests, oddly enough, had more to do with mechanics than with intimacy. I got him his children, and the price he paid. Well, a pound or more of flesh. Two days of exquisite suffering, Jane, along the banks of a lovely river. I had some children with me—bought in Bangkok at one hundred dollars each—and I had them do the honors. Layers of skin, peeled back, like some exotic rind. The fruit within was for me. Then, the children, for they had

253

already suffered much at Greer's own hands. I can't bear to watch children suffer more than a few hours. It's not yet an art for them; they're too natural."

"Lucy?"

He grinned. "She's still Lucy. I could crawl into his skin, but I was enjoying the game. She could not tell the difference because she didn't give a fuck, both literally and figuratively. Our whole trip down the river, only Jim knew, but he's a believer. Sweet Lucy, the most dreadful woman from Manchester, and that's saying a lot. I'll dispose of her soon, though. But she won't be much fun. Her life is her torture—anything else is redundant."

Jane wasn't sure how much of this monologue to believe. She said, "And me? What do you intend to do?"

Unexpectedly, he leaned into her, brushing his lips against hers, but not kissing. His breath was like jasmine flowers floating on cool water. He looked into her eyes as if he needed something that only she could give him. He said, softly, "That will be up to you. You have come to me. I am your servant."

He pulled away, stood, turned his back to her. He went to the wall and lifted a monkey skull candle up. He held the light along the yellow wall. "You think from what I've done that I'm a monster, Miss Boone. You think I thrive on cruelty, but it's not that way. Even Greer, in his last moments, thanked me for what I did. Even the children, their life-force wavering, and the stains along their scalps spreading darker juices over their eyes, whispered praise with their final breaths that I had led them to that place."

He held a light up to the papers stuck to the wall. His shadow seemed enormous and twisted as he moved the light in circles; he didn't look back at her, but moved from petition to petition. "Blessings and praises and prayers, all from the locals, the believers in Y-Cha. And I, Miss Boone, I am her sworn consort, and her keeper, too, for it is Nathan Meritt and no other, the Man Who Skinned A Thousand Faces, who is her most beloved, and to whom she has submitted herself, my prisoner. Come, I will take you to the throne of Y-Cha."

A pool of water, a perfect circle, filled with koi and turtles, was at the center of the chamber. Jane had followed Nathan down winding corridors, whose walls seemed to be covered with dried animal skins, and smelled of animal dung. The chamber itself was poorly lit; but there was a fire, in a hearth at its far end; she thought she heard the sound of rushing water just beyond the walls.

"The river," Nathan said, "we're beneath it. She needs the moisture, always. She has not been well for hundreds of years." He went ahead of her, towards a small cot.

Jane followed, stepping around the thin bones which lay scattered across the stones.

There, on the bed, head resting on straw, was Lucy. Fruit had been stuffed into her mouth, and flowers in the empty sockets of her eyes. She was naked, and her skin had been brutally tattooed until the blood had caked around the lines: drawings of monkeys.

Jane opened her mouth to scream, and knew that she had, but could not even hear it. When she stopped, she managed, "You bastard, you said you hadn't hurt her. You said she was still alive."

He touched her arm, almost lovingly. "That's not what I told you. I didn't hurt her, Jane. She did this to herself. Even the flowers. She's not even dead, not yet. She's no longer Lucy," he squatted beside the cot, and combed his fingers through her hair. "She's the prison of Y-Cha, at least as long as she breathes. Monkey God is a weak god, in the flesh, and she needs it, she needs skin, because she's not much different than you or me, Jane, she wants to experience life, feel blood, feel skin and bones and travel and love and kill, all the things animals take for granted, but the gods know, Jane. Oh, my baby," he pressed his face against the flowers, "the beauty, the sanctity of life, Jane, it's not in joy or happiness, it's in suffering in flesh."

He kissed the berry-stained lips, slipping his tongue into Lucy's mouth. With his left hand, he reached back and grasped Jane's hand before she could step away. His grip was tight, and he pulled her towards the cot, to her knees. He kissed from Lucy to her, and back, and she tasted the berries and sweet pear. She could not resist—it was as if her flesh required her to do this, and she began to know what the others had known, the woman with the scraped face, the

255

children, Greer, even Rex, all the worshippers of Y-Cha. Nathan's penis was erect and dripping, and she touched it with her hand, instinctively. The petals on the flower quivered; Nathan pressed his lips to Lucy's left nipple, and licked it like he was a pup suckling and playing; he turned to Jane, his face smeared with Lucy's blood, and kissed her, slipping a soaked tongue, copper taste, into the back of her throat; she felt the light pressure of his fingers exploring between her legs, and then watched as he brought her juices up to his mouth; he spread Lucy's legs apart, and applied a light pressure to the back of Jane's head.

For an instant, she tried to resist.

But the tattoos of monkeys played there, along the thatch of hair, like some unexplored patch of jungle, and she found herself wanting to lap at the small withered lips that Nathan parted with his fingers.

Beneath her mouth, the body began to move.

Slowly at first.

Then, more swiftly, bucking against her lips, against her teeth, the monkey drawings chattered and spun.

She felt Nathan's teeth come down on her shoulder as she licked the woman.

He began shredding her skin, and the pain would've been unbearable, except she felt herself opening up below, for him, for the trembling woman beneath her, and the pain slowed as she heard her flesh rip beneath Nathan's teeth, she was part of it, too, eating the dying woman who shook with orgasm, and the blood like a river,

A glimpse of her, not Lucy.

Not Lucy.

But Monkey God.

Y-Cha.

You suffer greatly. You suffer and do not die. Y-Cha may leave her prison.

She could not tell where Nathan left off and where she began, or whether it was her mouth or the dying woman's vagina which opened in a moan that was not pleasure, but was beyond the threshold of any pain she had ever imagined in the whole of creation.

She ripped flesh, devouring, blood coursing across her chin, down her breasts, Nathan inside her now, more than inside her, rocking within her, complete love through the flesh, through the blood, through the wilderness of frenzy, through the small hole between her legs, into the cavern of her body, and Y-Cha, united with her lover through the suffering of a woman whose identity as Jane Boone was quickly dissolving.

Her consciousness: taste, hurt, feel, spit, bite, love.

V

In the morning, the saint slept.

His attendant, Sunil, came through the entrance to the chamber with a plate of steamed vegetables. He set them down on the table, and went to get a broom to sweep up the broken ewer. When he returned, the saint awoke, and saw that he stared at his face as if he were seeing the most horrifying image ever in existence.

The saint took his hand, to calm him, and placed his palm against the fresh wounds and newly formed scars.

Sunil gasped, because he was trying to fight how good it felt, as all men did when they encountered Y-Cha.

His mouth opened in a small o of pleasure.

Already, his body moved, he thrust, gently, at first, he wanted to be consort to Y-Cha.

He would beg for what he feared most, he would cry out for pain beyond his imagining, just to spill his more personal pain, the pain of life in the flesh.

It was the greatest gift of humans, their flesh, their blood, their memories. Their suffering. It was all they had, in the end, to give, for all else was mere vanity.

Words scrawled in human suffering on a yellow wall:
Flesh of my flesh, blood of my blood
I delight in your offering
Make of your heart a lotus of burning
Make of your loins a pleasure dome
I will consecrate the bread of your bones
And make of you a living temple to Monkey God.

The servant opened himself to the god, and the god enjoyed the flesh as she hadn't for many days, the flesh and the blood and the beauty—for it was known among the gods that a man was most beautiful as he lay dying.

The gift of suffering was offered slowly, with equal parts delight and torment, and as she watched his pain, she could not contain her jealousy for what the man possessed.

Subway Turnstile

Walks through the turnstile, dropping tokens, grasping the boy by the elbow.

"Pull through," he says, but the little boy won't budge.

Glances at the others, behind them, waiting. A friendly woman behind him suggests that they hurry. "The train's coming. Please," she says.

"Come on," he says, and again grasps, and again, the boy manages to stiffen.

"Are you scared?" he asks, and glances up at the others. "He's not usually scared."

Gets a kind look from the woman behind him. She is wrapped up in a thick tan winter coat. A large handbag over her shoulder.

"Come on," he says, and this time reaches around and places his fingers against the child's throat. "Davy," he says. "People are waiting."

"Let's go," the woman says, on the edge of polite.

The train comes, and human noises of annoyance arise from a low grumble behind the woman who stands behind the man with the boy.

"Just push him," someone says.

The heat of the train against his face.

Davy looks up at him. Shakes his head.

"I know what to do," the wrapped woman says, and steps beside the man. She looks at Davy and smiles sweetly. Then, she lifts him up in her arms, and carries him through the turnstile. "See?" she asks. "It's not scary at all."

The boy whispers against her ear, "He's not my daddy. I don't know him. He grabbed me in a shop."

She feels a shock go through her. Lowers the boy to the platform. The man has come through, and grabs the boy's hand.

"Thank you for that," the man says.

The little boy looks up at her.

"Come on, Davy," the man says.

The boy looks back at her as the man tugs at his hand. They board the train.

The wrapped-up woman watches them, nearly about to do something. She glances at the others on the platform.

At the face of the boy through the smudged window of the train.

The train leaves the station.

She picks at her coat, unwrapping herself.

She finds a place on a bench and waits for the next train, but the heat of his whisper remains.

.

I am
Infinite; I Contain
Multitudes

I Am Infinite; I Contain Multitudes is kind of sick. Still, I kind of like Joe and his unwavering affection.

First off, I'll tell you, I saw both their files: Joe's and the old man's. I had to bribe a psych tech with all kinds of unpleasant favors, but I got to see their files. I want you to sit through my story, so I'll only tell you half of what I found. It was about Joe. He had murdered, sure, but more than that, he had told his psychiatrist that he only wanted to help people. He only wanted to keep them from hurting themselves. He wanted to love. Remember this.

It makes sense of everything I've been going through at Aurora.

Let me tell you something about Aurora, something that nobody seems to know but me: it is forsaken. Not just because of what you did to get there, or how haywire your brain is, but because it's built over the old Aurora. Right underneath it, where we do the farming. I heard this from Steve Parkinson, *right underneath it* is the old Aurora. I saw pictures in an album they keep in Intake. It used to be a dusty wasteland. The old Aurora was underground. Back then they believed it was better, if you were like us, to never see the light of day, to be chained like animals and have your food shoved to you in a slot at the bottom of your door. Back then, they believed that nobody in the town outside the fence wanted to know that you were there. But that's not why it's forsaken. You will know soon enough.

There was a town of Aurora once, too, but then it was bought out by Fort Salton, and 'round about 1949 they did the first tests.

I heard, from local legend, that there were fourteen men down there, just like in a bunker at the end of the war.

They did the tests out at the mountain, but some people said that those men in Aurora, underground, got worse afterwards.

I heard a story from my bunkmate that one guy got zapped and fried right in front of an old timer's eyes. Like he was locked in on the wrong side of the microwave door.

The old timer, he's still at Aurora; been there since he was nineteen, in '46. Had a problem, they said, with people after the war. He was in the Pacific, and had come back more than shell-shocked. That's all I ever knew about him, before I arrived. You can safely assume that he killed somebody or tried to kill himself or can't live without wanting to kill somebody. It's why we're all here. He's about as old as my father, but he doesn't look it. Maybe Aurora's kept him young.

He was always over there, across the Yard. He knew everything about everyone. I knew something about him, too. Actually, we all pretty much knew it.

He thought he was Father to us all. I don't mean like my father, or the guy who knocked your mother up. I mean the Father, as in God The.

In his mind, he created the very earth upon which we stood, his men, his sons. He could name each worm, each sowbug, each and every centipede that burrowed beneath the flagstone walk; the building was built of steel and concrete and had been erected upon the backs of laborers who had died within the walls of Aurora; the sky was anemic, the air dry and calm; he could glance in any direction at any given moment and know the inner workings of his men as we wandered the Yard, or know, in a heartbeat, no, the whisper of a heartbeat, where our next step would take us. There was no magic or deception to his knowledge. He was simply aware; call it, as he did, hyperawareness, from which had come his nickname, Hype. He was also criminally insane by a ruling of the courts of the state of California, as were most men in Aurora.

I watched him sometimes, standing there while we had our recreation time, or sitting upon the stoop to the infirmary, gazing across the sea of his men. His army, he called them, his infantry: they would one day spread across the land like the fires of armageddon.

The week after Danny Boy got out was the first time he ever spoke to me.

"Hey," he said, waving his hand. "Come on over here."

I glanced around. I had only been at Aurora for four months, and I'd heard the legends of Hype. How he only called on you after watching you for years. How he could be silent for a year and then, in the span of a week, talk your head off. I couldn't believe he was speaking to me. He nodded when he saw my confusion. I went over to him.

263

"You're the one," he said, patting me on the back. You couldn't *not* look him in the eye, he was so magnetic, but all the guys had told me not to look him in the eye, not to stare straight at him at any point. They all warned me because they had failed at it. They had all been drawn to his presence at one time or another. He was pale white. He kept in the shade at all times. His hair was splotchy gray and white and longer than regulation. His eyes were nothing special: round and brown and maybe a little flecked with gold. ("He milks you with those eyes," Joe had told me.) There were wrinkles on his face, just like with any old man, but his were thin and straight, as if he had not ever changed his expression since he'd been young.

"I'm the one? *The one*," I said, nodding as if I understood. I had a cigarette, leftover from the previous week. I offered it to him.

He took the cigarette, thrust it between his lips, and sucked on it. I glanced around for an orderly or psych tech, but we were alone together. I didn't know how I was going to light the cigarette for him. They all called me Doer, which was short for Good-Doer, because I tended to light cigarettes when I could, shine shoes for one of the supervisors I'd ass-kiss, or sweep floors for the lady-janitors. I did the good deeds because I'd always done them, all my life. Even when I murdered, I was respectful. But since there was no staff member around, I couldn't get a light for the old man.

Hype seemed content just to suck that cigarette, speaking through the side of his mouth, "Yeah, you don't know what it means, but you're it. Danny Boy, he would've been it, but he had to pretend."

"You think?"

He drew the cigarette from his mouth, and held it in his fingertips. "He was a sociopath, you must've recognized that. He had to perform for his doctor and the board. He studied Mitch over in B—the one who cries and moans all the time. Mitch with the tattoos?"

I nodded.

"He studied him for three years before perfecting his technique. Let me tell you about Danny Boy. He was born in Barstow, which may just doom a man from the start. He began his career by murdering a classmate in second grade. It was a simple thing to do, for they played out in the desert often, and it was not unusual for children to go missing out there. He managed to get that murder blamed on a local pedophile. Later, dropping out of high school, he murdered a teacher, and then, when he killed three women in Laguna, he got caught. The boy could not cry. It was not in him to understand why anyone made a fuss at all over murder. It was as natural to him as is breathing to you." He paused, and drew something from his breast pocket. He put the cigarette between his lips. He flicked his lighter up and lit the cigarette. Although we weren't supposed to have lighters, it didn't surprise me too much that Hype had one. As an old-timer he had special privileges, and as something of a seer, he was respected by the staff as well as by his men. It's strange to think that I was suitably impressed by this, his having a lighter, but I was. It might as well have been a gold brick, or a gun.

He continued, "Danny Boy is going to move in with one of the women who works in the cafeteria. She's never had a lover, and certainly never dreamed of having one as handsome as Danny Boy. Within six weeks, he will kill her and keep her skin for a souvenir. Danny Boy would've been it, but he wasn't a genuine person. You are. You know that don't you?"

"What, I cry, so that makes me real?"

He shook his head, puffing away, trying to suppress a laugh. "No. But I know about you, kid. You shouldn't even be here, only you come from a rich family who bought the best lawyer in L.A. I assume that in Court 90, he argued for your insanity and you played along 'cause you thought it would go easier for you in Aurora or Atascadero than in Chino or Chuckawalla. Tell me I'm wrong. No? How long you been here?"

"If you're so smart, you already know."

"Sixteen weeks already. Sixteen weeks of waking up in a cold sweat with Joe leaning over your bed. Sixteen weeks of playing baseball with men who would be happy to bash in your head just for the pleasure of it. Sixteen weeks hearing the screams, knowing about Cap and Eddie, knowing about how all they want is the taste of human flesh one more time before they die. And you, in their midst," he seemed to be enjoying his own speech. "You're not a sociopath, son, you're just someone who happened to kill some people and now you wish you hadn't, and maybe you wished you were in Chino getting bludgeoned and raped at night, but at least not dealing with this zoo."

The bell rang. I saw Trish, the Rec Counselor, waving to us from over at the baseball diamond. She was pretty, and we all wanted her and we were all protective of her, too, even down to the last sociopath.

"Looks like it's time for phys. ed.," Hype said. "She's a fine piece of work, that one. Women are good for men. Don't you think? Men can be good, too, sometimes, I guess. You'd know about that, I suppose."

"What am I 'it' for?" I asked, ignoring the implication of his comment.

He dropped the cigarette in the dust. "You're the one who's getting out."

265

I thought about what the old timer'd said all day.

In the late afternoon, I was sitting with Joe on the leather chairs in the T.V. room after we got shrunk by our shrinks, and said, "I don't get it. If Danny Boy wasn't it, and 'it' means you get out, why the hell am *I* it?"

Joe shrugged. "Maybe he means 'you're next.' Like you're the next one to get out. That old guy knows a shitload. He's God."

Joe had spent his life in the system. First at Juvy, then at Boy's Camp in Chino, then Chino, and finally some judge figured out that you don't systematically kill everyone from your old neighborhood unless you're not quite right in the head. But Joe was a good egg behind the Aurora fence. He needed the system and the walls and the three hots and a cot just to stay on track. Maybe if he'd been a Jehovah's Witness or in the army, with all those rules, he never would've murdered anybody. He needed rules badly, and Aurora had plenty for him. He had always been gentle and decent with me, and was possibly my only friend at Aurora.

I nudged him with my elbow. "Why would *I* be it?"

"Maybe he's gonna break you," Joe whispered, checking the old lady at the desk to make sure she couldn't hear him. "I heard he broke another guy out ten years ago, through the underground. That old man's got a way to do it, if you go down in that rat-nest far enough. I heard," Joe grabbed my hand in his, his face inches from mine, "he knows where the way out is, and he only tells it if he thinks your destiny's aligned with the universe."

I almost laughed at Joe's seriousness. I drew back from him. "You got to be kidding."

Joe blinked. He didn't like being made fun of. "Believe what you want. All's I know is the old man thinks you're it. Can't argue with that."

And then, Joe kissed me gently, as he always did, or tried to do, when no one was looking, and I responded in kind. It was the closest thing to human warmth we had in that place. I pulled away from him, for a psych tech was trolling in with one of the shrinks. Joe pretended to be watching the T.V. When I looked up at the set, it was an ad for tampons. I laughed, nudging Joe, who found nothing funny about it.

I wanted to believe that Hype could break me out of Aurora. I spent the rest of the day and most of the evening fantasizing about getting out, about walking out on the grass and dirt beyond the fence. Of getting on a bus and going up North where my brother lived. From there I would go up to Canada, maybe Alaska, and get lost somewhere in the wilderness where they wouldn't come hunting for me. It was a dream I'd had since entering Aurora. It was a futile and useless dream, but I nurtured it day by day, hour by hour. I could close my eyes and suddenly be transported to a glassy river, surrounded by mountains of pure white, and air so fresh and cold it could stop your lungs; an eagle would scream as it dropped from the sky to grab its prey.

But my eyes opened; the dream was gone. In its place, the dull green of the walls, the smell of alcohol and urine, the sounds of Cap and Eddie screeching from their restraints two doors down, the small slit of window with the bright lights of the Yard on all night. Only Joe kept me warm at night, and the smell of his hair as he scrunched in bed, snoring lightly, beside me, kept alive any spirit which threatened to die inside me. I had never been interested in men on the Outside, but in Aurora, it had never seemed homosexual between us. It had seemed like survival. When you are in that kind of environment, you seek warmth and human affection, if you are at all sane. Even if sanity is just a frayed thread. Even the sociopaths sought human warmth; even they, it is supposed, want to be loved. I knew that Joe would one day kill me if I said the wrong thing to him, or if I wasn't generous in nature towards him. He had spent his life killing for those reasons. Still, I took the risk because he was so warm and comfortable, and sometimes, at night, that's all you need.

The next morning I sought Hype out, and plunked myself right down next to him. "Why me?"

267

He didn't look up from his plate. "Why *not* you?" His mood never seemed to alter. He had that stoned look of one who could see the invisible world. His smile was cocked, like a gun's trigger. "Why not Doer, the compassionate? Doer, the one who serves? Why not you?"

"No," I said. "It could be any one of these guys. Why me? I've only been here four months. We don't know each other."

"I know everybody. I'm infinite. I contain multitudes. Nothing is beyond me. Besides, I told you, you don't pretend."

"Huh?"

"You don't pretend. You face things. That's important. It won't work if you live in your own little world, like most of these boys. You've got the talent."

"Yeah, the talent," I said, finally deciding the old fart was as looney as the rest.

"I saw what you did," he said. As he spoke, I could feel my heart freeze. In the tone of his voice, the smoothness of old whiskey. "I saw how you took the gun and killed your son first. One bullet to the back of the skull, and then another to his ear, just to make sure. Then, your daughter, running through the house, trying to get away from you. She was actually the hardest, because she was screaming so much and moving so fast. You're not a good shot. It took you three bullets to bring her down."

"Just shut up," I said.

"Your wife was easy. She parked out front, and came in the side door, at the kitchen. She didn't know the kids were dead. All she knew was her husband was under a lot of pressure and she had to somehow make things right. She had groceries. She was going to cook dinner. While she was putting the wine in the fridge, you shot her and she died quickly. And then," Hype shook his head, "you took the dog out, too. Who would take care of it, right? With everybody dead, who would take care of the dog?"

I said nothing.

"Who would take care of the dog?" He repeated. "You had no choice but to take it out, too. You loved that dog. It probably was as hard for you to pull the trigger on that dog as it was to pull it on your son. Maybe harder."

I said nothing. I thought nothing. My mind was red paint across black night. His words meant nothing to me.

He patted me on the back like my father had before the trial. "It's all right. It's over. It wasn't anything anyone blames you for."

I began weeping; he rubbed his hand along my back, and whispered words of comfort to me.

"It wasn't like that," I managed to say, drying my tears. Although we had been left alone, I looked across the cafeteria and felt that all the others watched us. Watched me. But they did not; they were preoccupied with their meals. "It was..."

"Oh. How was it?"

I wiped my face with my filthy hands. I was so dirty; I just wished to be clean. I fought the urge to rise up and go find a shower. "I wanted it to be me. I wanted it to be me."

"But you wanted to live, too. You killed your family, and then suddenly—"

"Suddenly," I said.

"Suddenly, your life came back into focus. You couldn't kill yourself. You had to go through all of them before you found that out. Life's like that," he said. "The bad thing is, they're all dead. You did it. You *are* a murderer. But you're not like these others. It wasn't some genetic defect or some lack of conscience. Conscience is important. You couldn't kill yourself. That's important. I don't want to get some fellow out who's going to end up killing himself. You need to be part of something larger than yourself. You need God. Tell me, boy: how do you live with yourself?"

I couldn't look him in the eye. I was trying to think up a lie to tell him. He reached out and took my chin in his hand. He forced me to look at him.

I remembered the warning: *He milks you with those eyes.*

"I don't know how," I said, truthfully. "I wake up every morning and I think I am the worst human being in existence."

"Yes," he said. "You are. But here's the grace of Aurora. You're it. You will get out. You will live with what you did. You will not kill

269

yourself or commit any further atrocities." He let go of my chin, and rose from the table. "Do you love your friend?"

"Joe?"

"That's right," he nodded. "Joe."

"Two guys can't love each other," I said. "It's just for now. It's surviving. It's barely even sexual."

"Ah," he nodded slowly. "That's good. It would be hell if you got out and you loved him and he was here. You must be careful around him, though. He is pretty, and he is warm. But he has the face of Judas. He will never truly love anyone. Now, you, you will love again. A man, perhaps. Or a woman. But not our friend Joe. Do you know what he did to the last man with whom he shared his bed? Has he ever told you?"

I shook my head slightly.

"Ask him," Hype said. He walked away. From the back, he didn't seem old. He had a young way of walking. I believed in him.

"Tonight," Hype said to me during Recreational Time. "Two thirty. You must first shower. You must be clean. I will not tolerate filth. Then, wait. I will be there. If your friend makes trouble, stop him anyway you can."

Joe could be possessive, but not in the expected way.

He was not jealous of other men or women. He simply wanted to own me all the time. He wanted me to shower with him, to sit with him, to go to the cafeteria with him. Our relationship seemed simple to me: we had met about the third week in, when he caught me masturbating in the bathroom. He joined in, and this led to some necking, which led to a chill for another week. Then, I got a letter from my mother in which she severed all connections with me, followed by one from my father and sister. I spent two days in bed staring at the wall. Joe came to me, and took care of me until I could eat and stand and laugh again. By that time, we were tight. I had only been at Aurora for two months when I realized that I could not disentangle myself from Joe without being murdered or tortured—it was a Joe thing. I didn't feel threatened, however, because I had grown quite fond of his occasional gropings and nightly sleep-overs. In a way, it was a little like being a child again, with a best friend, with a mother and lover and friend all rolled up into one man.

That night, when I rose from my bed at two a.m., Joe immediately woke up.

"Doer?" he asked.

"The can," I said, nodding towards the hallway. Because Joe and I weren't in the truly dangerous category, we and a few others were given free rein of our hallway at night. Knowing, of course, that the Night Shift Bitch was on duty at the end of the hall.

"I'll go, too," Joe whispered, rising. He drew his briefs up—he had the endearing habit of leaving them down around his ankles in post-coital negligence.

I tapped him on the chest, shaking my head.

"Doer," he said, "I got to go, too."

I sighed, and the two of us quietly went into the hall.

In the bathroom, he said, "I know what's going on." He leaned against the shiny tile wall. "It's Hype. Word went around. This is the night. Are you really going?"

I nodded, not wanting to lie. He had been sweet to me. I cared a great deal for him. I would be sad without him, for a time. "I'll miss you," I said.

"I could kill you for this."

"I know."

"If you leave I'll be lonely. Maybe it's love, who knows?" He laughed, as if making fun of himself. "Maybe I love you. That's a good one."

"No you don't." I knew that Joe was fairly incapable of something so morally developed as love, not because of his sexual leanings, but because of his pathology.

"Don't go," he said.

"For all I know, Hype is full of shit."

"He's not. I've seen him do this before. But don't go, Doer. Getting out's not so terrific."

"I want freedom," I said. "Plain and simple."

"I want you." Joe seemed to be getting a little testy.

"Now, come on, we're friends, you and me," I said, leaning forward to give him a friendly hug.

I didn't see the knife. All I saw was something shiny which caught the nearly-burnt-out light of the bathroom. It didn't hurt going in—that was more like a shock, like hearing an alarm clock at five a.m.

Coming out, it hurt like a motherfucker.

He pressed his hand against the wound in my chest. "You can't leave me."

"Don't kill me, Joe. I won't leave you, I promise. You can come too." This I gasped, because I was finding it difficult to breathe. I felt light-headed. The burning pain quickly turned to a frozen numbness. I coughed, and gasped, "Get help, Joe. I think you really did me."

Joe pressed his sweaty body against mine. I began to see brief tiny expolosions of light and dark, as if the picture tube of life were going out. Joe kissed the wound where he'd stabbed me, as blood pulsed from it. "I love you this much," he said.

Then, he drew his briefs down, a full erection in his hand. He took his penis and inserted it in the wound, just under my armpit. As I worked to inhale, he pressed the head of his member into the widening hole of the wound.

He pushed further into my body.

I passed out, feeling wave after wave of his flesh as he ground himself against my side.

272

I awoke in the infirmary three days later, barely able to see through a cloud of pain-killers. My stomach ached with the antibiotics that had been pumped through me. I stared up at the ceiling until its small square acoustic tile came into focus.

When I was better, in the Yard, I sought Hype out. "I tried to make it," I said.

He said nothing. He seemed to look through me.

"You know what he did to me," I said. "Please, I want to get out. I have to get out."

After several minutes, Hype said, "Love transformed into fear. It's the human story. The last man Joe befriended was named Frank. He grew up in Compton. A good kid. He tore off another man's genitals with his bare hands and wore them around his neck. His only murder. Sweet kid. Twenty-two. Probably he was headed for release within a year or two. He had an A+ psych evaluation. A little morbid. Used to draw pictures of beheadings. Joe latched onto him, too. Took care of him. Bathed him. Serviced him. Loved him, if you will. Then, rumor went around that Frank was getting some from one of the psych techs. Totally fabricated, of course. Frank was taking a shower. Joe knocked him on the head. Strapped him to the bed, spread-eagled. Don't ask me how, but he'd gotten a hold of a drill—the old kind, you know, you turn manually and it spins. He made openings in Frank. First, in his throat to keep him from screaming. Then, the rest of him. Each opening..."

"I know," I said, remembering the pain under my arm. Then, something occurred to me. "Where did he get the knife?"

Hype made a face, like he'd chewed something sour.

"The knife," I repeated. "And the drill, too. Everything's locked up tight. You're supposed to be God or something, so you tell me."

Without changing his expression, Hype said, "Joe gets out."

The enormity of this revelation didn't completely hit me. "From here?"

Hype nodded. "It's not something I'm proud of. I can open the door for about three hours, if I use up all my energy. Joe knows it. He was the first one I took out. But he didn't want to stay out. He only wanted out to get his toys. Then, he wanted back. He's the only one who manages to get back. Why he wants to, I couldn't say." For the first time ever, I watched worry furrow the old man's brow. He placed his hand against his forehead. A small blue vein pulsed there, beneath his pale skin's surface. "I created the world, but it's not perfect."

"Joe knows how to get out?"

273

"I didn't say that. I can get it open. I just can't keep him from going back and forth. And then, it closes again."

I wasn't sure how to pose my next question, because there was a mystery to this place where men got out. I had figured it to be down in the old underground, where Hype would know the route of the labyrinthine tunnels. "Where does it go?"

"That," Hype sighed, "I can't tell you, having never been through it. I just know it takes you out."

Back in my own bed that night, trying to sleep, I felt his hand. Joe's hand. On my shoulder. He slipped swiftly between the covers to cradle my body against his. "Doer," he said. "I missed you."

"Get off me." I tried to shrug him away. He was burning with some fever. A few drops of his sweat touched the back of my neck.

"No," he tugged himself in closer. I could feel his warm breath on my neck. "I want you."

"Not after what you did."

He said nothing more with words. His mouth opened against my neck, and I felt his tongue heat my sore muscles. All his language came through his throat and mouth, and I let him. I hated him, but I let him.

Afterwards, I whispered, "I want out."

"No you don't."

"Yes. I don't care if you stab me again. I want out. You going to get me out?"

I waited a long time for his answer, and then fell asleep.

I was still waiting for his answer three days later.

I cornered him in the shower, placing my hands on either side of him. I could encompass his body within my arms. I stared straight into his eyes. "I want out."

He curled his upper lip; I thought he would answer, but first, he spat in my face. "I saved you. You don't even care. Out is not where you want to be. In here's the only safe place. You get fed, you got a bed." He leaned closer to me. "You have someone who loves you."

274

I am Infinite; I Contain Multitudes

I was prepared this time. I brought my fist against his face and smashed him as hard as I could. His head lolled to the side, and I heard a sharp crack as his skull hit the mildewed tile wall. When he turned to face me again, there was blood at the corner of his lips. A smile grew from the blood.

"Okay," Joe said. "You want out. It can be arranged."

"Good. Next time, I kill you."

"Yeah," he nodded.

As I left the shower room, I glanced back at him for a second. He stood under the shower head, water streaming down—it almost looked like tears as the water streamed in rivulets across his face, taking with it the blood at his lips.

An hour later, Hype found me out by the crude baseball diamond we'd drawn in the Yard, under the shade of several oak trees which grew just beyond the high fence.

"Your lover told me we're moving up the schedule. Shouldn't do this but once every few years. You should've gotten out that night. Joe shouldn't have stopped you. Any idea why he did?"

I kicked at homeplate, which was a drawing in the dirt. Aurora was a funny place that way—because of things being considered dangerous around the inmates, even homeplate had to be just a drawing and not the real thing. The real thing here were the fences and the factory-like buildings. "No," I said. "Maybe he's in love with me and doesn't want to lose me. I don't care. He can go to hell as far as I'm concerned."

"I once tried to get out," Hype said, ignoring me. "It was back in the early fifties. I was just a kid. Me and my buddies. I tried to get out, but back then, there was only one way—a coffin. Not a happy system. I didn't know then that I'd rather be in here than out there."

"Make sense, old man," I said, frustrated. I wanted to kick him. The thought of spending another night in this place with Joe on top of me wasn't my idea of living.

"A little patience'll go a long way, Doer," he said. It felt like a commandment. He continued, "Then they started doing those tests—bombs and all kinds of things, twenty, thirty miles away.

Some closer, they said. Some this side of the mountain. We lived below back then. Me and Skimp and Ralph. Others, too, but these were my tribe. We were shell-shocked and crazy and we were put in with the paranoid schizophrenics and sociopaths and alcoholics—all of us together. Some restrained to a wall, some bound up in strait-jackets. Some of us roaming free in the subterranean hallways. Skimp, he thought he was still on a submarine. He really did. But I knew where we were—in the furthest ring of hell. And then, one morning, around three a.m., I heard Skimp whimpering from his bunk. I go over there, because he had nightmares a lot. I usually woke him up and told him a story so he could fall back to sleep. Only, Skimp was barely there. His flesh had melted like cheese on a hot plate, until it was hard to tell were the sheets left off and Skimp began. He was making a noise through his nostrils. It was like someone snoring, only he was trying to scream. Others, too, crying out, and then I felt it—like my blood was spinning around. I heard since that it was like we got stuck in a microwave. The entire place seemed to shimmer, and I knew to cover my eyes. I had learned a little about these tests, and I knew that moist parts of the body were the most vulnerable. That's why insects aren't very affected by it— they've got exoskeletons. All their softs parts are on their insides. I felt drunk and happy, too, even while my mouth opened to scream, and I went to my hiding place, covering myself with blankets. I crawled as far back into my hiding place as I could go, and then I saw some broken concrete, and started scraping at it. I managed to push my way through it, further, into darkness. But I got away from the noise and the heat. Later, I heard that it was some test that had leaked out. Some underground nuclear testing. We were all exposed, those who survived. Never saw Skimp or Ralph again, and I was told they were transferred—back in those days, no one investigated anyone or anything. I knew they'd died, and I knew how they'd died. There were times I'd wished I'd died, too. Every day. That's when I learned about my divinity. It was like Christ climbing the cross—he may or may not have been God before he climbed onto that cross, but you know for sure he was God once he was up there. I wasn't God before that day, but afterwards, I was."

I am Infinite; I Contain Multitudes

Hype was a terrific storyteller, and while I was in awe of that ability, I stared at him like he was the most insane man on the face of the earth.

"So I found a way out," he concluded.

"If that's true, how come you don't get out?"

"It's my fate. Others can go through, but I must stay. It's my duty. Trust me, you think God likes to be on earth? It's as much an asylum out there as it is in here."

I was beginning to think that all of this talk about going through and getting out was an elaborate joke for which the only punchline would be my disappointment. I decided to hell with it all: the old man could not get me out no matter how terrific his stories were. I was going to spend the rest of my life with Joe pawing me. I went to bed early, hoping to find some escape in dreams.

I awoke that night, a flashlight in my face.

Joe said, "Get up. This is what you want, right?" His voice was calm, not the usual nocturnal passionate whisper of the Joe who caressed me. He hadn't touched me at all. I was somewhat relieved.

"Huh?" I asked. "What's going on?"

"You want to get out. Let's go. You've got to take a shower first." I felt his hand tug at my wrist. "Get the hell up," he said.

The shower was cold. I spread Ivory soap across my skin, rubbing it briskly under my arms, around my healing wound, down my stomach, thighs, backs of legs, between my toes, around my crotch. Joe watched me the whole time. His expression was constant: a stone statue without emotion.

"It doesn't have to end like this," I said. "I'm going to miss you."

"Shut up," he said. "I don't like liars."

When I had toweled myself off, he led me, naked, down the dimly lit hall. The alarm was usually on at the double-doors at the end of the hall, but its light was shut off. Joe pushed the door open, drawing me along. The place seemed dead. Hearing the sound of footsteps in the next ward, he covered my mouth with his hand and drew me quickly into an inmate's room. Then, a few minutes later, we continued on to the cafeteria. He had a key to the kitchen; he unlocked its door. I followed him through the dark kitchen, careful to avoid bumping into the great metal counters and shelves. Finally, he unlocked another door at the rear of the kitchen. This led to a narrow hallway. At the end of the hallway, another door, which was open.

Hype stood there, frozen in the flashlight beam.

"Hey," I said.

Hype put a finger to his lips. He wore a bathrobe which was a shiny purple in the light.

He turned, going ahead of us, with Joe behind me. I followed the old man down the stone steps.

We were entering the old Aurora, the one that stretched for miles beneath the aboveground Aurora. We walked single file down more narrow corridors, the sound of dripping water all around. At one point, I felt something brush my feet—a large insect, perhaps, or a mouse. The place smelled of wet moss, and carried its own humidity, stronger than what existed in the upper world. For a while it did seem that Hype had been right: this was the furthest ring of hell.

But I'm getting out, I thought. *I'll go through any sewer that man has invented to get out. To go through. To be done with all this.*

Joe rested his hand on my shoulder for a brief moment. He whispered in my ear, "You don't have to do this. I was wrong. I love you. Don't get out."

I stopped, feeling his sweet breath on my neck. Even though I had only been in Aurora a little over four months, I had begun getting used to it. If I stayed longer, I would become part of it, and the outside world would be alien and terrifying to me. I saw it in other men, including Joe. This was the only world of importance to them.

"Why the change?" I asked.

"You don't want to go through. I want you here with me."

"No thanks." I put all the venom I could into those two words. I added, "And by the way, Joe, if I had a gun I'd shoot your balls off for what you did to me."

I am Infinite; I Contain Multitudes

"You don't understand," he shook his head like a hurt little boy.

Hype was already several steps ahead. I caught up with him while Joe lagged behind.

"I'm going out through that hiding place you talked about," I guessed.

"No," he said. When he got to a cell, he led me through the open doorway.

A feeble light emanated within the room—a yellowish-green light, as if glow-worms had been swiped along the walls until their phosphorescence remained. It was your basic large tank, looking as if it had been compromised by the several earthquakes of the past few years.

Joe entered behind me. "This is where Hype and his friends lived. This is where it happened." He shined the flashlight across the green light. I shivered, because for a moment I felt as if the ghosts of those men were still here, still trapped in the old Aurora. "Tell him, Hype. Tell him."

Hype wandered the room, as if measuring the paces. "Ralph had this area. He had his papers and books—he was always a big reader. Skimp was over there," he pointed to the opposite side of the cell. "His submarine deck."

"Tell him the whole thing," Joe said.

In the green light of the room, as I glanced back at Joe, I saw that he had a revolver in his right hand. "Tell him," he repeated.

"Where the hell did you get that?" I pointed to the gun.

"You can't ever go back," Hype said. "Once you're out, you can never go back. I won't let you back. Understood?"

I nodded. As if I was ever going to want to return to Aurora.

"Tell him," Joe said to Hype. This time, he pointed the gun at Hype. Then, to me, he said, "The gun was down here. I get all my weapons here. We get all kinds of things down here. Hype is God, remember? He creates all things."

"To hell with this," I said, figuring this bad make-believe had gone too far. "You can't get me out, can you?"

Hype nodded. "Yes, I can. I am God, Joe. Those underground tests, they made me God. They were my cross. I'm the only survivor. The orderlies, the doctors, the patients, I'm the only one. That's when I became God."

"You want to get out, right?" Joe snarled at me, "Right?" He waved the gun for me to move over to the far wall.

Hype turned, dropping his robe. Beneath it, he was naked, the skin of his back like a long festering sore. The imprint of hundreds of stitches all along his spine, across the back of his ribcage. To the right of this, a fist-sized cavity just above his left thigh, on his side.

"Tell him," Joe said.

The old man began speaking, as if he couldn't confess this to my face. "Inside me is the door. The tunnel, Joe. To get through, you've got to enter me."

The must vulgar aspect of this hit me, and I groaned in revulsion.

Joe laughed. "Not what you think, Doer. Not like what you like to do to me. Or vice-versa. His skin changed after the tests. Down here, it changes again. Look—it's like a river, look!"

At first, I didn't know what he was pointing at—his finger tapped against Hype's wrinkled back.

Then, before I noticed any change, I felt something deep in my gut. A tightening. A terrible physical coiling within me, as if my body knew what was happening before my brain did.

I watched in horror as the old man's skin rippled along the spine. A slit broke open from one of the ancient wounds. It widened, gaping. Joe came closer, shining his flashlight into its crimson-spattered entry. It was like a red velvet curtain, moist, undulating. A smell like a dead animal from within. The scent, too, of fresh meat.

Joe pressed the gun against my head. "Go through."

My first instinct was to resist.

Seconds later, Joe shot a bullet into the old man's wound, and it expanded further like the mouth of a baby bird as it waits for its feedings.

Joe kissed my shoulder. "Goodbye, Doer."

He pressed the gun to my head again.

The old man's back no longer seemed to be there; now it was a doorway, a tunnel towards some green light. Green light at the end of a long red road. His body had stretched its flesh out like a skinned animal, an animal hide doorway, the skin of the world...

With the gun against my head, Joe shoved me forward, into it. I pushed my way through the slick red mass and followed the green light of atomic waste.

Once inside, the walls of crimson pushed me with a peristaltic motion further, against my will. Tiny hooks of his bones caught the edge of my flesh, tugging backwards while I was pressed into the opening.

We are all in here, all the others who got out through him. Only "out" didn't mean out of Aurora, not officially. We're out of our skins, drawn into that infested old man. When I had rein of him for an afternoon, I got him to go down and bribe the psych tech on duty. I pulled up both of their files, Joe's and Hype's.

Joe was a murderer who had a penchant for cutting wounds in people and screwing the wounds. This was no surprise to me. Joe is a sick fuck. I know it. Everyone who's ever been with him knows it.

Hype was a guy who had been exposed to large amounts of radiation in the fifties. He had a couple of problems, one physical and one mental. The physical one I am well aware of, for the little bag rests at the base of my stomach, to the side and back. Because of health problems as a result of the radiation, he'd had a colostomy about twenty years back.

The mental problems were also apparent to me, once I got out, once I got *through*. He suffered from a growing case of multiple personality disorder.

I pulled my file up, too, and it listed: *ESCAPE.*

I had a good laugh with Joe over these files. Then, God took over, and I had to go back down into the moist tissues of heaven and wait until it was my turn again.

There are prisons within prisons, and skins within skins. You can't always see who someone is just by looking in their eyes. Sometimes, others are there.

Sometimes, God is there.

"I am infinite," the old man said, "I contain multitudes."

THE JOSS HOUSE

When I was a boy, my mother told me a story about something that happened up in the mountains out west that involved two children who stole something from a joss house. The name alone fascinated me. What was a joss house? I had to look it up. Was it a racist thing? What happened? These children went missing after they'd committed the theft, and no one really knew what happened to them. Additionally, I knew a man with several sons, and one of the sons did something terrible without meaning to. The man told me that he would've taken his son out in the woods and shot him if he had known the terrible thing the son had done. That is an extreme viewpoint on right and wrong, and I just had to write about it. Additionally, I wanted to write a little bit about the Old West without romanticizing it in the least.

This happened long ago, when things were different. Back then, mining towns were everywhere in the hills and mountains, and logging camps, too. Beneath the mountains, there'd be small towns cropping up here and there as fortunes waxed and waned with the discovery of gold and ore and sometimes nothing was discovered in the mines. Fair Corners didn't have much more than a town clock and the coffee shop at the depot. While it was several years into the 20th century, it's easy to forget that mountain towns are usually thirty years behind the times. Yes, it had Colson's Drug Store even then because Nicky Colson's grandfather had opened it after the big storm when property went cheap; and yes, even the Shop-It was there only back then it was just called Shep's Sundries. This was when old Joshua Turner was actually a little boy, and when it meant something that you knew scripture. The prison on the hill had not yet been built, and the river was not quite dry. The anglos lived within town limits, and on the other side of the tracks was that Chinese community that pretty much drifted with the winds once the mining was done up in the hills and once they had more opportunities upstate. Ben Durham ran a poker blind behind his wife Sophie's dress shop, and his games and track betting were legendary for a town that then held fewer than two hundred residents. But even so, Ben went to church and raised his two sons well. Ben was in many ways the closest thing to the Law in Fair Corners for a few years—at least before they got a regular lawman. It wasn't that Ben owned a lot of guns, or that he knew the law. He was just the man people came to if they needed to settle disputes. He believed in fairness. He believed in making sure that if someone was hurt unduly, there would be repayment just like a gambling debt. Although he was a church-going man, he was not beloved by the local preacher—his gambling operation was too well-known for that. But Ben Durham was the Law of the People, and when Fanny Bishop was compromised, the man who had been responsible was brought to justice; when a horse thief was found out, usually a quiet lynching was held up behind the mining camp; if one man took from another man's plate, Ben Durham was there to try and settle their differences.

His sons, Paul and Wes, both passed out the prayerbooks on Sundays and more than once they carried meals to widows along with the minister's wife. Ben Durham taught them respect for others, even those of lesser fortunes, and he taught them that when it came to a fight, sometimes you could not run away.

He taught them how to use a gun. They didn't have a rifle since their father had lost his in a poker game, but they had an old pistol.

"A gun can save your life," their father told them. "A gun can destroy your life. It's all up to you. You must be wise. You must use it for the good of others more than the good of yourself. You want to hunt, you hunt for your family. If you hunt for yourself, it will all come to no good." Wes and Paul nodded when he spoke, but both just wanted to shoot some birds as soon as the pistol was in their hands. "This was your grandfather's pistol, and now it's mine. Then someday, one of you will own it."

"I will," Wes said. "I'm the oldest. And I'll shoot all bad men."

"And how will you know the bad men from the good?"

"I'll just know," Wes said. "Because I can tell. And all bad men should die."

"When you own a gun," their father said, "you must follow the law. Not all laws are in books or are from judges. There are higher laws."

"Like church," Paul chimed in, and his father nodded.

"Like church. Like the good of the people, which can rise above the law."

"Like the law of the wilderness," Wes added.

Ben Durham shook his head. "No, son. The law of the wilderness is no law. We're not animals. We're children of God. We have responsibilities to community, to church, and to each other. You take the law into your own hands, and you will find yourself alone." And just to teach Wes that guns were not playthings, he shot the pistol so close to Wes' thigh that it left powder burns on him, and Wes cried like a baby even though there was no blood; that night, Paul heard his father tell his mother that Wes was going to be trouble because there was too much spirit in him.

Sure, the boys got up to no good sometimes. It was to be expected in a town that size with so little to do. Sure, once they rolled some logs down Baseline Road and blocked the tracks, but it was a sight to see those boys getting switch-whipped by their daddy right up by the War Memorial so that they'd never pull a stunt like that again. It's even possible that the stories were true that they stole candy sometimes, but what boy hasn't done that? Wes tended to be the instigator of these episodes, but even he wasn't all that bad–he would set a trap up of a cigar box and a stick, and catch a squirrel and then let it loose in school. That was as bad as he would get for the most part. Paul and Wes stole their father's pistol for a day and went and shot birds out in the ridge—for that, they got whupped, but the worst for Paul was watching a mockingbird that had been cut clean in half, and knowing it was somehow wrong to have done it.

And everyone knew that Ben and his Sophie had some problems of their own. It's like that in small towns—or at least it was back then, before the first World War, back when people minded their own business for the most part. People used to understand these things—the difficult births that left the women scared and cautious, and the men with their demons. Sin was completely accepted back then as something awful but true. No one looked when men like Ben Durham took a Thursday night stroll across the tracks to Little Hong Kong, barely more than a shanty with some laundries and one restaurant on the northside of town.

It would be twilight, and he'd find his way to a place where this one paper lantern that was red and pink swayed in the breeze…and the wind chimes, too, would tell any man where to find her, but no one could pronounce her name, so they just called her Little Kim. Ben practically owned her—it was said he took his winnings down there from some poker games and would lay it all out for her mother, who was happy to have food and clothes and all the things that she and her three children could never afford on their own.

Townsfolk looked the other way. It was understood about Ben, and the men wanted to keep it all private because even in wicked small towns there's an unwritten law that the human animal must hunt outside his own cave. But the problem was that when Ben's boys got to a certain age, they began to hear the stories. They began to notice that their father was missing some nights and that those were the nights when their mother was silent and feverish.

It was Paul who followed his father first. He reported back to Wes that he'd watched their father fall into the arms of some Chinese girl who looked like she was barely more than sixteen. Wes didn't believe his younger brother. Wes was thirteen, a year older than Paul, and knew more about life than Paul ever could.

The Joss House

So, Wes accompanied his brother on the following Thursday night, and saw the same thing. Even so, Wes would not accept that it was what it looked like. "He's helping the poor," Wes said. Then, another day, "He owes them money from a poker game." But he knew it was all a lie.

This led to silence all around the Durham house. Wes and Paul found themselves stealing more and more around town, and getting switched a lot at the War Memorial. Wes began talking bad about the Chinese in Little Hong Kong. Paul wasn't sure if they were all that bad, but Wes convinced him they were. "They don't even go to church, they don't worship God. They should all die. They worship the Devil."

"How do you know?" But Paul didn't even need to ask, because Wes practically dragged him over to the Joss House in Little Hong Kong that sat right at a crossroads. A Joss House was a little one-room shed in which the workers could worship, just like the townsfolk did in church. The smell of incense was always in the air around the House, and the inside was beautifully carved wood and filled with candles. No one begrudged them their worship, and even the minister showed some respect for their eastern demons.

Inside, there was a statue of a small fat man, on his head were snails, and the most amazing thing was that he seemed to be made out of gold. His face had an aspect of calm, as of one sleeping. "Remember the Golden Calf?" Wes asked. "This is like that. They worship idols."

Paul went up and touched the statue. "It's solid gold."

"That's right. From the mines. They steal bits and pieces of it," Wes said, and before Paul could stop him, Wes went right up and smashed his fist against the statue's face. Then he ran out to the dirt street and grabbed some rocks. He came back in and smashed it hard against the statue's face; he gave a rock to Paul. Paul laughed, and brought his sharp rock down hard on the head of the statue. Part of the face fell off. It was not solid gold after all, only gold leaf.

"You busted it," Paul gasped.

"You did it," Wes laughed. "I wish it was that girl. That whore!" He took the face and stuck it under his shirt. "This is the god of whores."

At home that night, silence ruled like the hand of a schoolmarm. Then word got back to Ben Durham that his sons had broken the Buddha face in the Joss House at Little Hong Kong. At supper, he said, "Boys, let's take a little walk," and when they were all three walking out by the river, Ben said, "Sons, I hear stories about things you've been up to."

"Like what?" Paul asked.

"Like going over to Little Hong Kong and getting up to no good."

"We're not the only ones," Wes said.

They walked a ways further. "The Joss House is a sacred place to those people," Ben said. "It's important to their happiness. You desecrated it."

"What does that mean?" Paul asked.

"It means you dirtied it."

Paul gasped.

Wes spat on the ground. "We know about you and that whore."

Ben said nothing for awhile. Paul thought his father might be weeping, but it was too dark to know. They sat by the river; Paul could tell that Wes was thinking mean thoughts just by the way he was quiet.

Finally, their father went up the bank and returned with a switch. "You know what I have to do, sons," he said.

Paul nodded, and began unbuckling his belt, but Wes snarled, "You go over there and whore around and we do one thing and we get switched. No more," and he grabbed the switch from his father's hand. "It's you who needs to be whupped, not us," and he raised the switch up over their father and brought it down so that the switch sang.

Paul watched his father take the switch across his face, and hands. The moonlight was like a magic lantern as the switch went up and down and up and down, slashing, but his father didn't try to take it from Wes at all, he just wept and let his eldest son attack him.

By the end, even Paul was crying. He didn't understand why his father let Wes beat him. He didn't understand why his father wept openly and sometimes cried out, "My boys! Why? My boys! My precious sons!"

Then, it was over. The switch was broken. Wes was exhausted from hurting his father. Paul watched the shadow of his father drop into a heap on the muddy ground and whisper, "I can't do it. I just can't do it."

After lights out, in their room, Paul thought he heard voices in the kitchen. He went to use the outhouse, and saw three men from town talking with his father. They all kept their voices low, and Paul wasn't sure what was being said, but it seemed serious. He heard words like "can't" and "must" and "not fair" and "not right" and "community," as he tiptoed out the side door. Walking on the flat stones to the outhouse, he thought he saw others in the woods— people standing among the trees as if waiting for something. Something frightened him about this, and he used the outhouse as quickly as possible and then went back to bed.

"Something's happening out there," Paul whispered to his brother.

"What do you think it is?"

"I don't know. But it looks like the time they caught the man who ruined Miss Bishop. It looks like that."

"Maybe someone got ruined," Wes said. He sat up and turned the lamp up next to his bed. "Maybe there's going to be a hanging."

They began whispering to each other all the possibilities for what this might mean. Then, Paul heard the footsteps at their bedroom door.

Ben Durham came to both of them in bed that night and kissed each of his sons on the forehead. Then he thanked Wes for the whupping. Wes began to cry, and his father said, "But you still desecrated their Joss House, Wes. You don't understand these people. I know why you did this, but they won't. This is like going into our church and throwing the cross in the mud. But it's worse." His father seemed different to Paul, then. Like he was made of stone, not flesh.

"Why?" Wes asked.

"It's worse because people died to make that statue. And you destroyed it."

"I don't care," Wes said.

"I don't think you understand the balance you upset. Everything is in balance, Wesley. Everything. And you can't do this to people." Ben's voice was calm and brittle, and he said the words slowly and carefully as if accepting something difficult with dignity.

"It's Little Hong Kong," Wes huffed. "They're all bad over there. Everyone says it. Who cares. I don't give a damn. I took a rock and I broke it and I will do it again. Paul broke it, too."

Ben glanced at Paul. "Is that true?"

Paul shook his head slightly. He felt as if snow were being pressed into the small of his back.

Ben returned his attention to Wes. "You're the eldest. You should know better."

Then, Ben Durham went over to Paul and touched his forehead. "You go to sleep, son. Your older brother and I need to talk some more." His father's touch was warm. Paul nodded.

Wes sat up in bed. "What?"

"You heard me," Ben said. "We need to talk some more, you and me."

"Why?" Wes said, glancing at Paul. His eyes glared with some mild alarm. Paul got worried, as well. This would mean another switching.

"Because you've done something very very bad. Something that can't be taken back. You took something from the Joss House in Little Hong Kong."

"I can take it back. I didn't mean to whup you so much," Wes said. "Paul's the one who broke it. Paul, tell him. I still got the face. It's here...Pa? I can give it back."

"Be a man, Wes," his father said. "Son, I have men here who can't abide what you've done. The people in Little Hong Kong, they make the mines work. We need them to make the mines work right. They work on the tracks, too. You know that. All of us pitch in to build up here so we can have a community, so we can prosper. And you've done something terrible."

Wes reached beneath his pillow and withdrew the face of the statue. "See? I can take it back."

"I'm sorry, son," Ben said. "I'm sorry. Let's go. If we don't go now, others will come for you at some point, and it won't be easy."

"Why can't Paul come too?" Wes' voice sounded small to Paul. Paul sensed the fear in the room, and wasn't sure where it had come from. The fear grew like a shadow from Wes. "Why can't Paul come? He was there with me. He's the one who broke it. Paul," he pleaded, looking at his brother.

"Paul is all I have left," Ben said. He went over and pulled the covers off Wes, and scooped him up in his arms like he was a baby rather than a boy of thirteen.

"Why? I can put it back," Wes said, struggling against his father's strong arms, arms like a bear wrapped around him.

"There are things that can't be put back," Ben said, "There are men who are very angry over what you've done. They saw you. Worse, you brought shame on us. Open shame." His father spoke gently, more gently than he had ever done before. But Paul still felt the coldness in his father; as if he'd changed in some mysterious way, as if the switching Wes had given him had turned him icy.

Paul watched as his father left the room carrying Wes, whose voice was faint as he asked why over and over again.

Paul threw off the covers and put on his coat. He climbed out the bedroom window, grabbing the oak tree's thickest branches and scrambled like a cat to the ground. He followed the shadows of his father and brother out to the railroad tracks, and then across the wooden slat road into Little Hong Kong. The lanterns were all lit, and Paul had to hide alongside the shanties, staying as much in the shadows as possible so as to avoid being seen.

291

He watched Wes, his arms around his father's neck, weeping and crying out, "I'm scared, I'm scared, please Pa, don't," and then finally Paul's father dropped him down on the ground, and several of the men from Little Hong Kong gathered around. But then Paul saw others too: men from town, men who ran stores and some of the miners, as well. Even the preacher was there.

Ben Durham held up the face of the statue. A man from the crowd took it, nodding.

Then, Paul watched as his father drew his pistol from his belt and aimed it at Wes. Wes looked up at his father, and Paul thought that Wes didn't really believe this was happening, Paul thought that Wes must have felt as if it were a dream. For how could this tribe of men gather here to watch Ben Durham shoot his eldest son?

Wes began crying and looking around to all the men, and to his father. "I didn't mean it! I didn't mean to do it," Wes wept. "It was Paul! Paul did it! I told him not to! Please, Pa! Please!"

"Son," Ben Durham said. "Say your prayers now. Say them."

"Oh God please forgive me," Wes said, his voice like a sheep bleating. "Pa, please forgive me. I didn't know what I was doing. I won't do it again. I promise. I didn't mean to."

Ben brought the gun to the edge of his boy's scalp. "I love you son. No one is above the Law."

And then, the dream was gone from Wes' eyes. In the next moment, lightning seemed to flash between Ben and his son.

Paul screamed, but the shot overpowered his voice. Just like the statue, Wes's face had been smashed off. Wes lay on the ground, no longer a boy. Now, a body. Paul wasn't sure if he himself were breathing; all he heard was his own heart beat.

Ben Durham dropped his pistol, and turned into the crowd, which parted for him. Little Kim ran up to him, but he pushed her away.

The men were quiet, and someone covered Wes with a canvas. Paul stayed back, so as to remain unseen. Sometime, before morning, he went home. His father was still up as the sun began to bleed purple across the eastern mountains. Ben Durham offered Paul a mug of coffee, and father and son sat down on the porch.

"I saw you there," Ben said. "I knew you'd come."

"Pa, he didn't do it."

"That doesn't matter, son. They needed someone. Wes was already ruined. He was already going to become something terrible when he grew older. I could see it in him."

"But I did it. I broke the statue."

"Boy, there are two things you'll never mention in this world again. First, is what you boys did. Second, is what you saw in the night. It's the business of men, and your mother—and when you're married, your wife and children—do not need to know of this business." After a few sips of coffee, his father continued. "Let's not speak of this again. The past is the past. There's no undoing. No man is above the Law. Your brother has moved on." There was no more weeping between them. Then, his father handed him his pistol. "It's yours now. It was my father's. When he was tired of the Law, it became mine. And now, I have made my last judgment. Here is your inheritance."

Paul held the pistol in his hand, thinking of the Law and his brother.

293

Back in those days, life was simple, and men did what men must do. Paul went to school the same as always. He sometimes got into trouble but he made sure it wasn't the sort of trouble that caused more trouble for anyone. The story went around that Wes had run away that night, that he had stolen gold from the Chinese and had run off to San Francisco and maybe hopped a boat to some faraway place. Paul's mother went about her work in the dress shop, and his father ran his poker games in the backroom. When Paul's mother wept for nights on end about her son—which she did much of in the first year—suddenly a letter would arrive with Wes' terrible handwriting, telling her that he was fine, that he was up in the Klondike seeking his fortune; or a parcel came, with candies and teas that Wes had bought for his mother. Paul let it go. He knew his father had arranged this somehow.

Paul went about the business of a boy growing to manhood, but one day curiosity got the better of him. He went, at dusk, over to Little Hong Kong, to the Joss House, and saw that the statue's face was fixed again, even if it had some cracks around the lips and forehead. The face seemed different than the one that he had smashed with stone—for the other face had seemed calm and placid. The god had a different aspect; Paul wondered how this could be. He became aware that the little golden god was laughing gently. The golden smile was open and warm, and there was nothing of judgment in its gaze. Paul began to see the world from that statue's eyes. It was very funny, this world of men and their Law and what a man would do to his son to keep the world and its gods happy.

This happened a long time ago, before the floods and earthquakes, before the malls and stores and houses sprouted along the mountain, before Fair Corners became a distant suburb of Sequoia City. Back when white people thought they were the most important people on the earth. Back when nobody respected different beliefs. The Joss House remained until the first World War, in which Paul himself died, at which point the Joss House fell apart, unattended, uncared for; the golden statue had long since been stolen; and it wasn't until the early 1950s that someone found the old bones of a little boy out in the woods, when they were digging to build another house.

Buried with the boy, the thin golden face of a statue.

Martha

Their daughter, freshly buried. They go in the car back to Martha's for drinks and consolation. Martha, her large arms engulfing them in an embrace, the weeping and the cocktails and the steam of summer rising.

Mother turns to Father, and says, "I wished she was still here. When we buried her. I wished it badly." She crumples against him. "So much. Oh God. Dear God. I miss her so much. So much."

"Me, too," he tells her and kisses her forehead.

"I wished all these people would go away. Martha, too. And it would just be the three of us again. And we'd be somewhere far away, together. Just you and me and...dear God, why isn't she with us? Why did this have to be? Why can't we go back for one second. One second and stop it from happening?"

"I know," he whispers. "I know."

Later, upstairs, on the large bed in the master bedroom, she lies looking up at the cracked ceiling, in her slip, and she wishes again that her daughter would come back to her. She wishes that she had the power of God and could raise the girl up from the grave, her face twisted from the accident, her body broken, but digging out of the warm dirt, and wandering out on the highway, heading home. She wishes so hard until her scalp hurts, and then she wishes that God would do something for once instead of just not being there.

Martha brings up a dinner tray later and tells her that Bob is sitting on the front porch just watching the cars go by. "You need to eat something. Keep up your strength."

"Who cares," she says. "I don't. Not really. Maybe I'll eat later, Martha. Maybe later. I've lost the only person I ever really loved. The only one. It's terrible. It's terrible. We put her in the ground. She's in the dirt. In a box. In a box, Martha. Oh God. I can't stand it. She's the only one. They took her away from me. The only one I've ever loved. I'd give anything. Anything. Oh God, I can't live without her. She was the only one. I can't go on. I just can't. I want to die, too. If she can't live, I don't want to live, either. I don't. I can't. She was everything. Everything."

"I know," Martha says. She sets the tray down by the bed, and goes to rub her mother's back.

Underworld

"Underworld" came out of getting lost in Manhattan too many times, hearing about some bizarre murders, and thinking I'd seen someone I knew through a window in a restaurant.

They say that love never dies. Sometimes, it goes somewhere else, to a place from which it may return transformed.

We were subletting the place on Thirty-Third, just down from Lexington Avenue—it was not terribly far from my job up at Matthew Bender, across from Penn Station, where I was an ink-stained drudge by day before transforming into a novelist by night. Jenny was getting day work on the soap operas—nothing much, just the walk-on nurses and cocktail waitresses that populate daytime television, never with more than a word or two to say, so it was a long way to her Screen Actor's Guild card. But she made just enough to cover the rent, and I made just enough to cover everything else, plus the feeble beginnings of a savings account which we affectionately named, The Son'll Come Out Tomorrow, because at about the time we opened the account, Jenny discovered that she was pregnant. This worried the heck out of me, not for the usual reasons, such as the mounting bills, and the thought that I might not be able to pursue writing full-time, at least not in this life, but because of a habit Jenny had of sleeping with other men.

It will be hard to understand this, and I don't completely get it myself, but I loved Jenny in a way that I didn't think possible. It wasn't her beauty, although she certainly had that, but it was the fact that in her company I always felt safe and comfortable. I did not want to ever be with another woman as long as I lived; I suppose a good therapist would go on and on about my self-image and self-esteem and self-whatever, but I've got to tell you, it was simply that I loved her and that I wanted her to be happy. I didn't worry if I was inadequate or unsatisfying as a lover; and she never spoke openly about it with me. I was just aware she'd had a few indiscretions early in our marriage, and I assumed that she would gradually, over the years, calm down in that respect. I felt lucky to have Jenny's company when I did, and when I didn't, I did not feel deprived. I suppose that until you have loved someone in that way it is impossible to understand that point of view.

So I wondered about the paternity of our child, and this kept me up several nights to the point that I would slip out of bed quietly (for Jenny often had to be up and out the door by five a.m.), and go for long walks down Third Avenue, or down a side street to Second, sometimes until the first light came up over the city. During one of these jaunts, in late January, I noticed a curious sort of building—it was on a block of Kip's Bay that began in an alley, and was enclosed on all sides by buildings. Yet, there were apartments, and a street name (Pallan Row, the sign said), and two small restaurants, the kind with only eight or nine tables, one of them a Szechwan place, the other non-descript in its Americanized menu; also, a flower stand, boarded up, and what looked like a bit of a warehouse. The place carried an added layer of humidity, as if it had more of the swamp to it than the city.

I am not normally a wanderer of alleys, but I could not help myself—I had lived in this neighborhood about a year and a half, and in that time had felt I knew every block within about a mile and half radius. But it was as if I had just found the most wonderful gift in the world, a hidden grotto, a place in New York City that was as yet undiscovered except by, perhaps, the oldest residents. I looked in the windows of the warehouse, but could see nothing through the filthy windows.

All day at work, I asked friends who lived in the general vicinity if they knew about Pallan Row, but only one said that she did. "It used to be where the sweatshops were—highly illegal, too, because when I was a kid, they used to raid them all the time—it was more than bad working conditions, it was white slavery and heroin, all those things. But then," she added, "so much of this city has a history like that. On the outside, carriage rides and Broadway shows, but underneath, kind of slimy."

On Saturday, I convinced Jenny to take a walk with me, but for some reason I couldn't find the Row; we went to lunch. Afterwards, I remembered where I'd led us astray, and we ended up going to have tea at the Chinese restaurant. The menu was ordinary, and the decorations vintage and tacky.

"Amazing," Jenny said, "look, honey, the ceiling," and I glanced up and beheld one of those lovely old tin ceilings with the chocolate candy designs.

The waiter, who was an older Asian woman, noticed us and came over with some almond cookies. "We usually are empty on weekends," she said, and then, also looking at the ceiling, "this was part of a speak-easy in the twenties—the cafe next door, too. They say that a mobster ran numbers out of the backroom. Before that, it was just an ice house. My husband began renting it in 1954."

"That long ago?" Jenny said, taking a bite from a cookie, "it seems like most restaurants come and go around here."

"Depends on the rent," the woman nodded, still looking at the ceiling, "the owner hasn't raised it a penny in all those years." She glanced at me, then at Jenny. "You're going to have a baby, aren't you?"

Jenny grinned. "How did you know?"

The woman said, "Young couples like you, in love, eating my almond cookies. Always brings babies. You will have a strong boy, I think."

After she left the table, we laughed, finished the tea, and just sat for awhile. The owner's wife occasionally peeped through the round port-hole window of the kitchen door, and we smiled at her but shook our heads to indicate that we weren't in need of service.

"When the baby comes," she said, "Mom said she'd loan us money to get a larger place."

"Ah, family loans," I warned her.

"I know, but we won't have to pay her back for a few years. Can you believe it, me, a mother?"

"And me, a father?" I leaned over and pressed my hand against her stomach. "I wonder what he's thinking?"

"Or she. Probably, 'get me the hell out of here right now!' is what it's thinking."

"Baby's aren't 'its'."

"Well, right now it is. It has a will of its own. It probably looks like a little developing tadpole. Something like its father." She gave my hand a squeeze. I kissed her. When I drew my face back from hers, she had tears in her eyes.

"What's the matter?"

"Oh," she wiped at her eyes with her napkin, "I'm going to change."

"Into what?"

"No, you know what I mean. I've been living too recklessly."

"Oh," I said, and felt a little chill. "That's all in the past. I love you like crazy, Jen."

"I know. I am so lucky," she said. "Our baby's lucky to have two screw-ups like us for parents."

Now it could be that I'm just recalling that we said these words because I want her memory to be sweeter for me than perhaps reality will allow. But we walked back up Second Avenue that Saturday feeling stronger as a couple; and I knew the baby was mine, I just knew it, regardless of the chances against it. We caught a movie, went home and made love, sat up and watched *Saturday Night Live*. Sunday we took the train out to her mother's in Stamford, and then as the week was just getting under way, I walked through the doorway of our small sublet, to find blood on the faux oriental rug.

Yet the door had been locked. That was my first thought. I didn't see Jenny's body until I got to the bathroom, which is where her murderer had dragged her, apparently while she was still alive, and then had dropped her in the tub, closed the shower curtain around her. It wasn't as gruesome as I expected it to be—there was a bullet in her head, behind her left ear, but she was lying face up so I didn't see the damage to the back of her scalp. She didn't even look like Jenny anymore. She looked like a butcher shop meat with a human shape. She looked like some dead woman with whom I had no acquaintance. I was pretty numb, and was thinking of calling the police, when it occurred to me that the killer might still be in the apartment. So I went next door to Helen Connally's and knocked on the door. Helen, in her sweats, saw my panic, let me in, and made me some tea while we waited for the police. I hated leaving Jenny there, in the tub, for the ten minutes, but if the murderer was still lurking, I had no way of defending myself.

After the police and the neighbors and Jenny's mother had picked my brain about the crime, it hit me.

I had not only lost my partner and lover, but also my only child. I cried for days, or perhaps it was weeks—it was like living, for a time, in a dark cave where there was no hour, no minute, no day, only darkness.

301

When I emerged from my stupor and weeping, the police had arrested a suspect in my wife's murder, and then the mystery unraveled: we had been subletting an apartment from a man who had several such places around the city, and each one was used, occasionally, by the man's clients, as a place of business on certain weekdays for drug dealing. The dealers' assumption had been that on a given day of the week, no one was home. Best the detectives could tell, Jenny had come home too early on the wrong Tuesday, a drug deal was in progress, and one of the men had killed her as soon as she'd come in the door. I was devastated to think that strangers could be in our apartment; but of course, it wasn't really ours. The renter of the apartment was arrested; he pointed the finger at a few associates; and within a year, the guilty were behind bars, and I was living in a place off Houston and Sullivan Street, over in the SoHo area. I was seeing, on a friendly basis, Helen Connally, my former neighbor—it was almost as if the tragedy of my wife's death had given us a basis on which to form a friendship. Helen was thirty-two to my twenty-eight, and, while I knew I would never love her the way I loved Jenny, she was a good friend to me through a most difficult time. We spent a year being slightly good friends, and then, we became lovers.

I was taking some out-of-town friends of ours on an informal sightseeing tour of the Big Apple, and brought them down to little Pallan Row. I thought the Szechwan place would be good for lunch, but when we entered the alley, both it and the cafe were closed; windows were boarded up. "Jesus," I said, "just a year ago, the woman running it told me that they'd had it since the '50s."

Helen took my elbow, "C'mon, we can go get sandwiches up at Tivoli. Or," she turned to the couple we'd brought, "there's a great deli on Third. You guys like pastrami?"

Their voices faded into the background, as I looked through the section of the Chinese restaurant's window that was clear, and thought I saw my dead wife's face back along the wall, through the round glass window of the door to the kitchen.

"Oliver," Helen said, looking over my shoulder, "what's up?"

"Nothing," I said, still looking at Jenny, her dark hair grown longer, obscuring all but her nose and mouth.

"It must be something."

"It's just an old place. It was once a speak-easy, back in the twenties. Think of all that's gone on in there," I said. Jenny's face, in that round window, staring at me.

"Cool," Helen said. She was originally from California, so "cool" and "bummer" had not yet been erased from her vocabulary of irony. She stood back, and her friend Larry whispered something to her.

I watched Jenny's face, and noticed that when her hair fell more to the side of her face, there were no eyes in her eye sockets.

"Let's go," Helen whispered, "they want to take a ride on the ferry before it gets dark."

"Okay, just a sec," I said.

Jenny moved away from the round window.

My heart was beating fast.

I assumed that I was hallucinating, but the thought of spending the rest of the afternoon escorting this couple around town when I had just seen my dead wife was absurd. I made an excuse about needing to be by myself—Helen always took this well, and I caught an understanding look from Anne, who nodded. I knew they would go on to a late lunch and talk about how I still hadn't quite recovered from Jenny's death; and I knew Helen would act the martyr a bit, because it was so hard to play nurse to me over a woman who had cheated constantly behind my back. I adored Helen for her care and caution around my feelings; I wished them a good afternoon, and stood there, along the Row, watching them, until they had rounded the corner and were out of sight.

After a few minutes, I took off my shoe and broke the windowglass, and tugged at one of the boards until it gave. Within half an hour, I stepped in through the broken window, and walked across the dusty floor to the kitchen.

The kitchen was all long shiny metal shelves and drawers, pots and pans still piled high. But it was dark, and I saw no one. I walked across the floor, back to the walk-in freezer, and looked through its frosty pane of glass. Although I could see nothing in there, I found myself shivering, even my teeth began chattering, and I had the sudden and uncomfortable feeling that if I did not get out of that kitchen, out of that boarded-up restaurant right then, something terrible would happen.

It didn't occur to me until I was on the street again that there should've been no frost on the glass pane at the walk-in freezer, that, in fact, there was no electricity to the entire building, perhaps to the entire block.

Helen noticed, over the next few days, that I was becoming nervous. We sat across from each other in our favorite park, me with the *Times*, and her with a paperback; I looked up and she was watching me. Another day, we went to a coffee shop, and she mentioned to me that my knees, under the table, were shaking slightly. She said this with some seriousness, as if shaking knees were an indicator of some deeper problem. But I doubted myself then, and I did not want to talk about seeing my dead wife in the Chinese restaurant kitchen on Pallan Row. Finally, my restlessness turned nocturnal, and I tossed and turned in my sleep. Helen, sleeping over, finally sat up in bed at four in the morning and flicked on the bedside lamp. Her eyes were bloodshot.

"You have not slept a full night for two days," she said, "you tell me what's going on."

I spent about an hour dodging the issue, until finally, as she pushed and pushed, I told her about seeing Jenny.

"She was blind," Helen said, speaking to me like I was a lying twelve year old.

"Not blind. She had no eyes. I felt she could see me, anyway. She was staring at me. She just had no eyes."

"And you went in there and no one was there..."

"But the freezer. Why would it be going?"

Helen shrugged. "I'm going to make a drink. You want something?"

At five-thirty a.m., she and I had vodka martinis, and went and sat out on the fire escape as all of Manhattan awoke, as the sky turned several shades of violet before becoming the blank light of day.

"I don't believe in ghosts," I said, sipping and feeling drunk very quickly. "I don't believe that the dead can rise or any of that."

"What do you believe?"

I watched a burly man lift crates out of the back of his truck down in the street. "I believe in what I see. I saw her. I really saw her."

"Assuming," she said, "that it was Jenny. Assuming that the freezer was running on its own energy. Assuming you saw what you saw. Assuming all those things as givens, what does it mean?"

"I have no idea. I thought at first maybe I was just crazy. If I hadn't seen the frost on the freezer window, I don't think I would've believed later on that it had been Jenny at all. Or anything but an hallucination."

Helen was obstinate. "But it's got to mean something."

"Why?" I asked.

I slept through the next day fairly peacefully, and when I awoke, Helen was gone. I watched television, and then called a few friends to set up lunches and dinners for the following week.

Helen walked through the door at six thirty in the evening, and said, "Well, I found that alley again. I pulled back one of the boards."

When she said this, I felt impulsively defensive—it was my alley, it was my boarded-up restaurant, I felt, it was my hallucination. "You didn't have to," I told her.

She halted my speech with her hands. "Hang on, hang on. Oliver, the windows are bricked up beneath the boards."

"No they're not."

"Yes," she said, "they are. You couldn't have gotten in there."

We argued this point; we were both terrific arguers. It struck me that she hadn't found the right alley, or even the right Pallan Row. Perhaps there were two Pallan Rows in the city, near each other, perhaps even almost identical alleys. Perhaps there was the functional Pallan Row and the dysfunctional Pallan Row.

This idea seemed to clutch at me, as if I had known it to be true even before I thought it consciously.

The idea took hold, and that night, on the pretext of going to see a movie which Helen had already seen twice with friends, I took a cab over to Pallan Row.

It was colder on Pallan Row than in the rest of the city. While autumn was well upon us, and the weather had for weeks been fairly chilly, down the alley it was positively freezing. My curiosity and even fear took hold as I peeled back one of the window boards, the very one I had pulled down on my last visit. Helen had been right: the windows were bricked-up beneath the boards. But then, I had to wonder, why the boards at all?

I touched the bricks; had to draw my fingers back quickly, for they seemed like blocks of ice. I remembered the owner of the Chinese restaurant telling Jenny and me that it used to be an ice house. I touched the bricks again, and they were still bitingly cold—it hadn't been my imagination.

I walked around the alley, but saw no way of getting into the buildings again, for all were bricked up.

And then I heard it.

A sound, a human sound, the sound of someone who was trapped inside that old ice house, someone who had heard me pull the board loose and who needed help.

I am no hero, and never will be. For all I knew, there were some punks on the other side of that wall torturing one of their own, and if I walked into the middle of it, I would not see the light of day again.

And yet I could not help myself.

I found that if I kicked at the bricks, they gave a little. The noise from within had ceased, but I battered at the bricks until I managed to knock one of them out. It seemed to be an old brick job, for the cement between the blocks was cracked and powdery. After an hour, I had managed to dislodge several.

To my surprise and amazement, there was a light on within the old restaurant. I looked through the sizable hole I'd made, and saw the former proprietress of the Chinese restaurant standing behind the bar, dressed in a jade-colored silk gown, talking with her barman. A few people sat at the tables, eating, laughing. None of them had noticed my activity at the window.

As I put my face to the hole, I breathed in air so cold that it seemed to stop my lungs up.

I moved back, and stood up. I was sure that this was a delusion; perhaps I needed some medication still, for immediately after Jenny's death, I had begun taking tranquilizers to help blot out the memory of finding her dead. Perhaps I still needed some medical help and psychological counseling.

I crouched down again to look through the opening, and noticed that at one of the tables, facing the other way, was a woman who looked from the back very much like Jenny.

I noticed the ice, too. It was a shiny glaze along the walls and tables; icicles formed teat-like off the chocolate-patterned tin ceiling. I watched the people inside there as if this were a television set; I lost my fear entirely, all my shivering came from the arctic breezes that stirred up occasionally from within.

I thought I heard someone out in the alley behind me, and turned to look.

Helen stood there in a sweatshirt and pants, my old windbreaker around her shoulders; she held a sweater in her arms.

"I figured you'd be here. Look, it's getting chilly." She passed the sweater down to where I sat on the pavement. She noticed the bricks beside me, and the light from within the building. "I see you've been doing construction. Or should I say, de-construction."

"Do you see the light?" I asked her.

She squatted down beside me. "What light?"

"I know you see it," I said, but when I glanced again through the hole, the place within had gone dark.

"What is it about this place for you?" she asked. "Even if you did see Jenny here, or her ghost, whatever—why here? You and she only came here once. Why would she come here?"

"I think this is hell," I said. "I think this is one of those corners of hell. I think Jenny's in hell. And she wants something from me. Maybe a favor."

"Do you really believe that?"

I nodded. "Don't ask me why. There *is* no why. I think this is a corner of hell that maybe shows through sometimes to some people. I don't even think maybe. I know that's what this is."

"You may be right," Helen said. She stood up, stretched, and offered me her hand to help me get up. I took it. Her hand was warm, and I felt a rush of blood in the palm of my hand as if she had managed to transfer some warmth to me.

And then, the sound again.

A human voice, indistinct, from within the walls.

Helen looked at me.

"You heard it, too," I said.

"It's a cat," she said. "It's a cat inside there."

I shook my head. "You heard it. It's not just me. Maybe Jenny can only show herself to me. Maybe hell can only show itself to me, but you heard it."

"Wouldn't Jenny's ghost be in your old apartment where she died?" Something like fear trembled in Helen's voice. She was beginning to believe something that might be dreadful. It made me feel less alone.

"No. I don't think it's her ghost. A ghost is spiritual residue or something. I think she is in here, it's really her, in the flesh, and I think there are others in here. I need to go back in and find out what exactly she wants from me."

The noise again, almost sounding like a woman weeping.

"Don't go in there," Helen said. "It may not be anything. It may be something awful. It may be somebody waiting in there the way somebody waited for Jenny."

I took her face in my hands and kissed her eyelids. When I drew back from her face, I whispered, "I love you Helen. But I have to find out if I'm crazy. I have to find out."

We went and sat in an all-night coffee shop talking about love and belief and insanity. Because I was beginning to convince myself that Pallan Row was a corner of hell, I waited until the sun came up to investigate further within its walls. Helen returned with me, and between the two of us, we managed to break enough bricks apart and away from the wall so that the hole grew to an almost-window-sized entrance.

I asked her to wait outside for me, and if anything happened, to go get help. I went in through the window, scraping my head a bit. The room on the other side was empty and dark, but that unnatural ice breath was still there, and, through the kitchen portal window, there came a feeble and distant light.

Helen asked, every few seconds, "You okay, Oliver? I can't see you."

"I'm fine," I reassured her as often as she asked.

I walked slowly to the kitchen door, looked through the round window pane. The light emanated from the freezer at the other end of the long kitchen. I pushed the door open (informing Helen that this was my direction so that she wouldn't worry if I didn't respond to her queries every few minutes), and walked more swiftly to the walk-in freezer.

The freezer door was unlocked. I opened it, too, and stepped inside.

The light was blue and as cold as the air.

Through the arctic fog, I could make out the shapes of human beings, hanging from meat hooks, their faces indistinct, their bodies slowly turning as if they had but little energy left within them. I did not look directly at any of these bodies, for my terror was becoming stronger—and I knew that if I were to remain sane as I walked through this ice-house of death, I would need to rein in my fear.

Finally, I found her.

Jenny.

Ice across her eyeless face, her hair, strands of thin, pearl-necklace icicles.

She hung naked from a hook, her head drooping, her arms apparently lifeless at her side.

Her belly had been ripped open as if torn at with pincers, the skin peeled back and frost-burnt.

I stopped breathing for a full minute, and was sure that I was going to die right there.

I was sure the door to that freezer, that butcher-shop of the damned, would slide shut and trap me forever.

But it did not.

Instead, I heard that human sound again, closer, more distinct.

I heard my heart beating; my breathing resumed.

The sound came from beyond the whitest cloth of fog, and I waved my hands across it to dissipate the mist.

There, lying on a metal shelf, wrapped in the clothes which Jenny had been buried in, was our baby, his small fingers reaching for me as he began to wail even louder.

I lifted him, held him in my arms, and wiped the chill from his forehead.

Someone was there, among the hanging bodies, watching me. I couldn't tell who, for the fog had not cleared, neither had the blue light increased in intensity. I could not see to *see*. I felt someone's presence though, and thanked that someone silently. I thanked whoever or whatever had suckled my child, had warmed his blood, had met his needs. The place no longer frightened me. Whatever energy the freezer ran on, whatever power inspired it, had kept my child safe.

I took my son out into the bright and shining morning.

"This was why I was haunted," I told Helen, upon emerging from the open window. "This is what Jenny wanted to give me."

I can only describe Helen's expression, through her eyes, as one approaching dread. She said, "I think you should put it back where it belongs."

"Babies aren't 'its'," I said, and recalled saying this to Jenny once, too, at this very place. Or had Jenny said it to me? We had been so close that sometimes when she said things, I felt I'd said them, too. I glanced down at my boy, so beautiful, as he watched the sky and his father, breathing the vivid air.

Across his forehead, I saw a marking, a birthmark, a port-wine stain, perhaps, which spread across his skin like fire until it became something other than what might be called flesh.

Medea

Chopping arms and legs
And their little heads
Tussles of hair flowing
Tunics torn
She sows the sea
With her brothers
And clings to one
Who will cut out her heart.

The Hurting Season

This is a weird one, and has to do with the little rituals that every family seems to have that keeps them just on the safe side of incestuous. It's about a boy who is learning that the secrets of his family are not necessarily going to jibe with anyone in the rest of the world.

The wind had a taste to it, for Leona hung out the wash on the rope strung between the willow and the sapling, down by the river, with the smell of shad, dead on the water's surface from running, and the clean of soap powder and bleach; the Sack was strung up and bounced with each windblow; and Mama was boiling meat in back before the flies would be up to bother her; and it was a rough wind, a March wind even in late April, coming ahead of a storm. The river was high, threatening flooding if the storms kept up, which they were wont to do, but Theron had done all the clearing, and the chairs and table from the levee were already in the spring house, the old spring house that no longer flooded, and he was almost to the shed, now, because the horses were kicking at the stall. The sky was its own secret blue, unnatural, with blue clouds and blue winds and blue sun, all signaling a squall coming down from off-island. He could see the oyster boats rocking across the bay, two miles from the house, just like mosquito larvae wriggling, and he wondered how it was on Tangier, of that girl he met at Winter Festival—he was fourteen, and she was nearly seventeen, but he had seen it in her eyes, those flatland island dull eyes, a flicker of what could only have been fire when she had let him touch her the way Daddy touched Mama.

The horses, prophesying storm, kicked the wood, and the shed trembled. Mama cried out at the noise, surprised, but Leona, in her earthly wisdom, just kept hanging sheets and shirts as if the impending storm mattered not one whit, for it would come and go quickly, a final rinse for the laundry. Theron kept buttoning his shirt; the screen door banged with the wind; the blue sky turned indigo and then gray, with flashes of lightning between. First drops of rain, sweet and cold.

He ran like a horse himself, back to the shed, for he loved the horses and could not bear their distress. The ground was damp, but not muddy, and he galloped across it barefoot in spite of the biting chill. He could feel the rain spitting at his back as he got there, to the door, which he drew back. The smells of the horses, the manure, the cats, too, for they roamed mongst the piles and hay for mice and snakes, strong but not unbearable.

His father was there, at the mast which centered the shed, around which the horses were knocking and frenzied. The mast had a great length of chain hanging from it, and the leather strops of discipline, too, wrapped about its middle. Carved notches marked the days of the season, from Winter Festival to May Day, the days when Daddy did his penance, the hours of his atonement for a sin long ago forgotten. His father wore no shirt; his chest was covered with kudzu hair which sprawled across his shoulders and connected to his belly like inflamed moss; trousers were dirty, shit-stained; boots, too, with blood near the toes for they were tight and he would wear them all during the hurting season.

"You got Naomi upset," Theron said, not meaning to scold, but it was hard to avoid. Naomi was not yet a year, and needed gentleness; the old horse, her sire, Moses, was used to the season, the frantic pain that Daddy put himself through, but Naomi was barely more than a foal.

His father's eyes were not even upon him, but gazing through him, beyond him, to some richer meaning, listening to the words, but decoding them. The man's face was yellow jaundice, and the hunger was showing in the sunken cheeks; the thin blond hair, cut short like a monk's Theron thought, was slick and shiny, the sweat, pearls of mania. "That's not good," his father said, "you take her out, then, take her out, boy."

Theron nodded, glad, and ran around the mast to grab Naomi's bit. He tugged at her, but her eyes were still wild. Theron looked around the shed. "It's the chain, Daddy," he said, for he knew that a horse, unless tempered to a rope, would take fright at anything that resembled one; the silver chain swung lightly about the thick wood. On its end was a rusty hook, from one of the oyster trawlers that had dry-docked over in Tangier, and there was blood on it. He registered this, for a moment, wondering what his father did with the hook that drew blood from him. It was frightening, sometimes, the hurting season, at least to him; he was sure it frightened Mama, too, for she was moody during those months; Leona, older than Daddy or Mama, didn't seem to notice or care; and Milla, being so young, accepted it the way Theron had up until he'd become aware that it was only *his* Daddy who did it, that when he went to Tangier, nobody else had a mast or the chain and strops, nobody else had a Daddy that slept with the horses from February to May.

The boy brought the horse out of the shed, into the slapping rain; the smell of bleach and soap stronger, and he looked up to see the wash swimming in the wind, but their stays holding tight to the rope; Naomi tugged away from him, but he kept his grip, watching for the horse's teeth. He spoke to her, calmly, and led her over to the spring house. It would be small for the horse, but she'd be safe and fairly dry, and the darkness of it would calm her. He tied her to the upturned patio chair, and wiped at her forelock and nose with the red bandana the girl over at the Festival had given him, smoothing down the horse's mane, and withers, to settle her. The horse had the thick hair of the island horses—it was said that they could be traced back to the Spanish ships wrecking off the islands, and his father had told him that the harsh winters in the wild had developed the breed to the point of hardiness and hairiness. Something Theron had learned in school, too, a phrase, "survival of the fittest." That had been the island horses, for they swam every spring around the time of May Day from Tangier over to Chite Island, which was here. *Here, beneath my feet. Centuries of horses coming to mate on Chite in the spring, and to swim back in October when winter came too harsh here first. Here.* Chite was a small island, although the river that ran through it connected it through the wetlands to the Carolina Isthmus, so it had not been a real island since sometime long before Theron was born. Old Moses, he had been a Chiter, and his dam, a wild horse that had never been tamed on Tangier, had died and left the one foal, Naomi. *Mine.* Naomi had a bad fetlock, the back left, and she raised it a little, so he squatted down beside her and massaged it. The wind through the cracks in the old gray wood bit around his ears, but the whistling sound it made seemed to steady his horse. "Good girl," he said, and wrapped the bandana around his neck the way the girl had. It smelled of horse, now, and perfume, and fish, as all things on Tangier smelled of fish.

Theron waited out the storm in the spring house, and when it was over, in just a few minutes, he led the horse out to the rock-pile road that spanned the wetlands to the west of the house, and took her at a canter.

The horse slowed towards the middle of the rock-pile, for it became less smooth here, and there were small gaps in the rocks. The sky cleared, but the sun was still not up in the middle of it, but back in the east, over Tangier. A red-winged blackbird flew up and out from the mesh of yellow reeds and dive-bombed at Theron's hair. "Hey!" he shouted, "Didn't do nothin' to you!" He flapped his hands at the descending bird, and dug his heels into Naomi's side until she galloped some more. His butt was sore from the pounding, for he didn't have his seat yet, at least not with Naomi, for she was an erratic bounder, but he rose-fell-rose-fell with her, his leg muscles feeling stronger, and he tried to pretend that he and the horse were one animal, just like his Daddy had taught him. The bird left him alone once he was out of its territory, and he guided Naomi down to some fresh water for a drink. He saw their reflection, the horse's long neck, its thick shaggy mane hanging down, and then his own face in the cold brown water—the red bandana tied smartly just under his chin, and some whiskers on his upper lip. He smiled at himself; she had liked him, that older girl in Tangier, the pretty one. She had brown eyes just like everybody else on the islands, and brown hair, and freckles. Her hands were like little brushes on his, for they scratched and tingled and smoothed when she had slid them across his palms. "Lookit," she'd said, after she'd done it, and he had looked at his hands. At the palms of his hands. All red, the palms, like they were blushing and warm. "You got skin like water," she said, "see-through hands. I can see you through your skin, boy. Boy." She said boy like it was a dare, so he had kissed her behind the booth, where nobody could see them. He had known what the other boys did, the ones in school, even over in the Isthmus, for they bragged about tit touching and pussy stroking and diving and plunging and gushing. He had felt the electricity in his body, and in hers, and her lips were—*gold warm hot sting bite taste smell wet mud*—sensations had gone through him that words did not even come near, for it was his first kiss ever, and she had seen his excitement when she drew back from it. She had looked down at his trousers and said, "I guess that means you like me."

Embarrassed, he had dropped a hand in front of him, and clasped it with the other, "Huh?"

"Rising like that. In your pants. It means a boy likes a girl. It's nature," she had said, the teacher of his flesh. She drew a line with her finger down his belly to his pants, and circled the knob that thrust forward from the denim. It grew wet, a spot. She grinned. He leaned forward and kissed her again, but she pushed him away this time, and said, "Nuh-uh." But it led him, this feeling, just like the boys had told him it would, it led him without a thought in the world to anything else.

The horse leaned down, disturbing the water, and Theron's reflection whirled and broke in the water. She had liked him, that girl, that day. He had changed since then, he knew it.

He was a man now, even if the others called him boy.

The rock-pile road ended at the Isthmus Highway, rising out of reeds and swamps and curly-down trees like an altar of the true religion. Theron wasn't supposed to take Naomi up on it, for even though few cars traveled it until summer, when the summer people from the cities came down, and when Daddy blocked the rock-pile road to keep them off his property, the highway could be dangerous, for an occasional truck roared through in nothing flat, and a girl's mother got hit a long time ago trying to push her daughter out of the way and to safety. But Theron, a man now, and cocky, rode Naomi up the brief, steep hill, batting back the sticks and dead vines that had not yet greened since the winter, and clopped up onto the pot-holed blacktop. Naomi was faster on the highway, riding down the center line, for it was completely flat, and where it dipped could be seen, and avoided, for several yards.

As he slowed her down at a bend in the road, there was a car stuck in mud on the shoulder. Theron was not big on cars, not like the others boys, but this one was pretty and sporty, a two-seater. A man stood beside it, kicking the bumper and cursing to high heaven. He was a lot younger than Daddy, but maybe only Mama's age. He wore a tan suit, and had rolled his slacks up almost to his knees, which were black with mud. He was soaked head to toe, caught, no doubt in the storm. His eyeglasses were fogged in exertion and frustration. Cars were like that, which is why Theron's family didn't own one.

Theron dismounted, and led Naomi up to the man. "Mister, 'scuse me, but what kind of car is that?"

The man looked at Theron as if he could not hear. Almost like his father in the shed. Then, he said, "It's a Miata. Mazda, kid. Right now it's a shitkicker."

"Pretty nice. Never seen one before," Theron nodded. "You're stuck."

"You must be the local genius," the man said, and then grinned. "Sorry, but you ever get so pissed-off at something you can't see straight, kid?"

"I guess."

"So, kid, you live nearby? You got a phone or something?"

"Yeah, only we don't let strangers use it."

"Okay. Anybody else around here? A drugstore?"

Theron laughed, and covered his mouth to keep from making the man feel too bad. "Sorry—sorry—don't mean to laugh. Don't mean to. But you're twenty five miles from town center." He pointed toward the direction that the man must've already come.

"That piss-hole? Christ, kid, that's a town? I thought it was a mosquito breeding ground. Nothing the other way? You sure?"

Naomi whinnied, and Theron patted her nose. "She's shy. Just shy of biting, sometimes, I think." Then he tugged at the bandana around his neck, self-consciously. There was something about this man he didn't feel comfortable about. "You're not from around here."

The man shook his head. "No, kid, I'm a damn Yankee. Make that a goddamned Yankee. But don't hold it against me." The man said his name was Evan, and was from Connecticut, and that he wrote magazine articles and was supposed to meet his wife up in Myrtle Beach, but he was doing some kind of article on Lost ByWays of the South.

"You write," Theron said, smiling, "that's wild. Wild. Me, I barely read. I watch T.V. Anything you write ever get on T.V.?"

Evan shook his head, "Yeah, I once wrote for the T.V. news. CBS."

"I watch that. Dan Rather. My Daddy thinks he's from another parish, if you know what I mean, but Daddy thinks anybody on T.V. is."

"Well, kid, I don't know about that, but I know I hated it. I hate this. What a way to make a living, huh?"

Theron shrugged, "Survival of the fittest, I guess."

The wind, which had died, picked up again, rattling the dead reeds, shagging at the budding trees, dispersing the petals of those that had blossomed early. He could smell honeysuckle already, up here on the Isthmus, and it wasn't even May. The man had a kind look to him, a wrinkled-brow honesty, and Daddy had always told him that when someone needed help, there was only one thing to do. "Look, Mister," Theron said after watching the man pace his car, "if you don't mind walking down there." He pointed down the gulley, over the wetlands, to the stand of trees that separated Chite from the mainland. "It's about two miles. I'd let you ride her, but she's shy. My Daddy's got a phone, only I got to warn you about one thing."

Evan said, "What's that, kid?"

"We keep to ourselves most of the time. I go to school up in Isthmus, but we don't really mix. My baby sister Milla, she's never even *seen* a mainlander."

The man named Evan seemed to grasp this immediately. "Let's go."

Evan got a camera and a tape recorder out of the back of his car, and strung both of them around his neck like ties. His shoes were brown and would be uncomfortable for the trip—Theron smiled inside himself when he thought of crossing the land on the other side of the rock-pile road, where the mud would surely suck him to his ankles if he wasn't careful. Evan asked, as they descended from the highway, down to the road between the wetlands, "Are there snakes down here?"

"Too cold still. There'll be plenty by June. I once saw a man from Tangier bite the head off a cottonmouth. You ever see that? He just chomped, and spitted it out like it was tobacco." Theron rode Naomi, but walked her slow so the man could keep up with them. He wasn't sure how Daddy or Mama, or even Leona for that matter, would take having a stranger over; Daddy was normally friendly with outlanders, but this was the hurting season, and it might be embarrassing for someone to walk right into the middle of that. Theron assumed that other fathers had their own hurting seasons, although he'd been too awkward to ask any of the boys over in the high school, both because they always seemed smarter than him, and because he was already teased enough as it was for being so different.

The sun was just past noon when they reached sight of the house, and the wind had pretty much died. The sky was white with cloud streaks, and the earth was damp, the moss that hung from the trees sparkled with heaven's spit, as Mama called rain when she was feeling poetic. Naomi tried to pick up speed, for the shed was close by, but he kept her slow out of courtesy to the stranger. "How you doin'?" he asked Evan.

Evan wagged his head around, and said, "Hey, kid, can I get a picture? You and the horse and the house and that thing—what is that? Some kind of bag?"

Theron looked in the direction where Evan indicated, as the man unscrewed his camera's lens cap. Dangling from the willow, with the wash, was the Luck Sack. "It's for good luck," Theron said, "it keeps away hurricanes and floods in spring."

"How's it work?"

"So far, so good." He posed for a picture, sitting up proudly on his horse, keeping his chin back so the man could get a clear shot of the red bandana that girl in Tangier had given him. Theron wished he had a hat—his father had a hat, and now that Theron had crossed the border between boyhood and mandom, he would've liked something brown with a broad brim to keep the sun out of his eyes, to make him feel like a horseman.

"So," Evan said, snapping several pictures, "you have other good luck charms?"

Theron struck pose after pose, attempting a masculine look for this one, a shy look, a rugged, tough pose, "We're not much into good luck. It's what we call tradition. Say, how much film you got in there?"

"Lots." Snap—snap—snap. "What's in that sack, anyway?"

"One of the cats. We got seven. Kittens on the way," Theron said, "I love kittens, but cats I ain't so fond of. You gonna put my pictures in a magazine or something?"

"Maybe," Evan said, lowering the camera. He let the camera swing around his neck. He reached beneath his glasses and rubbed his eyes. His face glowed with sweat—the two miles had been hard on him, because he was a Yankee. The man seemed to be taking in the house and the river, maybe even the bay if his eyesight was any good with those thick glasses. "Are you people witches or something?"

Theron straightened up and grunted, "Nahsir," his pride a little hurt by such an assumption. "We're Baptists."

"Ronny, honey," Leona said, her eyes lowering, not even looking at the stranger; she kept the screen door shut, and her massive form blocked the way. "I don't think you should be bringing people home right now."

"This's Evan. He's a Yankee," Theron said, "he needs to use the phone."

Leona looked at Evan's shoes. Theron saw the squiggle vein come out on her forehead, like when she was tense over cleaning. "Mister, our phone's out of order," she said lightly, delicately, sweetly. Then she looked him in the eye.

Evan blinked. "That's okay," he said, patting Theron on the shoulder.

Leona arched her eyebrows, and stared at the small tape recorder and camera around his neck. "You a traveling pawn shop, mister?"

"Nah'm," Theron butted in, "he writes for magazines. He's a famous writer, Leo, he used to write for Dan Rather."

"Not really," Evan said.

"I'm sorry, sir, but you can't come in the house. The little girl's sick, and like I said, the phone's not working. We had a big storm this morning. Always knocks out the power lines and such." She kept her hands pressed against the screen door as if the man would suddenly bolt for it. And then, to Theron, "Now, Ronny, why'd you bring this nice man all the way out here when you knew the line was down?"

Theron said, "'Cause I thought it'd be up by now," turning to look up at Evan who kept staring at Leona, "it's usually up in a hour or two," and, as if this were a brilliant idea, he clapped his hands, "I know, Evan, you can stay and have some sandwich and pie, and then maybe the phone'll be up."

A groan from the shed out back, and Evan and Theron both glanced that way. It was Daddy with his hurting. Leona groaned, as much to cover up the other noise as anything, and she clutched her stomach. "I tell you, Mister, what little Milla's got, we all seem to be coming down with. You'd be wise to get on back up to Isthmus."

"Some kind of flu," Evan said.

"That's right. That one that's been going around," she nodded, looking pained.

Evan grinned, as if this were a game. "Had my flu shots, ma'am. And anyway, even if I hadn't, I'll survive it."

Leona lost all semblance of pretend kindness. "Just get off this property right now, and Ronny, you take him back up to the highway." She stepped back into the gray hallway and shut the big door on both of them.

"She always this sweet?"

Theron shook his head. "I don't know what's wrong with her today. She's almost a hundred but all age done for her is make her ornery." He went and tied Naomi around the sapling.

"I thought you had your marching orders," Evan said, following him.

"I don't listen to Leona. She's just the hired help. You take orders from servants, my daddy says, and you end up a shit frog. We got them in the spring house. You ever see a shit frog? They go from the stable to the river, but they still can't get it off them." Theron grabbed the laundry rope with both hands and clung to it, letting his knees go slack. "You gonna take more pictures?"

"I don't know," Evan said, but he lifted his camera again, snapped some more of the boy, and then of the river, and the house, and the tire swing, and the Lucky Sack hanging on the willow. He looked all around, through his camera, as if trying to see something else worth photographing, when he seemed to freeze. He lowered the camera, and turned to face Theron.

Theron shivered a little bit, because of the man's look, all cold and even angry, maybe.

"Where are the lines?" he asked.

"Huh?"

"Kid, if you got a phone, where's the pole? Where're the lines? If the line's down, you got to have a line in the first place, kid, what kind of game is this?"

Theron didn't have an answer, not yet anyway. He said, "Dang."

From the shed, a series of shouts, cuss words as strong as Theron had ever heard from the boys at Isthmus.

The stranger named Evan turned around at the sound, took in the whole landscape, the house, the river, the shed, the springhouse, the laundry rope, the bay, the boats, the way the grass was new and green and damp. He walked over to the Lucky Sack, and Theron shouted, "Mister! Evan! Hey!"

But the man had already opened the sack, his face turning white, and he looked at Theron, his eyes all squinching up, and Daddy began screaming at the top of his lungs from the shed, and Old Moses, the horse, started thumping at the wood.

"You sick fucks," Evan said, weeping, "you sick fucks, you said it was a cat, you sick..." But the sobbing took him over, racking his body, the convulsions of sadness shaking him.

Theron blurted, "It's bad luck to look in the Sack, mister."

"Who is it, you sick fuck, who is this?"

Theron tugged at the red bandana around his neck. "It's private."

"Listen, you," Evan raised both fists and brought them down on the boy, knocking him to the ground.

Theron was angry, and knew he shouldn't, but told him anyway because he hated keeping the secret, "It's the first girl I ever kissed. It's the part of her that's sacred. It's the part that made me a man!"

But then Mama was there, behind the man, and hit him with the back of the hoe, just on his skull, and the glasses flew off first, and then his hands wriggled like nightcrawlers, and he crumpled to the ground.

Milla held on tight to Mama's skirt, her brown eyes wide, her hair a tangly weedy mess. She looked like an unmade bed of a baby sister; when Theron got up from the ground, he went and lifted her up. "It's okay, it's just fine, Milla-Billa-Filla." He bounced her around. She was only three, and she looked scared. Theron loved her so much, his sister. He had prayed for a brother when the birthing woman was in their house, but when he had seen Milla in the shed, laying there in his mother's arms, while the birthing mother screamed as Daddy tied her to the mast, he knew that he would love that little girl until the day he died, and protect her from all harm.

Mama said, in her tired way, "Ronny why'd you bring him down here?"

Theron kissed his sister on the cheek, and looked up to his mother. He was always frightened of his mother's rages, for they, like the hurting season, came in the spring, and lasted until mid-summer. "I—I don't know."

"That ain't good enough. And don't lie to me, or you shall eat the dust of the earth all your days and travel on your belly."

"I—I guess…I guess because I wanted Daddy to stop hurting for awhile. I want us all to stop hurting for awhile, Mama," and then he found himself crying, just like the man named Evan had been, because he didn't like the hurting season, and he didn't completely understand the reason for it.

For a moment, he saw the temper begin to flare in his mother's eyes, and then she softened. She bent down, dropping the hoe at her side, and gathered him up in her arms, him and Milla both, hugged tight to her bosom. "Oh, my little boy, you may be a man now, but you will always, always be my little boy." She threatened to weep, too, and Theron figured they'd be the soggiest mess of human in the county, but Mama held back. Daddy was silent in the shed, no doubt exhausted.

Theron thought it might be the right time to ask the question he'd had on his mind since he first discovered about the hurting season. "Why, Mama?"

"Ronny?"

"Why does it have to be us?"

"You mean about the season?"

"Not just the season," he said, drying his tears, "but us here, and them." He looked across the bay to Tangier. "Over there. We don't mix."

325

His mother reached over to his forehead, and traced her finger along the brand that had been put there, a simple *x*. He felt her nail gently trace the lines of the letter. "It's our mark," she said, "from the beginning of creation. Passed through the fathers to the sons."

Theron looked at Milla, "What about the daughters?"

"Uh-huh, that, too, but no birthing, no creation. Our womb must not bear fruit. You remember the scripture."

He did: *And your seed shall not pollute your womankind, but shall be passed through the women of the land to bring your sons and daughters into lesser sin. And of your daughter, the fruit of her womb shall be sewn shut, and neither man nor beast may enter therein. Behold, you and your seed shall sin that the world may be saved.* But when he told the lines to one of the boys in Isthmus, the boy laughed and said he knew the Bible by heart and that wasn't in it. But in the hide-covered Bible that Leona kept above the bread-box, it was right there, in Genesis.

The man on the ground began to stir, his hands twitching.

"I'm gonna take him to the shed," Theron said, pulling away from the warmth of his mother's arms.

The man was heavy.

Dragging him through the mud was made more difficult because of the way he was moving, for the legs now kicked a bit, and the man was groaning, but the blood had stopped from the wound on the top of his skull. Theron felt muscles in his arms and legs begin to plump with this effort; he was sore from riding, too, which didn't help, and when he was halfway to the shed, he wished he'd been smart enough to have just thrown the man over Naomi and get him to the shed that way. He smelled the stewpot, for Mama let it cook all day long, and then when the men, meaning him and Daddy, were hungry, they could just ladle out a hefty portion into the bowl themselves, for men were too busy with work to sit down at table until supper time. When he got to the shed, Evan looked up at him, although the glasses had fallen somewhere along the way. Theron could tell by the way he was squinting that he wasn't seeing much right in front of his face.

"It's okay, mister," the boy said, "don't worry."

Evan, scrunching up his face, not quite sure where he was, coughed up some spit, which dribbled down the side of his chin. "Uh-awh," was the noise he made.

Theron rapped on the shed door, not wanting to let go of the man's shoulder with his other hand. "Daddy!" he called, "open up, Daddy!"

The door opened inward, and his father seemed to know what to do. He bent down on one knee, cradling Evan's face between his hands. His father's face was slick with greasy sweat, and there was blood around his eyes where he'd driven the fish-hooks beneath the lids. He brought his face close to Evan's, and kissed the sputtering man on the lips.

Theron knew then that he had done the right thing, for it would mean that spring would come fast now, and that Daddy didn't have to suffer through the hurting season alone. While he kissed the man, Daddy brought the oyster boat hook with its length of chain down beside their lips, and began pressing its rusty point into the man's forehead to carve the *x* of their mark upon him so that the transfer of hurting could begin.

327

Laundry dried by three, with Leona taking it down, and laying it out across the basket. Milla was playing on the tire swing, head first through it, her small fingers clutching desperately at the black sides as she twirled around on it. Mama was napping, as she did in the spring afternoon, and the horses were calm again, after the first wave of screeching. Theron sat out on the dock, twiddling his toes in the icy water, and soon, Daddy came and sat down beside him.

"Give him some rest," Daddy said, but the pain was gone from his eyes, for the first time since Winter Festival.

"No more storms I reckon," Theron said, feeling the weight of his father's arms around his shoulders. A bird was singing from one of the trees, and there were ducks bickering out on the river. Across the bay, the solitary Tangier, so close, so distant.

"You may be right."

"Daddy?"

"Boy?"

"Why does it have to hurt?"

"What do you mean?"

"This life. Why does there have to be a hurting season?"

His father had no reply.

That was what disturbed him about life, the very mystery of it, the deepness of its river, where on the surface all was visible, but beneath, something tugged and grabbed and drowned, and yet the current flowed, regardless.

"Look there." His father pointed off toward Tangier.

Theron squinted, but could only see the island and the emptiness beyond it.

"The curvature of the earth," his father said. "Why does it go in a circle? Who knows? It's for God to decide. But we have our task here. We follow the rituals so the circle remains unbroken."

Theron was fourteen, a man now, he had been kissed, he had helped his father with the serious work of life, he had the mark, but he thought, looking at the eastern horizon, that one day he would go beyond Chite and Tangier and even Isthmus, and see the places that the Yankee had seen, in some yonder springtime. He would take what he knew of his task, of his mark, and show the world what it meant.

The Fruit of Her Womb

Ever move into a new house and find something that the last owners have left? Or even the owners before them? I have, too many times. Growing up, we moved through a few homes, and it was always a treasure hunt to find the strange little things that people left behind when they moved. They seemed magical to me, full of their own stories.

1

I woke up one morning, after a nightmare, and turned to my wife. "I feel like there's no hope left in the world," I said. I felt all my sixty years seeping through in that one sentence.

Her voice was calm, and she held me. "Old man," she said, sweetly mocking, "you need to get your joy back. That's what you need."

After several such mornings, she and I had to make some decisions. We had some savings, and the leftovers of my inheritance, and I felt it was time to retire to the country. When my first pension check came, I told Jackie it was time for the move while we were still fairly young and able, and she went along with it because she always adapted herself to whatever was available. The truth was, I had lost my love for life, and I needed a plot of earth; I just didn't know where or when I would need to be buried in it. I wanted a small town, with woods, with groves, with jays bickering at the window and the sound of locusts in the summer evening—and then, when I turned seventy or so, I wanted to die. These were my projections, and having been an actuarist, I knew that given my height, weight, and predilection for tobacco, that death by stroke might come in the next decade.

And we found all the birds and gardens and quiet in Groveton, not two hours out of Los Angeles, and more, we found a house and I found a reason to wake up in the morning.

The house was beautiful on the outside, a mess within. It had a name: *Tierraroja*, because one of the owners (there had been nine) was named Redlander, and decided to spanish it up a bit in keeping with the looks of the place. An adobe, built in the '40s, it had been a featured spread in *Sunset, The Magazine of Western Living* in 1947, as "typifying the California blend of Spanish and Midwestern influences." Its rooms were few considering its length: three bedrooms, living room, kitchen, but enormous boxcar corridors connecting each chamber around a courtyard full of bird-of-paradise, trumpet-flower vine, and bougainvillea. Beyond the adobe wall to the north, criss-crossed thatches of blackberry vines, dried and mangled by incompetent gardeners, providing natural nests for foxes and opossums. Beyond this, a vast field, empty except for a few rows of orange trees, the last of its grove—ownership unknown, the field separated the property from a neighbor who lived a good four acres away.

We loved it, and the price was reasonable as we'd just moved out of a house in the city that was smaller and more expensive. Jackie had a carpenter in to redo the kitchen cabinets the same day escrow closed. I asked the realtor about the empty field, and he reassured me that the owner, who was a very private person, had no wish to sell the vacant lot. We would have the kind of house we had dreamed of, where I could relax in my relatively early retirement (at 60), and where Jackie could put in the art studio she'd dreamed of since she'd been twenty.

The Fruit of Her Womb

It was on the third day of our occupation of the place that we found the urn. It was ugly, misshapen from too much tossing about, a bit of *faux* Victoriana, dull green nymphs against a dark green background. Jackie found it at the back of the linen closet, behind some old Christmas wrapping papers that had been left behind, presumably by a previous resident. The urn was topped with a lid that looked as if it were an ashtray put to a new use, and sealed with wax.

My wife shook it. "Something inside."

"Here," I said, and she passed it to me. I gave it a couple of good shakes. "Rocks," I said. I sniff everything before I let it get too close to me; this is an odd habit at best, annoying at worst, and applies to clothes, my wife, the dog, and especially socks — a habit acquired in childhood from observing my father doing the same, and feeling a certain pride in a heightened nasal sense as if it were an inherited trait. So, I put the urn to my nose. "Stinks. Like cat vomit." I looked at the pictures. Not just nymphs, but three nymphs dancing with ribbons between them. On closer inspection, I saw that the nymphs had rather nasty expressions on their faces. In one's hand was a spindle of thread, another held the thread out, and the last held a pair of scissors. "It's the Fates in some young aspect," I told my wife, remembering from my sketchy education in the Mediterranean myth-pool. "See, this one spins the thread of life, this one measures it out, and this one cuts it. Or something like that."

Jackie didn't bother looking. She smiled, and said, sarcastically, "You're such a classicist."

"It's pretty ugly," I said. I was ready to take it out to the trash barrel, but Jackie signaled for me to pass it to her.

"I want to keep it," she said, "I can use it for holding paint brushes or something." Jackie was one of those people who hated to waste things; she would turn every old coffee can into something like a pencil-holder or a planter, and once even tried to make broken glasses into some unusual sculpture.

My wife turned the garage into her studio. The garage door opened on both sides, so that while she painted, she could have

331

an open-air environment; the fumes would come up at me, in the bedroom, where I stayed up nights reading, waiting for her to come to bed. But she loved her studio, loved the painting, the fumes, the oils, the ability to look out into the night and find her inspiration. I played with my computer some nights, called some buddies now and again from the old job, and read every book I could on the history of the small California town to which we had come to enjoy the good life. I was even going to have a servant, of sorts: a gardener, named Stu, highly recommended by our realtor, to tend the courtyard, and to keep the blackberry bushes, ever-encroaching, in check, and to bring in ripe plums in August from the two small trees in the back. I was happy about this arrangement, because I knew nothing about dirt and digging and weeding, beyond the basics. And I didn't intend to spend my retirement doing something that I seemed incapable of. Stu and I got on, barely—he was not a man of many words, and we seemed to have no common ground to even begin a conversation. He liked his plants and bushes, and I liked my books and solitude.

Within weeks of being settled, I knew I had nothing to do with my time. I found myself going into town on small, useless errands, to get paper clips, or to see if I could find *The New York Times* at some newsstand within a fifteen mile radius. The town, while not worth describing, was less planned than it was spontaneous: it had been a citrus-boom town before the second world war, and after, it was a town for people to find cute places in, but to not do much else. From the freeway, it looked like stucco and smog, but from within, it was pretty, quaint, quiet, and even charming on a cool October afternoon. The library captivated my interests, since I had been a history teacher, and was an avid reader. It was full of documents about the town and its architecture, fairly unique to southern California, because most of its buildings were a hundred years old rather than built since 1966.

I found our house, *Tierraroja*, had at least one story about it. This I learned, briefly, at first, from a local newspaper account from 1952. It seemed the Redlander family had left suddenly, and the house was empty; no one could discover the mystery of their whereabouts.

When I went to the librarian, a man named Ed Laughlin, he asked me why I was so interested in the house.

"I live there," I said.

He smiled. "Yeah, right."

"No, really. My wife and I moved in the middle of September."

He chuckled, "Who's your realtor?"

I told him the name.

Again he laughed, "Should've known. She's been trying to unload that place for two years."

"Are there ghosts?" I asked, hoping that there might be just for something different.

He shook his head. "Nothing that unbelievable. Just that old Joe Redlander chopped up his wife and kids one night. Nobody knew it until about a year after they were gone. The new owners found body parts all over the place, hidden in secret places. They found Joe eventually up in Mojave, but he claimed he didn't do it. He'd found them like that, he said, but the police weren't buying because first off he ran and second off his prints were all over the ax. Heard he blew his brains out up in Atascadero or someplace like it."

333

2

I parked in front of my wife's studio; the doors were open, letting in the last of October sun, almost a light blue sunlight, through her canvases and jars, making her brown-gray hair seem almost cool and icy. I went up to her, kissed her, and looked at the painting she was doing. It was from memory, of the pond that had been behind her mother's house back in Connecticut. She had just put the light on the water; and it wasn't New England light, but sprays of California light. I waved to Stu, our gardener, who was trimming back what had, in mid-summer been a blossoming trumpet vine, but which was becoming, as winter approached, a tangle of gray sticks.

"He's so dedicated," Jackie said, "I think I'm going to ask him to sit for a portrait. His face—it has those wonderful crags in it. He's just about our age, but he looks older, and then, those lines. And the way he holds the flowers, sometimes." She shook her head in subtle awe, and I wondered if my wife was in the throes of a schoolgirl crush on our gardener.

"We had some murders in our house," I told her, figuring it was the best way to make her think of something other than Stu.

She grinned, shaking her head at me as if I'd been a bad boy. "Good god, you'd think you'd have better things to do than make up stories just to frighten me."

"No, really. I was down at the library. The guy who named our house killed his family. You're not afraid, are you?"

She gave me what I had come, through the years, to call her Look Of False Brain Damage. Then, she set the large flat board she used as a palette down on the cement floor, and began dipping her brushed in turpentine. "Well, I'm finished for the day," she said, "you making dinner, or me?"

I shrugged. "I guess I can. Spaghetti or chicken?"

"Spaghetti's fine," she said, and then, bending over, picking something up. It was the urn. "I still can't get this lid off. I've been prying and prying. Think my Mister Strong-Man can do it?" She passed it to me.

I tried, but could not get the old ashtray off the urn. "You tried melting the wax?"

She shook her head. "Not yet. You're so smart and strong," mocking me, "I'm sure you can get it open for me."

I gave the urn a good shake, and heard that thing inside it again. Hard. Like a large rock. "You know," I said, "this guy Redlander chopped his wife and kids up—there were three—and then put their body parts in weird places in the house. Maybe they didn't find all of them. Maybe one of them's in here. Maybe it's the missing hand of little Katy Redlander."

Jackie made a face. "Don't you dare try and scare me."

"Maybe," I said, "it's Mrs. Redlander's left breast, all hardened around the mummified nipple."

I didn't bother trying to open the urn until after dinner. Jackie went into the living room to watch T.V., and I stayed in the kitchen. I turned on the gas stove, and put the edge of the urn's top near it. Wax began dripping down into the flame, making blue hisses. When the wax seemed to be loosening enough, I pulled on the ash-tray, and it made a sucking sound. Then, I twisted it, and it came off. I wondered if, in fact, little Katy Redlander's missing hand might not be inside the urn. I sniffed at it, and it smelled of tobacco. I held the urn up and tipped it, and out dropped a smoking pipe.

I picked it up off the floor, setting the urn on the edge of the counter. I sniffed the pipe. Smelled like cherry tobacco. A very uninteresting find, although the pipe was quite beautifully carved in rich red wood, a satyr's face. A satyr, I thought, to chase the nymphs of fate on the outside of the urn. Carved clumsily, as if by a child, into the base of the satyr's bearded chin, were the initials, J.R.

Joe Redlander.

"So that's why it's covered with an ash-tray," my wife said when I showed her. "Somebody was trying to quit smoking."

"So he seals his pipe up and hides it."

"Or has someone else hide it for him."

"Joe Redlander," I said.

"Who?"

"The guy—you know, the guy I told you about."

"Oh, right. The Lizzie Borden of Groveton, California."

I paced about the room, holding the pipe in one hand, the urn in the other. Jackie kept shooing me around so she could watch T.V. in peace, but I kept crossing in front of her. "His wife wants him to quit smoking the pipe. But he wants it. So she seals it up, and hides it. He begs her for it. He begs the kids, maybe even bribes them, to show him where Mommy put it. But the kids know better, or else they don't have a clue. And then, when it gets to be too much, he gets the axe he's chopped up all the wood with, that afternoon, and he says, 'Dolores.'"

Jackie interrupted, "Dolores?"

"Whatever," I said. "Joe says, 'Nancy, if you don't tell me where my pipe is, I'm taking you and the kids out.' And she thinks he's joking, so she laughs, and he," and here, I mimed whacking my invisible wife with the pipe.

As if she had a moment of supreme victory, Jackie said, "Ah, just like you and your Baskin-Robbins Pistachio ice cream?"

"I never chopped you up for that, did I?"

"You would've liked to. You were going to become a blimp the way you ate it, it was a kindness to throw it out. The way you whined for days after that, you'd think I took away your soul."

I made a Three Stooges eye-poking gesture at her and an appropriate noise. "Okay, anyway, so then he goes to the kids, and they're screaming, so he does them, too. And to think, if he'd only looked behind the old wrapping paper..."

"The paper was old," Jackie said, "but I don't think it was from the fifties. And that pipe could've belonged to anybody. Jesus, Jim, you need a hobby."

"Look at the initials," I said, to further prove my case, passing the pipe to her.

She looked at the pipe, its carved face, and then squinted at the satyr's beard.

"J.R.," I said, "Joe Redlander. The man who killed his family."

"Your initials, too, Mister Smarypants. Could be James Richter," she reminded me, "maybe the pipe's meant for you."

Later, I put some tobacco in the pipe (for I was an inveterate smoker), and lit it, as if this would give me some inspiration.

3

I found the old crime, and the pipe and urn, occupying my thoughts after that. The wrapping paper wasn't from the '50s, I discovered, but a kind that was sold by Girl Rangers in the mid-seventies. So, I figured, someone else had found the urn, too, and had hidden it. Maybe someone else knew of its secret. I went to the linen closet, and looked back at the cubby hole where the urn had been secreted; I reached back to it, and found, that by pushing one of the shelves aside, there was another hiding area. I moved the towels around, and brought the shelf out. I leaned forward, and reached back into this newfound hole, and only came up with a wadded scrap of note-book paper. It was wrapped in a spider web, which I dusted off, and then, unfolded the paper. It was yellowed, and the kind that had large gaps between the thin red lines—the kind of paper elementary-school age children use before they've become adept at rocker curves and the like. In scraggly block letters in ink, it had several figures written across it. It actually looked like a pictographic language, until I realized that it was not some ancient tongue recorded, but the doodlings of perhaps a six-year-old. At the bottom, an initial "K." I folded it neatly and put it in my pocket. I would ignore it; perhaps throw it out. I didn't even tell Jackie about finding it, because I didn't want her to know the extent to which I was fascinated by the story of the Redlander family.

I went back and read the obituaries of the old local newspaper, *The Groveton Daily*. For 1952, March 17, it listed Virginia Redlander, and her children, Eric, 11, May Lynne, 9, and Katherine, 7. So, there was a Katy Redlander, after all, I thought, how clairvoyant of me to have guessed it, considering I couldn't predict weather or my own wife's mood with anything greater than five percent accuracy. So little Katy had written what looked like a highly-stylized hieroglyphics and had put it back in her secret place, not far from the urn.

"Or maybe you're just bored to death, " Jackie said, when I finally showed her the wrinkled piece of paper that had occupied my mind for three nights in a row.

We were in bed, and she was feeling amorous, while I was being indifferent to sex. "These diagrams," I said, pointing to the one that looked like it had an eye in the middle of it, with some kind of strange animal (a unicorn?) in its iris, "You think a second-grader really did this?"

"My exact question to you," my wife said, turning over, finally. "I think, Jim, maybe you need to go back into teaching at least part-time or as a substitute, because you're driving yourself and me crazy with all this weirdness."

I hadn't even noticed how weird I had become in the past few nights. I looked around my side of the king-sized bed, and there were books on Egyptology, and Runes, and Greek mythology. I had checked out half the local library's classical section, because those diagrams of Katy's resembled a mix of mythic-images, and I wondered if there were some key to it all.

But I was being weird. So, I leaned into my wife, kissing her neck. "I love you," I said.

"I was sure you were enamored of Katy Redlander's ghost."

"I'll throw those things out tomorrow," I whispered, and she turned her face so I could kiss her, and we made love that night, but it was not like it had been when I'd felt more vital. I knew, at my age, I was still fairly young, but I did not believe it, and as my wife and I held each other afterwards, I wondered why it was not as interesting as when I was twenty, or thirty, or even forty, why sex and even food were pleasures that were losing their taste for me; and I wondered why life had to slip like that, why, I thought, looking out the window at the few deciduous trees in the yard, their leaves having turned the pale yellow of California autumn, why can't we be like leaves, more beautiful when we are closer to the ends of our lives?

I thought I saw something there, as I looked at the trees, something dark against the floodlights, not quite human, trotting away from the window as if it had just watched us.

4

In the morning, I went to check the window, as if I would see footprints, but there were none. Jackie skipped her painting that day, and was going to drive into Los Angeles to visit with a friend, so I took to wandering. The empty field that bordered us beckoned me with its orange trees, for they held small but juicy yellow-green fruit, and I decided it was high time to pick an orange right from the tree. The grass in the field was just turning green again, because of a recent rain, and I waded through it, mindful of snakes and fire ants. When I approached the fat orange trees, I glanced back at my house: it seemed tiny, like a house on the edge of a toy train track. The trees were powerfully aromatic, for some tiny white blossoms still clung to the branches; most of the oranges were wrinkled and inedible, but there were a few, at the highest branches, which were plump and only just mature. I got a stick and knocked on the uppermost branches until I managed to bat one down. It rolled into the rich earth that was dark and grassless between the several trees, and I went to retrieve it.

There, on the ground, someone had drawn, with a stick, one of the same diagrams I had seen on Katy's paper.

The eye with the unicorn.

I looked around the other trees, and by each of them, another drawing or diagram. A sketch of a dog? Or a pig? And then, several lines with forked endings—snakes?

But something else, too, there, in the dirt, beneath one of the orange trees: an animal, torn up beyond recognition, the size of a small dog.

Dressed as if for a celebration with dozens of tiny orange blossoms stitched with a gay red thread through its mouth and arounds its eyes, and sutured along its guts.

5

It was a pig, as best I could determine, because in spite of its mutilations, its corkscrew tail was intact, and rather than stink of slaughter, it smelled fragrant with orange and just the scent of mint and sweet pepper—both of which grew wild in any direction across the field.

Children, I thought, and then: Katy Redlander.

The conflicting thought: but she's dead.

Then, a playmate.

Some friend of hers from 1952, who giggled over arcane rituals they'd found in—a book? *The Golden Bough*? Or Jaspar's *The Birth of Mythology*?

Some friend who grew up—would be, what? Forty-nine or so now? And still believed in ritual sacrifice in a sacred grove?

I had read reports of Satanic cults in surrounding towns, and of fringe fundamentalist groups which held snakes and drank poison—how far from that was this?

I left the animal there, and went to spend the rest of the day in the library. I looked up pigs in both the Frazier and Jaspar texts. In Frazier, pigs were associated with the Eleusian Mysteries, the rites of Demeter and the loss of Persephone for half the year—a resurrection cult. But it was in Jaspar's *Birth of Mythology* that I struck gold. In the fifth chapter, on mystery cults, Jaspar writes:

"...what 20th century man fails to realize about these so-called 'cults' is that these rites brought the god or goddess closer to man, so that man, in his ignorance, would be inducted into the mystery of creation. The virgin would be buried with the other offerings for a moon, during which time the participants would dance and sing themselves into a frenzy, and fast, and often commit heinous acts as a way of unleashing the chaos of the human and divine soul, intermingled—all in the name of keeping the world spinning the correct way, of keeping it all in balance. Thus, when the virgin was buried alive, it was not an act of cruelty, but of unbound love for the child and for the very breath of life, for the virgin represented the eternal daughter, who died, was buried, and then resurrected into the arms of the Great Mother after a time in Hell. This is not so different from the rites of crucifixion, and burial of Christ, after all? And in this act, the young woman who was sacrificed mated with the God, and returned to impart wisdom to the other participants in the Mysteries..."

Beneath this were the diagrams I had found in the wadded paper.

On the following page, a color plate showing an urn, of which mine was an obvious replica, of what I had thought were the three fates, dancing.

The caption beneath it read:

The furies in disguise, dancing to lure youths into their circle, so that they might torment them into eternity.

I remembered a quote from somewhere,

Those whom the gods would punish, they first make mad.

And the story of Orestes, who had brought tragedy and dishonor down upon his House, tormented by the Furies in their most horrible aspect.

Joe Redlander with an ax in his hand, holding down little Katy's neck while he went chop-chop-chop.

I could picture the house in disarray, the walls splattered with red, the boy trying to crawl away even while his father slammed the ax into his skull; and the mother, dead, cradling her other daughter, as if both were sleeping on the small rug in the hallway.

I closed my eyes, almost weeping; when I opened them, I was still in the armchair of the reference room of the library. Ed Laughlin, the librarian I'd spoken with before, stood near me. He wore a pale suit which hid most of his paunch; his hair was slick and white, drawn back from the bald spot on top of his head. He squinted to read the cover of the book I had in my hands.

"You feeling okay?" he asked, then, before I could answer, he said, "ah, the ancient world. Fascinating. Coincidentally, I hope you noticed who donated most of our reference works on mythology, particularly fertility cults."

He gestured for the book, and I handed it to him. He flipped it closed, and then opened it to the inside cover. He passed it back to me.

I was not surprised.

The bookplate read: From the Library of Joseph and Virginia Redlander.

"He kills his family and then donates books?" I asked.

Ed didn't smile. "Believe it or not, Joe was a smart man, well-read, quiet, but strong. Admired, here in town, too. When a man cracks, you never know where the light's gonna show through. I guess with Joe it just showed through a bit strong."

"Did you know them well?"

He shook his head. "Barely. I was involved in the library here, but also the county museum over in Berdoo. Joe was always nice, and careful with books. That's about how well I knew him. A hello-goodbye-nice weather kind of thing. It bothers you, too, though, huh?"

I assumed he meant living in the house, knowing about the murders. "Not too much. I find it more fascinating than frightening."

"Well, always got to be some mystery in life, anyway, stirs the blood up a little, but it seems strange to me she never showed."

I asked, "Who?"

"The oldest one. Kim. She was sweet and pretty. Fifteen. Some say she ran away about a year before the killings—she may have had a boyfriend here, met on the sly because her folks were real strict about that kind of thing. Maybe she ran off with him. Maybe she did the killings, gossip was. But I don't think so—she was fifteen and sweet and small, like a little bird. Me, I think she got killed, too, only Joe, he did it somewhere else. I hope I'm wrong. I hope that pretty little girl is all grown up and living across the world and putting it all behind her best she can."

6

My wife was sitting at her canvas, painting, and I arrived swearing, as I went through the area packed with art supplies that surrounded her. "Damn it all," I said, "this is the only garage in creation without garage things."

"Damn right," she responded, "now take your damn language and get the hell out of here." All of this in a calm, carefully modulated voice.

I gave a false laugh, and slapped the inside wall with my hand. "Now, where in hell would a shovel be when I need one?"

Jackie pointed with her paintbrush to the courtyard. "He'd know, Mister Brainiac." She looked more beautiful now, with the late afternoon light on her hair, her face seeming unlined, like she always had to me, and it amazed me, that moment, how love did that between two people: how it takes you out of time, and makes you virtually untouchable.

I turned in the direction of her pointing—it was to Stu, our gardener, kneeling beside the bird-of-paradise, trimming back the dying stems that thrust from between the enormous, stiff leaves. I went out into the yard. "You have a shovel I can borrow?"

He didn't hear me at first.

He was humming; then, he saw my shadow. He turned.

He was only a few years younger than me, but he actually looked older. Not on the surface of his skin (except in laugh and smile lines) but in something I'd seen mainly in cities: a hard life. Not difficult, for all lives are difficult to varying degrees, and some people suffer with more relish than others, but hard, as if the lessons learned were not pleasant ones. I had always thought the gardening life would be a fairly serene one: the planting, growing, flowering, seasonal, balanced kind of thing.

"I need a shovel," I repeated.

"No problem," he said, and stood. He led me out to his truck, and reached in the back of it, withdrawing a hoe and a shovel. "I assume," he said, "you're planting."

"Just digging," I said.

He nodded, handed me the shovel, and set the hoe back down.

"You've done a good job around here," I said.

He almost smiled with pride, but another kind of pride seemed to hold him back. "It's my life," he said, simply, and then returned to work.

I watched him go, his overalls muddy, the muscles in his back and shoulders so pronounced that he seemed to ripple like something dropped into still water. Then, I turned. I didn't know if I was going to bury a dead animal, or to dig something up, something that had been in the ground for four decades. I used the shovel to press my way through the blackberry bush fence that had become thin with autumn, and headed into the field.

343

The stink of the dead pig came back to me, along with the scent of its orange blossom garlands. There was a wind from downfield, and it brought with it these and other smells: of car exhaust, of pies baking, of rotting oranges and other fruit ripening. It almost made bearable the task I was about. When I got to the brief clutch of orange trees, I saw the flies had devoured much of the dead animal, but, oddly, the local coyotes had left it alone.

Behind me, a man's voice, "You planning on burying it?"

I turned; it was Stu, the gardener. He shrugged. "Decided to follow you out here. Figured you could use some help."

He reached up to a branch of one of the trees and plucked off a small blossom. He brought it to his nose, inhaled, and then to his lips. It seemed, to me, that he kissed the blossom before letting it fall.

"Do you know anything about this?" I asked, indicating the pig. "Local kids?"

Stu shook his head. He had kind but weary eyes, like he'd been on the longest journey and had seen much, but now, only wanted sleep. "You won't be burying the pig, will you, Mr. Richter?"

"No," I said.

"What the hell," he said. "I know you know all about it."

"What's that?"

"I hear her, sometimes," he said, "when I touch the leaves."

"Who?"

He looked dead at me, almost angrily. "I don't have nothing to hide. I didn't put her there." He pointed to the ground beneath the dead pig.

"The dead girl."

He whispered, "Not dead." His eyes seemed to grow smaller, lids pressing down hard, like pressing grapes for wine, tears. "I don't believe it."

"You were her friend," I said.

"I love her. I always will love her." Stu wiped at his eyes. "Look around. This field, used to be nothing. Dirt. Nothing would grow. No orange trees. And your house, dead all around, a desert. But she's done this." He spread his arms out wide, as if measuring the distance of the earth.

"Did you do it?" I asked, even though I didn't want to.

"I killed the pig, if that's what you're asking. It's an offering."

"To whom? To Kim Redlander?" I glanced at the ground, wondering how deep she had been buried; buried alive for a Mystery more ancient than what was written down in a book.

"To the goddess," he said.

We went out into the field, as two farmers might after a long day of work, and spoke of the past.

He said, "I have faith in this. I have faith. It wasn't strong at first. He told me he and her mother went all crazy and it was their festival time or something, and what he did...to the other kids...and to Kim...it was 'cause she didn't come up that spring. He went wild, Joe did. I read all the books, later, and I came to a kind of understanding. I spoke to Joe before he killed himself. He lost his faith, you know? He didn't believe anymore. But I had nothing *but* faith. I know she's there. Look." He showed me the palm of his dirt-smeared hand. "She's in the earth, I can see her, there."

Joe Redlander and his family buried their daughter alive, I thought.

For the Mother of Creation, buried her in the earth, Persephone going to the underworld to be with her sworn consort, and they must have expected her to return in the spring. A family of religious nuts, and one teenaged boy, hopelessly in love with a girl.

In love forever.

"It never happened," Stu said, "that's what her dad told me. They waited in the spring, and she didn't return. But I knew she was still here. I know she'll come back, one fine spring day. 'Til then, gardening seems to bring me closer to her."

"She's dead, Stu. I know you weren't responsible. But she's dead. It's been over forty years." I was shivering, a little, because I sensed the truth in his story.

He looked across the land, back to the orange trees. "She's in everything here, everything. You may not believe, but I do. I've known things. I've seen things. She's down there, fifteen, beautiful, her hands touching the roots of the trees. She's going to come up, one day. I absolutely know it."

As we both stood there, I knew that I was going to have to fire Stu, because there was something unbalanced in his story, in his fervor. I didn't think I could bear to look out the windows and see him gardening, thinking of love and loss as he tended flowers.

I knew I would lose sleep for many nights to come, looking out at that field, wondering.

345

7

Then, one night the following April, someone set fire to the field, and, in spite of the best efforts of the local firemen, my wife and I awoke the next morning and found we were living next door to a blackened wasteland. I got my morning coffee, and went to the edge of the field, near the road. The orange trees were standing, but had been turned to crouching embers. I walked across dirt, stepping around the bits of twig that continued to give off breaths of fugitive smoke.

Where the girl had been buried: a deep gouge in the earth.

I watched the field after that, but saw nothing special. In a month, new grass was growing, and by summer, only through the dark bald patches could anyone tell that there'd been a fire at all.

And today, while my wife painted a picture of the courtyard, I went into the garage and found an old tool, a scythe. I took it up and went out into the field to mow. This action was not taken because of some fear or knowledge, for the Mystery remained—I didn't know if some animal had been digging at the hole where Kim Redlander was offered to the world, or if Stu himself had dug her up days before, moving rotting bones to another resting place. I didn't go to the field with any knowledge. I went singing into the field, cutting the hair of the earth, propelled by an urge that seemed older than any other.

Some have called this instinct the Mystery, but the simpler term is Stu's: *faith*.

I swiped the scythe across the fruit of her womb, and gave thanks and praise to the Mother all that day, for I could feel Her now, walking among her children; I spilled my own blood in the moistened dirt for Her.

My wife called to me, waving from the yard, and I turned, holding fast to the bloodied scythe, while I heard a young girl whisper in my ear that faith demands sacrifice.

Life was precious, for that moment, full of meaning, and wonder.

The Fruit of Her Womb

I walked wearily but gladly across the field, and when I reached my wife, her face brightened. "You've found it," she said.

"What's that?"

"Your joy," and she seemed truly happy for me.

"I have." I thought of Joe Redlander, and Stu, and Kim, the believers who brought me to this place.

The scythe seemed to shine like a crescent moon in my hand as I brought it across my wife's neck.

The Ripening Sweetness of Late afternoon

This story is a mytho-hallucinogenic dream. I just loved this world, with its curfew and unusual creatures.

Sunland City was the last place in the world Jesus was ever going to come looking for Roy Shadiak.

He returned to his hometown in his fortieth year, after he felt he could never again sell Jesus to the rabble. Something within him had been eating him up for years. His love for life had long ago dried up, and then so had his marriage and his bitter understanding of how God operated in the world. He'd gotten off the bus out at the flats, and brushed off the boredom of a long trip down infinite highways. He stood a while beside the canals and watched the 'gators as they lay still as death in the muddy shallows. He'd been wearing his ice cream suit for the trip because it was what his mother liked him to wear, and because it was the only suit of his that still fit him. And it fit Sunland City, with its canals and palmettos and merciless sunshine. It was a small town, the City was, and they would think him mad to arrive on the noon bus in anything other than creamy white. He would walk down Hispaniola Street and make a detour into the Flamingo for a double-shot vodka. The boys in there, they'd see him, maybe recognize him, maybe the whores, too, and call him the King, and he'd tell them all about how he was back for good. He'd tell them that he didn't care what the hell happened to Susie and the brats and that doctor she took up with. He'd tell them he was going to open a movie theater or manage the A&P or open a boat-rental business. He'd tell them that anything you really needed, and all you could depend on in this life, you could find in your own backyard. Didn't need God. Nobody needed God.

God was like the phone company: you paid your bill, and sometimes you got cut off, anyway. Sometimes, if you changed your way of thinking, you just did without a phone. Sometimes, you switched companies.

Oh, but he still needed God. Within his secret self, he had to admit it. Roy Shadiak still needed to know that he could save at least one soul in the world. His feet ached in his shoes. He only brought one suitcase. He had just walked out on Susie. It was in his blood to walk. His father had walked, and his grandfather had walked. They probably got tired of Jesus and all the damn charity, too. Even Frankie had walked, as best he could. All leaving before they got left. Roy had blisters on the bottoms of his feet, but still he walked. He passed beneath the Lover's Bridge, and the Bridge of Sighs, with its hanging vines and parrot cages. He walked along the muddy bank of the north canal, knowing that he could close his eyes and still find his way to Hispaniola Street. All the street names were like that: Spanish, or a mix of Indian and Slave, named like Occala and Gitchie and Corona del Mar. Sunland City was a many-flavored thing, but in name only, for its inhabitants would've been pale and translucent as maggots if not for the sulfurous sun. All the canals were thick with lilies, and snapping turtles lounged across the rock islets. The water was murky and stank, but beautiful pure white swans cut across the calm surface as if to belie the muck of this life. Roy saw three men, old-timers, with their fresh-rolled cigarillos and Panama hats, on a punt. He waved to them, but they didn't notice him for they were old and half-blind.

After climbing the steep steps up to the street level again, he was surprised to observe the stillness of clay-baked Sunland City. As a boy, it had always seemed like an Italian water town, not precisely a Venice and something less than a Naples, thrust into the Gulf Coast like a conqueror's flag.

But now it seemed as ancient as any dying European citadel: it looked as if the conqueror, having pillaged and raped, had left a wake of buildings and archways and space. It had been a lively seaport once. It was now a vacant conch. The hurricane that had torn through it the previous year had not touched a building, but it had cleaned the streets of any evidence of life. When he found the Flamingo, he kissed the first girl he set eyes on, a wench in the first degree with a beer in one hand with which to wipe off that same kiss. A teenage boy in a letterman's jacket sat two stools over. The boy turned and stared at him for a good long while before saying anything. Then, suddenly, as if possessed, the boy shouted, "Holy shit, you're King!"

"And you, my friend, are underage."

The boy stood up—he was tall and gangly, with a mop of curly blond hair, a face of dimming acne, and cheek of tan. He thrust his hand out. "Billy Wright. *I* swim, too."

"Oh."

"But you're like a legend. A fucking legend. The King. King Shadiak."

"Am I?"

"You beat out every team to Daytona Beach. You beat out fucking Houston."

"Did I? Well, it was a long time before you were born."

"You ever see the display they got on you?" Billy pressed his palms flat against the air. "The glass cabinet in the front hall, near the locker room. Seven gold trophies. Seven! Pictures! Your goggles, too. Your fucking goggles, man."

"If they do all that for you at your high school, you should really be something, shouldn't you?"

Billy made a thumbs up sign. "Fucking-A. You *are* something, man."

"I'm nothing," Roy said, downing his drink, and slamming the glass on the bar for another. "No, make that: I'm fucking nothing, man."

"What you been doin' all this time, man?" Billy asked, apparently oblivious to anything short of his own cries of adoration.

"Selling Jesus."

"Who'd you sell him to?"

Roy laughed. "You're all right, boy. You are all right."

"Thanks," Billy said, then glanced at his watch. "I better get going. Curfew soon. Listen, you come by and see me if you got car trouble. I work at night at Jack Thompson's. You know him? I can fix any problem with any car. I'm not the King of anything like you, but I may be the Prince of Mechanics."

"Why would anyone care if his car got fixed around here?"

The boy laughed. "That's a good one."

When Roy arrived at his mother's house a half-hour later, he was three beers short of a dozen.

"The great King comes home." His mother's voice was flat, like the land. "You had to get drunk before you saw me. And you couldn't shave for me, could you?" Alice Shadiak asked. His mother wore khaki slacks and a white blouse. She had lost some weight over the past few years, and seemed whiter, as if the sun had bleached her bones right through her skin. A sun-visor cap protected her face. She had seen him from the kitchen window, and had come to greet him on the porch. "I suppose you need a place to stay."

"I can stay downtown."

"With your whores?"

"They all missed curfew, apparently," he attempted a light note. "Must've heard I was on my way."

His mother sighed as if a great weight had just been given her. "Some man of God you turned out to be. I just wish you'd've called ahead. I'd've had Louise fix up your old room. Lloyd's in Sherry's old room. The house is a mess. Don't act like such a foreigner, Roy, for god's sakes. Give me a hug, would you?" She moved forward. In all his life, he could count the times she'd hugged him. But he knew he needed to change, somehow. He had not hit on precisely how. He would have to listen to his own instincts, and then disobey them to find out how he might change. He held his mother, smelled her saltwater hair. When he let go, she said, "Susie called. She wants to know when you're going to forgive her."

"Never," Roy said.

"What are you going to do?" Alice asked.

Roy Shadiak said, "Mama, I had a dream. It came to me one night. A voice said—"

His mother interrupted. "Was it Jesus?"

"It was just a voice. It said, 'Set your place at the table.' Something's trying to come through me. I know it. I can feel it. Like a revelation."

"It was just a dream," Alice said, sounding troubled. "What could it mean? Oh, Roy, you're vexing yourself over nothing."

"This is my table. Sunland City. I have to set my place here," Roy said. Then, he began weeping. His mother held him, but not too close.

"A man as big as you shouldn't be crying."

"It's all I have left," he said, drying his tears on the cuffs of his shirt. "You live your life and make a few mistakes, but you lose everything anyway. Everything I ever had, it all came from here. Everything I ever *was*."

Alice Shadiak took a good hard look at her son and slapped him with the back of her hand. "You did it to yourself, what you are. Who you are. Don't blame me or your father or anyone else. All this big world talk and wife-leaving and crying. Don't think just because it's been twenty-two years that you can just walk back in here and pretend none of it ever happened." She raised her fist, not at him, but at the sky, the open sky that was colored the most glorious blue with cloud striations across its curved spine. "No God who takes my boys away from me is welcome in my house."

"I told you, I don't work for God anymore," Roy said. He went past her, into the house. He found the guest bedroom cluttered, but pushed aside his mother's sewing and the stacks of magazines on the bed. He wrapped the quilt around his shoulders, and fell asleep in his suit.

353

In the morning, he took a milk crate down to the town center. He set it down and stood up on it just like he would in other towns when he had preached the gospel. Folks passed by on their way to work, and barely noticed him. He spread his arms out as if measuring Sunland City and cried out, "I am King Shadiak and I have come here to atone for the murders of my brother Frankie and his friend, Kip Renner!"

A woman turned about as she stepped; a laborer in a broad straw hat glanced up from the curb where he sat with a coffee cup; an old Ford pick-up slowed as its owner rolled down the window to hear.

As Roy Shadiak spoke, others gathered around him, the older crowd, mostly, the crowd that knew him, the people who had been there when he'd drowned the two boys at the public swimming pool over on Hispaniola Street, down near the Esso station, by the railroad tracks.

"No need, Roy," one of the men called out. "We don't need your kind of atonement. We been fine all these years without it."

"That's right," several people added, and others nodded without uttering a word.

"No," Roy said, pressing the flat of his hand against the air in front of him as if it were an invisible wall. "All these years I've squandered my life in service to others. I owe Sunland City an atonement."

"You want us to crucify you, King?" Someone laughed.

Others chuckled more quietly.

"That is exactly what I want," Roy Shadiak said. "Two atonements, two murders."

A woman in the crowd shouted, "Two atonements for two murders!"

"Two atonements! Two murders!" Others began chanting.

"Frankie Shadiak!" Roy shouted. "Kip Renner!"

"Two atonements! Two murders!" The crowd became familiar now—Roy saw Ellen Mawbry from tenth grade, Willy Potter from the corner store, the entire Forster clan, the Rogers', the Sayres', the Blankenships', the Fowlers'—as he chanted and as they chanted as the day loped forward, they all gathered—labor stopped, activity ceased, schools let out for a spontaneous holiday, until the town center of Sunland City was a sea of the familiar and the new. All turned out for the returning hero, their King, who passed among them to offer his life for their suffering.

"Two atonements!" they cried as if their voices would reach beyond that Florida sky.

It was what Roy expected from a town that God had turned his back on twenty-three years before.

And then Helen Renner, her hair gone white, stepped out of the crowd, towards him. She wiped her hands on her apron, as if she'd just finished baking, and went and stood at the foot of the milk crate.

Roy crouched down, and took her face in his hands.

"Don't do it," she said. "Roy Shadiak, don't you do it. Neither one of them was worth it. We all let it happen. We're all responsible. It may not even fix anything, Roy. There's no guarantee."

His kissed her on her forehead. "I've got to. It's something inside of me that needs room to grow, and I've been killing it all these years. I've been killing every one of you, too. Two atonements," he repeated, "for two murders."

355

Joe Fowler was a crackerjack carpenter. He and his assistant, Jaspar, were at the Shadiak house within an hour of Roy's leave-taking of the makeshift podium. He stood on the porch in paint-spatter overalls, his khaki hat in his hands, looking through the screen door at Roy's mother. "We got some railroad ties from out the Yard," he said. "They got pitch on'em, but I think they gonna be just fine for the job." His voice quavered. "We'd like to offer our services, Alice."

Alice Shadiak stood like stone. "You and your kind can get off my porch. I don't mean to lose two sons in this lifetime."

Roy came up behind her, touching her gently on the shoulder. "Mama, it's got to be done."

"Where is it written? Where?"

"On my soul," he said.

"Our kind has no soul," she said, pulling away from him. "I don't need God's forgiveness on my house. I don't want sweet Jesus' tears."

"It's Jesus that keeps you here."

"He doesn't even look on us, Roy," his mother said. "He doesn't even come to our churches. What does it matter? Does anyone in Sunland really believe there's a Jesus waiting to shine his light on us?"

"That's because of me."

"It's because your brother and his sick little friend were unnatural and perverted, and God cared more for them than for decency or nature or for any of us. I don't mind burning for that, Roy. I don't mind that sacrifice."

"I do," Roy said. "I saw Jesus out in the fields up north, and in the alleys of the fallen. Nobody else did. And you know why? Because Jesus was laughing at me, he was showing me that he was not going to be mine. He was going to belong to every fool who walked this earth."

Joe Fowler nudged the screen door open and stepped inside. "He's right, Alice. We ain't had Jesus or God for all this time, only those...things." He shivered a little, as if remembering a nightmare. In a softer voice, he said, "I'm getting tired of this life."

"I would advise you to get out of the light, Joe," Alice Shadiak said, sounding like the retired schoolteacher that she was. "I heard about your little Nadine."

All of them were silent for a moment, and Roy thought for a second he heard the cry of some hawk as it located its prey.

"Your boy knows what he's doing," Joe said, spreading his hands like he could convince her with gestures. Still, he glanced briefly up at the empty sky. "We can't keep on like this." Then, Joe grinned, but Roy could tell he was tense. "I'm prouder of you now, King, than I was when you won all those ribbons at the championship. Why don't we get on with this business?"

"Yes," Roy said, feeling an ache in his heart for Susie and the kids, but not wanting to retrace his steps. He glanced out on the porch, and beyond, to Joe's truck. "That's a sturdy looking piece of wood, Joe."

"From the old Tuskegee route, before tracks got tore up. We're going to have to balance them good. That's why I brought Jaspar here." He nodded towards his assistant who stood, mutely, on the porch. "We can get this going now, you like."

"Why wait?" Roy shrugged.

His mother retreated into the shadowy parlor. She called to him, but Roy did not respond.

Jaspar suddenly pointed to the sky and made a rasping sound in his throat.

Calmly, Joe Fowler said, "Come on in Jasp, come on, it's okay, you'll make it."

As if too frightened to move, Jaspar stood there, sweat shining on his face. He stared up at the sky, pointing and shaking.

"Jaspar." Joe opened the screen porch slightly, beckoning with his hand.

Roy shoved Joe out of the way, and ran out to the porch. He grabbed the young man by his waist.

The cry grew louder as the great bird in the sky dropped, blackening out the sun for a moment.

357

The smell was the worst thing, because they got it on their talons sometimes, from an earlier victim, that sweet awful stink that overrode all other senses.

Roy hadn't slept a night without remembering that smell. He couldn't get it out of his head for the rest of the afternoon.

"Where do they take them?" Roy asked.

Joe, who was still jittery, helped himself to the vodka. "Down to the shore. There's at least a hundred out there. And the rotting seaweed, too, and the flies, all the crawling things...it turned my stomach when I had to go down there to try and find Nadine."

"That's where it has to be."

"No, King. No. I won't go down there, no matter if it's midnight or midday."

"But how can you abandon her?"

Joe turned his face towards his glass. "She ain't her. I saw her. I risked my sanity, and I saw her. It ain't her. It's an It, not a little girl. I told her not to go out between two and four. All of us know about the curfew. All of us know to stay inside. And you," Joe shook his head. He raised his glass, as if to toast Roy. "You're the luckiest son of a bitch alive, you can get out, and instead, you decide to come back. You fucked up once, King, you don't need to keep on doing it."

"How many are left?"

"First, have a drink." Joe pushed the glass across the kitchen table.

Roy picked it up. Downed the remainder. Set the glass down. "How many?"

"Twenty-six in one piece. The rest in as many as they leave us in. Some morning, you take a walk down there. Only, if any of them calls your name, you just run, you hear? You don't want to know who it is, believe you me."

Roy reached across the table and pressed his hand against Joe's shoulder. "That's where we need to do it."

"I ain't never going down there again."

"You'd rather all this continued?"

"Than go down there? You're damned right."

"I'll find someone else, then."

Joe stood up, pushing his chair back. He said nothing. He stomped out of the kitchen, and went to sit with Jaspar and Alice.

Roy drank some more vodka. He glanced out the bay window. On the roof, two houses over, three of them had a woman pressed against the curved Spanish tile. Their wings had folded against their bodies, and they were digging with their talons into the soft flesh of her stomach.

He was sure that one of them saw him spying, and grinned.

That night, he found the teenager working at Jack Thompson's garage on the south corner of Hattatonquee Plaza.

"Billy?" Roy asked as he stood beneath a streetlamp.

The Ripening Sweetness of Late Afternoon

The boy dropped the wrench he was using, and bounded out to the sidewalk. "Hey, it's the King. How you doin'?" He snapped his fingers several times as if he was nervous.

"I'm doing just fine. And yourself?"

"Hey, any day you get through the afternoon here's a good day. So I heard you're going to try something."

Roy nodded. "Let's go for a walk, Billy. Can you get off work?"

"Sure, let me just tell Mr. Thompson, okay?"

Several minutes later, they were walking down along Hispaniola Street towards Upper Street. Roy had been doing all the talking, ending with, "And that's where you come in. Joe'll give me the ties, but I need someone to help."

"I don't know," Billy said. "You ever see how big those suckers are?"

"Yep. But we won't be out that late. We can do this at nine or ten in the morning. Hell, if you want, we can probably do it tonight."

"I heard the beach is really a bad scene. My dad got taken down there. I heard this guy at school say that they're like cracked eggs or they're all ripped up, only not quite dead yet. If I think about it too much I get sick."

"It must be strange."

"What's that?"

"Well, you grew up in it. You never knew what the world was like before. You don't know what the rest of the world is like."

Billy stopped walking. "I thought it happened everywhere."

Roy shook his head. "Only here. Because of what I did."

"I don't believe you."

"Other places, you can walk around any time of the day or night and those things don't attack. Honest. When I was the King here, I used to skip classes at two and take off with my friends to Edgewater to the McDonald's. Didn't anyone tell you? Not even your dad?"

Billy shook his head. "Well, if God did this, why didn't he do it just to you?"

Roy shrugged. "Who knows? It may not even have been God. I've never seen Jesus. Maybe there's just those things. The way I figured it, it's not just because of me killing those boys. It's because everybody here thought it was okay, no big deal. Nobody made a fuss."

"You loved your brother?"

"I did, but I didn't know it then. I wanted him and his friend to go to hell, back then. I was the King back then. I thought I was God, I guess."

They came to the end of Upper Street, which stopped at the slight dune overlooking the stretch of flat beach.

The full moon shone across the glassy sea. The sand itself glowed an unearthly green from the diatoms that had burst from the waves.

On the sand, the shadow of slow, pained movement as a hundred or more mangled, half-eaten Sunlanders struggled to die in a corner of the earth where there was no death.

Billy said, "I saw one of them up close. When they got my dad. She had long hair, and her eyes were silver. She had the fur, and the claws and all, and her wings, like a pterodactyl. But there was something in her face that was almost human. Even when she tore my dad's throat open, she looked kind of like a girl. Boy," he shivered. "I'm sure glad I'm up here and not down there. Down there looks like hell."

Roy said, "From down there, up here looks like hell, too. And it won't just end by itself."

Billy seemed to understand. "You swear you're not lying about what everywhere else is like?"

"I swear."

"Okay. Let's go down there. But in the morning. After the sun's up. I still can't believe it." Billy cocked his head to the side, looking from the moon to the sand to the sea to Roy. "I'm standing here with the King."

"Is that enough for you?"

"I guess. I got laid once, and that was enough. Standing here with you, that's enough." Billy pointed out someone, perhaps a woman, trying to stand up by pushing herself against a mass of writhing bodies, but she fell each time she made the attempt. "When

I was little, we used to come down here and throw stones at some of them. But it's kind of sad, ain't it? Some of the guys I used to throw stones with, they're down there now. Some day, I'm going to be down there, too, and if there are any girls left, they'll have babies, and they'll start throwing stones at me, too. Where does it end?"

"Now," Roy said. "In the morning. You and me and a couple of railroad ties."

"There's going to be lots of pain though, huh?"

"There's always pain. You either get it over with quick, or it takes a lifetime."

Billy rubbed his hands over his eyes. "I'm not crying or nothing."

"I know."

"I just want to get my head straight for this. I mean, we're both going to hurt, huh?"

"You don't have to. I do. I can find someone else to help."

"No. We'll do it. Then I'll be a legend, too, huh? Maybe that's enough. We just drag those ties down there and set it up. One way or another, we all end up on that beach, anyway, huh?"

It was easier said than done, for they had to borrow Joe's truck to get the railroad ties to the beach, which was the easy part. Lugging those enormous sticks across the burning sand, sliding them across the bodies, the faces...it made a mile on a Thursday morning at nine a.m. seem like forty or more. By the time they'd arrived at a clearing, Billy was too exhausted to speak. When he finally did, he pointed back at Sunland. "Look."

Roy, whose body was soaked, his ice cream suit sticking to his skin, glanced up.

There, on the edge of Upper Street and Beach Boulevard was the entire town, lined up as if to watch some elegant ocean liner pass by. The chanting began later. At first the words were indistinct. Gradually, the boy and the man could hear them clearly: *Two murders, two atonements.*

"Roy?" Billy asked.

"Yes?"

"I'm scared. I'm really scared."

"It's okay. I'm here. I'll go first."

"No. I want to go first. I want you to do me first. I might run if I go last. I can't do it right if I go last—I mean, I'll fuck it up somehow."

"All right." Roy went over and put his arm across Billy's shoulder. "Don't be afraid, son. When this is over, it'll all change again. Atonement works like that."

"I wasn't even born when you did it. Why shouldn't one of them do it with you? Why me?"

"Now, Billy, don't be afraid. If they could've done it before, they would've. I think Jesus brought you and me together for this."

"I don't even know Jesus."

"You will. Come on." Roy lifted up one of the smaller spikes and placed its end against Billy's wrist. "This one'll fit. See? It's not so bad. It's just a nail. And all a nail can do is set something in place. It's so you won't fall. You don't want to fall do you?"

"Tell me again how you'll do it?"

"Oh, well, I set this rope up around my hand so I can keep it up like this...and then I press the pointed part of the nail against my hand and pull on the rope. My hand goes back in place, see? Like this, only I have to push a little, too."

"You won't leave me, will you?"

"No, I won't. I'm the King, and you're the Prince, remember? I won't abandon you. Now why don't you just lie down on it, like that, and your hand, see? It's going to pinch a little, but just pretend its one of those things with the claws. Just pretend you won't scream because you know they like it when someone screams. Okay? Billy, don't be afraid, don't be afraid..." Roy spoke soothingly as he drove the spikes through Billy's wrists.

By two, they'd both gotten used to the pain of the crosses. Roy tried to turn his head towards Billy to see how he was holding up, but his neck was too stiff and he could not.

"When's it going to happen?" Billy's voice seemed weak.

The Ripening Sweetness of Late Afternoon

"Soon, I guarantee it. I had a dream from God, Billy. Something inside of me knew what to do."

Billy began weeping. "Just because of a couple of queers. What kind of God is that?"

"It's the only God."

"I don't believe it," Billy whimpered. "I don't believe that God would punish everyone just because of what you did. I don't believe that God would punish the unborn just because of what you did. It's all a lie, ain't it? We just did something stupid, building crosses and crucifying ourselves. Look at that, look up."

Roy tried to look up, but he couldn't. What he could see was the endless sea, and the shimmering sky as the sun crisped the edges of the afternoon. The smell was growing stronger from the bodies.

"I don't believe in God!" Billy cried. "Somebody! Get me down! Get me down! He's crazy! Somebody help me! Somebody get me down! Jesus!"

Roy tried to calm him with words, but Billy didn't stop screaming until an angel dropped from the sky and tore into him.

Roy remained, untouched, on the cross, amidst the writhing bodies on the shore of the damned. He waited for some sign of his atonement, but only night came, and then day, and then the long afternoon set in.

THE MYSTERIES OF PARIS

1

We become what we are most afraid of, it's true. I don't need to tell you the stories about the man terrified of fire who becomes a fireman, or the woman terrified of aging who grows old; neither do you really need to hear about the boy afraid of going bald, who, of course, grows up to lose his hair. Fear is often the crossing signal, the flashing light, before the train of inevitability; but fear is Cassandra, and she heralds what will be, and still we try to look the other way and pretend it will not come to pass.

But sometimes the lights are out and we cross the tracks unheeding.

Let me tell you about a town called Paris, not in France or Texas or in its dozen other namesakes with which you might be familiar, but Paris, Arizona, not far across the Colorado River from California. In fact, if you lived in this Paris, you might cross the state line just to get a decent Big Mac at McDonalds, or if you came through late one night, you might need to turn around just to get diesel if you owned an old shitkicker '83 Mercedes, which you bought for five hundred dollars not six months ago from a mule skinner on his way to Mexico.

You learn all this when you stop for gas in Paris, and you find there is no diesel, and you are just about on empty.

But best of all, you learn the secret of fear.

2

"We been out of diesel for a week now, won't get filled up till maybe Monday afternoon. I tell you, there's a diesel place back in Blythe—maybe second, third stop back over the California line," the boy said—he was about seventeen, and heavily into the black leather look, which always made the man think of nerds he had known in high school, those who wore clothes to up their images. The boy looked at the dent on the front of the Mercedes in the fluorescent light by the pumps. He walked around the car. "Bad accident, mister?"

The man shrugged, craning his neck farther out the window. "Before I bought it. I got it cheap from this old desert rat who had to move to Mexico."

"What's cheap?" the boy asked.

"Five hundred."

"No shit? I don't believe you—no shit?" The boy blinked, and dug his hands into the pockets of his leather jacket. "Jesus, what I'da given for this. Four, five thousand, end of story. That's if I had it to *give*."

"Yeah, but the problem is, it's diesel. Hard to find these days, especially out here."

"Blythe's only twenty miles back."

The man shook his head. "It's on empty. I don't want to get stuck between here and there. Don't like dark roads. Makes me think of psychos and serial killers."

The boy half smiled and said, "This is one of their highways, apparently."

The man blinked. "What do you mean?"

"Well, you know, for some reason every damn serial killer seems to come through here at one time or another. Seems that way to me, anyway. I know this cop, and he helped catch one of 'em, not ten miles t'other side of town. Said the man had a woman helpin' him murder too, just like looking two rattlesnakes in the eyes, this cop said." The boy's mouth dropped from a grin into a straight line. "I don't like working graveyard because of it. This town's so dead, sometimes I think, when I walk home, that somebody's come right off the highway, someone like you, mister, even, and he's killed everybody in town, and I'll go home and my folks'll be dead too, and then I can't call nobody for help."

"Jesus," the man said.

The boy brightened again, giggling. "And then I think, Chad, you dick, you got the most active imagination and no serial killer'd even bother to stop in your sorry-ass gas station…Look, I can give you a lift, mister. I get off shift at midnight. Cooter—he's graveyard—he sometimes comes in late, but no more'n half an hour. Look, I can give you a ride to Blythe, be back here fast, you got your gas, and I don't get my ass fried. End of story."

"I don't want to put you out. Really. That's a lot of trouble."

"It's either that," the boy said, "or you stay up with Cooter all night and drink coffee and wait for the three-fifteen bus from El Paso to come through for a fill-up and give the riders a place to pee."

"Well, to be honest, I think it might be a better idea if I just go get a room at the local Motel 6. In the morning I can either call Triple A or try and make it back to Blythe. I have this thing about night."

"The dark?" The boy leaned forward, placing his hands against the car door. He drummed his fingers on the metal.

"Not particularly, just night. Like you said, anyone can come off this highway. I heard a whole family got killed by a hitcher near Indio. And it was someone they knew. I just don't like thinking about it. It's always at night, those things. If I'm going to get stuck somewhere without gas, I'd prefer it be in broad of daylight."

The boy added a bit of Arizona wisdom, "That's true everywhere else but here, mister. Here you don't want to get caught in the sun at noon, believe you me. This is the deadest place on the planet."

"I guess I'm just tired," the man said, not wanting to tell the real reason that he didn't want to ride with the boy. "I need a good night's sleep. I can figure the headache of diesel out in the morning."

The boy chuckled at the turn of phrase. "Headache of diesel, ain't it the truth. Oh. Yeah. That's a good idea. I mean, if you don't want a lift," the boy said, and pointed his thumb at the tow truck that was parked behind him. "We got a company truck and all, though, filled with gas, we can be in Blythe before twelve-thirty, and back before one. You could just keep on driving. I'd do it."

"Well," the man said, "thanks anyway. Can you point me in the direction of the nearest motel?"

The boy grinned. He was innocent in a way that the man had not experienced since maybe 1962, and this was '95, January seventh, and teenage boys of his age were supposed to be sullen and rude and helpless. But not this one; the man accounted for it by the small town. Paris, Arizona, and the sign had read (unless he imagined things) Population 65. Someone had crossed it out with bullet holes, a sign on the highway that was used for target practice. Population 65. Sixty-five people, living in a town with a single all-night gas station, a town of what appeared to be a smattering of one-story two-bedroom houses, vintage World War Two, with flat roofs and barracklike precision to the arrangement of the downtown area—the man had had to go through Main Street, all of three blocks, to get to the light of the gas station. And then this boy, like a beacon of innocence. The boy had squinty eyes and lots of dark hair, falling neatly on either side of his forehead. The man had always lived in cities, big cities like Los Angeles and New York, and found it refreshing on these occasional jaunts to find youth that seemed to harken back to his own green days, unaware of urban problems and of the difficulties of modern life. This boy looked as if his furthest horizon was Blythe to the west, maybe Phoenix to the east, and to the south and north, just the river as it snaked along. He probably had a nice nerdy girlfriend who was going to get pregnant before the winter was over, and he probably was going to pump gas for the rest of his life.

Not a bad existence, all things considered, the man thought.

The boy said, "We don't exactly have a Motel 6 or nothin', but there's the Miller's Motor Coach Inn two miles up, just when you're leavin' town. It's usually pretty vacant because we don't get a lot of snowbirds comin' through, not the way towns right on the river do. I think it's about twenty bucks a night." He leaned into the window, close enough for the man to smell his breath, which was sweet, like he'd been chewing on orange blossoms all night. "I take my girl over there now and then. It ain't the best place, mister, but it does the job."

"Great, sounds good," the man said, and started his engine up again.

The boy in black leather stood away from the blue Mercedes and leaned against one of the pumps. He grinned again. "You see the lady who runs that place, you tell her Phil's boy sent you."

"Will do," the man said.

As he drove out of the gas station, he glanced in his rearview mirror, and noticed that the boy just stood there, watching him go, leaning against the pumps.

It was a circuitous route to get back on the highway, but he finally did, and saw the green sputtering neon of Miller's Motor Coach Inn—the sign was lit to read MILL MOT R OACH IN. There was a buzzing yellow neon sign that read *Vacancy* out front, although he would've been more surprised if the place was full. The man wondered what he was getting into, but hoped it was a nice firm bed and maybe seven hours' sleep before he'd have to deal with all that called to him the following day. He parked near the small front office. The lights were down inside, but he got out of the car and went up and rang the bell by the door.

RING BELL FOR NIGHT MANAGER, the sign read. In fact, he noticed a sign plastered everywhere inside the dimly lit little office. He rang the bell twice more, but no one came. There were three cars in the parking lot, over near the rooms, so he knew that the place was operational.

Then the man got the strangest feeling. It was a feeling of being watched, not just by one person, but by several. The hairs on the back of his neck stood up, or it felt like they had. He glanced around the motel, and then down the dark street, lit with feeble lamps for only a few yards beyond the motel.

Headlights from the highway as several trucks passed by.

369

No one came to the office door, and he was about to go back to his car when the phone in the office began ringing. It was a bell-ringer, the kind of phone that the man missed, the kind that made a rather nice sound rather than the computerized electronic annoyances that phones emitted elsewhere.

So, he thought, someone will come to answer the phone.

He noticed a coffee mug and a half-eaten doughnut on the counter, and a ball of yarn sitting next to the phone.

The boy's words haunted him. *Somebody's come right off the highway, someone like you, mister, even, and he's killed everybody in town.*

The phone rang twelve times before it stopped.

The man had already gotten into his car. He was feeling uncomfortable, and he wasn't sure why. The place was so dead, he told himself, that was the problem. He had always liked cities, because there were always lights and people around, someplace, even if it was the train station, which was always open. Not that he ever ventured down to Union Station in Los Angeles at four in the morning, but just the thought had been a comfort to him. The thought that there was life and light. He swallowed. *Don't think about it.* Where to go next? His choices were to either drive back to Blythe, hoping that his gas tank would hold out, or sleep in the car.

Or go find that kid and get him to drive you to Blythe and back.

On a lark, he switched on the light in the Mercedes and drew the Triple A *Guide to Arizona* (from 1984) out of the glove compartment. He flipped pages to try to find Paris, and when he did, all it said was:

Paris, Arizona. Pop. 71

So, six smart people got the hell out of here.

He turned on the radio; nothing but static. Turned it off again— static and country music, all the way from Indio, and now just the idiot airwaves of confusion. *Like me.* Something about the static made him sweat a little. Keep it down, keep it down, he thought. Now, the man, if he could, would've kicked himself right smack in the butt. He owned another car, a good old Honda Prelude, but he had put it in the shop for repairs, and then, when this conference came up in Phoenix, he had thought: What the hell, take the Mercedes, even with the dent in it, it'll be a novelty for all those old farts with their spanking new Beamers and Porsches. Don't call the shop to get the Prelude back early, just drive the diesel, you moron.

3

It took him ten minutes to get back to the gas station—he stopped every street or so in order to curse his sorry fate, and to calm down. The town was empty, the lights off in stores, even most of the streetlights were off. A few stores had GOING OUT OF BUSINESS signs up in their windows; others were too dark to see into. It was Thursday night, just about midnight, and this was a place where even the kids didn't run wild. Good lord, deliver me from small towns, the man thought.

The boy was sitting on a chair in front of the gas station office. He was leaning his head back, drinking a bottle of Yoo-Hoo. He looked up when the Mercedes pulled up and parked. He shook his head, smiling, and set the bottle down. He jogged over to the car just as the man got out, stretching his legs, yawning.

"Don't tell me that place was full-up," the boy said.

"No. Just nobody came to the door."

"That's weird," the boy said, "the woman who runs it, she don't sleep much, she's a what you call…"

"Insomniac."

"Thank you, and she usually is right up front where you can see her, knitting. Ain't that weird? I mean, it's been so silent tonight all over town too, now I think of it. She wasn't out front knitting? Weird."

The man remembered the yarn by the phone. "She was probably in the bathroom or something."

"How long you wait?"

"Ten minutes. But I rang the bell the whole time, and then the phone rang and nobody answered it."

"Ain't that strange, I was just, earlier tonight, talking to her, when…" The boy seemed briefly lost in thought, and then thrust his hand out. "Name's Chad Partridge, never introduced myself, my mama'd say where'd your manners go, young man, and I'da told her, after midnight, they always seem to go into hiding."

The man said, "Hello, Chad, I'm Bill."

"You got a last name, don't you?"

The man laughed. "Yes, I do. Mudd. People make fun of it, though, so I'm loath to admit to it."

The boy said, "That's a nice one. I sorta collect names, you know, when I'm workin' late, like I could tell you the name of everyone in Paris, backward, forward, I got that kind of mind, even though I ain't too smart in other ways. We got a woman named Hogg livin' here, and the great part is her first name and middle initial, Sue E. Pretty good, huh? And my uncle Jack, his last name's Coffman, and if you put those together, you got a pretty dirty joke, you was to ask me."

Bill Mudd laughed good-naturedly. "Amazing. Listen, is your friend—what was his name?"

The boy's expression changed. It almost looked like he was blushing.

"Cooter?"

"Oh," the boy sighed, "lordy, I didn't know what you meant for a sec, *Cooter*, he ain't been in yet, and it's"—the boy held his arm out in front of him and glanced at his wristwatch—"twelve-fifteen. Let me go call him, Bill, wait just a sec."

Bill went over to use the rest room while Chad went to make his call. The rest room was clean, and after using the urinal, Bill went to wash his hands and then his face at the sink. The soap powder smelled like Ajax, but it was nice to get some of the road stink off of his skin. He looked at his face in the mirror. *You stupid idiot, what the hell are you scared of? A nerd in black leather, a town on the edge of a vast nothing? Of all people, what the hell are you scared of?*

But he knew what he was scared of, it was a fear he'd had since as far back as he could remember. Totally irrational, but something that he'd had since he'd seen a *Time* magazine when he'd been seven, and in it a man had gone on a killing rampage. They'd showed the dead woman, one of the six, in *Time*. And then, growing up, how many others had he seen? Movies, too, that were totally unreal, and then he had been at a party and someone had mentioned another bout of...

He just didn't like naming it.

Unlike Chad, who could apparently name everything he'd ever come in contact with. (Like a collector, that boy was, only he collected the labels, and not what was behind them.)

He couldn't name it, and he knew everything there was to be studied about fears. Bill Mudd was no psychoanalyst, but he had spent his spare time reading every book, every article, he could get his hands on, about specific phobias, only he never found his, never precisely found the word that captured the fear he held inside, held on to tightly and could not deny.

He could put it in a phrase, of course.

It was a fear that someone near him was a psycho killer.

(He knew how inelegant and stupid that phrase sounded, but it was the best he could do.)

373

If they were in institutions, like Darden State, in L.A. County, it bothered him less, because then he knew. He *knew* they were psychos. He didn't need to second-guess someone on the psych ward. They had their labels.

But people on the outside...they were different. You couldn't always know. They could look just like a kid at a gas station who wanted to take you for a ride to get gas.

But what if a psycho killer, a serial killer in the making, looked just like anybody? Any ordinary person?

This was not precisely paranoia, but a close cousin.

It was a persistent fear for him, not a heightened awareness, but something that attacked him only in its most extreme incarnations. In Los Angeles he could read the newspapers and watch television—in fact, keep it on at his home 'round the clock—because he wanted to cure himself by glutting his life with information. What they looked like, their foreheads, their eyes, the way they walked, haircuts, clothes, everything...Bill wasn't stupid. (He could tell himself this a thousand times, but when he ended up in Paris, Arizona, at midnight with no gas and an empty motel, he didn't believe it.) Bill Mudd could spend days without the fear presenting itself directly to him, although it was there at the periphery of his existence, hovering, all the time.

Whenever he met a stranger, it was there.

He looked at the face in the mirror, drops of water under the eyes.

A knock at the rest room door.

"Bill? Mr. Mudd?" It was Chad.

"It's open," Bill said.

Chad opened the door and gave a nervous grin. "I don't like this john much. Makes me all weird."

"Oh?"

"A guy tried to get me in here once. You know. The way they like to do, those people."

"Oh." Bill didn't bother pursuing this further.

"Well, Cooter's not answering his phone, so I'm just gonna shut the station up for a while, and you and me, we can trot on over to Blythe and get back before he gets his sorry ass in here."

"Apparently, nobody's answering phones tonight," Bill said, drying his hands with a paper towel.

Chad brightened, clapping his hand together. "Not true, Bill, I called my girl, Betsy, and she picked up on the first ring so's her mother don't wake up. Let's go, hoss."

Something in the boy's manner made the man think that he could not refuse this offer.

4

Chad passed him a cup of coffee when he got in on the passenger's side of the tow truck. "It's on the house, a Little Debbie oatmeal cookie, if you want one. It's got cream filling, Bill, you might not want to pass on it." Chad held the large cookie in its wrapper up near Bill's face. "I love these things. Don't you love Little Debbie? With her little hat and her little smile. And then, you get to eat her cookie."

Bill took the coffee, sipped it, grimaced because of its bitterness, but drank some more.

Chad unwrapped the cookie before he started the truck. "Cooter's father owns the station, so Cooter gets away with murder sometimes, being late and all. He's the kind of guy who wipes his ass with a whole roll of teepee and then expects you to run get another roll for him. A practical joker, that dude is, always trying to put something over on someone. His name's actually Coolidge, his middle name, but he's been called Cooter since we was kids."

"You grow up here?"

The boy nodded. "All my life. All my life with everybody watching your every move and thinking whatever they like. You musta heard of Paris before? No? Hell, Mrs. Paladino, she ended up on Sally Jessy Raphael one time, using the name Crystal—which is funny since if you knew her, it's her little girl's name—she was on TV 'cause she was always terrified of things. Even Cooter used to scare the hell out of her."

"She's not scared of things now?" He was trying to make some polite conversation, but everything the boy said just made him sweat.

Chad shook his head. "Don't think so." He was silent for a moment, as he turned the truck out onto the narrow road that led to the highway. Houses were dark along the street. "She was a celebrity for nearly a month after she come back. I never want to be on TV, though, I mean, too many fags on TV, you ask me. That guy, what's his name, the guy on the show with the Mustang…" He mentioned the name of an actor, but not just his stage name, also his real name. "He's a fag, I think, at least he looks like one."

"What does one look like?"

"Oh, I can't describe it, but I know one when I see one. We're gonna take a little shortcut, Bill, is that okay?" Chad didn't wait for an answer, but steered the truck to the right at a railroad crossing, right up onto the tracks. He started laughing as the truck bounced along the tracks.

"Is this wise?" Bill asked, the last of his coffee spilling down the front of his shirt.

"Oh, I don't know 'bout wise, Mr. Mudd, but it's the best way to get you to pee in your pants—just joking, just joking, come on, how often do you get to see the desert from here?" Chad nodded his head at the passing scenery. "Look at it, it goes on forever."

"I can't see a thing," Bill said, his jaw tense, his voice jittery from the bouncing of the truck as much as from nerves.

Chad laughed even harder. "Okay, okay, fun's over," and he spun the steering wheel to the left to get off the tracks.

The truck stalled.

Chad pressed his foot on the accelerator.

Bill was getting just a touch frightened by this, although he saw by looking up and down the tracks that no train was coming from either direction.

"Shit, Cooter told me this was gonna happen one day," Chad said, and beat his fist against the horn as if the noise would free the truck. "Looks like we got to get out and see what's the holdup."

The man and the boy spent the better part of an hour trying to get the tow truck off the tracks. Bill had to do most of the pushing, and Chad had a crowbar he was using to try and get the tire up from where it was caught, but nothing seemed to go. There was no flashlight in the truck, and only one headlight was working; it illuminated only the vast expanse of desert. Bill Mudd wasn't even sure in what direction the highway lay. Chad did a bad imitation of Stan Laurel. "This is a fine mess, you've gotten us into, Ollie."

Bill would've cursed and kicked the truck, but he knew it was futile, and he was starting to feel strange again too, something about Chad he didn't like, beyond the boy's foolishness at driving up the tracks. Something about the way he was acting, like this was planned, getting stuck on the tracks. Bill kept a false smile on his face and pretended the shivering was from the cold.

"It does drop at night, don't it?" Chad zipped his leather jacket up. "It can be hot as a griddle at noon, but come midnight, and you got yourself an icehouse."

"You're too young to know about icehouses," Bill said.

Chad's face was in darkness. "We used to have one in Paris. It was kind of a train stop, this town was. Had a nice beer place, and a Harvey House. Or something like it. The old icehouse is just a pit now. My granddaddy, he used to deliver ice. He was a nasty man, though, used to whip me but good when I just was doing nothing wrong, mind you, just what boys do." He clapped his hands together. "But he's dead and rotting now, he is, end of story. Now, what say we walk back down the tracks—they'll take us into town and we'll get there fast if we hustle."

"Aren't you worried about the truck? I mean, what if the train comes?"

Chad giggled and came over to Bill, almost leaning into him. Again Bill smelled that orange blossom breath, only now it had a tinge of beer in it. *He must've had a beer when I went to check out the motel.* Chad whispered, "There ain't been a train through here since maybe 1962, which was a long time before I appeared in this one horse-dick town."

Bill stepped back. There was more than one beer in that breath; he was amazed he hadn't noticed it before. *Great, stuck in bumfuck with a drunk kid.* "I thought you said you were born here," Bill said.

"That's right, sir, my first appearance: birth. Son of Lolita Jane Hamer and Phillip Arthur Partridge, April first, 1977. An April Fool. Now, let's go, if we walk fast we can get to Cooter's place in fifteen minutes, twenty tops, and get his car so you can get your diesel."

5

"That's weird," Chad said, leaping off the porch and back onto the sidewalk where Bill stood. "Cooter's not answering. His old man neither."

"Maybe you need to knock harder," Bill said.

Chad, whose face was clearly distinguishable in the porch light, looked a little ticked off. "Maybe I need to FUCKING BLOW THE DOOR DOWN, BILL!"

Bill said nothing. The boy would calm down. He'd had a few beers and was probably all wound up worrying about his boss's tow truck. He was excitable, seventeen, wanted to go see his girlfriend. Didn't plan on spending Thursday night with some passerby who needed diesel.

The boy began stomping around the yard, reaching up and knocking his fists into his forehead. "That fucker Cooter, he's probably over in Blythe right now, with his suck-ass old man, doing inmates at Chuckawalla Prison, that's where they are, damn it."

Bill began to walk up the street. If he walked fast, the boy might not notice him, and he might make it to the gas station within twenty minutes. He could take his Mercedes and get out of Paris, and head toward Blythe and maybe sleep on the side of the road if he made it at least ten miles out of this town, at least ten miles away from this kid. He was halfway up the block when he heard Chad shout, "WHERE THE HELL DID YOU GO, BILL?"

6

All right, he could admit to himself, it was an irrational fear, but that was the great thing about phobias, you knew you were overreacting, you knew your anxiety was more than a bit excessive. But that boy was really making him nervous, shouting like that so late at night, in such a small town, you'd think even the dogs would've been up and barking, but no such luck. The place was so quiet, and the boy's voice seemed to echo throughout the universe, that he wished *somebody* would open their window or go to the bathroom so there'd even be a flush, even the tiniest flush somewhere. He thought he heard the sound of footsteps, but he knew they were Chad's, and he really didn't want to deal with that kid anymore—he was bad news, and worse, he reminded Bill of some of the patients he worked with back at Darden State. He had been a psych tech for ten years, and the boy reminded him of what some of the patients must've been like when they'd been teenagers, before they'd killed their first human. A lot of the patients were doped up at Darden, but the newer ones, they were usually just like Chad, kind of stupid and bright at the same time, kind of sane too, the way they talked about how their wives and kids kept talking to them even after they'd chopped their heads off.

Bill Mudd vowed to do anything he could not to run into Chad again.

He walked a zigzag route through the narrow streets, hoping he was heading in the general direction of the gas station. The houses were flat-roofed and small, and the only trees in the town were tall palms, so it was not hard to find out where Main Street lay. The highway was to his right about two miles, so he knew that if he just kept heading east, he'd make it to his car. If the boy was still knocking on Cooter's door for another ten minutes before giving up, maybe he wouldn't even go back to the gas station yet.

You may even be wrong, Bill, he may not even be one of them, he may be an ordinary, high-spirited boy.

But something in Chad's grin had bothered him.

One window of one house had a light on, and just for the comfort of it, Bill walked by that house. He peered in the window, for it was facing the sidewalk, and what he saw made him stop.

On the other side of the window was a beautifully preserved Formica and chrome early sixties kitchen, in sparkling condition.

379

And there, on the kitchen table, a complete meal set out as if a family had, earlier, been sitting down about to have dinner. He checked each plate: it looked like ravioli, and some kale, and maybe apple sauce on the side. Two glasses of milk, an open beer can, and a can of Coke. Bill looked above the table, to the wall clock: 2 A.M.

Who would have their dinner this late? Two glasses of milk. Flies were wandering the edges of the plates. A Barbie doll next to one of the plates—a little girl's.

Flashing through his mind the images of: a little girl on the stairs, her face beaten in; a woman just beneath the window, inside, cut open from neck to stomach; a boy and his father, in the living room, still bleeding to death.

Chad's words in his head: *This town's so dead, sometimes I think, when I walk home, that somebody's come right off the highway, someone like you, mister, even, and he's killed everybody in town, and I'll go home and my folks'll be dead too, and then I can't call nobody for help.*

Bill tried to peer into the hallway, but it was dark.

And then someone touched his shoulder.

He turned and froze as Chad stood there with a flashlight turned on full blast into his face.

"Looky what I found," Chad said. "God, Bill, can you believe it? Just what we needed—it was in the work shed out behind Cooter's place—but why the hell'd you take off like that?"

Chad flicked the flashlight on and off, on and off, and then drew light-streak circles against the sidewalk.

"I just wanted to get to my car," Bill said. "I thought I'd get it and come get you and then we could maybe get help for the truck."

"No you didn't," Chad said, flicking the light off. The two stood in the light from the kitchen window. "You wanted to get in your car and drive out of here, because you're scared of me. End of story."

Bill said nothing.

He stared at the boy.

Chad stepped closer and tapped him on the chest with the flashlight. "Don't you be scared of me, I ain't gonna hurt you, not like I did that geezer in the john who kept wanting to...well, you know."

And then, looking over Bill's shoulder, at the kitchen window, Chad said, "Oh, my God."

Bill didn't glance back. He didn't want to take his eyes off Chad. He was trying to figure out a way that he could stop this boy from doing any harm to him. The flashlight seemed like a weapon now, as the boy tapped him a bit harder on the chest, and maybe it was only Bill's imagination, but it seemed like the boy was beginning to smell bad, like his body chemistry was changing.

Chad said, "The Bradshaws left their supper out. Ain't that weird? Jesus to Christ, ain't that like something out of *Twilight Zone*, Bill?"

While Chad was preoccupied with the window, Bill took the opportunity to grab the flashlight and hit the boy hard on the head; the boy reeled back for a second, and then came at him; Bill hit him with the flashlight in the forehead as hard as he could; the boy still kept coming, and pushed Bill down to the ground; Bill kept thrashing at the boy, and finally took his own fist and socked the boy in the jaw as hard as he could, and the boy slumped down on the sidewalk. Hit him one more time for good measure.

But he'd be up in just seconds.

Bill got up and just started running.

Funny thing was, what he was noticing as he was running was not his fear, or the houses passing by, or even that his feet ached because he was running in his street shoes, but what he noticed were the stars—on the desert, they were like optical illusions, there and not there at the same time, pinholes in the fabric of night. He thought he was going to die there, in that town, and his last memory would be nothing other than a starry night.

But he made it to his Mercedes.

And, even though he fumbled with his keys, he got the door unlocked and started the engine, and drove the hell out of Paris, Arizona.

7

The car came to a shuddering, shaking stop about seven miles on the road back to Blythe, and he managed to get it to the shoulder of the highway. He flicked the hazard lights on. Always kept a bottle of aspirin in the glove compartment. He retrieved it, opened it, and popped three in his mouth, swallowing them dry.

It was 2:25 in the morning. Trucks went past him, blowing their horns, but none stopped. He locked the doors. Thought he'd get out and try to thumb down a truck, but what if it was another Chad behind the wheel? Who could be sure? What idiot would hitchhike at two in the morning anyway?

Bill tried not to, but fell asleep within an hour, and only awoke when someone was tapping on his window.

He awoke, sweating.

It was a highway patrolman.

Bill rolled down his window. "Officer?"

Morning hit him like the blast of a horn. He must've slept several hours. His clothes were soaked; his head ached.

"Are you all right, mister?" the policeman said. "Need some help?"

381

Bill coughed, and nodded. "I ran out of gas. Couldn't find any diesel."

"Paris is only five minutes down the road. They got one diesel pump. I'll give you a lift."

"No," Bill said, "I was there. I stopped there. The diesel pump was out of order."

"Mister, I don't know where you were, but I live in Paris, and I know for a fact that they got diesel because my son works in the gas station, and my wife's family owns the place."

Bill looked at the policeman's eyes and noticed a resemblance. "He said it was empty."

"Cooter said that?"

"I didn't...meet Cooter. I met Chad."

The policeman shook his head, laughing. "Oh, mister, that boy of mine, Cooter *is* Chad. My boy been pulling your leg? I get after him about that all the time, and he still spends his time pulling folks' legs, boys will be boys, huh, mister. You got to forgive the boy, mister, there's only four families living in the whole town. He gets bored, I guess."

Bill remembered the sign: population 65. "But, I thought...I mean, all those houses."

"Oh, I know, all set to be condemned, we're gonna have to move back to Quartzite or someplace with a little more life to it. It was the work, it all dried up in the area—we used to have a lot of date farming, but it went a while back. The stores just went one after another. It's been the gas station and the motel that's kept us there. Oh, gosh, mister, he didn't do the thing where he sets a table to look like the Bradshaws still live in their—oh, no, I'm so sorry, mister, sometimes I think he belongs in Juvy. My wife got a shock when he tried that one on her, but he got a bigger one later on that night when he was grounded for three weeks. I will tan his hide, mark my words."

Bill was stuttering over thoughts and words. "I went there...to the motel. There was no one around."

"Well, last night, mister, my wife's sister, she had her baby over in Blythe, and we packed up and went over—Cooter had to watch the gas station, 'cause some of the truckers, you know, depend on us. So, can I give you a lift back to get gas? I'm sure Cooter owes you some kind of apology. I know, I know, in some places they'd strangle that kid, and in others, well, he'd be making millions coming up with commercials, or making movies or something. Hope no major damage is done? His ass is gonna be grass, you can count on that. Damn, but we were all boys once, huh. Jesus, what else is a boy supposed to do all by himself in a town like this? Didn't see him when I got back today, but it's only seven—he won't be off shift till nine. What say?"

The man named Bill Mudd sat there for a minute, staring at the highway patrolman, and wondered if he was still asleep.

Then he went with the policeman in his car back down the road about six miles.

8

It didn't surprise Bill Mudd when they returned to the gas station and Chad, also known as Cooter, was not there. Bill noticed that the diesel pump, indeed, did not have an out of order note on it. Cooter's father, whose name really was Phil, got a spare gas can and filled it with diesel, "on the house, and you come on back and I'll make sure my boy fills up your whole tank. If you hang on a sec, I'll just go in and use the phone and see if Cooter's up at his mama's."

The policeman took a set of keys out of his pocket and walked toward the glassed-in office.

Bill knew that Cooter was dead, lying on the sidewalk outside the Bradshaw's place where the boy had played a practical joke.

So, Bill thought, this is how my friends back in the hospital for the criminally insane start. It's just like they say, it's all an accident, you didn't mean to do it, not the first one, and then you do the second one because you need to make sure he doesn't find out about the first one. And then it just snowballs.

He looked at the patrol car, with the keys in the ignition.

The policeman with his hand on the phone.

What was the smartest thing?

He could just pretend he'd last seen the boy at midnight, at the gas station.

But there would be fingerprints on the flashlight.

Maybe he could just steal the policeman's car, and figure something out later.

But the policeman was on the phone. He might tell his wife to get someone else out on the highway to stop him, Bill thought.

The Big Question, the million dollar one, was how do you kill a policeman who has a gun on him?

Think, Bill, think.

And then he looked at the police car, with the engine running, the keys in the ignition, just waiting for him. The policeman would come out, not see him behind the wheel at first, and he would gun it.

And pray that the car would smash into Cooter's father before he could draw his gun.

End of story.

384

9

And so, you manage to drive out of Paris, finally, changing cars on the railroad track—Cooter was lying about that too, because the tow truck was not stuck. That boy had just tricked you so he could play his bizarre little game. You don't think too much about being tricked, neither do you think about your conference in Phoenix, because that's where everybody's going to think you're going. Instead, you head back to California, maybe you'll hide out in the hills, the Big Bear area. California seems to draw you back, as it does your brothers and sisters.

And you know the best part?

You're not afraid of them anymore, the psychos of the world or the games of life, because you know what the secret is, you've crossed the tracks of fate.

And you embrace the fears of this world with joy and gladness.

The Skin of the World

This is one messed up little story. I still have no idea what provoked it. I wrote it in my early 30s, and had visited a little ghost town gas station out on the desert. It's a slip of a story, and I've never felt it was ready to send out to a magazine. I'm including it here because something is in it that I like.

1

"I gotta go, anyway," my brother Ray said.

He had a look on his face that I only now understand, a look of wanting to do something without regard to consequences. He had a face like a raccoon, dark-encircled eyes, and a need to get into things he wasn't supposed to. I remember that face with fondness, not for his smile or his wildness, but for what came after.

It was 1969, and a man had landed on the moon the day before which is why we'd been staying at my uncle's. My uncle had a color television set and my father didn't believe in them until the day a man walked on the moon. It had been an unpleasant family outing, and my brother was giving my father some lip. We drove past the sign that said Vidal Junction, and my father turned to my older brother, Ray, and told him to just keep it shut tight or he'd be walking from there back to Prewitt. As if to show he meant it, my father slowed the car to ten miles an hour, and pulled off on the shoulder. My mother was quiet. She kept facing forward, as she always did, and I pretended I wasn't even there. Vidal Junction was just a sliver of a gas station and maybe an old diner off the railroad tracks, but it had been abandoned back in the thirties. When I was much younger my mother and I had stopped there to collect some of the junk she took to her junkshop dealers, like old telephone pole insulators and bits from the gas pumps. It had looked the same since I was four, that junction, a ghost place, and that sign just sitting up there: VIDAL JUNCTION, as if it would continue, lifeless, into infinity.

"It's damn hot," my father said, parking the car so we could all look at Vidal Junction, and so my brother Ray could get good and mad about my father's threats to make him walk. "Look at that big heap behind the pumps."

My mother was trying to remain silent, I could tell. But she wanted to say something—she ground her teeth together so as not to let anything out.

"What do you boys think it is?"

"I don't know," I said. It looked like a piece of a car, but I didn't know cars too well, and it could've just as easily have been a piece of a rocket. I smelled something from my cracked window, something sweet like an early memory of candy or perfume.

"Maybe you can sell it to one of your junk shops," my father said to my mother.

"Antique stores," she said.

"This place is strange," my father said, "you'd think somebody would plough it over and put up some stores or maybe grow something. Maybe that thing's from outer space. Or Russia. Or maybe it's like space trash. Everything's space-something these days. Right, Ray? That's right, Ray? You think it's from Mars?"

I heard a click, and there was my brother Ray opening the door on his side of the car. "Maybe I will walk from here," he said, "just maybe."

"Just maybe my ass," my father said, "it's a sure thing."

Ray got full out of the car and left the door hanging open.

"Coop," my mother said. She reached over and touched my father gently on his shoulder. He shrugged. "Coop," she repeated, "it's twenty miles home."

"Only fifteen, by my estimate," my father said. "He's old enough. Or is sixteen still a baby?"

My mother was silent.

Ray walked across the steamy asphalt on the highway, over to Vidal Junction and I wondered if he was going to burn to a crisp. As if he sensed this, he took his shirt off and rolled it up and stuck it under his right armpit. He was so bony that kids at school called him Scarecrow, and I swear you could read the bones of his back, line by line, and they all said *up yours*.

My father started up the station wagon.

"Coop," my mother said. Coop wasn't my father's name, but it's what Ray used to call him before I was born and my father was a Corporal and wanted to be called Corporal but Ray could only say Coop. My mother had called him Coop since then. To my father it must have been the kind of endearment that reminded him that he was a father after all and no longer a Corporal. My mother probably figured it would soften him, and it probably did.

"He wants to walk, let the boy walk," my father said. "I didn't make him walk. I didn't. His choice."

That was the end of that, and my father started up the car, and as we drove off toward Prewitt, I looked out the back window and saw Ray just sitting down by one of the old gas pumps and lighting up a cigarette because he knew he could get away with it.

We crossed the railroad track, and the road became bumpy again because nobody in the county much bothered to keep up this end of the highway, and it would stay bumpy until we got out of this side of the valley.

"Fifteen miles," my mother said. We were sitting on the front porch, just sweating and wondering when Ray would be home.

"Daddy said he used to run fifteen miles every Saturday."

My mother looked at me, and then back to the road.

387

"Used to," she said under her breath.

"Ray walked ten miles in the rain last March."

My mother stood up and said, "Oh." I thought at first it was because she saw Ray coming up the road, but there was nothing there. We had four neighbors back then, before the development came through, and the nearest house was a half-mile down the road. Across the road was a pond and some woods, and beyond that the mountains and the Appalachian Trail. It was pretty in the summer, if the temperature dropped, to sit on the porch and watch the light fade by slow degrees until the sun was all but gone by nine-thirty and it was past my bed time.

My father looked out through the screen door and said, "Well, you do a little math. They still teach math? At a slow pace, given the sun and other factors, you can figure on maybe three miles an hour. So he won't be home 'til eleven. Maybe midnight. Ray's stubborn, too. Got to factor that in. He may just sleep out back of Huron's, or by the river."

"Mosquitoes'll eat him alive if he does," I said.

"He's done this before," my mother said, more to herself than to anyone.

My father said, "Huron said he might carry some of your junk."

"Oh," she said. She walked out into the yard and called for the collie to come in for the night. I wondered what Ray was thinking right now, or if he was sneaking a beer at Huron's, or if he was just out of sight but almost home.

Seven days later, I was fairly sure we would never see Ray again, and we eventually moved, when I was twelve, to Richmond, where my father got a job that actually paid, and where I was sure we had arrived because it was so different from Prewitt. I thought of Ray often, and what our family would've been like if he had ever returned from his walk that day when I was ten and a half.

I have to admit that our family was the better for his loss. My father became a tolerable man, and the violence which I had known from early childhood transformed into a benevolent moodiness, an

anger that took itself out on, not his family, but his employer, or the
monthly bills, or the television set. No longer did he throw furniture
against the wall when he and my mother argued, and never again
did he raise his voice to me. I missed my brother somewhat, but he
had never been kind to me, nor had he been my protector. Ray had
always dominated things for me, and had even gone so far, once,
to piss on my leg when I was five (and he was just about eleven) to
prove that he was the brother with the power. Although my mother
suffered greatly for a few years after Ray disappeared, I think even
she finally blossomed, for Ray was a difficult child, who, according
to her, since birth had been demanding and unreasonable and quick
of temper. I think that Ray did a great service by walking the other
way from Vidal Junction, or wherever I assumed he had marched
off to, for my mother had the tragedy of loss, but over the years
she drew strength from the thought that Ray was, perhaps, living in
some rural Virginia town, and functioning better without the burden
of his family. Perhaps he was even happy. Never once did it cross
anyone's minds that Ray was dead. He was a cuss, and cusses don't
die in the South. They become the spice of the land, and are revered
in the smaller towns the way unusually beautiful women are, or
three-legged dogs.

389

2

When I grew up, I moved around a bit, and raised a family, and
then got divorced. When my own son was five, we were going to
drive to his grandma's for a belated visit—I had custody of Tommy
for six whole days, which was generous of my ex-wife—I took the
surface roads of the towns, and thought it would be nice to drive
to Prewitt and show him the failed horse farm. But my memory
of the area was bad, and I was too proud to stop at gas stations for
directions, so we got a little lost. Tommy wanted lunch, and so we
pulled off at a coffee shop that looked like it was made of tin and
was shaped like an old-fashioned percolator. The waitress was cute
and told Tommy that he was the red-headiest boy she had ever seen.
The place smelled like rotting vegetables, but the ham biscuits were
good, and I taught my son the lost art of see-food with the biscuits

and some peanuts thrown in. His mother would hate it when he returned to Baltimore and kept opening his mouth when it was full of food.

"You know which way to Prewitt?" I asked the waitress.

She went and got a road map for me, and I moved over so she could scootch in next to me and show me the route down past Grand Island, and off to the south of Natural Bridge.

"All these new highways," I said, "got me confused."

"I know what you mean," she said. "They just keep tearing the hills up. Pretty soon it's gonna look like New York."

Because I wanted to keep flirting with her, I began the story of my missing brother, which never ceased to interest Tommy whenever I told him. While I spoke, I watched the girl's face, and she betrayed nothing other than interest. She was years younger than me, maybe only twenty, but it was nice that she enjoyed my attentions at least as much as I enjoyed hers. I ended, "...and to this day, we don't know where he went."

She looked thoughtful, and reached over, combing her fingers through Tommy's hair to keep it out of his eyes. "Well, I've heard about that place."

Tommy asked for more milk, and the girl got up to get him some. When she returned I asked her what she'd meant.

"Well," she said, her eyes squinting a bit as if trying to remember something clearly from the back of her mind, "they don't call it that, anymore, Vidal Junction, and the railroad tracks got all torn up or covered over. But it's still there, and people have disappeared there before."

"You talk like it's a news story," I said.

She laughed. "Well, it was one of those boogey-man kind of stories. When I was a kid."

You're still a kid, I thought. It struck me then, that she reminded me in some way of Anne, my ex. Not her looks, but the girl in her.

"What's a boogey-man?" Tommy asked.

"Someone who picks his nose too much," I told him.

The waitress looked very serious, and she spoke in a whisper. "There was a girl in Covington who ran away from home. My cousin knew her. She got to that place and she didn't get further. My aunt said she was taken by her stepfather, but my cousin said that was just to keep us all from getting scared."

"It's one of those stories," I said, but then I started to feel uneasy, as if the child in me were threatening to come out. "You know, like you hear from a friend of a good friend about a dead dog in a shopping bag that these punks steal, or the hook in the back of the car."

"What's a hook in the back of the car?" Tommy asked.

"Fishing hook," I said by way of calming him. His mother had been telling me that he had severe nightmares and I didn't want to feed them.

But the girl went ahead and scared him anyway, by saying, "Well, folks around here I grew up with think it's something like the asshole of the universe."

I paid our bill, and I raced Tommy to the Mustang, because the girl had finally given me the creeps and convinced me that Tommy would have more nightmares—for which I would be rewarded with fewer and fewer weekends with him.

But, instead, Tommy said, "I want to go there."

"Where?"

"The asshole."

"Never say that word again as long as you live."

"Okay."

"She was weird, huh."

"Yeah," he said. "She was trying to scare you."

"I think she was trying to scare *you*."

He shrugged, preternaturally adult, "I don't scare."

I didn't hunt Vidal Junction down intentionally, but we happened to come upon it because of my superb driving which, at the rate we were going, would set us down at my mother's in Richmond at midnight. It was only five-thirty. I didn't recognize the Junction at once. It had changed. The sign was gone, and the old gas pumps, while they were still there, were surrounded and almost engulfed by abandoned couches and refrigerators, and the chassis' of old rusted-out clunkers like trees growing along the roadside. The highway was itself worn down to a gravel groove, and I would've just driven by the place if it were not for the fact that Tommy told me that he had to pee. He could not wait, and what I had learned in my five years of fatherhood was that my son meant he had to go when he said it. So I pulled over and got out of the car with my son, and told him to pee behind one of the couches. I didn't stand near him just because I was afraid of the waitress' apocryphal warning, but because I worried about copperheads and perverts. I glanced around the junction, and noticed that the girl in the coffee shop had lied: the railroad tracks were very much in evidence.

"Lookit," Tommy said, after he had zipped up. He grabbed my hand and pointed to the bottom of the torn-up old couch.

"It's asphalt," I said. *Or oil,* I thought.

Or something.

"Don't touch it," I told him, but I was too late. Tommy stooped over and put his fingers right into it. "I hope it's not doggie doo."

I pulled him up and away, but as I did he let out a squeal, and then I saw why.

The skin of his fingers, right where the pads were, appeared ragged and bleeding. The top layer of skin had been torn off.

"Owee," he said, immediately thrusting his fingers in his mouth.

The asshole of the universe is right, I thought.

"Hurts bad?" I asked.

He shook his head, withrawing his fingers from between his lips. "Tastes funny."

"Don't eat it, Tom, for God's sakes."

He began crying as if I had slapped him (which I never did), and he got away from me and went running across the drying field of junk. I called to him, and jogged after him, but something made me move slowly, as if the earth were not dry at all but was made of mud. "Oh, Tommy, get back here right now."

THE SKIN OF THE WORLD

But all I heard was a truck on some other highway, and then a screen door slamming. I went toward the sound, behind the old gas station, and there stood a man of about forty, with long hippie-style hair, and a white cotton t-shirt and jeans on, covered head to toe with dirt. "Tried to stop him," the man said. "He went in, and I tried to stop him."

"Tommy!" I called, and heard something that sounded like him from inside the gas station. The man blocked my way to the doorway, which had, in its last life, been the gas station restroom. It was odd that it had a screen door, and it seemed odder that this man standing there didn't move as I came rather threateningly towards him.

He had a puzzled look, and he nodded to me as if we knew each other. "It's a kind of attraction they smell. I don't smell it much now, but at first I did. The younger you are, the more you smell it."

From the restroom, I heard my son cry out, but not as if he'd been hurt.

"You don't want to go in there," the man said. He remained in front of me, and I felt adrenaline rush through my blood as I prepared for a fight. "I tried to stop the boy, but it's got that smell, and kids seem to respond to it best. I studied it for three years, and look," he said, pointing to his feet.

And then I understood why he stood so still.

The man had not feet, but where his legs stopped, his shins were splinted against blocks of wood. He squatted down, balancing himself against the wall of the building, and picked up a small kitchen knife and a flashlight, and then slid up again.

"Be prepared," he said, handing me the knife, "I was smart, buddy. I cut them off when it started to get me. Cauterized them later. It hurt like a son-of-a-bitch, but it was a small sacrifice."

Then he moved out of the way, and I opened the screen door to the restroom, and was about to set foot inside when he shined a flashlight over my shoulder into the dark room. I saw the forms, and the beam of the light hit the strawberry-blond hair of my son, only it was not my son but something I can't even give a name to, unless it can be called skin, skin like silk and mud, moving slowly beneath the red-blond hair, and from it the sound of my boy as if he were retreating somewhere, not hurting, and not crying, but just like he was going somewhere beyond imagining, and was making noises that were incomprehensible. Skin like an undulating river of shiny eels, turning inward, inward.

Knife in my hand, I stood on the threshold, and the man behind me said, "They go in all the time. I can't stop them."

"What in god's name is it?"

"It's a rip in the skin of the world," he said. "Hell, I don't know. It's something living. Maybe anything."

I felt something against the toe of my shoe, and instinctively drew back, but not before the tip of my Nike was torn off by the skin. The toes of my left foot were bleeding.

"Living organism," he said, "I don't know how long it's been here, but it's been three years since I found it. Could've been here for at least a decade."

"Maybe more," I said, remembering my brother Ray and his cigarette in front of the gas station, and his words, "I gotta go, anyway." He would've gone around back to take a leak, maybe smelled whatever you were supposed to smell, and then just went in.

The skin of the world.

"Does it hurt them?" I asked.

The man looked at me, startled, and I wondered for a moment what I had said that could startle a man who had cut his own feet off. And it occurred to me, too, what I had just asked. *Does it hurt them?* The man didn't have to say anything, because he knew then what I was made of. That I could even ask that question. And what that question meant.

He looked like he was about to tell me something, maybe advise me, but he knew and I knew that only a man who had given up would ask that question.

Does it hurt them?

Because, maybe if it doesn't hurt, maybe it's okay that my son went in there, and got pulled through the seam of the world, the asshole of the universe. That must be what a man like me means when he has to ask.

"How would I know?" the stranger said, and hobbled across the grass, moist with the sweat from the skin of the world.

3

I stood in that doorway, and could not bring myself to call to my son. I shined the flashlight around in that inner darkness, and saw forms rising and falling slowly, as if children played beneath a blanket after lights out. Soon, the evening came, and I was still there, and the man had gone off somewhere into the field of junk. I thought of Tommy's mother, Anne, and how worried she would be, and perhaps the need she would have that I could respond to. I began to smell the odor that the man had spoken of: it was gently sweet and also pungent, like a narcissus, and I remembered the day after my brother Ray had not come home, and how my mother and father held each other so close, closer than I had ever remembered them being before.

I remembered thinking then, as now, *it's a small sacrifice for happiness.*

Why My Doll is Evil

She came from Japan
In 1963
My father, on business, saw her in a shop window
With her fan and her obi
And her curious smile
She stood on a chest of drawers

I could not sleep some nights
Looking at that placid face,
So shiny and white in the nightlight's halo.
She beckons and repels with her gently curved hand.
Her lips move at night,
But she has no voice

Things happen in houses
Where families live
She watched,
And I watched her watch.
She smiled as it happened,
Held her fan close,
But her gaze told me nothing.

Douglas Clegg

I watched her lips move,
But she remained silent
While it happened.

Now, in the attic,
She rests,
For she knows more than she can say.
Her black hair is ragged
Her obi torn
Her perfect feet, tucked into wooden sandals,
Arthritic at her age.
But she smiles,
Holds her fan just so,
Without voice,
Reminds me of things that happened
In families
While she stood
Watch.

398

Piercing Men

If I were to tell what this story is based on in real life, I'd probably disrupt at least two lives. So, I won't tell. But when I was young, I learned things about suburban people–and it's all great fodder for writing horror stories.

1

"Sex is aggression," Sam said.

"Aggression is aggression," Danny laughed. "Once I got so mad, I put my fist through a window. When I was a kid. Maybe I was fourteen. Fifteen."

"Yeah? That must've hurt."

"Weirdly enough, it didn't."

"Once, I got so mad," Sam said, "I took it out on someone I really cared for."

They both laughed about this.

"Once I got so mad, I *wanted* to," and then they laughed louder.

"You like to fish?"

"How'd you know?"

"The fishing poles." Sam nodded toward the open garage door. "In the garage. Dead giveaway."

"You like to swim?" Danny laughed. "The pool. In your back yard. Dead giveaway."

"Sometimes, I swim buck naked back there," Sam grinned. But it was an innocent comment.

It had rained for six days in a row, and southern California had that feeling of quicksand by the time the sun had come out. Then, dryness like a pagan bonfire, the barbeque was lit and spitting with steaks and burgers, and the wives had already noticed the house down the block where no one seemed to live anymore, and which Bonnie, who dabbled in real estate, could not sell for the life of her.

He and Danny were standing on the front lawn in Summerland, and Danny's wife Faith was over by the oleanders with Sam's wife Bonnie, pointing out where they'd found the dead cat after the coyotes had gotten to it. Faith had a look on her face that was not her best—she hadn't really liked moving out to Summerland from the city, and now they had to contend with coyotes and the murder of small animals. Still, Danny shot her a smile, and she acknowledged it with a slight, quirky one of her own, ice goddess that she was.

It was mid-summer, the sky hazy with an approaching sunset; the house was older than the one that Danny and Faith had just moved from, and, as Sam, their new neighbor had told them the week before, "It's gonna take a lot of digging to get the crap out of that place." Sam was a fast friend, Danny noticed. First, he'd swung by in the minivan with his four-year-old son in the backseat, and a hello that had lingered into a "let's all go for pizza, the wife'll love meeting you," to bringing over a local gardener to work on the rose garden that had gone to hell under the previous owner's neglect. Then, a beer or two out back by the plum tree, and "a word to the wise, don't get to know the Bartlett's down the street," for reasons that weren't entirely obvious to Danny. But it was good to know another soul in Summerland—it was small town life, which meant Danny and Faith were not yet part of it, but still outsiders waiting for acceptance.

Back to the roses, another day, Sam had advice. "You've got to put bags over them, and water them with a hose, right into the ground, at dawn, and then at sunset. Don't water mid-day, and never spray. Get the hose right into them," Sam had said, demonstrating by squatting down and pressing the garden hose almost into the dirt. For the barest second, in the harsh sun, Danny had thought that the hose looked like a snake—and he had a fear of snakes, especially in Summerland where there were legends of rattlers.

The conversation that day had gone from gardening to football to another beer in the backyard to Sam commenting on the master bedroom when Danny gave him the tour, "I can already see where Jeff—the guy who lived here before—had done things to this place to ruin it. But the walls are sound," and then, within two and a half weeks of the move-in, Danny and Faith were having Sam and Bonnie over for steaks. That was how great friendships were begun, Faith told him, in places where the sidewalks rolled up at seven, and where the only town drunk was married to the only town tramp.

And Sam—standing in the cloudy smoke of the barbeque, watching the wives talk by the oleanders—somehow had worked the conversation from where in town you could get the best steaks to how, when he'd been twenty, he'd decided sex was a sport, and then he found out that it was fertility later on, only now, in his mid-thirties, it was pure aggression.

401

"What about you?" Sam asked. "I see you and Faith. You're both young. Good shape. Both of you pretty and smart and on your ways up in the world. Has it died yet?"

Danny took a breath and nearly smiled. He glanced over at his wife who seemed to notice him, and nod, as if giving permission from nearly an acre away to reveal some intimacy. He chuckled. "Sam, that's private."

"Oh, come on," Sam said. "We're all men here. I've been married thirteen years. You've been married, what, five?"

"Six."

"All right, six. I know what happens by the sixth year, Danny. The friendship develops and then, zip-zap, out the window with sex. It has to transform right about then, or the marriage never lasts."

"If you say so," Danny said, turning one of the steaks over. Then, he laughed again. "You're joking. You joker."

Sam shrugged. "You meet Faith in college?"

"Right after grad school. Long story."

"Love at first sight."

"Pretty much."

"You know," Sam said. "I noticed something about you, that first day. Not when I drove up here to say 'hi,' but before that. You and Faith came out to look at the house. She wore jeans and a sweater and pearls. You wore khakis and a striped shirt."

Danny squinted. "What?"

"A white shirt with red stripes. I remember details," Sam said. "That steak looks done." He went to the cart by the barbeque to get the long china plate. "Let's start piling 'em on."

2

After supper, they had a really good desert wine and some boysenberries in small saucers—Bonnie had picked them from the bushes out by the field at the back of the neighborhood.

"These are delicious," Faith said, her lips berry-stained. "I don't think I've had them before." Faith always seemed to say the right thing at the right time. She had a knack—Danny had noticed this right away with her. She was direct, and didn't flinch, and she knew how to compliment. These were all the things he first noticed about her, and they were the things she still had. She was going to make a friend in Bonnie, he thought. That would be good.

Bonnie laughed. "Gordie calls them poison berries."

"You should've brought him."

"Please, we like to have at least one night a week with just the two of us."

"You should have kids," Sam said, too bluntly. He was sitting there, his shirt open, and Danny wished he would just button the damn thing, but he was too polite to say so. Sam was in good shape, but Danny didn't like to eat berries and see so much flesh from a neighbor. He thought of making a joke of this—maybe it was the wine that made it seem funnier, the wine on top of the beer—but decided it was best to just keep quiet.

A momentary silence. They were in the courtyard, the summer sun still not gone, sitting on the cheap lawn furniture that Danny had managed to grab for this, their first barbeque together.

"Problem is," Faith said with a straight face. "I'm barren."

Then, she laughed, and they all did, and it was a funny, funny shock of a joke.

Then, Danny said, "I think we'll wait until we're thirty for kids."

"That's smart," Bonnie said, pointing her finger at him. She glanced at Sam, still pointing at Danny. "This is one smart cookie." She was a bit drunk. They had gone through three bottles before the desert wine. Bonnie had hair like a nest, all short and wispy and crackling and wrapped around her face, the baby bird.

Danny had his arm around Faith, who nestled further against him, spilling wine and dropping berries. "I want to have three kids," Faith said. "Two girls and a boy."

"That's too many," Bonnie waggled her finger. "Go for one boy and one girl. The perfect family."

"We once had a daughter," Sam added, and then said nothing more. Danny, feeling woozy from the sweet wine, felt as if music had suddenly stopped, and before he knew it, the barbeque was over, and he was in bed with Faith and it was two a.m. and he woke up needing a glass of water. He went to the kitchen, and looked out the window, over at the house across the street. His head pounded.

403

You can't drink anymore, he thought. Gettin' old.

He glanced two houses up the street, and saw Sam and Bonnie's stucco house. Their boy's tricycle was in the driveway under the garage light. For a moment, he thought he saw Sam standing there, the red circle of a cigarette in the shadows. Just standing there.

He went and fell asleep on the sofa in the living room.

3

"Sex is aggression," Danny laughed, as they ran.

He and Sam had taken to jogging on Sunday mornings in early September. Sam wanted to keep his weight down, and Danny just liked jogging. Danny had always jogged, since he'd run cross-country in high school, and now, at twenty-eight, he was still in good shape. This made him happy and comfortable, because he'd been an uncoordinated kid and had always been a little plump and too attracted to food. To attract people, he wanted to look good, and he liked the feeling of running rather than team sports. So, here he was, late 20s, still jogging, up and down the sloping hillsides of suburbia wasteland. Sam was older and couldn't keep up—he had just enough weight around his middle to qualify as a love handle, but not enough to ruin his looks; Danny slowed down to keep pace, but the sun threatened along the edge of the distant mountains. Once the sun was out, there could be no more running, because the sun brought the desert down like God's fury.

When they rounded the curve on Baseline, Sam said, "All sex is aggression. I notice that you lost your edge."

"My edge," Danny chuckled. He slowed to a walk when they reached the edge of the orange grove. He stepped off the pavement, and onto the dirt. It felt good beneath his sneakers. They always ended their run with a cool-down walk through the town's groves. The orange groves were the only wilderness left to Summerland— once tended, they now grew wild. The town maintained them to some extent, harvesting oranges for local markets, but they were not farmed as they once were—but they provided shade and privacy to wanderers, and free fruit to anyone who wished to break the local law and grab it.

"Yeah, your edge. Most guys lose it early," Sam added later, after he'd plucked an orange ("That's illegal," Danny had chided gently). "Not all. Just most."

They shared an orange, Sam hogging the larger segments, and Danny didn't like the way Sam had held the orange sliver up to his lips like he was a baby, but then he felt that heat, and the look that Sam gave him—as if he could see into him, as if he knew his secrets—and Danny took the bite of orange in his mouth, the juice biting him.

Danny felt a gentle shiver as he stood there, among the orange trees, and smelled his own sweat from the run, and knew better of it than to stand there with this man who had created such intimacy so quickly, just as the man had in Los Angeles, the one who brought the overnight package, causing that shivering, that cool darkness

404

within him, that overwhelming feeling of helplessness that Danny only rarely felt in the presence of other men.

When Sam took his hand, Danny felt it was okay, but he couldn't look at Sam. "You're sure?" Sam said, leading him back into a bamboo thicket that grew beneath a clutch of palm trees at the center path between the groves. The thicket was like a child's fort, it could not have been designed better by nature, and who would look there, for two men as they pursued their secrets?

"I guess I've been expecting this."

"It's in the eyes. We always know each other."

"Don't talk," Danny said. And it had begun. "Don't say anything. Don't."

4

The second time, again in the groves, but this time at night, Sam said, at the height of Danny's arousal, "Let go, let it all go, let it out, whatever you have, open it, let it go, release it,"

And Danny felt a wildness come out, like the fist through the window, and it was as if his movements in the throes of this uncontrolled heat were part of some primitive rhythm he had never before known.

405

5

It wasn't until after Christmas that Sam mentioned the college kid. "He's beautiful."

They took a drive into the hills overlooking Summerland, and Sam's son was strapped into the backseat. Danny kept glancing at Gordie, but Sam laughed. "Oh, Gordie isn't going to understand this."

"It doesn't seem right."

"Gordie," Sam said, looking in the rearview mirror. "Whatcha up to back there, peanut?"

"I see birds, Daddy," Gordie said, pointing a wobbly finger out the side window.

"He sees birds," Sam grinned, sweetly. "Okay, so here's the thing. I think the three of us."

"Three?"

"Yeah, you, me, and Joe."

"The college kid?"

"Well, he's nearly 21. He's hardly a kid. Not much younger than you."

"I sort of thought what we have is special."

"Crap. Don't start moralizing. Jesus. What we have is special. This is about sport, baby. We talked about this."

"Not like this. Not like it was real."

"All right, in the throes of fucking," Sam was decent enough to say this one word in a low voice, "you said that you could imagine another guy with us. Wouldn't it be great?"

"It was a fantasy," Danny said. Then, he began feeling ugly. "Pull over."

"What?"

"I want to go for a walk. I'll walk back into town."

"No, you won't," Sam said. But still, he pulled the van to the side of the road. Once the car was parked, he turned in his seat to face Danny. "Here's what you are going to do, Danny. You're going to go invite this young man to your house when Faith goes to her mother's on Sunday, and you and I are going to have a party with him. Just like you fantasized."

"That's ridiculious. You can't tell me what to do, Sam. That's complete and utter bullshit."

Sam turned to glance back at Gordie. "Gordie, cover your ears, please."

"Okay," Gordie said, gleefully pressing his hands against his earlobes.

Sam reached across the seat, pressing his hand against Danny's stomach. It created an uncomfortable warmth, and Danny tried pulling away. He wanted to reach for his shoulder harness and seat belt, but didn't. "You will do this, Danny. For us."

"Get your hand off me."

"How's Faith going to feel when she finds out about us?"

"You *said…*" Danny couldn't finish.

Somewhere in his mind, he had already begun to accept this. Accept that Sam somehow dominated him. Sometime between that first time in the bamboo, to the motel out by the freeway, to the Saturday up on the high desert, to the night in the swimming pool in Sam's backyard, practically under Bonnie's nose, somewhere between knowing who he was on the inside and being unwilling to let it out into daylight, Danny already had accepted Sam's complete ownership.

His protestations were merely for show.

Finally, Danny said, "All right."

Only later, when Danny had gotten a room over in San Bernardino, did Sam cuff him to the bed and begin to slap him too hard, all the while telling him that if he was going to own him, body and soul, then Danny had better get used to doing what he was told.

6

"Well, good news," Faith said, when he picked her up down at the drugstore. She looked great that day, very relaxed, which was a relief for Danny, since Faith had seemed agitated and suspicious—for no apparent reason—since before Thanksgiving. She had pulled her hair back, and he was sure she had gained a small amount of weight, which looked good on her.

"How good?"

"So good it's hard to believe."

"Wow. Something at work?"

"No," Faith said, suddenly losing her cheer. "Oh honey, let's go grab dinner out tonight."

"Okay. What's the good news?"

"It'll wait. How was your day?"

"Uneventful. The usual usual. Too much to do, too few hours, and wishing I was back home the entire time."

She kissed him on his cheek. "That's so sweet. Chinese?"

"How about Mexican?"

"How about Italian."

"All right, baby," he said. "Italian it is."

Over pizza, the noise unbearable with all the teens in the pizza parlor, Faith leaned into him and said: "We're going to have a baby."

7

The college kid looked nearly like Danny, but with shorter hair—nearly a buzz cut—and spindlier legs. He wore a white button-down shirt and jeans and sandals.

"Jack." His voice was scratchy and full of hormones.

"I thought it was Joe."

"Sam calls me Joe. He says I remind him of a Joe."

"Where's Sam?"

"Aren't you gonna invite me in?" Jack asked.

"Yeah, sure," Danny said. He drew the door back, allowing Jack to enter his house.

"You're married."

Danny shrugged.

"Happy?" Jack asked, with a bemused look on his face. He was brash and arrogant. Danny could already tell. In fact, Jack reminded him of some of his frat brothers, who were generally pricks.

Jack walked around the living room as if he were in a showroom picking out furniture. "So this is the place."

"Where's Sam?"

"He's running late. He beeped me. He wants you to make me feel at home."

Danny felt nervous. Danny had run marathons, sat on board meetings with corporate honchos who ate people alive, had gone on Outward Bound and survived a forest for weeks, had taken a journey on a sailboat from Florida to Venezuela through rough weather, but with a young man of 20 in the living room of his own home, he felt as if he were a child about to go to the dentist for the first time.

"How do you know Sam?"

Jack glanced back at him. "How do you think I know him?"

"I…" Danny wasn't sure where to go with this. Better to just wait for Sam to show up. "Want a Coke?"

"How about a drink?"

"All right. Want a beer?"

"How about a shot of vodka?" Jack grinned. Then, he went to sit on the sofa. He was almost a pony of a guy—sturdy and tight and strong and yet very small in some way. Not short. Not compact. Then, Danny knew what Jack reminded him of: a pony ride. He nearly laughed out loud thinking of it.

Danny returned with two vodka martinis; he set one down for Jack, and sipped from the other. "Maybe I should call Sam."

"That your wife?" Jack pointed to the picture on the wall.

"Yeah," Danny said.

"Have a seat." Jack patted the cushion beside him.

Danny went and sat next to him. He gulped most of his drink, setting the glass down on the coffee table.

Jack leaned back, sinking into the sofa a bit. He put his feet up on the coffee table, stretching. "Nice place, Danny boy."

"Thanks."

"You're probably wondering where Sam is."

"I guess he'll be here."

"Actually, he won't. He wanted the two of us to get acquainted."

"Yeah?" Danny said, meekly. "Cool."

"I can tell you're nervous. I'm a little nervous, too," Jack glanced sidelong at him. Jack was very, very cute. Sweet. Handsome. A pretty boy who was a bit masculine. Danny had noticed his shoulders and his ass, and then could not help but see the outline of thick penis pressing against the front of his jeans. It was a substantial mound.

"I bet I'm more nervous," Danny laughed. The alcohol was beginning to warm him.

"Maybe. So, where's your pretty woman?"

Danny looked at Faith's picture. "She's seeing her mother. Every few Sundays she goes over to Redlands to see her."

"You never go?"

"Her mom and I don't see eye to eye."

As an after-thought, Danny added, "She stays for hours. And hours."

"Nice," Jack said, but it was a different kind of word from his throat than most people made it out to be. It sounded sexual. *Nice*.

Then, Jack unbuttoned the top two buttons of his shirt. Danny looked at Jack's throat. He was a muscular young man. He was pretty and muscular and he was already aroused, just by the vodka and the picture of Faith and the sense that he was in this suburban home about to do god knew what but it would involve men's bodies.

That was enough.

"How long have you known Sam?"

"Not long. Long enough. You know."

"Sam's a good guy," Danny said, but hadn't really meant it.

"Oh, he's not too good," Jack said. "So, Danny, am I going to have to get you really drunk before you reach into my jeans and grab my dick?"

"Umm…" Danny began, wondering what he could respond.

Then, Jack leaned over and whispered something so vile in Danny's ear that it made Danny feel cold and on fire and as if every part of him were melting into some kind of thick liquid, and he saw darkness at the edge of his vision as this demon named Jack whispered these things, over and over again, about what he wanted Danny to do to him, how he wanted it, where he wanted it, how much it would hurt him but the hurt would give him so much pleasure that Jack would beg for mercy and even that turned Danny on; and he felt as if he had become more of a man.

8

"Was it good?" Sam asked. They met for a squash match at the Bally's in Riverside, but Sam didn't really want to play squash. He wanted to sit in the Jacuzzi and find out about Danny's Sunday with Jack.

"It was great," Danny said. "Just great."

"What'd I tell ya?"

"Wish you'd dropped by."

Sam grinned. "I was there."

"You were?" Danny asked, suddenly feeling as if maybe Sam had been hiding somewhere, watching what he had done to Jack, what he had made Jack experience and do and how he had humiliated him and forced him and dealt with him as if he were less than nothing and how it had completely turned Danny on.

"In spirit," Sam winked. "Next time, the three of us, Danny."

"Yeah," Danny said, and that's as far as it had gone until the next time Faith had gone out of town, this time for two days. Her father—who lived in Ojai—had recently remarried, and Faith had to go patch things up between them, but didn't want Danny coming along. "It needs to be me and my dad," Faith told him.

"All right," Danny had said.

"You'll be fine. One weekend alone. You and Sam can drink beer and talk like old bachelors or something."

But, in fact, what Sam and Danny did was invite Jack over again, and this time, it got a little out of hand, because they had two days with Jack, who was more than willing to keep the pain going, the humiliation, even the terror—that's how Danny had begun to think of it, as a kind of reign of terror on this 20-year-old who had seemed so innocent, who was just starting life, really, who was not much younger than Danny, just seven years or so, this Jack who could withstand a candle flame and pincers and a large instrument that Sam called the Cradle of Judas—and somehow, Jack was inflamed, and Danny was out of control, and Sam was there, a shadow, goading, encouraging, suggesting, but it was Danny's hands on the ropes, Danny's hands tightening the apparatus, Danny's hands reaching in and around and beneath and above until all the openings seemed to split and separate and Danny felt as if he were entering a vast cavern through a sleeve of human flesh and in that cavern, a beast waited for him.

411

9

"Jesus," Sam said.

"What?" Danny awoke to Sunday morning light through the one open slat of the blinds in the rec room. His face was pressed to the carpet. His hand rested across Jack's back, ridged slightly from welts.

"Jesus, Danny, what did you do?" Sam said.

Danny glanced up. He could barely see Sam at all.

"Jesus, Danny."

Danny glanced over at sweet Jack, waiting for the young man's grin, but saw the bubble of blood from the edge of his lips, the eyes nearly sewn shut with fishing line.

And then, the nauseating smell.

10

Sam held his hand over Danny's mouth for what seemed like a half hour. Finally, when Sam had assurances—given by nods—that Danny would not cry out, he released his hold.

"I didn't do that."

"I went home last night at three," Sam said, measuring his words carefully. "You had Danny in the stirrups, and the wax melting, but his eyes? Danny?" Sam held Danny's face in his hands. Danny's eyes were tearing up so he could barely see. "Did you lose it last night?"

"I swear, it couldn't have been me," Danny said. "Christ. Poor Jack. Poor Jack."

"Look at him. Jesus, Danny. The barbed wire? Was that from out back?"

"I don't know. I didn't do it. I couldn't have," Danny pleaded, sure of his innocence.

Sam held Danny's hands up. They were scored in shallow red lines, the flesh torn up.

"And that other thing, the way he—"

"Please," Danny wept, pressing his face into Sam's chest. "I couldn't have. I know I couldn't have. You were there."

"It's all right, baby. It's all right. Jesus, Danny, I think you went too far. I think you went over the edge," Sam whispered, and Danny didn't want to ever go back into the rec room or see what had become of Jack, he didn't want to see the fishing line through the eyes, or the wire wrapped around his thighs, or the other devices and instruments—the household items, the things from the garage—the way Jack had just been taken one step beyond what he had desired.

By someone.

It could not have been me, Danny told himself, and believed it. It had to be Sam. Or Jack himself.

But now, they had to deal with concealment.

11

"You took care of it?" Danny asked.

"Don't go into this, Danny. You don't want to know," Sam said.

They were jogging on Sunday night, and Danny had taken Sam's advice and stayed away from his house for the entire day – he had gone to the movies in town, but had a fever the entire time. As they came to the orange groves, Danny tried to take Sam's hand, but Sam would not let him.

"Jack was a good guy," Sam said.

"I'm sorry," Danny said, and it seemed stupid to say it.

"He was a fine specimen," Sam added. They walked through the groves in silence.

12

When Faith was six months pregnant, she finally began showing. "You bitch," Bonnie laughed, patting her stomach, "I was showing in two months. I got so fat. Didn't I get so fat?" She turned to Sam.

The sun was high, and they all sat at the edge of the pool, feet dangling in the water. Faith sat in a chair, and wore a big straw sunhat and movie star sunglasses. Danny slipped into the pool to cool off.

"Yeah, you got fat," Sam said, "but I knew that was good. Too thin and pregnant can't be good for a kid."

"I wish I could hide it," Faith grinned. "But part of me just wants to get really fat and happy with this baby and maybe deal with aerobics classes after it comes."

"You look beautiful," Sam said.

"She does yoga every day," Danny said.

Danny swam to the diving board, and then slowly swam back to the shallow end. He walked up the steps, out of the water, and watched as Sam put on Gordie's water wings.

Faith said, "I'm glad we moved here. I think it helped me get pregnant."

"It's in the water," Bonnie giggled, like a schoolgirl, and Danny grinned and went over to help Sam because Gordie was struggling to get his flip-flops off his feet.

13

When they were alone, after Gordie was in bed, and the wives had gone for a long walk up to Sunset Heights, they took a shower together to rinse off the chlorine. Danny said, "How did you know him?"

"Danny," Sam said, soaping his back. "Don't."

"I just don't know anything about him."

"That's as it should be."

"Who was he? Sam?"

Sam kissed his neck, and began drawing his arms behind his back, which hurt slightly, but Danny felt he deserved some hurt. "He's gone now," Sam said, kissing his shoulders. "He was just somebody pretty. That's all. He was just somebody pretty."

Only Connect

1

Watch the scenery awhile. It'll take your mind off the pain. I'll tell you all about him, if you'll just listen. You must never breathe a word of this to anyone, but I can tell you're simpatico—you won't betray me.

His name was Jim, and he worked at the train station taking tickets. He grew up in Hartford, but moved to Deerwich-On-Sparrow, called Deerwich by most, on the Connecticut coast—in his early twenties, the job had seemed good. He'd begun his career riding the rails taking tickets and cleaning the cars, but he'd moved up so that at twenty-nine he could sit behind the glass and say, "Roundtrip to Boston leaves at 9:15. That'll be $49.50." His head often pounded when it rained, and he was prone to popping aspirin as if it were hard candy, and just sucking on it until the headache went away. The sound of the train as it arrived in the station aggravated his condition, but Jim had begun to think of the headaches as normal. He'd long ago forgotten that they had never existed before working with the railroad.

It was the train wreck that had begun his journey towards discovery. One night, fairly late for the train—which had been due in before midnight—there was an awful screeching, from some great distance along the track. The old-timers knew what this meant, and they all ran out to see the spectacle. All except for Jim, who stayed back.

He went to grab another bottle of aspirin from beneath his perch. He felt around, but all his fingers found was a completely empty bottle. He stood from his stool, stretching, yawning. Outside, he heard the scraping of metal—the train, he would later learn, went over an embankment, into the river, and some child somewhere would be blamed for playing quarters on the tracks—the shouts of onlookers as the train tossed like a restless sleeper from its bed—but Jim took the opportunity to walk across the street to the drug store for aspirin.

Inside the store, the fluorescent lights flickered. The old man who worked the pharmacy stood up on his platform behind the white counter, measuring his nostrums and philters. Jim walked the aisles, glancing briefly at the magazine covers and the greeting card displays. Finally, he turned the last aisle, and saw the large bottles of aspirin.

The fluorescent light above his head flickered in a dark way, as if it were just about to go out. As Jim reached for the aspirin bottle, he watched as his hand seemed to go through water and touch—not a bottle of aspirin, but a green tile on a bathroom wall. As the light flickered again, he sensed that he was no longer in a drug store down near the train station in Old Deerwich, but in a small bathroom with lime-green tiles and a large mirror above the toilet. He glanced in the mirror and for a moment thought he saw the aisles of the drugstore behind his reflection, but this faded, and all was green tile.

He almost said something, as if someone stood near him, but he was most definitely alone.

He turned about, facing a door. He pushed at the door, and it opened out onto a room that was all green and white and smelled of rubbing alcohol with an undersmell of urine. Flowers on the windowsill. The window looked out on a courtyard and garden, and there, as he went to look out it, were a half a dozen or more patients. He knew they were patients by their bathrobes and by the nurses that pushed some of the wheelchairs, or stood beside a patient who used a walker or cane to get around. Across the courtyard, a silver-metal building, probably precisely like the one he occupied at the moment.

"Mrs. Earnshaw," someone said at the door. British accent. He knew he was in a British hospital.

Jim turned, sensing others in the room.

The fluorescent lamp flickered a liquid green.

Jim glanced up at the light overhead—a large brown water blotch spread like the profile of a face next to the ice-tray lamps.

"It's terrible," someone said, as he glanced down again.

He was in the drug store, holding a bottle of aspirin in his hand. A woman looked up at him queerly.

"I can't imagine anyone survived."

Jim had to squint a moment to focus on his new environment. His head throbbed now. He calmed himself with the thought that the pain in his head had caused the brief and vivid hallucination of the hospital room.

The little old woman, half bent over, reached for a box of arthritis pain reliever. "Did you see it?"

"No," Jim said. Then, "See what?"

"The crash. I was in my car and driving down Water Street and I heard it. It was terrible. It's so unsafe."

"Yes," Jim nodded.

"Travel is always dangerous. To get there from here, one must risk one's life these days," she said, nodding as if they'd understood each other.

Jim stood there a moment. Then, feverishly, he opened the jar of pills and grabbed three. Tossing them down his throat.

When he paid for the bottle, the pharmacist said, "Finally found what you wanted."

"Excuse me?"

"The aspirin. I saw you standing there reading labels for nearly half an hour."

"Half an hour?"

"Bad headache, huh? You probably drink too much caffeine."

417

Jim walked out into the rain, feeling as if he still vibrated with his hallucination. He remembered his brief romance with peyote in college, and began to worry that this might be the flashback from that. He forgot about it for days—the hospital—and buried himself in work.

The photograph in the local papers showed all angles of the train crash. It had fallen on its side, plunging seventy-nine people into the river, all of whom died. Another two hundred and fifteen people were injured.

What struck Jim most about the pictures of the fallen train was that it looked—if you squinted at the photos—like a sleeping person made entirely of metal, lying on a gray blanket.

The flashes began a week or two later.

The first time, when he tried to unlock his car, a small Honda Civic, and found that the lock was jammed. He twisted the key so hard that it broke off in his hand. Again, the headache kicked in, and he saw the aspirin bottle on the passenger seat inside the car. He felt angry suddenly—angry at the car for not opening, angry at his job for its dullness, angry at his parents for not really preparing him for the world in the way he'd wished.

Then, the flash—he thought it was heat lightning. In the same moment, he was in the hospital again. This time, he sat in a wheelchair in the courtyard as a light rain fell.

"You all right, now?"

"Yes," he said, adapting quickly to his new environment. "It's only a little rain."

"A little rain," the pretty nurse beside him smiled. "Yes, that's all it is. But all the others have gone inside."

He looked about the path through the garden with its iris and hibiscus, and saw that they were indeed, alone. The silver of the buildings dulled in the gray rain, but he liked the fresh smell of it.

"What's your name?" he asked her.

"Nora," she said, glancing up from her magazine.

"Your reading's going to get soaked," he nodded.

"I don't mind. It's only a little rain after all." She had a warm smile, and her eyes were a toasty brown. "Been feeling good today then, have we?"

"Very," Jim said. "The pains are gone."

"A few days is what they said."

"Yes, and they were right," Jim said.

Then he bit his tongue slightly. "Where am I?"

"Holyrood," she said.

"What town?"

"Oh, you," Nora laughed. "More tricks. Is this like that dream you told me about? The one where you're a railroad man taking tickets in some little town in—where was it?"

"Connecticut."

"That's right. Connecticut. The effects should've worn off by now," Nora said, glancing at her watch. "You're only on the IV for two hours before ten. It's nearly three." Then, she reached over, patting Jim's hand. "All of this for just a little information. It does seem daft, doesn't it? You holding up? No more weeping at midnight?"

"No," Jim said, feeling more lost and yet extremely comfortable. "Was it the aspirin?"

"Or lack thereof," Nora said. "Do you ever read these?" She held the magazine up. It was the *London TellTale* magazine. "All these royals and celebs knocking each other up. You'd think they'd have other things to occupy them, don't you?"

"What town are we in?" he asked.

"Why," Nora shook her head, glancing at the magazine. "Just look at what the Prince is up to today." Then, "What, dear? Town? Does it matter?"

"Yes."

"I'm sorry, I'm not supposed to tell too much. You know that more than anyone, Mrs. Earnshaw."

Jim felt a warm salty taste in the back of his throat. He glanced down at the hand that she had just finished patting. It was the hand of a middle-aged woman, and the hospital bracelet he wore read, "Catherine Earnshaw."

When the lightning flashed overhead, and the rain began coming down in earnest, Nora said, "Oh, dear, let's get the two of us in out of this nasty weather, shall we?" But then, there was no Nora, and

419

she faded, and all that was there was the Honda and the rain and his headache and a man who was not sure why he was going mad at the age of twenty-nine.

2

You didn't think he was married? Well, of course Jim was married—they'd tied the knot at twenty-four, almost got divorced at twenty-seven, but managed for a couple of more years because their jobs put them at opposite shifts so that every weekend was a honeymoon. Her name was Alice, and she worked at the sandwich shop on Bank Street. When she got off work at five, she went first to the library, since she was an avid reader, and then to the video shop. Her evenings, while Jim worked late, were mainly spent with the cat and a good book and a mediocre movie nine times out of ten. She'd slip into bed around midnight, fall asleep with a glass of wine, and then feel him next to her just before she got fully awake at 7:00 in the morning. She'd cuddle with him, unbeknownst to Jim, and then get up to make a pot of coffee and begin the day again.

The movie that night was to be an old musical, and the novel, a light romance to take her mind off her worries. She slipped into the tub at about 7:15, and while she dried herself off, the bathroom door opened. At first, Alice was frightened, but she saw quickly it was her husband.

"Jim? What are you doing home?"

"Called in sick," he said. "I've been napping since six."

"Migraine? Poor baby."

"It's not that," but he nodded anyway.

"Come here," Alice said, reaching her hand out. Jim approached her, his head down. She touched the back of his neck, squeezing lightly. "You're tense."

"Baby, I think I'm going nuts," he said.

"You've been nuts a long time."

"I mean it," he said, and his tone was so serious it almost shocked her.

Later, by the fire, she held him and told him it would be all right and he wept.

Then, he told her.

At first, she had a hard time not laughing.

But when he told her the woman's name, she cackled.

He looked hurt.

"Oh, honey, that's a name from a book. Catherine Earnshaw. It's from *Wuthering Heights*. You must have seen the movie."

He shook his head. "Was she in a hospital?"

Alice grinned. Her grin was not as warm as Nora's, but it was familiar. "No, no. It must be some kind of dream brought on by those headaches. Let's get you into the doctor's for a check-up."

"A head exam?"

"So you're an invalid woman in a British hospital with silver buildings and your name is Catherine Earnshaw. What an imagination," Alice said, kissing his forehead. "My big baby. It's your job. It's getting to you. I told you you needed to finish your degree and maybe get into computers or something."

Jim smelled her hair—like petals on a wet bough—and glanced at the fire as the flames spat and curled and flickered. He closed his eyes, his head beginning to pound, but he was going to fight it off, the pain, the throbbing, the near-blindness that the headaches brought with them when at their worst.

When he opened his eyes, he was sitting in a large white room with no windows. In an uncomfortably hard chair. In a circle, with others. Some men, a few woman—nine in all. The nurses stood towards the back, sitting on chairs, crossing and uncrossing their legs, looking at their watches now and then, seeming to reach into their breast pockets for cigarettes or mints or something they needed desperately but were unwilling to give themselves.

A man sitting across from Jim was talking, and gradually Jim began to understand what he was saying.

"It's not as if we all aren't going through the same thing. What did they call it? Adjustment?"

A woman laughed. "Mine told me to get used to it."

Someone else chuckled at this. "I was told it was a period of containment."

421

"Well, it's been working for me to some small extent," the man continued, his voice slight and nervous as if he were afraid of being overheard or of making a mistake in what he said. "At least in the mornings. The mornings are good. It's only about now."

"Yes," another man said, just to the left of Jim. "At about three everyday. Sometimes as late as four. These flashes."

"Flashes of insight," a woman said.

"Hot flashes," another woman said, and they all had a good laugh. "Not that you can't have those, Norman."

Norman, the man who had originally been talking, blushed. He was handsome, mid-forties, and reminded Jim a bit of his father. Actually, the more he spoke, the more Jim was becoming convinced that Norman was related to him in some way. The thin, tall frame, the thick black hair, the nose a bit beaky and the chin a bit strong and the teeth a bit much. "Well," Norman said, "since we're all in this together, and since they," and he nodded backward, to the row of nurses behind him, "Seem to want us to get it all out in these groups, I think we should tell everything we know."

"Not everything," a man said. "I couldn't. It'd be too much."

"All right then," Norman said. "Whatever we feel comfortable with."

"You'll have to begin then, Norman. Mine is rather embarrassing," the laughing woman said. "It involves me and another man and I can't tell you what we seem to do all day long."

More laughter.

"Mine is not that...invigorating," Norman smiled. "I'm just a little boy of ten, perhaps eleven. I live in a small village in Morocco."

"Good lord, not Morocco," the woman said. "Are you a Berber bed-warmer?"

Norman lost his smile. "No, I just help bring water to the house and do a bit of feeding of animals and cleaning and running errands. I'm constantly hungry, and I can't seem to talk with others there, but I can understand them."

"Oh!" the woman gasped, "So interesting compared to mine. I'm the wife to a man who hallucinates."

Jim almost laughed, something in him told him to laugh a bit. He glanced down at his hands and saw the wedding ring on the left hand. He drew it carefully off his finger as the woman told her story. He looked inside the ring. *Cathy and Cliff Forever.*

"Yes, and while he's at work in his dull job, I go have mad affairs up and down Main Street," the woman continued, "only...it's not called Main Street. I find this entertaining if disconcerting. My husband really is a fool. He surprised me a bit today, however."

Jim reached up and felt his neck. It was slender. He drew his fingers across his throat and up around his chin—a small slightly round chin—up to his fullish lips, his small nose, around his eyelashes which seemed long and feathery.

"Dear," someone whispered behind him, "you'll smudge your make-up."

He recognized the voice; it was Nora.

He put his hands down.

"You should listen to the stories," Nora whispered. "It might help your condition?"

Jim nodded, glancing over to the woman who was just finishing up hers.

"He hasn't a clue," she said. "He lies constantly himself. It's easy to fool a liar." She looked over at Jim. "Mrs. Earnshaw, you never told yours, have you?"

The woman seemed to look at Jim with a special knowledge. He began to feel his skin crawl a bit. A coldness seeped into his voice as he spoke.

"There's not much to tell, really. To be honest, I think I'm more there than here." Laughter across the room. "This feels less me than the other. I know so much about him."

"Him?" the woman laughed. "Oh, lord, you got to change sex. Do you play with it much?"

"Juliet," the man named Norman exclaimed, "What a filthy mind you have."

Jim felt slightly offended, particularly for Mrs. Earnshaw, who he imagined to be a very circumspect and polite woman of fifty-two. "Really," he said. He reached down, smoothing the lines of the bathrobe. "Even now, sitting among you, I feel more him than me."

"Tell us about him," Norman said.

"Yes," another chimed in.

"Perhaps I will." Jim paused a moment, wondering where to begin. "He's a nice young man in his late twenties who works for the rails in a little New England town. He is happily married, drives some kind of Japanese car, an older model, and likes rock and roll music from the 1950s. He has terrible headaches..."

After a moment, Jim continued. "Actually, I am more sure I'm him than I am sure that I am me."

Norman's eyes lit up, as he nodded. "That's how it's supposed to be, isn't it? They said you get a gleam at first."

"A glimmer," the woman named Juliet said. The smile on her face grew impossibly wide. "They called it a glimmer. It feels like... like..."

"A warm rain," another said.

"Yes, and then," Norman nodded as if feeling a religious transformation, "the warmth spreads over you."

"Like you've been rewired," another said.

The woman next to him said, "Well, Mrs. Earnshaw's certainly been rewired if she's a man now."

"He's not just a man," Jim said, and for the first time noticed that he spoke with Mrs. Earnshaw's voice. "He's a special young man. He doesn't know it yet, but he's very special."

Behind him, Nora touched his shoulder. She whispered, "I knew you'd be the first, Mrs. Earnshaw."

Jim leaned his head back slightly. "The first to what, dear?"

"The first to cross the bridge," the nurse said.

3

When Jim next recollected anything, he was in bed with Alice, his wife, in their small apartment on Hop Street, the peppermint smell of the nearby toothpaste factory assaulting his senses. Alice was snoring lightly, and as Jim glanced around the darkness, moonlight and the summer steam pouring in through the open window, he saw evidence of sexual abandon—the packet of condoms, open, on the dressing table, the clothes strewn about the floor in a trail, the half-empty glasses of red wine, one spilled on the carpet. Had they been animals? He wished he could remember. Because of their schedules, they didn't make love all that often, and now he had been in some kind of dream support group in a British hospital rather than in his Alice.

Then a disturbing thought occurred to him: was someone else occupying his own body while he occupied Mrs. Earnshaw's? Did Mrs. Earnshaw herself enter his skin and make love to Alice, drink his wine?

He sat up most of the night, just watching Alice as she slept. Sweet Alice, lost in some dreamworld—she stirred, her fingers curled, once, her hand went to her throat, once, she seemed to weep but it was like a puppy sound—a puppy at the door to a room that she wanted to be set free from.

She awoke in the early morning, her eyes opening wide. "What are you doing?"

"Nothing," he said. "Just watching you."

"Why?" she wiped her face with her hands as if washing off a mask of sleep. "You scared me for a moment."

"What was it like?"

"What?"

"What we did last night."

"Weren't you there?" she grinned, giggling.

"I'm not sure."

"Oh stop it. It's too early for jokes." She looked across the bed to the clock. "It's only 5:30. I can sleep some more. That is," she arched an eyebrow, "if you'd quit staring."

She turned over, facing the window. The sunlight had crept up. "Can you close the curtains," she said. "I need some dark."

4

Jim wandered downtown, walked along the river, along the railroad tracks, alongside the boatslips and the chemical factory—miles of walking at dawn, when the town seemed to wake like a baby—from a gasp to a full cry. When the sun was fully up, he got a cup of coffee from the doughnut shop and walked out to the pier, watching the ferry as it crossed to Newburyport.

The 7:15 blew its whistle, coming into the station, and he turned to watch it—remembering the train crash of a few weeks earlier, and the first time he remembered being in the silver British hospital as Mrs. Earnshaw.

Then it came to him. That had not been the first time. That had been the first time he'd remembered it so vividly. Closing his eyes, he recalled an incident when he'd been four or five, and he'd been in a hospital—was it the same one? Only it was not in England. It had been in Massachusetts, when he'd been taken to visit Grammy Evans, her drinking out of control—the white and green rooms, the silver flask she hid even there to take a nip now and then when the nurses weren't looking. "Hold this," she'd said, passing him the silver flask. "Don't let them see it." So, he'd hidden it in his shorts, feeling the cold metal against his thighs. Then, he'd wandered the halls of the hospital while the grown-ups talked and did not notice him missing. He began playing "Spy" and decided that the doctors were Secret Agents. When he came across one, he'd run up some stairs, and down some others, and through double doors and hallways with words written in bright red and yellow along them. And then, he'd come to a room where four men in green masks stood about a table. On the table, a naked old woman who was probably dead. Jim had kept himself hidden away, and he watched as the four doctors injected something terrible into the old woman so that she sat up screaming.

It had made Jim scream, too, and one of the four men turned and saw him and before he could get out the door, someone else grabbed him.

"What in god's name is this kid doing in here? Where the hell is security?" a man said.

The woman screamed again, and then began coughing.

Jim, sitting on the pier, sipped his coffee, trying to remember more, but that had been all.

What he knew without a doubt was that the woman on the table had been Mrs. Earnshaw, and that she was dead when he was a little boy and that somehow this was all a hallucination caused by a traumatic incident.

The coffee grew cold as he closed his eyes, and determined to go into Mrs. Earnshaw in the hospital. He willed a headache to come on, he tried to simulate the pain that arrived, and the flickering lights.

After an hour, he gave up.

Several days later, while he was sitting on the toilet, he arrived into Mrs. Earnshaw again, who was sitting in the garden with Nora. Nora was reading one of her magazines, and Jim was doing a little needlepoint.

"Nora. Tell me about myself," he said.

The nurse glanced up. "All right. I suppose this is good."

"It seems I'm losing bits of me," Jim said, nodding as if to the will of the universe. "I'm not sure where I fit in with all this."

"Well, that was the issue, after all," Nora said. She set her magazine aside, and crossed her leg. "Mind if I light up?"

"Go right ahead, dear."

Nora drew a cigarette from her breast pocket, and struck a match along the edge of the low brick wall she leaned against. After the first puff, she said, "You're a psychiatrist from Bristol who worked with NASA and spent a good deal of time in Belize working on the Arc Project."

"Whatever is that?"

Nora shrugged. "I wish I knew." She said this warmly and without a trace of deception. "All I know is my end of this."

"The Arc Project doesn't even sound familiar to me."

"All of you were involved with it. That's all any of us knows." Another long drag on the cigarette. "You have the mind-link to this man named Jim, as do the others to various people. And you're dying."

"I had no idea," Jim said, setting his needlepoint on his lap. "Why am I called Catherine Earnshaw? That's obviously not my real name."

427

"You picked it. All of you picked names from books and movies. You liked the name Cathy."

"Do you know who I am, really?"

Nora closed her eyes for a minute. Smoked. Scratched a place just above her eyebrows. Opened her eyes. "Not really."

"Doesn't all of this seem inhuman?"

Nora sighed. "We have to trust that this is saving something important for us."

"Saving from what?"

Nora dropped her cigarette to the ground, stubbing it out with the toe of her white shoe. "From loss. The information has to be retained, and it's not like you're a computer that can just be downloaded."

"I wish I could remember the information you're talking about, but really, I can't. There seem to be great gaps in my memory."

"It's just the connection," Nora said. She stepped over to the wheelchair and crouched down before it. She placed her hands over Jim's and looked up into his eyes. "I know that Mrs. Earnshaw is leaving us. I know that you're this other person, this Jim. I can see you when you come into her."

Jim trembled, and felt sweat break out along his neck. "Really?"

Nora nodded. She glanced about, slightly nervous. "I have to tell you something, Jim. There's someone here who is an Intruder from the Arc Project. I'm not sure who, but Mrs. Earnshaw is in danger."

Jim shivered. "What is this all about? Am I crazy?"

Nora grinned. Then, she grew serious again. "Maybe. I never would've thought I'd be involved in this, too. None of us really thought it would work. But someone is after you Jim, not here, in this hospital. But the Intruder is already trying to track you down."

"Who is the Intruder?"

"Someone who is inside one of you. Someone who wants to sabotage the entire operation. A very bad person," Nora said.

"Do you have any idea who it might be?" Jim leaned forward.

But Nora grew silent. An old man in a white jacket walked up beside them.

"Dr. Morgan."

"Here, the rain's coming again," the doctor said. "Let's get Mrs. Earnshaw inside for another series of shots, shall we?"

As Nora wheeled Jim across the path towards the door, as the first drops of rain fell, Jim whispered, "She's already dead, isn't she? Mrs. Earnshaw?"

Nora put her hand on his shoulder, squeezing slightly. She waited until they were in the corridor before she said yes.

5

And that was the last of it for Jim. He returned to work the following day, sitting behind the glass, selling tickets for the train. He tried to induce the headaches, but they seemed to be gone for good. His aspirin bottle stayed full, and he had a feeling of well-being that he almost despised. Occasionally, when he didn't even realize he was doing it, he glanced at his hands, half-expecting to see Mrs. Earnshaw's in their place, her wedding ring on her slightly wrinkled left finger.

A woman said, "Two plus a child for Penn Station."

"One hundred and fifty-two," he said, typing the information into the computer.

She passed him the money, he counted it out. As he passed her the three tickets, he said, "Boarding on the river side, the train's delayed by ten minutes. Arrive Penn Station at 7:30."

She said, "I wanted to get there by 7:00."

He looked at her. She was forty, trim, brown hair cut short and left to fly like a halo around her face. "It won't happen."

The woman looked slightly tense. "It has to happen."

"You could try the airport."

She shook her head. "Damn it," she muttered. She reached for the tickets, grabbing them. Her husband and little girl stood back, near the benches. She turned away, and then turned back. "Is this the same Deerwich where the train crashed once?"

Jim chuckled. "Everyone asks that. Yep, it is. Just to the north, when it crossed the bridge over the river."

429

The woman frowned. "It's dangerous to cross bridges. I hope there aren't too many bridges between here and Manhattan. I never fly and I don't like to cross a bridge that's already had a crash on it. Bad luck."

She and her family went to wait for the train, but Jim sat there with his mouth open. She'd said it, and it felt like a secret code. *It's dangerous to cross bridges. I don't like to cross a bridge that's already had a crash on it. Bad luck.*

On his break at 9:30, he took a walk out along the tracks, trying to remember the night of the train crash when he'd first had the experience. He followed the track up to the bridge over the Sparrow River. He saw the place where it had been repaired, where the train had cut loose and gone off.

They'd blamed it on kids playing quarters, or on a faulty switch. The investigation was on-going. Maybe they'd never know what had malfunctioned with the train on the tracks.

430

He stood there, staring at the tracks, and thinking about the woman complaining about the danger of travel, and remembering Nora's words: *the first to cross the bridge.*

And then he knew, even before he found the list of names in the newspaper of several weeks earlier.

It read like a joke list of names from books and movies, the names of the dead:

Juliet Capulet, Norman Bates, Paul Bunyan, Zazu Pitts, Ramon Navarro, Silas Marner, Gregor Roche—the list of the dead included, he believed, every one he met in that group in the hospital room. Every single one.

In that list, too, was the name Catherine Earnshaw.

All just happened to be in the one car of the train in which all passengers were killed.

Another name, too, that he recognized: Nora Fitch.

He sat down in the library with the newspaper and wept. He drank too much that night, and went wandering along the docks and backstreets, as if somehow the answer would be revealed to him if he searched hard enough. Finally, after 2:00 A.M., he ambled home.

As he lay down next to his sleeping wife, he wrapped his arms around her, wanting to feel safe from a world he did not understand, another world he'd somehow been thrust into, whether through madness or design.

Alice's skin was almost hot to the touch, and he realized she was burning with fever. She moaned slightly in her dream, and he let go of her, for her fever seemed to spread.

She woke with a start, and said, "What are you doing?"

"Sorry," he said, his breath a blast of whiskey. "I just needed to touch you."

She rolled onto her back, staring up at the ceiling. "You're drunk."

"Sure am," Jim said, wanting to touch his wife so badly, wanting to wrap himself around her and be part of her so he would not feel so alone in his madness, in his fears.

"Go to sleep," she commanded, "in the morning you'll be sober and we can talk about things."

"What things?" he asked, reading to fall in the coma of drunken sleep.

"Things about us. Things we should talk about. Things we need to talk about," Alice said. She sat up. Switched on the bedside lamp. He looked at her naked back, wishing it could be pressed against his chest and stomach.

"I love you," he whispered hoarsely, unsure whether or not he had really said it aloud or had only wanted to say it.

"I'm not who you think I am," Alice said, still not facing him. "Not anymore."

"Yes you are," he said. "Of course you are. You're my wife. You're Alice."

But he hadn't said Alice, had he? As he lay there, the fear washing over him like a warm bath, he knew he had said "You're Juliet," because something within him knew it was Juliet, the Mrs. Earnshaw part of him knew, had known, and had been trying to tell him in her own way, had been trying to tell him that this was no longer the woman he loved but a woman who called herself Juliet

431

Capulet and might not even be a woman at all or even a human being as far as he knew.

The Mrs. Earnshaw part of him let him know that this was the Intruder in his bed.

He lay there, feeling his heart beat accelerate as Alice slowly turned in the lamp-light, a half-grin on her face. As her smile curled up, and her eyes glimmered with a dark onyx that might have been shadow, might have been stone, she said, "We have to have a long talk, you and I, about what really is going on inside that mind of yours."

"Juliet?" he asked.

She smiled. "I'm Alice. Alice. Remember? Your Alice."

She sat there, watching him, and he could not sleep.

In the morning, she rose and went to shower.

Jim lay there, frozen, waiting for what was to come. Remembering the woman on the table surrounded by doctors and realized that in some respects he was still there in that room watching Mrs. Earnshaw—or whomever the body had been—being brought back to life, or some form of life, some kind of intelligence within the skin that had so recently been shed.

How he had felt a presence in that room when he was only four, a presence that was not entirely human, not entirely like a middle-aged woman whose heart had given out and who now was going to have another being within her.

Just as he had felt that being, briefly, within him.

When the water stopped, he heard Alice sing as she toweled off, and then she opened the bathroom door and something that was not entirely Alice moved like silver liquid towards him.

But even as he felt something warm and metallic inject itself into his throat, he had the sense that he was not Jim at all, but something that lived within the skin of a nice lady sitting on a moving train as it headed down the New England coast.

6

You mustn't pass this on, because I know who you are on the inside, but you haven't crossed the bridge fully, have you, dear?

432

Only Connect

You're still only halfway across, feeling the warm rain, the glimmer as it warms you, but it has not burst within you yet.

Mustn't make this worse than it is. It's only a train after all, and travel by rail is so safe these days.

Look at that little town we're coming to now.

Isn't it lovely?

Across that river.

Across that bridge.

Get ready, dear. Our connection's coming up shortly.

The Little Mermaid

The beach-house was large, and an entire glass wall looked out
upon the flat brown sand below the hill, to the brief line of pavement
for the boat landing, down where the pelicans and gulls cracked their
clams and oysters and crabs.

Alice didn't see the birds or the beach much. That first year, she
kept the curtains drawn shut. Sometimes, she opened them, standing
at the window, smoking a cigarette. The ocean was a haze most of
the winter, but that was fine by her. She wasn't an ocean person. She
could not even swim, and she never waded. She considered herself
more of an isolationist, and that is precisely what the beach-house
offered. She drank a lot of her father's stored wine (a woodbin had
been converted into a wine cellar), and only left the house twice a
week to go see a therapist in Nag's Head.

Molly came down for a visit that lasted approximately six hours
before the mother-daughter anger got out of hand; Molly still didn't
understand the divorce, and being a mother now herself and perhaps
(Alice surmised) in a bad marriage, Molly was young enough to still
believe in staying together for the sake of family.

Alice read a lot of books, particularly long fat ones that took
her mind off life and her miserableness at it. When she thought of
it, she practiced her own brand of yoga based on having watched a

morning television show once. When the hangovers from the red wine became unbearable, she slacked off drinking, and became a coffee addict. This prompted her to frenetic activity, in the winter; she began jogging on the beach, finally unable to avoid the outdoors and health (which she kept in check by smoking and drinking coffee sometimes into the wee hours) and thus, she met the old man who collected shells.

He was, at first, barely a face to her, for while her jogging was slow enough to distinguish features on the few beachcombers who came down her way, she had stopped looking anyone in the face. She noticed his hands, actually, and the cracked, worm-holed shells he held in them. His hands were tanned and rough. Then, another day, she noticed his knees: rather knobby, with fat blue veins down the sides of them. Finally, she met him the day she sprained her ankle at a place where the sand sank. She sat on a large piece of driftwood—moving the red kelp to the side—and rubbed her ankle.

He walked right up to her. "You okay?"

She nodded. She still could not bring herself to look at his face. She looked at his feet: he was barefoot, as was she, with a particularly nasty looking ingrown toenail on his big toe.

"If you run, you should wear shoes," he said. "The sand tugs at your heel. It's very bad for your arches. It's made for crabs and seaweed, not people, this beach is."

"I'll take that into consideration next time," she said, testily. She rubbed her foot.

"Here," he said, dropping to his knees. She could no longer avoid his face. He was probably in his late sixties; old enough to be her father by a hair. He had brown eyes and thin lips. He must've been handsome, but it had turned to sand, his skin had, and his nose, the shiny red of a lifelong drinker.

He took her foot in his hands, and rubbed.

"Please," she said, pulling her foot back. It hurt when she did it.

"I'm a doctor," he said. "Retired now, but I know something about feet. We'll just massage it a little."

"Well," she said, non-committally. No one was around to watch, and it did feel good. He pressed his thumbs into the soft flesh at her ankle; the sensation burned at first, but then, as he continued, it felt warm and pleasant. She had had a headache; it melted.

He watched her. "You need to keep off this for a few days. I can wrap it for you, if you like."

Because she was financially broke from countless therapy sessions and the divorce itself and would not be able to afford any medical expense if her foot's condition worsened, she agreed to this. She leaned against his shoulder, and he guided her back to her house.

In the master bathroom, he heated torn rags of old towels in the sink with hot water. Then, he squeezed them, and tied them around her ankle and foot. "The heat," he said, "it helps. They say it's ice that helps, but not for this. It'll swell up from the heat, but it needs to."

Alice, who knew nothing of medicine, nodded as if she did.

"Sometimes we need fluids to collect. They carry away the bad stuff."

She almost laughed. "Sorry, sorry," she said, "it's just that it sounded so undoctorly."

He grinned. He was a warm man, she decided. Not like her ex. This old man, he was a good country doctor who cared. He was a housecall kind of doctor. He said, "I try my best. I find that all that medical jargon gets in the way of patient care. Sometimes nature knows best."

"I couldn't agree more."

He continued to massage her foot through the warm wet rags.

"You collect shells?" she asked, not wanting him to stop.

"I'm rather aimless these days. Since my wife died."

"I'm sorry."

"Oh, we had quite a life together. Life, while it lasts, has its own secrets."

Alice didn't quite understand him, but she really didn't want to get into the dead wife as a topic of conversation any more than she wanted to start prattling on about her husband.

"So I walk the beaches like I'm waiting for a ship to come in or something. Like an old salt. Do you believe in mermaids?" His eyes glistened a bit, as if he practiced this question and its anticipated response.

"No."

"I used to, when I was a boy." He grinned dopily. "Do you know that when a man becomes old, he begins to remember what he believed in as a child and it all comes back to him?"

Something sweet in his voice; that boy that was him thousands of years before, that little boy, was still there in his eyes. She smiled. He rubbed.

"I believed that out in that ocean was a lovely mermaid. She and I knew each other, and when I was four, I would go down to the beach early in the morning, before anyone else was up, and stand on the edge of the land and sing mermaid songs to her. I imagined her fins and her tail, how if she were on land, I would carry her to a safe place and how she would tell me all the secrets of the sea. And I, in turn, would tell her how much I loved her, how much I wanted to be with her," he said.

438

Alice began weeping upon hearing this. She could not control it, and it was not just about the pathetic little four-year-old who sang to the non-existent mermaids; it was about everything she'd wished for as a child, all within her grasp, gone now, like sand, like sea-water, the way memory always left her bereft and longing for innocence. He slid his hands from her feet and placed them on either side of her face. They were comfortingly cold.

"A beautiful woman should never cry," he said.

"I'm sorry."

"No, don't say that, either. Your tears are like the mermaids."

She opened her eyes to him, and felt that lustful heat of first love again, just as if he were not old and she were not middle-aged.

He caressed her, and they fell across the bed, her ankle's throbbing becoming a distant and occasional pinching. They kissed, weeping, both of them, and then he kissed her every arch and turn and curve.

Afterwards, she fell asleep.

When she awoke, the pain was excruciating. The room, shrouded in darkness. The curtains were still drawn shut. She gasped; a light came on.

Her doctor-lover stood over her.

The pain was in her foot. She wasn't thinking clearly because of the pain.

She reached down to touch her foot, anticipating a throbbing ankle.

But her hand, sliding down her leg, ended at a stump.

She touched the air where her foot should've been.

He said, "I had to operate, Alice." He knew her name now, even though she didn't know his.

His words seemed meaningless, until on the third try to find her foot where it should've been, she suddenly understood.

Her screaming might've been heard, had the night surf not boomed, had the winter not brought with it a tree-bending wind.

The operation was not completed for six days; it was a blur to Alice, for he kept her drunk and on painkillers.

When she awoke, clear-headed, she felt nothing but a constant stinging all up and down her spine, as if her skin had been scraped and she'd been rolled in salt.

There was dried blood on the sheets. Several hypodermic needles lay carelessly beside her. Fish scales, too, spread out in a vermillion and blue desert, piled high, as if every fish in the ocean had been skinned and thrown about. The smell was intolerable: oily and fishy, and the flies! Everywhere, the blue and green flies.

She tried to sit up, but her back hurt too much. She fought this, but then parts of her body, including her arms, felt paralyzed. She wondered what drugs he'd been administering to her—strangely, she felt euphoric, and fought this feeling.

439

She lay back down, closed her eyes, willing this dream to depart.

She awoke again when he came back into the room.

"One last thing," he said, holding the serrated knife up to her neck, "one last thing."

The blade had been warmed with the fire on the gas stove. She felt no pain as he took the knife and scored several slits just below her chin. Afterwards, she could not even speak or scream, but could only open her mouth and emit a bleating noise.

He lifted her up into his arms, kissing her nipples like they were sacred, and carried her out to the beach. "I will take you out to your city, my love, and set you free," he said, as he laid her down in the bottom of a small boat. She could only stare at him. She felt resigned to death, which would be better than the results of the torture he had put her through.

Out to sea, he rolled her over the edge of the boat.

440 At first, she wanted to drown, but something within her fought against it. She managed to grasp hold of some rocks out beyond the breakwater. She held onto them for over an hour as the freezing salt water smashed against the back of her head.

She grasped at the edge of a rock; it cut at her hands, but she held on. *If I just hang on for another minute*, she thought, *just another ten seconds, I'll be fine. God will rescue me. Or someone will see me. Will see what he's done to me, this madman. I haven't lived all my life to come to this. I know something will happen. Something will pull me out of this.*

The waves crashed around her, like glass shattering against her face. *Please, God, someone, help me.* All she could taste was the stinging salt. Something animal within her was clinging to all that she knew of life, now, not her marriage or her family or her career, but this serrated rock and this icy sea.

From the shore, she heard him, even at the distance. His boat already docked. The old man stood there, singing.

Alice held onto the rock for as long as she could.

Then, she let go.

The old man stayed on the shore for hours, his voice faltering only when dark arrived. He had a great and lovely baritone, and he sang of all the secrets of the sea. A couple, walking along the beach that evening held each other more tightly, for his song sparked within them a memory of love and regret, and such beautiful and heart-rending longing.

They watched him from a distance, as the old man raised his hands up, his songs batting against the wind, against the crash of the surf, against all that life had to offer.

441

The Night
Before Alec Got
Married

1

You can never be too sure or too stupid, but you can be too horny—Alec DelBanco, he was smart, but men are never very smart in that one area, and it got him right where you don't want to be got, not if you're twenty-four and on the run because something's after you, only it doesn't have a name and maybe it doesn't even have a face but you can see it sometimes in *their* faces looking out at you like it's some kind of tourist on a world cruise and you're one of the Wonders of the World to It. You call it an It because you don't know if It's been noticed by anyone else, and you can't really talk about It, because if you did, maybe that's when It would get you.

It got Alec that night, and he didn't even have to talk about It. Boy, was he smart, he was practically Phi-Fucking-Beta Kappa from Stanford, and then the job with Kelleher-Darden with an eighty-thousand-a-year salary for a twenty-two-year-old asshole you used to get drunk with—well, everybody figured Alec had just grabbed the golden ring and had not let go. And handsome! He'd been a stud since the age of twelve, if you remembered far back enough when every girl you'd ever had a crush on seemed to only want to get near you so they could get within breathing distance of your friend. Still, Alec DelBanco never forgot a friend, and you got some fringe benefits from knowing him all those years, beautiful girls who wouldn't normally give you the time of day all around you — you couldn't touch them, of course, not in the light of day, not with them in the room, that is, but, oh! when the lights were out and you were alone in bed with your hand and a little imagination — you had them all every which way but loose! You loved Alec, though, really loved him. Like a brother, I mean, because you'd practically grown up with him since you could remember. He was better than a brother, too, because your own brothers were kind of missing something in the compassion department. I wouldn't fuck a guy, no way, but if I had to fuck a guy — I mean like the Nazis had me in this torture rack and told me I'd have to fuck a guy or get it cut off, well, I couldn't fuck just anyone — it would have to be Alec, and not just 'cause he was pretty, but because I have feelings for him — but not like you think. Once, in the showers after gym, he was leaning around to get his towel, and I swear to god this is true, I thought he was a girl, from the back, he's all lean and muscular, but I thought he looked like, you know, one of those Olympic women swimmers, taut and strong but kind of attractive, too. So, yeah, if pressed into it, I guess you could say I'd do him.

444

But this isn't about me or what I would do if the Fourth Reich came along — and it just might if you read the papers — it's about Alec and the night before he got married. His girl, Luce, was out with a whole gaggle down at the Marina getting toasted on margaritas and opening cute little presents, while you and me were over on Sunset trying to find just the right pro to come in and do a little dance over Alec's face when he least suspected it. I didn't like Luce too much — she was always kind of a bitch to me, almost like she thought I wanted Alec more than she did. I've got to be honest here, I would've preferred Alec to marry a hooker and at least be happy rather than wed Lucille C. St. Gerard, a fifth generation Californian from Sacramento who debuted at every second-rate cotillion north of Bakersfield.

So we cruise Sunset, all the way from, say, La Cienega up to Raleigh Heights, and it's getting close to nine — you'd think every working girl in the world would be out by that time — Saturday night, party night, but we only see a bunch of tired old dogs pounding the pavement. You and me, we're doing St. Pauli Girl, but keeping the bottles low so the cops don't notice, when I see what I think is just about the most beautiful piece of work this side of the Pacific and I slam on the brakes and cross a lane to park.

"Look at her, holy mother of fuck, look at her," I say, and barely remember to put on the parking brake. I leap out of the Mustang—it's a convertible—and practically dive right over to her. She's got everything, and packed tight: a nice rack of tits, thin waist, and child-bearing hips. But what really gets me are the lips on her, big fat suckers that make me wonder if her labia's like that, too.

"Hey, little boy," she says, "you want some sugar in your coffee tonight?"

I've never picked up a whore, so I feel real tongue-tied.

"You want a date?" She's got teeth all the way down her throat, it seems, big white flashy teeth with a couple of gold caps in the way back. She's practically steaming there like an oyster out of the fish market, and I start to feel like a twelve-year-old of rage hormones and dripping wick.

"Listen," I say, "I got this friend. Alec."

She looks at you in the car, "That him? He's cute."

"No, no, that's not him. We're throwing a bachelor party tonight. We need a stripper."

"I can do that. I can do all of you boys."

"Well, more than a stripper," I say.

She shrugs, "I can do that, too."

"We want you to get him alone and you know," I say.

She smiles. "A dance and a fuck? It'll cost you."

"Not just a dance and not just a fuck, okay? We want the Dance of Seven Veils, like Salome did, we want you to really get him to want you, and then it's got to be more than fireworks, more than an explosion, it's got to be the Big O."

"The Big O?"

"You know, the Orgasm at the End of the Universe. The Big One. The kind that guys dream about in their sleep, the kind that most of us never get."

445

She looks at me sideways, like maybe I'm some kind of creep with diarrhea of the mouth. "You just talking, ain't you? You don't really want the Big O, nothin like that, do you?"

I shake my head. "Every trick you got. Think you can do it?"

She has a look in her eyes like she's thinking, but cagily—she has a few secrets, I guess, and she guards them. Her eyes are muddy brown, and when she looks back at me, they look like tiny little pebbles, hard and round. "Baby," she says, "I think *I* can do *anything*. You pay, I'm gonna make sure it happens." She glances down the street. There's a big fat guy wearing a Hawaiian shirt—he looks less like a beach boy and more like a beached something else. "My manager," she says. "You need to talk with him, I think. I ain't too good at the business side of things."

Because I don't want to talk to him, I get you to do it, and the whole thing's arranged, even though it's going to cost us: four hundred bucks, plus whatever she makes in her dance, and if it goes over two hours, another four hundred. Two hundred in advance, so I pay the pimp, and we give him the address, to be there at eleven, all that shit, and then we head on back to the party.

Now, this is the part where I'm really stupid I guess, but you can't have a stripper come to the party without giving somebody an address. But I guess this pimp looks at the money and figures there's more where that came from—so he must've gotten this idea—and I'm only assuming. You and me, we look like nice preppie kind of guys, shit, we practically have ties on from work, and I'm wearing $500 Italian shoes. So he decides that when he takes his girl over, he better pack something, because you never know how much cash you can get out of rich, scared, drunk guys at a bachelor party. I don't know a thing about guns, but this pimp probably had the automatic kind, and I figure that's how you got two of your fingers shot off before midnight.

2

But I'm getting ahead of myself—it's easy to do when you're spilling your guts and you can't always remember the sequence of events; especially if you're trying to second-guess everyone around you. The thing with your fingers, it didn't happen until about eleven fifty-five, and the thing with Luce, that happened just before ten, after we'd gotten back, hoisted a few more St. Pauli's and watched Long Jean Silver and her amazing stump-screwing of another woman in one of the six videos you rented from that scuzzy video store down in Long Beach. But something happened before even that, and that was when we stopped for more beer at 7-11, and I bought a bunch of multi-colored rubbers, all fancy, and then pricked them full of holes and you and I laughed our heads off thinking about Alec and Luce on their honeymoon, thinking they were doing some family planning by wearing the rubbers. I don't think I've ever laughed so hard.

So I stuff the rubbers in my jacket pocket. As I'm pulling out of the 7-11, a car almost hits the Mustang, and then swerves and crashes into a wall; the front half is all crushed, but the driver seems okay. "Should we call for help?" you ask, and I say, "oh, right, like the cops are gonna love the beer in the car and all." So we pass this woman in the car, and she looks at us for a second, and I got to tell you, I will never, as long as I live forget that look. Women are like this swamp, or something, all dark and mysterious, but still you got to explore 'em, it's a guy thing. You know, I always say that if you were to put some fur around a garbage disposal, we'd all still take turns at it, even if it was turned on. But women, they have this power, that woman in the car, it was like she'd cursed us, you and me both. But we drive on, get to the house, ring the doorbell like twenty times before you remember you've got a key, and we get up to the party just in time to hear one of Ben Winter's dumb blonde jokes. Billy Bucknell had been throwing up since about eight o'clock, and the bastard is still drinking. MoJo keeps stuffing his fat face with Cheetohs, every now and then burping or farting; three guys I don't know are there, too, not that into the flicks, more into the poker game and cigars; Alec's little brother Pasco is sneaking peeks at the t.v. screen, but pretending to be more into a bowl of pretzels. And Alec—where the hell is he? Back in the can, ralphing his guts out—he's not too good at mixing the finer

447

liquors with the baser variety, but our motto through college had always been that if you boot then you can keep on drinking. Alec was going to become a severe alcoholic, by the look of things, because within ten minutes of coming out of the bathroom, he's already mixing Zombies with Todd Ramey ("from Wisconsin," he kept telling everybody who gave a fuck). So Alec is battered and sloshed from the twin bombs of imminent marriage and bad booze, but he still has the classic smile and his dark hair still parts perfectly to one floppy side. "Hey, you," he flags me down with an overflowing plastic cup, "get it over here, man," he says, putting his arm out for a big hug, "dude, you should've seen the mud getting flung at dinner, her sister's a major twat."

When I get close to him, his breath is like a toilet bowl; I pull back a little to let a breeze from the ocean beyond the open window protect me. You keep looking at your watch; you're nervous, I guess, about the whore. I say, "So, Lec, I saw Pasco. Getting tall these days that boy is."

This brings a tear to Alec's eye. "My baby brother. Gettin' older. Already he's climbed into more panties than me. HEY!" shouting across the room, "PAQUALE!"

His brother glances over, shakes his head, maybe even rolls his eyes, and looks away.

"He's pissed 'cause he's taking her side in this," Alec makes some obscure but definitely obscene gesture towards his brother.

"Whose side?"

"Luce's. She and that sister, Jesus is all I can say. Just Jesus. Hey, you wanna get stoned? C'mon, please? Wanna get stoned?"

I shake my head, but I can tell that you, you want to get stoned 'cause you're all shivering, and I'm afraid you're about to blow it and tell him this whore's coming from the city, the kind with a pimp. But you don't blow it; you go over to get another drink, and I think that's a good idea. "What's up with Luce?"

"Ah, that bitch. Thinks she owns me. God, this is a good party, all my friends." Alec begins crying; he was always verging on the sentimental, ever since I'd first met him. It was some Italian thing, I guess (he always said it was), about not needing to keep a tight rein on emotions, all the stuff. I kind of liked him for it, because I've never been a good one with the tears and open with anger. So, anyway, he tells me all about this thing with Luce, how she heard some story from her sister about Alec and this girl at a party from about a week back and suddenly she's claiming that he's doing everything that walks the earth. "She has this trust thing, it's something I don't understand," he says, "I mean, I trust her, hell, I'd trust her even if she was jawing some guy right in the backseat while I was driving, why the hell doesn't she trust me? It's not like I was unfaithful to her or anything, I was just, well, pursuing a little."

"Women," I shake my head, amazed that yet another woman failed to understand a man so completely, "and it's not like you were even married."

We both crack up at this, drunk as we are. "She even called me an asshole," he says, and we laughed some more.

"Of course," I say, coming down from the laughing high just like those kids in *Mary Poppins* when they came down from Uncle Albert's ceiling, "it's true. I mean, we're all assholes. Basically. All men are assholes."

449

"Basically," he concurs, and we crack up again.

As if this were the greatest cue in the world, the French doors open—we're at your folks' house at Redondo, with the cliff and the balcony and the moonswept Pacific just out there—*out there*—and it's the door to the balcony, so whoever it is has to have climbed up the trellis or something to get to the second floor, and who do you think's standing there with a tight green dress and a big old ribbon tied around her waist looking like Malibu Barbie on a date, but Luce, more Nautilized and Jazzercised than when I'd last seen her, and she just keeps coming like a barracuda right towards Alec and spits in his face.

He's still laughing from the joke, too, so now he's all shiny and laughing and hiccuping like he might start throwing up again.

Luce looks at me, "When he sobers up, tell him there won't be a wedding, tell him I know all about it, and tell him he can go to hell."

Then, she turns, and sort of flounces out of the room, down the hall stairs, presumably to go out the front door now.

"What," Alec says, shaking his head, "she fly up here on her broom?"

"Must've," I say, "so, wedding's off?"

"Jesus, if I listened to her, the wedding would've been off for the past six months. Trust me, man, she's gonna be there tomorrow, it's costing her dad too much and her ego way too much—she'd rather wait and get divorced later on, I know her, I know my Luce." And it was true about Luce—she'd rather worry about divorce in a couple of years than NOT GETTING MARRIED, she attached a lot of status to Alec—his family was rich, he was rich, and they were going to be living in Palos Fucking Verde Estates and have a house big enough for the two of them and any lovers that snuck in the back door.

But with love, who knows? Could be once that ring was on his finger, he'd be the most faithful little lapdog the world has ever known. Could be she would be, too, and then they'd sink into the marriage trap where sex is an outmoded idea, and lust gets swept between the rug and the floor.

But not the night of his Bachelor Party.

You keep drinking those Zombies, and I say to Alec, my arm around him, his arm around me, "We got this girl, Alec, oh, Christ is she a girl. She's got a nice rack of tits."

He giggles, and then dissolves into weeping again, "You're my best friend, you know that? You are my fucking-A best friend in the whole snatch-eating world."

"Yeah, yeah," I say, and the doorbell rings—I don't quite hear it, but you do, and you go to the door downstairs—I see you bounding down the stairs like a kid on Christmas. I decide to check out the poker game, but I can tell Alec's all hot for this stripper, and he watches the stairs expectantly.

You come up a few minutes later, the pimp and stripper in tow, and there's like dead silence—even the music stops, like the Bruce Springsteen CD knew when to end.

The stripper's changed clothes—she's in a kind of party outfit, something that Luce herself would wear, in fact, at a casual, by-the-sea kind of affair: it says glitz and glamour, but it also says, throw me in the pool. Alec calls that kind of dress a French maid's outfit, a short skirt to show off legs, and lots of poofy ruffles, and those kind of fluffy short sleeves like the Good Witch had in Wizard of Oz—in fact, she looks a little like the good witch, but with a very short dress and a nice rack of tits. But she's changed more than her clothes. I could swear her eyes had been brown when I'd spoken with her on the street, only now, they're Liz Taylor blue, and her skin seems sort of peaches and creamy, instead of the tanned and beat look she had before. But I know a good contact lens can do a lot, and maybe with make-up—I mean, women are so into changing their faces with paints and brushes, like they're all afraid we won't want to see their true faces (and I've seen a couple of chicks without their mascara and gloss and stuff, and let me tell you, it gets pretty scary when you're prettier than your date at four a.m.) Alec, he looked more fetching than Luce when she didn't wear a lot of make-up—I don't think I'm more into guys or anything, but give me Luce without make up or Alec, and I'd rather see Alec's baby face down on my bone any day.

So the whore looks almost completely different than she had on the street. She looks like she could fit right in with the house and all of us, and I was thinking, boy, you did this right, you got the right girl.

I look over at you, and you wink at me, because we know that even if this girl costs us a thousand bucks or more, it's all worth it for Alec's last night before his doom.

Her pimp, who's still dressed like one of the Beach Boys on acid, is casing the place in a fairly obvious way, and I realize at this point that you and I have made a colossal mistake. We should've just got a stripper out of the phone book, but stupid me, I wanted a girl who would, for a little extra, take Alec into one of the empty bedrooms and sit on his face. The pimp sees me, comes over, grabs my drink out of my hand and drinks it. Fairly turns my stomach. "Nice place," he says, his voice half-gravel and half-belch. "Name's Lucky. You boys gonna have a good time tonight?"

"Yeah, yeah," I say, wishing we'd wiped him off on the doormat out front.

Then he whispered, "You be careful with her, now, boy, 'cause she's one of a kind, and I don't want nothing funny to happen to her. If there's gonna be sex, it's got to only be head or hand, no tail, you got me? It ain't safe for my girl to do tail, not with everything going around."

It dawns on me, drunk as I'm getting, that in some sewer-rat way, he cares for this girl. "We will, don't worry, man. Get yourself a drink, sit down, enjoy!"

"Naw," he says, "it's time to let the games begin."

I notice he's packing something under his flappy shirt—just the glimpse of some kind of revolver. I think, well, he's in a rough business, but I know he's got to protect himself. He sees me see the gun, and we stare at each other, but he says nothing. He's got eyes like a snake, all perverted looking and squinty—sometimes I think people with squinty eyes have squinty brains, and this pimp, if anyone has one, hell, he's got the most squinty-ass brain on the planet. I'm thinking of maybe turning the revolver into a joke, by saying, "So's that a gun in your pants or are you just happy to see me," but I know people with squinty brains aren't going to chuckle at that old stand-by. I keep my mouth shut.

And then, the girl punches up a CD of Rod Stewart's song Hot Legs or whatever it's called, and she started a routine.

But you don't want to hear about how she writhed and spun, how she took everything imaginable off, lifted one leg above her head, how Alec played the Golden Shower game with her—drinking Molson Golden Ale from her pubes, how she squatted on my face and took a rolled up fifty from between my lips just using her snatch—those are all the basics of a good party stripper.

What you want to hear about is how your fingers got on the floor in the bathroom, with you screaming bloody murder, and how she screamed even louder, right?

That's what you want to hear.

3

I guess I'm going to digress a little here, but only for clarity's sake—the night before Alec got married was one of those nights where you have to piece a few things together later on. Like Pasco, Alec's little bro, giggling and blushing when the girl sat on his lap naked and beat his pretty face silly with her tits; or when MoJo got pissed off because she wouldn't sit on his face for a lousy ten bucks; he said, whining, "doesn't she know any cheaper games?"—see, the girl was so hot and we were so loaded, that we were dropping hundreds and fifties on her like she was a bank. Cigar smoke was the only veil she had around her, in the end, just that stagnant smoke that stinks and sits in the air like it doesn't have anywhere to go, and all of us, through its mist, looking like ghosts. That's what I thought at the time: we were enshrouded by the gray smoke, and we looked like ghosts, or maybe old men with wrinkly skin, testicular skin, pale and blurry of feature. Horny bastards all, MoJo licking his lips like he was trying to taste her from three feet away, and Billy Bucknell grabbing his crotch without even knowing he was doing it. She really had us going, that girl did. You even kept trying to get your hand up her, and she kept pushing you away, until her pimp had to come over and tell you to knock it off, that nobody, but nobody touches her kitty. That's what he called it, her kitty. Might as well have called it her flesh purse, since she was making so much money out of opening it up. The pimp and I had a nice convo about how prostitution was a victimless crime, and all that; his name was Lucky Murphy, a nice Irish boy as it turned out, from Boston, who had once been a fisherman off Dana Point, and as he spoke I could practically hear someone's Irish mother singing, "Danny Boy," until I looked him in the eye and knew he was a fucking liar through and through, that he was Hollywood scum and if he could, he would've been peddling all our preppie asses for the twenty bucks per corn-hole he could make.

And we keep looking at her kitty, too, all our eyes drawn back to the unholies of unholy, "little pouty petals," you called it. You were pretty adamant about getting your fingers up there, weren't you, you horny son of a bitch? It wasn't the pastrami labia of Penthouse magazine, or the mu-shu pork-dripping-with-plum-sauce of other, nastier skin mags—it was pink and sweet, almost like a Portuguese Man-of-War turned on its back.

And finally, when it was over, all her dances, she took the party boy into the bedroom, and all I can say is, he didn't come out for over an hour.

In fact, by 1:15 he hadn't come out at all, and that's when you and I decided to storm the room.

4

Now, I had seen this room once before—it was your folks' master bedroom, and it was a good size, with kind of a faggy bed, if you were to ask me, lots of silk and brass; a nightstand that looked like it was out of the Versailles; green-gold wallpaper, shiny and clean like they'd just had it put up the day before; a wall that was nothing but mirrors; and two walk-in closets, the sizes of my apartment in Westwood; a bathroom, all gold-plated fixtures, something I always thought was tacky about your folks—and I told you this a few times, too—with a big round Jacuzzi bath and a window so you could take a bath and watch your neighbors at the same time.

The door is locked, of course, but you know how to take a dime and very simply unlock it. So we get in, and the bed is perfectly made; no sign of hooker or trick. You go into the bathroom to look for them, giggling as always both of us are, because we think we're going to find them with her ass bent over a sink and his schlong pumping in like an oil drill; I check out the walk-in closets, but there's nothing but tons of Armani and Valentino and the smell of Red and L'Air du Temps.

As I'm about to go into the second closet, the pimp comes running in, out of breath because it's quite a hike up those stairs in your folks' house. "What you boys doin?"

I cackle—sometimes, when I'm really bombed and in a party mood, I do this laugh that's like "snort-cackle-pop," and it sounds like I hurt myself or something.

Then I notice, he's got his revolver out.

Oh, shit, I'm thinking. I sober up real fast. "Looking for the party boy."

He just stares at me with the gun drawn, and that's when I hear the girl in the bathroom, kind of moaning, and you, too, still giggling, and that wet sound like rubber and lubricant.

And another sound, while the Irish pimp from hell is staring at me, a sound in the walk-in closet.

My hand is on the door.

But someone else's hand is on the other side of the door.

"Alec?" I ask the door.

The sound that comes back isn't entirely human, but it's human enough. It sounds like the noises Alec used to make when he was doing like a feeb imitation: like his tongue got cut out and his lips are shredded. So I think maybe it's some kind of set up and joke on me, so I give the door a good pull, and it opens.

Dresses and coats, hanging, rustling, in a dark closet.

The sound of slow dripping.

I can smell the pimp's breath: he's real close to me.

I can tell he's a little scared, too, and he still has the gun out.

He's pointing it at the dresses, hanging.

Something clear and dripping from the corner of a full-length mink coat.

I switch on the closet light, but the pimp, very quickly switches it off again.

But in that one second of light, I see something in the corner.

Something that left a trail of slime and human waste in its path.

Its ribs quivering.

Open, and quivering, like the skeleton of a boat, a slaughter-house boat with the flesh and innards of animals dripping from its deck.

It's always through the eyes that you know someone. I once took care of a friend's dog when I was eight; and then, when I was nineteen, and had long ago moved away from that friend, I was in New York, in Central Park, and I saw in the eyes of a dog an old friend, and sure enough, it was the dog I had known when I was eight, and in Orange County. It's always there in the eyes, the person, the animal, the creature, not in the skin or voice or the movements: it's in the eyes.

So, I had seen in the brief light, his eyes, Alec's eyes, left in their sockets long after the skin had been torn from bone and skull to make the rest of him resemble a skinned 'possum.

455

And when it registers on my brain that it's Alec, that this girl did something to Alec, something inhuman, I hear your scream from the bathroom, and I turn and the pimp turns, and the girl screams, too, and there's the sound of breaking glass.

The pimp gets to the bathroom first, before me, and I hear him fire two shots; I'm just behind him, and when I see you clutching your hand with all that blood coming out, I figure the pimp shot your fingers off. For just a second, I see her, too, not as she was, pretty and tall and sexy, but some small tentacled thing, like a sea urchin, dropped from between her legs, released from the empty and ragged socket that had been her vagina, with a cut umbilical cord, loping on its worm-like feelers across the bathtub rim, out the broken window, into the night.

The pimp yells, "Goddamn it, that fucking bitch," and then drops his gun, grabs me by the collar, "you bastards, you asked for it, you ain't supposed to get her down there, that's what she wants, you sons of bitches, you're supposed to get head or a hand-job, didn't she tell you? She tricked you, and she was the best, you sons of whores!" He's weeping, and I'm thinking: Christ, he's in love with...that thing.

"Is that a fucking alien?" I'm screaming, "You brought some fucking outer space—"

But, he cuts me off, spitting a wad of slime on my face, "I fished her out of the sea, asshole, down at Santa Monica pier, she got caught on my hook and she does things to you, she gets boys like you, but not like this, it's up to you, your buddies wanting to put it there, but I told you that ain't allowed! She's the best, but you can't touch her there, it's so hard to trap her, and now, look what you done!"

But you, you start screaming again and turning blue, so the pimp lets me go and goes running out of there in search of his escaped sea creature. That's when I figure it's time to call an ambulance.

5

So now I know it wasn't the pimp shooting at you, but at that thing, that thing that you stuck your fingers up into. It was hell cleaning up the mess in the bathroom, getting rid of her skin. Funny thing about her skin and guts—they looked like they'd been spun with a fine silk, but they were all sticky, just like she was some kind of tar baby out of Uncle Remus. You were lucky to lose only your fingers. Think of what Alec lost, the night before he got married—not that he ever did get married. He's sort of a vegetable now, living off of machines at his folks house, and Luce got married to Billy Bucknell last year, that scheming son of a gun.

You and me, we're rooming together these days. My new nickname for you is Fingers, and in the morning, when you bring me coffee, it's kind of nice, just the two of us. We get by. I tried to do it with a girl again, after that, but what if she's up inside there, what if that girl's just spun out of her silk, what if she's waiting to take me to the Big O and rip my skin right off my back and end up like Alec with wires and tubes all over him and his eyes, so weird and sad, like he had it, that orgasm at the end of the universe, like maybe it was worth it, what she did to him, but I got to tell you, Fingers, I got to tell you, I'm never getting close to one of those things again as long as we both shall live.

I keep seeing it in their faces, their eyes, the It that was the whore's core, the creature in the flesh purse, and I feel like It's coming for both of us, maybe to finish off the job. Alec, too, maybe even Billy Bucknell, and MoJo, and Pasco, and Ben Winter. Sometimes at night, when I can't sleep, I hear It's sloppy wiping at the windows, and I pull the covers up over the two of us just to feel safe. You and me, we'll take care of each other, we don't have to go out much, at least not 'til we get evicted, and then we can hide under the sewers or in the alleys, and if we see her, if we still got legs, we can run, you and I, I will not abandon you to It, and I promise, for better or worse, good buddy.

In sickness, and in health.

457

O, Rare and Most Exquisite

"What is human love?" I have heard my mother ask, when she was sick, or when she was weary from the rotted wood dams of marriage and children. It's a question that haunts my every waking hour. I, myself, never experienced love, not the kind between a man and a woman. I once learned about it second-hand. When I was seventeen, I worked in a retirement home, in the cafeteria, and on my afternoons off I went up to the third floor. This was the nursing facility, and I suppose I went there to feel needed; all the elderly patients needed attention, often someone to just sit with them, hold their hands, watch the sun as it stretched down across the far-off trees heavy with summer green. I don't know why I was so taken with the older people, but I felt more comfortable around them than I often did around my peers. One day, an old man was shouting from his bed, "O, rare and most exquisite! O, God, O God, O, rare and most exquisite creation! Why hast thou forsaken me?" His voice was strong and echoed down the slick corridor; his neighbors, in adjacent beds, cried out for relief from his moans and groans. Since the orderlies ignored all this, routinely, I went to his room in order to find out what the trouble was about.

He was a ruffian. Bastards always lived the longest, it was a rule-of-thumb on the nursing floor, and this man was a prince among bastards. Something about the lizard leather of his skin, and the grease of his hair, and the way his forehead dug into his eyebrows as if he were trying to close his translucent blue eyes by forcing the thick skin down over them. He had no kindness in him; but I sat down on the edge of his bed, patted his hand, which shook, and asked him what the matter was.

"Love," he said. "All my life, I pursued nothing but love. And look where it's gotten me." He was a rasping old crow, the kind my brother used to shoot at in trees.

"Did you have lunch yet?" I asked, because I knew that the patients would become irritable if they hadn't eaten.

"I will not eat this raw sewage you call food."

"You can have roast beef, if you want. And pie."

"I will not eat." He closed his eyes, and I thought he was about to go to sleep, so I began to get up off the bed. He whispered, coughing a bit, "bring me the box under the bed."

I did as he asked. It was a cheap strong box, the kind that could be bought in a dimestore. When I set it beside him, he reached under the blankets and brought out a small key. "Open it for me," he said. I put the tiny key in the hole, turned, and brought the lid up. The box was filled with what appeared to be sand. "Reach in it," he said, and I stuck my hands in, and felt what seemed to be a stick, or perhaps it was a quill. I took it out.

It was a dried flower, with only a few petals remaining.

"Do you know about love?" he asked me.

I grinned. "Sure."

"You're too young," he said, shaking his head. He took the dried flower from my hand, and brought it up to his nose. Dust from the petals fell across his upper lip. "You think love is about kindness and dedication and caring. But it is not. It is about tearing flesh with hot pincers."

I smiled, because I didn't know what else to do. I wondered if he were sane; many of the patients were not.

He said, "This is the most rare flower that has ever existed. It is more than sixty years old. It is the most valuable thing I own. I am going to die soon, boy. Smell it. Smell it," he pressed the withered blossom into the palm of my hand, and cupped his shaking fingers under mine. "Smell it."

I lifted it up to my nose. For just a second, I thought I smelled a distant sea, and island breezes of blossoming fruit trees and perfumes. Then, nothing but the rubbing alcohol and urine of the nursing floor.

"I will give this to you," he said, "to keep, if you promise to take care of it."

Without thinking, I said, "It's dead."

He shook his head, a rage flaring behind his eyes, a life in him I wouldn't have expected. "You don't know about love," he grabbed my arm, and his grip was hard as stone, "and you'll live just like I did, boy, unless you listen good, and life will give you its own whipping so that one day you'll end up in this bed smelling like this and crying out to the god of death just for escape from this idiot skin so that the pain of memory will stop."

To calm him, because now I knew he was crazy, I said, "Okay. Tell me."

"Love," he said, "is the darkest gift. It takes all that you are, and it destroys you."

And he told me about the flower of his youth.

461

His name was Gus, and he was a gardener at a house that overlooked the Hudson River. The year was 1925, and his employer was an invalid in his fifties, with a young wife. The wife's name was Jo, and she was from a poor family, but she had made a good marriage, for the house and grounds occupied a hundred acres. As head gardener, Gus had a staff of six beneath him. Jo would come out in the mornings, bringing coffee to the workers. She was from a family of laborers, so she understood their needs, and she encouraged their familiarity. Her husband barely noticed her, and if he did, he wouldn't approve of her mixing with the staff.

One morning, she came down to Gus where he stood in the maze of roses, with the dew barely settled upon them, and she kissed him lightly on the cheek. He wasn't sure how to take this. She was wearing her robe, as she always did when she brought the coffee out to the men, although it revealed nothing of her figure. She was the most beautiful woman he had ever seen, with thick dark hair, worn long and out of fashion, a throwback to the long Victorian tresses of his mother's generation. She had almond-shaped eyes, and skin like olives soaked in brandy—he had never seen a woman this exotic in Wappingers Falls, which was his hometown. She smelled of oil and rosewater, and she did not greet him, ever, without something sweet on her lips, so that her breath was a pleasure to feel against his skin. She drew back from him, and with her heavy accent, said, "Gus, my handsome boy of flowers, what will you find for me today?"

Gus had girls before, since he was fourteen, but they had been lust pursuits, for none of the girls of the Falls, or of Poughkeepsie, or even the college girl he had touched in Connecticut, stirred in him what he felt with Jo. He called her, to his men, "My Jo," for he felt that, if things were different, she would not be with this wealthy man with his palsied body, but with him. Gus and Jo, he wrote it on the oak tree down near the river, he carved it into a stone which he had placed in the center of the rose garden.

When she kissed him on the cheek, he waited a minute, and then grabbed her in his arms, for he could no longer contain himself, and they made love there, in the morning, before the sun was far up in the sky.

He knew that she loved him, so he went that day to find her the most beautiful flower that could be had. It was a passion of hers, to have the most beautiful things, for she had lived most of her life with only the ugly and the dull. He wished he were wealthy so that he might fly to China, or to the South of France, or to the stars, to bring back the rarest of blooms. But, having four bits on him, he took the train into New York City, and eventually came to a neighborhood which sold nothing but flowers, stall upon stall. But it was mid-summer, and all the flowers available were the same that he could grow along the river. As he was about to leave, not knowing how he could return to his Jo without something very special, a woman, near one of the stalls said, "You don't like these, do you?"

Gus turned, and there was a woman of about twenty-two. Very plain, although pretty in the way that he thought all women basically pretty. She was small and pale, and she wore no make-up, but her eyes were large and lovely. "I've been watching you," she said.

"You have?"

"Yes. Do you think that's rude? To watch someone?"

"It depends."

"I think it's rude. But then," she said, smiling like a mischievous child, "I've never been ashamed of my own behavior, only the behavior of others. I'm ashamed of yours. Here I've watched you for fifteen minutes, and you barely took your eyes off the flowers. How rude do you think that is? Very. You like flowers, don't you?"

"I'm a gardener. I take care of them."

"Lovely," she said, wistfully, "imagine a life of caring for beautiful things. Imagine when you're very old, and look back on it. What lovely memories you'll have." Although she seemed forthright, the way he knew city people were, there was something fitful in the way she spoke, almost hesitant somewhere in the flow of words, as if all this snappy talk was a cover for extreme shyness. And yet, he knew, city women were rarely shy.

463

He had not come all the way to the city to flirt with shop-girls. "I'm looking for something out of the ordinary."

She gave a curious smile, tilting her head back. She was a shade beautiful in the thin shaft of daylight that pressed between the stalls. She was no Jo, but she would make some young man fall in love with her, he knew that. Some city boy who worked in the local grocers, or ran a bakery. Or, perhaps, even a junior bondsman. She would eventually live in one of the boxcar apartments in Brooklyn, and be the most wonderful and ordinary bride. She would have four children, and grow old without fear. Not like Jo, who was destined for romance and passion and tragedy and great redemption, not Italian Jo of olive skin and rosewater. The woman said, "I know a place where you can find very unusual flowers."

"I want a beauty," he said.

"For a lady?"

Because Gus knew how women could be, and because he detected that he might get further along with this girl if he feigned interest in her, he lied. "No. Just for me. I appreciate beautiful flowers." He felt bad, then, a little, because now he knew that he was leading her on, but she seemed to know where the interesting flowers were, and all he could think of was Jo and how she loved flowers. Gus was considered handsome in his day, and women often showed him special attention, so he was used to handling them, charming them. "I need a beauty," he repeated.

"I'm not saying beautiful," she cautioned him, and began walking between the stalls, through an alley, leading him, "but unusual. Sometimes unusual is better than beautiful." She wore a kind of apron, he noticed, the long kind that covered her dress, and he wondered if she were the local butcher's daughter, or if she were a cook. The alley was steamy; there was some sort of kitchen down one end of it, a Chinese laundry, too, for he smelled the soap and the meat and heard someone shouting in a foreign language, but nothing European, for Gus knew how those languages sounded, and this must've been Oriental. The woman came to an open pit, with a thin metal staircase leading down to a room, and she hiked her apron up a bit, and held her hand out for him to steady her as she descended. "My balance isn't too good," she told him, "I have a heart problem—nothing serious—but it makes me light-headed sometimes on stairs."

"There're flowers down there?" he asked, as he went down the steps slowly.

"It's one of my father's storage rooms. He has a flower shop on Seventh Avenue, but there's an ice house above us, and we get shavings for free. They stay colder down here," she said, and turned a light up just as he had reached the last step. "There's another room three doors down, beneath the laundry. We keep some there, too."

The room was all of redbrick, and it was chilly, like winter. "We're right underneath the storage part of the ice house." As the feeble light grew strong, he saw that they were surrounded by flowers, some of them brilliant vermillion sprays, other deep

464

purples and blacks, still more of pile upon pile of dappled yellows on reds on greens. "These are all fresh cut," she said, "you can have any you want. My father grows them underneath the laundry, and when he cuts them, we keep them on ice until we ship them. Here," she said, reaching into a bowl that seemed to be carved out of ice. She brought up tiny red and blue blossoms, like snowballs, but in miniature. She brought them up to his face, and the aroma was incredible, it reminded him of Jo's skin when he pressed his face against her breasts and tasted the brightness of morning.

The woman kissed him, and he responded, but it was not like his kiss with Jo. This woman seemed colder, and he knew he was kissing her just because he wanted the blossoms. He remembered the cold kiss all the way to the big house, as he carried his gift to his beloved.

Jo was shocked by the tiny, perfect flowers. He had left them for her in a crystal bowl of water on the dining room table so that she would see them first when she came to have breakfast. He heard her cry out, sweetly, and then she came to the kitchen window to search the back garden for him. She tried to open it; but it rained the night before and all that morning, so it was stuck. She rushed around to the back door, ran barefoot into the garden and grabbed his hand. "Sweetest—precious—blessed," she gasped, "where did you find them? Their smell—so lovely."

He had saved one small blossom in his hand. He crushed it against her neck, softly. He kissed her as if he owned her and he told her how much he loved her.

She drew back from him then, and he saw something change in her eyes. "No," she said.

When the flowers had died, he ventured back into the city, down the alley, but the entrance to the pit was closed. He rapped on the metal doors several times, but there was no response. He went around to the entrance to the ice house, and asked the manager there about the flowers, but he seemed to not know much about it other than the fact that the storage room was closed for the day. Gus was desperate, and had brought his month's pay in order to buy armloads of the flowers, but instead, ended up in an Irish bar on Horace Street drinking away most of it. Jo didn't love him, he knew that now. How could he be such a fool, anyway? Jo could never leave her husband, never in a thousand years. Oh, but for another moment in her arms, another moment of that sweet mystery of her breath against his neck!

He stayed in the city overnight, sleeping in a flop house, and was up early, and this time went to the Chinese laundry. The man who ran it took him to the back room, where the steam thickened. Gus heard the sounds of machines being pushed and pressed and clanked and rapped, as a dozen or more people worked in the hot fog of the shop. The owner took him further back, until they came to a stairway.

"Down," the man nodded, and then disappeared into the fog.

Gus went down the stairs, never sure when he would touch bottom, for the steam was still heavy. When he finally got to the floor, it dissipated a bit, and there was a sickly yellow light a ways off. He went towards it, brushing against what he assumed were flowers, growing in their pots.

Then, someone touched his arm.

"Gus," it was the woman from the week before. "It's me. Moira."

"I didn't know your name," he told her. "I didn't know how to find you."

"How long did the flower last?"

"Six days."

"How sad," she said, and leaned against him. He kissed her, but the way he would kiss his sister, because he didn't really want to lead her on.

The mist from the laundry enveloped the outline of her face, causing her skin to shine a yellow-white like candles in luminaria, revealing years that he had not anticipated—he had thought she might be a girl in her early twenties, but in this steam, she appeared older, ashes shining under her skin.

"I loved the flowers."

"What else do you love, Gus?"

He didn't answer. He pulled away from her, and felt the edges of thick-lipped petals.

She said, "We keep the exotics here. There's an orchid from the Fiji Islands—it's not properly an orchid, but it has the look of one. It's tiny, but very rare. In its natural state, it's a parasite on fruit trees, but here, it's the most beautiful thing in the world."

"I never paid you for the last flower."

"Gus," she said, and reached up to cup the side of his face in the palm of her hand, "whatever is mine, is yours."

She retreated into the mist, and in a few moments, laid in the palm of his hand a flower so small that he could barely see it. She set another of its kind into a jewelry box, and said, "this is more precious than any jewel I know of. But if I give it to you, I want you to tell me one thing."

He waited to hear her request.

"I want you to tell me—no, promise me—you will take care of this better than those last ones. This should live, if cared for, for over a month. You do love flowers, don't you?"

"Yes," he said, and, because he wanted this tiny flower so much for his Jo, he brought Moira close to him and pressed his lips against hers, and kissed around her glowing face, tasting the steam from the laundry. He wanted it so badly, he knew this flower would somehow win his Jo. Somehow, she would manage to leave her husband, and they would run away together, maybe even to the Fiji Islands to live off mango and to braid beautiful Jo's hair with the island parasite flowers.

Yet, there was something about Moira that he liked, too. She wasn't Jo, but she was different than any woman he knew. When he drew his face back from hers, her face was radiant and shining, and not the middle-aged woman he had thought just a minute ago. She was a young girl, after all, barely out of her teens, with all the enthusiasm of fresh, new life. He wondered what his life would be like with a girl like this, what living in the city with her would feel like, what it would be like to live surrounded by the frozen and burning flowers.

There were tears in Moira's eyes when she left him, and he sensed that she knew why he wanted the beautiful flowers.

And still, she gave him the rare and exquisite ruby blossom.

The tiny flower died in fourteen days. Gus could not return to the city for over six weeks, because a drought had come down the valley, and he had to take special pains to make sure that the gardens didn't die. Jo did not come and see him, and he knew that it was for the best. She was married, he was merely the gardener, and no matter how many gorgeous flowers he brought to her, she would never be his. He thought of Moira, and her sweetness and mystery; her generosity was something he had never experienced before in a woman, for the ones he had known were often selfish and arrogant in their beauty. He also knew that the old man must suspect his over-familiarity with Jo, and so, his days would be numbered in the Hudson River house.

One afternoon, he took off again for the city, but it took several hours, as there was an automobile stuck on the tracks just before coming into Grand Central Station. He got there in the evening, and went to the Chinese laundry, but both it and the ice house were closed for the day. He remembered that Moira had mentioned her father's shop, and so he went into the flower district and scoured each one, asking after her. Finally, he came to the shop on Seventh Avenue and there she was, sitting behind a counter arranging iris into a spray-like arrangement. She turned to see him, and in the light of early evening, she was the simple girl he had seen the first day they had met. How the mist and the ice could change her features, but in the daylight world, she was who she was!

"Gus," she said, "I thought you weren't coming back. Ever."

"I had to," he said, not able to help his grin, or the sweat of fear that evaporated along his forehead, fear that he would not find her. It was like in the moving pictures, when the lover and his beloved were reunited at the end. He ran around the counter and grabbed her up in his arms, "Oh, Moira, Moira," he buried his face in her neck, and she was laughing freely, happily.

She closed the shop, and pulled down the shade. "Gus, I want you to know, I love you. I know you might not love me, but I love you."

Gus sighed, and looked at her. Here he was, a gardener, and she, a flower shop girl, how could a more perfect pair be created, one for the other?

"There's something I want to give you," she said.

"You've given me—" he began, but she didn't let him finish.

"Something I want to give you," she began unbuttoning the top of her blouse.

When she was completely naked, he saw what was different about her. "I could never give my heart freely...knowing I was... different...like this..."

469

He stepped back, away from her.

"Who did this to you?" he asked, his voice trembling.

She looked at him with those wide, perfect eyes, and said, "I was born this way."

The threads.

There, in the whiteness of her thighs.

He was horrified, and fascinated, for her had never seen this before.

Her genitals had been sewn together, you see, with some thread that was strong, yet silken and impossibly slender, like a spider's web. She brought his hand there, to the center of her being, and she asked him to be careful with her. "As careful as you are with the flowers."

"It's monstrous," he said, trying to hide the revulsion in his voice, trying to draw back his fingers.

"Break the threads," she said, "and I will show you the most beautiful flower that has ever been created in the universe."

"I can't," he shivered.

Tears welled in her eyes. "I love you with all my being," she said, "and I want to give you this...this...even if it means..." her voice trailed off.

He found himself plucking at the threads, and then pulling at them, until finally he got down on his hands and knees and placed his mouth there, and bit into the threads to open her.

There must have been some pain, but she only cried out once, and then was silent.

Her labia parted, curling back, blossoming, and there was a smell, no, a scent, like a spice wind across a tropical shore, and the labia were petals, until her pelvis opened, prolapsed like a flower blooming suddenly, in one night, and her skin folded backwards on itself, with streaks of red and yellow and white bursting forth from the wound, from the pollen that spread golden, and the wonderful colors that radiated from between her thighs, until there was nothing but flower.

470 He cupped his hands around it. It was the most exotic flower he had ever seen, in his hands, it was the beauty that had been inside her, and she had allowed him to open her, to hold this rare flower in his hands.

Gus wondered if he had gone insane, or if this indeed was the most precious of all flowers, this gift of love, this sacrifice that she had made for him.

He concealed the bloom in a hat-box, and carried it back to the estate with him. In the morning, he entered the great house without knocking, and his heart pounded as loud as his footsteps, as he crossed the grand foyer. He called to the mistress of the house boldly, "Jo!" he shouted, "Jo! Look what I have brought you!" He didn't care if the old man heard him, he didn't care if he would be without a job, none of it mattered, for he had found the greatest gift for his Jo, the woman who would not now deny him. He knew he loved her now, his Jo, he knew what love was now, what the sacrifice of love meant.

She was already dressed, for riding, and she blushed when she saw him. "You shouldn't come in like this. You have no right."

He opened the hat box, and retrieved the flower.

"This is for you," he said, and she ran to him, taking it up in her hands, smelling it, wiping its petals across her lips.

"It's beautiful," she said, smiling, clasping his hand, and just as quickly letting go. "Darling," she called out, turning to the staircase, "darling, look at the lovely flower our Gus has brought us, look," and like a young girl in love, she ran up the stairs, with the flower, to the bedroom where the old man coughed and wheezed.

Gus stood there, in the hall, feeling as if his heart had stopped.

"It was three days later," he told me, as I sat on the edge of the nursing room bed, "that the flower died, and Jo put it out with the garbage. But I retrieved it, what was left of it, so that I would always remember that love. What love was. What terror it is."

The old man finally let go of my arm, and I stood. He was crying, like a baby, as if there were not enough tears in a human body to let go of, and he was squeezing his eyes to make more.

"It's all right," I said, "it's just a bad dream. Just like a bad dream."

"But it happened, boy," he said, and he passed me the flower. "I want you to keep this. I'm going to die someday soon. Maybe within a month, who knows?"

"I couldn't," I said, shaking my head. "It's yours."

"No," he said, grinning madly, "it never was mine. Have you ever been with a woman, boy?"

I shook my head. "Not yet."

"How old are you?"

"Seventeen. Just last month."

"Ah, seventeen. A special time. What do you think human love is, boy?"

I shrugged, "Caring. Between people. I guess."

"Oh, no," his smile blossomed across his face, "it's not caring, boy, it's not caring. What it is, is opening your skin up to someone else, and opening theirs, too. Everything I told you is true, boy. I want you to take this dried flower—"

I held it in my hand. For a moment, I believed his story, and I found myself feeling sad, too. I thought of her, of Moira, giving herself up like that. "She loved you."

"Her? She never loved me," he said. "Never."

"How can you say that? You just told me—"

His voice deepened, and he sounded as evil as I have ever heard a man sound, "Jo never loved me."

I looked again at the dried flower. He plucked it from my fingers, and held the last of its petals in his open palm.

He said, "You thought that was Moira? Oh, no, boy, I buried her beneath the garden. This is Jo. She finally left her husband for me. And then, when I had her...O, Lord, when I had her, boy, I tore her apart, I made her bloom, and I left her to dry in sand the way she had dried my heart." He laughed, clinging more tightly to my arm so that I could not get away. "Her flower was not as pretty as Moira's. Moira. Lovely Moira." He sniffed the air, as if he could still smell the fragrance of the opening flower. "I made Jo bloom, boy, and then I stepped on her flower, and I kept it in darkness and dust. Now, boy, *that's* what love is." He laughed even while he crushed the dried blossom with his free hand.

"O, rare and most exquisite!" He shouted after me as I pulled away from him, and backed out of that madman's room.

"O, why," he laughed, "why hast thou forsaken me?"

472

The Virgin of the Rocks

This one is not a story. I had a dream that was so vivid I wrote it up. Names have been changed to protect the guilty and the innocent. I don't know what the dream meant, but it was quite a dream. And this tale came of it, and makes no sense to me, which is why I like it so much.

1

This is the story about the two miracles in Paul Howard's life, which came after the age of forty. The first had to do with death; the second, with transformation. It was after his first marriage, also, and the end of that union opened the door for a union of another kind. The first marriage, while not perfect, had taken up both of their lives to an extent that the wife had not anticipated; she was almost forty when she decided to end it. She borrowed money from her parents, and took the beat-up Volkswagen rather than the Honda, which was in better shape. Julie and Wes fit in the back with the two cats, and she found herself almost crying when she realized that she'd put nothing in the front seat beside her—she was so used to Paul filling that space. She did not intend to revert to her maiden name, but would keep the name Alice Howard to give her children continuity of some sort. These are the things that Paul learned two years later, after the ill-wind of divorce blew across his desk, and with it a newfound, and not altogether disagreeable, state of loneliness. Alice told him about it herself, the tears in the Volkswagen, the ten thousand she owed her parents (who were notoriously tight with a buck), and the most unusual bit of information—

"One of the children isn't yours, anyway," Alice said. She had grown her fingernails long, and had lacquered them professionally with a dark red. She had taken to wearing black. Black tight-fitting pants, black shirt, black vest, black beret. On seeing her like this, versus her generally bright skirt and pastel blouse mode of dress, Paul felt he knew what Patty Hearst's parents must've felt upon seeing the photographs in *Time*.

Paul took her all at a breath: the coffee-house look, the information that one of his children was a bastard. He tried to read her face for the trace of a prank; but she was like a cat, meditating. She was drinking Sambuca (which she never touched during the fifteen years of marriage), and he wondered if she might be suffering from a multiple personality disorder.

474

Or worse: if she were sane.

The first question, in his head and out from his mouth, "Which one?"

She shook her head, slightly. "I won't play that game."

"I knew about Jim. You didn't hide it well."

"It wasn't Jim Watson. It wasn't anyone you know. It was a total stranger."

Paul guessed. "The trip to San Francisco. The convention. You came back looking very mysterious."

She shrugged. "That was after Julie was born. Trust me on this, it only happened once."

Then, he knew. Positively. "It's Julie." Now, he was the smug one. He sipped his beer. Score one for the underdog, he thought.

"Please," she said, "I told you, I'm not going to tell you."

"Well, it couldn't've been Wes. You got pregnant on the honeymoon."

A look crossed her face that he could not decipher. That was the damnedst thing about marriage, how one could know the other, intimately, after a decade and a half, and still not know what a change of face might mean.

Finally, she grinned. "Did I? You sure it wasn't the week after the honeymoon?"

He was fed up with her mystery—which he didn't completely believe to be true. "I won't sit here and count months, if that's what you want. In times not so long ago, men would kill the child that wasn't his, or turn it out in the street. I love both of them, Alice, but this is really unfair. What do you want, anyway?"

After the drink, she asked him to walk her to her car. It was no longer a Volkswagen, but had blossomed, somehow, into a Volvo. He looked at the car; he looked at her. He didn't need to say it—she had met someone new and was in love and living with him. Paul wanted to tell her that was all right, and that he was happy for her, but he couldn't. He noticed the air had a bite to it, like crisp wine. It was already dark, and only six. For a moment, he couldn't remember what city he lived in.

"This is it, Paul," she said, and leaned into him to give him a peck on the edge of his lips.

"It?"

"I'm moving tomorrow. I need a new start."

"You got a new start."

"Newer than this."

"What about Wes?" *Funny,* he thought to himself, *I don't seem to care about Julie. Sexism, or is it a deep knowledge that for the eleven years of her life on this earth, I've known she wasn't mine?*

"They'll see you on holidays and in the summer. Just like the lawyers said."

"Are you allowed to take them out-of-state?"

"How do you know for sure we're going out-of-state?"

"With Mr. Volvo?"

Alice didn't answer. She waved goodbye, as if he were a half-mile away, and as if she were getting on some country bus to nowhere. Out of his life completely. She got into the car, and started it, and drove down the street. He watched as she went; she wasn't used to drinking, and he knew she'd drunk a lot of Sambuca sitting with him in the bar, so he wanted to see just how bad off she was.

She didn't even make it past the first stop light before the six-ten, coming from Fredericksburg, entered the intersection at the same time, and Alice, making an illegal left-hand turn, got hit less than a quarter into her turn, and although he knew that Volvos were probably the safest car on the market, he was aware that Alice might not survive an accident that seemed to him like a fire-storm blazing across the small, cobblestone street of the historic district.

That was the first miracle in his life.

They were leaving the funeral, Paul and his two children, returned to him via the graces of the state and his lawyer, when he met the man in question. The man who owned the Volvo. Paul thought he'd met him once, and said so.

"I don't think so," the man said. He didn't extend a hand, and neither did Paul. Paul searched his face for similarities to either of his children. He had no good feeling toward Alice, because he felt that she was the soul of deception. He wished that somewhere, in the world, there was a woman of purity and grace, someone who was above reproach. He had thought, once, that Alice was that woman, for she was better than most. But he realized, too late, that she was as dark in her heart as any.

He spent some nights sitting up in bed, wondering which child was not his. He knew that this was a pointless exercise, but he couldn't help himself. He tried to see if he could find a nose other than his or Alice's on either child, or if Julie's blue eyes were inherited from the mother's side of the family, or if Wes' crooked teeth (pre-orthodontia) were part of the clue. He knew he loved his children, both, but each time he saw them, he wondered. Damn her for doing it. Paul was somewhat of an old-fashioned man, and had not suspected through his whole marriage to Alice that she might betray him, and in such a way as this. He now wondered, since her death, if she had been deceiving him about other things in their lives together. He had been an upstanding lover and husband and father, insofar as he had been able, and if that had not been enough for Alice, what was he supposed to have done? He began to think about women very differently after the revelation; he would've liked to ask Alice all kinds of questions, but death had silenced her possible responses quite effectively.

Mysteries and guessing games might be able to go on indefinitely, but human beings find that, if a solution is not forthcoming in a reasonable period, they will bury the questions or put them on their wish lists for Judgement Day, alongside the mysteries of what really happened with the dinosaurs or what books and pictures are contained in the Profane Library of the Vatican, or what the nature of the cosmos is. A man can only stay up for so long, before his sleep returns, and with it, everyday normal life, routine, and perhaps, even love.

477

2

Paul remarried.

This time, a girl of twenty-three, named Barbara, who was dazzled by his experience, and his job, and was a virgin. This last part had become important to Paul in the half-year since Alice's death, because he had decided that fidelity was the most important thing to him now. Who better than a young virgin to attach to a man who wanted to believe that there were still values in the world? Barbara was less than beautiful, but pretty in the natural way that all girls of twenty-three might be to a man of forty-two. He liked the man-girl equation; he could be strong for her, and she could be sweet. Like coffee, with sugar. She professed such an ignorance of sex and sexuality, that he mistook this for virtue rather than a general lack of common sense and socialization skills. Although Paul lived on the edge of a small man-made lake, with woods off to the side, masking the suburban development beyond them, Barbara proved to be an indoor kind of girl. The children were not the problem that Paul had anticipated. Wes was now almost eighteen, and liked Barbara on sight; while Julie was a little put off, but she was getting into her teens and was awkward and shy and barely spoke to anyone new.

The courtship had been quick; the honeymoon a delight, for Paul had not bothered with sex, but had held her night after night and felt her warmth like a new sun. Then, after she fell asleep, Paul would sneak off to a local cantina where the girls could be had for cheap, and in that way, he didn't sully Barbara's reputation. He would return to the motel room, his ass caked in sand from beachfront screwing, and would shower, pretending to have just arisen for the new day. He napped between noon and five on the beach. He knew this wasn't the best behavior for a husband, but he wanted something from this marriage that was more than the usual.

He said it to his colleague, Dave, while they were jogging one afternoon. "I want a saint."

"Huh?"

"A saint. A woman beyond reproach."

"You got one helluva girl in your pocket right now."

"I don't want you to talk about her that way," Paul told him, "she's not like other girls. Barbara is—somehow—better. Nature is so ugly, how it rips them up, makes them have babies, and we poke at them, no wonder they take their vengeances on us and set our mattresses on fire and shoot us and castrate us with wit, look what we do to them. The ugliest act on earth, sex, and yet we're compelled to repeat it over and over."

"In my dreams," Dave said.

"We have these organs and we have to prod between legs, to force women into giving up the normal shapes of their bodies just to keep the species going. Doesn't that seem dumb? God must be dumb. He must be an idiot. He must be the King of Fools. Why couldn't children come into the world through the pleasure of music, or of dancing?"

"Last time Sally and I did it," Dave said, "I seem to recall some music and dancing. So, Paul, never knew this about you not liking sex and all."

"Oh," Paul said, "I love sex. I just wouldn't do it to someone I cared about."

The Virgin of the Rocks

The Virgin (for that was how Paul thought about her within months of their marriage) slept late in the mornings, and had no intention of working. That was fine; he could hire a maid, and he could well-afford to pay all the bills. She was inordinately attached to the house; she had been a dependent twin whose sister had moved to Asia when they were nineteen—since then, the Virgin had lived just this side of agoraphobia and disliked going out. He had only met her by chance, at a friend's dinner party, and he had had to pry her like an oyster from her shell. All of these things were for the good; Alice had been much too outgoing and independent to make a good wife.

Paul was up by 5:30, off for a quick jog, and then a clean up before commuting to his office in town. But first, before he left, a touch of that lovely skin of hers. The Virgin had skin that was so white he thought at times that she was made of pure ivory; she looked at him sleepily, smiled without showing her teeth, and then closed her eyes. He kissed them, right on the lids, and then kissed her forehead. She turned her face into the pillow, and Paul left for work.

When he returned, at six in the evening, she was barely up—just taken a shower, dressed, smelling of hyacinth and sandalwood. She wore the cotton gown with the small roses embroidered on its edges. Her breasts were ripe; her waist small, her hips a healthy width. He would like, sometimes, to grab her and take her, but knew that this would change the whole equation of their relationship. The Virgin sat opposite Wes.

Wes was sitting in the dark in the living room, staring at the lightning that played across the far sky above the lake.

Paul flicked on a light.

"No, the lightning's so pretty," the Virgin said.

Paul turned the light off. He looked at Wes and then at his wife. Wes was a handsome boy, athletic but not outgoing, a brooding muscle-bound boy. Paul began to get an indistinct but uncomfortable feeling. He'd been looking at his children differently ever since the Alice Crash day. He tried to find himself in either of them, and was having trouble. He had never been terribly athletic, and there was Wes, a hulking side of beef. There had been a butcher at the local market who looked like that. Had he been Wes' real father? Sometimes Paul thought that Alice might've lied about the whole thing just to drive a splinter into his brain; Wes looked enough like him in the face.

"Anything the matter?" Paul asked. He could see his wife's face flash brightly when the lightning came up. She was beautiful. No worries troubled her features.

Wes kept his eyes on the window.

The Virgin said, "Wes had a bad wrestling match."

"Wes?"

Paul's son acknowledged this with a shrug.

"Is Julie home yet?"

The Virgin said, "She's still at band practice. I'll go pick her up in half an hour."

Paul looked at the Virgin for traces of betrayal, but she seemed to shine with her inner spirit. Untainted by human intercourse. She was the absolutely perfect woman, and as long as he could keep her here, with him, nothing from the outside would touch her.

Still, he had that weird feeling when he looked at the two of them, a tableau, sitting there across from each other, the lightning streaking across their faces.

He woke up in the middle of the night in a cold sweat.

He'd been dreaming that his son was making love to his wife, and the look of indescribable ecstasy on her face made him shiver. Her skin so white and shiny with lust-sweat, not like the women he had sex with, whose skin was porous and tanned and obviously tainted.

But the worst was at the end of the nightmare:

Alice, burnt from her accident, laughed at him as he watched the coupling of his son and young wife. She had her snifter of Sambuca, too, which she raised to him. After the couple climaxed, Alice whispered to Paul, "You're not even his father, what do you care?"

He took Wes out to the woods that grew in a great clutch along the river. It was Saturday, and Wes was looking guilty. He wore no shirt; Paul noticed how beautiful his son was. It pained him.

"Something I have to tell you," he said.

His son raised his eyebrows. Shivered, a little, too. "How bad is it?"

"Pretty bad."

"Shoot."

"I don't want you living here anymore."

Wes accepted this just fine. He looked at the trees across the water, and tossed a rock in the river. "I figured you didn't want me here."

"It's not me," Paul said, "it's Barbara."

Wes gave his father a sidelong glance.

"She's dying," Paul said.

"Oh, god," Wes gasped with genuine surprise. "What do you mean?"

"It's an inherited illness. She doesn't want me to discuss it much. She's very weak."

481

"I don't believe it," Wes said, and Paul held his breath wondering if his son would catch the lie, but then his son continued, "no, wait, wait. She coughs sometimes. Too much. She said it was asthma. Oh, my god. Dad." Wes had tears in his eyes. He hugged his father. Paul felt the tears on the back of his neck. After Wes had calmed down, he said, "I can live with Pete Lewis. He's got an extra room. And then after graduation, I can get a place of my own."

"I'll see you financially, Wes, don't worry. There," his father put his arm around Wes' shoulder. "Oh, my boy, you've been through so much in such a short period of time."

Wes said, "I just miss Mom. I don't want Barbara to die. I want you to be happy, Dad."

"I know, so do I. So do I."

Julie was a little more savvy than Wes, and ran off with a boy from school by summer; she sent a postcard from North Carolina, so he knew she was all right.

3

Then, one morning, Paul awoke and reached out to touch his wife. He felt something cold and still.

He sat up. The light was dim; he turned on the bedside lamp. "Barbara?" he asked.

She lay there, very still. He could hear her breathing, but it seemed weak. In the lamplight, her skin was mottled, like bastard marble. Paul drew himself back from her sleeping form. Her eyes were open. She was staring at: nothing. Her grayish eyes had turned dark. He called her name again, and he felt that something stirred in the stiff form. As if she were beneath this outer layer of stone, the way a pupae might wriggle within its cocoon.

A sound like a gasp came from the vicinity of her mouth.

Because Paul could not believe his eyes, he touched her (cautiously) again. Cold.

He got out of bed and turned on all the bedroom lamps.

Her skin reflected the light.

She was a statue. One arm placed behind her head, one arm over her breasts. Beneath her nightclothes, hard rock. She had fallen asleep, and had been awakened by something—thus, her opened eyes. It was a transformation; he had never witnessed this kind of thing before, and at first wondered if it might be some rare disease.

A tear slid from the corner of her left eye, and froze halfway down her cheek, turning to stone.

Later, after the doctors and the police and the scientists had thoroughly examined her (and Paul, too), he came to think of her as a miracle, the second one of his lifetime.

4

She was set just on the edge of his property, by the lake, on a brief promontory that, in the spring, would be the nesting area of several species of duck and goose. She was propped up—for she had transformed in a sleeping position—with several rocks, strategically placed at the back of her legs and around her feet until she was well-anchored. He clothed her with a sheet, wrapped about her to allow her the highest degree of modesty. A religious group camped out on the edge of the shore for a few weeks—they believed that she was a manifestation of the Mother Mary. Paul had no specific religious sensibility, but felt proud that his Virgin would be so exalted by those who possessed such sensibilities.

Paul did, however, have a spiritual side to him, long buried, which emerged daily as he took his walks down to the Virgin's place.

Finally, his love for her overpowered him, and he quit his job and spent his days at her side, on the rocks, overlooking the water.

Years passed; Wes came home to sell the house because his father was behind in mortgage payments; Julie tried to have her father institutionalized.

Paul finally went away, taken by force, to spend several weeks in the state hospital. Because of legal difficulties, and a failure of various drugs to raise him out of his fixation, he spent the better part of three years there.

The statue turned green, perhaps from algae creeping off the lake, or from years of birds lighting upon her fair arms, or in her hair, leaving excrement behind. The new owners of the house thought she was rather creepy, and, not understanding the Virgin's history, sold her to an eccentric art collector.

483

The collector's name was Jaspar Fine, and he was not aware that the Virgin had once lived in the flesh at all, but he prized mottled beauty in image and word above most other considerations—he rarely sold from his collection unless he felt the new buyer would share the same affection for the piece in question. She stayed in his house for several months, but then, owing to lack of funds, he had to sell off some of his collection. She was one of the least expensive items, for the abstracts seemed to fare better in the market-place. But a young man named Don bought her, and brought her to his home in the city. There, he placed her in his garden, surrounded by vines and flowers and ripening tomatoes.

5

Paul was finally released, and went in search of his wife.

The amount of time it took, and the money, too, which he had to borrow from his son, was much, but he came, at last, to the garden in the city.

Don answered the door. Paul assessed him immediately: only in his late twenties, but already going downhill. He was overweight, slovenly, with an untucked shirt, and sweatpants. In one hand, he held a beer. "Can I help you?"

Paul could barely get his breath out. "I understand you have something of mine."

Don invited him in. "I buy lotsa junk. You like art? I like it. I buy a painting of yours or something?"

"I believe you bought my wife."

"Excuse me?"

"The Virgin. A Mr. Jaspar Fine informed me that you purchased her for a hundred and fifty dollars two years ago."

Don took a sip of beer. "Oh, yeah, the statue. In the garden. Worthless piece of shit."

Paul wanted to deck him for this comment. "What do you mean by that?"

"Two weeks ago, maybe three, I barely touched it and it fell apart."

Paul felt his mouth go dry. "How—how did you touch her?"

Don glanced at him slyly, "You're a pervert, are you? Nothing like that. I was moving it from one end of the garden to another, and dropped one end of it, and it fell, broke into five, six pieces."

"What did you do with them?"

Don shrugged. "Hate to let anything that pretty go to waste. Made kind of a funky barbeque out of it." He took Paul into the backyard of his townhouse, through the garden, to its edge. A small patio had been built of brick, and tucked against the corner wall, the gray-green arms and torso and legs and head of the Virgin configured in the shape of a barbeque. Her head and torse provided the back; her limbs, the sides and base of the pit. On her lap, dusty gray coals, and a steel rack, burnt from a recent dinner. To look at her, in her new incarnation, you might think that the place where the barbeque pit was situated was her vagina.

Within it, ashes.

Paul imagined, with pain, the fire burning there between her legs, the meat thrust across her lap, the flame rising to char the meat, the cook standing by to prod the coals with a long fork to get the fire to rise even higher.

"You can buy it back if you want," Don said, seeing Paul's anguish, "I didn't know it was so important to anyone."

Paul borrowed his son's truck, and the barbeque was loaded into the back. He was living, now, in the apartment above his son's house. Wes had gotten out into the world and had made a quick success of himself; within another year or two, he had built his father a small guesthouse in back. Wes married, and he and his wife raised three children together.

The barbeque went unused, of course, for Paul did not want to subject the Virgin to the pain and degradation which she'd had to submit to at the hands of the awful Don. He made garlands of flowers for her, and draped her hair and neck with them. She became a sort of goddess for him, and then, one day, Wes and his firstborn, Joe, were taking a walk out to see Joe's grandfather. When Wes couldn't find him at the guest house, they wandered back to where the barbeque stood, in an arbor, hidden by flowering vines.

Paul lay there, dead. He was only in his late fifties, but Wes knew that he had died of something that must've been like a broken heart.

The barbeque was gone, but there were footsteps and bits of chipped rock, going up the side path that led to the street.

Someone reported that a most unusual young woman was walking naked up Arden Street. There were several such sightings within a few hours of each other.

At Paul's funeral, Wes recognized the Virgin standing in back. He went up to her, astonished.

She was more beautiful than he had ever remembered.

She smiled, kissed him, and drew back.

He was still close enough to her to feel it.

A heat.

A burning passion, that seemed to emanate from her hips.

Something animal, uncaged.

485

He found himself, without remembering where he was or why he was doing this, pressing his mouth against a fire that could no longer be contained.

She held him there, for a long time, even in the midst the funeral crowd, with a grip of steel.

The Rendering Man

1

"We're gonna die someday," Thalia said, "all of us. Mama and Daddy and then you and then me. I wonder if anyone's gonna care enough to think about Thalia Inez Canty, or if I'll just be dust under their feet." She stood in the doorway, still holding the ladle that dripped with potato chowder.

Her brother was raking dried grass over the manure in the yard. "What the heck kind of thing's that supposed to mean?"

"Something died last night," Thalia sniffed the air. "I can smell it. Out in the sty. Smelt it all night long, whatever it is. Always me that's first to smell the dead. 'Member the cat, the one by the thresher? I know when things's dead. I can smell something new that's dead, just like that. Made me think of how everything ends."

"We'll check your stink out later. All you need to think about right now is getting your little bottom back inside that house to stir the soup so's we'll have something decent come suppertime." Her brother returned to his work; and she to hers. She hoped that one day she would have a real job and be able to get away from this corner of low sky and deadland.

The year was 1934, and there weren't too many jobs in Moncure County, when Thalia Canty was eleven, so her father went off to

Dowery, eighty miles to the northeast, to work in an accountant's office, and her mother kept the books at the Bowand Motel on Fourth Street, night shift. Daddy was home on weekends, and Mama slept through the day, got up at noon, was out the door by four, and back in bed come three a.m. It was up to Thalia's brother, Lucius, to run the house, and make sure the two of them fed the pigs and chickens, and kept the doors bolted so the winds—they'd come up suddenly in March—didn't pull them off their hinges. There was school, too, but it seemed a tiny part of the day, at least to Thalia, for the work of the house seemed to slow the hours down until the gray Oklahoma sky was like an hour-glass that never emptied of sand. Lucius was a hard worker, and since he was fifteen, he did most of the heavy moving, but she was always with him, cleaning, tossing feed to the chickens, picking persimmons from the neighbor's yard (out back by the stable where no one could see) to bake in a pie. And it was on the occasion of going to check on the old sow, that Thalia and her brother eventually came face to face with the Rendering Man.

488

The pig was dead, and already drawing flies. Evening was coming on strong and windy, a southern wind which meant the smell of the animal would come right in through the cracks in the walls. Lucius said, "She been dead a good long time. Look at her snout."

"Toldja I smelled her last night." Thalia peeked around him; scrunched back, wanting to hide in his lengthening shadow. The snout had been torn at—blood caked around the mouth. "Musta been them yaller dogs," she said, imitating her father's strong southern accent, "cain't even leave her alone when she's dead."

The pig was enormous, and although Lucius thrust planks beneath her to try and move her a ways, she wouldn't budge. "Won't be taking her to the butcher, I reckon," he said.

Thalia smirked. "Worthless yaller dogs."

"Didn't like bacon, anyways."

"Me, too. Or ham."

"Or sausage with biscuits and grease."

"Chitlins. Hated chitlins. Hated knuckles. Couldn't chaw a knuckle to save my life."

"Ribs. Made me sick, thought a ribs all drownin' in molasses and chili, drippin' over the barbecue pit," Lucius said, and then drew his hat down, practically making the sign of the cross on his chest. "Oh, Lord, what I wouldn't give for some of her."

Thalia whispered, "Just a piece of skin fried up in the skillet."

"All hairy and crisp, greasy and smelly."

"Yes," Thalia sighed. "Praise the Lord, yes. Like to melt in my mouth right now. I'd even eat her all rotten like that. Maybe not."

The old sow lay there, flies making haloes around her face.

Thalia felt the familiar hunger come on; it wasn't that they didn't have food regularly, it was that they rarely ate the meat they raised—they'd sold the cows off, and the pigs were always for the butcher and the local price so that they could afford other things. Usually they had beans and rice or eggs and griddle cakes. The only meat they ever seemed to eat was chicken, and Thalia could smell chicken in her dreams sometimes, and didn't think she'd ever get the sour taste out of her throat.

She wanted to eat that pig. Cut it up, hocks, head, ribs, all of it. She would've liked to take a chaw on the knuckle.

489

"She ain't worth a nickel now," Thalia said, then, brightening, "you sure we can't eat her?"

Lucius shook his head. "For all we know she's been out here six, seven hours. Look at those flies. Already laid eggs in her ears. Even the dogs didn't go much into her—look, see? They left off. Somethin' was wrong." He shuffled over to his sister and dropped his arm around her shoulder. She pressed her head into the warmth of his side. Sometimes he was like a mama and daddy, both, to her.

"She was old. I guess. Even pigs die when they get old." Thalia didn't want to believe that Death, which had come for Granny three years before, could possibly want a pig unless it had been properly slaughtered and divvied up.

"Maybe it died natural. Or maybe," and her brother looked down the road to the Leavon place. There was a wind that came down from the sloping hillside, sometimes, and coughed dust across the road between their place and the old widow's. "Could be she was poisoned."

Thalia glanced down to the old gray house with its flag in front, still out from Armistice Day, year before last. A witch lived in that house, they called her the Grass Widow because she entertained men like she was running a roadhouse; she lived alone, though, with her eighteen cats as company. Thalia knew that the Grass Widow had wanted to buy the old sow for the past two years, but her parents had refused because she wasn't offering enough money and the Cantys were raising her to be the biggest, most expensive hog in the county. And now, what was the purpose? The sow was fly-ridden and rotting. Worthless. Didn't matter if the Grass Widow killed it or not. It recalled for her a saying her daddy often said in moments like this:

"How the mighty are fallen." Even among the kingdom of pigs.

Lucius pulled her closer to him, and leaned down a bit to whisper in her ear. "I ain't sayin' anything, Thay, but the Widow wanted that sow and she knew Daddy wasn't never gonna sell it to her. I heard she hexed the Horleich's cows so they dried up."

"Ain't no witches," Thalia said, disturbed by her brother's suspicions. "Just fairy tales, that's what Mama says."

"And the Bible says there is. And since the Bible's the only book ever written with truth in it, you better believe there's witches, and they're just like her, mean and vengeful and working hexes on anything they covet." Lucius put his hand across his sister's shoulder, and hugged her in close to him again. He kissed her gently on her forehead, right above her small red birthmark. "Don't you be scared of her, though, Thay, we're God-fearin' people, and she can't hurt us 'less we shut out our lights under bushels."

Thalia knew her brother well enough to know he never lied. So, the old Grass Widow was a witch. She looked at her brother, then back to the pig. "We gonna bury her?"

"The sow? Naw, too much work. Let's get it in the wheelbarrow and take it around near the coops. Stinks so bad, nobody's gonna notice a dead pig, and then when Mama gets home in the mornin', I'll take the truck. We can drive the sow out to the renderin' man." This seemed a good plan, because Thalia knew that the Rendering Man could give them something in exchange for the carcass—if not money, then some other service or work. The Rendering Man had come by some time back for the old horse, Dinah, sick on her feet and worthless. He took Dinah into his factory, and gave Thalia's father three dollars and two smoked hams. She was aware that the Rendering Man had a great love for animals, both dead and alive, for he paid money for them regardless. He was a tall, thin man with a pot belly, and a grin like walrus, two teeth thrusting down on either side of his lip. He always had red cheeks, like Santa Claus, and told her he knew magic. She had asked him (when she was younger), "What kind of magic?"

He had said, "The kind where you give me something, and I turn it into something else." Then he showed her his wallet. She felt it. He'd said, "It used to be a snake." She drew her hand back; looked at the wallet; at the Rendering Man; at the wallet; at her hand. She'd only been six or seven then, but she knew that the Rendering Man was someone powerful.

If anyone could help with the dead sow, he could.

491

The next morning was cool and the sky was fretted with strips of clouds. Thalia had to tear off her apron as she raced from the house to climb up beside Lucius in the truck. "I didn't know you's gonna take off so quick," she panted, slamming the truck door shut beside her, "I barely got the dishes done."

"Got to get the old sow to the Rendering Man, or we may as well just open a bottle-neck fly circus out back."

Thalia glanced in the back; the sow lay there peacefully, so different than its brutal, nasty dumb animal life when it would attack anything that came in its pen. It was much nicer dead. "What's it anyways?" she asked.

"Thay, honey?"

"Renderin'."

"Oh," Lucius laughed, turning down the Post Road, "it's taking animals and things and turning them into something else."

"Witchcraft's like that."

"Naw, not like that. This is natural. You take the pig, say, and you put it in a big pot of boiling water, and the bones, see, they go over here, and the skin goes over there, and then, over there's the fat. Why you think they call a football a pigskin?"

Thalia's eyes widened. "Oh my goodness."

"And hog bristle brushes—they get those from renderin'. And what else? Maybe the fat can be used for greasing something, maybe..."

"Goodness sakes," Thalia said, imitating her mother's voice. "I had no idea. And he pays good money for this, does he?"

"Any money on a dead sow's been eaten by maggots's good money, Thay."

It struck her, what happened to the old horse. "He kill Dinah, too? Dinah got turned into fat and bones and skin and guts even whilst she was alive? Somebody use her fat to grease up their wheels?"

Lucius said nothing; he whistled faintly.

She felt tears threatening to bust out of her eyes. She held them back. She had loved that old horse, had seen it as a friend. Her father had lied to her about what happened to Dinah; he had said that she just went to retire in greener pastures out behind the Rendering Man's place.

She took a swallow of air. "I wished somebody'd told me so I coulda said a proper goodbye."

"My strong, brave little sister," Lucius said, and brought the truck to an abrupt stop. "Here we are." Then, he turned to her, cupping her chin in his hand the way her father did whenever she needed talking to. "Death ain't bad for those that die, remember, it's only bad for the rest of us. We got to suffer and carry on. The Dead, they get to be at peace in the arms of the Lord. Don't ever cry for the Dead, Thay, better let them cry for us." He brought his hand back down to his side. "See, the Rendering Man's just sort of a part of Nature. He takes all God's creatures and makes sure their suffering is over, but makes them useful, even so."

"I don't care about the sow," she said. "Rendering Man can do what he likes with it. I just wish we coulda ate it." She tried to hide her tears; sniffed them back; it wasn't just her horse Dinah, or the sow, but something about her own flesh that bothered her, as if she and the sow could be in the same spot one day, rendered, and she didn't like that idea.

The Rendering Man's place was made of stone, and was like a fruit crate turned upside down—flat on top, with slits for windows. There were two big smoke stacks rising up from behind it like insect feelers; yellow-black smoke rose up from one of them discoloring the sky and making a stink in the general vicinity. Somebody's old mule was tied to a skinny tree in the front yard. *Soon to be rendered,* Thalia thought. *Poor thing.* She got out of the truck and walked around to pet it. The mule was old; its face was almost white, and made her think of her granny, all white of hair and skin at the end of her life.

The Rendering Man had a wife with yellow hair like summer wheat; she stood in the front doorway with a large apron that had once been white, now filthy, covering her enormous German thighs tight as skin across a drum. "Guten tag," the lady said, and she came out and scooped Thalia into her arms like she was a tin angel, smothered her scalp with kisses. "Ach, mein leibchen. You are grown so tall. Last I saw you, you was barely over with the cradle."

Just guessing as to what might be smeared on the woman's apron made Thalia slip through her arms again so that no dead animal bits would touch her. "Hello, ma'am," she said in her most formal voice.

The lady looked at her brother. "Herr Lucius, you are very grown. How is your mutter?"

"Just fine, ma'am," Lucius said, "we got the old sow in the back." He rapped on the side of the truck. "Just went last night. No good eating. Thought you might be interested."

"Ach, da, yes, of naturally we are," she said, "come in, come in, children, Father is still at the table mit breakfast. You will have some ham? Fresh milk and butter, too. Little Thalia, you are so thin, we must put some fat on those bones," and the Rendering Man's wife led them down the narrow hall to the kitchen. The kitchen table was small, which made its crowded plates seem all the more enormous: fried eggs on one, on another long fat sausages tied with ribbon at the end, then there were dishes of bread and jam and butter. Thalia's eyes were about to burst just taking it all in—slices of fat-laced ham, jewels of sweets in a brightly painted plate, and two pitchers, one full of thick milk, and the other, orange juice.

The Rendering Man sat in a chair, a napkin tucked into his collar. He had a scar on the left side of his face, as if an animal had scratched him deeply there. Grease had dripped down his chin and along his neck. He had his usual grin and sparkle to his eyes. "Well, my young friends. You've brought me something, have you?"

His wife put her hand over her left breast like she was about to faint, her eyes rolling to the back of her head, "Ach, a great pig, shotzi. They will want more than just the usual payment for that one."

Thalia asked, "Can I have a piece of ham, please?"

The Rendering Man patted the place beside him. "Sit with me, both of you, yes, Eva, bring another chair. We will talk business over a good meal, won't we, Lucius? And you, sweet little bird, you must try my wife's elegant pastries. She learned how to make them in her home country, they are so light and delicate, like the sun-dried skin of a dove, but I scare you, my little bird, it is not a dove, it is bread and sugar and butter!"

After she'd eaten her fill, ignoring the conversation between her brother and the Rendering Man, Thalia asked, "How come you pay good money for dead animals, Mister?"

He drank from a large mug of coffee, wiped his lips, glanced at her brother, then at her. "Even dead, we are worth something, little bird."

"I know that. Lucius told me about the fat and bones and whiskers. But folks'd dump those animals for free. Why you pay money for them?"

The Rendering Man looked at his wife, and they both laughed. "Maybe I'm a terrible businessman," he said, shaking his head. "But," he calmed, "you see, my pet, I can sell these things for more money than I pay. I am not the only man capable of rendering. There is competition in this world. If I pay you two dollars today for your dead pig, and send you home with sweets, you will bring me more business later on, am I right?"

"I s'pose."

"So, by paying you, I keep you coming to me. And I get more skins and fat and bones to sell to places that make soap and dog-food and other things. I would be lying if I didn't tell you that I make more money off your pig than you do. But it is a service, little bird."

"I see," Thalia nodded, finishing off the last of the bacon. "It seems like a terrible thing to do."

"Thay, now, apologize for that," Lucius reached over and pinched her shoulder.

She shrugged him off.

The Rendering Man said, "It is most terrible. But it is part of how we all must live life. Someone must do the rendering. If not, everything would go to waste and we would have dead pigs rotting with flies on the side of the road, and the smell."

"But you're like a buzzard or something."

The man held his index finger up and shook it like a teacher about to give a lesson. "If I saw myself as a buzzard or jackal I could not look in the mirror. But others have said this to my face, little bird, and it never hurts to hear it. I see myself as a man who takes the weak and weary and useless, empty shells of our animal brethren and breathes new life into them, makes them go on in some other fashion. I see it as a noble profession. It is only a pity that we do not render ourselves, for what a tragedy it is to be buried and left for useless, for worm fodder, when we could be brushing a beautiful woman's hair, or adorning her purse, or even, perhaps, providing shade from the glare of a lamp so that she might read her book and not harm her eyes. It is a way to soften the blow of death, you see, for it brings forth new life. And one other thing, sweet," he brought his face closer to hers until she could smell his breath of sausage and ham, "We each have a purpose in life, and our destiny is to seek it out, whatever the cost, and make ourselves one with it. It is like brown eyes or blond hair or short and tall, it is there in us, and will come out no matter how much we try to hide it. I did not choose this life; it chose me. I think you understand, little bird, yes. You and I know."

Thalia thought about what he'd said all the way home. She tried not to imagine the old sow being tossed in a vat and stirred up in the boiling water until it started to separate into its different parts. Lucius scolded her for trying to take the Rendering Man to task, but she ignored him. She felt like a whole new world had been opened to her, a way of seeing things that she had not thought of before, and when she stepped out of the truck, at her home, she heard the crunch of the grass beneath her feet differently, the chirping of crickets, too, a lovely song, and a flock of starlings shot from the side of the barn just as she tramped across the muddy expanse that led to the chicken coops—the starlings were her sign from the world that there was no end to life, for they flew in a pattern, which seemed to her to approximate the scar on the left hand side of the Rendering Man's face.

It was like destiny.

She climbed up on the fence-post and looked down the road. A dust-wind was blowing across to the Grass Widow's house, and she heard the cats, all of them, yowling as if in heat, and she wondered if that old witch had really poisoned the pig.

2

Thalia was almost twenty-nine, and on a train in Europe, when she thought she recognized the man sitting across from her. She was now calling herself just Lia, and had not lived in Oklahoma since she left for New York in 1939 to work as a secretary—she'd taught herself shorthand and typing at the motel where her mother had worked. Then, during the war, Lucius died fighting in France, and her mother and father, whom she'd never developed much of a relationship with, called her back to the old farm. Instead, she took up with a rich and spoiled playboy who had managed to get out of serving in the military because of flat-feet, and went to live with him at his house overlooking the Hudson River. She went through a period of grief for the loss of her brother; after which, she married the playboy in question. Then, whether out of guilt or general self-destruction, her husband managed to get involved in the war, ended up in a labor camp, and had died there not two weeks before liberation. She had inherited quite a bit of money after an initial fight with one of her husband's illegitimate children. It was 1952, and she wanted to see Germany now, to see what had happened, and where her husband of just a few months had died; she had been to Paris already to see the hotel where her brother supposedly breathed his last, suffering at the hands of the Nazis but dying a patriot, unwilling to divulge top secret information. She was fascinated by the whole thing: the war, Paris, labor camps, and Nazis.

She had grown lovely over the years; she was tall like her father and brother had been, but had her mother's eyes, and had learned, somewhere between Oklahoma and New York, to project great beauty without having inherited much.

The man across from her, on the train, had a scar on the left-hand side of his face.

It sparked a series of memories for her, like lightning flashing behind her eyes. The stone house on the Post Road, the smokestacks, the mule in the front yard, an enormous breakfast which still made her feel fat and well-fed whenever she thought of it.

It was the Rendering Man from home.

On this train. Traveling through Germany from France. Now, what are the chances, she wondered, of that happening? Particularly, after what happened when she was eleven.

Not possible, she thought.

He's a phantom. I'm hallucinating. Granny hallucinated that she saw her son Toby back from the First World War walking towards her even without his legs.

She closed her eyes; opened them. He was still there. Something so ordinary about him that she knew he was actually sitting there and not just an image conjured from her inner psyche.

He spoke first, "I know you, don't I?"

She pretended, out of politeness, that he must not be talking to her. There was a large German woman sitting beside her, with a little boy on the other side. The German woman nodded politely to her, but didn't acknowledge the man across from them. Her little boy had a card trick that he was trying to show his mother, but she paid no attention.

497

"Miss? Excuse me?" He said.

Then, it struck her: he spoke English perfectly, and yet he looked very German.

He grinned when she glanced back at him. "See? I knew I knew you, when I saw you in the station. I said to myself, you have met that girl somewhere before. Where are you from, if I may ask?"

"New York," she lied, curious as to whether this really could possibly be the Rendering Man. How could it? He would have to be, what? Sixty? This man didn't seem that old, although he was not young by any stretch. "I'm a reporter."

He wagged his finger at her, like a father scolding his child. "You are not a reporter, miss, I think. I am not saying you are a liar, I am only saying that that is not true. Where is your notebook? Even a pencil? You are American, and your accent is New York, but I detect a southern influence. Yes, I think so. I hope you don't mind my little game. I enjoy guessing about people and their origins."

She felt uncomfortable, but nodded, "I enjoy games, too, to pass the time."

She glanced at the German woman who was bringing out a picnic for her son. Bread and soup, but no meat. There was not a lot of meat to go around even six years after the war.

The man said, "You are a woman of fortune, I think. Lovely jewelry, and your dress is quite expensive, at least here in Europe. And I heard you talking with the conductor—your French is not so good, I think, and your German is worse. You drew out a brand of cigarettes from a gold case, both very expensive. So, you are on the Grand Tour of Europe, and like all Americans with time on their hands, you want to see the Monster Germany, the Fallen."

"Very perceptive," she said. She brought her cigarette case out and offered him one of its contents.

He shook his head. "I think these are bad for the skin and the breathing, don't you?"

She shrugged. "It all goes someday."

He grinned. "Yes, it does. The sooner we accept that, the better for the world. And I know your name now, my dear, my little bird, you are the little Thalia Canty from Moncure County, Oklahoma."

She shivered, took a smoke, coughed, stubbed the cigarette out. She had white gloves on her hand; she looked at them. She remembered the German wife's apron, smeared with dark brown stains. She didn't look up for a few minutes.

"I would say this is some coincidence, little bird," the Rendering Man said, "but it is not, not really. The real coincidence happened in the Alsace, when you got off the train for lunch. I was speaking with a butcher who is a friend of mine, and I saw you go into the cafe. I wouldn't have recognized you at all, for I have not seen you since you were a child, but you made a lasting impression on me that morning we had breakfast together. I saw it in you, growing, just as it had grown in me. Once that happens, it is like a halo around you. It's still there; perhaps someone might say it is a play of light, the aurora borealis of the flesh, but I can recognize it. I followed you back to the train, got my ticket, and found where you were seated. But still I wasn't positive it was you, until just a moment ago. It was the way you looked at my face. The scar. It was a souvenir from a large cat which gouged me quite deeply. No ordinary cat, of course, but a tiger, sick, from the circus. The tiger haunts me to this day, by way of the scar. Do you believe in haunting? Ah, I think not, you are no doubt a good Disciple of Christ and do not believe that a circus cat could haunt a man. Yet, I see it sometimes in my dreams, its eyes, and teeth, and the paw reaching up to drag at my flesh. I wake my wife up, at night, just so she will stay up with me and make sure there is no tiger there. I know it is dead, but I have learned in life that sometimes these angels, as I call them (yes, dear, even the tiger is an angel for it had some message for me), do not stay dead too long. Perhaps I am your angel, little bird; you must admit it is strange to meet someone from just around the bend on the other side of the world."

She looked at him again, but tried not to see him in focus because she felt the pressing need to avoid this man at all costs. "I'm sorry, sir. You do have me pegged, but I can't for the life of me place you."

He smiled, his cheeks red. He wore a dark navy coat, and beneath it, a gray shirt. When he spoke again, it was as if he had paid

499

no attention to her denial. "My wife, Eva, she is in Cologne, where we live, and where I should be going now. We came to Germany in 1935, because Eva's parents were ill and because, well, you must remember the unfortunate circumstance. I was only too glad to leave Oklahoma, since I didn't seem to get along with too many people there, and Germany seemed to be a place I could settle into. I found odd-jobs, as well as established a successful rendering business again. And then, well," he spread his hands out as if it were enough to excuse what happened to Germany. "But I knew you and I would meet again, little bird, it was there on your face. Your fascination and repulsion—is that not what magnets do to each other, pull and push? Yet, they are meant to be together. Destiny. You see, I saw your brother before he died, and I told him what was to come."

She dropped all pretense now. "What kind of game are you playing?"

"No game, Thalia Canty."

"Lia Fallon. Thalia Canty died in Oklahoma in the '30s."

"Names change through the years, even faces, but you are the little bird."

"And you are the Rendering Man."

He gasped with pleasure. "Yes, that would be how you know me. Tell me, did you run because of what you did?"

She didn't answer. "What about Lucius?"

The Rendering Man looked out the dark window as a town flew by. Rain sprinkled across the glass. "First, you must tell me."

"All right. I forgave myself for that a long time ago. I was only eleven, and you were partly responsible."

"Did I use the knife?"

She squinted her eyes. Wished she was not sitting there. "I didn't know what I was doing, not really."

"Seventeen cats must've put up quite a howl."

"I told you. I didn't know what I was really doing."

"Yes you did. How long after before you ran?"

"I ran away four times before I turned seventeen. Only made it as far as St. Louis most of the time."

"That's a long way from home for a little girl."

"I had an aunt there. She let me stay a month at a time. She understood."

"But not your mama and daddy," he said with some contempt in his voice. "A woman's murdered, we all called her the Grass Widow. Remember? Those Okies all thought she was a witch. All she was was sad and lonely. Then, all she was was dead. She and her cats, chopped up and boiled."

"Rendered," she said.

"Rendered. So they come for me, and thank god I was able to get my wife out of the house safely before the whole town burned it down."

"How was I to know they'd come after you?"

He was silent, but glaring.

"I didn't mean for you to get in trouble."

"Do you know what they did to me?" he asked.

She nodded.

He continued, "I still have a limp. That's my way of joking; they broke no bones. Bruises and cuts, my hearing was not good until 1937, and I lost the good vision in my right eye—it's just shadows and light on that side. Pain in memory brings few spasms to the flesh. It is the past. Little bird, but you think I am only angry at you. All those years, you are terrified you will run into me, so when you can, you get out for good. I was sure that little town was going to make another Bruno Hauptmann out of me. Killing a sad widow and her pets and boiling them for bones and fat. But even so, I was not upset with you, not too much. Not really. Because I knew you had it in you, I saw it that day, that we were cut from the same cloth, only you had not had the angel cross your path and tell you of your calling. It is not evil or dark, my sweet, it is the one calling that gives meaning to our short, idiotic lives; we are the gardeners of the infinite, you and I."

"Tell me about my brother," she pleaded softly. The German woman next to her seemed to sense the strangeness of the conversation, and took her son by the hand and led him out of the cabin.

"He did not die bravely," the Rendering Man said, "if that's what you're after. He was hit in the leg, and when I found him, he

501

had been in a hotel with some French girl, and was a scandal for bleeding on the sheets. I was called in by my commander, and went about my business."

"You worked with the French?"

He shook his head. "I told you, I continued my successful rendering business in Germany, and expanded to a factory just outside of Paris in '43. Usually the men were dead, but sometimes, as was the case with your brother, little bird, I had to stop their hearts. Your brother did not recognize me, and I only recognized him when I saw his identification. As he died, do you know what he told me? He told me that he was paying for the sins that his sister had committed in her lifetime. He cried like a little baby. It was most embarrassing. To think, I once paid him two dollars and a good sausage for a dead pig."

Lia stood up. "You are dreadful," she said. "You are the most dreadful human being who has ever existed upon the face of the earth."

502

"I am, if you insist. But I am your tiger; your angel," the Rendering Man said. He reached deep into the pocket of his coat and withdrew something small. He handed it to her.

She didn't want to take it, but grabbed it anyway.

"It is his. He would've wanted you to have it."

She thought, at first, it was a joke, because the small leather coin purse didn't seem to be the kind of thing Lucius would have.

When she realized what it was, she left the cabin and walked down the slender hall, all the way to the end of the train. She wanted to throw herself off, but, instead, stood and shivered in the cold wet rain of Germany, and did not return to the cabin again.

She could not get over the feeling that the part of the coin purse that drew shut resembled wrinkled human lips.

3

"He's here," the old woman said.

She heard the squeaking wheels of the orderly's cart down the corridor.

"He's here. I know he's here. Oh, dear God, he's here."

"Will you shut up, lady?" the old man in the wheelchair said.

An orderly came by and moved the man's chair on down the hall.

The old woman could not sit up well in bed. She looked at the green ceiling. The window was open. She felt a breeze. It was spring. It always seemed to be spring. A newspaper lay across her stomach. She lifted it up. Had she just been reading it? Where were her glasses?

Oh, there. She put them on. Looked at the newspaper. It was *The New York Times*.

March 23, 1994.

She called out for help, and soon an orderly (the handsome one with the bright smile) was there, like a genie summoned from a lamp. "I thought I saw a man in this room," she said.

"Mrs. Ehrlich, nobody's in here."

"I want you to check that closet. I think he's there."

The orderly went, good-naturedly to the closet. He opened the door, and moved some of the clothes around. He turned to smile at her.

"I'm sure I saw him there. Waiting. Crouching," she said. "But, he may have slipped beneath the bed."

Again, a check beneath the bed. The orderly sat down in the chair beside the bed. "He's not here."

"How old am I? I'm not very old, really, I'm not losing my wits yet, am I? Dear God in heaven, am I?"

"No, Mrs. Ehrlich. You're seventy-one going on eleven."

"Why'd you say that?"

"What?"

"Going on eleven. Why eleven? Is there a conspiracy here?"

"No ma'am."

"You know him don't you? You know him and you're just not saying."

"Are you missing Mr. Ehrlich again?"

"Mr. Ehrlich, Mr. Vane, Mr. Fallon, one husband after another, young man, nobody can miss them because nobody can remember them. Are you sure I haven't had an unannounced visitor?"

The orderly shook his head.

She closed her eyes, and when she opened them, the orderly was gone. It had grown dark. *Where is my mind?* She thought. *Where has it gone? Why am I here at 71 when all my friends are still out in the world living, why, my granny was 88 before senility befell her, how dare life play with me so unfairly.*

She reached for her glass of water, and took a sip.

Still, she thought she sensed his presence in the room with her, and could not sleep the rest of the night. Before dawn, she became convinced that the Rendering Man was somewhere nearby lurking; she tried to dress, but the illness had taken over her arms to such a great extent that she could not even get her bra on.

She sat up, half-naked, on her bed, the light from the hallway like a spotlight for the throbbing in her skull.

"I have led a wicked life," Thalia whispered to the morning. She found the strength at 5:30 to get her dressing gown around her shoulders, and to walk down the hall, sure that she would see him at every step.

The door to Minnie Cheever's door was open, which was odd, and she stepped into it. "Minnie?" Her friend was nearly ninety-three, and was not in bed. Thalia looked around, and finally found Minnie lying on the floor, on her way to the bathroom. Thalia checked her pulse; she was alive, but barely. Thalia's limbs hurt, but she used Minnie's wheelchair to get Minnie down the hallway, onto the elevator, and down to the basement, where the endless kitchen began.

They found her there, two cooks and one orderly, like that, caught at last, Thalia Canty, all of seventy-one going on eleven, chopping Minnie Cheever up into small pieces, and dropping each piece into one of several large pots, boiling with water, on the stove.

She turned, when she heard their footsteps, and smiled, "I knew you were here, we're like destiny, you and me, Mister Rendering Man, but you'll never have me, will you?" She held her arms out for them to see, "I scraped off all the fat and skin I could, Mister

Rendering Man, you can have all these others, but you ain't never gonna get my hide and fat and bones to keep useful in this damned world. You hear me? You ain't never gonna render Thalia, and this I swear!" She tried to laugh, but it sounded like a saw scraping metal. The joke was on the Rendering Man, after all, for she would never, ever render herself up to him.

It took two men to hold her down, and in a short time, her heart gave out. She was dead; when her body was taken to the morgue, it was discovered that she'd been scraping herself raw, almost to within an eighth of an inch of her internal organs.

It was a young girl, a candy-striper named Nancy, going through Thalia's closet to help clean it out, who found the dried skins beneath a pile of filthy clothing. The skins were presumably from Thalia's own body, sewn together, crudely representing a man. Thalia had drawn magic-marker eyes and lips and a nose on the face; and a scar.

Those who found Thalia Canty, as well as the candy-striper who fainted at the sight of the skin, later thought they saw her sometimes, in their bedrooms, or in traffic, or just over their shoulders, clutching a knife.

She would live in their hearts forever.

An angel.

A tiger.

505

Chosen

1

When it was over, he remembered the picture.

Because of living in the big city all his life, his first hand knowledge of nature had come from PBS documentaries, or Time-Life Books, or Mutual of Omaha's Wild Kingdom.

But he had forgotten about the picture all those years.

The caterpillar, its skin green and translucent and wet.

The wasp.

The bumps beneath the caterpillar's skin.

The caption: *As paralysis sets in, the wasp has proven her superior power.*

He remembered what he thought, too, of the picture: that in some awful way, it radiated a beauty beyond conscience.

This was what he kept coming back to, later, when it was over, in his mind. Not his emotional life or his education or even his work, but that picture from a book he'd seen at the public library when he was only nine or ten. How, even in his forties, it could come back to him with so strong a memory.

2

Rob Arlington awoke one morning, and thought he felt something on his hand. He brushed at it, but saw nothing there. A sensation left over from a dream, perhaps. He took a quick shower, crawled into his suit (he was so tired from being up late the night before), and grabbed his briefcase on his way out the door. It wasn't that he was late for work, it was just that for the fifteen years of his life that he had lived alone, he hated it. Not life, not work, not his loves and losses, but just the fact of knowing he was alone in the morning, that, at his age, there was no one human being who shared his home with him.

The hallway, when he stepped into it, was hospital green, and smelled of paint. He locked his door, and then thought he heard a noise from inside it. As if something were moving around in the kitchen. He looked at his door: *to open or not? Could be just an echo from another apartment.* Glancing down the hall, he saw, just this side of the fire doors, the super, papers in one hand, a dripping paint brush in the other.

"Exterminator comes on Thursday," the Super said; he was taping notes to doors; he came up to Rob, and slapped a note to his door. The Super, with his fat glasses, and balding pate with its twin sprays of hair, looked like a large worker ant going about its business. Rob shot him a friendly grin—*never hurts to be on good terms with management*—and lifted the note off his door. It read: *exterminator comes on Thursday. 10 a.m.* He wadded the note up.

"I don't want the exterminator," Rob said, still vaguely listening for the thing that might be moving around in his kitchen. Was it a rat?

"You don't got roaches?" The super, his glasses magnifying his small button eyes to enormous disks of glare, thrust out his lower lip in a middle-aged pout which meant disagreement. "Everybody in New York's got roaches."

"None that I've noticed," Rob lied. Of course he had roaches, but he also didn't like the idea of the super and his wife going into his apartment, looking through his things. He already had evidence of their last visit when he'd been on a business trip to California, how they'd gotten in and used his tea kettle. He'd known it was the super, or perhaps Fanny, his wife, because they'd left behind a set of skeleton keys, which Rob returned to them hoping that embarrassment would be enough incentive to keep them from going through their tenant's homes again. "Look," Rob told him, "I've been fogging."

"You been what?"

"Fogging the apartment. I buy these foggers — you know — and it kills them. I don't have roaches. Or spiders, for that matter."

Then, 6C opened her door. She was clunky and large, like an old piano, with hair in her eyes from just washing, and an enormous towel wrapped around her middle, barely keeping her breasts bound up. "I don't want one, either," she said. "A bug-killer. Don't let him into my place. Let me chance being beloved of the flies, but I don't want no bug-killer coming through my place. I like my privacy."

The Super looked at her, then back at Rob, "Pretty soon, everybody's gonna tell me they got no roaches. Why in hell did I call up the exterminator if suddenly nobody's got no roaches?"

The woman in the doorway glanced at Rob. Her eyes were wide and glassy, like she'd just had great sex and was now a zombie. She was not pretty, but still looked freshly plucked, which, to a man of Rob's years was just this side of alluring. She was less overweight than stocky, and her skin was pale from staying inside too much. When the super had gone on down the hall, through the fire doors, she said, "Do you really fog?"

She'd been eavesdropping at her door, he figured. "No," he said, "I just don't like the nosy couple going into my apartment without me around."

She let slip a smile, and blushed, as if she'd just dropped an edge of her towel. "They do anyway. I'm here all day, and I see them. They go through all our apartments. All except mine. 'Cause I'm here all the time."

Then she drew herself back through the doorway, hands clutching the door and frame, as if her legs weren't quite strong enough. She seemed to drag them with her, one after the other.

On the weekend, Maggie came up. When she and Rob lay after the Great Event, him feeling sticky, and her feeling exhausted, he mentioned meeting the neighbor for the first time. Maggie said, "I've talked to her on the elevator. She seems nice. It's too bad about the accident, but I guess we all get smashed about once or twice before life is up."

He moved his arm around, because the back of her head seemed to cut into it at an uncomfortable angle. "She get hit by a car or something?" Remembering his neighbor's legs, how she barely moved them.

"She told me she's agoraphobic. Stays in all the time. Lives on disability. Sad little thing."

"Sad hefty thing. How the hell does she afford that apartment on disability?"

"That's not nice, the hefty part. It's her grandfather's old apartment—he had it since the building was built in 1906. He knew the Lonsdale family, in fact, when they were designing the place. And she's sweet, even if she is strange. She's only thirty-four—can you believe it? It's life that's aged her—in that apartment, all her grandparents' things around, antiques, and dark windows, and old shiny floors, she just sits there and collects her checks and...well, *ages*."

"Like a cheese left too long under glass," he joked. "She claims she's beloved of flies."

Maggie was beginning to look stern; she didn't appreciate disparaging comments about women. "Oh, stop, you. She's had a terrible life. She worked at a grocers, but her back bent or something. And then, she finally works up the courage to get out, into the marketplace, as it were. She went out one day, she told me, to see her mother, who's in Brooklyn, and when she was coming up from the subway, two men took her purse and pushed her down the steps. Twenty steps, she said. She woke up in the hospital, and couldn't move for three months. She's only been back in her place maybe two weeks. She said she had terrible nightmares in the hospital. She's scared of people, I think."

"No wonder I never see her. You heard all this in the elevator?"

510

"You'd be amazed how much information she can fit in between the fifth and second floors." Maggie paused, and looked at the wall beside the bed. "You don't think she can hear us, do you?"

"Not unless she has a glass to the wall. Hey," Rob said, rapping his knuckles along the wall, "No spying."

Somewhere, beyond the wall, the sound of shattering glass.

Then, after Maggie left at eleven, he took the elevator to the basement, putting the weekend's laundry in the machine, and counting quarters out. He thought he heard a noise. Figuring it was a mouse, he ignored it. There were cracks in the lower parts of the walls, right where wall met floor, all along the basement. He had seen fat roaches run into these hidey holes when he'd flicked the laundry room lights on. Always gave him the creeps, *but they're only bugs*, he told himself.

He put his quarters in the machine, and switched it on. He leaned against it, listening to the gentle humming as water sprayed down on his clothes. Rob always took a book with him when he did his laundry—and he never left the room while his wash was going, because the one time he did, his clothes had been taken out, in mid-cycle, and left on the dusty cement floor. At some point in his reading, above the sound of the machine, he heard a series of ticks, like a loud clock ticking. Assuming the laundry had set the machine off-balance, he opened it; rearranged the soaked clothing; closed the lid. But the ticking continued. He lifted the machine's lid again, and while it turned off, the ticking kept going. He identified the area of ticking as one of the cracks along the wall. Then, he thought it might be coming from over by the trash dumpsters, down the hallway—sometimes the noises in the shafts echoed through the basement. He walked down the narrow, dimly lit hall, its greenish light humming as if about to extinguish from unpaid utilities, and looked around the trash.

Something was tapping from inside one of the disposal shafts. Rob hesitated at first, wondering if a very large and angry rat might be inside it, but the tapping continued, and seemed too steady to be a rat. He went, and lifted the hatch up—

Something living, wriggling, wrapped in gauze and surgical tape, dropped, and he instinctively caught it, because he saw a bit of pink, like a human hand, from an undone section of the gauze and he knew as he caught it that it was a baby.

3

He had the sense to call the police before he unwrapped the gauze, and was spared the sight of the dead infant.

"I think it was alive when I found it," he said. "I felt movement. Not for very long, though."

The officer, named Gage, shook his head. "Nope, she wasn't alive when you found her, Mr. Arlington. She'd been dead at least a half-hour."

"I heard tapping. I think the baby was moving."

"It wasn't the baby," the officer told him.

The next morning, he read about it in the *Daily News*.

"Must be a slow week," he told one of his co-workers. In the paper, they detailed the story: newborn baby, wrapped in gauze, skin chewed up by roaches, apartments under investigation, related to similar cases of babies left in dumpsters and thrown down sewer drains, left in parks wrapped in old newspapers, covered with ants or flies or roaches or whatever scavenger insect had lucked into finding the fresh meat. There was his name: Rob Arlington. Advertising man. There was the building: *The Lonsdale*, Central Park West, where they refused to let the most famous rock stars live, even the ones who could pay the rent. It had another picture, older, of a man in his fifties, in the style of the turn of the century, a stern looking man with a Rasputin beard and glaring eyes. The caption read: *The Original Lonsdale scandal of 1917, Horace Grubb and his Theory of Nature*. But nothing in the brief article elaborated on this photograph.

Maggie came by that night with wine and fresh salmon. "I thought you could use some cheering up," she said, whisking past him in the doorway, with her packages. She smelled like gardenia, which he loved, and wore a bustierre under a short jacket, a translucent skirt, and boots. He knew she would seduce him so that he would feel better, and he loved her for the thought.

"You heard," he said.

"Yep. Did you actually talk to the *News?*"

"What do you think?"

She didn't answer; he realized that he was sounding grouchy. She opened the kitchen drawers in search of the corkscrew.

"It's in the basket on the fridge," he said. "My guess is some poor bastard junior reporter is stuck down at the precinct waiting for the dirt on a rape or riot, and he looks at the schedule of events and sees a baby in a dumpster story. My name's right there. He can't file the story he's after 'cause nothing's in on it. So he ties this in with all those other dead babies left out to die stories and voila—an urban legend begins. With my name attached to the most recent one. The Man Who Found A Dead Infant In The Laundry Room Of The Famous Lonsdale Apartments Right Off Central Park West."

"You're a star," she said, pouring the Merlot into two glasses.

"I didn't know about the bugs, about how they'd been...doing that to the baby's skin," he said, shivering a little, going over to her, taking the wine, reaching around her back with his free hand, between the jacket and her skin. "You smell good. Like a garden of earthly delights."

"Yeah, I've been gargling with cologne. It's not too strong?"

"Not at all," he said, smiling, loving her little insecurities because they made her seem less perfect, more human. He drew back, sipped wine, rotated his head around to relieve tension in his neck. "God, Maggie, a baby. They said it was less than a day old."

"It's a rough place, this world," she said, and drew him to her. "You ever wanted a baby, Robby?"

He almost was going to cry, thinking of the dead thing in his arms, whatever brief and terrible life it had to endure; but he held back. Kissed her with gentleness. "I don't know," he said.

"Someday I want a baby, but (don't get that fearful bachelor look) not yet, and probably not from you, unless you play your cards right."

After dinner, they watched television, and as he lay on the couch with her, he saw a roach on the wall. He picked up his shoe and threw it across the room, but missed it. The shoe made two loud thuds as it hit the wall, and then the floor.

A few seconds later, the phone rang. He leaned over her head ("massive hair," he murmured, "like a scalp jungle,") and lifted the receiver. "Hello?"

"6D?"

He didn't recognize the woman's voice.

"Who's this?"

"6C. Your neighbor. I got your number from the Super. You all right? I heard a noise."

"Oh, hello. Yes. I lobbed a Bass Weejun at the wall."

She seemed to accept this.

Maggie looked up at him, her eyebrows knitting.

He shrugged and mouthed: *next-door neighbor.*

The woman on the line said, "It scared me. After all the news."

"Oh," he said.

"It was you who found it," she said.

He felt drained. "Yeah."

"Were they hurt?"

Rob pulled his ear from the phone and looked at it. *What the hell?*

"Were what hurt? You mean, the baby?"

But she'd hung up the phone.

"My neighbor lady is spooky indeed," he said, as he rested the phone back into its cradle.

After midnight, he had a craving for frozen yogurt. There was this place down on the corner that made the best cappuccino nonfat yogurt, a favorite spot of his. So, while Maggie slept, naked except for her panties, her breasts creamy and lovely above her small, indented belly, her dark hair obscuring one side of her face, he slipped on his jeans and tucked his cotton shirt in, stepped into his shoes, and tiptoed out of the apartment. He forgot to lock the apartment from the inside, so he stuck the key *(three strikes and you're out, bubba,* he thought as he finally got the sucker in the key-hole on the fourth try) into the door on the outside, and turned it so it was locked twice over. *Never be too sure, even in a building like The Lonsdale, seventeen-hundred-a-month for a junior one-bedroom, even if you've been here for ten years. Babies in the garbage chute, roaches on the wall, anything can happen.* He was a little drunk from the wine, and the thought of frozen yogurt, even with the October coolness outside, sobered him a bit; by the time he got to the elevator, he was standing up straight, and wiped the grin of requited lust from his face.

He had to stand in line behind six others, all frozen yogurt fiends like himself, and by the time he'd gotten up to make his order, he decided on the largest size possible. He got two plastic spoons, and tasted the treat on the walk back to the apartment. He fiddled with his pockets, because he couldn't locate the keys. Had he left them upstairs? *Damn it.* He'd have to wake Maggie up after all. He buzzed the apartment. Three times. The last one, a long sustained buzz. Finally, she picked up the intercom.

Her voice was sleepy. "Rob?"

He giggled, high on Merlot and frozen yogurt, "Hey, sweetie-pie, I locked myself out getting some dessert for the one I love and me."

As if she couldn't hear him, she asked again, "Rob?" She was still waking up, he could tell. He looked at the small black plastic of the intercom as if he could maybe see her through it if he concentrated. "Is it you?" she asked.

He pressed the button on his side. "Yeah, yeah, I got melting yogurt, Maggie, and I'm starting to feel a draft."

"Rob?" she asked again, weakly, and it sounded, for just a second, like she wasn't sleepy at all, but about to pass out. About to cry, or something, something almost whimpery and breathless. Not like sleepiness at all.

And then, he remembered: he'd left the keys in the door to the apartment.

Don't panic.

Pressed the button. "Maggie? You okay? Buzz me in, okay?"

He let go of the button.

Waiting for her buzzer. The intercom finally got pushed, but there was just the *ch-ch-ch* sound of dead air.

He pressed the button for the Super. "It's Rob Arlington, 6D. I left my keys inside."

The super, ever vigilant, buzzed him in with no further identification required.

Rob ran to the elevator, and, luckily, it was on the first floor. He got on, and pressed 6. The elevator gave its characteristic lurch. He realized that he was clutching the frozen yogurt cup so tightly that it was all twisted, with dripping cappuccino yogurt spreading down his hand. He dropped it in the elevator. When he reached the sixth floor, he sprinted down the hall, tried the door. No keys. Locked. He rapped on it several times. "Maggie? Maggie! Maggie!"

He heard a noise, and glanced to his right.

The woman in 6C stood there, in a navy blue bathrobe. "She left."

"What do you mean she left?"

"She knocked on my door about ten minutes ago. She told me she had to go home, and she didn't know where you went. Here," the woman held her hand out. "she just left a second ago."

In her hand, his keys.

He looked at her, at the keys. "I just talked with her on the intercom. I came up on the elevator. I would've seen her."

The woman looked annoyed. "She comes banging on my door at god knows what hour and tells me you left the keys in the door and then we hear the buzzer go off and she goes back to the apartment, and mister, I can't tell you what else she did, because I came back inside kind of pissed off that I now have to wait up for you because your girlfriend wants to split. If she takes the stairs or something, I can't help it. She's a nice lady, seems like, but I can't read her mind. You want these or what?" she asked, finally, tossing the keys to him. As she stepped back inside her apartment, he noticed the light blue bruises like polka-dots on her pink legs.

Maggie's answering machine picked up for three days, and then he stopped calling. He dropped by her place one night, with flowers, but she didn't answer the door. Even though the lights were out in her apartment, he sensed that she was standing behind the door, looking through the peep-hole.

Then, on Monday morning, she called.

"It's me."

"Jesus, Maggie, I've been worried sick. What happened to you?"

"What do you mean, what happened to me? What happened to you?"

"I went out for some yogurt. You were asleep. I didn't want to wake you."

Silence on the line.

"Something frightened me."

"What?"

"Oh, Rob," she sounded close to tears, "I can't talk about it. Not like this."

"Will you meet me somewhere? Café Veronese?"

He heard her slow breaths, as if she needed to calm down.

She whispered, "Okay. After work. Six."

When they met, she moved away as he tried to give her a friendly hug. Her eyes were circled with darkness, and blood-shot. Her lips were chapped. Something about her skin was shiny, as if she had a fever. They sat at a booth in the back, and she, uncharacteristically, withdrew a cigarette from her purse and lit it. "I didn't know where you went. The door was wide open. The lights were off. Someone was inside with me. I knew it wasn't you."

He noticed that she kept glancing down at her fingers; and then, he knew why. She was afraid to look him in the face.

He said nothing.

"I was just about naked, and scared. I reached for my jacket, but...it...it grabbed my arm."

"A man," he said.

She shook her head.

"A woman?"

Maggie laughed once, bitterly. "None of the above. It crawled up my arm."

He looked at her, and couldn't help grinning. "It was a bug?"

She glanced up, saw his look, and her lips became tight. "Fuck you," she said.

"Sorry. But you got scared by a bug?"

"It wasn't just a bug. Robert. I knew I couldn't talk to you."

He sipped his coffee, she smoked her Camel. Her fingertips were yellow-brown from smoking.

As if suddenly inspired, she rolled the right hand sleeve of her sweater up, and thrust her arm under his face.

Dark bruises, in a diamond pattern.

He touched along them, and felt thin blisters, also.

"It attacked me," she said.

"Jesus," he gasped, "Maggie, you've go to see a doctor. This isn't just some bug."

"Exactly," she said, triumphant. Tears shone like jewels in her eyes. "It's like a disease. It feels like a disease. It's taking me with it. Whatever it is. Inside me. It did something. But this," she nodded toward the diamond bruise, "this was only where it held me. The others..."

"Others?"

Maggie's expression turned again to stone. "You don't believe me."

He said nothing.

She said, "They opened me up."

4

"She doing okay?"

Rob was checking his mailbox. He glanced around the corner, and there was the woman from 6C. It was eight o'clock, and he had walked Maggie home, put her to bed with a stiff drink, made her promise to see a doctor in the morning, and then walked home. He was hoping to just go to bed early, himself.

The woman said, "Your girl. I heard from the Super she got attacked. He said it was a spider from South America or something. He started talking exterminating again—sounded like Adolf Hitler, you ask me."

"Better," he said, "she's doing better. I haven't talked with her since Monday, though. I think maybe she just needs to be alone for awhile."

"You think she imagined it, don't you?"

"I don't know."

"She seemed nice. I don't think she'd lie. I seen spiders as big as birds at the Natural History museum. She doesn't seem like the lying type, your girlfriend."

"I didn't say that. Something definitely happened."

"You was thinking it, though. Hard for guys to deal with things like that, I don't know why, happens every day in this city—bugs and thugs. You probably don't believe about the gators in the sewer, but I know two cleaning women who swear by them. Guys, they never believe it til it hits them butt-first in the face. But you ain't like that, right? You half-believe her, don't you?" The woman gave a hopeful smile. "I got attacked in the subway three months ago. My hip still ain't too good. You give me a choice between getting bit by a spider or jumped by a hoodlum, I choose spiders every time."

He managed a smile.

"My name's Celeste. Celeste Pratt. We talk a lot in halls and junk, but we never been introduced." She extended her beefy arm. It was the first time he'd actually seen her dressed, and it was all in black like some East Villager, but it made her pale face sparkle a bit. "I didn't know she got bit that night. I'm sorry I ragged on you so much. I was tired. Friends?"

519

He nodded, "Sure."

"Glad to hear she's doing better. You think it was a black widow or something?"

"I don't know. She won't see a doctor."

"I don't like doctors, neither," Celeste said, shaking her head, "I believe in homeopathy and stuff like that. The mind, Rob. The power of the mind. And nature. It's weird to believe in nature when you live in a city like this, ain't it? But I always lived here, all my life, and you look for nature where you can find it. The law of nature, way I see it, is we got to sometimes give ourselves up to it, like we're part of this big system, and your legs, like say mine, get bashed, but you just let the pain of healing take over, you let nature run its course. It's like Grubb's Nature Theory, about survival and adaptation. Know what I mean? You tell your girlfriend I hope she gets better, okay? Do that for me? She's always been so nice and friendly to me, I hate to see nice people get hurt, but in this city, you know, it happens every day, but better some spider or something instead of a guy with a butterfly knife, right?"

Rob stared at her as if he could not quite believe she existed. He blinked twice.

"What's wrong?" she asked.

"Nothing," he said, and then departed for the elevator. Celeste got on it with him, and smiled, but didn't volunteer another river of conversation. On their floor, he let her off first, and then got off, stood just on the other side of the elevator door, and watched Celeste go to her apartment.

When she had put her key in the lock, and turned it, he said, "Excuse me, Celeste."

She turned to him, beaming.

"Downstairs, did you mention something about someone named Grubb?"

"Grubb's Nature Theory. Yes."

"Is that Horace Grubb?"

She nodded, blushing.

"My grandfather," she said.

She invited him into her apartment, to show him her grand-father's books. Rob accepted out of curiosity, as much to see the large apartment as the texts. The apartment was a three-bedroom, "although it was once this entire floor, a fourteen-room affair, but it was divided up in late '29, when everyone with anything lost it. My grandmother was from New Orleans, and redecorated accordingly," Celeste pointed out the French touches, "and the apartment, what's left of it, has largely remained as she left it in 1964, when she died. 'Course, she ruined the floor, the beautiful dark wood floor, what with her wheelchair scraping along, it's why I have the oriental carpets and runners all over the place. My mother never wanted to live here ever since she married back in '48, to my dad, Rice Pratt, but Grammy left it to me, because she knew I'd take the right kind of care of it. But I ain't much of a housekeeper. The bedrooms are disaster areas—I do all my crap in them—but, here, we can have a nice martini at the window." She guided him over to the kitchen, which was dark and wooden like the rest of the place; the floors were dark with a layer of dust and crumbs, as if she never cleaned up after herself; the windows were dark, too, painted black, supposedly because her grandmother, at the end of her life, could not abide light because of an ocular problem. But, Celeste pressed the small latch to the left, and then pushed the larger of two windows open.

521

The view was of the park, shrouded in night, and was not blocked by the Cavanaugh Building, as it was from Rob's small apartment.

When both martinis were made, she sat down opposite him, and raised her glass. He clinked his to hers, and sipped. Strong.

He said, "I saw in the papers a picture of your grandfather."

She rolled her eyes, and flapped her hand in a gesture of dismissal. "Oh, god, that business. Grampy's book was called *De Naturis,* and it basically expounded his theory. Oh, right, right, you want to know about it, don't you? It was that man's role in nature was as a farmer and facilitator. We ain't here to enslave nature, he said, but 'cause we got to ease the birth, so nature can keep on keeping on, or something like that."

"How'd he get in trouble over that?"

"It was about the time of World War I, and it had something to do with soldiers going to France, and some literature Grampy gave out. It was a mob thing. Terrible. Would've killed him, too, but things worked out, eventually. But it made the news here for about ten minutes before the war took over. Put the Lonsdale on the map, too."

"Was he anti-war?"

"Oh, no," she said, her breath strong and gin-soaked, "just the opposite. He supported war, he said, 'cause it meant more human flesh got put in the ground, which was good for crops throughout the world. He believed that the best use of human beings was as compost or incubators. That's really where the trouble was, in his big fat mouth. He cheered the deaths of soldiers, because he felt the death of a youth was the best food nature knows. He had people, you know, who agreed with him, listened to him, and stuff. Wrote a lot of pamphlets. They called themselves Grubbites. He was definitely weird. He wasn't a cannibal or anything like that, even though they said he was. He was a what do you call it?"

"Misanthrope?"

"Yeah, in a big way." She drank down the rest of her martini and went to get another. Her back to him, she said, "Maybe something different, too. He had this whole spiritual side to him, like he believed there was a god in everything alive, trees, birds, even the air."

"Sort of a pagan transcendentalist, then," Rob amended.

She was drinking her martini at the sink, half-turned to him, looking out the window. "Everything. Even unto the smallest," she whispered.

Rob noticed that there was a trail of ants running from a crack near the top of the kitchen wall, all the way down beneath the sink. *No wonder,* he thought, *she leaves crumbs and scraps everywhere.*

She was watching the ants, too, but she made no move to kill them. As he followed the trail from its highest point, he noticed that the ants went down to the corner of the shelf where the sink was, and were trooping across the shiny tile to within an inch of her hand.

He lay in bed that night with his reading light on. He thought about Maggie, which was pleasant after the martini, about her gardenia smell, garden of earthly delights—and somehow this reminded him of the ants in Celeste's apartment, for he wondered what kind of urban garden they made their nest in. Finally, he turned out the light, and fell asleep.

He awoke, sometime in the night, hearing the sound of a woman moaning from nearby.

Through the wall.

Celeste. Having a nightmare. But the moaning continued, escalating to muffled cries, and he knew it was not a nightmare, but a private pleasure. He heard the humming buzz of what could only have been a vibrator, and he thought: *good for her.*

Strangely, it aroused him, and the more he listened, the less aware he was of his own left hand slipping down beneath the elastic of his jockey shorts.

Just as he was closing his eyes, dreaming about a faceless but beautiful woman, the moaning from the other side of the wall turned into a scream.

The screaming went on for nearly a minute, and then died.

523

He threw on his bathrobe and dashed to the hall, but by the time he was knocking on Celeste's door, it was silent. The hallway light flickered and buzzed; the bulbs would need replacing. He stood there, looking around at the other apartments, wondering if anyone else had heard the woman's screams. He started knocking again, and this time he heard her moving around, as if drunk, knocking things over as she made her way to the door. Maybe she'd had another martini or two after he'd left; she'd certainly gulped them down fast enough.

He saw her shadow beneath the space between the floor and the door. She was standing on the other side of the door, looking through the peephole at him.

"Celeste? Are you all right?"

She must've been scraping her nails on the door.

"Celeste?"

The shadow beneath the door vanished; he heard noises as she moved back down the corridor.

From within the apartment, the chime of a clock.

Two a.m.

He turned to go back to his place, shaking his head.

As he climbed back into bed, he thought he heard the buzzing of her machine, again, just at the wall. A little louder than before. He closed his eyes, wondering if he should investigate further. Maybe she'd just tripped on something and screamed, maybe she was drunk, maybe she didn't even scream with pain, maybe it was the way she climaxed, who the hell knew?

He was asleep, probably dreaming, he knew, but he imagined that a big cockroach was riding Celeste's ass, its feelers stroking the back of her neck, and its face turning slowly to look at Rob as it diddled with his neighbor, its face all brown and callused, with flecks of dirt across the broad platform between its eyes, and its eyes looking just like the Rasputin eyes of Horace Grubb.

The phone rang, both in the dream and out of it; in the dream, Rob went running down a long corridor in search of the phone; in reality, he snarfled himself awake, and reached to the table by the bed.

"Hello?"

He heard static on the line.

Then, "Help me."

A woman's voice.

Its very weakness shocked him awake.

"Celeste?"

"Help me," she said, and then a sound like high-pitched humming, like the Vienna Boys Choir humming one note without taking a single breath filled the phone, and it felt like a needle thrust in his ear.

He dropped the receiver.

5

The door to 6C was open.

The sun was still not up, although he could hear the honkings and screechings of morning traffic.

Her apartment was lit with red lights, like a bordello, and he thought of Celeste's grandmother decorating the place with her New Orleans touches. The furniture seemed bloodied by the light, and it made him queasy as he walked through the front hallway. He had a sense that there was movement all around him, just on the periphery of his vision, but every time he glanced at the red-shrouded furnishings, there was nothing out of the ordinary.

The phone, off its hook, lay in the kitchen.

A smell, too, there, like clothes that had been sweated in and discarded in a heap to rot for months. The window that had formerly held the view of the park had been blackened over with dark cellophane.

Again, he sensed a slithery movement, and glanced around the floor, but saw nothing.

525

He glanced down the slim hallway that led to the three bedrooms.

"Celeste?" he asked.

A sudden noise, as of someone rushing to a door, and throwing herself against it, sliding down to the floor. Sobbing. Muffled, as if a mouth were taped over.

His first instinct was to walk back to the door, go to his apartment, and call the police.

He took one step back, and stood still when he heard another sound: a repetitive vibrating sound, like monks chanting *aum* over and over.

But it was a woman; it sounded like a synthesis of a woman and a machine, for the vibration of her voice seemed to increase beyond what a human might be able to, and he felt the vibrations in the floor and walls.

Someone threw herself at the door again.

Door Number Three.

He could not turn around and run for cover.

It was Maggie's voice that was humming, louder until he wanted to cover his ears.

Then, it was as if he were being swept along with a tide, for he found himself moving toward that door, that dark red-stained door, moving smoothly straight forward, moving his feet, not one after another, but together, as if he were in a dream and was not touching ground at all. His heart was beating loud; it was not his heart, but her humming; his mouth had dried up; he swallowed dryness.

When he reached the door, he twisted the knob, opened it.

The room was dark.

The stench came at him in waves of heat; it smelled like a compost pile.

He stepped into the darkness, and reached for a light switch.

The switch was low, as if made for someone in a wheelchair (her grandmother had been in a wheelchair, she'd said, and had left tracks all along the floor.)

The light came up, also red, from the solitary bulb that dangled from a thin chain in the center of the room.

The room was small, and covered with dark earth and wet leaves.

Maggie lay in mud just a few feet in front of him.

She was naked.

She stared at him, and he could see the vibrations of her lips as she hummed.

Bruises, too, all along her arms, stomach, breasts, legs.

Her humming increased to a shattering pitch.

There was a twitching, almost, no, a wriggling of skin along her arms and belly, too, and as he leaned forward to touch her

As the humming seemed to vibrate the entire building,

He felt the edge of an antenna stroke feather-like down the back of his neck.

Celeste whispered in his ear, "Isn't she beautiful?"

He turned around, and Celeste was dressed in a gown made entirely of wasps, all with wings twitching, diamond heads, their thousand legs clinging to her, "I am their chosen, Rob, for what my grandfather did for them, his many kindnesses, I got chosen as their midwife. They won't hurt you, Rob, I wouldn't let that happen, as long as you don't try to hurt me, you're gonna be fine."

The wasps moved along her shoulders, over her breasts, her living clothes shimmering in the light.

He gasped, "What did you do? What in god's name?"

"Nature is God," Celeste said, "we are here to serve. People build cities like this, and what, do you think it's all for us? It's for them. It's all for them. We're just part of the colony, Rob. God's a maggot, Rob, turns the flesh to earth, we're less than maggots, don't you get it?"

"What about Maggie? What did you do to her?"

Celeste shook her head, clearly disappointed that this was his interest. "It ain't like she's in any pain, you know, one of the mothers paralyzes her while they lay their eggs under her skin. I ain't gonna make anybody go through pain. Not what's not natural, anyways."

The scream on the other side of the wall.

Maggie's scream.

Maybe. Maybe.

Maybe it was Celeste, maybe she was mating with a wasp, maybe the scream was pleasure, maybe it's her eggs inside Maggie's body.

It was then that Rob felt his mind leaving his head, as if it were leaking out of his ears, and drifting smoke-like to dissipate in the hall. Something short-circuited for him; he could not easily remember words or how to make his arms or legs move right; for a moment, he wondered if he knew how to breathe.

Celeste reached out and took his hand in hers. He watched her do this, and felt like an infant, unable to make sense out of the world in which he'd found himself. She stroked his hand. "If I want, they'll choose you, too, to help. I want you to help. I feel like you're a friend," she said, drawing his hand to her bosom. "It's so lonely sometimes, being chosen. It's so lonely sometimes being the one that the gods pick."

He watched the wasps travel from her hand to his, and then up his arm, sometimes biting, but it didn't bother him, he didn't mind, he didn't mind. He felt them everywhere, all over his skin, and when he listened carefully he began to understand what they were saying, all of them at once, through their vibrations and feelers and bites.

6

The season was a hard one, for the earth needed turning, and there needed to be others, for once these young came up, the mothers would need to lay more eggs after the mating time.

When it was over, he remembered the picture.

He remembered the picture when he looked at Maggie as they were coming out.

The caterpillar, it's skin green and translucent and wet.

The bumps beneath the caterpillar's skin.

Beauty beyond conscience.

The cruel face of nature.

But as he was watching it happen, Maggie's eyes on him, her humming at a pitch, he knew it was the most glorious and selfless act that any human being could ever perform, he wept with the intense and silent beauty as her shiny skin ruptured with conquering life.

The Dark Game

"The Dark Game" is really meant to be read after having read my novel, The Hour Before Dark. I'm assuming, however, that if you're reading this collection in its Cemetery Dance Publications form, that you probably are a reader of my fiction already, and it's likely that you either own or have read The Hour Before Dark. If you haven't, go read it now, and then come back to read this story—which is a kind of prequel to the novel.

1

I saw a painting once, by an artist unknown to me. The painting was of a man's hands, bound together. The title was "Victory is freedom of mind and body." I believe that is true. I would go further and say that victory is freedom of mind from body. Separation from the thing that imprisons us. Flight. Perhaps freedom from life itself. That is victory.

Life is brutal. It is like this whip and these ropes. It hurts. It scars. But we must take it.

We must find some pleasure and solace within this terrible lashing.

You want to hear it all? You want me to tell you how it went, in the prison camp? Why I like the ropes? You want to play the game with me?

First let me tell you this: youth is something you put in a drawer somewhere, you lose the thought of it behind socks and letters and medals and old passport photos and keys that no longer fit locks. You wear it when you're of the right age, and you do things that you ought not to, and then as you gain perspective with age, you put it away, and you close the drawer.

And you lock it.

Then, you live the life you've built toward, and no one needs to see what's in that drawer.

A secret is something to be hidden, and if it is hidden well enough, it never becomes a fact. It is just something that is not there when you go to look for it. It is the thing missing, but the thing that is not missed.

That is how I feel.

That is why I don't revisit those times, often. The camp.

Or the motel room.

Or the smokehouse.

But since you have me here, like this, I'll tell you. Maybe you'll leave after that. Maybe you won't want to stay here once you know about me.

2

Before the war, I was in a motel room with a girl I met outside the base, and for fun she tied me up and when she did it, I went someplace else in my head. My hands tied, my feet bound. I remember she smelled like orange blossoms, and she enjoyed tightening the thin ropes around my hands. But my mind was just gone—drifting upward into darkness, into another place. Back to Burnley Island, I guess, and that's where I've always ended up—my memories, my family, my home.

I was just not there anymore. The game had taken me over.

It had become automatic for me.

It was second nature.

The Dark Game

My name is Gordon Raglan.
Gordie, to my friends.
Captain to folks on Burnley Island.
In the war, things got worse for me.
The game got worse.
But it wasn't so bad when I was a kid.

3

Early memory: winter.
Bitter cold.

Wind whistling around me, boxing my ears, as I trudged through three feet of snow to get out to the smokehouse. I was ten, perhaps. Heavy with a burden. It was the dog I'd had since he was a foundling of two or three years old, and I was too young to remember bringing him home from a walk in the woods. He was dying now, of some undiagnosed malady. In those days, you didn't take the dog to the vet when it was its time. You took him someplace and you shot him. And this freezing February day, that was what I was to do. My father marched behind me. I could not bring myself to turn and look over my shoulder to see how he kept pace. I was weeping, and it would be the first and last time I would weep for years. I held my dog—a small mutt, no bigger than my arms could carry—and he looked up at me as if he understood that something not wonderful was to come.

At the smokehouse I stopped and prayed. I wished that God would intervene, just this once. I would trade, I promised God, my life for this dog's. I would do anything God wanted me to do if he would just take a minute and breathe new life into my dog's body. I would build a chapel. No, I would build a cathedral.

The snow bit at my cheeks and nose.

My dog, whose name was Mac, whimpered and groaned.

"Go on, son," my father said.

He called me son more than he called me Gordie or Gordon. Sometimes I thought he wasn't sure of my name. That I was just another son to him. Another child to deal with before I became a man.

I reached up, and opened the door to the smokehouse. I barely kept my balance, for the dog had grown too heavy for me.

My father lit the lantern inside the smokehouse—it was old-fashioned, and my mother felt it was a fire hazard, but my father insisted on using it. A yellow flickering light filled the small room.

When I'd set Mac down on some straw, I kissed him on the muzzle and kept my prayers going—my deals with God to change this, somehow.

Then, my father handed me the pistol and told me to get it over with quickly. "Misery is terrible. That animal is in misery. When you brought him home, you promised to take care of him. That is a commitment. This is a way to take care of him, so he won't be in any more pain. You can stop his pain. He won't get better, son. He won't."

"I can't," I said.

"You have to. You promised. You promised me. And you promised that dog when you brought him home. He has had a good life here. But now he's sick. And he needs to be taken care of."

I looked at my dog's face and saw the terribleness of all existence in his eyes. In his shivering form.

And that is when I learned about how life doesn't matter at all. Not one bit. It is a misery. A wretchedness foisted on us by a God who turns His back on all. We live on a planet of ice, and the only thing we human beings can do is endure it and try to make sure that we don't add to the misery too much.

4

Here is my life. I was born on Burnley Island, in a house called Hawthorn, and I grew up in a family called Raglan that had a history on that island. We were shepherding people, I'm told, originally. We came with Welsh and Scots and English in our blood, and we were dark and swarthy, as I am, a perfect descendant of the Raglan clan. My father was a brute, and I don't say that lightly. He was a man more likely to lash with a belt or a switch than to scold with words. He was quick to judge, and hot-tempered, and I suppose I joined the army to get away from him more than anything else. I went off to see the world and fight the good fight, and found myself one dawn in the heat of a jungle, in the boredom of a company that was lost, our communications screwed beyond all measure, and I had a "fuck all" attitude toward the war and the jungle. I was nineteen, and the last place I wanted to be was in that miasma of heat, humidity and the stink of swamp.

And then, before much time had passed, the enemy got us.

No need to go into specifics. It was ugly. There were a dozen of us originally, but by the time I regained consciousness, tied like a pig to a stick, there were only eight or so—counting me and my buddy, Gup (short for Guppy, which was a kinder name than his original nickname, which was Shrimp), Davy, who seemed too young to be a soldier, a man I had no liking for named Larry Pastor, and Stoddard. I knew what to do if captured—name, rank, serial number, and nothing else, but the truth was, I was scared spitless and we'd all heard the stories of the POWs and how no Geneva Convention was going to stop our enemy from torturing us and then dropping us in some mosquito breeding ground, dead, when it was all over. None of us was commander. We were just soldiers, and we had no valuable information at all, and no reason for a negotiation with our commanders.

533

But hope is the last thing to go, and so we had it—I had it, and Gup had it, although Stoddard had already told me that he knew he'd die in the jungle and he didn't give a damn because his girl was already pregnant by some other guy and his folks had disowned him for some reason he wouldn't say, and what the fuck was the point? That was his attitude, and even though I felt we lived on Ice Planet and life was a hurdle into chaos, I still hoped. For the best. For life. For good to come out of bad.

I woke up later on, pain running through my arms and legs like they'd had nails driven into them, in a dark hole in the ground that smelled like feces and had just a grate at the top so I could see a little of the sky.

Luckily, I still had a pack of gum on me—I kept it in this small pouch at the back inside of my skivvies that my mother had sewn for me to hide money. Instead, I hid Wrigley's gum, and I took a sliver of a piece and began chewing it just to feel as if I were still an American and that things mattered even if I was in a hole in the ground.

5

I was a little boy when my mother taught me the game, only it wasn't really a game the way she told me about it. It was a way to get calm and to try and get through pain. I guess I was probably four when she taught me it. She said my grandmother had taught her, and that her grandfather knew about it, too. It was like make believe, but when I had scarlet fever as a kid, I really needed something to help me get through it. I was sure I was going to die, even though I didn't know what death was at four. But scarlet fever gave me an inkling. I was feverish and delusional, and I remember being wrapped in blankets and taken in the car to Dr. Winding over in Palmerston, and lying naked on his ice cold metal table while his nurse drew out the longest needle I had ever seen in my life and they told me it wouldn't hurt, but I screamed and screamed and my mother and father had to hold me down while that needle went into my butt. Even though I still had fever, it wasn't quite so bad. But my butt stung, and, wrapped in blankets on the way home, I was in my mother's arms, a baby again. She whispered to me to try the game, that's what she called it. I named it the Dark Game later on. When it got to me.

At home, in my room, she sat beside my bed and told me to close my eyes despite my moans and groans, and she told me to take her hand. But I couldn't close my eyes. I kept opening them. Finally she took a handkerchief and put it over my eyes like a blindfold so I couldn't see. She started the rhyme, and I said it along with her in a singsong kind of voice, and after a bit, she and I were somewhere else, in the woods, in darkness, and I could not feel the pain or the fever at all.

She told me that it was a way the mind worked that was like magic, that it got you out of yourself and out of where you were.

When I began to teach my friends how to do it as a kid, she pulled me aside and told me that I should keep it to myself.

"Why?" I asked.

"Because it can be bad, too. It's important to stay in the world. To not delve into that too much. If you need God, there's church. If you need friends, don't go off into your head too much."

But I didn't understand what she meant then, and I'm not sure I do now.

Or maybe I do and I just don't want to look at it.

"It's a daylight game," she said. "Between you and me. It's a Raglan game. It's just to make things easier when they're rough."

I played it, all by myself, my eyes closed, that wintry day in the smokehouse when I shot my dog, too.

I played it in that hole in the middle of the jungle without a hope in hell of getting out of there alive.

6

The first day and night, They watched me.

They, being the enemy. I don't want to call them what we called them back then. It was racist. It was nasty. It was a nasty place to be. I hated their guts. They were Enemy. They were They. We were Us. My boys—that's how I thought of Gup and Stoddard and Davy— screamed at night. I heard them clearly. I'm pretty sure Stoddard died right away. That's what I heard, anyway. I could picture him working hard to piss off the Enemy, even if his nuts were being nailed to the wall. Gup might hang in there. Davy, I worried most about. He was practically just a kid.

I began to discover my darkness in my dirty pit of a bedroom. I began to feel my environment. I guess I was about twenty feet down. Some kind of well. Maybe it was dug for water. Or prisoners. I don't know. It was deep but not wide. I had just enough room to sit with my knees nearly touching my chest. It was dirt and rock, and they lowered water down after midnight, just a cup on string. Half the water had dropped out of the cup by the time it reached me. Not even a cup, I discovered. A turtle shell. Drank out of it because I was damn thirsty, and I soon discovered that if I didn't drink out of it fast, they yanked it back up.

They.

Sons of bitches.

I stared up through the grate, trying to see the stars or at least something that meant the hole was not just an o in the earth that had no beginning and no end.

7

Memory: back to Texas, back to the night I got tied up, back when I was barely more than a kid and out on an adventure.

The girl who tied me up was named Genie, and she could be had in that heat-stroke town in Texas for less than twenty bucks. I was too young to be sure what I could do with a girl like that—I had left my sheltered island a virgin of eighteen, and knew that I would have six months or so before getting my orders overseas into the heart of the war. I didn't want to die a virgin, and I doubt there has been a virgin in existence—who wanted to die in that state of being untouched by another. So, when my buddies and me went out to the local rat bar called The Swinging Star, playing pool and downing too many beers, I let down my guard a bit when one of my friends, named Harry Hoakes, slapped me on the back and whispered in my ear with his sour mash breath that he and a couple of the guys were going down to Red Town, a part of the desert where the whores were cheap and fast and you could buy a few for a good deal less than a week's pay.

I look back with shame, of course, upon this youthful episode in my life. I do not proudly admit that my first experience with a woman was at the hands of a seasoned pro of twenty-six, but it is what it is—or, it was what it was. I was drunk, stupid, pretty sure I was going to die in some distant jungle, so I went with my compadres out in a truck that some townie drove—no doubt the pimp for the Red Town girls. Then, we unloaded outside yet another bar, and went in, and there they were, like glittery fool's gold, or broken glass mistaken for diamonds on a moonlit highway. Harry Hoakes looked like a movie star and was from L.A. and had this air of magic around him, no matter what he did. He died in the war, within a year. I heard he stepped on a mine and it just ripped him up. But that night, he was completely on and alive like lightning—all around you and illuminating the landscape. This landscape was alien to me—slovenly, lazily pretty girls who looked the way whores are supposed to, not quite unhappy yet with their situation, not quite sure of how they landed in that desert canyon, not quite hardened to the way their lives would surely go. When you're 18, and in the army, whores don't seem sad or needy or even lesser. They seem like angels who don't ask for the reasons of your interest. They know you want them, and they're perfectly fine with that.

Harry Hoakes introduced me to the girls like they were his sisters. The one who sidled up to me was named Genie. "I'm like that old movie star, Gene Tierney. From *Laura*. You ever see *Laura*? It's a beautiful movie. I'm gonna be a movie star someday. I am," and she was a big brunette with big teeth, from the Midwest, she said, a farm-girl who wanted adventure, and intended to wind up in Hollywood in a couple of months—some producer had discovered her already and she was just waiting to hear from him, she told me so fast it made me laugh—and she asked me what I wanted to do. I told her that I didn't want to do all that much. We got a bottle of Jack Daniels and went back to the motel and plunked down the few bucks for a two-hour stay, and then she brought out those ropes.

She told me that since I was a virgin, she wanted to make sure I didn't do any of the work. That's what she called it, and I guess it was her work.

But when the ropes went on, I went off, and I was no longer in a rundown motel with a big toothed girl, but was back on my island, back on Burnley Island, and it was winter, as my memories of it often are in a hot, dry, desert place, and my father tied me up to the post that sat at the center of the smokehouse. He told me that I had been bad to do what I had done, and that he had to teach me a lesson. I was, perhaps, fourteen, my shirt had been torn off my back, and I felt the sting of his cat—a cat-o-nine-tails that he kept to discourage my brothers and me from doing the bad things we often did. But in my Dark Game memory, I didn't feel pain from the stings—I felt myself glowing, and becoming a powerful creature beneath the lashes. I felt as if I were commanding my father to whip me, to

537

torment me with the bad things I'd been doing. I felt as if I were a god, and he were merely my servant.

And soon, in the Dark Game, it was my father with his shirt torn, tied to the post, and I had the whip, and I was lashing at him and telling him that he was a bad, bad man.

When I opened my eyes, the game done, I found that I was tied to that bed in the motel in Texas. Outside, the sound of trucks going by.

In a corner of the room, Genie, the whore, lay like a crumpled rag doll, her face bloodied.

8

Harry Hoakes came a-knocking at the motel room door. I was tied up in Room 13, which made it lucky, I guess. He was drunk from his own bottle of Jack Daniels, and he nearly busted down the door to get to me. Inside, he looked at me, tied up and naked on the dirty bed, and then at Genie, her big teeth all but knocked out, lying in a corner, her eyes wide.

He stared at me, then at her.

"I passed out," I said.

"Jesus," he scratched his head, dropping his nearly empty bottle. His fly was open from his time with his girl. He was too drunk to process everything. "Jesus. What the hell?"

"I don't know. I passed out. We didn't even do anything."

"Must've been her pimp," he said.

"She's got a pimp?"

"What, you think she's a nice girl from Iowa?"

"Maybe she's not dead," I said.

"If she's not dead, then she's the greatest actress in the world. Because she's dead like I ever saw dead."

"She thought she was going to be like Gene Tierney."

"Who?"

"That pretty actress with the overbite. In *Laura*. You ever see *Laura?*"

He looked at me kind of funny, and then shook his head. "We are up the legendary creek, my friend. You got a dead whore in your room, and you're…well, nekkid as a jaybird tied up." Then, he let out a laugh. "Christ, you could not have made this up if you wanted to."

"Help me out of these ropes," I said. "Houdini I ain't."

9

In the hole, in the prison, the enemy would sometimes stand over the grate and spit. They did this a lot, and now and then, they'd take a leak down on me. I'd hear Them laughing up above. This might've been over a few days or a few weeks. I barely saw the sun in that time, because the grate got covered by a board during the day. They didn't want me to get that Vitamin D from the few rays of the sun, I guess. It was like living in a cave, and time seemed to evaporate. I lived in endless night.

They'd pull me out of there sometimes, too. Usually when it was dark out. They'd send a rope down, and I was to bind my hands to it. They'd pull me up. Why did I go? They fed me during those times. Fed me much better than if I stayed in the hole and ignored the rope. They brought me up and gave me fish or frog or some kind of large maggot cooked with thick flat leaves around it that didn't taste half-bad to a starving guy. They pretended to be friendly, and the one who spoke English, who I called Harry Hoax, after my friend from Texas, because he sounded a little like Harry, he made light jokes with me about my situation that actually were pretty funny.

So Harry Hoax took me aside into the mud-brown cell where I'd get the sumptuous feast, and he told me that he was my only friend. "Your men already betrayed you," Hoax said. "They have told the commander everything. The position of other companies. The plans of the General."

I looked at him, grinning. "I bet they have. Good for them."

"Yes," Hoax said. "It is good. How are you feeling? I see sores on your shoulder."

"I'm fine."

"You seem in good spirits. Are you praying to your god?"

"God has more important things to worry about than me."

"I bet you are thirsty."

"Somewhat."

"Good. We have some pure water for you. And even a small cup of wine. Specially for you."

"To what do I owe this sudden bout of hospitality?"

"We are not primitive people. We may live and fight among the trees and swamps, but we have a sense of culture. You are important to us. We want you happy and healthy."

"That's why you put me in a hole in the ground."

"War is evil. I know that. We know that."

"Am I talking to 'I' or 'We'?"

He laughed. "Very good. Here," he said, glancing at the doorway.

A young attractive woman in the garb of the local peasants entered, with a wooden tray. On the tray, a small porcelain cup, and beside it some palm leaves. Atop the leaves, more of the fried grub I'd had before, and then what looked like a rabbit's leg, also cooked. After setting this down in front of me, she left and returned moments later with a jug of water.

"You see? We treat you well," Hoax said. "All we ask is that you tell us a few things. They are minor, unimportant questions, really."

"I thought my friends told all. I certainly don't know more than they do," I said.

Suddenly, like a brief shock to my body, I heard a wail from one of the other cells.

I tried to place the voice as one of my team, but I could not. I wasn't even sure it was human.

Hoax closed his eyes for a moment as if he didn't enjoy the sound, either. Then, he nodded to the girl with the jug, and she rose and poured water into the cup.

I brought the cup to my lips and drank too fast. She refilled the cup, and while I sat there with Hoax, she made sure I always had water.

"There is a small bit of opium in the water," he said, softly. "You have pain, and it will help with it."

"You're drugging me?"

He sighed. "I feel bad for the state you're in. It is just a distillation of the poppy. Not enough to make you crave it. Just enough to ease any physical torment you might be feeling."

After a moment, I nodded. "That's kind of you."

"You are different from the others," he said. "You are not like other Americans, Gordon. You have a deeper quality. We do not want to hurt you. We want to bring you into realignment with truth."

"Ah," I said, feeling a bit blurred around the edges. I assumed this was the opium.

Hoax began the routine questioning that had been done before, and I gave him the standard answer, which was no answer at all. At the end of this, and the end of my meal, he sighed, and told me that he wished me no harm but that the war would end with Their victory and Our defeat and that all my pain would be for nothing.

"Perhaps," I told him. "But perhaps not."

And then, two interrogators came in, and I recognized in their eyes the sadism I'd seen before. These were pleasure-torturers, and I would be their toy for the night.

Hoax left the cell, looking a little sad.

The interrogators bounds my hands and ankles, and began to play a game that I believe is called, in torturing circles, the Thousand Scratches.

But it didn't matter what they did to my body.

I closed my eyes, and I could begin the rhyme I'd learned as a child:

Oranges and lemons say the bells of St. Clemens.

And then, my mind eroded into darkness, and I returned to the smokehouse, tied to the post, with my father's cat-o-nine-tails slapping hard at my scarred shoulders.

10

My father and I had good moments, too. He took me hunting and fishing. We spent idle summer Sundays out on a skiff that he'd borrowed from a friend down in the harbor, and he told me of his abiding love for the sea. He took me on his occasional deep sea fishing voyages, and he brought me closer to him when my sister

Nora drowned off the island, coming home from the mainland on a small boat when a storm had hit. My father took me aside and wept with me, the closest he'd ever come to showing genuine softness and true compassion.

If I felt something other than love for him, it was no doubt honor.

I hated him for the whippings, but I knew that some demon drove him to it, and I was willing to take it for the building of my character. Perhaps in these days, people might call the police if a boy was being whipped by his father. But in those days, not long ago, it was considered nobody's business outside the family.

My father's demons were many, but he seemed to have an overzealous Christian sense of the Devil and of Angels and of saving his children from the Burning Fires of Hell. He was too good a Catholic, perhaps, and felt that I was not quite Catholic enough. He'd shout at me, while he whipped, that this hurt him more than it hurt me, and that angels and Jesus wept as the lash ripped against my skin, but that if I were to go to heaven, I must repent of my sinful ways, of the bad things I had done, and I must turn to Jesus and the Queen of Heaven, Mary, and to God's grace and his iron will.

I was, he told me, of the Devil.

11

Oh, the bad things I'd done, they were truly bad, I suppose. I smoked a bit, and I drank sometimes when I was far too young to drink liquor. Once, I tried to set fire to the smokehouse, but only managed to burn most of the field nearby and many of the small thorny trees.

He had also caught me in the woods, in a way that a boy doesn't want to be caught, and that too was part of my sin.

I deserved the whippings, and took them, played the game to get through them, and then would spend a feverish night with my grandmother's salve all over my back to help the healing.

I honored and respected my father, even then, and I also thought of ways I might kill him someday.

But I never did.

12

After I awoke from the game, after the interrogators—my impersonal demons—had left their scratches all over my too-thin body—I was returned to my pit, to my endless night.

Sometime later—days, perhaps—I was brought out again.

This time, Hoax was not happy with me. It seemed that my comrades had not said as much as they'd wanted. It seemed that none of us was behaving.

This time, I was to have a night of theater, he told me.

"Might I have a bit of that opium water?" I asked. I might've begged. I liked the stuff and I wanted to make my time in this Hell as pleasant as possible.

"Perhaps after," he said, rather sadly.

I was brought into a cell lit by wavering candlelight, and there was my buddy Davy, nineteen years old but looking like he was sixteen. Sixteen and in hell. His eyes swollen from beatings. His jaw cracked. A festering wound on his scrawny arm.

Ropes again. This time, on his wrists and ankles.

Four men had the ends of the rope.

"This is a play we call the Tug of War," Hoax told me.

Then, he began asking me questions.

Tears came to my eyes, but I had nothing to tell them.

The four men tugged at the ropes and I heard Davy's bones pop, one by one, as they pulled, and his jaw dropped open, slack, but he was still alive.

Until one of the men pulled what seemed to be his forearm right out of Davy's skin.

Oh, but the game kicked in again, you see, at that point, and I missed most of the evening's entertainment by flying off to Burnley Island, by going somewhere I would be punished for my sins, but they were my sins alone and it was my punishment and no one else's.

When I came out of the game, I was missing a finger and had no memory of it being taken, or of the burning metal that had cauterized it to keep it from bleeding.

Hoax, however, told me the next time I was hauled up that I was a man of iron. "You didn't make a sound. You seemed..."

"To be someplace else," I said.

He nodded. "Where did you go? The one you call Axeman was using a dull small scissor to cut off your finger. Why didn't you flinch?"

"Magic," I told him. "What's on the menu for tonight?"

"Menu?"

"Bugs? Rats? Frogs?"

"Oh," he said, smiling. "Supper. Well, tonight, we have a special treat. Tongue."

"Cow?"

"Pig. But it's very good. Wild pig makes a wonderful dish."

When I was finished with supper—and it truly was sumptuous compared to my previous ones—they brought another from my company, the scrappy little guy we called Gup. Like the previous show with Davy, he had obviously been beaten, and perhaps his left leg was broken, also, for he hobbled in and nearly collapsed when the interrogators let go of his arms.

"Your friend cannot speak," Hoax whispered in my ear, like a mosquito circling. "He has, unfortunately, just this afternoon, lost his tongue under the Axeman's blade."

Now, Hoax didn't say that the tongue I had just eaten was my buddy's. He didn't have to. Maybe it was, and maybe it wasn't. But he obviously wanted to give me that message, no matter what the truth of it might be.

I didn't eat for a few days, but finally, pulled out of the hole again, I gobbled down the food they brought me—stew of strips of meat and leaves that tasted terrible but completely satisfied the gnawing in my gut.

Again, Gup was brought out, this time missing both hands, cauterized and bandaged at the wrist.

"His hands fell like leaves from a dying tree," Hoax told me.

"Very poetic," I said, trying to keep my mind from thinking about Gup and the Axeman too much, and forcing myself to keep out of playing the Dark Game. To remain in the moment.

"Have you ever tasted human flesh?" Hoax asked.

I didn't answer. I looked at poor Gup's face. I wished him to die right there. I prayed to God. I prayed to the Devil. I prayed to the Queen of Heaven, Mary, the Mother of God, Blessed is the Fruit of her Womb, Jesus.

I prayed that his spirit would be pulled from his body before another night passed.

This entertainment of Hoax's went on for several nights, but each time I refused to answer his questions. I will admit with nothing but shame that I began to crave the meals brought to me, and I convinced myself—no doubt for survival's sake—that this was not the body of Gup that I slowly consumed, sliced from him day after day and cooked up with spices and jungle flowers to make dishes that I began to love.

This was simply meat that had been taken from the body of pigs and rats and snakes and lizards and frogs and fish and other creatures of this Enemy's country.

This was not Gup's foot, sliced into slivers, swimming in fragrant soup. This was not a bit of flayed skin from Gup's buttocks, wrapped within a palm front that had been buttered and baked into a moist but crunchy crust.

Yet, nightly, Gup was there, soon an eye was gone, then his nose, his ears, toes and left foot, his lips sliced off, until I saw him no longer as a man at all, as a friend, as a former buddy, as one of the team.

I saw him as the supplier of my life.

In a dream, in the hole, I saw the great snake of life, devouring its own tail. Life eats life, the image of the snake seemed to tell me. Life devours itself. You are part of this, and so is Gup. The snake is the whip in my father's hand. The whip is in my hand and reaches from my bloodied back to whip my father's hand. The torturer and the tortured are each playing a part and cannot be without the other.

So, I awoke from this dream and knew then that life was neither beautiful nor perfect nor magical.

Life was simply the gutter of heaven, the place where offal and waste was spilled.

545

I began to love my suppers with Hoax, and even when the Axeman came to me, a razor in his hand, and my mind shooting off to the game, I began to enjoy my contact with these cosmic barbarians and I looked forward to whatever they had in store. I had forgotten my army, my country, and my friends. There was only my hole and my cell, and my smokehouse back on Burnley Island. It was the whole universe, and I could not tell whether it was heaven or hell.

Then, coming from the Dark Game, out into the cell again, it was pain in my crotch that had me screaming, yet I felt distant from the scream. I felt I could measure the scream and how it flew along the cell walls, bouncing up and down and back again.

They took another one of my fingers, but worse, one of my nuts that night.

The Axeman had done it, with his little razor.

I hadn't answered the questions, and they had taken my left ball after slicing off my next finger down from my already-torn-off pinkie.

When I came around, I was in the cell, screaming, and one of my guys, Larry Pastor, sat across from me, watching, his face trembling as if with an impending storm of sobs.

I had become the new entertainment for someone else now.

I was the star of the show.

The next night, I had the best supper yet, with Larry staring at me from across the room, his face a grimace.

What was I eating? My finger? My testicle? Or simply some specially sliced rat over a bed of rice and plantains?

"It's all right," I told him. "It tastes good. It really does."

13

I was unsure of what I ate most nights, but the strangest thing of all was that I had begun gaining weight. I still drank a bit of the opium water—Hoax would bring in barely a thimbleful. I guess he wanted to keep me pliable and still sober enough when necessary.

I attributed my gain in bulk to a combination of the fatty meat they fed me, as well as sitting in a hole in the ground for days on end. Hoax commented on it, and I could see it in Larry Pastor's eyes—while he got thinner and thinner, no doubt refusing to eat any meat offered him, I was beginning to put on the pounds.

Truth was, I felt better. I felt as if my mind had adjusted to the hole and the cell. I began to realize that, contrary to what Hoax might've thought, I never even felt I was going to escape. I just refused to tell Hoax or his beloved Axeman any military plans or secrets because I knew that once I told, I was as good as dead. The meals would stop. They'd leave me in the hole and either forget about me completely, or fill it in with dirt and rocks.

I began to see my imprisonment as a kind of luxury hotel—a fancy five-star place. I began living in my head a lot, believing that I went on adventures when I was in the hole. I used the Dark Game to get out—I began to see the world again. I was in Paris, briefly, for a moonlit walk along the Seine with a beautiful girl who reminded me of a teacher I'd once had a crush on. I had breakfast on the Champs Elysee, buttered almond croissant and a demitasse of espresso while watching traffic as it headed toward the Arc de Triomphe. Another voyage out, I sat on a striped blanket on some tropical island, surrounded with bare-breasted beauties, feasting on mango and coconut milk, feeling the warm breezes as the shadows of palm trees cast thin lines along the pumice-strewn beach. In the cell, I'd go to Burnley Island, to a moment in the past, but in the hole, I'd be somewhere magnificent, off on some adventure that was like a wish fulfillment of my boyhood.

Perhaps this saved me. Perhaps it damned me. In my rare moments of lucidity, I'd try to stay grounded by chewing on a small bit of the Wrigley's gum – the little I had left. A tiny infinitesimal piece. It reminded me of who I was, where I was, why I was there.

I began to talk to Hoax, without even knowing that I might be giving away secrets.

I told him all kinds of things. Not military secrets. I didn't really know any. Just about my life. About my nocturnal adventures.

Hoax became my best friend, and I suppose months passed. Other soldiers were captured. Sometimes I saw their faces, and now and then I recognized their faces.

547

But they were part of the Show now. I watched the show, or they watched me. But Hoax didn't let the Axeman cut from me again. I was valuable. I was telling things. Nothing important. If I told anything important, I was as good as dead.

No, I was telling Hoax about life outside of the jungle, and he loved my stories. He had studied the works of Shakepeare, so now and then we'd talk about Macbeth or about Othello, and I told him about Moby Dick and how my island was somewhat like Nantucket and had been part of the whaling trade. He loved American movies, too, so we talked about them at some length, and he offered up critiques that were quite well-thought-out about how Americans approached movies as opposed to other cultures. He also enjoyed discussing famous wars, and warriors of the ancient world.

These conversations often went on during the torture of another.

I watched a man weep as the Axeman sliced off both of his ears, and then held them high.

548

I am loath to admit that, deluded, and not really as sane as I should've been, I clapped for this performance because I thought it was some kind of special effects magic. The Axeman was good at his job.

I had no idea what Hoax had in store for me, but soon enough, he brought me into a lower level of Hell with him.

14

Here's the thing about the Dark Game: by itself, it's simply a mind trick. It's a way to open doors inside you and to escape. Pain. Hurt. Sorrow.

That's all it is.

But in that prison camp, with the techniques they taught me purely by trying them on me, I learned how to add another level to the game.

How to make it go deeper.

And when it did, something truly magnificent came of it.

15

"Brainwashing." It sounds like some medical experiment.

But it's really simple.

You just put the subject in a position of separation from every sensory detail.

And then you go to work on him.

I had been prepared for it, in my training.

But I guess you're never really prepared for this kind of thing, not after months in a hole in the ground, not after watching your friends get their noses and eyes and ears and hands cut off in front of you.

Not after they feed you what might be your left ball.

16

Hoax had me tied up, hands in front of me, but tied to another rope that went to my ankles. They had positioned me, standing, in the middle of a cell. Plugged a fan into the wall. I guessed that this was to help block out any noise beyond the cell wall. Then, each wall was covered with a dark cloth to block out even the cracks of light that might come in.

549

Additionally, Hoax tied a blindfold around my head.

Plunged into absolute darkness, I felt Hoax touch my hands. "You are going to be here for several hours," he said. "You are not going to touch the wall. Or sit down. Or fall. Should you fall, you will be strung up so that you are dangling from the ceiling with a stick thrust between your arms to keep you balanced. So, do not fall, that is my advice, my friend. You are to keep silent. If you cannot keep silent, Axeman will cut out your tongue and sew your lips together. Understood? This is for your betterment. We find that you are truly a patriot to the world, to freedom, and to honor, and we want you to realign yourself with nature and man's true calling, instead of with this monster you have served in America. You have been deluded by your country, and we intend to help you recover. You are special to us, and to me, Gordon. You are worth realigning."

And that was the last word I heard for many hours, during which my bones ached, my bowels let loose without my being able to control them, and after awhile, I felt as if I were floating.

The sound of the fan—a buzzing like a thousand black flies—seemed to take over my mind, as if it were what my brain generated: the noise of a cosmic buzzing.

And somewhere beneath it, after awhile, I heard Hoax's voice again, only I could not make out what he was saying.

I was fairly certain, however, that he was inside my head now, doing the brainwashing, planting ideas and truths known only to the Enemy, trying to make me over into one of their servants.

But I went into the Dark Game, and there I met Hoax, and I heard him clearly, and I understood how this brainwashing could serve the Dark Game—and how it could help me survive. It wasn't getting into your brain that's the problem. It's making your mind separate from your body so completely that your body becomes a servant to someone else's mind. That is the goal of brainwashing. They are not cleansing the brain. They are turning it off, and switching on another brain, imprinting another set of memories and values and thoughts so that your past is no longer there. It is wiped out, but not so completely—you think you are the same person. But someone else has invaded you. The Other. The one who has turned off one switch has juiced you from another one.

And you are that person's mind now. You are that person's imagination.

That is what I learned. That is how I began to understand that the Dark Game was not just for one to go off on flights of fancy. To protect you from some pain of life. It could be changed, using this brainwashing. It could become a way to turn a switch in another—to implant your own mind into another's mind, so that he no longer had his own perception but might, at least briefly, have yours.

I knew there was a way I could use this on Hoax. On the Axeman. I knew that there was a way I could put the Dark Game into them so that I might escape.

17

They told me later that I stood there for 20 hours.
They told me later that I had been realigned.
But I had not been.

The Dark Game had saved me. It had protected me. It had kept me from letting their words and thoughts press into my gray matter.

When they brought me out into the sunlight—for the first time in many months—they rejoiced and called me Comrade and Friend and Healed One.

But, on the inside, I had already begun planning how I would destroy them and set their camp on fire, and sow the ashes with salt so that those demons might never rise again.

18

But I've got to pull you back to that night when I was eighteen. Remember? Me tied to the bed, the whore dead on the floor, and the real Harry Hoakes, my buddy, my pal, untying me, his breath all whiskey and perfume absorbed from his girl for the night.

"She thought she was going to be like Gene Tierney," I said, and then, "Jesus, I'm going to end up in jail for this."

"Or you'll be in the jungle. In the goddamned war. Which do you want?"

"I choose the goddamned war."

Harry grinned, slightly, despite everything. "You didn't do it. You were tied up. I'm a witness to that."

I got up and got dressed as fast as I could, tripping over my trousers as I yanked them up.

"You let her tie you up?"

I shot him a glance that shut him up.

"What are we going to do?" he asked.

"We ain't gonna get caught, that's for damn sure," I said.

Next thing I remember, we're dragging that body out to Harry's car, and we plop her in the trunk.

I looked at her once, in that fizzling little light of the trunk, before we shut it down on her.

Her face.

She was somewhere else.

That's what Death was, I thought. It's going into the Dark Game for good.

I had no feeling for her. She was no longer there.

But the drive out to the mesa, thirty miles away from Red Town, the whole way I kept wondering how she had been murdered, and why I had awoken from the Dark Game with the strange feeling of pleasure in my loins as if I had truly lost my virginity that night.

But it is a Mystery with a capital M.

Part of me has felt all these years that I had untied myself, had beaten her to death, and then had somehow wrapped myself up in the ropes again.

Houdini, after all.

We buried her in a desolate spot, so deep that the coyotes and scavengers wouldn't be able to dig her up.

I heard, years later, that Red Town eventually flourished and became more than a saloon and whorehouse railroad stop. It expanded out into the mesa, and I think a shopping mall was built near the spot where we buried her.

Harry said to me, at four that morning, driving back to base, "No matter what happens, we can't ever say we met her. Or were even there. The other girls won't tell. They don't like cops. But you and I have to be clear on this. We were never there."

"Where?" I asked, and then Harry muttered, "Jesus," and I knew our friendship was over that morning.

When I heard he died later, in the war, I felt bad for him. I missed him, too. We had done our time together, and that's a bond even after it passes.

I wonder if he ever got over the sight that had greeted him when he stepped out of the ordinary world of red light night and into that motel room of me tied up and a dead woman on the floor.

But now, he's in the Dark Game.

19

Suddenly, like an overnight celebrity, I became revered among the Enemy in the camp.

No longer made to sleep in the hole, I had a straw mattress beneath me, and I ate regular food with some of the lower officers. More of my own countrymen arrived at the camp, and I saw them as they trooped in, proud and wounded, through the barbed wire at the edge of the jungle. The camp was in a flat wetland area, but with long planks connecting marshy islets, until you got to the end of the swampy part, and rose onto higher ground. The commander's headquarters was at the highest point, and I got to calling it Mount Olympus. The pits and holes where the Americans were kept, I called Tartarus. I taught Hoax, who now accepted his nickname happily from me, about the various levels of Hell, and he and I cooked up a scheme to begin a new set of torments for my countrymen.

We would take Dante's Inferno, which was easy enough to find, even with the supposed anti-European sentiment of the Enemy, and create elaborate Rings of Hell for the prisoners. Next, I talked about the Cannibal Torture. I suggested a whole new way to do this. Why even use the Axeman, despite his pleasure in the act of cutting off flesh and bone from a live victim?

Why not me, their countryman? What would be more horrifying than a well-fed compatriot slicing off the lips of his fellow American in front of the remnants of a once-proud platoon? A USO show from Hell, I called it, and it took Hoax several days to see this as the less grandiose and more intriguing idea. Dante's Inferno went on the back burner, as it were. Instead the USO Show from Hell would begin.

We'd have beautiful girls dancing for the boys. Then, we'd have the main event. I'd do a comedy routine, I told Hoax. I'd strip them of their dignity. I'd cut off bits and pieces of the happiest, sweetest guy they knew, the youngest of their friends, the one they thought of as a mascot.

Right before their eyes.

"They'll tell you what you want to know," I said. "They'll divulge their mother and father's addresses if you want, once we do this."

Hoax, not suspicious in the least, was thrilled. Yet, he still didn't completely trust me, for he felt the Axeman should be there to do the slicing. I wasn't handed knives or razors. I was still a prisoner, albeit a Friend of the Enemy, as they proclaimed loudly, nightly, into the pits and holes of Tartarus.

20

The prisoners built the stadium, first. I oversaw its construction, and they worked tirelessly and swiftly, for I told them that it was a monument to their Dead. That it was their Memorial, and that they must take pride in it. I spent some nights with them, talking of how we were going to be well-treated by our captors, and that for them to trust me, despite appearances. They did not trust me at all, I could tell, but they had the resignation of those who wait for freedom to come from outside their sphere. The helicopters raiding from the sky, perhaps. The end of the war itself, perhaps. They had lost the will to escape. They had lost the will to resist. They were broken, yet capable men.

They did as I told them to do.

I also spent nights with them, playing the Dark Game.

I needed their minds. I needed to bring them into a state of calm and of service.

I needed for them to hear only my voice.

21

The bleachers went up, the theater backdrop created. Within two weeks, it was, by the standards of the jungle, a beautiful imitation of an amphitheater, and could seat forty or fifty men.

The night of what I called The Most Magnificent Show in the Universe, finally arrived. A banner announcing this, painted from human blood, hanging on the wall.

The celebrities of our Damnation were there: the Commander, with his long face and inscrutable gaze; my friend Hoax, a chubby, round-faced fellow who whispered in the Commander's ear, no doubt about the show to come; the Enemy soldiers, dressed as if for an evening at the theater. No doubt the women with some of them were not wives, but girlfriends who lived in the nearby Enemy Town, just beyond our Doom City. The girls had fine red or blue dresses on, as if they would go to a celebration after the show. The men were dressed in full military garb. Cocktails were served, a rarity at this outpost, but the liquor had been distilled from a local flower, and had a jasmine-like scent. The air fairly crackled with the electric moment to come.

I felt as if we were going to stage a great Broadway show. Or a spectacular Fourth of July fireworks demonstration.

It would be, I was certain, the inauguration of some wonderful event that might be remembered and talked about for years to come.

The usual excitement of opening night spread, even among my countrymen. They were brought in, roped at the hands, shackled at the legs, shuffling to their seats, although I kept a contingent backstage, the actors in the drama to unfold. Footlights consisted of small fatty candles laid in a semi-circle around the stage floor. The backdrop, an enormous canvas that had once been an officer's tent covering but was now painted with scenes of the Enemy's Great Leader, stepping on all things American. Just seeing the backdrop made the Enemy guard cheer and raise their glasses.

What they didn't know, of course, was that I had made sure that a bit of the opium water that I had grown to know well had been stirred into their drinks, and as I led them in their national anthem, as they stood and sang bravely and happily, they drank—all, including the girls—I could tell from their expressions that they had begun to go into a slight blurred state—the strong alcohol and the poppy had some effect.

The opium would help me with what I needed to do. First, I said, "We are here for a momentous occasion! This is the inauguration of a great moment of historical significance! We are all the proud and the brave who have learned so much from our Enemy, who is really our Friend and who wishes to teach us the errors of our ways and the true path of life! Here, on this very stage, you will see the wonders of transformation! You will see the magic of the ancients! The famous tricks of the fakirs of India! The secrets of the alchemists of old Europe! The mystical wonders of the sorcerers of ancient Mesopotamia!"

I spouted all the bull I could, and Hoax stood up and translated every word for the Enemy. They laughed, and brawled as I had some of my countrymen portray our President, and our Army foibles.

They tripped, and simulated intercourse with each other, at my command, and the laughter from the stadium was enormous, even from Americans, whom I had brought into a state of the Dark Game just for this evening.

Hoax probably laughed the hardest, and once, when I glanced up at him, I saw the Enemy Commander slap him on the shoulder and whisper some approval in his ear that made Hoax beam.

The dancing girls came out next—they writhed and gyrated for the men. I had given them unhealthy doses of the local drink, and they began touching each other and taking off their clothes until they were nearly naked. This got the Enemy to cheer further, and the girls threw garments up to them.

My own countrymen sat quietly, as I had commanded for them to do in the Dark Game. I could see that their eyes were glazed over, and they awaited my word.

Finally, I announced the evening's entertainments. "Tonight, good gentlemen and ladies, for your pleasure, the Axeman and I will carve up several Americans before your eyes. They will devour one another, as that is the way of our kind, and you will see how corrupt in our very beings we truly are. But first, I ask for volunteers from among you. For I want you to participate greatly tonight. Do I have any takers?"

The Enemy ranks roared approval, and many leapt from their seats to volunteer. But I wanted a special man to come forward. I wanted an important man.

"Commander!" I called out.

"Yes!" cried my countrymen, "Commander!"

Hoax laughed, clapping his hands, turning to his leader. "Commander!" he said.

The Commander shook his head violently, laughing the entire time.

While he resisted coming forward, I brought the few remaining men from my own company out on the stage. They were further along in the Dark Game than the other prisoners. Each was blindfolded, and they held each other's hands. I had spent four nights with the three of them to make sure that their minds were switched into another realm, so that my voice and my mind was their only guide.

"Commander!" I cried out again, and even the Axeman, coming up beside me, raised his glinting blade as it caught the last of the sunlight and called the Commander by full name.

Finally, goaded, blurred from drink, the Commander came down from the bleachers. I raised a hand and called out a word of cheer, and all the Americans began clapping for him, and soon the Enemy guard clapped as well, whistling, as the Commander went on stage.

"We have a magic show tonight!" I shouted to the noisy audience. "But we must have silence, now! Absolute silence!"

Within a minute or two, those in the bleachers quieted.

I glanced up at Hoax who smiled and nodded as if watching his prize protégé.

I thought of my friend Harry Hoakes, blown to bits by a land-mine. I thought of little Davy, tortured in front of me, tortured until his last breath left him.

I went up and blew out more than half the candles. The sun was going down, and darkness surrounded us. Only six or so candles lit the stage. It was an effect I'd worked on—the backdrop now seemed ominous and evil—the Commander's face on the backdrop seemed to have gone in shades into a diseased, corrupt form rather than the healthy look that backdrop had when sunlight was upon it.

The crowd quieted even further, although I heard murmurs among the Enemy that set my teeth on edge—they had begun to feel uneasy.

The Commander stepped up next to me, and he even patted me on the shoulder. He announced to the crowd that I was a shining example of the realignment procedure that had been developed in the Great City. I told the Axeman that it was time to begin the carving of the Americans. He brought the blade up to the ear of one of my boys. I stopped him, and announced, "Why an ear? Can you make a good purse from it, ladies?" A tittering from the women in the bleachers as if this were the cutest of jokes. "I think not! Why not flay him alive? Right now? But even better, see, how his friends—" I pointed to the other two men, "—do not know what is to come? Their ears are stuffed with wax. Their eyes are covered! Why not have them skin their friend for the delight of the Commander?"

Cheers went up, as I had expected. In the dark, of course, it was the Americans who began the cheer, but in a stadium, cheers and claps become contagious. People want to be enthused about a show, and so the Enemy began clapping and cheering.

Then, when they quieted, I asked the Axeman for his blade.

Now, this was the point when my nerves nearly destroyed what I was about to do.

The Axeman gave me a strange look, but his Commander, the Supreme Leader of the camp, nodded to him, and told him in a not-friendly tone, to go on. The pressure of an audience watching did exactly what I wanted it to do—the Commander was caught up in the magic of the theatrical moment. He wanted the show to go on as planned.

Reluctantly, the Axeman passed me the blade.

It was heavy, and its edge was sharp.

"You will now see," I announced, "one of the Evil Americans be skinned before you, and before your Commander, by his own compatriots!"

The audience went silent as I passed the blade to one of the blindfolded men.

Quickly, however, I took it back, and whispered to the three men who whose ears were not, in fact, blocked, "Now. To your left."

I turned with the blade, and stabbed the Axeman in the groin, and then cut my way up into his belly and sternum—

As the audience began to gasp—

And the three men, blindfolds still on, grabbed the Commander, and tore at him as if they were wild dogs.

In their heads, they were wolves, in fact, and they believed that they were tearing at a stag in the hunt.

The commander screeched, but the men were strong, and in the darkness of the stadium, the Enemy rose, panicking, but it was too late.

They had drunk the opium and liquor, and my countrymen had already risen up with gnashing teeth and a strength that they had never known they'd had in their bodies.

I wanted to see Hoax one last time, to see the look on his face when he knew that this had not gone his way. That he had misplaced any trust he had in me. But it was too dark, and knowing him, he probably died too quickly.

I heard what sounded like wolves tearing at bleating sheep in the dark.

22

The beauty of the escape of my men—men from various platoons who now thought of me as their hero—was that none could remember the show at all.

By dawn, not all the prisoners had survived. Many had died in the fight.

But those who lived, blood on their faces and blotching their clothes, awoke without memory of the past year.

They didn't know the atrocity committed against them, neither did they know of their own savagery, which had killed the Enemy in the camp.

I returned home, eventually, a hero.

The surviving men believed they had escaped the camp, not that they had, in and of themselves, eaten those who had imprisoned them.

By dawn, I commanded the men, still under the influence of the Dark Game, to set fire to the last of Hell.

23

An old memory: I was sixteen, and my father lay dying in his bed.

My mother, who had to take up work now, needed me home to help nurse him while he was in pain.

I sat each day with him, and one morning, when I brought him his breakfast, which he barely touched, he told me, "You're an evil son-of-a-bitch, Gordie. You show the world how good you are, but I know who you are on the inside. I've seen it since you were a baby. You have the Devil in you, and you spend your time hiding it."

I sat with him, patiently, nodding so that I might not appear to be the bad child.

Then, when he was through talking about my evil and how I was going to Hell, I offered him a glass of water.

He drank it, greedily, and passed the glass back to me.

"I still love you, dad," I said.

"I know you do," he said.

In the afternoon, he died, peacefully, in his sleep.

I missed him terribly.

His lifeless body, in that bed, made me remember the day he had me shoot my dog and had taught me about how sometimes, Death was a friend.

24

There. I've told you it all. I've told you about the war, and the girl named Genie, and my father. My youth, pulled from the drawer, so you can look at it and judge me.

I should be tied up. Bound. Whipped. It is the only way for me to go out of this body, the freedom of my mind to wander. It intensifies the Dark Game for me.

I don't want to remember anymore.

I want to close the drawer now.

I want to lock up the past.

I give to you, my wife, Mia, the key.

THE WORDS

for Bentley

"What he touched was, according to his account,
a mouth, with teeth, and with hair about it, and,
he declares, not the mouth of a human being..."
—M.R. James, from "Casting the Runes"

Part One:
The Night and
Before

The end is like this:

After the last match goes out, he mouths the words to the Our Father, but it brings him no comfort. He remembers The Veil. He remembers the way things moved, and how the sky looked under its influence. He doubts now that a prayer could be answered. He doubts everything he has come to believe about the world.

The echo of the last scream. He can hear it, even though the room is silent. It seems to be in his head now: the final cry.

Hope it's final.

The scream is too seductive, he knows. He understands what's out there. It's attracted to noise, because it doesn't see with its eyes anymore. It sees by smell and sound and vibration. He has begun to think of it by its new name, only he doesn't want to ever say that name out loud. Again.

Your flesh won't forget.

Prickly feeling along the backs of his hands, along his calves. In his mind, he goes through the alphabet, trying to latch onto something he can work around. Something that will give him a jump into remembering the words.

He presses himself against the wall as if it will hide him. Rough stone. *No light. Need light. Damn.* He thinks he must be delirious because the goofiest things go through his mind: Michelle's phrase, *Unfrigginlikely, Spaceman Mark. Those aren't the words. Spaceman Mark. Hey, Space! What planet you on today? Planet Dark, that's what I'm on. Planet Midnight.*

And out of matches.

The wind dies, momentarily, beyond the cracked window.

The damn ticking of the watch. Someone's heartbeat. The sensation of freezing and burning alternately—a fever. The sticky feeling under his armpits. The rough feeling of his tongue against the roof of his mouth. The interminable waiting. Seconds that become hours in his mind. In those seconds, he is running through sounds in his head—*the words? What are they? Laiya-oauwraii...no. That's the beginning of the name. Don't say it again. It might call it right to you. You might make it stronger. For all you know. What the hell are the words?*

He clutches the carved bone in his left hand. It's smooth in his fist. Like ivory, a tusk from some fallen beast. Slight ridges where the words are carved. Like trying to read braille, only he's never studied. *If only I could read them. Need to get light. Some light.*

Distracted by the smell.

That would be the first one it got.

Over in the corner, something moves. A darkness against darkness.

Someone he can't see in the dark is over there.

Eyesight is failure, Dash once told him. *Perception is failure. All that there is, all that there ever will be, cannot be perceived in the light of day. At night, the only perceptions turn inward.*

The words? he thinks. *The words. Maybe if you remember them, you can stop it.*

Maybe it reverses. Or maybe if you just say them...

Moves his lips, trying to form vowel sounds.

The dry taste. Humid and weather-scorned all around.

In his throat, a desert.

Every word he has ever heard in his life seem to spin through his mind. But not the words he needs. Not the ones he wants to remember tonight.

THE WORDS

A beautiful night. Dark. No light whatsoever but for the ambient light of the world itself. Summer. Humid. Post-storm. One of those rich storms that sweeps the sky with crackling blue and white lightning, and the roars of lions. But the storm has passed—and that curious wet silence remains. Taste of brine in the air from the water, a few miles away.

He remembers summer storms like this—their majesty as they wash the June sky clean, bringing a gloom on their caped shoulders, but leaving behind not a trace of it. The smell of oak and beech and cedar and salt and the murky stink of the ponds and bogs. Their years together, all in those smells. All in the dark.

The night, summer, perhaps just a few hours before the sun might rise.

Might.

He wonders if he'll ever see another storm. Another summer. Another dawn.

Those damn words.

"Your flesh will remember the name even if your mind forgets," *Dash had told him, and he had still thought it was a game when* *Dash had said it. "The name gets in your bones and in your heart.* *Just by hearing it once. But the words are harder to remember. They* *don't want you to know the words because it binds them. So, listen* *very carefully. Listen. Each time I say them, repeat them exactly* *back to me."*

He's shivering. Sweating. Nausea and dizziness both within him, the pit of his stomach. Something's scratchy around his balls—feels like a mosquito buzzing all along the inside of his legs. Twitching in his fingers. Tensing his entire body. Afraid to take another breath.

A conversation replays in his head:

"It's not that hard. Watch."

"I can't. I just…"

"All you do is take the thing and bring it down like this. Think *of it as a game."*

"I can't do it."

"Don't think of it like that. Pretend it's a game. It doesn't *mean what it looks like. You've been trained to think this is bad by*

church and school and your parents. And the world outside. But it is not real. It is just a game, only none of the rest of them know this. They're stupid. Nobody's going to get hurt. Least of all one of us. Least of all you or me. I would never let it happen. You're like my brother."

"I know. But I can't."

"All right. I'll do it. I'll just do it. Just remember what you're supposed to do. As soon as it happens. As soon as my eyes close. Promise? Okay?"

"Okay, okay."

"And the words. After. If it's too much. You know what to say. You remember?"

"Yes."

"You know how to pronounce them? You have to know. If this gets out of hand, you can stop it. The name for me, and the words to stop it. If it's too awful."

"I know, I know."

"'Cause it might get too awful. I don't know."

"Sure. Of course. I remember how to say them."

"And the name?"

He has no problem remembering the name. He'd like to blot it out of his mind. The name is on the tip of his tongue, and he can't seem to forget how to say it, how to pronounce it perfectly. The words have somehow vanished from his mind.

He tries to remember the words, now. How they sound. The language was foreign, but he couldn't read them off the bone. Especially with no light. But even if he had some light, he knew the letters looked like scribbles and symbols. They didn't look like sounds. All he can remember is the name, and he doesn't want to remember that.

A name like that shouldn't be said in a church.

A New England church. *Saint Something. Old Something Church.* Older than old, perhaps. Nearly a crypt. Made of slate and stone. Puritanical and lovely and a bit like a prison, now. Church of punishment. Rocky churchyard behind it. He remembers the graves with the mud and the high grasses and the smell of wild onion and lavendar, like it was years ago rather than the past hour. Smell of summer, wet grass, and that fertile, splendid odor of new leaves, new blossoms.

The smell of life.

He is inside the church. In a room. The altar is at the opposite end.

Danny had the lighter, he thinks. *If I get it, maybe I can at least save her.*

He wasn't sure if the shape in the doorway was Danny, or the thing that he didn't even want to name. *Not Dash. Not anyone he had ever met or known. An 'It'. A Thing. A Creature. Something without a Name.*

But it has a name. He know the name, but he does not intend to ever say it again. He knows the name too well, but it's the words he keeps trying to remember. The ones that are on the bone. The words that might stop it from continuing.

He tries to lick his lips, but it's no use. His mouth is dry.

Dry from too much screaming.

567

Nearby, there's a very slight noise. A sliver of a noise. He is sensitive to sound.

In the Nowhere.

Someone might've just died outside. He doesn't know for sure. Who? He just heard the last of someone's life in a slight moaning sound. The open window. No breeze. Just that sound. A soft but unpleasant *ohhhhhh.*

The puppy is whimpering. Somewhere nearby.

Other sounds, barely audible, seem huge.

Branches against the rooftop. Scraping lightly.

His heartbeat. A rapping hammer.

In the dark, the ticking of his watch is too loud. He slowly draws it from his wrist. Carefully, he presses it down into the left-hand pocket of his jeans. The watch clinks slightly against his keys. He holds his breath.

Needs to cough.

Fight it. Fight it. Swallow the cough. Don't let it out.

Closes his eyes, against the darkness. Closes his eyes to block it out. To make it go away.

Holds his breath for another count. The cough is gone.

Brief sound.

Someone's breathing. Over there. Across the room. Small room. More than closet, less than room.

Her? Thank god. Thank god. He licks his lips. Mouth, dry.

After a few minutes, he can just make out her shape.

He's staring at her, and she's staring at him, but they can't really see each other. Just forms in the dark. *Michelle?* Ambient light from beneath cracks in the walls creates a barely visible aura around her as he stares.

Dead of night. Dread of night.

The dread comes after the knowledge. He remembers the line from the book. That awful book that he thought was fiction.

But the words do not come to him. The sounds of them, just beyond his memory.

Breathing hard, but as quietly as he can.

Smells his own breath. The stink of his underarms. Glaze of sweat covering his body. Shirt plastered to him. Hair wet and greasy against his scalp.

The chill that hasn't left him, not since he came up out of the earth. Burning chill.

She's going to do it.

Or I am.

One of them is going to scream again. He knows it. He wasn't even sure if he had stopped screaming a half hour before.

Problem is, when the screaming starts, it happens.

And neither of them wants it to happen.

But the puppy is okay.

It doesn't want the puppy.

That's what someone said before. How many minutes ago? Did he say it? Had he said it and just not remembered it? "*It doesn't want the puppy.*"

She whispers something. Or else he imagines she whispers.

Or it's the sound of the leaves on the trees, brushing the rooftop.

If it's her, it's wrong for her to whisper. Neither of them know what decibel level it needs to find them, but she whispers anyway, "Please say it's a game. Please god say it's a game."

He's not close enough, but he wants to hold her. Hold her tight. Rewind the night back to day, back a year or more, so he can undo it all. He wants everything to turn out okay, but he knows it won't.

Most of all, he wants her to shut her mouth up. He wants to hold her and press his lips or his hand against her mouth and keep in whatever she's trying to let out.

Silence. Come on, silence. Don't...

Even her whisper is too loud.

And it hears her.

And it wants to make her scream.

If she screams, it's all over.

Not just the game. The game will never be over.

If we can just hold out 'til daylight, he thinks.

But the noise begins. From her throat. He wants to shut her up, but he can't. He can't. She's over there in the dark, and he's on the other side of the room from her.

The scream is coming up from her lungs in a staccato gurgle. A hiccuping gurgle.

She can't hold it in.

That's when he hears the sound.

Not her scream.

Dear Sweet Jesus, do not let that noise out of your mouth. Do not scream. It is inside here. With us.

He hears the sound it makes as it moves. Wet, popping sounds, like bones springing free of joints, and then that stink of overripeness. Rotten. Steaming. Then that awful thumping begins again.

And the steady hissing, as if dozens of snakes trail behind it.

He leans back against the wall, wanting to press himself into the wood as far as he can go. Wanting his molecules to change and move through the wood so he can just escape. He's praying so hard he feels like his skull is going to crack open, only the prayers are

569

all messed up and he's sure they don't work if you get them wrong. *Dear God, Dear Jesus, please help this poor sinner, Hail Mary, full of grace, Hail Mary, full of grace and the fruit of thy womb, Jesus, Our Father who art in heaven, hallowed be thy name.*

Then, it whispers something in the darkness.

He begins shivering when he hears the words.

The girl in the corner finally begins to scream as if she already knows the game is up.

It sweeps toward her. Sweeps.

He can't stop it. He's too scared. He's so scared he's afraid he's going to pee his pants and start giggling because something inside his head is going a little haywire.

And then, he feels the wet fingers–he hopes they're fingers— along his ankles.

He tries to remain perfectly still.

Perfectly still.

Like a statue.

Like I'm not alive.

Like I'm not even here.

Remember. Come on. Remember. Remember.

Damn it, the words.

One:
Before the
Night

1

All that screaming and darkness happened one night when they were eighteen, but the truth was, it started long before, at least for Mark.

The longest day of the year; the shortest night of the year. But they didn't take off for the party until the dark had fallen. No one in his right mind went to a party early.

But that was the end of it.

The beginning was a game. A game within a game.

The game was about darkness.

2

There was a history of minor corruption between Mark and Dash that began when they were thirteen. Dash was named, he told Mark early in their friendship, for Dashiell Hammett, a writer. Dash refused to read anything Hammett had written. Mark was called the Spaceman because, he assumed, he must've seemed spacy at times. He didn't do any illegal drugs, but other kids were sure he did. Dash only called Mark "Marco." "Names have power," he told him. "Only I can call you Marco."

Douglas Clegg

Back when they were a bit younger, Mark was completely unnoticeable. He had few friends, and tended to mumble in school. Like the other students at the Gardner School, he had been pulled from public school for one mysterious reason or another. He had arrived, newly thirteen, at the Gardner School in Mannosset Sound, at a spur in the Massachusetts coastline. It was nearly a forty minute drive from his home, which was in an outer suburb of Boston. Some nights, he slept over at the boarding department, but most, he went home. Sometimes, his mother or father drove him to school; sometimes he carpooled with another older student who had a car. The Gardner School was the only school that would take him after the little incident with the knife.

"I found it out on the blacktop," he'd told the guidance counselor at his previous school. "I did not bring it to school. I didn't threaten to kill anyone. And I didn't stab him. I held it up and I wanted him to get away from me. He was a bully. He tried to push me. He got cut because he pushed me on the blacktop and then he was about to hit me and I put the knife up between us."

Dash told Mark that he was at the Gardner School for something fucked up, too. "I have an IQ of 180, so I'm apparently really smart only I'm bored with school already. Why don't they get better teachers here? It costs a fortune to go here. You'd think they could hire a better group."

They'd bonded immediately. They both turned up in French class, sitting next to each other in eighth grade. Then, they found themselves with lockers side by side. Mark was an altar boy at St. Peter's, and as he got his robe on one Sunday, there was Dash, inside one of the confessionals, his head craning out from behind the narrow doorway.

"Wanna smoke?"

"How'd you get out here?" Mark asked. Dash lived closer to school than to Mark's neighborhood.

"Bus."

"I didn't know you were Catholic."

"I'm not," Dash said. "I don't believe in that stuff. I was just waiting for you to get off-duty. And have a smoke. I saw you smoke

572

in the stalls at school. I like to hang out in graveyards, and there's a nice one behind this god place. I was having a smoke, and I saw you troop in with all the other god people." Dash had a funny rhythm to his speaking voice, even then. As if he were preparing lectures, an old professor in the body of an adolescent.

"We're too young to smoke," Mark said. "And it's bad for you."

"Like I said, I saw you smoke at school. Or at least, I thought it was you. Do you have vices? Self-destructive ones?"

Mark only hesitated a moment. He had never smoked a cigarette before in his life. "They might catch us in there."

"Nope. Confessional's all empty. Come on," Dash said. He held up a pack of Marlboros. "This is the slowest way of killing yourself. One cigarette at a time, but if you start young enough, it'll help."

"Not everyone dies from that," Mark said.

"Everyone dies from something. That's the problem of life. You're just going to die," Dash said. "Me, I'll get hooked on any number of things if I can. It's always good to improve the odds if you want to succeed."

"That's like suicide. That's a sin."

"For you. You're Catholic. You have that whole resurrection of the body thing and the life everlasting, choirboy," Dash said. "Not that I don't find that appealing. I'd love to die and then come back. Conquering death should be the alternate goal if dying is the common one. I'd love to be a messiah. It would suit me. Now, come on, let's have a smoke."

3

In school, they went into the janitor's closet—a deep broom closet that had stacks of *Playboys* beneath a pile of cleaning supplies. The closet stank of Comet and bleach and oil.

"Just shut off the lights."

"Why?"

"Just shut 'em off."

"Okay."

Off went the lights.

"Listen," Dash said.

"To what?"

"Just listen. Hear my breathing? Now?"

Mark mumbled something about bad breath.

"See? This is the Nowhere," Dash said.

"This definitely is nowhere."

"*The* Nowhere. It's a different place than when the lights are on," Dash said. "Different rules apply. Hell, there are no rules. With the light on, it's all rules and regulations and laws and order. But with the dark, it's a different world. When you're dead, you're in the dark."

"When I'm dead, I'll be somewhere else."

"You think so?" Dash asked. "Now here's the thing. I know these people who believe they talk to the dead."

"Psychics?" Mark said.

"No, none of that crap. I mean people who actually believe they talk to the dead. Who call them up from corpses. They believe it. I don't know if I believe it yet."

"Are they in school?"

"Don't be ridiculous. I met them in a graveyard. Manosset has more than just the rocky beach. There's the Old Church. They were there. Doing a ceremony. They were sacrificing a turtle."

"Gross."

"It wasn't as gross as you'd think," Dash said. "They told me all about the Nowhere. How it changes the world. Darkness. Night. Absence of light. And in the dark, they think they talk to the dead. They have an old religion. Older than, well, yours. One of them told me that people still practice it, only no one ever talks about it. Bands of believers, basically. It's not so much different than yours. Only, they believe in a messiah of darkness. A savior who comes by night."

"You making this up?"

"I wish I were. I don't really believe it. But they do. I find it a very attractive kind of belief system. It's this interesting idea. And you know how I like interesting ideas. And you've got this absolute connection between death and life. Bringing back the dead," Dash said this last part in full old professor mode. Then, he asked, "Do you believe in God?"

"Of course."

"Well, then you might as well believe in the Nowhere. I mean, virgins and miracles and raising from the dead. It's not so far from what they believe."

"You mean your made-up people who sacrifice turtles?"

"Not just turtles," Dash said. "Other stuff, too. Goats sometimes. Chickens. I'll introduce you to them one night. Did you know that a man named Crossing actually wrote several stories about their group? More than a hundred years ago. He was one of them. People thought he was writing fiction, but apparently, none of it was made up. I'll loan you one of his books sometime. He said that the darkness has a reality to it that lets illogic through. Isn't that a cool way of saying it? The darkness lets illogic through. He called it The Veil." He paused. Smoking. "It's not so different than anything else. It's *almost* logical. There aren't any virgins in it. But there are some miracles. Take the streets, lights on. It's normal. Boring. At night? Lights out. No light. No moonlight even, it's a place where you make up the rules. You define the space. You create what's there and what's not," Dash said, his breath all warm. "You create what's there. And maybe it creates what's there."

"It?"

"The Nowhere. There's something out there. In the dark. And if you're in it long enough, it comes out. That's why they had to do the sacrifices. They told me it stops worse things from happening. You know about eastern philosophy?"

Mark did not.

"Some of it is about how it's all an illusion. Everything we think we see. It's not what's really there. And if that's true, maybe what's really there is something else. Only we don't see it because we're too busy perceiving the crap we expect to see. We're taught from an early age to see things a certain way, and we name things so that they stay that way. But the darkness is fluid. It defies perception. You know how your eyeball works? How everything you see, you're really seeing upside-down, only your eye somehow adjusts it back again?"

575

Mark had never heard of this before. Sometimes, Dash's ideas went right over his head; or else they hit him square in the head and gave him massive headaches.

"Or a rose. They're not really red. How it's the absence of some pigment, and how all the other colors are there, and it somehow makes it red? But if you turn off the light, is the rose still red? Or is it no color? Is it even a rose? Does it become something else in the dark? And do you become something else in the dark?"

"Cool," Mark said. "But, I mean, I'm...me. I'm me even now. Even in the dark."

"Are you? Are you sure?"

Mark laughed a little.

"I'm not joking. Are you the same you in the dark as you were when the light was on?" Dash asked. "Would you do the same things in the light of day that you'd do if no one could see you? Do you ever wonder why people have sex in the dark?"

Mark didn't answer.

"Maybe it's 'cause they can be something different in the dark. Or maybe they really are something different in the dark," Dash said. "Maybe right now, you're not even Mark. Maybe you're something else. Do you believe in life after death?"

"Well," Mark fumbled with his thoughts. "I'm sort of Catholic."

"Sorta?"

Mark shrugged. "I believe some things and not others."

"The only thing I believe about Christianity is the resurrection of the body. I mean, I think dead bodies still have somebody in them. Maybe we do them a disservice by burying them."

"What, you mean if you didn't bury a body it would just be fine?"

"Not saying that," Dash said. "If you can't think deeper than that, Marco, I don't know about you. I just don't know. I mean, what are those caskets for? They're like little traps. What if we could all roll the stones away from our tombs after we die. Maybe there'd be more messiahs around. Who knows? Let me give you a rundown on deity. First, God's name is not God. Second, in the Old Testament, they called him Yahweh or Jehovah. In Greek, Deus. The Greek name for the top dog god was Zeus. Pretty close to Deus, don't you think? And Jehovah is pretty close to the Roman god, Jove, alias Jupiter. I won't even go into what I learned about the goddess Ishtar and her relationship to your Queen of Heaven. You don't want to know what the word Easter comes from, trust me. It would blow you out of that little churchworld you're in. God, Yahweh, what have you. And none of these are the names of God, and even with God, there are other gods. That's why you have this commandment, 'Thou Shalt Have No Other Gods Before Me.' It's because there are other ones. And people can't say their names because no one really knows how to say the names. They used to. That's what priests in ancient times used to do. That was their power. They knew the real names of the gods. And naming them means bringing them. Invoking them. And that's what these people in the Nowhere have. For centuries, they've kept alive the name of a particular god. Maybe it's 'the' God. I don't know. But the name of the god is the power. And the god of the Nowhere is all about death and resurrection and darkness."

577

Dash had been reading a lot. He claimed to have read the Bible three times til he knew it backward and forward, and a book called the *Aegyptian Book of Darkness*. He spoke of Kierkegaard and Kant and Buddha and Hesse and Yeats and Eliot and someone named Robert Graves and someone named Colin Wilson and about quantum something, and about transformations and chiaroscuro and shadows. He loaned books to Mark, and asked him questions about what was in them.

Mark found it irresistible, although he found the books tough going. Only the short stories by Wacey Crossing seemed to be any fun. In them, Crossing wrote about ancient practices that called up creatures of beauty and malevolence. He even mentioned Manosset Sound by name, as if these practices happened there in the 1800s. T.S. Eliot and Robert Graves were a little more rough going, although Mark loved a book called *Demien* by Herman Hesse.

Dash told Mark that, in the dark, everywhere was Nowhere. And it was better to be in the Nowhere than in the Somewhere. Particularly if you were like one of them. A bit outcast. A bit funky. A bit eccentric. A bit different.

"Nowhere guys," Dash said. Their favorite song became "Nowhere Man." They loved to say to their parents, when asked, "Where are you going?"

"Nowhere. Honest. Just Nowhere."

And the Nowhere was always dark, and always somewhere else.

4

But Mark didn't ever get to meet these "people of the Nowhere," as he began thinking of them. Dash mentioned them now and again; he acted as if he was getting close to them in some way that wasn't expressed. He became secretive about some of the goings-on when Mark wasn't with him. "There's a ceremony they have called the Tempting. Each of them cuts his left arm open and spills it over a newly dug grave. They say some ancient words, and begin chanting something I still can't make out. They have these stones and they put the words on them, and dip them in this syrupy mixture, and then put the stones under their tongues, and the words are always inside them after that. Their bodies memorize them or something. They don't even use their minds. It's weird. And then, one of them becomes possessed by the dead person."

Mark assumed it was made-up, stolen from Wacie Crossing's stories, and as a year or so passed, he grew to appreciate Dash's offbeat and dark sense of humor.

Once, together again in some dark place, hanging out, Dash asked, "Do you love me?"

"Excuse you?"

"I don't mean that," Dash said. "I mean, do you love me. Like a brother. Like we have a bond?"

Mark thought a minute, feeling uncomfortable with the question. "Sure. Like a brother."

"We've got to have that bond to make any of it worthwhile. I mean, we'll get married to some babes someday and do all kinds of stuff, but if we love each other like that—like brothers—than we can move mountains."

"Sure," Mark said, but decided to turn the light on the back porch at his parent's house.

He was surprised by what he saw.

Dash sat next to him, but he had a hypodermic needle in his arm, just withdrawing it.

"What the hell is that?"

Dash held the needle up. "It's not for you. Don't worry."

"You a junkie? Dash? What the hell is that?"

"It's not heroin. Jesus, it's The Veil," but Dash would not explain further. He took the the needle, covered it, and pressed it into a plastic case that looked more suitable to a toothbrush. "See? I'm not tripping out or anything. Don't freak."

Dash reached up to shut the light off. Dark again. Mark sat there in the dark wondering if he shouldn't end the friendship or talk to someone at school about what seemed to be Dash's latest self-destructive habit.

5

579

But he didn't. He did what others probably did when their best friends were on drugs—he somehow just put it out of his mind, because Dash never seemed high or wired. And Mark didn't see much evidence of the hypodermic needle again. Nor did he look for it. After a few months or so, Mark had blocked that moment from his mind. Everything seemed normal, in its own messed up way.

Dash was his only real friend at school, anyway.

6

On a night-smitten country road, Dash would flick the headlights off.

Suddenly, it was as if the world had disappeared. They were in a car with the world gone around it. With just a sense of "road." A sense of "nowhere."

Dash started doing the headlight trick before he even had his license. This was back when he had managed to steal his brother's Mercury Cougar and sneak out in the night. He'd pick Mark up down the hill from where he lived. Always after midnight.

Mark would be out there waiting for him, waiting for the adventure. "I waited here forever," he'd say.

"Forever must last about fifteen minutes," Dash said, giving him a gentle punch to the shoulder.

They'd go to parties, or sneak off and grab a burger, or find out where some of the other guys were hanging out, smoking, drinking, making out with a girl or just watching others make out.

Neither one of them did much wild stuff. Not real wild stuff. Mark even wrote down what he called the Nowhere Manifesto, but he tore it up one afternoon, worried that his mother might find it. At the end of most evenings, they just called it a night and Dash dropped Mark off at his house.

But, on some nights, Dash took Mark to the graveyard behind the old church. Mark never saw him draw the needle out again, but he knew that when Dash asked him to wait in the car a second, that he might be going into the darkness to shoot up with whatever he used. *The Veil.*

But Mark could ignore it. It didn't matter. They were friends.

Mark got out of the car, and Dash, up near the church, whistled to him to come on up the path to the graves.

7

It was not Mark's church, nor was it Dash's. It was older and more of a historic landmark than a functioning church. It was made of stone. All Mark knew about it was that the founding fathers of the area had built it, or built the original building that no longer existed. The graves behind it had those names like Goody Something and Sir Walter John Something, but most of the gravestones were rubbed smooth and coated with a slimy ooze of moss and yellow-green muck. A bog, just the other side of a thin line of trees, had flooded the area recently, so they walked in mud and damp weeds.

"This is where I saw them," Dash said. "This is where they spoke to me. They showed me The Veil for the first time. Here."

Mark glanced around, but they were alone together.

"They asked me to tell them my heart's desire," Dash said. He went over and sat on a long flat stone. He patted the area beside him.

Mark went over and joined him. "They told me that the Nowhere needed guys like me. Maybe like you, too."

"Are they some kind of witch cult?" Mark asked, his chin in his hand. He stared across the expanse of field and wood beyond the old church. "Do they worship Satan?"

Dash grinned. "No. Not witches. Not Satan. That's all fairly new stuff. This is older than that. Long before. They're wise people, though. They know things. They believe that they talk to the dead. They believe the dead tell them things. They know the name of twelve different gods. The real names. The names of power. I don't know how they do. They knew things about me that even my mother wouldn't know. Even you wouldn't know."

"Like what?"

"You don't want to know," Dash said. "There are some things I wouldn't want people to know. But they knew."

"Is it about why you had to leave the other school?"

"Want to know something funny?"

Mark shrugged.

"They told me about you. This was before we met. They told me about that thing you did. When you were eleven."

"What thing?"

"You know," Dash said. "With the knife. Don't worry. It's kind of cool."

Dash put his hand on Mark's shoulder. Felt his breath against his ear. "I did something terrible when I was twelve," Dash whispered. "Something you can't ever tell anyone else in the whole world, or I will hunt you down and kill you and tear out your heart and cut the eyes out of your face. Understood? We're fifteen, but when you're a kid, I mean a kid-kid, you do things without really knowing why. You're changing. Everything is changing. You have these impulses. You do things because something inside you tells you to do them. I once saw the most beautiful dead woman in the world, lying on the ground. She had killed herself, but it left no marks on her because she took pills. She was naked. I was caught doing something to her. But it wasn't what you think. Nothing perverted. She was so beautiful I didn't want to hurt her, even when she was dead and was beyond hurting. And they knew about what I did. They had spoken to her. The Nowhere people. After she died. They had gone to where she was buried, and they'd dug her up from the grave, and she told them about me, about what I did, and they think I'm some kind of messiah because of it, like it was a sign that I was the golden child or something."

8

On the phone, the next afternoon, a Saturday. "I made it all up. None of it's true," Dash said to Mark, and then hung up.

9

Mark didn't see Dash for awhile, but eventually, Mark saw Dash's car idling on the street beneath his bedroom window. Mark was furious with his father for taking away his stereo because of a drop in grades, and he snuck out the back of the house and got in the Cougar and told Dash, "It's about time you showed your sorry face."

10

Once, they narrowly missed being hit by a car that was following the Mercury Cougar too closely. They followed the car for miles just to annoy the driver. They planned raids on some of the guys' houses, too. When a family was out of town, Mark and Dash would go out in the dark, late as they could stand and still feel awake. They'd break in, out in some suburban enclave. They wouldn't take anything from the home. They'd just get in through some window—it was easy to jimmy one of them open—and just see what the house was like on the inside. They wouldn't disturb anything. They just kept the lights out, and wandered the house. Dash said he wanted to see how the people in suburbia lived, what they owned, what they had. Dash once said it seemed psycho to do it, but Mark reassured him that they weren't doing any harm.

Sitting there, on someone else's sofa, Dash would sometimes say some words that weren't English, and they weren't any kind of language that Mark had ever heard. He would say a few words, and if Mark asked about them, Dash would say that he hadn't said anything at all.

Sometimes, they'd move a book around on a bookshelf. Or they'd put a CD out of its case and put it on a windowsill. Just enough that it might seem curious to the family, returning from a weekend away.

But this was the worst of what they did together, and it really wasn't much. Some of the other guys at school regularly shoplifted. Others were smoking marijuana half the school day. Others were doing much worse. Mark reassured himself that what he and Dash did was fairly innocent. It really hurt no one. He tried not to think about that needle that Dash had. He didn't really see it, although sometimes he noticed the plastic toothbrush carrier inside Dash's green army jacket.

Mark and Dash loved girls and talked about them as much as any other guy in school, they really adored each other. They could've been brothers. Before they'd met—at thirteen—nobody would've thought they resembled each other. But by fifteen, they could've been twins.

Dash made Mark promise to be his Best Man at his wedding, whenever it happened; Mark asked Dash to be the godfather of his first kid, whenever it came into the world.

In the Nowhere, sometimes, Mark would say things to Dash that he never told anyone else. When Mark got dumped by Emmie, he told Dash first.

When Dash decided he was going to kill himself rather than grow up, he only told Mark. "That's right," Dash said. "Why turn into some corporate robot and end up like our dads? I'd do it with a knife. I'll become one with the Nowhere. You?"

"Hanging. The front staircase."

"Do it at my folks' place. In the foyer. From the chandelier," Dash said. "In the dark."

They had a good laugh about it, and then shared a cigarette.

"What about those people?"

"What people?"

"The ones," Mark said, grabbing the cigarette from Dash's mouth, "that were in the graveyard. The ones you told me about."

Dash flicked on the light. Regarded Mark with a nearly mistrustful look. His eyes were bloodshot. "Listen, they're dangerous, sometimes. They showed me some things that were kind of nasty."

"Like what?"

Dash shivered slightly, but Mark couldn't tell if he was just joking or not. "Just some really bad shit," he said. "They have these ceremonies that you have to study. I've been studying them for a long time now, and I still don't completely understand them."

"Why haven't I met them?"

"They decide who meets them and who doesn't," Dash said.

"I thought you made them up," Mark laughed again, puffing on the cigarette. "Back in eighth grade. To scare me. You told me you made it all up."

"No," Dash said. "I made up the other thing. The priests of the Nowhere are real. They're practically holy. They're really good people, but they do some nasty shit. I'm sort of into what they do."

"Sort of philosophically," Mark added.

"Maybe," Dash said. "Give me that cig back, or go buy a new pack."

11

Dash would end the night out in the middle of godforsaken nowhere, spinning the car in the mud, or glide down an icy patch of road, the back-end of the car fishtailing. All around them, the dark, like they were driving inside their own minds, and the world existed around them only for them.

The connection between them came with it. They could talk about their deepest thoughts, argue philosophy, their sense of the meaning of life and if there was one at all. They determined that there was no meaning to life, but to truly enjoy life, they each must act as if there were a meaning to it. Their understanding of girls became legendary, as they discussed sexual availability versus the sacred virgin as it applied to the girls they knew; misunderstanding of other boys in school, which manifested in an open contempt for jocks and their football parties; they shared their love for Herman Hesse's novels and Joan Armatrading albums and this writer with the unusual name of Wacey Crossing, who wrote *When Nowhere Comes*, and other books in the 1800s, that Dash swore were true. He had three Wacey Crossing books, all short stories, and their bindings were leathery and cracked like old Bibles, and inside, people had written messy illegible notes all in the margins and drawn what looked like dirty pictures of naked women with huge breasts in the front and back of the books. The Crossing stories were about a mystery cult that had survived centuries of persecution, misshapen creatures that lived beneath graves, and ancient ones that prowled the darkness. Mark borrowed each of them, and read them thoroughly, enjoying the terribleness of the punishments meted out to those who treated the Nowhere people badly. There were six primary deities in the Crossing stories, all with nicknames: the Devourer, She Who Befouls The Night, Hallingorianang-the-Eater-of-Souls, Oliara-the-Sword-of-Fire, The Swarmgod of the Thousand Stings, The Pope of Pestilence, and Julaiiar the Conqueror. Mark began calling Dash the Devourer, and he in turn might call Mark Swarmgod. It definitely sealed their fates within weirdohood, and Mark was perfectly happy with that. They dreamed together, aloud, of what they'd do if they had the powers of Julaiiar the Conqueror who came in Shadow and cut the heads off friend and foe; or if She Who Befouls the Night decided to make it with Oliara-the-Sword-of-Fire, what kind of kid they'd produce.

585

It all happened when the lights went out.

Heading down some lonesome road, the headlights off. They'd light their cigarettes, and the world would change from its unsubtle self to some kind of dark wonderland.

Even though Mark might be in the backseat with Emmie, making out and doing everything two teens can do with each other while still keeping most of their clothes on, it was Dash who made him feel as if it were just their world: in the car, on a dark road, with nothing but the unexpected wonders of night around.

And one night, Rachel Cowan had a big party out at the country place her folks had, a few weeks after graduation, and everybody they knew was going. Michelle and Danny needed a lift, and even though Dash and Rachel used to date and now didn't get along very well, Mark convinced him to go. "This is a perfect night for this," Dash said.

"Yeah?" Mark asked, grabbing a cooler of beer. Checked his watch: *10:15*. "I figured the party'll be hoppin' by eleven."

"It's a sacred night to the Nowhere. It's a night they call Lifting the Veil."

"Oh," Mark said, used to Dash's tales of the Nowhere and its priests.

Dash whispered to him, as Mark slid into the front seat next to him, "Let's have some fun with them. Okay?"

Mark couldn't reply, because Danny had already opened the backdoor, and Michelle rapped at Mark's window for him to unlock her door. In her arms, a plastic and wire cage. She had brought a stupid puppy from her sister's kennels as a surprise birthday gift for Rachel, who had just turned nineteen, and whose dog had recently passed away.

"Just a little fun," Dash said. "For a sacred night."

Then, he reached around to unlock the door for Michelle.

TWO:
THE NIGHT
Begins

1

Dash flicked the headlights off. The night came up like veils of shadow against shadow—purple darkness, black darkness, and the curious ambient light of the earth itself—particles of illumination from unknown sources. Reflections of slivered moonlight off distant ponds. It was beautiful, Mark thought. The narrow, winding road was ripe with pot-holes and wounds, and the June-fat trees hung low over it—it was a beautiful world as far as Mark was concerned, and he felt comfortable there with Dash in the front seat, their world, their Nowhere surrounded them.

Mark glanced over at Dash, beside him. Dash in his green army jacket, with holes throughout it. Beneath, he wore a black t-shirt. Even in the summer he wore the jacket, his emblem of weirdohood, of not abandoning his outcast nature. Smoke from his mouth. The red glow of the cigarette lit Dash's features. His hair had gone from brown to dark blue with fiery tinges where it flopped around his eyes. His eyes seemed to have a light of their own. He smiled, showing all his teeth.

It was not pitch black quite yet, for the moon half-lit the world. Its light, diffuse behind scalloped clouds, hinted the outline of a dilapidated farmhouse with its property cut in a ragged square from the encroaching forest, and a balding fringe of dead trees at the edge of the road before the property. A single light was on in the house, and it somehow made Mark think about loneliness, despite being there with his friends. He wondered what he would do—now that college loomed, and he and Dash would probably grow out of their friendship, as all friends seemed to after high school. He didn't want it to happen, but there was an inevitability to it—they would move on and stay friends, but lose that closeness, that brotherhood they felt. The farmhouse became a blur as Dash recklessly swung the steering wheel to negotiate a curve in the road.

Then, the woods appeared again, thick and dark, and another turn, another break in the woods cut by a stream and ditch to the left. They passed what seemed at first an empty, desolate field, and there came the moon across it, a white sickle of moon. It was not empty, but was some kind of cemetery—Mark didn't recognize it at first, but then knew he had been there before—*of course,* he thought, *it was here, the Old Church is here. Saint Something.*

They had been mostly silent in the car—*me and Dash in front, our world, our night world.* Mark grabbed another beer from the back, and nearly stuck his hand down Michelle's shirt—she was sure Mark was making a grab for her, but Danny already had his hand halfway down her shirt, and suddenly something stank like a dead animal in the car, and Mark knew it was the puppy, in his crate. It was whimpering. Michelle, after nearly slapping him, reached back and thrust a finger through the small Kari-Kennel opening and mur-mured, "That's okay, baby, that's okay," then, she reached up and flicked on the car's interior light. "Some light in here would be nice. What's this thing with darkness."

"Darkness is cool," Mark said.

"Friggin' Goth," Michelle said; but Mark was not a Goth. He was just a guy who felt better in the dark. With friends. In the car. It was his comfort zone.

"Are you sure Rachel wants a new dog?" Dash asked. "She can't exactly take it to college with her."

"I already talked to her mom about it. Her mom's going to keep it while Rachel's at Smith."

"She got into Smith?" Mark asked.

"Last minute," Michelle said.

"Where are you two going?" Danny asked, fairly innocently. With the question, came the unspoken: they were a couple to some extent. Mark and Dash were paired in the minds of their classmates.

"How could you not guess?" Michelle huffed. "They've practically been talking about it since sophomore year."

"Oh, yeah," Danny said. "I thought maybe Mark might go to Georgetown."

"I didn't want to go to Georgetown," Mark said. Then, he added, "Really. I didn't."

"U-Mass for us," Dash said.

Mark sniffed at the air. "Who farted?"

"That dog crapped," Dash said. "He needs to go outside. Not in the car."

Mark laughed, popped open the beer, and reached for the radio buttons. Dash rolled down a window, and the humidity poured in—a gentle steam. He switched the air conditioning up to a higher level.

589

Michelle began lecturing Dash on why the puppy was in the car in the first place, and how Rachel had wanted the puppy ever since her last dog was hit by a car out on the highway; and how, even though we were headed for "what no doubt is going to be some kind of brawl," the puppy would be fine, and when they got to Rachel's house, she'd let it out to do its business in the wild.

"Whoa!" Dash cried out, "that was close!" Another pair of headlights, in the opposite lane from them, fast approaching and crossing the invisible line in the road. Dash swung the car to the right a little too hard, and they all felt the car leaning into the ditch on that side.

Then, back to normal, driving in the dark.

"Do you really want to hurt me?" Mark began singing along with the radio, which he'd very wisely turned up slightly to drown out Michelle's whine. "Jesus, nothing but oldies." He punched the radio buttons, but the best he could find was a heavy metal.

Briefly, he turned the sound up high; Dash reached over and

switched the radio off. Then, he switched it back on, and a voice came up that was nearly monotone, "And the angel carried a crown and a burning sword, and sayeth unto…"

"'Jesus' radio. I love it. Selling God on the airwaves without really knowing all about God," Dash said, switching to a soft rock station. "I like oldies better."

"Look," Danny said, rising from the back seat. "I think that's Carbo's truck over there. Hell, did Rachel even invite the dropouts?"

"That redneck," Michelle whispered, as if no one would hear her. "Carbo is such a hillbilly. I'm surprised he ever even got into Gardner." She drew the little yellow puppy from the crate into her arms. She let it lick her all over her face. Her shirt was still unbuttoned, and she wore no bra. Mark could make out the roundish mounds of her breasts, glancing back at her for a second too long. He found them unappealing. They weren't as big as they looked when covered up.

2

Perhaps it was because it was Michelle, who Mark found generally unappealing.

She had a well-bred look, as if her parents had never been in love, but had known that between their checkbooks, their inheritances, and their basic health, they should mate and produce offspring with equally good checkbooks, inheritances, and health. Like some alien lifeform that must have progeny in order to conquer the earth. Michelle was the natural product of this loveless but purposeful union. He had seen her type throughout high school—she was not a prototype the way Dash was, or even Rachel, who was a true original. She was just one of the herd. Dash had a thing for her, but he said that his interest didn't go much past the flesh. "She's a copy of a copy of a copy. But with an especially nice rack," he'd said at some point.

Michelle was mass produced. She was one of many rich girls with not a lot going on other than her birth certificate and her trust fund. She had teeth—and a lot of them—and hair, and a strangely seductive little jaw of determination that waggled side to side when she was pissed off. She dressed like she was hot stuff, even in her khaki shorts, with visible panty line, and white top wrapped for maximum breastage. Mark supposed there were boys with the low expectations of a Danny who found her completely irresistible.

But she was no Rachel.

She wasn't even an Emmie, Mark's girlfriend who had dumped him on Prom Night right after they'd made love on the golf course at the Country Club. Right after he'd lost his virginity. Just dumped him, and left Mark on the moist morning grass as the turgid sun rose somewhere—Mark, there, near the seventh hole, his tux jacket somewhere else in the world, cumberbund lost, shiny black shoes in a sandtrap, and carnation shredded from passion. Still, he had his cufflinks, and a hazy memory of his first time. Emmie had given him that, and she was more of a human being than Michelle could ever hope to be.

Unfortunately, Michelle and Emmie were best friends, so Mark knew that Michelle knew about his getting dumped in that way; she probably knew about how badly he'd fumbled with Emmie's shiny blue prom dress, how he probably was less-than-perfect at the whole sexual thing, and how he may have said something stupid in the throes of coitus that really made Emmie dislike him once and for all.

3

"You know, that dog has worms," Mark said to her, in the car, still looking at the sloping mounds of her breasts through her open shirt. "And you letting him lick your face could put wet puppy spit full of miscroscopic worm larvae on your skin, and from there, they could get inside you. And when they do—"

"Only someone like you could come up with something that disgusting," Michelle said.

"I want to hear," Dash said. He drove the Cougar with one hand; he had a cigarette in the other.

"The puppy has roundworms, and maybe tapeworms," Mark said. "Almost all puppies have them. The puppy will get wormed soon, but right now, that poop inside that little crate probably has tiny strands of spaghetti—that wriggle."

"God!" Michelle shouted, kicking at the back of his seat. "Stop, now. Just stop."

"I want to hear it," Dash said. "So what do they do?"

Mark shrugged. "Well, to dogs and cats, a lot, but worming pills will take care of it, most likely. But when they get into people, it's harder. They make little canals under the skin. They like to go for the eyes."

"You're making that up," Danny said.

"No, for some reason, the roundworms can't mature into adults in people. So the larvae just make do, and they seem to really like getting the tissue around the eyes."

"If," Michelle said, slowly but with her usually dominating force, "You. Do. Not. Shut. Up. Right. Now."

"I won't even go into the tapeworm possibility."

"Jenny Patterson had tapeworm when she was twelve," Dash said. "Remember?"

"No," Mark said. "I didn't know her back then."

"She had it, and she lost twenty pounds practically overnight. She was sick for a long time. She said it was pretty nasty."

"They grow inside you," Mark said. "They grow as long as they can. They can fill your intestines, and just eat at you."

"I once saw a dead body that was opened up and it was full of worms," Dash said. "I almost took a shit when I saw them in her mouth."

"Shut up!" Michelle shouted; the puppy began whimpering; Dash laughed and accidentally dropped his cigarette; Michelle cried out something that Mark thought was "What," and that's when they hit something in the road.

THREE: THE DEER

1

The car didn't just hit something in the road.

It slammed into something like a brick wall. The car made a squealing sound, and the sound of glass breaking filled Mark's ears. He felt the world spin a bit, and his head knocked back into the headrest of his seat. He was thrown against the glove compartment, to the front of the car, almost to the windshield; something flicked against his scalp; Michelle screeched, or else it was the tires screeching; Danny made a noise like he'd had the air knocked out of him. Dash whooped as if he enjoyed the ride; Mark wondered if the puppy was going to be okay.

But it was over in a second.

Mark opened his eyes and saw something dark and liquid covering the windshield.

Not the windshield.

His eyes.

He reached up. "Shit." He was bleeding. Something had cut his forehead.

Someone touched him on the scalp. "Not much, Marco." It was Dash. "Just a little blood. It just seems like a lot to you." Then, "Everybody okay back there?"

No answer.

Whatever they'd hit had darted out in front of the car from the edge of the bundle of trees at a bend in the narrow road. It was dark, but even so, Dash didn't turn the headlights back on. Perhaps they didn't even work. Mark wondered if something awful was going to happen now. If one of them was dead. Or if they'd killed an animal. Or if Dash's parents would ground him and take away all his privileges for the summer and beyond.

Mark wiped his face. It was a lot of blood for a little cut, but he felt the irregular slice at the top of his scalp, and it was, indeed, not much of a wound.

"Lots of bleeding at scalp level," Dash said. He took a facial tissue and daubed it on Mark's forehead. "See? All better. You knocked it on the dashboard."

"I thought I was dead."

"Maybe you are," Dash said. "Maybe we all are. Maybe we're dead but doomed to stay right here in this wreck and never leave the dark road."

"Hmm," Mark said. "I think I saw that old *Twilight Zone* episode."

From the backseat, Danny gasped, "Oh my god, we hit a deer."

Michelle shouted out "Fuck!" The word seemed to stretch into an eternity of several seconds.

Outside the car, the world was dark.

For just seconds, they were all silent again. Mark closed his eyes and wished it away. When he opened them again, he was still in the car, feeling bruised, a throbbing at the front of his scalp.

A few seconds, which felt like minutes.

Complete silence.

"Is everybody okay?" Dash asked a second time, breaking the quiet. He didn't bother turning around to check. He adjusted the rearview mirror, and glanced back.

"I guess I'm ok," Mark said, although the back of his neck hurt from the way he'd slammed back against the seat. His scalp stung.

"Just a little upside down back here," Danny said. "More beer, please."

"I'm fine. The puppy's fine. As if you care," Michelle said, coughing. "My arm hurts a little. And ow. My knee."

Dash began cussing up a storm. When it subsided, he looked at Mark, tapped him on the shoulder and gave a slight squeeze. "Shit, and I forgot to pay my goddamn insurance this month. I am so screwed."

2

It wasn't a deer.

At least as far as they could tell, although Danny insisted it had antlers, and since he was the drunkest of them, he was the least believed.

3

Mark got out last, generally pissed off that they wouldn't make it to Rachel's party at all. They were somewhere between school, and the Sound, and it was a section of road he couldn't quite identify. There were no lights in the distance. There was no sound of traffic on some nearby highway. Trees all around, thick with leaves; the moon existed somewhere, but not where Mark stood. It seemed darker than dark.

But Dash had a flashlight and was waving it around the front of the car.

"This car is fucked," Dash said. He spat out some more choice words, and Mark thought it was a bit like watching a three-year-old have a temper tantrum, the way Dash stomped around in a circle, muttering and shaking his head.

"It is, truly," Danny said. He hoisted a beer to his lips, and seemed to drink the entire bottle in one gulp. Then, he belched.

The damage to the Cougar was extensive. The front end had completely smashed inward, practically wrapped around the engine; the front axle was bent; and Danny made a joke that it was a miracle none of them was hurt. "Even the puppy," Danny said. "Man, that was a hell of a deer."

"I didn't see a deer," Michelle said. She had put the puppy on a short leash and walked around the front of the car. "I saw some people. A few of them."

595

In the flashlight's beam, she looked like like a doll that had been through a windstorm. Pale white, her shirt half unbuttoned, her hair a mess. For a second, Mark thought her lip was cut, but it was just an odd shadow.

"Well, they'd be lying here," Danny began, but Michelle gave him a harsh look that shut him up fast.

"I saw these people. I didn't see their faces or anything. I just saw a group of them. Maybe three. Maybe more." She had begun crying a little, only not so much that anyone could notice. When the half moon came out from behind a cloud, beyond the trees, casting the slightest amount of light across the road, Mark noticed.

"Somebody hold me," she said.

Danny obliged; his arms wrapped around her. "No, babe, it was a deer. I'm sure it was."

"We killed some people," Michelle said, but even as she said those words, it didn't sound like she really believed it now, seconds after saying it. "They all had shaved heads. They might've been monks or something. I know. It sounds crazy. Maybe it wasn't people."

"We're not far from the old church," Danny said. "Maybe it was some monks."

"I didn't see any monks," Mark said.

"Monks, skinheads," Michelle said with a bit of venom in her voice. "I saw faces. And maybe one of them had antlers on." Then, she laughed. "Oh, my god, it sounds ridiculous. I've had two beers exactly and I sound ridiculous." She looked at Mark and Danny. "You would've seen it if it was people, wouldn't you?"

"Antlers?" Mark grinned.

"What?" Dash let out a huge laugh, like a ballon popping.

"Okay. Something on his head."

"It was dark," Mark said.

"Maybe," Michelle began. Then, seemed to change her thought. "All right. If I had seen them, they'd still be around."

"Well," Dash clapped his hands together. "Mystery solved. You got bounced around back there. Maybe it jogged some memory or made you hallucinate."

"Well, I guess you three have talked me out of my mania," Michelle said.

"It was pretty dark, 'chelle, and it happened pretty fast," Dash said. He shook his head, chuckling. "Antler hats. Pretty good. Skinheads in antler hats."

Mark looked at Dash, but couldn't read anything in his face.

4

It was only later, when Dash went to take a leak with Mark, that Dash said, "It was them. The priests of the Nowhere. This is the night." They stood at the edge of a mossy embankment that encircled what looked like a bog. Thin trees all around. Mark had the uncomfortable feeling that they weren't alone. He kept looking off in the woods as if he would see Danny or Michelle standing there.

Mark toggled his zipper and let loose a stream onto some twigs.

"This is fun, no?" Dash asked. "We're going to be part of a ceremony."

"What are you talking about?" Mark zipped up.

"I guess I didn't tell you. This is Midsummer's Night. A sacred night. Remember in the Wacey Crossing story?"

Mark did. There was a Wacey Crossing story about midsummer's night, and how it was the weakest point of darkness in the world, so the Nowhere gods had their moment to come into the world of Man. It was a bit of a shivery tale, and Mark had a few nightmares after reading it. "It was just a story," Mark said. "You nut."

"Everything Wacey Crossing wrote was true," Dash said.

Mark nearly looked at Dash straight on, but didn't. It looked like Dash was pulling that toothbrush case-that-didn't-hold-a-toothbrush out of his inside jacket pocket.

Mark didn't want to see the needle come out.

Or see Dash use it.

5

Excerpt from "The Night of Changing" by Wacey Crossing, from the collection, In The Grave of the Devourer & Others *published 1882, N.M. Quint & Sons Press, New York, NY. Used here with permission.*

...The one called Rowen motioned to Petra, a flourishing movement of hands that reminded me of fish, swimming. Petra left my side, and I was loathe to let drop her hand, for fear, for the terror I had begun to feel in my heart. She was my beloved, and she was too innocent for this night of madness. Her mind would become twisted from their heathen perversions and dark callings. I looked upon her in the shaded and sickly moonlight, upon her luxurious dark hair, her figure so lovely and dress of gossamer. I was afraid of what this Unholy Man would do to her, what he might take from her, as he had taken my peace from me.

But it was too late. She had persuaded me to bring her, for she longed to speak again to her father. She had begged me with tears and cries and silence, until finally, weak man that I am, I allowed her to come with me to this ceremony.

Gudrun took her hand, and brought her into the sacred circle, drawing down her cloak, and painting strange figured upon her face and neck.

I did not know what to expect, for although I had been an initiate for nearly a year, I had not borne witness to this highest of their Holy Days, the shortest night of the year at Midsummer. From my studies, I knew that this was the sacred veil that flowed the thinnest between the world of the Nowhere and the world we human beings occupied. The gods were at their most powerless to resist human intervention in their affairs. I was well aware that invocations would be made, that the Names would be said, and the seven words of power would be intoned over the exhumed grave of one of the early Masters.

The bones of the Masters had been given, relic-like, to the handful of followers left in the world—one some distant European shore, hundreds of thousands of years ago. Each bone, whether a toe-bone or knuckle or entire skull, had been held in secret, and buried with one of the followers, and the circles of belief arose around the grave that held the relic.

I had known that this particular spot of worship held a rib from an early Master. On the rib, were the runes of Boediccaeringon, the last words uttered in a time of famine and torture in the west of the British Isles centuries previous. It was used, they said, to ward off the invasions of Romans and Norsemen. I had never seen this sacred rib, but now, Gudrun held it.

In the darkness, I saw only its knife-like appearance, curved slightly at the end.

Then, Rowen drew close to her. I saw their shadows nearly touch, and it filled me with both jealousy and dread.

And I knew what he was about. He had lied to me about what this ceremony was—yes, there was truth to his lie. But I knew in that instant that I would forever regret bringing Petra to this bloodthirsty tribe of worshippers.

He was telling her the Words, and the Words were sacred and known only to the few.

And the Words were the names of the Gods, the TRUE NAMES, THE NAMES OF TERRIBLE AND SWIFT POWER, THE NAMES THAT SHOULD NEVER HAVE BEEN REVEALED TO MANKIND!

To know the secret names of the gods, to be able to say them aloud, had been brought by one who had come back from the dead thousands of years ago. The legend of the Words was that the one who brought them could not get rid of them. They were accursed to the one who knew them, for he could not resist saying them. Could not resist intoning the names of the gods, and this brought terror and panic into the world, and with it, disease and ill-begotten monstrosities. So the first Masters had found a way to put a lock upon them, so that only part of the Names could be said by one, and the Masters knew the completion of the Names—but no Master knew the entire Name to himself alone. The priests that followed the Masters shared the Names as well, and for each gathering, two priests or priestesses would know the Names, and could perform the ceremony if times were needed to invoke the Wrath of Gods. The flesh of the one who heard the Words could not resist saying them, for the Words went wormlike not into the brain, but into the lips and the throat, and remained there until the point of Death.

Only in the last throes of Death would the Words emerge.

I knew then to what end they used my beloved Petra.

God have mercy on my soul that I had ever taken the woman I loved into their corrupt circle! Petra had been living within a world of despair since her dear father had died so horribly! Had I but known the lengths she would go to in order to reach him, in order to be with him again!

She herself took the sharpened bone and thrust it into her breast, and as she died, I heard her utter some insane language, a string of vowels and consonants that made no earthly sense. She fell; the others held me back, though I fought them dearly to get to her.

Rowen crouched down, a lion over its kill, and leaned into her ear to whisper something.

I struggled free and escaped my captors. I fled deep into the bogs and woods, ran from the terror and the evil of it all. The visions of what I'd seen in the dark, of the dancing and singing of the priests and their minions, their shadows against the darker shadows of night, and within their circle, Petra, dying—and with her last breath, the demonic language!

At my apartment on Broad Street, I locked the door, and shuttered the window from the night. I lit candle after candle and lamp after lamp, to bring the brilliance of day into the late hours.

I heard a rapping at my door at nearly three in the morning.

She had found me. She had returned to me.

How could I resist her? She was my heart. She was my soul.

For her, I snuffed the candles, and turned down the lamps.

I left the Nowhere into my room. My soul.

Petra found me, before the morning had come.

And she showed me the true visage of a god whose true name should have been destroyed millenia ago, in the ancient tongue of the Chaldeans and Babylonians, a savage, devouring god whose hunger for children and the innocent is never-ending…

Four: Shelter

1

They found nothing in the ditch on the side of the road—neither were there any people—or deer—moaning in the woods.

"Whatever it was, it was big and strong."

"Brilliant deduction," Michelle said.

"A bear, maybe," Dash said.

"We got bears out here?" Danny asked.

Michelle flipped out her cellphone. The green light came up, and she began punching in numbers. "You have triple A, Dash?"

"No."

"Who you callin'?" Mark asked.

Michelle turned her back to them.

Then, she said, "Rachel? It's 'chelle. Listen, Dash wrecked his car out—no, we're okay. Oh my god, I know," she said, her voice dropping to a whisper as she said stuff that Mark was sure had to do with what geeks they were and how she'd been stuck riding with them because Danny was too drunk to drive. Then, her voice returned to normal. "No, no idea. We're not far from some farmhouse. And a graveyard. Yep. We have a special gift for you. I am not telling. Can you send your brother out to Route—Rachel? Rach? You're breaking up. Damn it," Michelle said, slapping her phone shut. She spun around. "You guys have a cell phone?"

"I'm technologically challenged at the moment," Dash shrugged, and went to grab a beer from the back of the car. When he got there, scrambling around the backseat, he shouted, "Jesus, Danny, did you drink two six packs?"

"I don't think so," Danny said, looking at both Michelle and Mark with the look of an innocent puppy. "Did I?"

"Found one. Wait, found three. No, five. Who wants a beer?"

"I do!" Mark shouted.

"Yeah," Danny said.

Michelle opened her cell phone again, and tried dialing. "We're in one of those dead areas."

"Dead?" Danny grinned.

"Can't get through," Michelle said, practically under her breath. She went over and stood beside Mark, and touched him lightly on the shoulder. "I guess we can't just walk to the party? Jesus, Danny, you always have that damn cell phone."

"I have my beeper," Danny said.

"That'll help. Yeah."

"We can find another phone," Dash said. "There's that church."

"Or the farmhouse."

"Church is closer. There's either going to be a payphone or an office phone in there."

The sky began dripping with rain. The soft distant rumble of thunder.

"It's comin' back," Danny said. "One-one-thousand, two-one-thousand."

A few seconds later a flash of lightning so bright it seemed to illuminate the forest, and for a moment, Mark thought he saw some people standing there, behind some trees, just standing there.

Danny began counting again, and a louder rumble of thunder sounded.

The rain began coming down fast, and Dash called out, "Come on, this way," and Michelle put the puppy in the little carrier; Danny took it in his left hand and held her hand with his right, and they ran together. Mark jogged behind them all, down the now-slick road.

Within minutes, Dash ran to the right, up the grass-covered path that led to the Old Church. Mud sloshed all around. The rain came down in sheets, and Danny was laughing and running, and the puppy in the carrier was barking; Mark held the flashlight up so they could see their way up the path, and couldn't wait to get inside the church and be dry again.

As they got closer to it, Mark noticed that there was a flickering light from within the church.

2

"God, we should've just stayed in the car," Michelle said. She was soaked, her hair, dripping strings, her shirt pasted to her breasts. "This feels a little déjà vu in the junior high department. I can't wait to get out of this place and get to Northhampton. May this be my last rainy night in Manossett."

"Yeah," Danny said. Then, he added, "God, I feel wasted."

"I'm amazed you're on your feet," Michelle said, nearly cheerfully.

"I can always go down the road to that farmhouse, too," Mark said, not breaking eye contact with Michelle.

"No need, Marco," Dash said.

They huddled inside the arched doorway of the church, Mark pressed against the thick wooden door.

"This is more of a chapel than an actual church," Dash said. "It's one of the oldest in this area."

"It's locked," Danny said.

The windows were all shuttered and locked from the inside, as well—Mark had checked when they'd first arrived.

Lightning lit the night again, and Mark saw the rocky graveyard lit up. Again, he thought he saw people—a group of them there—but they seemed blurred to him, and he wasn't sure if perhaps he should not drink more than a couple of beers in any one night.

"This kind of place," Dash said, "has to have a key. This isn't the kind of place people worry about getting broken into. Not way the

603

hell out here." He felt around in the recesses of the arch as it peaked and then dipped, and cried out, "Gotcha!"

He held up a thin round key. "Ask and it shall be given to you."

"Thank god," Michelle said. "I just want to be somewhere dry."

Mark kept looking out through the heavy rain at the darkness of the graveyard. He heard the door open behind him. The puppy whimpered in its carrier, and Danny made baby noises to it as he lifted it and took it inside.

One-one-thousand, two-one-thousand.

The sky lit up with whiteness.

There, in the graveyard, there were several people, shadows of people.

And what looked like an open grave.

Then, darkness. Rain. The grumble and crack of thunder.

3

"The world's smallest chapel," Dash said. "You probably know its history."

The chapel was one oblong room, with angles cut into it to create recesses with shrines along its gray stone walls. Mark noticed the windows first—barely slits to let in light, with stained glass in them. The shutters outside were deceptive—they were large, and had made Mark think the place had large windows as well. When he and Dash had been in the graveyard before, they'd never thought to venture in the church itself. It was a plain, nearly bare church, with flat, long benches for pews. The altar looked very much like a wide flat stone of four or five feet in length, and two feet wide.

The light they had seen from the road had been from candles—there were fat long candles in brass holders up and down the aisles.

"If the windows were shuttered, how did you see the light?" he asked Dash.

Dash grinned. Winked at him.

"Well, there's no phone here," Michelle said. "At least it's dry."

"Yeah. And it's better than being out there."

"How's the puppy?" she asked.

Danny crouched beside the carrier and looked in. "Doing fine. Chewin' on his rawhide."

"Damn," Dash said. "My ciggies are ruined." He held his pack of Marlboros up.

"I have some," Mark said. He reached into his pocket, and drew out two cigarettes. "Got a lighter?"

"I do," Danny said, feeling in his pockets.

"I got matches," Dash said, withdrawing some from within his jacket. "And shockingly, they're dry. Five left." He struck one against the matchbook, and Mark passed him a cigarette. "You keep these," he passed the matches to Mark once he'd begun puffing on the cigarette. Mark thrust the matches into the back pocket of his jeans. "You got four more cigarettes and four more matches. Perfect, Marco."

"I hope Rachel appreciates the effort we go to for her birthday," Michelle said. She reached into her handbag and withdrew a comb. She ran it through her hair, her head tilting sideway. She wandered over to one of the pews near the front of the chapel. "So now what?" She patted the bench where she sat, and Danny hobbled over and sat down beside her. Soon his arm was around her waist, and she leaned against his shoulder, looking up at the candles at the altar. "This is one ugly chapel. Those puritans really—holy crap, look at that!" she pointed toward the curved wall behind the alter.

Mark immediately looked there. Behind the flickering candle, there was a painting that reminded him of something from his sophomore European History book. It was nearly medieval looking—a faded painting of what seemed to be several monks, their heads shaved in tonsure.

"Those look like the guys I saw," Michelle gasped, and then giggled. "How bizarre."

"Oh yeah, the monks we hit," Dash said, his voice brimming with contempt.

"Gives me the creeps, a little," Michelle said. "Now I *really* wish we'd stayed in the car."

"And risked getting hit from behind by another car. No thank you," Dash said. "What good would that do? Your cell phone won't work. I know this place. I'm sure there's a phone in it."

Mark said something about how seeing a painting of monks in a chapel was not the strangest thing in the world, but the whole time he felt like he was lying. Wasn't sure why, but there was something funny about the painting. He walked up the aisle to get a closer look. Stepped up the worn, uneven stone steps to the altar.

The monks had faces that were like softened inverted triangles, and large wise eyes. There were four of them. In one of their hands, there was what looked like a thin white flute or recorder that bore markings—*Hebrew? Latin?* Mark had no idea. As he gazed at it in the shimmering candlelight, he thought it might be the thin tusk of some wild animal rather than a flute. The monk next to him held a round stone in his hand, or perhaps it was a large wafer of some kind. Again, this had strange marking upon it. The third monk held both his hands out. The artist had painted in that flat style of Norman invasion paintings—that's what it had been—the picture in his history book of William the Conqueror invading England. The third monk's hands were merely presented as having nothing in them.

But the fourth monk in the group held a small human skull in his hands.

And the skull had small bumps along its scalp—two just above the forehead. And its front row of teeth seemed unusually sharp, nearly wolf-like.

"It's funny," Mark said.

Behind him, Michelle. She had gotten up and looked around the altar, too. "What?"

"I was sure I'd been in here once. A long time ago. Some time. But I guess I never have. I've been outside before. But never in here. I've never even seen anyone go in here before."

"Look at this," Michelle said. He turned, and she was reading something off the top of the altar.

He went to look. The stone tablet of altar was rough, and covered with a stubble of what might've been mold or some kind of dusty lichen. Michelle brushed some of it off. "Look at that, Mark," she said, pointing to something carved into the stone.

Mark thought the drawing was a squiggle of circles and lines intersecting—some abstract Christian imagery. He noticed that it had eyes.

"It's some kind of bird," she said.

"Or bug. Look at its wings. There are four of them," Mark said. In his mind, the words *Swarmgod of the Thousand Stingers* seemed to surface. Words beneath the carved figure. "Is this Aramaic or something?"

"It's Latin," Dash said from the back of the room. "Or Greek."

"I took Latin in ninth grade," Michelle said. "It doesn't look like anything I remember."

"Then it's Greek," Dash said. "I've been in here before. I got a guided tour. This is one of the oldest churches in New England."

"How old?" Michelle asked, idly, her eyes never leaving the altar top.

"I would guess the sixteen-somethings."

"No, wait, I know what language this is. This is just French," Michelle said. "It's just carved in the stone with such a strange script, I didn't notice it. Let's see, this means, no, maybe it's not French. It's something I recognize." She leaned against the stone tablet. "Why would the pilgrims write in Greek? Or French?"

"I'm sure more than just pilgrims have been using this in the past five hundred or so years," Mark volunteered.

"That's right," Dash said.

"This is Latin, this part of it." Michelle's fingers traced the engraving. "VE. DEU. VI. Well, it's all broken up. It could mean anything. And what the hell is that? It looks like a round mouth full of sharp teeth."

"Deu is probably Deus," Mark said. The words seemed to be in his head: *The Devourer. She Who Befouls The Night. The Pope of Pestilence.*

"Maybe," Michelle nodded. "These drawings are fascinating. They almost look like caveman paintings. This word—AMOR. That's easy. Unless it's part of a longer word—too bad it got rubbed away here. I just wish I could figure out the letters in between."

"I didn't know you studied Latin," Mark said.

"Two years, but I switched to French junior year. I stopped enjoying it," Michelle said. Then she arched an eyebrow. "What, you think I'm just some dumb rich girl skating through life?"

"No, no, really, I don't," Mark said.

"Well, there's always more to people than you think. Even you and your buddy," Michelle offered a sweet smile. "I'll probably major in comparative lit at Smith, if I can take German and handle it at the same time. Someday, maybe I'll translate great works of literature. Or be a foreign correspondent."

"Or a spy," Dash said.

Mark almost wanted to tell Dash to shut up. He had his own interest in language, and had been studying Spanish in school, but had wanted to learn French, too. He looked at Michelle carefully, as if seeing her for the first time. She noticed, and laughed.

"I guess it takes a car wreck and a storm for us to get along," she said, and he felt a warmth from her, just standing beside her. Connecting in some way that he never thought he could with a girl like Michelle.

"Well, obviously, there's no phone here," Dash said. "Maybe we better take a hike."

"Yeah," Mark said, feeling a bit more like a man.

"I'll be fine here. I'm going to try and decipher this stuff," Michelle said. "Danny, you want to go with them?"

Danny, the puppy in his lap, made a motion that seemed to indicate that the puppy needed him.

"Me and Mark will go to that farmhouse," Dash said. "You two stay here. What, it's maybe a mile down the road?"

Mark nodded. "Yeah."

"We can run."

"Sure," Mark said, but dreaded the rain.

"You two just continue the party here, dry off, and we'll be back," Dash said. "Feel free to chug the last beer, Danny."

4

The rain had slowed to a steady but light sprinkling. The lightning was off in a distant sky, barely lighting the path from the old church.

"Okay, now, here's what we do," Dash said.

"What's all this?" Mark said.

"Huh?"

"'Huh?' You planned this," Mark said. "I know you did. What is all this? The church. The crash. Huh?"

"Come on, Marco, I told you, we'll have a little fun."

"It's not fun. It's the opposite of fun. Fun would be the party. Fun would be anywhere but here."

They walked out among the graves. Mark kept the flashlight on the ground to avoid any rocks and stones.

"She's a bitch, you know that? Don't let her fool you with all that Latin shit. She spent half of high school thinking that guys like you and me are less than toads, so don't suddenly get all sugary just because she shows you her rack."

"Aw crap, maybe we are less than toads, sometimes, Dash. Maybe we are. Maybe all this weirdo Nowhere shit is just the kind of crap that toads do."

"Blasphemy," Dash spat, and reached over and slapped him hard on the face.

It stung. Mark reached up and touched his cheek. It was numb.

609

"What the hell?" Mark said.

"Tonight is the night," Dash said, and grabbed him by the elbow, and pulled him close to him. The flashlight fell from Mark's hand. Dash's breath was all beer. "Look, you've known since you were thirteen that you were going to be part of this. You knew. And tonight is the night. Just like in the book. It's the Night of Lifting the Veil. It is nearly midnight. It is midsummer's night. The shortest night of the year. The night when the veil between our world and the world of the Nowhere is thinnest."

Mark laughed. "Come on. Come on, Dash. Come on."

He pulled away from Dash, walking ahead on a narrow, scraggly path between gravestones. "Get real."

Then, Mark thought he saw something before him—some shape that was all shadow, and he saw that at the edge of the graveyard, like a gate, there were people standing there, in long coats or cloaks, he wasn't sure, but he could see them.

He heard Dash groan behind him. Sound of sudden movement. Mark was about to turn around to see what was wrong, when something hit him hard on the side of the head, and he was out.

5

Mark awoke a few seconds later, but felt dizzy. His vision blurred, but it was all shadows and scant moonlight around him. The rain kept coming down. He lay in mud.

He thought he saw others there, those people, those monks, whoever and whatever they were, and it seemed nearly natural to see them. He almost expected them. Had it all been true? Had everything Dash had been telling him about the Nowhere — all those stories — been true?

He lay there, blinking, in the rain.

Of course, a cult could survive. There were people who practiced witchcraft who believed their religion had survived despite burnings and centuries of torture and murder. There were all kinds of cults and religions in the world — he knew that. But right here? In Manosset, near the Sound, in the 21st century? And could they be so backward and ignorant as to truly believe that there were gods with such ridiculous names as She Who Befouls the Night?

But those were just nicknames. He knew that from the Wacey Crossing stories. All names for the gods were not their true names. Their true names were only known by those who held the power.

The back of his head throbbed.

He looked up into Dash's face, shadowed with night.

Were they alone? He felt alone.

"Here's the thing. You've got to listen very carefully, Marco. Very carefully. There are words, and they're on this," Dash pressed something into Mark's hand. His fingers curled around it instinctively. "Sometimes, the god that enters gets out of hand. And has to be stopped. The words will stop the god. The words are the only thing that stops the god. Listen. Just lie there and listen or I will hit you again so hard so help me god Marco you might never wake up. Listen! This is so important," Dash said. Was he weeping? Was it rain? Mark couldn't tell. "I have to fulfill something here. It is my destiny. I am chosen for something, and tonight is the night. When this happens — and it has only happened nine times since the dawn of recorded history, Marco, nine times, I will be the tenth. I will be the tenth, and this hasn't been arrived at lightly. They are very smart people. They have waited more than a thousand years in their religion to allow this to happen again. They feel it's time. And I am the one. But you have got to remember the words when you hear them, Marco. I can only say them once. You are the only one who can stop this with the words. Only the one I…I," Dash's voice broke. Then, strength returned. "Only the one I have given my heart to can stop this once it starts. And the words have got to be remembered. These others," Dash nodded to darkness, although Mark saw no one, "they have had their tongues cut out lest they utter the words. The one who told me, taught me, drilled me in this, is dead. I can say the words to you, but you must remember them. And with the words, I will tell you the names of the gods. This is an enormous responsibility. The world is corrupt. The time of human life is nearly over. The gods want to return and end the stupidity of this race of men. The names of the gods," he leaned into Mark's face, and pressed his mouth to Mark's ear, he began whispering something that Mark tried to remember as soon as he heard it.

"There's really a Nowhere?" Mark asked, pleading in his voice.

"Oh," Dash sighed. "Marco, wait til you see it. I mean *really* see it. There's something you need to drink. Here, sit up."

Mark felt Dash's hand slip behind his neck, pressing near the throbbing. "It's easier to see like this."

Mark moaned a little—the pain at the back of his scalp intensified. "You hit me too hard."

"Sorry." Dash withdrew the hypodermic needle from the plastic case.

"What—what are you—what—don't," Mark whispered.

"It'll take the pain away. And you'll understand. You'll see. You will really see," Dash said, and he held Mark's arm down, tore his shirtsleeve up to his bicep. Dash squeezed his bicep, and then Mark felt the needle go in, twisting into his flesh. "This isn't junk. This is ambrosia. Believe me," Dash whispered. "You'll have a taste of the Nowhere. What it really can be like."

611

6

The sensation of floating, but not floating.

Hands moved in bird-like blurs before his eyes.

It was already morning. The rain had stopped. The sun was out.

But the sun was white, not a warm yellowish gold, it was white— all the light was pure white in the sky. There was no sun. Mark sat up against the gravestone. The throbbing in his head was gone. The trees were funny, the woods seemed funny. Something moved along the bark of the trees. Snakes and worms wriggled along them.

The strange thing was: some things were missing. The trees themselves didn't move in a light wind; and there was no rain, although there had been second before.

Dash was there, only he was Dash with a difference: he seemed better looking. Color in his face. A rosy glow. His eyes were like a little boy's—all happy and expectant. Mark's eyes went in and out of focus, and he heard a strange humming in his head. He looked at his hands, and he saw them as liquid, contained within some invisible boundary that defined "hand." When he waved his hand, some molecules of flesh dispersed—just a few and seemed to form into an insect of some type in the air—a ladybug, flying off.

"Ain't it cool?" Dash asked. "It's like the world only different. If you stay still, you disappear. Watch." Dash closed his eyes and mouth, and clasped his hands together. Within seconds, he seemed to evaporate like steam.

Then, he laughed, and suddenly was there again. "The world we're used to has to move a lot or make noise for things in The Veil to see it. It's a strange place, no?"

Dash kept laughing, but it all seemed to move slowly, and Dash reached into his own chest, and drew back his black t-shirt, tearing it, only it didn't tear like fabric. It formed droplets of black goo that absorbed against his green jacket. Then, Dash pressed his hand against the skin of his pale, hairless chest and drew back the skin— not as if it were cut or scraped, but again, in that liquid medium, as if Dash himself were a bubble of soap, with the image of flesh and clothing poured into him—malleable and shifting, but within a boundary that kept the liquid in place.

The Words

Dash's fingers went deeper into his flesh, and drew out what appeared to be a pulsing mass of purple and poppy red. Smiling, Dash brought it closer to Mark's face. "My heart," he said. "My heart and your heart." Dash reached into Mark's chest, and it tickled. Mark laughed, and felt Dash's fingers inside his flesh, moving along the organs within his ribcage, and up. A feather like tickle of his heart. All the while, the liquid between their bodies, the floating droplets, merged and mixed, splashing together.

Dash held both hearts for Mark to see. "We're brothers," Dash said.

"The Veil," Mark murmured, feeling particularly good, as if he had never known what it meant in life to feel good.

Dash nodded. "Yep. The Veil. From a garden that existed thousands and thousands of years ago. A garden destroyed by mankind when it learned the secret names of the gods. But the wise ones who knew its value rescued this flower and its seed. And they've planted it and cared for it in secret all these years, Marco. And it shows you the real world. The Nowhere. If I told you this was Eden itself, wouldn't you believe me? Look, we flow. Look at the sky. This is night, Marco. Not daylight. This is true night. The blackness is an illusion. See? Look—" Dash pointed to the sky. An eel or snake of somekind wriggled in the white air as if it were moving through rippling milk. "This is the realm of the gods. This is what we're blinded from. This is what the Nowhere people know. And always have. We can't be here long. We can't take The Veil too much. It's addictive, but it can be horrible as well as beautiful. Do you see now? Marco? How beautiful? Marco, I've seen magnificent cities on the surface of the sea—I've seen creatures that have only been drawn in ancient texts—sea monsters, mermaids, all here, all within The Veil. And the gods, too. They cause what happens in our world, but we are blinded and cannot see—we see through darkness. The Nowhere is the true light."

"I feel a little sick," Mark said, reaching to his stomach. "Sick."

"It's your first time. But you'll get used to it. You'll enjoy it more. Right now, you can only tolerate a few minutes. But later, you'll be able to have more of it. I'll show you amazing things, brother.

Amazing. One more beautiful than the next," Dash said, and then he held something in the air. It looked like a white horn of some type. Writhing around it, tiny red insects, mites of some kind, thousands of them. "You'll come out of this in a minute or two, Marco. When you do, you must say the names as soon as I've said the first part. And if it gets too much out of hand, you can stop it. There's always a way to stop it. Just remember the words. They're here, on this bone. The names you can't forget, even if you try. Your flesh hears them once, and your molecules take the names of the gods in, and holds them. You have to say the names as soon as you see me die."

"Die?" Mark looked at him, uncomprehending. "You're going to die?"

"Not really. Not die like you think. You ready?" Dash held the bone in front of his chest.

He began saying what Marco realized were the first halves of the names of the gods of the Nowhere.

7

Alone, with Dash, in the rain. Out of The Veil. In the real world. The ordinary, awful world again. Mark sat up. Sky, black. The earth, sucking mud.

Taking the smooth thin bone, Dash pressed the sharpened end of it into his chest.

Mark reached for the bone, pulling it out. "No, Dash, please, no!"

As he let out a final breath, Dash whispered the beginning of the names of the gods.

When Dash's eyes were closed, Mark said the last half of the names. He didn't know how he could remember them—they were a long string of sounds and clicks and howls. They hurt his ears to say, like a strangely out of tune sound of pipes being played from his throat—or a saw twanging across the vowels of the names.

He almost wanted to say the words, as well, out of fear.

The words that could stop this.

But he hesitated.

Then, Dash opened his eyes again.

They glowed like the ends of cigarettes in the dark.

Five:
Church of the
Veil

1

Mark began shivering in the darkness as he watched what had been Dash rise to its feet. It no longer seemed to be Dash, not in the sense that he had felt Dash had been. It had the glowing eyes, and its teeth were sharp at the ends, small nails of teeth, and even in the moonlight, Mark could see the way spurs had burst from his joints—elbows and knees—and writhing worms, long nightcrawlers, moved along his fingers.

"Nowhere is here," Dash grinned, and for a second, Mark thought it was a trick. The drug, perhaps. Still lingering in his system. *Of course. The drug. The Veil.* The needle that had gone in his arm.

"Jesus," Dash said. "I'm hungry."

2

Dash turned, glancing toward the church. Then, back to Mark. "You're not going to understand this, Mark. If you could see what I see, you would." The red eyes burned and then seemed to fade into Dash's normal eyes.

Mark heaved a sigh—it must've been the drug. It must've been. He was still hallucinating. He still felt weak and dizzy, and he had to sit down again. His head was spinning. It was the drug. That's all it was. None of it had happened.

"Look, give me a minute," Dash said. "You need to rest. You're going through a lot. Shit, *I've* been through a lot."

Mark turned, and threw up onto a gravestone. He wiped his mouth; a sickly sweet taste lingered in his throat. *The Veil.*

When he turned around, Dash was gone; by the time Mark rose up on his feet, he thought he saw some enormous winged bird—almost a pterodactyl, given its wingspan—landing at the door to the old church; but it was a man—no, it was Dash.

Mark walked toward the church, lurching with each step, stopping every few feet to cough. *God, what if I die? What if that drug kills me?* He slid in the mud and had to pick himself up. His heart beat rapidly. *It was poison. I'm going to die.*

By the time he reached the door to the old church, he heard Danny's shout.

616

3

The candles along the altar were lit. It was warm and humid within the church, as if the summer storm had turned it into a steamroom.

"What the fuck?" Danny laughed. "Holy shit, what the hell have you been drinkin', Dashy? Or maybe it's me, maybe it's just me!" He was beer-soaked at this point; the last couple of bottles of beer lay beside him on the stone altar. Michelle glanced up—they were making out, which is what they seemed to do whenever they had five minutes to themselves.

"Dash, don't, just—just—get away," Mark shouted from the doorway. He stepped into the back of the church. "Just come outside!"

"Oh Danny boy, the pipes, the pipes are callin'," Dash began to sing, and practically skipped into the church. Danny had his pants off, briefs intact, button-down shirt still on with a few buttons missing; Michelle's shirt was open; she made an annoyed sound in the back of her throat.

"Sorry to interrupt, lovebirds," Dash said.

"Get the hell outta here," Danny said, but he began laughing—it must have struck him as funny to be caught nearly doing it with his girl on the altar of this rat-hole church.

Michelle pushed Danny away and began closing her shirt up.

"Enough," she said.

"Just a little fun," Dash said. Mark stood at the entrance to the church, watching Dash, unsure of what he was really seeing. Dash seemed to move with a grace he'd never had before, like a dancer or gymnast, and he went right up to the altar and pressed his hands down on two of the candles to snuff them out.

Only one left.

"Dash!" Mark called out. "Come on, let's go. This won't be fun."

Dash turned back to him, and in the final candle's glow, laughed a little—laughed the way he would when they'd first met, back in eighth grade, a let's-have-fun laugh, and said, "Oh, wait and see."

Then, he snuffed the last candle out. The room was plunged into darkness.

"Hey, who turned off the lights?" Danny shouted. Mark saw shadows against shadows. Michelle started cussing, and saying she just wanted to get the puppy and get to the party, and why didn't her cell phone work? Danny began laughing and telling her that it was going to be better in the dark, but Mark heard a strange groaning sound—perhaps a creaking of some door?

The door behind him slammed shut, as if by a great wind.

But there had been no wind.

And then, the screaming began.

The time moved swiftly, for Mark's first instinct was to run away; but he moved forward in the darkness, hitting against one of the long benches. He dug into his jeans for some matches, and drew them out. Only four left in the matchbook.

He lit one, and for a fizzing few seconds, the light lit up the room—there was Michelle, screaming, and something with enormous leathery wings, and crab-like appendages studding its body—it was Dash but it was no longer Dash—it had hold of Danny by the throat and was shaking him hard, side to side.

The match went out.

Another match; he struck it, and it flared up for a moment.

Michelle was halfway to him—her eyes were wide and seemed to have lost all intelligence—

A creature that seemed both insect and dragon—it was only an impression, like the flash of a dream—chewing on Danny's scalp—

Mark dropped the match, and was again in complete darkness.

Gurgling sounds followed, and then the tearing sound of meat and a cracking of bones.

Michelle ran past him. He felt a revulsion toward her, as if in her sudden madness, she were no longer human.

Dash's voice from the darkness:

"Yesssss," snakelike and hollow, "Marco, the Nowhere is here, you helped bring it, it's all true," and then the sounds of a dreadful slobbering and gobbling, as of a wild dog swiftly devouring some prey.

Mark drew out a third match, and struck it in the matchbook.

Dash stood so close to him that they were practically touching.

Shocked by the closeness, Mark dropped the match, and it went out.

In that second, he had seen the white and pink worms encircling Dash's throat and hands, growing in pulsating movements from his flesh, and soft fuzzy tendrils gently fluttering from his bare waist and ribcage.

His mouth painted a dark red.

In his arms, he cradled what was left of Danny's body. Torn and ragged and more meat that human.

"Any shape I desire," Dash said, and tossed Danny's remains to Mark when the darkness again engulfed him.

Mark felt the nausea sweep through him; he dropped the body, and turned to run, but fell to his knees instead.

"Pray to your little god," Dash said. "Pray like a good altar boy. But you're in the wrong place, Marco. This is the altar of the Nowhere. The Church of the Veil. Now, where do you think Michelle's run off to? Not outside. I made sure the door was shut tight and locked. She must be here. Hiding. Oh, yes! This makes it more of a game, doesn't it? But I can see with more than eyes now. You know that, Marco. You've been through The Veil. You know that it's a world of liquid white now."

Mark wanted to cry out, or scream, but his voice had abandoned him—or else he had screamed so much in the past few moments—without realizing it — that he had none left. He felt cold and hot at the same time. *The words. Remember the words.*

You can stop him with them. They're the words of ending. The god will return to The Veil. The words.

"I can hear her breathing," Dash said. "She is gonna love what I do to her. I hope you're there to see it, Marco. I hope you'll partake."

Mark thought he heard Michelle cry out from behind him.

"Run! Get out! Michelle! Just get out!"

The sound of her sobs echoed. "It's locked!" she cried out, banging on the door, "Somebody! Somebody help me! Help!"

"Michelle! Shut up! Just shut up!" Mark yells. "Stay still and shut up!"

It needs movement and noise. Maybe it will leave now that it had Danny. Dear Jesus help us. Help her.

The words. Remember them.

619

Part Two: The Ending

1

And so, in the room in the church, it feels his ankles. He has pressed himself against the wall, halfway between scared shitless and ready to do something—anything—to keep it from going after Michelle.

Slick and sticky and wormy, it seems to lick his calves with its feelers. Michelle by the door, moaning out little noises—and the thing that Dash has become is slithering and feeling its way over to her. In Dash's mind, he must be seeing the whiteness of the darkness. He must be seeing the liquid move and slosh, and the unseen things that move in the air and along the walls. He must see Michelle, too, not as a terrified young woman of eighteen, but as some collection of molecules to be devoured, to be fed upon, to increase its happiness and its mission as it moves through the world, but sees and feels all through The Veil that Dash has now destroyed within himself.

The last of the tendrils that Dash-thing drags with him, slides away from Mark's foot.

Leaving him. Letting him go.

Moving toward her.

She is groaning as if she can't contain her fear.

And then, she lets out a bloodcurdling scream—and another, and another in quick succession.

He hears the throaty laugh. "Come on, it's only me, Michelle, come on," Dash says, and for a fleeting instant Mark thinks that it might be a game. It might just be all fake. *The drug! Yeah! It's the drug!* That what he saw, the heap in the corner, wasn't Danny at all. That it was some kind of illusion. Some trick of light and dark. A bad acid flashback.

This is some kind of trip. This isn't the real world.

Michelle's sobbing, with screamlets in her voice, jagged shards of sound.

Get to Danny. In his jacket. A lighter.

It's afraid of light. The Nowhere can't exist where there's any light. Any genuine light. If darkness is light to it, than surely light is its own kind of darkness.

"You always wanted me, Michelle, you always did," the thing that Dash has become says. "Rachel used to tell me how you thought I was quirky and cool, and when she did, when she whispered those things to me, it got me so revved up, baby, and I knew that someday, you and I would have this moment." As he spoke, Mark heard the whirring sound again—a soft, rapid fluttering. He'd once had a junebug fly into his earlobe, and it was a sound very much like that.

If I just get to Danny's jacket, Mark thinks. *The lighter.*

"Please," Michelle is whimpering. "Dash, please. Don't hurt me. Please. Oh god. Please." Her "please" becomes the sound of bleating, and in a horrible way it's funny, it sounds like a joke, but Mark knows it's not.

Why doesn't she try to run? Is it blocking her way? Mark estimates that he can get to the doorway, to where Danny's body rests. He can grab the jacket, and thrust his hand into the pockets. He can get the lighter, flick it up, and scare it away.

Scare that creature away.

"Oh, Michelle, baby," it says. "I want to love you so badly. I want you to be my girl, don't you know that?"

"Please," she said in such an awful tone that tears came to Mark's eyes even as he took a step toward the opposite corner of the room.

"Take my hand, Michelle, don't be afraid," it says. "I want to love all of you in every way."

The sound changes—it feels like an alarm has gone off somewhere. A sound like hissing and spitting and the crack of a whip.

"No!" Michelle screams, "Oh my god, oh my god, god, god, god, god!" Her screams turn into giggles and jets of laughter. Mark races to Danny's body, pushing through the wetness, tearing the shorts from what remains of the lower half of him, sifting quickly through the pockets until he finds something cylindrical and hard.

The lighter.

Hang on, Michelle.

The sounds are wet and bubbling. Michelle is moaning, as if she has been swiftly gagged.

Mark turns, flicking the lighter. Doesn't light up.

Flick! Again no light.

Then, it lights.

A small flame erupts from the lighter.

He cups it in his hand, a yellow and rosy glow around his palm.

He calls out to it, but the noise the splattering noise and that whirring has begun again—

Mark brings the flame up to see—

Shadows cast against the old bare wall of the room.

He sees what looks like the spread wings of a shiny beetle, and long white and pink worms—or slender tentacles—moving between Dash's body, which floats barely a foot in the air—holding Michelle—caressing her—she struggles against it—the worms inside her mouth, her nose, tearing her shirt off, scraping at her skin until it is flaps hanging down—the wormy tendrils shooting and pulsing from Dash's mouth and eyes and ears—his ribcage opens like two doors creaking apart—and long feathery whips emerge and stroke her skin—Mark feels frozen in terror—the worms are wriggling, but they are from Dash's ribcage—boring out from

623

them, and feathery, barnacle-like fans—moving swiftly, tickling her breasts and sides—and her eyes are wild and the worm-appendages of the thing reach into her ears—and they are—

Mark shouts, "I have light! You have no power in the light!" He waves the flame around, his arm outstretches, his body taut. "I'll set you on fire."

He moves over to Dash, what Dash has become, to the beetle-like wings, four of them, spread wide, with a layer of nearly-transparent wings in between. Bone in one hand, lighter in the other, the flame shooting up high. He tries to read the bone, but he can't—not while Michelle is still…

But he tries—the symbols on the bone seem different than they did before. They seem to have smudged or moved around, and he can't quite see them for the flickering light.

With the light, he can see the markings—the sores and pustules along Dash's spine. Dash turns for a moment, his face covered with many small black eyes, and he says, his words rapid-fire and ripe with excitement, "The light has no power over me, Mark. Not once the incarnation has happened. All the world is white light. Once in the flesh, I'm indestructible. Unless you know the words. But you don't, do you? You will never know them. You will never read the bone, will you? How can you? Only the priests who have studied for decades can remember them, can speak them," and then the creature turns about to Michelle's beatific and glowing form, the blood shining along her body, and began devouring her like a spider feeding upon a wriggly fly caught in its web, "Oh, so delicious, such a del*ee*cious treat," Dash says, his mouth foaming with white and red. Then, his opening body, like a mouth, covering her, like a Venus flytrap, like a devourer.

Shivering, Mark moves toward him and thrusts the flame against his neck, but the worms shoot out from beneath the wings and tear the lighter from his fingers.

The creature turns—its face bubbling with sores, its eyes blinking in unison. It regards Mark with some interest.

The wings close, and it floats inches downward until it touches the floor.

Then, with the dark that encircles the small yellow flame like a cloak, it shoots tendrils around Mark's ribs. He presses against them, but he can't pull free. It lifts him up, and he feels the invasive, parasitic wormy fingers moving against the holes in his ears, pressing down onto his lips, forcing them open. Lower, his navel is stretching as the worms push inward. Wave after wave of nausea hits him.

The slick, wet tendrils pry the sacred bone from his fingers. What feel like bundles of worms thrust down the back of his throat. He feels the sharp jab against his stomach—

the bone—

Going into him.

Dash's voice, nearly sweet, whispering along with the dreadful humming of the wings as they move rapidly, "I won't let you hurt for long, Marco. I want you and me to be together. We can do anything now. Anything, and we'll bring the Nowhere into daylight. We'll tear The Veil."

2

Dying? Blood is pouring from his stomach and legs.

Dash, in the dark, seeming human, seeming not to have a thousand wormy and tentacles arms and barnacle feathers, lifts Mark up. Lifts him with two arms. Broken bones shift; freezing pain. No screams left in him. Mark is sure now that he screamed the whole time that the creature slaughtered Michelle.

Through the narrow hall. Smell of fresh air. Outside again. Sky is clear. Moonlight, very little, but enough.

Dash strips Mark's shirt off, and with his fingernails scratches markings on his chest and stomach. "You can be like this, too. Just like we said. We never have to be apart. We can be in the Nowhere."

"No," Mark tries to lift his head, but can't. "Please, I need help, Dash."

"The words," Dash says. "Just remember them. Your body will die soon." He lets out what can only be a sigh of contentment. "None of this has to change who we are. This is just the god thing. It's what gods have to do. Look, Mark, I know things now. I gained knowledge. Yeah, it hurts some, and part of me feels bad, but when it takes me over, man, you have got to experience this. It's like…like fucking life. Like there's no darkness at all. There's a whole other world you can see when you're like this. You can see things without your eyes. You have feelers. You have these parts of you that can stretch out and find things without even opening your eyes. And them? Michelle and Danny? Shit, they're in another place. Death isn't bad for them. They're the food of the gods, that's all, they're chow. Gods eat life. That's how it goes. The god of grass eats grass and the god of the flesh eats flesh, you can't have life without this. It's something we've all gotten away from, but the worshippers, the priests of the Nowhere, they've known. They've kept the ritual. They've put themselves at one with the gods to do this. We are anointed ones, we are gods in flesh, you can't be afraid, you can't look at this with the same eyes you had before, not once it's happened. It's stupid and human of you to do it. When you die, you're not going over there. You're going to come back here. Do you know what the gods are? Do you? Do you?"

A hiss that might've been contempt came from Mark's lips as he looks up at the dark figure.

"The gods are creatures, just like us, but they don't have boundaries. They reshape themselves at will. They let their hunger loose. Their lusts. Their wants. We think things happen because we do them or there are natural laws, but Marco, there aren't natural laws—the gods make things happen, they make it all go. But their names are power. I have the power. It's within me," Dash says, passion swelling in his voice. "I can be anything, Marco. Anything."

3

Mark, in the muddy grass, at the edge of the grave. He looks up at what once had been Dash.

What is still Dash.

The moonlight is soft around his face. Dash has a beautiful face. Dash has an ugly face.

Michelle. Danny. Gone. In less than an hour.

It still looks enough like Dash, with his hair, stringy from rain, matted with mud. His longish jaw and his eyes that seemed to shine even in the absence of light. Just two eyes. Two human eyes. No thousand eyes of some monster. Darkness around his lips. Blood?

"You're dying," Dash said. "Don't be afraid of it. Just say the name. Just say it, Marco."

"Mmm," Mark said. "Nuh. No."

"We never have to live anywhere but in the Nowhere again. Not ever," Dash said.

"You're dead," Mark whispered, but wasn't sure if Dash could even hear him. Mark felt so weak, with his life draining from him.

"The name," Dash said. "Remember? You say it as you die. The first part. I say the other half of the name after you breathe your last. I know all their names now, Marco. I know each of the gods, and their wonderful hungers and the way they look—I can see them all around us. We are their children. I have them incarnate within me, too. I can be a thousand different things. I can be a hornet or dragon, Marco. I can bring up a wind or burn with fire. I can see clearly, more clearly than I could in daylight, see with more than just these useless eyes. I can smell my sight, I can feel sight. You will, too! We can go to Rachel's party. We don't have to miss it. We can bring her the puppy. I'm not going to hurt the puppy. It's not like that. What's inside me now, it has meaning. It doesn't want puppies and turtles and goats and chickens. It wants more than that. Everyone will be there. Everyone from our class. And we'll show them that we're not just there for their pecking order and social put-downs. We'll be there to show them the faces of the gods. We could even bring some more of them back, if we're careful with their bodies. We could make all of us live forever, if you really want. I mean, yeah, it's too late for Michelle and Danny, but I let it out too much. I hadn't learned how to pull back on the reins yet. But I think I understand now. And the Nowhere is with us. They think I'm a messiah. They'll know you as my lieutenant. We'll change everything. Everything in one night if we have to. We'll pull back the Veil. You and me, both. After you say the name. And then you'll be here again. We can fly, now. We can swim underwater for hours. We can turn to liquid, or move within the bark of a tree. We can become the darkness. Or light. And it'll be you and me. Brothers. In the Nowhere. We'll be gods here, Marco. We'll do things we couldn't have imagined before. Before it was just a game. Now, it's real, and we're real, and the others, the people in the world, your mother and father and mine and the teachers at the Gardner School, they're the unreal ones. We can go on to Rachel's next. Just the name. Let me whisper it to you."

Mark closes his eyes.

Soft rain falling. Just drips of it. On his face. Cooling rain.

The feeling of Dash's wet slippery hand touching Mark's face.

"The name," Dash says, as gentle as the rain. "Just say it for me. I love you so much. Just say it." Dash may have had tears in his eyes, or perhaps it is the raindrops falling gently on Mark's face.

Opens his eyes. The shadow of Dash's face is all he sees. The smell of his breath—the same stink of the dead body, its flesh torn open.

Mark mutters something.

"Marco?"

Mark says it as loud as he can. It comes out a whisper. "You. Not my brother. I don't love you. I don't want to be with you after I die…far away from you."

All his energy in those words. He feels smug. Numb and smug. A worm of pain somewhere in his gut, but otherwise, he's ready to go. *In the arms of Death.*

Mark wants to close himself up.

To die without remembering the name.

To die without Dash's whisper against his ear.

The image of Michelle's face, covered with tears. Michelle, who was beautiful and wonderful, only Mark couldn't see it because he'd let Dash infect him all those years. Michelle who was not stupid. Michelle who was not trashy and snotty all at once. She was a beautiful human being, a shining human being, who had deserved more than eighteen lousy years on this earth. She had deserved a life after high school, a life after college. She might've become something magnificent if she'd had the chance.

He had loved her right then. That night. That moment of dread, of fear. He knew what love was. It wasn't sex and longing and a feeling. It wasn't the empty thing he had thought, of wants and needs and kindness. It was deeper than anything he had thought before—deeper than all the philosophies that Dash had spouted, the empty words, the babblings of Wacey Crossing, it was richer than any of that. It was the understanding that in the extreme of life, all of them were connected somehow. All of them were within the same skin. That was love. That was what love was. Not what Dash had sold him on. Not this...darkness...this death god. Danny and Michelle, swept from the earth as if they didn't matter. He had loved them, just because he had understood how he was brother to both of them. In that awful moment. He was connected to them by the invisible cord of humanity, a cord he had never felt tugging at him before, but now, it was all he felt.

Dash had trampled all that with his magic and words and runes. Stupid figures scratched on bones and somewhere in his mind. Words from some best-forgotten tongue. A tongue no doubt cut out by invaders and new religions that supplanted the darker ones, the ones that burnt children alive and devoured the innocent, and no matter what Dash said about cults and religions, they were more advanced than what was worshipped in the Nowhere.

The people of the Nowhere. Insane people who believed they were priests and worshippers, but they were merely spreaders of filth. They were like worms and flies themselves—traveling to shit and making a home within it. Dash had become some not-dead creature that fed on human flesh and had no conscience, followed by disgusting people within a perverse tradition, a twisting of the universal laws of brotherhood and sisterhood by which they were connected to all human beings, and by the ultimate law of life, to which every creature of flesh, every stalk of grass, was bound.

Dash had his high IQ twisted into triviality, into a monster's basic needs of hunger and domination. That was all. It wasn't God, or even god.

It was idiot and yes, evil, Mark thinks, *Evil*, as he fights for air—a heavy weight of something upon his chest, as if stones are

629

being piled upon him. *Evil. Nasty. Stupid. With the mind of Death, and nothing more.*

Dash is holding him now, cradling him, mouth to ear, practically kissing his ear as he begins to whisper something that Mark can't quite make out.

Dying. Please take me, God. Take me now. Break me out of life. Crush my spirit and body and slam me into another place. Or just cut off whatever it is that life is within me. Keep me from the Nowhere.

But even as he dies, Mark, without wanting to, without desiring this, parts his lips.

No! something within him fights against it. *Don't say it. Don't say the names!*

But his flesh is at war with his heart, and he realizes that Dash's remark had been true: *the flesh remembers the names.*

Mark utters the names. The unspeakable names of the gods of the Nowhere, of the Veil. Like the worst profanity coming from his tongue.

Permission to be called back.

He cannot remember the words that would stop this.

Only the names that would begin it.

His life slips away, just as if it were dropping into a pool. A rock in water, hitting the surface and slipping down into the murky depths. He's angry as he goes down to a place where the lights dim and flash and dim.

The lights are nearly out.

He can't even sense that he is breathing, or that Dash holds him now. Dash, singing some painful song in an unknown tongue as if he'd been singing it his whole life.

Mark has a sense of the others that are there—the priests and believers of the Nowhere. Standing in a circle around them both.

The part of Mark that still has a speck of thought and life feels terror and calm all at once, knowing that after he goes, that thing that Dash has become will hold him in his arms and intone the other part of the names, the response—*the litany* until Mark's eyes, once again, open.

Part Three: The Party

1

An hour or so later, and several miles away, a girl of nineteen, her arms around a boy of roughly the same age, says, "Oh my god."

The lights in the house go out, suddenly.

The boy kisses her again, his breath all beer. "Rachel, you know what? I hope we spend every night together this summer. Our last summer together."

"Damn, I'm not even sure where the fusebox is," the girl says, pushing her boyfriend away.

"It's a brown-out."

"It's just black-out."

"Lights!" someone shouts, laughing. "Somebody hit the lights!"

"What happened to the music?"

"Party must be over. Nice hint, Rachel!"

"Yeah, you want us to leave you can just ask us."

"It must be the storm," somebody says, drunken slur to his voice.

"Looks like somebody forgot to pay the bill."

"It must've been the storm."

"Yeah, or maybe a burglar."

"I love it in the dark. There's more to kiss."

"Perv!"

"Got a flashlight?"

"In my car. I'll get it."

"Jesus, it's nearly two. I better get home."

"We've got candles down in the basement, and some under the sink in the kitchen," Rachel says.

"Get your hands off me, Josh. And go get me some more beer."

"Somebody's knocking at the door. Somebody get it."

"No, something at the window. That a seagull? What the hell is that?"

"A bird hit the window."

"No, it's the front door."

"Come in!"

"Where are the candles?"

"The kitchen!" Rachel shouts. "Under the sink. There should be six of them."

"Here," some boy says. He flicks on a lighter. For a second, the small blue-yellow flame lit his face. The shadows of others, around him. In the mirror on the back wall the reflection of the light reveals more: the enormous living room is packed. "Everybody light your lighters."

"Don't be ridiculous. Just get some candles."

"Knock knock," a boy, a junior from the Gardner School, reaches the front door. He draws the door inward.

A gust of steam. Humidity has risen.

Two figures in the dark, on the front porch.

"You're late," the boy says, sleepily, not quite recognizing them in the dark. "Party's almost over."

For a split second, the boy who has opened the door has an instinct, but he ignores it. He thinks he should shut the door and lock it, but he doesn't know why he'd think that.

2

And then, it begins.

PURITY

"Vast, Polyphemus-like, and loathsome, it darted like a stupendous monster of nightmares to the monolith, about which it flung its gigantic scaly arms, the while it bowed its hideous head and gave vent to certain measured sounds..."
      —"Dagon" by H.P. Lovecraft

Prologue:
Why I Called
You Here

1

There is no madness but the madness of the gods.
There is no purity but the purity of love.

2

Someone once wrote that "the most merciful thing in the world,
I think, is the inability of the human mind to correlate its contents."

This describes my feelings perfectly. I correlate too much of my
own mind's contents. It's always troubling.

I don't live in the chronological moment; I doubt you do, either.
I live all at once in the past with only glimpses of the present. I live
mostly on that island, when it comes to me, when I think of my life
as it formed.

I live in darkness now, but the dark brings the memories back.
The dark brings it all back.
The dark is all I know.
I call the dark.
It's there that I find the god I met one day when I was just a child.
I remember that day; not the days of blood to come.
In the end, we were together.
In the beginning, we were not.

3

Here are the words I will never forget:

"Owen, I'm so sorry. I'm so sorry. I should never have come this summer."

Before that, the gun went off.

Before that, I looked into her eyes.

Before that is when it all began.

Dagon, bring it back to me.

Part One:
Summer Begins

Chapter One:
Who I am

1

These are the things I know:

Outerbridge Island has briny water running beneath its rocks, a subterranean series of narrow channels between the Sound and the Atlantic. You can see the entrances to these channels on the northern side of the island at low tide. These channels feed into the Great Salt Pond on the westerly side of the island before it empties into the sea. It was said that once-upon-a-time, a Dutch trading ship smashed up against the rocks, and local pirates fed upon the treasures found within the hold of ship. The treasure, it is said, was buried in the narrow caverns. To add to the chill of this tale, it was also said that the pirates fed upon the flesh of the survivors of the wreck for days.

I've actually swum into the caverns at times. I'm slender enough, and in good enough shape to maneuver in the darkness of the water, but I never found treasure, nor did I emerge in the Great Salt Pond by following the channels within that part of the island. I needed air, after all.

If you want something badly enough, there are ways to get it.

This doesn't mean that they are traditional means. It doesn't mean that pain is not involved. It doesn't mean that the cost may not overwhelm the need. It just means there are ways to get what you really want in this world.

If one has a conscience, one can be driven mad. Therefore, a conscience is a key to madness. Everyone is a potential madman. Everyone. The sweetest boy in the world can be driven to the most irrational of acts. The girl who has the world at her feet, likewise, could be driven to some act of desperation and tragedy.

And, in many ways, we want the irrational and the tragic and the desperate, because they bring meaning and life back into our existences.

Another fact: My mother prizes three things above all others:

The rose garden which my father planted for her before I was born. It runs in spirals along the bluffs and the small hillock behind our cottage. There are fourteen varieties of roses, with hues ranging from pale peach to blood red.

Her koi pond, which is really the Montgomery's koi pond, but it sits on our side of the property. It is largish for a pond, and narrow, nearly a reflecting pool. It was built deep for the harsh winters—the koi can survive a thick layer of ice as long as they can bury themselves down in the silt. My father covers the pool with a plastic tarp to further protect the fish.

And lastly, my mother prizes the gun.

My maternal grandfather had a small pistol that had been given to him by his mother. It was a small Colt pistol—what my grandfather called a vest pistol, but which I thought of as a Saturday Night Special. It had mother-of-pearl grips, and a clip that could not be removed from it. My grandfather had given my mother the pistol in the early years of her marriage for when my father would beat her. My father never beat my mother, but my grandfather would apparently not believe it. The pistol is useless, I heard my mother once say. Never been fired. I could barely shoot a cat with it, she joked. Someday, she told me, when she was weepy and bitter about life, she would go to Boston and sell it to a collector and take the money and go far, far away. When I first discovered my true god and his nature, I took the pistol.

Final fact:

Faith plays into all this. One must have faith that one can do what one sets out to do. One must have the courage of one's convictions. All the world's history teaches us this.

For me, it is that god I discovered.

I call it Dagon, although its name is unknown to me. It came from the sea, and I held it captive, briefly. I am its priest.

And Dagon, in a twisted and true way, upholds what I stand for.

One must stand for something.

For me, it is the force of love.

The undertow of love.

But that sounds romantic, and I'm not a romantic at all.

I've been called a lot of things since the day I was born; never romantic.

Schemer. Athlete. Brain. Manipulator. User. Common. Handsome. Shallow. Arrogant. Mad. Sociopath. Cold eyes.

All by my mother.

Jenna Montgomery once told me I had the most beautiful eyes she'd ever seen on a boy.

I had to catch my breath when she told me that.

She said it the same day I made the first sacrifice to the god I'd met.

2

Years ago, I came upon the god during a storm of late November, a frozen, bitter storm, in which I had gotten caught down at the caverns, taking a dinghy out to look for the famous buried pirate treasure. I was twelve and lonely, and when I saw the god thrust in between a rock and a hard place, as it were, I knew immediately who and what it was, and how I should please it. I read in my father's bible that Dagon was the god of the Philistines; the Fish-God. I found other books, too, with titles like *The Shadow Over Innsmouth* and *Dagon* that further told of the god and its worshippers and what was needed to feed the god.

Some may say it is just an abominable statue, a cheap and even grotesque trinket of some distant bazaar, brought by sailors or perhaps even the pirates. It is green with age, and made wholly of stone. Its eyes are merely garnet; its tail and fins carved with some exquisite artistry.

But when I bled a seagull over the cold eyes of the little god, while the storm raged around me, I felt a prayer had been answered.

I breathed easier then.

3

Breathing is essential to survival, and although this seems like a given, we know—scientifically—that it is not. Most of the problems of life are like that: simple, obvious, graspable, yet shrouded in a secret.

If one can breathe well—through any crisis, and exertion—then one will survive.

It is those who stop breathing who have let go of their wills to live.

I am what people in this world call a sociopath, although the idea of killing someone has never interested me. A sociopath is not necessarily a killer, and to assume this is to play a dangerous game. Just as not all famous people are rich, not all sociopaths are Jeffrey Dahmer. If Jeffrey was one at all. You must know this about me if you're going to understand exactly what went on at Outerbridge Island the summer I turned eighteen, the summer before Jenna Montgomery was to leave me forever.

They say that people like me can't experience love, but I find that a ridiculous statement. I'm fully capable of giving and receiving love, and it is monstrous to suggest otherwise. Even all those years ago I was, and love burned in me just as it did any boy who had fallen.

My mother would take her daily pain pill as I grew up—her pains being life itself and even her child — and tell me that there were two kinds of people in this world, the kind that give and the kind that take, and I knew I was neither, but somewhere in between the rest of the world: I was someone who observed, perhaps too coldly sometimes. I still observe, and observation has brought me to this place again.

Outerbridge Island, with its rocky ledges and glassy sea, the fog that came suddenly, the sun that tore through clouds like a nuclear explosion, the summers that went for years; the years that passed in a summer.

The storms that came and stayed and never left.

4

Let me turn it all back to the day I was born, since from what I've read about sociopaths, it's fairly genetic. My grandmother was probably the carrier of the gene, since she went crazy and ended up in what they called a nursing home over in Massachusetts, but which I found out—later in life, of course—was an impoverished sanitarium, the sort of which nightmares are born. My mother told me that it was my grandfather's fault for driving her to do things—again, not kill, for we have never been murderers—just things that caused people to believe my grandmother was insane. When I was born, my mother told me when I was eleven or twelve, I was a difficult birth and my own umbilical cord practically strangled me as I exited her body. She said I was blue in the face for nearly a minute from lack of oxygen before the doctor got me coughing. Then, I spent the first two weeks of my life in the hospital, for I was a month premature and no one thought I would live.

643

Sometimes I think this is why I'm a sociopath. I've seen documentaries on PBS about baby monkeys who are separated from their mothers for a short time, and this makes them seem without conscience (if that is truly what a sociopath is, although I don't believe it). My mother said she didn't touch me for the first month; she was terrified I'd die, and because she had already lost one child—two years earlier—in some kind of crib death scenario, she feared holding her first son, me. My father had to do all the touching and picking up, and even—my mother told me—when I had to nurse from her breast, she was too terrified. Instead, my aunt became my wet nurse—she who had, just five months before, given birth to twins and seemed to have milk enough for the entire population of the island. There were times, when I was older, that I wished my aunt had taken me back with her to her home on the mainland. Times when I hated the island. Hated my mother and father. Hated looking at the Montgomery house—the Montgomery Mansion, the Montgomery palazzo, the Big Place—staring down at us. But I suppose all this anger came about because of those first few days of life.

These things aren't spoken of much in families—how we each came to be. My mother suffered through bouts of depression, particularly in the winter, and she would stand in front of her bedroom window, looking out across the Sound, her face a shimmering reflection in the thick windowglass, and tell me all about myself.

She told me that when I was six weeks old, she realized I had never really cried, at least not the way babies were supposed to. Instead, I would turn red, and my mouth would open, and I'd scream. That's how she'd know I was hungry or needed changing. Because she was so grateful to have a child after she felt God had taken away her first in retribution for youthful transgressions, she tried not to think about what my lack of tears might mean.

As she'd tell this kind of story, I'd shift uncomfortably on her bed, wishing she'd release me from this kind of intimacy—the closeness of her depression, the morbid way her mind would pick over my birth and early years.

"I'm so sorry that you turned out this way," she said, once, her hands going up to her face. "I'm happy you're so smart. Not like your father. But this madness that comes over you...."

I remained silent, letting her have her feelings. I didn't understand then to what she referred—I was not mad. I took the ferry to go to school over on the mainland and did quite well in school. The ferry takes an hour and a half in the winter, and only runs twice a day—for school hours, since Outerbridge had no school of its own. Thus, I spent many nights with my Aunt Susan in Rhode Island, and learned more about my mother's mother than I had ever wanted to know. I also managed—through my cousin Davy—to make friends off-island, friends who believed I was like them. And I had a lot of friends as a child. Although I was not considered handsome at first—at least by my mother who found my hair to be too ominous in some way, my eyes too blue and perhaps too sharp, my manner arrogant (even as an eight-year-old, she'd called me that)—I began learning the secret of athletics early, and applied myself to molding my body the same way I went about molding my mind: I studied and read and found the boys who seemed to know what they were doing, and I gravitated towards them. I learned what they knew by nature. I was uncoordinated in most sports, until I realized that, as in all things, it was about breathing.

This is one of the secrets of life: it's all about breathing.

5

Voices in the dark:

"It's all right, I know you. I know what we both want."

"Shut up. Just shut up."

"Come here. Come here. Let me help you. It's all right. It feels good."

"No, not like this. No."

"I've been so lonely."

"Oh."

"Wanting this."

"Oh."

"Since the first time I saw you."

"Oh."

6

Have you ever felt that you would do anything to be with someone?

I almost feel sorry for you, if you haven't.

7

The purity of life is in the secrets—they're simple, they say everything, they are there for anyone, but we must wake up to the purity first in order to understand the secrets.

My pursuit of physical excellence began early. I tackled solitary athletics since this seemed best for my character. They were also cheaper. My family was poor—have I mentioned that? Not poor

poor. Not "out in the street with no food" poor, but poor nonetheless. My mother's first husband had been rich, but had been a gambler. My mother—I should call her Boston, for that's what my father called her even though her name was Helen—had been the fifth daughter in a wealthy family who had married well the first time around. But that man—someone I had never in my life heard of beyond knowing he existed—apparently lost all his and Helen's money, and soon she found my father, a good man one would suppose, who began his work life as a groundskeeper at the Smithsonian Museum in Washington, DC, but ended up working as a gardener for rich folk. It paid well enough—like I said, we weren't poor poor.

My father probably would've had more money, but he had a sister who was dying—for years—down in Annapolis, Maryland, and he was her only support. So, according to my mother, half of his income went to her upcoming. "She has the longest-lived cancer I've ever heard of," she'd say, sometime right in front of him.

Of course, this wasn't all there was to it, but if I tell you all the secrets of the world at once, you'll either be dazzled or overwhelmed, and there's no point in making it all explode right now. You'll want to know why breathing is one of the secrets of life.

All right, do you know how breathing is voluntary? I've heard that people with dementia sometimes end up forgetting how to breathe. That's a terrible way to die, although one would suppose that any method of dying would be awful. Well, breathing is the essential component of accomplishing anything.

I observed this early—I was on the school bus, and I noticed a little girl next to me who was terrified of an upcoming test we were about to take. She would, in fact, stop breathing for seconds at a time. I began to count her breaths, and I saw that for every four I took, she took one. I suggested to her that she try just concentrating on her breathing. After a bit of persuasion, she did. It didn't seem to work. I withdrew my father's pocketwatch—the one I'd stolen (yes, I stole things regularly around the house. I have reasons, none of which you want to know.) I had learned a bit about hypnosis, so I asked her to stare long and hard at the brass of the watch as the sunlight reflected on it. She asked me if I'd be putting her under. I told her no.

This was, after all, just suggestion, nothing more. I would suggest something to her and would hope that her mind would accept it. Of course, I was a child. I didn't say it that way. I said it in some little boy way. But eventually, staring at the watch so much that her eyes teared up, I began to help modulate her breathing. By the time we reached school, she wasn't half upset anymore about the test.

I began asking the other boys—the older ones who were good at softball and running—what their secrets were. To get their secrets, I entertained them with my modest ventriloquism skills—I could do bird calls and the sounds of crickets and even get brief sentences out without moving my lips.

Boys like entertainment—so they opened up and told me about athletics and sports. They all said screwy things, but what I noticed were two solid answers: breathing and imagination.

They made sure that they breathed through everything. They also imagined that they would win.

This was a huge revelation to me, since I had never felt that I could win anything. I realized that these other boys were winners in athletics because they in fact believed they were—whether from coaches, friends, family or whomever—and because they did not stop breathing. They used their breathing—without even knowing it—to help keep their bodies working.

647

All right, that sounds simplistic. I believe that the simplest things can lead to the strongest results.

So, I began working on breathing.

This was not merely inhaling and exhaling, but swimming at the beach in the icy spring and holding my breath under water. After all, if I were going to be lord of my own breath, I needed to master everything about it, didn't I? I wasn't sure that I'd ever be a great breath-holder, because I never seemed able to go much beyond a minute. I was holding on too much to my fear of dying. This is one of the first lessons about breathing—if you have breath within your lungs, you will not die. Death comes once there is no more breath.

Again, simple. Again, true.

"Owen," my mother said, pinning the laundry up outside the cottage that the Montgomery's housed us in. "What in god's name are you doing?"

I had come up after logging in a minute-and-a-half beneath the water, right at the rocky ledge. I had just leaned over and thrust my face underwater. I was eleven at the time. I tried to explain to her the principle behind my experiment, but she did not seem to understand. However, within a few short months, I had become best friends to the captain of the swim team in 7th grade, and by fall, I was running cross country. I would never be the best—this was not my goal after all. I would be a winner.

In fact, I knew I would close in on this with each sport or endeavor I tried—the other kids were lazy. Life and their families made them that way. I did not intend to let a day go which I could not claim was my own. I was going to own life in a way that neither of my parents ever had.

Academics slipped in my middle school years—but not enough for anyone to notice. I read studiously, and never for enjoyment, but to understand systems of thought that the world was trying to push at us. I learned quickly that an A+ in school sometimes meant a D- in life, and that in fact equal effort had to be made to excel in both spheres. Breathing helped. When I felt overwhelmed by it all, I practiced my breathing again. Even in December, when the island was desolate and the water was enough to drown, I would leap into the sea and stay beneath the water for as long as I could; I would, if possible, use the Montgomery's indoor swimming pool for my morning workout which began at six a.m.

8

That was the wonderful thing about the Montgomery's place:

They were usually gone all winter unless Mr. And Mrs. Montgomery were fighting, or Mr. Montgomery had gone off with one of his mistresses and Mrs. M was so angry she came to the island for a blisteringly cold February. I used to see Mrs. M in those cold Februarys, and I ran errands in town for her because she spent too much time staring at the walls or sitting along the indoor pool while I did laps. She enjoyed letting me swim there, and she sometimes even got in and did laps, too. Once, when I was twelve, Mrs. M told me, "You're turning into quite the handsome boy, Owen

Crites." She was in good shape for a woman of forty, and there were times when I was with her that she reminded me so much of Jenna it was almost like having Jenna there with me. When I watched her back, as she got out of the pool, bathing cap on, her narrow waist, the way the water beaded upon her skin—it was like seeing Jenna for a moment. This made me happy. Jenna meant a lot to me.

But the pool—dare I describe it now, how I remember it? It was vast. It was Olympic size. I could do real laps there as opposed to laps at the beach which ended with a summer lifeguard blowing a whistle for me to come to shore before I'd gone out twenty yards. It was off the southern wing of their estate, and had glass surround it, so that it was as if you were swimming outside, as if on the bluffs over the Sound, you owned the world as you went back and forth, breathing, carefully breathing so as not to wear out too fast.

Because, during those winters when the M's stayed down in Manhattan, my father and mother and I had the run of the house, I could swim naked in the pool, and rise to see the reflection of my body in the long mirrors that were in the small lockerroom off the pool. By my sophomore year in high school, I had created—and mastered—a beautiful, strong body, and what average looks I had were masked by health and physical near-perfection. I didn't admire this because I believed in beauty.

649

Beauty is for the lazy.

I admired it because I knew the world admired it, and I wanted to own the world.

Wrestling was my winter sport at school, and I did not excel at it, but I held my own. The girls loved me—and the boys, too. I never got too close to them, because I had to spend all my concentration on creating who I was. But the girls all cheered for me in the sweaty matches as I brought some great bull of a boy from a competing school down to the red mat. Because the psychological aspect to sports can't be emphasized enough, I would—with each match—create some threat to my opponent. Something I could whisper in his ear.

This took no small planning, as it meant I had to do research on those I wrestled, so I would know just what button to push to take away their psychological edge. Dagon helped me; my god took me to books and ideas and notions, if you will, that showed me just what other boys would be most hurt by. Usually, it involved their sense of sexuality. After all, even I knew that showering with other boys all day, wearing jockstraps, cracking jokes about everything from dicks to pussies, was a veil across homoeroticism among adolescents. And who but wrestlers were closest to puncturing that veil? So, I would whisper to my opponent something about him, something perhaps his closest friend had told me—his closest friend, drunk, being taken out to a parking lot—his closest friend who, with six beers in him, would finally admit to something that my opponent would be happiest to hide for a thousand years.

Sometimes, it was less interesting. My threat might be, "I know your little sister, Trey. I know all about her leg. I would hate for something to happen to her. I would hate for someone to do something to a little girl so sweet."

650

You may judge me for this if you like. It was a competitive edge, and this is what we, in athletics, were taught: to find our edge.

Skill alone never wins.

I wish it did, but lazy people think that way.

Faith is necessary, too. I had found mine. It had grown within me.

Now, this began rumors about me, but I had built up a loyal following of other boys and girls in school. I became head of the pep squad for the football team—team sports were never my thing, but I knew that I had to somehow attach myself to them. So, when kids from other schools began talking about me saying "crazy, psycho" things, I had friends who were willing to lay down and die for me rather than accept those lies. I really liked the kids I went to high school with; I liked the teachers. It was easy for me to like them. I think even being poor helped—teachers saw me as an underdog rising. I would tutor children in the local elementary school some afternoons; I took the coach's daughter to the junior prom, just because I was a nice guy and I felt bad that she wasn't pretty enough to get asked by any of the other guys. I was well-liked, and sometimes, that carries you.

But I haven't mentioned much about Jenna yet, have I? In all this talk of I, she has not yet entered—not in the way she should've. She was not at my school. She was not within my sphere. She was outer, she was beyond beyond.

How could I take her to the prom when she only arrived at Outerbridge Island in the summers?

I would count the days until Memorial Day weekend, when the Outerbridge Majesty would arrive in Quonnoquet Haven, heavy with tourists and summer people, and there, on the highest deck, I'd see her with my binos and I would lay back in the muddy grass and look up at the paling sky and think: please remember what we promised. Remember everything and don't leave anything out.

Remember why I came to you and why you let me and why it would make everything be the way it was supposed to, and why you're the reason for my every breath.

That's what had happened when I was twelve and dedicated my soul to the god of dark places. By the time I was seventeen, I was a dedicated servant to the one I worshipped.

And the only thing I asked of this divinity was:

Give me Jenna.

I found a cat over in town, and with just a pen knife, offered its soul to my god.

651

9

I'll tell you now, that it's safe, what really happened the summer that I discovered purity—genuine purity—in the shit of human existence. I can see myself as I was then, handsome, young, even pretty in a way with my thick hair falling to either side of my face, my blue eyes sharp, yes, but expectant. My shirt is an Izod, a preppie affectation—my mother never wanted me to look like the other islanders, she wanted something better for me, as did I. Khakis, no socks, Topsiders or sandals—my face burning from the beginnings of summer sun, my heart racing. It's no longer me as I am, it's that boy, that boy who is almost eighteen, a man at this point, a man who has nearly won in life.

I, he, you, it doesn't matter what I call that boy-man, he just is, I can feel his breath, I can smell the Old Spice on him, I can practically see the cap on his front tooth that cost his father a pretty penny after he fell and chipped it in sixth grade while he was running—I can practically see the fog lift between this day and that one.

He watches for her.

Chapter Two:
Memorial Day, Restless Nights, and an Open Window

1

Let me take you there.

Fly like a bird over the crotch of New England—that place where Rhode Island clutches at its small corner between Massachusetts and Connecticut, and out to the Sound, across the scattering of islands and islets and outlands until you see the One Man Rocks, the places where misanthropists going by the name of New Englanders lived two to three per islet—and then, beyond the beyond, as my mother would say, thar she blows—Outerbridge, Outerbridge, Outerbridge. The name conjures up older names, and for me—or for him, for the me who was, Owen Crites, the Dutch fighting the Indians, the pirates burying treasure beneath the land, and the people who built the walls. It even conjures all the names it must have had before, when the gods themselves had granted it some secret name. If Owen had known the secret name, he might have had power over it, but as it was, the island was master, and all who occupied its ground, servants.

The island's history began eons ago when some glacial giant swept the rocks and earth into the Atlantic and the world grew up around it. The Pequot and Narragansett Indians held it against the Dutch for as long as they could, and then the Brits wrested it for themselves. The island never provided much in the way of existence for any of its inhabitants; all that's left of the early English settlers were walls made of stone and foundations of cottages that speckle the northern end of Outerbridge (originally called a Dutch name that had sounded to the English like Outerbridge although there was a movement afoot among the summer residents to restore the old Pequot name for the place.) The largest beach, called the Serpentine by the British for its snaky shape, runs the western length. A Victorian Wedding Cake House called the Mohegan, converted in recent years to a twenty room hotel, sits perched on the main bluff overlooking the most public part of the Serpentine. On either sides are the summer homes—the large and the ordinary, and the woods all mixed in and winding through them. More than half the roads on Outerbridge were still dirt; there was no McDonald's, no 7-11, and only two stoplights between the three townships.

Spring shat out of winter in New England—and along the uneven row of islands called the Avalons that skirted Connecticut, Rhode Island, and a bare tip of Massachusetts, it was a heavy crap of rain and then sun and then rain and finally sun—the merciless summer sun which never left until two weeks after Labor Day. Outerbridge had it the worse, for the two other large Avalons—and the smaller rocky ledges called islets that formed part of the coastal barrier against the Atlantic—got the good weather first, or else no one much lived there to care.

Outerbridge, the furthest up the coastline was more narrow than wide—six miles long, two-and-a-half miles wide—with bluffs to the south and north, the Great Salt Pond at its center, the Wequetaket swamps in the lower points to the east; there are two hundred and fifty three summer residents; there are 75 in the winter, most of them over 60. At the height of winter's cruelty, helicopters come in with supplies. That sounds outrageous, but it's true, for Outerbridge is further from the mainland than even the Vineyard and Nantucket to the north—it is beyond beyond beyond, and there is no crossing easily. The historic landmarks are South Light and North Light, the two lighthouses that still work, sentries at either end of the island; Old Town, or Old Town Harbor as the old-timers call it, is at the southern tip; Quonnoquet Haven, with its bluffs and spectacular view of what they call the Big Nothing, where even the mainland is unseen in the distance, lays to the north of the island

This particular day was the glinting kind. Sun glinted off the Sound, and even the virgin leaves on the wet trees—and the bark, too—all of it spattered light refracted through the hangover of the night of rain so recently over. He hated it—he hated the end of winter, because it was usually the end of control within his parents house. His mother had been in bed for most of it, nursing imagined traumas, while his father had spent his hours away from home, either working as a handyman and gardener at the Big House, or in town or down to Old Town Harbor for drinks with his friends.

Owen Crites looked to summer for one thing, and one thing only. It would be the arrival of Jenna Montgomery, and that would mean that his misery, his feeling of loneliness would vanish.

It was a singular obsession of his.

She was purity.

655

2

"Hi," he said to her when he was six.

"Hi," she replied. But she hadn't needed to. She was six and all ringlets and ribbons and party dress.

"Owen," he said.

"I know. Hank's your daddy."

The fact that she called his father by his first name shocked Owen. No other child called a parent by the first name. It was taboo. And to call his father "Hank" and not "Henry" seemed far too familiar.

"I know where you live," she added, an afterthought.

"Here," he said, meaning her property.

"In my yard," she said. "You have the big goldfish pond."

"Koi," he corrected her.

"And all the roses my mommy loves," she said, and then took him by the hand and brought him into her world—the birthday party, the children from New York, the pony rides on the bluffs, the smoked turkey sandwiches, the games of pin-the-tail, and the dance. He had been woefully underdressed in a torn pair of jeans and a t-shirt. The other boys all wore white shirts and little ties; their hair glistened with gel. The girls were in puffy dresses and glittery shoes. He had no gift for her then. It had panicked him midway through the party.

He went and found a gift she had not yet unwrapped, and he threw away the other child's card. On the wrapping paper, he scrawled—*Hapy Birthday from Owen*. As it turned out, the gift was a small hand puppet, and Owen took it from Jenna and began doing something that he didn't even know he could do.

He threw his voice, so it sounded as if the puppet were speaking without Owen's lips moving.

When it was found out what he had done, he was punished, but even Mrs. M commented to Owen's mother about her son's delightful talent.

But forget that for now, forget it. Years passed; punishment was the result of knowledge. Smart people punished themselves, his older self knew. All people with brains received punishment.

He had only recently turned seventeen.

He knew better than to reveal secrets.

He waited for her, watching the Sound for the ferry on the Thursday before Memorial Day weekend.

3

His eyes turned to slits against the western sun; it was the last ferry of the day, and he couldn't find her or her parents among those on the deck.

Perhaps she wouldn't be coming until after the holiday—it happened before, but several years back. He didn't want to believe it because he never liked to consider the options that people had. His own life felt without option. He had created within himself the person who could most handle his life. He had worked his body, developed the grace of an athlete, he had tried to keep his face pleasant—and when the anxieties of his family or of studies became unbearable, he would go to the mirror and practice relaxing his facial features until he was sure he looked pleasant again. He did not want to seem anxious, even if he was. He wanted to give nothing away to those around him.

He ran down to the docks to see if she might be somewhere else on the ferry—perhaps she was sick and wanted to stay below. Perhaps she was taking a nap in the back seat of her family's Range Rover. Perhaps perhaps, he repeated to himself as he sloughed off inertia, and jogged down to the paved road near the marina.

The summer people were like ticks—they attached themselves to every aspect of the Haven, they drank all the beer, they ate the best the local cooks had to offer, they had all the accidents—more people would die from boating or swimming mishaps in three months than would die in six years in the other seasons of the island.

They were careless, they were bloodsucking, they were here to forget the venal world from which they came.

They, he thought. They. They debarked the ferry, bicyclists, clownish men and women in golfing outfits, or overly gilded women with poodles and wolfhounds and shih tzus, followed by weary overworked doctor-husbands; the college crowd, too, had begun filling up the local bars and the beach, and all these he hated with a passion. He had spent his life watching them come and be carefree in the summer. He had watched them spend more money some nights than his father could make in a month.

657

Dagon, he prayed, Dagon, hear me. Cast them down. Raise me up.

He ached for what they had. The lives they had. The freedom from this island. From the world he had mastered.

He read books on Manhattan; he learned about Jenna's family, how her great-great-grandfather had worked on railroads and then had gone on to own them, and how her great-grandfather had lost that fortune; how her grandfather had gotten into radio and television and magazines, owning several, selling them, building up a small but substantial media empire; how her mother had continued that work, married a great media magnate, divorced, married again, had Jenna and remained with Mr. M although the marriage ran hot and cold.

The story of Jenna's family was the story of all the summer people, and though they lived simply on the island for the three months, though they rode cheap bikes around the Big Salt Pond, though they dressed casually even for the one restaurant in Old Town Harbor (the Salty Dog), they were all overmoneyed as his father often said.

His father spoke of money as evil; his mother spoke of it like a lost child.

Owen felt it was something like fire—to be feared and mastered. It was what other people were given.

It's what he would be granted.

And these people tromping off the ferry had it. They lived it. They did not dream of getting off this island. They dreamed of things beyond what Owen could imagine.

4

She never arrived, and he walked the long narrow wooden staircase from the beach up to the bluffs; and then he ran along the fringe of pines to the dirt path the went further up the rolling cliffs; and he didn't look back down to the water until he was at their property.

At the house, he went and sat in one of them wrought-iron lawn chairs and leaned back to gaze up at the sky.

"Owen?"

He sat up, looking around. He rose from the chair, practically knocking it over, and there she was—at the third story attic window.

No, it was Mrs. M. Her auburn hair was swept back from her face, damp from the swimming pool; her robe fastened none too tight. She possessed the air of having enjoyed life too much that day. "Owen? It's good to see you."

"Yeah, Mrs. M, me too. I didn't think you had got here just yet."

"Oh, my husband still hasn't left his desk yet. I've been here since Wednesday. Good to be back. I despise the city."

"Survive winter okay?"

"Superbly," she said, but in a way that meant its opposite. Mrs. M was a woman full of irony; he had known it for years. Mrs. M. embodied the house: beautiful, classic, and rich. "Do you want coffee?" she asked.

5

"I saw you waiting for her," Mrs. M said. They were in the sun room off the kitchen, and Owen had just finished his first cup of cinnamon coffee. He got up to pour himself another, but Mrs. M interceded; she had a fresh cup, with cream, all ready for him. He sat down at the table again. She took the chair across from him. He saw her knee emerge from her robe. The hint of her champagne glass breasts, small but perfect. Mrs. M was in many way more beautiful than her daughter; but still, his heart belonged to Jenna.

He did what he could to look at her face, but something in her eyes bothered him. He looked, instead, at her silken arms.

"You're in love with my daughter. No, that's fine. I've known it since you were both young. Do you think it will lead anywhere?"

"Lead?" He said the word innocently, but she must've seen through this. "I don't know."

"Yes, you do. You're smart. I've watched you grow up. You're smart and handsome and wise. But, do you think that she will have you?"

"I haven't…I haven't considered…" he stammered.

"You're a remarkable young man," Mrs. M said. "She doesn't deserve you." Then, she put down her own untouched coffee, and stood up from the table. "She gets in tonight. After midnight."

"How? The ferry—"

"She has her ways," Mrs. M said. She brushed something from the edge of her eye, and combed her hands through her hair like a mermaid would. "Fancy a swim?"

"Not today," he said.

"Come on, just a nice long swim. Have you been practicing all winter?"

He nodded.

"I thought so. You ripple now. You don't move, you ripple. You're in better shape than he is," Mrs. M said, and then went to get her bathing suit.

6

Come midnight, he saw the shroud of some sailboat press beneath the lights of the harbor. He sat up on the bluffs and watched as she docked; as the sail came down. No one stepped off the boat at the jetty. Was it her? Was this what Mrs M had meant?

He fell asleep in the cool wet grass and awoke at dawn.

And he knew.

Jenna Montgomery had found another.

7

"Jimmy," the guy said, his face gleaming, tanned, teeth so much thoroughbred he could've been in Pimlico, his eyes squinty, his nose small, his hair honey-blond from too much sun, and his handshake strong and sure and arrogant. He looked rich without ever having to say it. He smelled rich. He probably tasted rich. "Good to meet you, Crites."

"Owen."

"You're not an Owen or a Crites," Jimmy said. "You're a Mooncalf."

"Mooncalf?" Jenna laughed, looking at Owen and then back at Jimmy. "That sounds ghastly." She wore a bikini, but had a long towel draped about her waist that ran all the way to her ankles. Her hair was wet and shining from a morning swim. For a moment, Owen imagined how it would feel to untie the bikini top and press his face against her breasts. For a moment, the image was in his mind; then, gone.

All Owen could think was: they'd slept together on the boat. Jenna and this Jimmy character. Jimmy had done it with Jenna.

Done it.

A sacred act if it was love.

A debased ritual, if it was lust and emptiness.

Which it had to be.

He tried not to imagine Jimmy drawing her legs apart, or the scent of passion that clung to them, the sweat and fever, as they joined together.

Tried not to imagine the thrusts.

"Mooncalf reminds me of upstate New York, or Pennsylvania," Jenna said with no little disgust. "Cows and chickens. Amish in carriages. Birthings and midwives. Owen can't be a Mooncalf."

Jim snorted. "No, it's a beautiful name. Mooncalf."

Owen remained silent, still numb from meeting the interloper.

"Well, if he's a Mooncalf then what am I?"

"Kitten," Jimmy laughed.

"If I'm Kitten, then you're Cat."

"All right, then I'm Cat. Now, what shall we call this island?"

"Outerbridge," Owen said. "Call it Outerbridge."

"That's not the game," Jimmy grinned, and damn if his smile wasn't dazzling. Anyone would fall in love with this guy, anyone, man, woman, or dog, he was so damn attractive and warm, it made Owen want to walk away and forget about Jenna completely. "The game is everything, Mooncalf. It doesn't matter what things are. You shape them into the way you want them. That's how you gain mastery."

661

"Mastery's the thing," Owen said, faking a sort of blissful—and very nearly nonchalant—take on all of it.

I'll beat you, he thought as he watched his rival, this apollonian boy with his golden hair and squinty green eyes and the way he had arrogance that was absolutely seductive.

I will beat you, Owen made the oath then and there. He glanced briefly up at the unfettered sun and prayed to God that if nothing else went his way in this life, he would beat down this Jimmy.

Then, Owen reached a hand out and gave Jimmy's shoulder a friendly squeeze. "Just not big on games I guess."

Jenna laughed, "Owen, the game is called Paradise. You rename everything to your liking. Jimmy invented it. Isn't it…marvelous?" She pecked the bastard on his ear. Owen noted: the kiss went to his earlobe, and Jimmy barely had an earlobe. His ear was smooth and rounded and touched down right behind one of his several dimples.

Jimmy laughed, shrugging, grabbing her around the waist and pulling her close to him. "Let's call the island Sea Biscuit."

"No," Jenna groaned. "That's terrible. Terrible. Owen, you name it."

"Outerbridge," Owen said.

It was noon, and they were at the jetty. The sailboat bobbed gently with the current, and Owen finally took his baseball cap off.

"There now," Jimmy said, approvingly. "You look less like a little boy than like a man. The Mooncalf has such pretty hair for a moody guy." He reached over and scruffed his hand through Owen's hair. His fingers felt electric. "I know the name for this island. I know. It's called Bermuda. We're in Bermuda," he laughed, leaning into Jenna, kissing her just behind her ear.

No, Owen thought. You're in the realm of Dagon.

8

A restless night came to him, and then another and another. He lay on his single bed, sheets pulled back, and a fever such as he had never before felt washed over him.

Whosoever has loved the way I love Jenna Montgomery, he whispered to the stars through his bedroom window, has known sacrifice and torture and days and nights of endless wanting, thirst without satisfaction, hunger without morsel. Whosoever has wept within themselves for what they could not reach, could not touch, has felt what I feel.

Whosoever has spent his life working his body, mind, and soul to its absolute limit to be the extreme candidate for the love of a beautiful and angelic girl as I have for her, as I have given myself to the shape that she would long for...

That man would not rest were a rival to steal the prize from him.

Dagon, he whispered soundlessly. Dagon. My god. Bring her to me.

Eventually, Owen Crites slept better imagining the world under the sea where the people who were part of the Dagon had dwelt, with their vast and imperious citadels, their large cold eyes and their wet shapeless forms, and he imagined the great sacrifice he would throw to them for their entertainment.

9

"How are you going to waste your last summer?" Owen's mother asked as she switched off the faucet, plunging her hands back into the soapy water. "Now, don't blot, Owen, dry. There's a difference." She passed him the first dish, which he sprayed down and then wiped with the green-and-white hand towel. The kitchen in the caretaker's house was as narrow as one of the closets in the big house; but the window looked out on a small sunken garden; behind which, the pine trees stuck out like crooked teeth. "Don't blot," his mother repeated.

Owen began stacking the dry plates carefully. "I need a job."

"You work for your father."

"Not this summer," he replied. "Hank'll do without me."

"Hank?" his mother said, nearly laughing. "Hank? Next you'll be calling me Trudy." Then, her mood darkened. "Show some respect." His mother reached down to pull the plug on the drain. She reached back to her hairpins, pulling them out so that her gray-streaked hair fell along her shoulders. She smoothed it back, and turned to watch him dry the rest of the plates and bowls from supper. "I know what you're thinking."

He glanced at her for the barest moment.

"You're thinking that you'll work down where she goes at night. The restaurant. The dock. You'll be there for the dances. I've seen the boys working at those places. They live here all year 'round. But in the summer, sometimes they get the rich girls. But those girls don't care about them. The boys are just part of summer to those girls. Just like the beach. Just like a walk."

He remained silent, and kept his eyes on each bowl as he carefully wiped the towel through them.

"I grew up in her world. I know what she'd have to give up. Don't ask her to do it. Not if you care about her," his mother said. Then, she nearly snickered.

"What's funny?" he asked.

"I remember your father at your age, is all. I remember him so well," she said. "He's working on the pump now. The pump and the well. Today he worked on the azaleas and the roses. Tomorrow, he'll probably check the pool. If I had only known then. Owen, you might as well go find that pirate treasure as think that a girl like that will be interested in you beyond these summerish flings."

Owen dropped the towel on top of the cutting board, and turned to walk away. "I know what you get up to," his mother called to him, but he had already stepped out of the house, letting the screen door swing lazily shut. "You're nearly a man, Owen. You need to grow out of all your imaginings now."

Her voice, behind him, was part of another layer of existence. The smell of fresh grass mingled with the slight scent of the roses which were just blooming in spirals and curves up on the bluffs.

He walked to the edge of the hill, feeling the late sun stroke him like a warm hand. At the rim of the koi pond, he knelt down and looked at his reflection in the green water. Soon, the patchwork fish came to the surface. He reached his hand into the murkiness, shivering with the chill, and found the god laying where he'd left it, behind the lava rocks.

He felt the edge of the god's face.

10

In a school notebook, Owen wrote:
Things Jenna likes.
1. She loves swing dancing.
2. She likes expensive perfume. The kind older women wear. Not like other girls.
3. She likes sandals.
4. She likes to let a boy open a door for her.
5. She likes clothes from Manhattan.
6. She likes to be complimented on how smart she is.
7. She likes someone who listens to her.
8. She likes holding hands.

Things Jenna hates:
1. She hates heavy metal rock.
2. She hates boys who look at her breasts.
3. She hates having to wait for anything. Ever.
4. She hates Julia Roberts movies. She reminds me of movie stars though.
5. She hates when animals get hurt.
6. She hates being treated like a piece of meat.
7. She hates boys who want to go all the way because she told me three years ago that she's going to wait for the right one.
8. She hates having to do things she hates.

11

He waited a week before going back up to the Montgomery place, and even then, it was after eleven, and the house was dark and silent except for the kitchen, where Mrs. M always kept a light on. At first, he intended to stand beneath Jenna's bedroom window and maybe toss a pebble at it to get her attention. He noticed that the window—on the third story—was open, and he decided he'd call to her.

Then, he noticed that one of the guest room windows was open, too.

That would be Jimmy's. The bastard.

Owen glanced along the trellis and gutters, and decided he'd try that route first. He climbed the trellis with the agility of a monkey, although it threatened to pull away if he didn't balance his weight just right. It wasn't much different from the rope climb in gym. When he worried that he wouldn't make it to the third story roof, he remembered the breathing trick and began inhaling and exhaling carefully. That was where the balance was: in the breathing. Then, he grabbed the raingutter, and scaled the slant of the roof. He crawled along it, slowly, cautiously, and went to look in on Jenna while she slept. He felt himself grow hard, imagining how he could hold her while she slept, imagining how he would smell her hair.

665

When he looked through the open window, he saw the other boy there, Jimmy, in bed with her, holding her, moving against her.

Owen caught his breath and held it for what felt like the longest time. He could hold his breath underwater for a few minutes, and holding it now while he watched Jimmy press himself into her, like a hummingbird jabbing at a flower, but not as pretty, just dark and murky, Jimmy's body rising and falling as he plunged into her, not gently the way she would want it, but like he was a jackal tearing apart some carcass.

666

Chapter Three:
The Morning Swim

1

"The Salty Dog," Owen said, lifting himself from the swimming pool. "Waiting tables. Since Memorial Day weekend. Lifting weights, too."

"That must be delightful," Mrs. M said. She stood near the changing rooms, swathed in a red bathrobe, dark glasses covering her eyes. She looked like a movie star. She had a cigarette in her hand, which she waved dramatically. "I imagine you meet lots of girls and boys your age at that dive."

"Some."

"You're still very young for your age," she said, and then caught her breath for a moment. "I'm sorry. I didn't mean that in a negative way. I meant it as…as…you're so innocent compared to the boys at that school she goes to. They've already begun those patterns they'll have for life." She exhaled a lungful of smoke. She was like a beautiful dragon, he thought. A jade dragon with sparkling eyes.

Owen drew himself up over the pool's edge. He exhaled deeply; coughing.

"My smoking bother you?"

"No," he said, swiveling to sit down more comfortably, his legs still in the water. "Just holding my breath. Trying, anyway."

"Trying to reach some goal? Underwater?" She took her sunglasses off, and dropped them carelessly on the tile.

He nodded. "To beat the Guinness Book of World Records. This guy, he held his breath. Thirteen minutes."

"That's impossible." She walked casually over to him. He could see her sapphire bathing suit top, and her sparrowish breasts cupped within it as her robe fell open. She stepped out of her sandals. For a moment, he thought of what she would look like with her suit ripped from chin to thigh, with him pressing into her—no, not him, Jimmy, the way he had torn into Jenna. Mrs M, a smile on her face, could not read his thoughts, he hoped. "No one can hold his breath that long," she said. "It must've been a cheat."

"If you believe in something, maybe you can do impossible stuff, Mrs. M."

"That's magical thinking, sweetie. And Mrs. M, good lord," she laughed, dropping her robe completely. She shimmered. "You're a man now. You'll have to start calling people by their first names, Owen. I feel like a schoolmarm when you call me that. Is that what you want me to feel like? A haggish old schoolmarm? I'm forty, not seventy. Catherine. Or Cathy."

"Oh, yeah, okay," he said, grinning. "Cathy."

As she walked along the edge of the pool to the far end, she pulled her hair back and tucked it into her white bathing cap. She lifted her arm in a certain way to him, like a salute. Then, Jenna's mother dove into the pool, graceful as a mermaid. He watched her do laps while he caught his breath.

2

When he went to shower off, Owen saw the other boy's towel hanging from the bathroom stall. Steam began to fill the changing room. He pulled his wet trunks down, and tossed them on a chair. He grabbed one of the long white towels that the Montgomerys' maid kept neatly rolled in the cabinet over the toilet. Then, he walked the narrow hallway to the large shower. All three shower heads were running, and the boy stood there rubbing soap along his arms, his face frothy with white soap foam. Owen ignored him, stepping beneath the furthest shower head, and grabbed a bar of Ivory from the holder.

"Mooncalf," Jimmy said, as the foam rinsed from his face. His hair stuck up high on his head. The smell of Ivory soap was overpowering. "Haven't seen you in awhile."

"I know," Owen said, his voice husky. He didn't feel the way he did in school with the other boys, not with this Jimmy, this eighteen-year-old who he had watched deflower Jenna. He felt disgusted. "Been busy." He turned his back on Jimmy for the rest of the shower, hoping the other boy would leave to go swim in the pool. But Jimmy toweled off, and began dressing just as Owen turned off the water. He slipped his shorts on, and reached for his t-shirt. "You've been working out a lot. Me, too. I run every morning. I play tennis."

"Swim," Owen said. He walked back to the toilet to take a leak.

"Swim?"

"I swim."

"Ah, a complete sentence out of the Mooncalf," Jimmy chuckled. "That's the first thing I noticed about you, you know."

Owen said nothing; flushed the toilet. Sat down on one of the chairs, and reached for his shirt.

"You talk in bits of sentences. Well, that and your hair."

Owen twisted back to look at him, his t-shirt shirt half over his head. "My hair?

"You've got pretty hair. It's soft, too. Most guys' hair is like bristles."

"Weirdo," Owen said, then, "Sleep in the guest room much?" He pulled the shirt down, and then went to grab his socks. Jimmy followed him, sitting down on a short bench.

"No. That bother you?"

"No. It's weird that her parents don't care."

"They don't. Well, her mother doesn't. Her father's still down in the city. And I thought you were hot for Jenna. That's the third thing I noticed about you."

"We're friends. That's all."

"Boys can't just be friends with girls."

"Okay," Owen said. He laughed, but it was a fake. It echoed off the turquoise tile and sounded less genuine as it went. He looked at Jimmy, who was watching him with a sort of paternal take—the way Owen's father would look at him when he didn't understand him.

"You know, Mooncalf, you comb your hair to the left a little more—make the part slightly higher, and you'd look top drawer. You really would. Your chin's strong, your body's in excellent shape. You need to get rid of these," Jimmy pointed at Owen's red t-shirt, "and start wearing some oxford cloths, button-downs. With sleeves. Short sleeves are for kids. It would show your best side. And maybe some khakis. When you grin, don't show all your teeth."

"Bite me."

Jimmy laughed, and reached out, pressing his hand against Owen's shoulder in what could only be a casual and friendly—even brotherly—gesture. "Good. Some spirit. I'm just trying to help. You look good, but you look too island. You need a little charm. All guys do. Swimming only goes so far, after all." Jimmy, ever-annoying, kept up the jabber. "I'm not much of a swimmer. I sail, but the idea of water, well, let's just say I do a passable dog paddle. But you've got those biceps. Amazing shoulders for such a Mooncalf runt. Pretty good. How much you bench?"

"Who cares?"

A brief silence.

Then, "I do."

"Well, not all that much," Owen said. "I just stack the weights on and push. I don't notice how much."

"Don't notice? My god, sport, you mean to say your goal isn't the weights?"

Owen shrugged. "I never think about it. I just want to be powerful. I mean strong."

"You said powerful."

"Same thing."

Another brief silence.

"You ever up for tennis?" Jimmy asked.

"Not really."

"I can teach you if you like. It would be fun to a doubles match one day. Early, before it's too hot. You, me, Jenna, and maybe you could find a friend to bring. We could have a good match. It's always fun to play doubles," Jimmy said. Owen noticed the combination of arrogance and nonchalance, as if none of this mattered. Even this small talk was something to fill some empty space. Jimmy probably screwed Jenna on a nightly basis. But he never thought about Owen, or Owen and Jenna. He probably lived in the moment. Completely.

"Saturday should be fun," Jimmy said, wiping the last of the spray from his shoulders as he pushed his feet into the cheapest sneakers that Owen had ever seen. "You bringing a date?"

Owen glanced up. "Her birthday?"

"Yeah, you know, the whole crowd's coming from the Cape, and then we'll just do tequila shots til dawn. You got a girl off-island?"

Owen began to lie, just to fill that emptiness between them. Yes, he had a girl. Yes, he was excited about Jenna's birthday party, even though he had not been invited to it. Yes, he was considering his options as to which colleges he was looking into—Middlebury looked promising, he didn't think he had quite the grades for Harvard, but his uncle had been a Dean at Middlebury, and yes, they could all go skiing in the winter up there in some distant holiday. The whole time, Jimmy reached into his shaving kit; went over to shave at the mirror, and then applied some kind of lotion to his face. He finished it off with a spritz of the most obnoxious cologne that Owen had ever smelled. While they small talked it, Owen knew, standing there in the diminishing steam of the changing room, he knew.

Owen knew just by standing there with Jimmy in the shimmering mist.

Jimmy had a weakness.

He began spending time, after that, thinking about that weakness.

Thinking about how he could get Jenna back.

3

Owen's shift at the Salty Dog began at three and lasted until eleven, six days a week. He emerged sweaty and stinking of grease, because half his job was cleaning out the fryers and grease pits at the end of the night, and when he got off shift in early July—it was nearly two a.m., and he went down to the jetty to stare out at the early morning mist of the Sound, smoke some cigarettes, and chill.

He didn't turn around when he heard the footsteps coming up behind him.

"Mooncalf."

"Hey Jimmy."

"Got a cig?"

"Take one," Owen tossed a cigarette back.

"Thanks. I guess you want to be alone."

"Didn't know you smoked."

"I don't. Not when anyone looks, anyway."

"That's nice. Anything else you do when no one's looking?"

"If I told, you'd know my secrets."

"How's Jenna?"

"She's okay. She fell asleep early. I just needed to wander a little. How's the job?"

"Good. You can smell it on me. You wander late. It's almost morning."

"In Manhattan, I wander at all hours. I like this time of night. I kind of miss work. I used to work summers in one of my dad's stores. It was fun sometimes."

"Seems like more fun to run around the island all summer. Like you two."

"It gets old. I take that back. Yeah, it's fun. I guess you want to be left alone."

"You guessed right," Owen said, cricking his neck to the left a bit.

"Your neck hurt?"

"It gets stiff. Leaning over a mop half the time. On my knees cleaning out all kinds of shit."

"Here," Jimmy said, and Owen felt hands at the back of his neck, gently massaging. "Better?"

Owen let him continue. "This fog depresses me."

"I think it's peaceful."

"You would."

"Mooncalf, you hate me, don't you?"

"Not really."

"How does this feel?" Jimmy pressed his thumbs into Owen's shoulders.

"Oh yeah," Owen said. "Right there."

4

Before dawn, he had gone to the pond. He knelt down beside it, and reached down among the algae and slimy rocks until he found it.

He drew the statue up, and set it down on the wet grass.

"I guess you're just made up," he said aloud. "I guess I'm just a screwed up guy who made you up. Maybe when I was twelve I was warped. But you're just some cheap souvenir someone lost. No one believes in gods."

But still, the itchy thought touched him somewhere between his eyes and scalp—he could practically feel the fire crawling on him.

But if you're not.

If you're real.

I'll do what needs to be done.

5

Mrs. M, in her own words

Here's what I thought of it all: my daughter Jenna had been trouble from the day she was born. She was pretty and plain at the same time, and I say that as a loving mother. She inherited her father's face, not much of mine, although I guess she got my eyes. Lucky her—my least favorite feature since my own mother always told me I had sad eyes. When Jenna was four years old, she told me that no man was going to do to her what her Daddy did to me. Definitely wise beyond her years, but just not special enough to handle what life would deliver to her, that's for damn sure.

It was her trust fund. It made her trouble.

Look, there's something that everyone pussyfoots around but no one ever talks about. That's money. Pure and simple. Money. When a girl has some, she can be elevated to the status of goddess. The most ordinary—even homely—creature can become ravishing with just a portfolio or a trust fund. That island—in summer—is full of trust fund widows who should by all rights be considered blemishes, but instead are constantly sought out for parties and gatherings and literary events. For Jenna, there's always been money. And I've watched it feed her in a way that can't be healthy; but what could I do? She has access to money. Lots of money. Money clothes her.

She was ruined because of it, basically. She could never learn how to survive. She could never learn how to rely on herself and her own character to get through a difficult or challenging situation.

She could always buy her way out of things.

This isn't true of me. I was raised solidly middle-class. My father had died when I was six, and my mother didn't have too many options, not back then. In many ways, I feel for Owen because of this. His life is a lot like mine was as a child. Yes, there was some inheritance later for me, but when you spend most of your childhood wanting things you never really get over it.

And money becomes a prison, too. When you know what it's like to live without it, and when it's within your grasp, then you know what it's like to not have it.

So, you cling to it. Pure and simple. You hang on for dear life.

I suppose people will say things about my marriage to Frank that reflect this, but my marriage is a different kettle of fish. We've got our way of living, and yes, you can assail it all you want, but it works for us nine times out of ten, and those times when it doesn't quite work, well, we have places to go where he can live his life and I can live mine, and the breather is well-needed. On both our parts.

I'm not the easiest woman in the world to live with.

And he's no saint.

I sat down with my little girl when she was just learning about sex, and I told her that men have different ways of dealing with love, and usually it's through the one part of their body that seems to cause others the most damage. "But it's just his body," I told her. She cried over all of this. She cried when she found out her father had another woman. A mistress. But you have to cry at first, don't you? To get all those little fairy tales out of your head about how life gets lived, about how there are a few good men, how some men don't cheat.

And it's not true. All men cheat, and all women marry cheaters, and to not look at that square in the face is like not looking at the good side of marriage, too.

So she cried off and on for a few years, and I held her sometimes; I was cold to her at times—I knew she needed to work this idea out in her mind.

When she fell in love for the first time, she told me that she was grateful for what she'd had to go through with her father. "I don't know why men do what they do," she told me.

"If you did, you'd have solved the greatest mystery of life," I said to her. Or something like that.

But for my money, she should've avoided that Jimmy McTeague. He was bad news. I know every little deb and sorority girl east of the Mississippi thought he was just the end of the world, but they were such goofy little virgins it was hard to have patience with them.

Jimmy McTeague is the devil incarnate. I know that's an over-the-top way of putting it. He wasn't evil, but he was cold. I knew a little about his family, and none of it was very good. His father had some bad business deals going, and even if he had all the stores, Frank told me some things that alarmed me.

With Jimmy, I felt it the first day I met him, which was sometime before summer. Perhaps some Easter break? She brought him by the house in Greenwich, and the first thing out of his mouth was, "Hello Catherine. I've heard so much about you, I almost feel like we've had an affair."

He thought that kind of thing was funny, that off-the-cuff jokiness. Within minutes, he'd given me some nickname, which of course he had to repeat five or ten times to truly annoy me, and within an hour of chatting with him, I knew more about that boy than I cared to know.

He is dangerous.

And so yes, I think it all has more to do with Jimmy McTeague than with anybody. At her birthday part in late July, he told me that he thought the world was meant to be owned by people like him.

I believe those were his exact words.

675

Yes, he had money. Yes, he was extremely good looking for a boy his age. Extremely. Only a fool wouldn't notice that. But he had no spirit. What he had was pure badness. He was absolutely pure in his badness.

I once had a dog like that. Beautiful. Completely bad.

Jimmy McTeague's like that.

I really began to hate that boy at Jenna's birthday party.

Chapter Four:
The Birthday Party

1

In the mirror, Owen combed his hair, parting it a bit higher, not to the middle of his forehead, but certainly an inch higher than his usual. He also brushed it back so it rose a bit higher. The summer blond-streaks looked better this way. He rubbed some gel into it, and made sure the part was clean. He smiled as naturally as he could. No, that wasn't right. He let his lips pull back slightly. He squinted his eyes the way that Jimmy did. It looked rich to do it. Like the sun was always on his face, even on a cloudy day.

Then, he rubbed some of his mother's Neutrogena face lotion on his face. It brought a shine to his cheeks and nose. He wasn't sure if he liked it, but it seemed to be what the rich boys had. That shine.

Hanging on the bathroom door: the crisp J.Crew shirt, pale blue, the tan chinos. He dressed, and then returned to his bedroom to get the gift he'd wrapped that morning.

"You're not going to that party," his mother said, glancing at his father. Both sat in the small living room in the dark, the television providing the only source of light. Their faces flickered.

His father laughed. "Oh, he'll have fun. The kids are really going to mix it up."

"Yeah. It'll be fun."

"You're not one of them," his mother said. "You can pretend. You always pretend." Then, she turned to his father, patting his shoulder. "Well?"

"Leave it alone, Boston," his father said. "It's the kids party. You used to go to parties."

"What's that you've got there?" his mother asked. She got up from the couch, setting her beer down on the coffee table. His father reached over, turning on the standing lamp. Light came up. His mother looked gray, despite the fact that she colored her hair. Even her skin seemed gray. His father looked like a wisp of smoke. It was all Owen could do to keep them from vanishing within the room.

Owen looked down at the box in his hands. "It's her birthday."

"You bought her something?" his mother asked, a grin spreading like blood on her face. He could imagine her dead, her skull cracked open like an egg. "You bought the Montgomery girl something? Working for tips at the Salty Dog and you bought the richest girl in the world something?" She shook her head gently. "Owen, you're always trying to impress someone with what you don't have." She said this sweetly, and he felt a tinge of love for her then. He almost felt bad for what he'd done. He almost felt bad for what he'd stolen from his mother to put in the box.

He almost felt bad for what he was giving Jenna.

Almost.

2

The party was in full swing by ten at night. Every Nancy, every Skip, every Jess and Sloan, they all were there, poolside. The great curtains were drawn back, and the glass doors had been removed for the party. White tents had been erected along the yard; lanterns of every conceivable hue strung along the walkway to the Montgomery place, and balloons flew with some regularity from the back acre. The smell of cigarettes and perfume and gin and beer and money were there, too.

Watching it, you'd have seen nearly fifty teenagers dancing, laughing, shouting, a tall blond girl with flowing hair and limbs soaked from having been thrown into the swimming pool, the fat drunk frat boy vomiting over by the birdbath, half-a-dozen homely young women shining under the spotlight of boy's gazes—for lust and money and breeding and privilege all attract beyond mere looks. The Sound sparkled with moonlight, and summer was at its peak, the sun had only just gone down an hour before, and the smell of salt sea air mingled with the foam of mermaids' souls, lost from true love.

All these things Owen thought.

3

"Did you see Jimmy at the nationals? God, I hear he's going to be at Wimbledon someday. Soon."

"If he's at Harvard—"

"When he's at Harvard, I'm going to call him Jimmy McTeague of the Ivy League. Isn't that cute?"

"I think what's cute is his father. Have you ever met him?"

"Well, I've been in the store."

"Sports superstores never interested me. It seems crass to sell that kind of thing."

"I read in Forbes that his dad is worth several billion."

"Dead or alive?"

"Dead; then Jimmy's worth that."

"Jimmy McTeague is shallow. He is. He's not smart either," one deb said, her party dress ruined because someone spilled a Bloody Mary down the front. "He's pretty but he's dumb. And my uncle went to Yale with his father, and let me tell you, that man was nearly kicked out for cheating and once that kind of thing happens, you never know."

Owen stood back, beyond the lights that had been set up along the tents, and watched them all.

The small gift in its box, in his trembling hands.

"Smooth. Just be smooth," he whispered to himself.

He wanted to make sure Jenna saw the gift.

Saw what it meant.

4

Jimmy McTeague held onto a bourbon and water as if for dear life, and he laughed with his jock friends, and he eyed the other girls, and he thanked Mrs. Montgomery for the excellent whiskey. "People who have whiskey like this should own the world," and even when he said it, he didn't know what it meant; and when he saw Owen standing just at the edge of the party, he raised his glass and shouted, "Yo, Mooncalf, get your ass over here!"

5

Jenna Montgomery, in her own words:

Here are things I've read about and I really believe:

The happiest of people don't necessarily have the best of everything; they just make the most of everything that comes along their way.

Happiness lies for those who cry, those who hurt, those who have searched, and those who have tried, for only they can appreciate the importance of people who have touched their lives.

Love begins with a smile, grows with a kiss and ends with a tear.

The brightest future will always be based on a forgotten past, you can't go on well in life until you let go of your past failures and heartaches.

Okay, before you think I'm just some rich bitch who gets sentimental and gooey over romance novels, the reason I think about those things is because when you are beautiful and you have money, it's those simple things you have to remember.

And I was pretty happy for the most part, right up until last summer.

This probably began because Daddy didn't want me to open Montgomery Hill on Memorial Day like we always did. Mom was already up there, a week or two early, and I'd only just come home from finals.

I have always gone to Outerbridge Island since I was about four, and I never miss a summer there. It's what I look forward to after a tough year in school, and since I would turn eighteen over the summer and I had just finished school—but I'd be entering Sarah Lawrence in September—I really wanted to enjoy what time I had left to just be a kid.

Daddy was in one of his moods, though, and I suspect that woman he knows was part of it. Mom told me all about that woman when she gave me the speech about sex and life and marriage when I was fourteen. "Men have problems with their bodies," she said, looking only a little embarrassed. "They all cheat. It's just something we put up with if we can. It's nothing about love. Don't even think that. It's just their biology. They have their good sides and their bad sides. And there are plenty of bad women, too," she added. "Like that woman."

That woman lived in Brooklyn, in a brownstone that my father had bought for her in the 1970s. I took the subway out to it once, and stood on the steps in front, looking through the windows. That woman had a nice chandelier and some paintings on the walls but it was a fairly plain house in Park Slope. I sort of think I saw a little of her, too, walking up the street. She wasn't even pretty, which was sort of what amazed me. She wasn't like my mother. She was tall, with big feet, and red hair that needed some kind of style. Her face was nothing like my mothers, nothing like the women I knew, she looked Irish, I guess, she looked sort of round and plain.

I don't really know if it was that woman I saw, but I suspect it was.

So, just after high school graduation, I was all ready to go to the island, but Daddy was just moody and told me that I needed to stay because of Jimmy, who was supposed to have been in town.

All right, Jimmy McTeague. He's a tennis player who goes to Wimbledon every year, he's practically a National champion, and his father owns McTeague Sports, the chain, although I never understand why they don't have stores in Manhattan. I met Jimmy when he was at Exeter, at some dance, and I was just thinking he was cute. Marnie called him the Leech for some reason which I didn't quite understand, but I knew there was something interesting about him. He lived a different life than me, and I never really saw myself with that kind of Midwestern jock-type. He was always sweating, too, which I guess goes with the whole athletic thing, but not something that's pleasant to be around an hour after a match.

Still, by the time I was seventeen, I really liked Jimmy. And no, I had no thoughts of marriage or anything like that. We hadn't actually even been intimate or anything, just held hands a lot and went to dances and out to dinner. When I debuted, Jimmy shared the drudgery of that awful debutante season by being my escort; when I was really pissed off over not getting in to Columbia, Jimmy actually flew in from the West Coast—where he had some important tennis match—and took me out to dinner.

Then, the night after I would normally go to the island, Jimmy told me we could sail there in this little boat he kept in Greenwich at the club. And that first night on the boat, I became a woman. We drank too many glasses of Chardonnay, and one thing led to another. Jimmy was never very aggressive in bed. He was kind of shy that way. So I pretty much had to seduce him, but once we both closed our eyes and let our bodies take over, we knew how to make love.

And it really was love. It really was. I felt it. We spent that first night on the boat. We got into the harbor at about twelve or one in the morning, and just slept together in the little bed. He snored sweetly. Not a hacking or sawing snore, but like a puppy dreaming. He did say something funny to me in the morning, something that struck me as odd, something about how maybe now we could think about the future more now that we'd mated, and I laughed at him and he looked a little angry when I laughed.

All right, I knew that maybe there would be trouble with Owen when I saw him on the jetty when we got off the boat the next morning. He looked like he'd been waiting there all night.

Like he'd been watching us.

The little turd. He really was. I care a lot for him, of course. We've known each other since we were both kids. He's the son of the gardener. His mother sometimes helps out with parties and laundry and other things. He's cute, which helps, too, because although I have nothing against boys that aren't very good looking, there's something about a good looking one that just makes you want him around all the time.

So I'm barely dressed, some tacky beach towel around me basically, and there's Owen at the shore seeing both of us coming up from the boat and the first thing he says to me is, "What happened?"

I felt all nervous and even giggly like I needed a cigarette. I told him I didn't want to see my mother for a day or two. And then Jimmy just took over, like he always does. He has this way with guys—he always gets them on his side. Jimmy gave him a nickname and acted like Owen was Jimmy's kid brother and they just seemed to get along fine. It was like they'd known each other all their lives, in about five minutes. Owen seemed to like all the ribbing and you know that sort of adolescent boy-talk they do. You know that. That way boys have of getting together and sort of sparring, and talking, and noticing each other's hair, or how one of them is sad, and they either peck it to death or get all brotherly. I saw it with Jimmy and his best friends at Exeter, too. The way they played like puppies. That's just what it was like—like watching two golden retrievers wrestle over a bone.

I didn't see Owen much during June. I guess he got the job down in town. Sometimes I saw him when we went to the Salty Dog, but he never waited on our table. Jimmy was virtually attached at the hip with me, which can get annoying no matter how much you care for a guy. I used to try and lose him in the mornings, after he'd go off to play his beloved tennis with one of the local pros or with my mother. My mother is excellent at sports, which are pretty much not my thing. I like golf a little, and sometimes I like to swim, but the whole girl-jock thing is beyond me.

So Jimmy would slip out of bed, and I'd just get dressed and go down to visit Marci and Elaine, and Elaine's brother, Cooper, down island. Sometimes we'd take whole afternoons just having brunch, or wandering the Cove by Big Salt Pond. Jimmy would get all pissed off at me. He was a little jealous. Well, a little more than jealous. He thought that since he was the first guy I'd slept with that he somehow should've had more ownership of me. Or maybe I should've been more attached to him. I mean, I was attached. And he was, technically, the first guy I'd slept with, although I let Ricky Hofstedter press his fingers up there sophomore year, and then there was that time that I got drunk at Hollis Ownby's party and wound up making out with Harvey Somebody (he was a Somebody. I just can't remember his last name) until I woke up with a hangover and a major pain down there and I hoped it hadn't gone too far beyond basic, you know, petting.

But Jimmy had all these needs, and some days, particularly in June and early July, I just wanted to chill and hang out with some friends without worrying about whether I was paying attention to Jimmy and all his issues.

I didn't think of Owen much except sometimes I remember how fun he was when I was younger and exploring the beaches, or how I'd take him out in one of my dad's small boats, and he'd tell me all about his plans. How he was going to slowly start investing in stocks. I'd ask him how? And he'd look at me funny, and laugh. Then, he'd tell me how his mother's father had been well-off and then when Owen turned 21, he'd come into a trust fund. I knew he was lying, but I sort of liked his lies. They made the days go by. Sometimes the summer seemed short when I was around him, and by the time I got back to school in the fall, I felt renewed. I owed a lot of that to Owen.

But this summer, I've been distant from everybody. Part of it is Jimmy. And yes, it's sexual, I guess. But since I'm paying you by the hour, I'd guess that you're okay with me telling you, right? Well, Jimmy seems to not be all that aggressive in bed. I know that must sound weird since I'm not terribly experienced in that arena, either, but I've watched movies, I've read books, and I talk with my girlfriends about this stuff. This isn't like twenty years ago when no one ever talked about sex. My friends all say their boyfriends seem to put the moves on them constantly. With Jimmy, I have to literally reach down and grab him. And then, he just sort of you know touches me here and there and then he—well you know—and then it's over and sort of unpleasant even though it's not ghastly or anything. It's just not what I expected.

And then there was that fiasco with my birthday party. Christ, it was embarrassing. Mind if I light up? I'm hungry for nicotine at the moment. Ravening.

Ah, that's better. I know everyone has to give up smoking at some point in their lives, but how nice to not have to give it up just yet.

So, the 17th was my big party, and I didn't even want Owen there—he didn't fit in with Jimmy's friends, and many of my friends found him a little cold. Plus, there was the whole problem of his mother, who's a force to be reckoned with. She's always looking at me like I'm the Whore of Babylon. She was helping us set up the party, and she kept giving me that look. You know that look. That mother look.

But Owen showed, and frankly, I was happy to see him. It was sort of a relief since I'd barely seen him all summer. Well, I saw him when he went swimming. In our pool of course. In our pool. I called him Leech (funny that he and Jimmy both have been called that, huh?) when he wasn't around because he really is such a leech. I mean it in a funny nice way, not some awful way. I once slipped off a rock into one of the little ponds on the property, and my legs were covered with leeches. They don't hurt. You'd be surprised at that, wouldn't you? You'd think that something that sucks your blood would hurt, but they don't. It's just the fact that they're there that makes them bothersome.

So it was my little joke: calling Owen Leech. I care a lot for Owen, actually. We grew up together practically. My island boy. My father laughs whenever I call Owen Leech behind his back, but my mother, well, she doesn't understand that kind of humor. That ironic kind of humor. I mean it as an affectionate term. Sort of like the way Jimmy calls him Mooncalf. It's a name. I guess it distances me from him or something. But it does get annoying when someone is always borrowing things or using your things or assuming things just because his father works in the garden. I like them. They're like family. I feel a lot for Owen, but really, he should've gotten over that Leech thing years ago.

I can hear my mother's voice in my head: that's cruel, Jenna.

685

I know. I know. I get accused of cruelty all the time. Not physical cruelty. My mother means it's cruel to fault poor people with using our things.

My mother has this thing for him. Well, for all young men. She won't acknowledge it, and she thinks Daddy's the bad one, but I know she likes the boys who hang around me. And no, I'm not jealous of her. Why should I be? She's old. Her time has come and gone. My time is only just beginning.

Anyway, eighteen-year-old boys do not want forty-year-old women. It's embarrassing, really.

Even at the party, Mom is sauntering around in that green getup she has that looks too glitzy for the island. We all go casual here, so she looked too much like Ginger on Gilligan's Island—too done up. Too too, as Missy Capshaw says. She's too too.

Missy came down from the Vineyard, and Shottsy had his cousin Alec with him, and pretty much the whole gang was there, except for the Faulkners who all went to Maine for the summer. I guess about sixteen of my friends came, and then six or seven of Jimmy's, and then Owen with his shirt that was so new it still had the wrinkles from the cardboard box, and Shottsy made a big point of letting everyone know that part of the plastic collar liner was still under the collar. Owen brought me this nice little gift, I mean that in an ironical way, and that's really the issue here.

But I was having some margaritas and just getting sort of high, and Marnie Llewellyn was regaling me with that story again, the one about her brother's professor and how him and two female students had gone off to Fenwick together and then got caught in the worst way, the very worst way possible.

And I saw what Owen was doing.

I saw that he had already cast a spell. Some kind of spell. Just like a witch.

Over Jimmy.

I saw Jimmy put his hand in Owen's hair, and I saw how they laughed, and I know it must seem irrational and paranoid, but the first thing I thought was:

That bastard is trying to steal my boyfriend.

You can imagine how I felt. I mean, I thought it was ludicrous. It wasn't like Skippy Marshall and that Donovan character from Harrow—they were both homosexual, and we all had known it since they got into the drama club and developed the perfect butts in the workout room doing squats.

This was different.

I thought it was absolutely ludicrous. But I grew livid as I watched them. Absolutely livid. Really, from the corner of my eye. I was working on my third or fourth margarita, and Missy kept talking and Alec kept eyeing my breasts like he always did, and I had my little circle, but they knew something was up, too. They knew that Jimmy was not fawning on me, and I didn't really enjoy that. Frankly.

I suppose if I had not been drinking, I wouldn't have caused a scene. But I kept my eye on the two of them, and I saw the touches.

Yes, that's right. Queerish little touches. Not the kind that boys do. Not normally. Owen touched Jimmy's elbow, and Jimmy looked at Owen's hand. And they laughed, and whenever one of them could, he took his fist and gently patted the other on the chest. Like old chums, yes, maybe. Certainly that's what I'd like to believe, but in fact, I saw Jimmy show him more genuine attention, not that needy attention he showed me, but the kind of attention every girl wants but never gets from a boy. That adoration kind of attention.

And Owen was milking it. I know he was. I asked Marnie later on, and she said I was imagining things, that Jimmy had been bedding girls since eighth grade, that it was just that boy thing. That's what she said, "That prep school boy thing where they get together and they touch each other and they tell dirty jokes and they check each other out. It's because they both want you. They need to check out the competition," she said.

But I don't know. I stood there, feeling embarrassed and humiliated, and at my party.

At my own party.

Finally I couldn't stand it.

Jimmy leaned forward and whispered something to him. It was like slow motion. I can remember it now like it's still in front of my face. I saw his lips move as he whispered, and I saw Owen lean into him, and Jimmy's hand was on Owen's shoulder, and maybe I was hallucinating or maybe I saw what I saw, but I think Jimmy McTeague placed the barest whisper of a kiss on Owen's ear, at my party, with me watching, with me having to bear witness to it. God, it's so gothic. It's so…Fire Island. It really hit me hard.

I began crying, without knowing I was doing it, weeping, just standing there, and Alec took my hand and said, "Aw, princess, what's up?"

And I shook myself free of that crowd, and I walked right over to those two horrible boys, that horrible Jimmy McTeague and I whispered, "If you embarrass me here, I will destroy you."

688

And then, of course, I had to go back to my party.

I had to.

I had an obligation to my friends. I was not going to let the boy who had been sleeping with me for nearly two months humiliate me in front of my friends.

It wasn't until the next morning that I opened the gift that Owen had given me, and that's pretty much why I freaked out, with my usual panache. I didn't want to see Owen again.

Ever.

But I knew that Jimmy would still be mine, no matter what we both went through to be together.

After all, remember these things:

The happiest of people don't necessarily have the best of everything; they just make the most of everything that comes along their way.

Happiness lies for those who cry, those who hurt, those who have searched, and those who have tried, for only they can appreciate the importance of people who have touched their lives.

Love begins with a smile, grows with a kiss and ends with a tear.

Purity

The brightest future will always be based on a forgotten past, you can't go on well in life until you let go of your past failures and heartaches.

When I think of all I've had to deal with, particularly with Jimmy, these words bring me comfort.

Oh yeah, what Owen gave me for my birthday.

It was a gun. A crap-ass gun at that. It was tiny. It had some pearly kind of handle, and the safety looked like it had rusted out, and I couldn't get the little clippy thingy off if I tried. I thought it was a joke at first, but I guess not. It looks like something that you'd buy from some little old lady in Brooklyn, some little old lady with a thousand cats and one of those old fox furs who chainsmokes and lives in a studio she's had since the 1950s.

Still, it was a gun, and I have to admit, it was the creepiest thing he could've given me.

He scares me a little.

I mean, what kind of psycho gift is that?

689

Chapter Five:
After the Party

1

Jimmy grabbed Owen's elbow, laughing, the smell of beer and tequila mixed in the air, and Owen giggled, too, and said, "Let's go to the jetty. It's beautiful there. You can see the north star."

"You know the north star?"

"Yeah. I know all the stars. I'm an islander. I know the dippers and Scorpio, too."

"You're a Mooncalf," Jimmy said, his grin big and goofy and not the controlled jock he'd once seemed. "God I wish I knew the stars like you. I want to just—just—look at the stars and know which ones they are, and where the earth is in relation to them."

The party spun around them, and Owen had a vague sense that Jenna's eyes floated around his every move. She'll understand, he thought. Someday, she'll understand. "She's a bitch," Jimmy whispered, as if reading his thoughts. "She and her friends and half these people here. All these quote unquote friends of mine, of ours, who are they? Damn it, who are they? And Jenna. Christ. Jenna."

"No, she's cool," Owen said. "Let's go. The jetty."

"God yeah, show me the stars," Jimmy said, and he kept saying it over and over again as they stumbled their way down the path along the bluffs, and every now and then Owen stopped and let

Jimmy take his hand. Jimmy's hand was warm, and above them, the sounds of the party spun, and the smell of pine and sea mingled.

The moon cut a path for them all the way to the jetty, and by the time they got there, Jimmy had already grabbed Owen hard and pulled him close to him until their chests pressed together, their thighs met, and he pressed his lips to Owen's mouth.

2

Voices in the dark:

"It's all right, I know you. I know what we both want."

"Shut up. Just shut up."

"Come here. Come here. Let me help you. It's all right. It feels good."

"No, not like this. No."

"I've been so lonely."

"Oh."

"Wanting this."

"Oh."

"Since the first time I saw you."

"Oh."

"Does this feel good?"

"Ah."

"Will you let me take you?"

"Oh."

"Ask me."

"Oh."

"Ask me."

"Owen, take me? Owen? Take me."

3

Owen takes control.

I had found my way to Jenna.

It wasn't much different than kissing a girl, and once I allowed Jimmy to feel as if he had seduced me, that I was the unwilling partner, it was easy to hold his attention. He told me to close my eyes and pretend he was a girl, to just let him do things to me, to just keep the image of a beautiful girl in my mind while he did things.

Jenna was the only face I saw.

I knew that once I had Jimmy McTeague of the Ivy League in my arms, once I had pressed myself into him, owned him, dominated him, that Jenna would be mine.

I look at the boy that I was then: Owen Crites. Mooncalf.

He mounts the rich boy and he drives his point home.

And no, I'm not gay. I had no thrill from what I did to Jimmy McTeague, how I made him feel tenderness and acceptance and release that night. It felt less like sex to me than stabbing someone over and over while they curl around you.

How I caressed him as no one ever had, to the point that he wept against my chest.

It was purely because I thought of Jenna.

My love for her.

Love is purity.

My next decision, as I lay there with that puppy whispering his soul into my ear, was just how I was going to murder him.

PART TWO:
THE LAST OF SUMMER

Chapter Six:
Jimmy McTeague
Keeps a Diary

1

1. Need to train better. Work on backswing, damn it. Wake up an hour earlier every morning. Run two miles. Then practice. Then row.
2. July was a waste. Feeling like I'm getting lazy. More strength training. Check out the sucky gym in town.
3. Jenna's a bitch. She thinks she knows. She doesn't know. She'll never really know.
4. Need to get back with Jenna. Need to figure this out.
5. I can't resist him. It's awful what we're doing. But I know I can stop. I know if I just stick with the program I can stop. I think he's evil.
6. What we did was wrong. I know that. What Jenna and I can build is right.
7. Call the Padre and Madre for more money.
8. Become a better person. Quit all the lying. Lying is bad. There's no reason. If you feel the way you feel, let it all out. Don't keep holding it in. Doesn't matter what dad thinks. Doesn't matter if you know what you need from life. You can let it out. Other people do. Other people need those things, too.

9. Maybe it's not real. Maybe it's just sex. Maybe I shouldn't let it happen. But now all I think about is him.
10. Jenna and Mooncalf.
11. Mooncalf.
12. He told me something really smart. Just shows that you don't need all these prep schools and universities to be smart. He said, "Love is purity." It is so true. It's something I couldn't say out loud. But it's so true. But there's more to life than love. You can't survive on love. You can't have the important things in life just because of love. No one pays for three houses and European vacations and clothes from Italy and Rolls Royces with love.

2

My name's Jimmy McTeague. It's safe to assume you know that because you are me sitting here reading my diary. Since after all no one else is going to read this if I can help it. It's also probably safe to assume that you'll burn these pages someday to make sure no one else reads them. But for now, writing it down seems right. My favorite movie is probably still the *Little Mermaid* which I saw when I was nine years old and I still watch it on video once a year at least. Why? Because it was about sacrifice for what you wanted. I've always sort of believed in that. My dad doesn't understand why I watch a cartoon to inspire me. Sometimes I watch it before a match because it gets me going. I don't see why being smart and grown up has anything to do with abandoning the things you believed in when you were a kid.

I've wanted to keep a diary since I was about nine, about the same time as I saw that movie, but I didn't start til I was 12, and then I threw it all out, so after another brief attempt at sixteen, I've decided now that I'm about to enter Harvard, it's time for me to keep one. I'm not only about tennis, anyway. I get tired of that dumb jock image. My SATs were through the roof. I get good grades and am totally wrapped up in Medieval History, which I figure I might pursue even after I graduate. If I graduate. If I make it through. If all the bad things that I've found out about don't happen in the meantime and it all ends.

This part of the diary is about my summer. Jenna and I were having a great year together, although I wasn't always there for her, I suppose, because of the matches I had in England and out in California, and then she spent Spring Break in Aruba, so that last week in May was really our first full week together, which is why I took the *Karenina* out of the yacht club and we sailed lazily up and down the coast for a few days. I was so pissed off at Dad over a lot of things. First and foremost was the talk he gave me, about how I needed to uphold the family and how I needed to look at life differently, not as a kid but as someone who had responsibilities and wanted to live a certain way with certain kinds of people. I didn't forget about Chip, but I guess that's one of those things I have to put aside. My dad says so anyway. Chip was really aggressive anyway, and the time we spent together wasn't really very meaningful because the whole time I kept thinking to myself: where will this go? Two guys can't marry. I'll lose everything. And Chip was all about loins, anyway. I shouldn't even write about it here. What if someone finds out? I'm not really gay anyway, I just get in these situations. I suppose I fall in love with people. And Chip turned out bad anyway. All that mess about fighting and arguing and him claiming I broke his arm when I didn't break it and if he fell it was his fault anyway for standing in my way and not letting me pass. He did that sort of blackmail thing too, but I showed him that I wasn't going to put up with that kind of shit.

699

I fell for Jenna pretty hard. I mean, who wouldn't? She's gorgeous and full of life and her brain is just amazing. And the money. To pretend it's not there is like not noticing her bra size. All the guys seem to want her, and I really had to fight off that bulldog from Choate with the Ferrari, but it wasn't too hard to dazzle her on the courts. She's a big fan of tennis, which helps, and that night we went for a walk back in the city really turned things around for me. I mean, we were walking down Fifth Avenue, and she was talking about what she wanted from life, all the wonderful things, to see the world and experience the best of everything, and how her trust fund was huge and she intended to always have the life her parents had, and my mind was turning a hundred little things around. I was walking with her under cloudy skies, and I was thinking about how this was right. Being with Chip was wrong because it was based on that one thing, that physical thing, and I thought, all right, I know where this will go with Jenna. We'll marry, we'll have children, we'll build something really solid. She has all this family land and properties and I'm really good at handling investments, so we'll be perfect together. And she wants kids really badly. So badly that she told me she wasn't even all that interested in college, and she wanted to just get out from under her parents and be on her own and make her own life. She has millions from her grandmother, and it's earning more millions every year, she said, so why should she have to go through college? She wanted to do some magazine work, one of those Conde Nast magazines, and her family has huge pull in that area, and she was smart enough.

It hardly bears comparison with a night spent on a dirty mattress in the back of some studio apartment in Chelsea with Chip, who fell on hard times after prep school. That sleaziness he had, like an air, like marijuana smoke in the back of a bus—that's what his place was like. He was slumming, he was degrading himself. His parents had cut him off, and he was willing to live like that. Hardly any furniture, a job that barely paid him per month what a reasonable man can live on. And still, he was willing to live like that for the sake of the feeling in his organ. I am never going to let that happen to me. I am never going to let people know how I am on the inside if I can help it. I got so mad at Chip I guess I ended up roughing him up a little, but he kept trying to ruin things, and I just won't let anyone do that. My dad is ruining things as it is, and pretty soon other people are going to know how he's ruining things, and I do not intend to be in that spot with him.

I remember clasping Jenna's hand, and listening to her optimistically go on about the life she intended for herself.

So I knew that if I just kept my eyes on her, it would all go in the right direction. When we made love for the first time, it even felt right. She was overheated on the inside, it was like lava or something, it felt so natural.

I thought it would all turn out all right up until I met Mooncalf.

I tried to fight it, too. I looked at him and tried. I tried not to look at his body. So well developed. The way he spoke, almost sullenly. I didn't want him then, but I knew he had it in him to take me over. And I suppose he has.

There's even a dangerousness to him I enjoy. I find myself looking over Jenna's shoulder, when we're at the beach, or bicycling, hoping he's there, just out of reach.

And then, the party. It was like waking up for the first time. It was like knowing that I'd been telling myself lies for years.

That I'd been foolish and wrong.

Now, all I think about is Mooncalf and I wish we were in a different world, not one of secrets and half-truths, but one where we could just be together.

I know he feels the same.

I'm sleeping pretty much on the boat now. I can't stay with Jenna. Not in her room. And her dad gives me those looks, which aren't pleasant, either. Jenna's been cold. Can't blame her. I know somehow it will all turn out okay. I know it will because I know life is not meant to be bad, and it's not meant to be confusing, and if we can all just get through this summer, it'll somehow work out because life is supposed to work out.

Sometimes, I get so lonely I want to just hold Jenna. As a friend.

I want to see him again, but he's been avoiding me since the party. I've had two weeks now, seeing Jenna and her family, playing a little golf, some tennis, taking the boat out when I can. Jenna's been good about this even if she's turned icy. She seems to handle my silences well. She really is a friend. I'm glad we can be this close and that she can be so understanding.

Most of the time, she seems to act as if the night of her party never happened, that I didn't go off with him. She won't really understand what it means, anyway. She'll think she'll know, but

I'll let her know it was nothing. I'll get her thinking about us again, which is what she really wants, anyway.

Chapter Seven:
The Hurricane
Approaches

1

There he is again: I see him. That boy Owen. He's been running down on the beach; swimming too much for his own good; working on his oxygen intake because breathing is the key; and he's felt a strength grow within him to match his body's power.

2

The weeks after the party went in a blur of moments and flashes in his brain—the sky clouded and then became unbearably sunny, the humidity soared and then dropped and then soared again; a tropical storm to the south had been upgraded to a hurricane but it would not strike so far north as Outerbridge; and once, in the dead of night, Owen lay in bed convinced he'd heard a gun go off somewhere on the island.

August was like that sometimes.

3

"Owen. Why?"

"Why what?" he asked, shielding his eyes from the sun.

Jenna had emerged from the deck all wrapped in a big yellow towel, and yet to him it was as magnificent as a summer dress. The smell of the pool was intoxicating. He had just finished his morning laps, and felt cleaner and stronger. Chlorine stank on his skin. He looked up at her. He wanted to kiss her; he wanted to touch her. They stood so close.

"Why the gun?"

"It's just a pistol. It's an antique."

"Why?"

"I thought you'd want it. I thought you'd like it."

"I'm not a fan of guns."

"No one is. But it has that inlay. It's mother of pearl. It seems feminine."

"You must be out of your mind. To give me that as a gift. On my birthday."

"It was my grandfather's."

"Well, I'm giving it back. God, I don't want it in the house, let alone in my hand."

"You need protection."

"From what?"

"Jimmy," Owen said. He sucked a breath in briefly. It was time to let it begin. He felt a curious shiver sweep through his body, as if he were on the verge of some delightful pleasure. "He told me…"

"Told you what? What did he say? Was it about me?"

Owen paused. He wanted her to feel the words as he said them. He wanted to make sure that she was completely focused on him. On his lips as he spoke. "No, it's nothing. I just think you should keep the gun."

"No, he said something," she nearly snarled. "Tell me."

"I'm sure he didn't mean it," Owen said.

"It made you think I needed a gun?" she asked. Her face went blank. She looked down at her feet for a moment. Then, she glanced up and looked him in the eye. "What's been going on between you two?"

"Nothing," Owen whispered.

"Owen, what's going on?" she said.

He looked at her and said, "Jenna, I want you to be safe. That's all. Look, I know you don't care for me, and that's fine. I can't make you like me. And I know I can't make you…care for me…in a way I happen to care for you. No one is magician enough for that. I've thought about you since we were both little kids. I've always considered you someone special."

"What?" she asked in a voice that was barely more than mouse squeak.

"I know that you'll go on to some really great college and you'll meet lots of guys like Jimmy and you'll come back to the island during the summer and be friendly with me but you'll see me as the island townie who paints houses for a living, or perhaps works on boats. And you'll have a different life."

"What is this all getting to—" Jenna gasped, and then her eyes lit up. "You lost the island accent. You talk like one of us now."

She said it as if it was one of the most dreadful things imaginable. As if the "one of us" was the worst thing that could happen.

"That isn't true," Owen said. Then, he glanced away from her, at the house and the beginnings of the roses his father so lovingly tended. "Look, I know I'm nothing to you. Just consider the gun some kind of protection. He's dangerous."

He walked away from her, his body barely dry from the swimming pool.

She called after him, but he didn't turn. He walked from the pool to the back lawn, and then disappeared down the path.

4

Another morning, he helped Mr. M with his golf clubs and luggage, driving the truck up from the ferry. Mr. M had almost missed the summer on the island. "Business takes a man over," he told Owen on the way up the hill to the house. He was the biggest man Owen had ever seen—like a bear, but slick, too, and shiny. He had on dark glasses and a rumpled blue oxford cloth shirt; his skin was like pink snow. When Owen got to the door with the last of the bags, Mrs. M (he had to start thinking of her as Cathy if he was going to ever grow up) kissed her husband lightly on the nose. "How's the summer?"

"Quiet," Mrs. M said.

"Where's that boy?"

"Which?"

"McTeague," Mr. M said.

"I think it's over. She's gone to Dr. Vaughan three times in two weeks. That's a record for her," Mrs. M said, and then turned to Owen. "Sweetie, can you go grab the mail?"

Owen nodded, feeling far too obedient, feeling his heart beating too fast, feeling too much within his frame, as if his muscles were about to twist and untangle and he was afraid for a moment that he had not heard what he thought he'd heard.

5

Owen sat by the koi pond, absorbing the last of an afternoon sun on one of his days off—the weather had gone back and forth, between brief bouts of showers and then sudden sunbursts. He was about to reach for Dagon beneath the placid green water, when he noticed a shadow reflection move across the water.

He didn't turn, but knew that Jimmy had come up behind him.

"Aren't you ever going to talk to me again?"

Owen shrugged.

"I thought...I thought we could...we could at least be friends," Jimmy said. "I think about you. All the time."

"Don't come here again," Owen measured his words carefully. The shadow withdrew, and Owen had the sun again.

6

Owen lay back in the grass and closed his eyes to the sun. As the violet darkness of his inner mind grew, he began to see the shadow sea of Dagon's realm. From the dusky waves, a form emerged, a magnificent sea god, its eyes round and without mind, like those of a shark, its body slick as oil with thousands of fins sprouting along its back; and as it grew, Owen knew what the god asked of him.

7

"I said peel the potatoes," his mother said, but he could see the look in her eyes. Her lashes wavered, she didn't look directly at him. His mother was afraid of him. A little. Just a little fear. That was good.

"Don't use that tone of voice with me," Owen said almost politely, as he lifted the first potato and brought it to the small sharp knife.

"Something's missing in the house," she said, but his mother had begun saying strange things the past few weeks—sentences that didn't go together, phrases that meant something only in her mind.

"You probably misplaced whatever it is," he told her almost non-chalantly. "You've always been like that, haven't you?"

8

And then, the storm came.

When storms come to Outerbridge, they usually have loss most of their power, they usually have been downgraded from hurricanes by the time they hit Bermuda to tropical storms when they reach Long Island, and by the time they make it past Block Island and start heading to the Avalons, it's usually high winds and warm rains but not much damage. The islanders who are over sixty remember the storm of '53 that "took the hats off houses," as they said, and generally made a mess of the summer homes.

707

The storm that arrived the last week of August was not a terror, nor did it threaten to take the hats off houses. It was a warm palace of rain and wind and it changed the geometry of the island with its shifts and movements.

The sky became a hardened gray, and the rain was constant, and the koi pond overflowed. Owen ran outside with his father, newspapers curled over their heads, to try and save the fish as they flip-flopped along the mud and grass, their patchwork colors seeming to melt beneath the downpour.

9

Owen was on his way to work, using his father's truck to get to the Salty Dog, when he saw the figure standing in the pouring rain of afternoon down by the docks. Owen pulled the truck to the edge of the road and parked. He got out in the rain, opening his dark umbrella. The smell of fish was overpowering—it was a stink he was used to, but with the storm it was worse.

Jimmy looked otherworldly: he wore a shiny parka, and his face was pale beneath it. He nearly galloped over to Owen, and reached out to touch him on the shoulder, but Owen pulled back. Owen slammed the truck door shut.

"I'm going to work," Owen said.

"Mooncalf?"

"Leave me alone."

"I thought you—"

"You thought wrong."

"I've been waiting for you. At the boat. Every night, I watch you leave the restaurant and walk home. Every night I wish you'd come to me."

"You disgust me."

"Stop it. I know that's not true." Jimmy's shoulders began heaving. The sound of the rain became thunderous and sheets and blocks of it seemed to dump right down around them. "God. God!" Jimmy cried out, his arms going up to the sky like some clown, like some revival preacher clown; the rain pouring against his face. A thunderclap hid the sound of his bleating. "If only you knew! If only you could grow up inside me! Knowing how I've been pushed and pulled, first my father forcing me into tennis and basketball and soccer since I was six years old, the camps I've gone to every summer, and these schools I go to, and what it all means when inside…inside Owen… you know something about yourself that's like a doorway into a different world. Something that's like…I don't know…like a doorway out of this torture place and into this garden. When I was nine I had this garden that I helped create. It had vegetables and flowers in it, nothing pretty and nothing special, but it was mine. My dad dug it up in the middle of the night. He dug it up and told me that no son of his was going to be a goddamn gardener. That's what this feels like. Like someone is trying to dig up the garden I need to grow. And you know you need to go to that garden but every single human being from your mother to your father to your coaches to your teachers to your friends to even strangers—every single human being—wants you to keep away from the one garden where you know you can just help things grow and where you'll feel calm for once in your life…where you will feel that what you have known inside your body, inside your heart, inside your mind, is the way God and nature and whatever it is that moves things within any human being—meant for you to be."

Owen nearly gasped, when Jimmy had finished.

"Jim, Christ, I know," Owen said, feeling as if he'd rehearsed the lines. He attempted a feeble smile. Part of him felt removed within his body. He was watching himself—Owen—react, seem gentle, seem kind. "It's just like that." Then, he looked around at the tourists coming off the ferry, their black and clear and red and green umbrellas all blossoming above their heads, and there, beyond the Crab Shack were six of the island guys he'd grown up with; and when he looked through the thick rain, he saw other people he had known all his life. "Look, we can't do this here," he said. "Get in the truck."

10

Owen drove in silence through a rain-shattered world—and followed the slick black island roads until they were nearly to the Great Salt Pond. Jimmy seemed content with the quiet of the drive. When Owen glanced over, he noticed that Jimmy pressed his forehead against the window beside him, reminding him somehow of a puppy. Finally, they came to the end of road-break that looked out over the enormous pond. When he'd turned off the ignition, Owen reached over and took Jimmy's hand in his.

"I know. It's difficult," Jimmy said. "I'm not like this either. Not really. There are things I want out of life. Things that have nothing to do with this. But right now. Christ, right now, this is it."

"Other people can do this kind of thing, but I can't. It wouldn't be right."

"No, it wouldn't be. But we can go somewhere that it'll all be all right."

"Where?" Owen laughed. "Where would it be right? My god. Where?"

Jimmy recoiled as if he'd been slapped. "Out to sea. In the boat."

"For how long, Jimmy? How long before your dad cuts you off, or before we move on? How long before you need to go off to your Ivy League school and then marry and meanwhile, I live in some kind of shame on this island. I'm not like you. I'm not like the kind of men who do this with other men. I'm just...Just."

"Just?"

"Just not sure what I feel right now."

It was easy to lie once Owen knew what he would do with Jimmy. How he would destroy him. How it would go easy once everything was in place.

"Oh, baby," Jimmy moaned, leaning over, into him, pressing his scalp against Owen's neck. Owen felt wetness along his throat. "You don't know how long I've hoped you'd say it."

"We don't need Jenna do we? Or girls like her," Owen whispered. "God, if I could, I'd kill her."

"Who? Kill? Owen?"

"I didn't mean that," Owen said, and kissed him on the top of his head.

The rain beat down in great sheets around the truck, and the great clouds roiled, and Owen knew that he had him now.

He had Jimmy right where he wanted him.

Where Dagon wanted him.

CHAPTER EIGHT:
Dagon

1

"Owen?" his mother asked, holding it in her hand. The statue. It had always seemed enormous to him, but in her hand, it was only a foot in length. The base was cracked, some of its teeth had fallen out, and all it was, after all, in her hand, was something that someone had carved and had left behind.

"Where'd you get that?"

"Where you left it," she said. She hefted it in her hand. "Where did it come from?"

"I...I found it."

"You found it?"

"Yeah, I did. It's mine." He held his hand out.

"Did you buy it?"

"That's none of your business," he said. "That's mine."

"Why did you put it in the fish pond?"

"It's an ornament. It looked nice there. Give it back."

"It's terrible looking. It's eyes. The skin on it. Whoever made this thing was sick. I think some kind of animal was used. It smells, too."

"Mother."

"Don't mother me. You may be a young man, but you have a thing or two to learn. I know you, Owen. I know how you think. I saw you that morning."

"What are you talking about?"

"I saw you. You cut your arm and let it bleed on this…this thing."

"That's crazy. Why would I do something crazy like that? Like—what—like cut myself? And what—did you say—bleed?"

"It's some kind of awful thing, isn't it? This thing. It's some awful thing for you. The way your mind works." She looked at the small statue in her hand, and then back at his face. She squinted as if trying to see him more clearly. "You've never been quite right. You know that, too. You know how you're different from other boys, don't you? Yes, you're crafty and you look good in a suit and you can make your muscles talk for you. But I know you better than you know yourself, Owen Crites. I know how cold you are on the inside. I know how you believe different things." He felt her closing in on him as she moved toward him. "What exactly is this thing? Is this a toy? Is this something else? Is this something you talk to? Is this…is this…some kind of devil god? Do you worship graven images now?" She said it in a half-joking manner, and that was the worst of it. She wasn't taking Dagon seriously. He could feel it in her tone.

Owen felt as if his tongue had been cut out. He felt a heat rash along his neck. He looked from the statue to his mother and back again. Then, he grinned. "Don't be ridiculous. You have such a small mind. You're so quick to judge me when you yourself are the one with the cold heart. You set a trap for dad and now you punish him for that same trap. You can't even love your only child. And your imagination—your paranoid imagination—finding some carved art in a koi pond, something that you claim you watched me bleed over, did you ever for a moment think that perhaps I hated myself so much that I wanted to slit my wrists? But something made me stop. Something kept me from hurting myself. But it wasn't the thought of you, was it? It wasn't the love of my mother that saved me, was it? It was the thought that maybe one day I'd have a moment just like this. A moment when dad is out of the house. A moment when

you're at your worst. And then, do you know what I am going to do
with you?"

"What are you talking about? Owen? Owen?"

"Give me that," he said, snatching it from her hand. "It's mine.
Not yours."

She stood before him, trembling.

Owen cradled Dagon in his arms. He closed his eyes, and
whispered a brief prayer.

When he opened them, he said, "Here is something I hope you
think about until the moment you die. I am going to be your dutiful
son as long as your years continue. But the moment that I get an
inkling that you are old and feeble, I will come to your bedside one
night, and I will press my hands over your nose and mouth until you
smother to death. And in those last moments, you will look at me
and know that everything you were ever afraid of was true."

His mother pressed her hands to her lips, but was unable to
speak.

It was the power of Dagon, of course. It was there, in the room.

The god was there with him.

Dagon whispered within his blood, "You will die like the bitch
that you are."

Or had Owen himself said it aloud, in a whisper, to his mother?

713

2

This is how it will happen, the voice came to him. You will tell
her things. You will tell him things. He harbors a madness. He is
breakable. Then, she will kill him. You will save her. She will kill
him and you will have her.

He slept that night with Dagon next to him in bed, and dreamed
of the great realm beneath the sea, and he no longer felt his age, but
felt as if he were again a child, and Jenna was with him, the Queen
of the Deepest Fathom.

3

"Hello sweetie," Mrs. M said. She had just finished the Sunday
crossword puzzle, and looked up from the paper. "You all ready

for four more days of this…this tempest?" The kitchen was like a brilliant day compared to the murky rain outdoors.

Owen had come in through the back, his towel in his arms. "Up for a swim, Cathy?"

Mrs. M shook her head. "Feeling a bit downtrodden from the rain. Ask Frank, he'd probably love a race with you."

"Mr. M's around?"

"He's enjoying the summer here after all."

"That's great. I would've thought with the rain…"

Mrs. M didn't seem to notice his comment. She crossed her legs, one over the other, and Owen thought for a moment that it was the most luxurious movement he had ever in his life seen. "You here for Jenna?"

"I doubt she wants to see me."

"Owen," Mrs. M said, setting the paper down on the kitchen table. She arched an eyebrow. "Something's changed about you. What is it? Turn around."

Dutifully, he turned about and then back to face her again.

"You're different now. What's that all about?" She said it with a sweet amazement. "Are you in love?"

"No," he said, too quickly.

"Jenna's in her room. She sleeps later and later. Go call her if you want. She should get up. It's nearly ten. No one should sleep this late. Not at her age. Not in summer." Then, Mrs. M leaned forward, her breasts dropping slightly out of her robe. "Between you, me, and the wall, Owen, I think she's really depressed over something. But I'm the last person she'll confide in. I imagine it's about a boy," she whispered. "That McTeague character."

Then, she said, lightly, "I always thought there was something not right about him."

4

"Oh. It's you," Jenna said. She was sitting up in her bed, the covers around her white cotton nightgown.

"Hi," he said from the doorway. The room smelled of sandalwood and vanilla.

"It's the rain. It does this to me," she said, wiping her hair back from her face. "I hate storms." She added, idly, almost as if he wasn't listening, "It's like my summer got stolen."

He remembered the love that he had nearly forgotten. He remembered why he loved Jenna so much. She was there for him, always. She had always been there for him.

"Okay if I come in? You know, like I used to?"

"Sure," she said, drawing her knees up. Then, "What is it between you two?"

He went into the bedroom, and sat down on the chair near her desk. "Who two?"

"Don't be coy," she said unpleasantly. "Jimmy. Is it just sex?"

"Oh. That."

"Yes. That."

"I don't want to talk about it."

"I think you do."

"No, I really don't." And then, something within him opened up. It was like feeling a heat—a fire—in his chest, near his heart. It was Dagon. Dagon would inspire him. He felt that strength, suddenly, just when he thought he would falter. Without even trying, tears poured from his eyes.

"Owen? Owen?" she asked, but he was nearly blind from the tears. She lifted the blanket, and patted a space next to her. "Come here. What's wrong? Owen?"

He bawled like a baby, and without knowing who—or what— had moved him, he found himself in her bed, her arms around him.

"Aw, Owen, what's wrong? What's wrong my precious, precious, precious baby boy?" She held him close, and Dagon was there. He felt it. He was not alone.

Dagon was there.

The voice that came from his throat didn't feel like his. It was some small boy's. Some crybaby who shivered and spilled emotion across the girl he loved.

"He…I didn't…I didn't want…I can't talk about…I didn't…he just kept…he just kept…he kept…he…I tried to…fight…fight… fight…push…hit…but…he just kept…he just kept…he just kept."

715

"Oh my god," Jenna said, her voice chilled and haunted. "No. He didn't. No. Did he? Owen? Did he rape you? Did he?"

"He just kept...oh god, Jenna, I can't face this...I wanted to...I wanted to...I wanted to...kill...myself...I wanted to..."

And so it began, and she said all the things that she was meant to say; and Owen told less than he needed to tell, because she made the connections herself, and he sat with her for hours in her arms, and then, they made love.

5

He went to the boat that night.

It was over now. It was all over. Dagon was still within him, and he had won. He wanted to take it to Jimmy. He wanted Jimmy to suffer from it. If he could, he would've videotaped the afternoon, he would've tape recorded Jenna's voice saying over and over again that she loved him, that it was all her fault, that Jimmy should never have come to the island, that he was bad, he was evil, and they should call the police, they should do something. She even told him that if that bastard ever set foot on her property again, she would take that gun and shoot him right between the eyes.

The storm continued to rage, but in muted anger, across the gray mood of sky. The Sound and the distant islands that could be seen were like watercolor images, fuzzy and melting in the rain. Owen wore a bright yellow raincoat that belonged to his father. He was a fire in the darkness.

"Mooncalf, you look like a fisherman," Jimmy said. He wore cut off jeans and a striped rugby shirt that was already soaked through, and his hair was like seaweed, hanging in his eyes. In his hand, a green bottle of beer. "Like, you know, a real New England Clam Chowder Fisherman!" He had to shout over a roll of thunder and a crack in the sky; then the world lit up for a moment; it returned to gray.

Owen laughed, shaking his head. "You're drunk, boy."

"Want a beer?" Jimmy asked.

"Sure," Owen said. "How many you drink already?"

"Four. Maybe five. Who's counting?"

716

"Let's get out of the rain!"

"I like the jetty," Jimmy said, tossing him a small bottle and then leaping to the dock. He grabbed Owen's free hand. "No one's looking. We can hold hands, all right?"

"I don't know," Owen tugged away. He twisted the top off the Rolling Rock bottle, and took a swig. "God, I'm sick of rain!"

"Me, too!" Jimmy tried to kiss him, but Owen stepped back to avoid it.

The rain lightened slightly; it was a warm rain; it washed across their bodies. "She's sort of expecting us," Owen said.

"Who?"

"Jenna."

"Jenna?" Jimmy laughed, and then looked sidelong up the hill to the Montgomery place. "What for? I thought it was you and me tonight."

"She's...she's pissed. I guess that's what it is," Owen shrugged. "She's pissed and she wants us to talk to her. I told her."

"You...you told her?"

"After yesterday, in the truck, Christ, Jimmy, I can't not tell her. I've known her all my life. She's one of my closest friends. I told her about us. About how we're going to go away together. How you love me now. How everything's all right."

"You...you..." he stammered. The bottle in his hand dropped to the rocky ledge, shattering. "You told her."

It was coming out now. The madness that they all had within them. Owen wanted to smile, but knew that if he did, he would give himself away.

6

The rain thinned. Minutes had passed while Jimmy had taken in what had just been said. Owen could practically see the thoughts in the eyebrows as they squiggled around, flashing anger and confusion, and the way he chewed his lip, and his eyes wouldn't stop blinking. Owen reached over and touched his scalp. "Sometimes I think I see a halo around your head. I do. I think you're some kind of angel," Owen said, and then scruffed his hair.

"You fucking told her?" Jimmy growled. "You goddamn fucking son of a bitch told her what we've been...what we've..."

"Do you think she didn't see?" Owen set his bottle down on the jetty, and put his hands on Jimmy's shoulders, pulling him into him. "Do you think she's stupid? We're her friends, for Christsakes. She can see. She told me she watched us that first night. She saw us. There was enough light to see our shadows, puppy. She told me it upset her, but she understood. She wasn't sure if it wasn't just one of those drunk boy things...or something else. I told her it was." Then, he added hesitantly, "Something else."

"You fucking goddamn son of a bitch gardener's son living in your goddamn peasant fucking world you don't even know what you've done!" Jimmy shouted. His face had contorted until it was more mask than face, a mask of pain and fury. It was no longer human. "You fucking think that," spit flew from his mouth, "that... that...you, you, with nothing to lose can just throw what we have in front of her, in front of—you know what you're playing with? You're playing with things you can't even understand!" Jimmy began stomping around in a circle, alternating his shouts with lion roars.

When he finally quieted, Owen said, "What happened to yesterday? You looking up at God and telling me how this all felt, how you felt on the inside. How you felt you needed to let this out? What happened to that?" He kept his voice low.

Jimmy's eyes lit up. "Don't you, you son of a bitch, use my words against me! I wasn't born to lose everything because I'm sleeping with some island townie pervert, I wasn't born to have this get out, to have this ruin everything I've ever built."

"Listen to yourself. It's practically a whole new century. You talk like it's 1950. You won't lose everything just because—"

"You think so? You little bitch, you think I won't lose everything? You don't even understand what is going on here, do you? You think it's about me wanting you. The stakes are higher! I'll tell you something, boy, I want you, but I don't want you. You don't even understand why I have to be with Jenna, do you? Do you?"

Owen turned and began walking toward the strip of beach. "I don't want to hear."

"Well, you need to. Maybe living in some little caretaker's house gives you no perspective on this, but Jenna Montgomery means I will not be some poor shit like you."

Owen glanced back. "You're rich."

"Ha!" Jimmy cried. "You don't know the half of it."

"You're an heir to some fortune. Some sports store chain."

Jimmy shook his head. "It's not like it looks. My father has these stores. That's all he has. But the business is changing. It's changing, and he's had some setbacks. He isn't a good businessman, Mooncalf. Never has been. All this stuff, this boat, the houses, all of it, will be gone in a few years. It's coming. He's going to be in jail someday, my father, and the IRS is going to eat him alive. And I do not intend to live like that. I do not intend…"

"Jesus," Owen gasped, and then began laughing. "Jesus. You're just a golddigger. You just are after her money. Jesus!"

Owen dropped to his knees on the wet sand.

"What's wrong with you?" Jimmy snarled, coming over to him. "You feeling bad now?"

"I thought you loved me," Owen said.

Jimmy's voice had grown cold. "It's not about whether I love you or not. It's not about that. But you've ruined even that now."

He grabbed Owen under his armpits, lifting him up to a standing position. "You've destroyed something for me, Mooncalf. You really have."

Then, he looked up the hill to the house. The lights were on along the pool, and the upstairs light—Jenna's bedroom—was dim.

"I need to set this right," he said.

"No, don't, Jimmy, it's—"

"I need to," Jimmy said. "I'll tell her that it was weakness. I'll tell her I love her. I love her more than anything on the face of the earth. I'll tell her that I couldn't help myself with you, but that it was nothing. That you were nothing." He nearly laughed, but it had a cry within it. "You're just a little manipulative piece of trash. She'll understand. She's not like you. She'll understand."

Then, he took off in the rain, bounding up the wooden steps that crept like a vine along the side of the hill, and Owen began following, but slowly.

He heard the shots ring out before he had reached the top step. Five distinct shots, and soon dogs down in town were howling, and lights came up along the waterfront.

7

The house was dark and silent when he went in through the glass doors by the pool. He walked past the shimmering water, flicking up the lights as he went. Entering the kitchen, he saw Mrs. M, lying in a pool of blood, and then Owen found himself moving more swiftly, his heart pounding—

—she resembled nothing of the mermaid she had once been; death had robbed her beauty; blood took away the magic of her form; her eyes were open, and fish-like—

Dagon, what is this? This isn't what was promised. This isn't what I prayed for—

—And he ran up the stairs to Jenna's room, and found *him* standing there, the Colt in his hand—

On the bed, Jenna, bleeding, an enormous hole in her neck. Her hands moved as if she were trying to reach up to her neck to stop the blood, but could not.

She opened her mouth to cry out, but all that came was a rasping sound, and blood pulses from her throat. He felt himself burning as he watched the last light flicker in her beautiful eyes.

Then, her eyes closed.

8

"Mooncalf, what did I do?" Jimmy said, his skin red, his eyes narrow slits, his shirt torn and bloody. Tears and sweat shone like diamonds on his skin. "What did I do? I...I came up...I wanted to talk...and she...she had this..." He held the pistol up. "She...she threatened me...and then her mother came up...I had grabbed it from her...I was going to leave...but they said things...her mother, too…they said things about me…and her father…About something…some lie…something you told her…something…"

"All of them?" Owen asked. "You killed. All of them."

Jimmy shrugged. "I guess so. It's kind of a blur. Funny thing is," he giggled in a way that seemed uncharacteristic, "it didn't really feel like me at all. It felt like something else. Like I got taken over. Maybe if she hadn't pointed this gun. Maybe if I hadn't been drinking. I don't know. It happened fast. I was about to leave, but her mother saw me with the gun. She saw me and she was saying these things. And then I just wanted to shut her up and this thing was inside me. This feeling. Like something wanted me to point the gun at her mother. Just to scare her. And then: kabang."

"Jimmy?"

"And then her father starts shouting upstairs, and I feel this… this wild thing inside me," Jimmy said, and now the giggling was becoming annoying and seemed to increase between words. "And I just go running back up the stairs and down the hall and there's her dad, and I think of my dad, and I think of all the things I'm never going to have, and suddenly the gun is going off, and then Jenna's screaming and she's picking up the phone in her room because I hear that beep beep noise and I have to stop her, I have to tell her not to call, that there'll be a way to work this all out. And then, I feel it in me again. I'm moving faster than I'm supposed to—the rest of the world is moving slow—and I'm in her room and she has a look on her face like she doesn't understand how I got there so quickly and I'm feeling this—power or something—and then I press the gun against her throat to shut her up."

Then, he calmed slightly. He pointed the gun directly at Owen. "It's something you said to her. Isn't it? It's because you told her. But you said something terrible, didn't you?"

"Jimmy," Owen said. "Now, I know you're upset. I know this is difficult right now. But I want you to breathe. Take a few deep breaths. Come on. Just breathe."

Jimmy looked at him curiously for a moment, blinking. Then he opened his mouth and let the air in. Then, out. Then, in. Slowly, carefully.

Epilogue:
Belief

1

I can look at this past summer now and see that it was all Dagon. Dagon was there, I had brought Dagon into our world, and Dagon had gotten loose. There is no madness except the madness of the gods. There is no purity except the purity of love.

Here is where he took me—down to the sailboat—and out to sea.

2

We sailed around Outerbridge, its cliffs and caves, around the Montgomery palazzo, shining green and white with the flashing of the lighthouse nearby, north and then east, beyond the Great Salt Pond, out into the diamond night where sea and sky met, and the storm howled around us, and Jimmy, gun to my head, calling me Mooncalf over and over again, forced me to whisper an incantation to Dagon of the purity and madness of human love.

Mooncalf, he said. Mooncalf.